SHATTERING
THE LEY

DAW Books proudly presents
the fantasy novels of
Joshua Palmatier:

SHATTERING THE LEY

The Throne of Amenkor:
THE SKEWED THRONE
THE CRACKED THRONE
THE VACANT THRONE

SHATTERING THE LEY

JOSHUA PALMATIER

DAW BOOKS, INC.

DONALD A. WOLLHEIM, FOUNDER

375 Hudson Street, New York, NY 10014

ELIZABETH R. WOLLHEIM
SHEILA E. GILBERT
PUBLISHERS
www.dawbooks.com

First printing, July 2014

1 2 3 4 5 6 7 8 9

*The book is dedicated to
my two brothers,
Jason and Jacob,
both SF&F enthusiasts,
and both writers.*

Acknowledgments

This book would not have been possible without the dedication of DAW to its authors. In particular, I'd like to thank my editor, Sheila Gilbert, for continuing to believe in me and for pushing me to make my books the best they can be.

This particular book went through the wringer with my local writing group, which has (unfortunately) since fallen apart as its members moved to various other locations. Thanks to Patricia Bray, Tes Hilaire, and April Steenburgh. I miss the wine, chocolate, and snark.

One beta reader in particular provided invaluable feedback throughout the production of the book and deserves a special mention. David J. Fortier, I couldn't have done it without you and your vicious red pen.

Of course, none of this would be possible without the support of my readers. I hope this book lives up to your exceedingly high expectations. But I also hope it's one wild, scary ride. *grin*

And lastly, thanks to my partner, George, for bearing with me during my crazy writer moments, meltdowns, and exuberant highs.

PART I

One

"I SHOULDN'T BE HERE," Kara Tremain murmured to herself, even as she turned the final street corner and came within sight of the stone walls of Halliel's Park. She halted and bit her lower lip, her body trembling with a strange mixture of apprehension and danger and excitement. The leather belt that held her schoolbooks hung heavy on her shoulder and she twisted the strap beneath her hand. She glanced up and down the street, catching glimpses of the park's open gate through the throng of people and wagons that passed by as the city of Erenthrall bustled around her. One of the ley-powered floating carts skimmed by, Kara's skin prickling with ley energy, and she frowned after it, distracted—the carts weren't typically seen in the Eld District; no one here could afford them—but her attention didn't waver for long. A flash of power from one of the lit globes above the park's entrance drew her gaze back to the gates.

It was midafternoon. Her morning classes had ended nearly an hour before. Her father had wanted her to come directly home to help him with one of his projects. But the park. . . .

The stone walls called to her with a low, persistent hum. They drew her, pulled at her, as if she were flotsam caught in the river's currents. She didn't understand what it was, but knew that it made her different—from her fellow classmates, from her friends, even Cory. She didn't want to be different . . . but the hum thrilled her at the same time, made her catch her breath, made her feel alive.

With a huffing sigh she edged down the street until she was opposite the gates, then halted again. The globes above, hovering over the edges of the rough stone arch, brightened as she drew closer. The arch had been carved ages ago, when Erenthrall had been nothing more than a Baron's keep at the confluence of the two rivers and a few scattered homes for the villagers, but Kara knew the area had been considered special long before that. Without asking so many questions that she'd draw attention to herself, she'd tried to find out as much as possible about the park from her instructors at school and her parents. As far as anyone she'd asked had known, the park had always been there, even before the Barons took control of the surrounding lands. It hadn't always been walled in, hadn't even really been a park, but it had been considered sacred.

Inside the heavy wrought-iron gates were the same paths and stone sculptures she'd seen the last hundred times she'd come to stand outside the entrance. One of the gardeners—a man with a short, trimmed, brown beard streaked with gray like his hair, wearing worn gray robes stained heavily with dirt—knelt in the earth, stones piled around him on all sides. Kara stepped back until she struck the stone of the building behind her, books gouging into her side, and watched as the man arrayed the stones before him, then straightened and stared at them with a frown before shaking his head and tearing them apart again, stacking them in a different pattern.

On his fourth try, as he turned and reached for a fist-sized stone behind him, he caught sight of Kara.

She froze, her heart thudding—once—hard in her chest as the man's eyes caught hers. Creases appeared in his forehead as he leaned back, stone in hand, and considered her. His lips pressed together tightly. He began to raise one hand, but a shudder of apprehension ran down through Kara and she lurched to one side, back scraping against the granite of the building as she pushed away and joined those walking along the street. She didn't know what he'd intended to do, but she knew she should be getting home, that her father would be surprised she was so late, perhaps even angry. She hurried down to the far corner, the pull of the park lessening with each step, but before she turned she glanced back, expecting to see the gardener coming after her, or at least watching her from the gate.

He wasn't. He stood at the entrance of the gate, but his gaze was locked on the white ley globes floating up above.

They'd dimmed again.

Before he could turn and catch her watching, Kara slid around the corner and headed toward the marketplace. People jostled her from all sides, the streets of Eld District narrower than nearly all of the rest of Erenthrall except for East Forks, Tallow, West Forks across the rivers, and Confluence where the two rivers met. Kara brushed up against one of the brown-skinned women from the Demesnes to the west, the tassels of her finely embroidered shawl catching in Kara's hair as she passed. The woman glared, tugging her shawl back into place, but her expression softened as she realized Kara wasn't a thief. Then she was lost to the crowd as Kara skirted a group of black-clothed Temerite men. The scent of their cologne hit her like a brick and Kara dodged farther away, nose wrinkled.

Then she reached the market.

Hawkers shouted into the afternoon sunlight, holding up beaded necklaces, swaths of cloth, or skewers of meat as the buildings fell away into an open square. Patrons—mostly people from Erenthrall and the Baronies, but also from the western Demesnes, the mustachioed Gorrani men from the south, and more of the eastern Temerites—touched the wares with doubtful grimaces, questioning the quality of the cloth or the origins of the pottery before beginning to haggle. The peddlers had tents or carts and were generally respectable, so only a few of the Dogs—the Baron's guardsmen—patrolled the square. Near its center, a lone man in the white robes of a follower of the Kormanley railed against the Baron's continued desecration of the ley, begun over fifty years ago with the creation of the Nexus. Everyone cut a wide path around him, leaving him isolated near the remains of the old stone fountain. Even as Kara passed, ignoring his tirade, she caught sight of three Dogs converging on the man, their dark brown-and-black uniforms standing out in the crowd. She ducked her head as one of them brushed past her, scarred face set in a scowl. She didn't look back as the Kormanley priest's shouts escalated and were cut off. Everyone around her averted their eyes as the sounds of the Dogs beating him filled the plaza.

An old woman, mouth pressed into a thin line of distaste, murmured bitterly under her breath, "The priests know the Dogs will find them. Why do they continue to defy the Baron?" She shook her head and made a clicking noise with her tongue, but kept her back turned from where the Dogs had pulled the priest to his feet and were hauling him off.

"It's the sowing of the new tower tonight," the produce monger before her said gruffly. "That's what's brought them out. They've been riled up for weeks now."

"The Baron won't stand for it," the old woman said. "He'd kill them all if he could find them."

Kara paused, the muttered words sinking into her gut with a cold shiver of uneasiness. She glanced back toward the man in white, hanging slackly between the arms of the two guards as they dragged his limp body through the throng. His black hair obscured his face, but she could see a string of drool and blood hanging down from his mouth. Blood stained his white robe in strange splatters, bright in the sunlight. The Dogs hauled the priest into a side street and they vanished.

Everyone on the square went back to haggling, errens and wares exchanging hands.

Kara turned to find the old woman watching her through squinted eyes. "Oh, don't let it worry you, poppet. I'm sure he'll be fine."

But Kara could hear the lie in her voice. When she reached out as if to stroke Kara's hair, Kara ducked and pushed past a Gorrani, the hilt of his ceremonial sword gouging into her side. He shouted at her in his own guttural language, angry and harsh, Kara catching only a few words, but she didn't stop. Her chest ached and she didn't know why. She'd never thought much about where the Dogs took those that they grabbed. Her father had told her they were taken to the Amber Tower, to the Baron's court where they were judged and held accountable for their crimes. But that wasn't what Kara had heard in the old woman's voice. She'd spoken as if the priest were already dead.

Kara fled the square, slowing only when the raucous noise of bartering faded and she found herself on the streets near her home. The crowd thinned as the storefronts of the market area succumbed to residential buildings, the granite facades of the shops becoming the smaller brick houses of the laborers and servants that dwelled in Eld. Kara turned the corner and headed down her own street. She could see the myriad buildings of the University from here, surrounded by high stone walls, nestled on the top of the hill in Confluence. The slate expanse of the Tiana and Urate Rivers cut toward it from the northwest and northeast. Beyond, East Forks and Tallow were a dark cluster of docks and cramped buildings covered over with a fine gray haze, the Butcher's Block filled with smoke farther south. West Forks and Tannery Row hung with a similar haze, all of the districts beyond hidden from sight by the smoke and the rises in the land. Only a few steeples and the ley towers that marked the nodes of the ley network broke through the layers.

She hesitated on the steps of her apartment building, gazing out over the lower end of Erenthrall. She knew her father was waiting for her, but even now, the park pulled at her, faintly. A mere whisper. And there was the disturbing image of the priest, blood trailing from his mouth, the words of the old woman. . . .

What *did* happen to the priests after the Dogs captured them?

Sighing, she pulled her schoolbooks off her shoulder and stepped up to the door of the building, shoved it open, and trudged up the stairs beyond the small foyer inside to the third floor, pausing only momentarily on the second floor where Cory lived. The door to her own flat was open and she could hear her father humming to himself as he worked. He sat at his desk, two small ley globes—all they could afford—hovering over him. One of them flickered fitfully, but he didn't seem to notice, his attention caught by the gutted clock, its gears and intricate metal workings spread out on the black cloth that covered his workspace. The main housing of the clock—a darkly-stained cherry piece that gleamed beneath the lights, its face white, surrounded by a band of gold—sat to one side. Its hands had been removed and its face looked barren, even though it was decorated with silver clouds.

Tables and chairs filled in the rest of the main room of the flat, with an open arch leading to the kitchen area and another door to one side where Kara and her parents slept. A few battered and misused clocks stood on the tables or were mounted on the wall, although nothing like the quality of the one her father was currently working on. Kara listened a moment, but the rest of the flat was silent; her mother hadn't returned yet from her position as a servant at the Baron's personal estate in Grass. Her father must have started cooking already, for the heady scent of roasting meat drifted out from the kitchen.

Kara tossed her books on the table inside the door, removed her shoes, and turned to find her father watching her, his face stern. The humming had stopped.

"I thought I told you to come home immediately after classes today. Your friend Cory's been home for almost an hour already."

Kara shuffled in place. "I came home through the marketplace."

Her father frowned, creases appearing in his forehead beneath the patch of gray hair that had cropped up over the last few years. His hazel eyes caught her own, held them for a long moment, searching, and then he grunted.

Kara heaved a mental sigh of relief. He wasn't truly angry.

"So," he said, half turning back to his table. "I'd wanted you to help me with this clock. Some of the pieces are so small I thought your nimble fingers would be helpful, and then I thought you and I could take a special trip, but now. . . ."

Kara took an involuntary step toward her father, then caught herself. "Where?" she asked, trying to sound casual, even though she could feel her blood pulsing in her arms, tingling in her fingers. She almost asked if he would take her to Halliel's Park. She knew people could visit, that's why the gates had been open, but she'd never dared to enter on her own, not with the gardeners constantly watching. If her father went with her, maybe she could see what was inside that pulled at her.

But her father shook his head. "I don't think we'll have time now. I need to get this clock finished." He turned back toward her, put on his narrow working glasses, and looked at her over their thin metal rims.

"I'll help," Kara said, and grabbed one of the chairs from the table in the kitchen. Her father made room for her at his side, muttering, "Careful!" as she bumped the table. Then she leaned forward and stared down at what seemed like hundreds of pieces, most gleaming in the ley light. They'd been arranged in a clear pattern and had already been polished, gears and arms of all sizes and shapes. In the center sat the metal case that would slide into the back of the wooden house. Numerous gears had already been set in the case, which rested on its face, and after a quick glance at what remained, Kara could see what needed to be done next. This one was fairly basic, completely mechanical, without relying on any use of the ley at all.

Reaching out, she said, "This one goes in next."

It hadn't been a question, but her father nodded. "If you can get the next few gears and the arm into the casing, I'll screw it into place."

Kara reached out and picked up one of the many-sized tweezers lying off to one side, then carefully plucked the gear from the smooth black silk and slid it into the casing. Her hands shook slightly, but when she let go with the tweezers, the gear slipped into place on the small metal post. She had to nudge it to get the teeth to mesh correctly before it dropped down. Her breath fogged the bright metal of the already assembled clock as she reached for the next gear and she realized she'd been holding it unconsciously. Behind, her father grunted once in approval, then moved into the kitchen. She heard pots clattering, the scent of cooked meat and vegetables growing strong enough to make her stomach growl, and then she became absorbed in the inner workings of the clock. Her father came by once in a while to check on her, but she barely noticed.

She was vaguely aware of her mother returning, standing over her as she worked. Then her mother kissed her on the side of the head and joined her father in the kitchen. Kara listened to the soft background murmur of their conversation without really listening. The ley globe above her flickered again and, frowning in irritation, she reached out and touched it, the pale light steadying and strengthening. Leaning over the casing again, she began twisting a screw into place but realized that her parents had fallen abruptly silent.

She glanced up to find them standing in the door to the kitchen, watching her intently. Her mother's mouth hung slightly open, eyes widened, but it was her father's troubled frown that sent a sliver of fear into her gut. "What did I do wrong?" She glanced down at the gears of the nearly finished clock, then back at her parents. If she'd ruined the clock, the patron who'd hired her father to fix it would make him pay for it and they couldn't afford that.

Her father grabbed her mother's hand and squeezed it reassuringly before smiling and stepping forward. "Nothing, Kara, nothing. Everything's fine. Are you almost finished?"

Kara glanced back at her mother—mouth now closed, but worry lines still surrounding her pale gray eyes—and then her father put his hand on the top of her head and drew her attention back to the clock.

"Ah, only a few more pieces left to go," he said. "It looks like we'll be able to go on that little trip after all. Let's get this finished up, and then we can all have some dinner."

At the thought of the mysterious excursion, Kara dismissed her mother's concern—she was always exhausted after returning from work—and with her father's help, placed the last of the inner workings of the clock inside the casing. They slid the casing into the wooden housing, attached the hands and spun them to the appropriate positions, then set the clock in motion before screwing the flat metal plate into place on back. Her father mussed her hair, then retreated to the kitchen with her mother and a final, "We can't leave until your home-work is done."

Kara rolled her eyes, sat for a long moment listening to the clock's motion, imagining the hidden gears inside ticking in precise, rhythmic steps. But finally she sighed, slid off her chair, and grabbed her books.

She had most of her work done—all except the rote mathematics—when her mother called her in for dinner. Her parents chatted as she wolfed it down, barely tasting it, watching the tension ease from her mother's shoulders, until at one point her father said something stupid about the Baron's court, his arms thrown wide as he flourished a mock bow while still sitting at the table, and she burst out in laughter, shaking her head. Her father caught her eye and she leaned over and kissed him lightly on the cheek before rising and setting her plate and utensils in a bucket, to be washed at the public fountain.

"Will you be coming with us?" her father asked.

Her mother considered for a moment, turning to catch Kara's eye, then smiled and shook her head. "I don't think so. I'm too tired. The Baron's steward had us working like dogs today to get ready for the ball tonight. Most of the outlying lords are attending, as well as a few other Barons, which meant we had to get the tower and the surrounding grounds into tip-top shape."

"I'm surprised they didn't need you for the events tonight."

"Ha! I'm glad I pulled the short stick on that one. I get to prepare for it, sleep during the celebration, and then clean up afterward." She made a face and sighed dramatically. "No, you two go and Kara can tell me all about it afterward."

"All right, then," her father said, glancing toward Kara with raised eyebrows and a stern expression. "Homework all done?"

Kara hesitated, but knew she could handle the mathematics easily tomorrow if she got called to recite answers, so she grinned in excite-ment. "All done."

"Then let's go."

Kara jumped off her chair and skipped toward the door, her father following more sedately behind her.

"Take a jacket!" her mother called from the kitchen. "It'll get cold up there tonight!"

"You heard your mother," her father said gruffly, then shooed her into the bedroom.

She flung back the lid of the trunk containing her clothes and rummaged through the layers, pulling her gray jacket free and slipping into it as she half ran back to the open door. Her father ushered her out, then down to the street, heading uphill, away from the University and Confluence and northward toward the new heart of Erenthrall and the Stone District. Away from Halliel's Park. Kara hid her disappointment, frowning as she tried to figure out where they were going. Others were on the street, headed in the same general direction—parents with their children who were screaming and chasing each other through the streets. Her father nodded to a few of the other adults, chatting quietly. The Baron's Dogs stood at every corner, eyeing the growing crowds, but generally hanging back. Kara thought of the priest in the market square that afternoon and shivered, pulling her long jacket tight against herself, but she didn't see any of the white robes of the Kormanley anywhere.

A moment later, she caught sight of Cory's dirty-blond hair and small form next to his own father ahead of them. She shouted, "Cory!" and caught up with him as he turned.

The look of confusion on his face broke with a smile as he saw her and, as their fathers shook hands, he urgently whispered, "Do you have any idea where we're going?"

"No idea. But it must be outside since my mother demanded I wear a jacket."

Cory snorted and tugged at his own short coat. "I think it has something to do with the sowing of the tower. My parents have been talking about it for days. They haven't sown a new tower in twenty years."

Kara smacked her forehead, even though her parents hadn't mentioned the tower much. "I should have thought of that! My mother's been working her fingers to the bone at the Amber Tower. If it is the tower, then that explains why we're heading toward Stone. We wouldn't be able to see into Grass from Green or Leeds." And of course they wouldn't be able to get into Grass and see it close up, not with the lords and ladies from across the plains coming to the city to witness the event. Kara felt her excitement escalating, heightened by Cory's and the general feel of the crowd around them, like the energy in the air before a storm. She practically bounced on her toes.

Everyone was converging on Minstrel's Park, situated at the top of the highest hill in Eld, at the border of the Stone District. Her father wormed his way through the crowd, trying to reach the highest point possible, although it was already packed with people, blankets thrown out on the ground, some with picnic baskets and wooden folding chairs or stools. The park was riddled with trees and a few of the kids Cory's age had shimmied up the branches and were perched with legs hanging down from above. Low stone walls divided the park into sections, with obelisks at various points reaching to the darkening sky. It was nearing sunset, clouds skidding toward the east now tinged a burnished yellow.

Her father halted near one of the obelisks and Kara and Cory climbed up onto the wall so they could see above everyone else. The excitement built as the sun sank into the horizon and night settled, broken by the ley lines scattered throughout the city. From atop the wall, Kara could see the white bands of light forking in all directions, like a spiderweb, its center in Grass beneath the heights of the Amber Tower and the myriad other towers that had been sown around it since it was first raised. They couldn't see the Nexus, but they could see the reflected white light from the towers. Even from this distance, it hurt to look directly toward the source, the light too intense. That light radiated outward, from ley tower to ley tower throughout the city and beyond, to Tumbor and Farrade and all of the other cities across the continent.

As the sun burned itself out in the west, the light from the ley lines intensified, flaring once before settling back to normal. Kara followed the rivers of light with her eyes for a moment, then turned her attention back to the still visible towers in Grass. "Where do you think the new tower will be sown?"

"I don't know." Cory craned his neck, eyes darting back and forth across the distance, face anxious. He was at least half a foot shorter than Kara, and at ten, a few years younger. "Do you see anything yet? Have they started?"

"Calm down, Cory," his father growled. "You'll know when it starts, trust me."

And then, abruptly, the light of the Nexus intensified even more, forcing Kara to shield her eyes with one hand. A collective gasp went up from the crowd when the ley lines throughout the city's districts fluctuated and dimmed, as if the Nexus were drawing energy toward it. Cory reached out and grabbed her upper arm and squeezed, but her own adrenaline dulled the pain. Her heart throbbed in her throat, in her arms, and her skin prickled, all of the little hairs on the back of her neck standing on end. A tingling sensation washed through her from head to toe, as if energy were passing through her and being sucked into the ground. She shuddered, drew in a sharp breath, tasted something on the air, thick and metallic, coating her tongue like molasses or blood. She fought the urge to spit it out, even as the energy spiked, feeding down and down into the earth—

Far out in Grass, the light of the Nexus flared, a fountain of white light spewing skyward, cascading back down, throwing all of the myriad towers in all shapes and sizes into stark relief, windows and balconies and terraces like black orifices in their sleek, multicolored sides. Kara saw people—lords and ladies and the upper echelons of Erenthrall—on some of the balconies, tiny figures ducking back and away from the sheaths of light seething upward like a geyser.

Then Cory shouted, "Look!" He jerked forward, dragging Kara with him, his fingers digging in even deeper on her arm. Everyone around them stilled, drew in a collective breath, and held it.

From the depths of the ley light, a thousand tendrils spiraled upward, writhing like vines stretching toward the darkness of night. As they rose, they wove together, the base growing more and more solid. Leaves sprouted from the vines, growing thick and large, and as the furious speed of the growth began to abate, the leaves began folding inward and flattening themselves against the outside of the forming tower like a skin. It rose, higher than most of the towers around it, but not as high as the Baron's Amber Tower, the top bulging out as the tendrils wove together, forming what looked like a giant seed pod with holes pierced through its center. Leaves began encasing the seed pod, leaving the holes empty. As the growth halted, the top of the tower solidifying into a thin spire, Kara thought she saw a bluish glow emanating from the holes, pulsing like the coals of a banked fire.

And then the gouts of white fire surrounding the towers of Grass began to abate, sinking back down into the depths of the inner city, the network of ley lines throughout the districts increasing in intensity as it did, until everything had returned to its regular glow.

The crowd in Minstrel's Park remained silent for a long moment, the newly sown tower shimmering a light forest green, appearing smooth from this distance, but threaded with veins, like those of a leaf held up to sunlight. Then, as if at some unspoken signal, people began to clap, men slapping each other on the back, conversations breaking out everywhere, punctuated by laughter.

Kara's father turned to her, smiling widely, then said in a muffled voice, as if he were speaking through layers upon layers of cloth, "What did you think? That's not something we're likely to see again in my lifetime."

Kara opened her mouth to tell him she could barely hear him, but a sudden wave of weakness passed through her. The tingling sensation against her skin had halted, but she felt drained, as if the stone and earth beneath her feet had sucked the life out of her. She felt her knees buckle, heard her father gasp in horror, heard Cory cry out, her arm wrenching as his hand was pulled away.

Her vision began to darken into a narrow tunnel of pulsing, jagged, yellow light, and the world receded. But before she could collapse, her father's hands caught her and drew her to his chest.

Two

ALLAN GARRETT GLARED down from the balcony in the Amber Tower, the sounds of the Baron's Ball spilling out from behind him, light glowing in the intricate detailing of the solid amber railing he leaned over. Far below, the main gates of the Baron's estate had been flung wide open and the ley carriages of the rich glided into the immense inner courtyard and gardens. They circled the stone fountain spewing jets of water skyward, jostling for position at the base of the wide steps radiating outward from the tower's base like ripples in a pool of stone. From this height, nearly halfway up the Amber Tower, Allan couldn't see individual crests on the carriages, but he could see the other Dogs lined up near the gates and outside on the streets and the wide square. They were inspecting the carriages as they approached, keeping the crowds of people in the square in check. Everyone in the city wanted to be near the Nexus during the sowing of the new tower, and everyone with an ounce of influence felt they deserved to be here in the Amber Tower, whether they'd been invited by Baron Arent Pallentor or not.

Forcefully, Allan shoved himself back from the railing. He deserved to be down there, containing the crowd, dealing with the rioters and protestors like the Kormanley, not trapped up here babysitting the rich and affluent as a useless honor guard. This wasn't even the main party, where the Baron presided over his most influential guests. He was a Dog, damn it, not the gods-cursed city watch!

"There you are, Pup," a voice growled.

Allan spun and glowered at his newest alpha's scarred face. He'd only been assigned to Hagger's pack that afternoon. "I'm not a pup," he snarled.

Hagger's eyebrows shot upward. "Oh, really? You're all of what, seventeen?"

Allan narrowed his eyes. "Sixteen."

"And you've been a Dog since . . . ?"

"Spring."

"And I can tell by your accent that you're from outside the city. A little bit of a slur on your S's. That would be one of the western towns. Bandoley?"

Allan shifted awkwardly. "Canter."

Hagger whistled. "That far west? Let me guess, you placed in the annual bout in swordsmanship and thought you were good enough to come to the city and become a Dog."

Allan bristled. "What of it?"

Hagger snorted, straightened where he stood in the glass doorway of the balcony, and crossed his arms over his chest. His face was shadowed—backlit by the thousands of ley globes that lit the open hall behind him, the Baron's lesser guests milling about—but Allan could still see the crisscross pattern of scars over his cheeks and neck. Not all of them were from blades; some had come from beatings, others from the practice pit, still others from skirmishes between the Barons' armies on the battlefield. The scars contrasted oddly with the formal black, red, and brown of the Dogs' dress uniform.

"Listen," he spat. "I've served more than sixteen years as a Dog. More than twenty. More than you're likely to survive. To me, you will always be a pup, Pup. Now straighten your uniform and get in here. The lords and ladies need supervision. The sowing is about to start."

"How can you tell?"

"I can feel it. Now move!"

Allan didn't feel anything, but tugged on the collar of his uniform and followed Hagger into the main hall.

It burned with white light, ley globes of every shape and size floating near the ceiling. The semitranslucent amber walls and floor reflected the light harshly as the guests flowed from one end of the rounded Great Hall to the other. Dressed in every style of clothing imaginable, they jostled and danced and mingled, the rumble of their conversations throbbing on the hot air, drowning out most of the music provided by the string quartet in the center of the room. As he entered, those guests nearest the balcony turned, caught sight of his uniform, and quickly turned away. But not before Allan saw their smiles falter, the shine in their eyes dim. Most tried to hide the reaction by sipping at their wine or with a forced laugh. Only one man, an older gentleman—back stiff, black vest and pants contrasting harshly with a pale blue shirt and vibrant yellow handkerchief tucked into one pocket—dared to look Allan in the eye. He nodded solemnly, glass raised as if in a toast.

Disconcerted by the direct look, Allan pulled the formal vest of his own uniform down to smooth the creases, then caught a hand motion from Hagger commanding him to move left and edge toward the black glass of the windows on the far side of the tower. Allan began circling the room, sticking close to the wall, where tall plants in urns and a few assorted chairs set up beneath huge tapestries interrupted the flow of the crowd. Nearly everyone shifted out of his way as he approached, the motions subtle. He wasn't certain what Hagger wanted him to do except circulate. The Dogs were there in case the guests got rowdy, and to keep them from wandering outside onto the balcony overlooking the Nexus when the sowing started. But it was only a formality; no one wanted to draw that kind of attention to themselves, especially not the Baron's. Allan scanned the guests as he moved, noting numerous minor lords from every part of the lower plains, as well as a few from the high Steppe, judging by the cut of their clothes. A boisterous laugh jerked his attention toward Baron Leethe, from Tumbor, Erenthrall's closest rival. With a frown, Allan watched the Baron for a long moment—this party was for the lesser dignitaries, Leethe should have been at the main function with Arent and the other Barons—but then he caught sight of the dark skin, thick mustache, and trimmed beard of a Gorrani. A quick glance toward the man's sheath found the usual blade absent. He sighed, then silently berated himself; the Dogs at the gates would never have allowed the Gorrani into the Tower with his saber.

He continued toward the windows. Another round of servants wove among the guests, trays of drinks and cut sandwiches held out before them, the excitement in the room escalating steadily as more of the influential members of Erenthrall arrived. The heat generated by so many bodies packed so close together caused sweat to run down Allan's back. He wiped at his face, then turned—

And collided with a servant carrying a large wooden crate.

The crate fell, jostled from her grip, the woman biting back a curse as she tried to catch it. It hit the amber floor with a loud crack and splinter of wood, one side splitting and spilling a few long, white, tapered candles across the floor beneath the guests' feet.

"Clumsy oaf!" a lord said as a candle rolled to a stop by his foot. "The Baron should dismiss you immediately for that!"

"I apologize," the woman said, ducking her head before kneeling and scrambling to pick up the loose candles.

The lord snorted, then caught Allan's dark frown. A look of horror crossed his face and he slid away without glancing back, lost in a heartbeat.

Allan knelt down, grabbed one of the escaped candles, and handed it over to the servant. She'd already gathered up the rest, stuffing them back into the box. "I didn't see you," he said as she took it. "I hope that lord didn't upset you."

"Oh, certainly not," she scoffed, waving her hand. "I deal with that every day." But Allan noted she was trembling as she stood, crate balanced in her arms so that none of the candles would fall out. He stood as well.

With a careful look, she said, "You're new to the Dogs, aren't you?"

Allan stiffened. "Since the spring."

She smiled at him, one hand brushing her black hair back from where it had fallen forward over her face. "I thought so. You wouldn't have stopped to help if you weren't. Or been concerned if I'd been upset." Her pale skin shone in the amber light, a small scar near the corner of one eye. A single gold hoop earring dangled from her ear. Her servant's dress was amber, like all of the rest, simple but elegant, designed to blend into the background of the tower itself. But Allan couldn't take his eyes off of the fine lines of her face.

When the moment stretched too long and her brow wrinkled in slight confusion, he glanced down toward the crate, frowning at the contents. "Why are you carrying around candles?"

She laughed, the creases in her brow vanishing. "They're for the guests. I need to hand them out before the sowing begins." She motioned toward the rest of the room and Allan saw other servants dispersing through the crowd. Nearly everyone accepted them with a small giggle or gasp.

"How quaint!" a woman nearby exclaimed. "The Baron must have something special planned."

The man beside her snorted and took his taper reluctantly, holding it as if it were a particularly virulent snake. "I hope he doesn't expect us to actually use them. I haven't held a candle since I was a child."

Allan turned back to ask the black-haired servant what the candles were for—Hagger's short briefing hadn't mentioned them—but all he caught was a flash of her hair as she vanished into the growing crowd. He swore under his breath, pushed forward after her, but she was gone.

Before Allan could begin a more serious search, a respectful hush fell over the room, the music cutting off sharply. He spun toward the darkness of the windows, expecting to see the first part of the sowing, his heart quickening in his chest—he'd wanted to be at the edge, where he would have the best view—but the windows were still dark. Nothing appeared to be happening outside at all.

Then he noticed that everyone's attention was focused inward, toward the center of the room.

He shifted forward through the still crowd, until he saw where the guests were parting to allow three Prime Wielders to pass through. The men strode forward with purpose, ignoring everyone—lord, lady, and servant alike—intent on the closed doors opposite the entrance that led to the restricted higher levels of the tower. Their black robes swished about their feet, their hands hidden in the folds of the robes in front of them. They ranged in age, although the youngest couldn't be less than forty, his hair streaked with gray.

They passed through the room without a word, only the youngest glancing to one side, catching Allan's gaze, his mouth pressed tight, face lined with intense concentration. As they reached the far doors, opening them and slipping through, one of the guests stepped forward as if to follow them, eyes filled with hatred, then halted abruptly as if catching himself. The man—dressed in a loose green shirt with white ruffles near the neck and sleeve—darted a glance to either side to see if anyone had noticed. The silence broke, the quartet launching into a new aria, conversations resuming with a low murmur that steadily rose back to the same level as before, nearly everyone eyeing the doors where the Primes had gone. The man in the green ruffled shirt cast one last look around, then smiled and began speaking to a woman in a white gown who was holding a bamboo fan.

Allan's hand slipped toward his sword hilt before he remembered he was wearing the ceremonial uniform and didn't have a sword, only a knife. He settled back, shifting as the guests drifted around him, keeping the man in the green shirt in sight while he listened in on conversations. But the man appeared to be just another guest, talking to numerous courtiers, flirting with the women, joking with the men. Yet Allan couldn't help feeling that he was moving with purpose, that he was maneuvering himself into position for something.

The man had stationed himself near the center of the wide bay of windows, Allan a discreet distance to the left, when a woman beside Allan gasped and held out her left arm. "Look! It's starting! The Wielders have started the sowing!"

Allan frowned down at the woman's arm, where gooseflesh had broken out, the fine hairs standing on end. The woman next to her shuddered.

"I feel it, too!"

"I only feel a prickling at the base of my neck," a man said with a disturbed frown.

The first woman smiled and said, smugly, "Some of us are more sensitive to the ley than others."

Gasps and small shrieks echoed throughout the room as the guests quieted, most edging toward Allan's position. Allan snorted in derision and glanced down at his own arms surreptitiously. He hadn't felt anything, but he couldn't explain the gooseflesh on the woman's arm or the reaction of the other guests either.

And then it didn't matter, because the white ley globes hovering above suddenly dimmed. Men cursed, glancing up, and someone cried out, voice strained with fear.

"What's happening?" someone asked.

A man standing to Allan's right answered, voice calm, as the ley globes flickered again. "The Primes. They're using the energy of the Nexus to sow the tower. It's interrupting the general flow for the network that feeds the city." He held up his candle. "That must be why they handed out these."

As he spoke the last word, the ley globes died completely, the entire room plunging into darkness. More than a few of the gathered gentry shouted in consternation, cursing or muttering under their breath. But even as Allan's eyes adjusted to the sudden darkness, he caught the flicker of flames spreading throughout the room. Servants appeared with lit tapers held protectively behind cupped hands, extending them to those who had taken candles. The tension brought on by panic subsided, women chuckling shakily as they used their own candles to light others, a few of the men looking sheepish as the flickering orange light—so different from the steady white of the ley globes—began to fill the room. The flame made the amber of the walls and ceiling glow as if lit from within, pulsing like a heartbeat. Lords and ladies marveled at the transformation in the room, voices hushed as they held their candles aloft, faces suffused with childlike wonder.

Outside, in the darkness beneath the tower, the first glow of ley light pulsed upward. Another gasp spread through the room, this one solemn, and everyone, including Allan, shifted toward the glass windows. Below, the ground between the myriad towers that made up the Grass District glowed with ethereal ley light, concentrated beneath the faceted glass structure that was the Nexus. Except the light of the ley was too fierce, too intense, obscuring the Nexus itself, as if somehow the light had broken free and spilled out into the surrounding land. The Dogs had cleared the paths and roadways below earlier in the day, setting up a restricted zone around the Nexus. Allan checked to make certain the doors leading out to the balcony were closed and locked. As he pressed closer to the glass, he noticed other people outside on the balconies of the towers across from the Nexus and shook his head. Idiots. Hadn't they been warned? They were too close to the ley!

Then, a gout of light shot upward from the Nexus, like spume against a cliff, or the jets of water in the fountain at the base of the tower. It was followed by more, each higher than the last, until they rose higher than the windows of the Great Hall. Across the way, the figures on the balcony outside panicked, most fleeing inside their tower, but not before one of the spumes cascaded down over the ledge, catching two people in its light. It poured down from the balcony like water, leaving two bodies crumpled behind it.

The activity of the light shifted, the focus of the energy concentrating toward a section of Grass that had been cleared and prepared for the new tower.

When the first thick tendrils shot forth from the ground, those pressed closest to the windows jerked backward, stumbling into the people behind them. The vines grew unnaturally fast, stretching into the sky, twining around each other as they rose. Leaves burst from nodules, unfurling in the space of a heartbeat; leaves so large they'd engulf the entire room of lords and ladies whole. The foliage began enclosing the tower, forming its walls, the head rising into the night sky like a bud on a flower. Allan watched in awe, struck dumb by the sheer immensity of it, the raw power he could see but couldn't feel. Nothing like this had ever occurred in Canter; nothing like this ever would. This was why he'd left, why he'd journeyed to the city, the hope of joining the Dogs burning inside him. In Canter, the most he could hope for was life as a guard for a local merchant. In Erenthrall. . . .

In Erenthrall, he could be anything he wanted.

"Sacrilege!"

Allan turned as the shout broke through the awe that held the group at the windows. He glared around at the surrounding people, most still transfixed by the sowing of the tower, their faces awash in the white light from the Nexus below. But near the center of the windows, people were stepping back, eyes wide in shock.

"It's a desecration!" a man's voice bellowed, roaring out above those gathered. "It's blasphemy! We are cavorting with a power that we cannot control and it is not natural!"

Allan shoved forward through the press of guests, thrusting lords and ladies alike aside as a sickening sense of foreboding drove daggers into his gut. Men cursed and stumbled out of his path, wax splattering from their candles, and women shot him black looks. But he focused on the window, where the crush of people had opened up into an empty circle. He couldn't see the man, but he could hear him as the tirade continued and he knew who it was, knew it even before he caught sight of his green shirt.

"The ley was not meant to be harnessed," the man cried, his voice rising. "It was not meant to be leashed. We are subverting a natural power, one tied to the earth. Even our ancestors knew this! We can see it in the stones, in the sacred grounds that our ancestors worshipped! They revered this power, gave it the respect it deserves! We abuse it!"

Allan reached the edge of the circle where the press of bodies became too great for him to charge through. He barked, "Dog! Out of my way!" and tried to press forward, but the lords and ladies didn't move. He could see the green-shirted man now, could see him as the deranged man paced back and forth before the window, the white blaze of the ley behind him as it fountained higher, the writhing vines of the tower struggling upward. He flung his arms wide, and as he did, Allan caught sight of something odd beneath his loose shirt. But the dagger the man suddenly produced distracted him, filling him with a sense of dread. He didn't have time to wonder how he'd managed to get the blade past the guards, didn't have time to react at all. The man's face was strained with righteous anger, eyes blazing with rage as he gestured toward the sowing with the blade in his hand.

"This is the latest desecration, the latest folly of our Baron! The Wielders pervert nature to our needs, twist the ley to their own purposes, suppress the land and its natural laws to build this city, to give us comfort, to provide for us, and it is time to stop! It is time to halt the sacrilege! It is time to return the ley to its proper course!"

Allan heard someone shout his name over the man's fervor and caught sight of Hagger and two other Dogs on the far side of the room, farther away than Allan and trapped by the crush of bodies. Hagger's face was livid with pure rage. The Dog snapped his hands in a short, final gesture whose message was clear: "Stop it! End it now!"

Allan spun back to the green-shirted man in time to see him slash down across his own chest with the dagger.

Women screamed, two fainting, and men cried out as liquid spilled outward, splattering the floor, drenching the front of the man's body. The crowd surged backward and away, the space between the man and the lords suddenly widening. Allan was thrust back, someone's elbow catching him hard in the side, but with a deep, low growl, he roared again, "Out of my way, damn it!" and grabbed the man before him by the shoulders, hauling him back and to the side. The man fell with a harsh, panicked cry, taking two more guests with him, but opening up a space into the circle. Allan leaped over the fallen lord, even as the green-shirted man lifted his head and arms skyward, even as the sharp scent of oil slammed into Allan's nostrils with gagging force and he realized that the liquid coating the man's front wasn't blood.

"For the ley! For the Kormanley!"

Allan surged across the small space between the lords and ladies and the green-shirted priest of the Kormanley. But the priest ignored him, caught up in the rapture of the moment. He fell to his knees, reached down with his free hand, grabbed one of the white tapered candles that the servants had handed out earlier, and brought the dancing flame to his chest.

Allan heard the whoosh of the fire as it caught in the oil, felt the heat of the flames burn his face as the man was engulfed in the space of a breath. The man screamed, the orange-red fire of the oil in sharp contrast to the still seething white fire of the ley outside the tower windows. Allan counted one heartbeat, two, felt the air sucked from his lungs by the conflagration, noted that the newly sown tower had almost neared completion outside, its bulbous top slowing in its ascent, the leaves folding gently to the tower's sides—

And then he tackled the pillar of flame the priest had become.

Fire seared his face and hands as they crashed to the amber floor and rolled. He tasted smoke and ash, felt heat through the layers of his uniform, smelled burned flesh and grunted at the beginnings of pain, and then he stopped trying to breathe, held everything tight—his eyes, his chest, the body of the priest—as he rolled back and forth on the floor trying to smother the fire. Screams and shouts filtered through the sizzle and snap of flame. The buttons of his uniform heated up and burned into his skin. His lungs began to ache for air and he caught himself trying to whimper as tears squeezed from his eyes.

And then someone was beating at him with a heavy cloth. He heard Hagger bellow, "Let go! He's almost out!" and he broke free of the priest and rolled away with a gasp, inhaling harshly. The air reeked of char and oil, but he didn't care. Hagger smothered him in a heavy tapestry—one of those from the walls—but turned toward the priest, leaving Allan to put himself out. He'd barely moved when the servant from earlier knelt at his side, grabbing the tapestry with two hands and beating it against him where his clothes still smoldered.

"Stop," Allan murmured. When she continued, her motions frantic, her eyes too wide, he grabbed one of her flailing arms and said, louder, "Stop!"

She tried to pull out of his grasp, then caught herself, some of the panic draining from her gaze.

"I think I'm out," he said. He tried to smile, but winced and groaned instead. His skin felt waxy and hot in patches, and his entire body throbbed.

The servant snorted, then dropped the tapestry.

"He's out, too," Hagger said. "Permanently."

He stood over the priest's body, glaring down at the man's shirt in disgust. Kneeling, he pulled back the charred remains of the clothing, some of the skin peeling back with it. He grimaced.

"He had skins tied around his chest," he said, lifting one of them so that Allan could see, "filled with oil. He intended to kill himself." He glanced around at the guests, all staying a good ten paces back, some of the women sobbing into their companions' shoulders, others tending to those who'd fainted. All of their faces were grim or troubled. In a voice pitched so low only Allan and the servant could hear, he said, "And perhaps kill some of the others as well."

Then he stood, moved to stare down at Allan. He considered him for a long moment, his face unreadable, then nudged Allan's still smoking arm with one foot.

"Perhaps you'll make a Dog after all, Pup."

Three

THE ROOM FULL OF DOGS, Wielders, and assorted servants and dignitaries stilled when the double doors that had been opened wide the night before to allow the guests into the hall were flung back by Baron Arent Pallentor. He paused in the entrance, accompanied by Daedallen, captain of the Dogs, and Prime Wielder Augustus. The Baron's eyes swept the room once, passing over Allan without hesitation, settling on one of the numerous higher-ranking Dogs in the center of the windows where the charred remains of the Kormanley priest still lay. As the Baron strode forward, flanked by Daedallen and Augustus, Allan shifted forward, but Hagger's hand closed tight on his wrist. Allan winced. His skin was raw from the burns he'd received trying to subdue the priest. His uniform had protected most of his body from serious damage, but his face and hands had been exposed. As he grimaced, he could feel the tightness of the skin beneath his jaw and across his left cheek. The healer that had been called had rubbed in some type of unguent that would help, but he'd said there would be scarring. Allan's hands had fared slightly better.

Sympathy flashed across Hagger's face as he caught Allan's reaction, but he didn't let go of Allan's arm. In a voice that would not carry beyond the corner where they stood, he said, "You don't approach the Baron unless he asks you to, Pup."

Allan settled back against the wall and Hagger released his grip.

Trying to ignore the cool yet spicy scent of the unguent, Allan focused on the activity near the blackened body. This was as close as he'd ever been to the Baron, the Lord of Grass himself, and he was not what Allan had expected. A few inches shorter than Allan, he was thinner and lankier, his clothes cut to emphasize the angularity of his body. The shirt was a subtle dark blue, stitched with gold thread, his breeches a sleek black, much simpler in style and form than anything the minor lords and ladies had worn the night before. The only ostentatious part of his attire was the gold belt and scabbard, with the rather plain hilt of a short sword visible in the sheath. Allan watched as the Baron moved, fluid and precise, and realized the sword wasn't an affectation; the Baron knew how to use it. And even though he'd ruled Erenthrall for over sixty years, he appeared to be no more than fifty.

The Baron stood over the body a long moment, spoke softly to the captain of the Dogs at his side, then listened to the response. They were too distant for Allan to hear the words, but Prime Wielder Augustus made a comment when Daedallen had finished, one hand motioning toward the body, and the Baron frowned. Augustus didn't react to the glare, his attention fixed on the body.

Baron Arent called one of the other Dogs forward, a blond-haired man twice as broad as Allan.

"That's Terrence," Hagger murmured, "one of Daedallen's seconds. He's the one my alpha reports to and gets his orders from."

"I know. I've seen him in the yard."

Hagger's eyebrows rose slightly. "And you learned who he was?"

"He seemed important."

Hagger stared at him a long moment, the expression on his face unreadable, then he grunted. "You're more dangerous than I thought."

Across the room, Baron Arent, Daedallen, and Augustus glanced toward both of them and Allan straightened, his burnt clothes crackling. A servant headed toward them at a word from Arent.

"Ah," Hagger muttered, and took one step forward, his demeanor and stance altering from bored to formal with a shift of his shoulders.

The servant halted two paces away. "The Baron requests an audience," he said stiffly.

"Lead the way."

The servant spun, Hagger following a few steps behind, Allan last. Allan's heart quickened as they halted a few steps from the Baron and the others, the Baron's eyes on Hagger. When he turned to look at Allan, Allan sucked in a sharp breath.

And instantly regretted it. The stench of burned and blackened skin, even hours old, slammed into him and he choked on his own breath, suppressing it to nothing more than a faint snort. Swallowing rapidly, he fought the urge to keel over and vomit, like some of the others had done the night before upon seeing the body. The Baron's eyes lanced into him, a muddy brown with hints of gold and green that left him exposed, naked and raw. Allan felt certain that the Baron understood everything in that one look, realized that he'd probably noted Allan and Hagger when he entered, and had dismissed them.

Then the Baron turned toward Terrence. Allan exhaled, and found himself trembling as if he'd been weakened.

"These are the two who interceded last night?" Baron Arent asked. His voice was mild, almost casual.

Terrence nodded. "They were stationed inside the room, among others, to watch over the guests and to make the Dogs' presence known."

"And none of those stationed outside noticed anything remarkable about this man?" He didn't gesture or glance toward the body, but nearly everyone looked down, including Terrence. A few grimaced and turned away immediately.

"No. He had the appropriate credentials, an invitation addressed to a Lord Pickerell of Ovant, with all of the required markings."

"And no one noticed anything else amiss?"

Terrence drew breath to answer, but Allan interrupted. "I did."

Allan flinched when Baron Arent turned to him. He saw Hagger shift slightly forward out of the corner of his eye but didn't dare turn. Both Daedallen and Augustus shifted their attention to him as well. Allan's skin prickled under the black glare of the captain of the Dogs, but it was Augustus who spoke, his voice scathing.

"And you did nothing?"

Daedallen bristled and annoyed anger flashed across the Baron's face.

Allan felt heat flare upward from his neck. "There didn't seem to be a threat—"

"No threat!" Augustus boomed, cutting off his stuttered response. "He somehow managed to get into one of the Baron's parties carrying not only a knife but enough oil to immolate himself! What if he'd had a different purpose? What if he'd managed to bring in something more deadly, something seemingly innocent, something that could have interrupted the sowing of the tower? All he would need to do is upset the balance of the sowing enough to release the ley from its controls and there would have been hundreds, perhaps thousands of deaths. We lost over twenty to sheer stup—"

"Prime Augustus."

The Prime's tirade shut off abruptly at the Baron's words, as if severed with a blade, even though Baron Arent had not shouted. Augustus spun to face him, but stilled at the Baron's raised eyebrow.

"While I applaud your concern over the success of the sowing," the Baron said, the words twisted with anger and irony, "and my general health and well-being, I'd like to ask him a few questions myself."

Augustus struggled with himself a moment, then stepped back. "Of course. You are the Baron after all."

Baron Arent's eyes narrowed and Allan sensed an undercurrent between them that he didn't understand, but then the Baron turned toward him again, the anger slipping from his face. Allan suddenly realized he hadn't been angry with him a few moments before, but with Augustus, and a tension in his shoulders eased. He tried to calm his racing heart and felt the heat in his face and neck recede slightly.

"Now, tell us what you noticed."

Allan swallowed once. "When the three Wielders arrived and stepped through the room, heading toward the tower heights, I noticed this man step forward as they passed, as if he wanted to follow them. And his face was . . . enraged. But he stopped himself. By the time the Wielders had left, he'd collected himself and returned to the party as if nothing had happened."

"Why didn't you report this to Hagger, or to one of the other Dogs?"

It was the first time Daedallen had said anything. His voice rumbled, like the low growl of distant thunder.

"It was just a look. I didn't think it was important."

"Yet according to Hagger's report, you followed him after that."

Allan nodded, shooting a quick glance toward Hagger. He hadn't noticed the older Dog watching him, following his movements. "I wanted to see if he did anything else odd, but he didn't. He merely drank and spoke to the guests. And then the sowing started and—"

"And you were distracted," Baron Arent finished for him. Allan didn't hear any judgment in his voice, but he lowered his head and said nothing.

After a long moment, the Baron said, "It's my understanding that Baron Leethe was in attendance as well. Did you find this odd?"

Allan nodded. "Yes. I wondered why he wasn't at the main party, with you and the other Barons."

"He should have been. Did this man—the priest—did he speak to the Baron at all?"

Allan thought back to the night before, then shook his head. "Not that I saw."

Baron Arent frowned in disappointment and exchanged a look with Daedallen. "Very well." He caught Augustus' eye. "And you're certain that there was no use of the ley involved in any of this? The priest was not attempting to disrupt the sowing?"

Augustus straightened. "There is no indication he used the ley, no."

The Baron glanced down at the body and anger crept into his voice. "Then this was simply a protest, like those on the streets."

"It was more," Daedallen said. "On the streets, they simply talk. This is an escalation. I don't like where the Kormanley's protests are headed. If they are willing to kill themselves for their cause, it is only a small step toward killing others. They may begin targeting Dogs, or Wielders, or even you."

Baron Arent frowned, creases appearing in his forehead. "Have you learned anything from those we've arrested around the city? Did any of them have knowledge of the immolation?"

"None. The priests of the Kormanley do not appear to know many other members of their own group by sight. It appears they meet in secret, using coded markings to call meetings where they wear hoods under cover of darkness, only five members or fewer at one time." Daedallen's voice had grown rougher in annoyance. "It is impossible to determine who else is a member based on the descriptions we are getting from those arrested."

"Have you tried the Hounds?"

Daedallen shook his head. "Not yet. I didn't feel the Hounds would be required. The Kormanley did not seem that dangerous. However, now. . . ." He glanced toward the Baron. "Do you want me to call them out?"

Baron Arent considered a long moment, staring down at the body, Daedallen, Hagger, and the other Dogs close by tense. "No," he said finally. "Calling out the Hounds will draw the attentions of the other Barons. See what the Dogs can find out first. Increase the patrols in the areas where the Kormanley appear to protest most—the Stone District, perhaps Leeds and Green—and continue the interrogations of those we have." He turned abruptly toward Allan. "And give this Dog something more meaningful to do besides watch over guests at parties."

Then he stepped over the charred body at his feet, moving swiftly toward the doors, Augustus hesitating before following. Daedallen stared at Allan a long moment before nodding. "You heard Baron Arent," he said to Terrence. "Assign this Dog's pack to the patrols."

"Very well."

Allan turned toward Hagger as Daedallen departed with Terrence and a few other Dogs at his heels.

The old Dog grunted. "Much more dangerous."

⌁

"Have you heard?"

Dalton halted in the doorway at the demanding question, quelling a burst of irritation. He hadn't even set foot inside the sanctity of the meeting chamber yet and already he was being pummeled with questions? He shot a baleful glance over the five members already inside, letting it fall on Tyrus, the one who'd spoken, last.

"It's why I came," he said, then purposefully knelt and genuflected before the door, drawing his hand across its entrance, leaving a faint trail in the dirt among several others. He muttered a short prayer beneath his breath and tried to center himself before rising and stepping into the room.

Tyrus waved a hand in dismissal and began pacing. "They've taken this too far," he growled. "I knew this . . . this splinter group would be trouble the moment we heard about it. I can't believe we allowed them to continue once we found out they were meeting on their own in secret. We should have forced them to disband—"

"And had them regroup and meet again, with more precautions?" Dalton asked with a raised eyebrow. "Disbanding them would only have made them angrier. At least now we know who they are and what they are up to."

"Do we?" Tyrus rounded on him as Dalton settled into one of the high-backed chairs surrounding the rough-hewn oak table in the center of the chamber. "Did you know what they planned at the Baron's party?" He stalked toward Dalton, his fervor altering as he approached, hand outstretched, his words now edged in horror. "One of them lit himself on fire, Dalton! He immolated himself in protest! The Kormanley is peaceful. We have always been peaceful."

Tyrus leaned forward onto the oak table, as if he'd used up all of his energy to get there, then fell back into the chair next to Dalton. "What have they done?"

Dalton listened to the low murmur that arose from the other members present, heard the strained fear in the tone of their voices, then cleared his throat.

Everyone fell silent. Dalton had been the nominal leader of their small group for at least a decade. He'd been a member twenty-four years, recruited at the age of fourteen. The chamber where they met—more of a cavern, with its rounded earthen walls smoothed by time and its dry scent of earth—felt more like home than his own rooms above ground in the city. It was, literally, his sanctuary, where he sought peace and a stronger connection to the ley. The *natural* ley, not the monstrosity that Prime Wielder Augustus and the Baron had built in the center of Grass.

But the peace he and the others had always found here had been broken in the last decade. It had begun as a mere grumble of discontent within the group, easily ignored, especially when Dalton agreed with the misgivings at their heart. Complaints about the abuse of the ley, about the Baron, and in particular about Augustus. But the grumbling hadn't stopped. In fact, it had escalated, picked up by the younger members, kept active by Dalton and a few of the elders. Until it had reached such a pitch that someone had finally taken action, had taken that discontent to the streets.

That's when Dalton had realized the splinter group needed to be kept separate and secret from those of the Kormanley who were peaceful at heart, who did not condone such active protest. Members like Tyrus. When they'd discovered the group's secret meetings, they'd been outraged, but Dalton had managed to calm them.

He wouldn't be able to calm them after this. What Michael had done at the Baron's party sickened him. When he'd first heard of it, his legs had given out on him. Immolation! He couldn't imagine going to that extreme. The heat, the intensity of the pain . . . it must have been unbearable. No one in the splinter group had known what Michael intended, Dalton had made certain of that before coming here, but he suddenly realized that the splinter group was more dangerous than he'd thought.

Aware that the eyes of the gathered members were still on him, expectant, he shifted forward. "They have not yet stepped over the line—" he paused at Tyrus' snort of disgust, then continued, "—because no one aside from one of our own was seriously hurt."

"I disagree," Tyrus said harshly. "They *have* hurt us. Before they began preaching in the streets, the Baron and his Dogs left us alone. Now, we risk beatings—or worse, an arrest—if we wear the white robes in public, whether or not we are preaching of the natural order. We live in fear."

"They took Eredrus in the Eld plaza yesterday."

Dalton shot a glance toward Priem. "Eredrus? Where did they take him?"

Tyrus answered with a sneer. "The Amber Tower, of course. Where else? With this immolation, the Dogs will be after us with greater force, greater numbers. It will no longer be safe to wear the white robes on the streets at all. This splinter group has harmed us irreparably."

Dalton shifted uneasily. "Perhaps this is an isolated incident. Perhaps the splinter group had no knowledge of it. We didn't hear of it until now, after all."

"Can we take that risk? We need to know what this group intends. We can no longer afford to be left in the dark. They have become too large, too disordered, and too violent. I'm afraid that it won't end here, regardless of how the Baron and his Dogs react."

Dalton sat back and drummed his fingers against the arms of his chair, staring at Tyrus as he contemplated. He saw the determination in his fellow Kormanley's eyes, and the fear. Without looking, he knew that the others wore similar expressions. Tyrus was right, the Dogs would crack down on the Kormanley—peaceful or not. They were all in danger, and no matter how fervently he agreed with the splinter group that more significant action was necessary, he didn't want to put the original Kormanley at risk.

The splinter group needed to be controlled. They needed a leader. And they couldn't go on meeting as they did. They'd have to break away from the original Kormanley completely, go into hiding, work from the shadows. He wasn't certain how that could be done—that it even *could* be done—but he needed to find a way if the splinter group was going to continue. It would have to be split into even smaller groups, no one group knowing the members of the others. They'd have to scatter throughout the city, spread out. But then how would he communicate with them? How would he keep each group in check? He'd need someone in each group to act as his eyes and ears, informing him of what was being discussed, what each group was doing, and allowing him to coordinate the groups without any of them knowing who he was. He wanted to keep random acts of violent protest like Michael's under control, although perhaps violence would be a way to make the Baron pay more attention to their cause. Michael's act—Dalton shuddered again thinking about it—had certainly forced a reaction.

He could see the shape of the Kormanley reforming even now.

"Very well," he said abruptly.

Tyrus frowned in confusion. "Very well what?"

"We have allowed the splinter group to go on without supervision long enough. What happened at the Baron's party last night is a clear sign of this. Someone must become a part of it so that we can better monitor what they are planning, and we must halt any additional violent acts, if possible."

Tyrus swallowed, uncertain now that a decision had been reached. "Who did you have in mind?" he asked weakly.

Dalton smiled. "You."

⌇

"—don't think there's anything seriously wrong with her."

Kara woke to the sound of the strange man's voice, her head throbbing with a headache that pulsed with her heartbeat. Her mouth tasted like ash, dry and sooty. She glanced around the bedroom where she and her parents slept, but it was empty. The voices were coming from the front room, where her father worked on the clocks.

"What about the ley globes? And the other . . . incidents we told you about." Her father's voice was creased with worry and Kara froze, coldness settling into her stomach. What other incidents? Were they still talking about her?

"Has she been tested yet?"

"She's only twelve. They won't test her or the others at the school for another few years."

Someone grunted. "I'd say she's simply manifesting some talents early. Don't worry, it's not unheard of. Sometimes the talent—whatever it may be—simply appears off and on ahead of time, as early as five years before testing. If it continues, bring it to the attention of someone at her school."

Kara heard movement, some more conversation too muffled for her to make out, and then a door closing.

A moment later, her father appeared in the door to the bedroom, his hair wild, his eyes haunted and hollow, bruised with lack of sleep. Kara gasped and tried to rise, but couldn't; her arms felt leaden. She could barely raise her hands off the blanket that covered her, and after a few moments holding them in the air, trembling as if palsied, she let them fall back into place. She stared at them in horror, then, with effort, turned her head toward her father.

"What's wrong with me?" She nearly choked on the words, her throat suddenly thick and tight. Tears burned at the corners of her eyes.

Her father stepped to her side and knelt, placing a hand on her forehead as if checking for a fever before brushing her hair back from her eyes with a tight smile. "There's nothing wrong with you, Kara. The healer was here and he checked everything out. He says that the excitement of the sowing of the tower overwhelmed you and wore you out, that's all."

Kara could hear the doubt in his voice. "I can barely move my arms."

Her father frowned. "Do they hurt?"

She shook her head weakly. "They just feel . . . heavy." She tried to move her legs, but they merely shifted beneath the blanket. She could wiggle her toes and make a fist with her hand, but anything more and her body barely reacted.

What if they never moved again?

Something seized her chest and began to tighten. It suddenly became hard to breathe, her throat constricted, but before she could completely panic, her father leaned over and kissed her forehead. "Hush. Don't try to move. The healer said everything was fine, remember? You're exhausted, that's all. You'll get your strength back. I bet you can even move your arm more now than you could a moment ago, right?" He sat back and motioned for her to try.

Kara frowned and tried to raise her right hand again. It came off the blanket much easier than before, and she could hold it in the air longer, but eventually it began shuddering and she had to lay it back down.

"See?" her father said. "You're already recovering." He squeezed her shoulder with one hand as he stood. "I have some of the stew from last night warming in the pot. It should be well-flavored after a night out on the windowsill in the cold."

He left, moving into the kitchen where she could hear him rummaging around. She waited for him to start humming to himself, but he didn't, so she knew he was still worried about something. She didn't hear her mother, but the light coming in from the direction of the kitchen meant it was just after midday. Her mother would still be at the tower.

She spent the next few minutes concentrating on her arms and legs, lifting them until she couldn't hold them up any longer, moving her hands, her feet, twisting her head around. The initial panic eased, although it still prickled her chest when her limbs collapsed, or her wrist sagged, too tired to hold her hand upright. The weight she'd felt since she'd woken still pressed over her body, as if she'd run and run and run until she couldn't run any farther and had collapsed, drained and empty.

Leaning her head back against her thin feather pillow, she thought about what she'd heard the healer say. She knew about the testing of talents at school, although she hadn't thought about it much since it wasn't supposed to happen for another two years. Everyone was tested, and then they could choose where they wanted to apprentice after that. Except for those that showed some significant talent. They were sent to the University in Confluence to study . . . or to the ley nodes and the Wielders. Cory and Brandt and some of the other boys whispered and snickered and dreamed about being chosen to become a Wielder, play-acting in the school's courtyard as they manipulated the ley for their own purposes, arms waving in wild, dramatic circles. But it was just playacting. Nearly everyone tested showed some trace of talent, but rarely was it strong enough to be selected to attend the University. Fewer still were taken off by the Wielders. And those that were taken by the Wielders never spoke of their training in the use of the ley. So everything that Cory and Brandt and the rest made up in the courtyard was simply . . . imagination. It wasn't real.

She frowned and stared down at her hands, clutched now against her chest. She thought suddenly of Halliel's Park, of the ley globes hovering above the gate brightening and dimming—

But then her father returned, a bowl of steaming stew held in one hand, a glass of water in the other. He dragged a stool close with his foot, and set the bowl and glass on the floor. "Let's get you into a better position," he muttered, helping her to sit up, rearranging the pillows at her back so she could lean against the wall that served as a headboard. He moved the bowl to her lap and handed her a spoon. She managed to raise a few spoonfuls to her mouth before her arm became too weak and he took over for her. The stew spread warmth through her stomach and chest and even though she still felt weak, the last vestiges of her panic subsided.

She'd eaten half the bowl when her father drew back and ruffled her hair. "Feeling better?" When she nodded, he stood. "Good. I need to get to work on this new clock. You stay here and rest. I'll be in the next room."

"Da?"

He turned at the door, bowl of stew cupped in one hand. He didn't look as weary as before. "What, Kara?"

She bit her lower lip, then blurted. "I was at the park, at Halliel's Park. That's why I didn't come straight home from school, why I was at the marketplace. I wanted to see the park."

"I know." He smiled. "And I'm glad you told me. Now you should get some rest, so you can go back to school tomorrow. Besides, your mother should be home shortly and you'll want to let her know you're fine by helping out with dinner, right?"

Kara made a face and scrunched back into the pillow. Her father chuckled, the sound fading as he settled into the outer room, the chair before his desk creaking with his weight. She wondered how he knew she'd been going to the park all this time, and why he hadn't said anything to her about it before.

Then she heard her father humming in the outside room, the sound barely audible, and the tension drained from her body and the weight that made her arms and legs leaden faded and she drifted off to sleep.

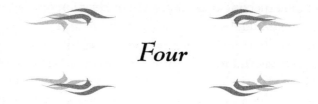

Four

"WHERE ARE YOU HEADED?" Cory asked Kara as soon as he emerged from the iron gate that served as the entrance to the school's courtyard. Their fellow students streamed out around them, screaming, laughing, and shoving each other as they dispersed toward their respective parts of Eld and whatever chores their parents had for them.

"Home," Kara said, and hefted the leather strap holding her schoolbooks onto her shoulder. It had been two weeks since the sowing of the tower, now visible from any of the hillocks in Eld and fast becoming a familiar sight. She finally felt as if she'd regained all of her strength; Cory had had to carry her books for her the first week. "You?"

Cory sighed. "The same. My father wants me to help him with the candles. Ever since the sowing, the local lords and ladies have ordered hundreds of them. The Baron used them during the ceremony somehow and now they all want them." He scowled. "I hate working with tallow."

Kara drew breath to point out that his father expected him to take over the business once he'd been tested, but then Justin caught her eye.

The eight-year-old had finally emerged from the main building into the courtyard, the younger students released later so that older brothers and sisters could meet them if necessary. Head lowered so that his dirty-blond hair covered his face, he plodded across the yard to the gates, books dragging across the cobblestones behind him.

As soon as he reached the gate, he looked up and searched the street. His gaze swept over Kara and Cory with only a flicker of recognition. Then it locked on something farther down the street and his entire body went rigid with tension, his gray eyes widening in fear, hand clenching tight on the strap holding his books.

Kara spun, expecting to see some of the older boys waiting down the street in a small huddle, punching each other in the shoulder and eyeing the students as they left. Her shoulders tensed, her eyes narrowed with rage, but she had to swallow the bitter words that rose in the back of her throat. The bullies weren't there. Some of the other students were still hanging around—a few older ones waiting impatiently for their younger siblings, a group of two or three chatting—and a few adults were going about their daily errands, but no one else.

Kara turned back to Justin, who still stood in the same place, body trembling slightly. She moved to his side. "What is it, Justin? What's wrong?"

Justin jumped at her voice, hand jerking his books closer with a thud. His terrified eyes latched onto hers, but for a long moment he said nothing. Then, in a soft, ragged voice, he said, "That man. He's watching me again."

"What man?" Cory said from behind them, body bristling with anger. "It isn't Brent, is it? I told him to leave you alone."

Justin shook his head. "Not Brent. Him." He pointed, Kara and Cory glancing down the street, then toward each other, Cory frowning.

"I don't see anyone, Justin," Kara said.

Justin's arm lowered. "He's not there anymore." His gaze darted back and forth across the street and he took a step toward Kara as if for protection. "He's waiting for me. He's been here every day for the past week."

"Well, he's gone now, right?"

Kara glared at Cory, who shrugged and mouthed the word, *What?* over Justin's head. "Were you walking home by yourself today? I don't see your mother."

"She's at the lord's manse. Lady Carlsing wanted new curtains." He edged closer still to Kara as he spoke.

Kara heard Cory sigh, but she ignored him. "We can walk with you, can't we, Cory?"

He rolled his eyes, but said, "Of course."

Cory started up a running conversation with her and Justin almost as soon as they left. Justin kept his eyes on the street, face twisted up into a tight frown of worry, but as Cory distracted him, drawing him out with stories from school and rude jokes, the tension that tightened his body relaxed. Kara watched the street as well, catching sight of a group of three Dogs headed toward Stone, another of five Temerite merchants talking rapidly in their own language, but nothing else out of the ordinary. Certainly no strange men watching them or following them. She wondered briefly if Justin had imagined him. He'd always been a little odd, quiet and prone to standing in the shadows of the courtyard while everyone else tussled in the grass off the main cobbles or watched the training in the practice yard. That was why he'd caught the attention of Brent and his group.

But when they reached the steps that led to Justin's flat, and he darted up to the door and glanced hurriedly in both directions before ducking inside, a shudder of unease coursed down her back.

"What do you think that's all about?" Cory asked. "Do you think he's just being . . . well, Justin?"

"I don't know. At school, he seemed terrified."

"And it didn't go away, no matter how awful my jokes were."

She snorted, then glanced up and down the street one last time . . . and suddenly realized where they were.

Halliel's Park was only a few streets away.

Even as she thought it, a different kind of shudder ran through her, from the roots of her hair down into her toes. It centered there, coursing through her feet and into the ground. She could feel the pull of the park again. She'd managed not to think about it since the sowing, had focused on recovering from whatever had drained her strength, but now the pull had returned, stronger than before. She thought about what the healer had said to her father, about the way the ley globes in the park had brightened and dimmed, about the testing at the end of each school year, those of age gathering in the Great Hall with the Master of the School, the teachers, staff, and students, a Prime Wielder, and the Head of the University. The Head of the University usually tested each student first, placing two glass globes, one each, in the palms of the student's hands. Most of the time nothing would happen and everyone present would release their pent-up breaths in a low sigh, accompanied by murmured conversation as the student stepped to the side and was presented to the Prime Wielder. Sometimes, one or both globes would flicker with colored light, usually only a spattering, as if the globes were struggling to catch fire on the inside.

Only once had Kara seen the globes flare with light, then steady into a cool, vibrant blue. That student had been sent to the University the following day.

The test by the Wielder was less dramatic. He or she would place a hand on the student's head, close his or her eyes, wait for a long moment, and then proclaim the student unworthy. Kara had never seen anyone proclaimed worthy during any of the tests she'd attended.

She suddenly wondered what the globes from the University would do if she held them. Or what the Wielder would say after his moment of silence.

"Kara, what's wrong?"

Kara gasped and jerked away when Cory placed his hand on her arm. He gave her a sharp frown. "What's wrong? Is it happening again? Are you getting weak?"

"I'm fine." The words came out too quick, but they were true. She could still feel the pull of the park, her feet tingling against the earth, but she didn't feel the prickling sensation that had coursed through her the night of the sowing. She drew in a deep breath and smiled. "It's all right, Cory, I'm fine. We should head back home."

He eyed her carefully, awkwardly concerned, then nodded. "Let's go. My dad will be furious if we don't get the candles done tonight."

Kara hung back, letting Cory make a path through the people on the street, following in his wake. When he turned onto the street that ran along one side of Halliel's Park, she nearly called out to stop him. But the pull of the park had increased, had tightened in a band across her chest, tight enough it had grown hard to breathe. She could feel the blood pulsing in her throat, in her arms and fingers. Her feet had grown heavy, yet at the same time her body felt light. The sensations increased as they drew near the park's entrance and she glanced toward the ley globes above the ends of the stone arch, catching sight of a gardener— the same man she'd seen before—working within. The globes brightened as she drew near and the gardener's head snapped up to stare at them, then out toward the street. He stood as he searched, moved to the threshold of the park—

And then his gaze fell on Kara.

Kara flinched and ducked her head, realized she'd slowed, that Cory was now a good twenty paces in front of her. She increased her pace to catch up, but a hand fell on her shoulder and a voice said, "Wait."

She knew it was the gardener even before she turned. Not because he'd seen her, or because his voice sounded exactly like she'd imagined it would—rough with age, yet still gentle. She knew it was the gardener because she'd felt him approaching through her feet, his presence like a pressure against her back.

She swallowed against the tightness in her chest. "Yes, sir?"

The gardener stared at her a long moment, glanced back toward the two globes, now slightly dimmed, then back to her. Something flashed through his eyes, something sad, although he smiled and knelt down before her. He didn't release his hold on her shoulder, though.

"You were here the other day, weren't you? Before the sowing?"

She nodded. She could feel something through the man's touch, an energy, streaming out from her, passing through him and into the ground where he knelt. Energy coursed from him into her as well, but it wasn't as strong, its flow sluggish and weak.

The gardener sighed, then squeezed her shoulder in reassurance before struggling to stand. As soon as he released her shoulder, the flow of energy cut off, although she could still feel him, as if some small part of that flow still remained, nearly undetectable.

He nodded toward Cory, who'd halted a few paces distant and was eyeing the gardener suspiciously. "I think you, along with your friend, should take me to your father. We need to speak. Right now."

When Kara opened the door to her family's apartment, her father was working at his desk, the ley globe pulled in close. It brightened as soon as she entered, the gardener trailing behind her. Cory had escaped as soon as they reached his apartment, casting her a worried look as he closed the door.

"Ah, Kara, I'm glad you're home," her father said without turning. "Someone dropped off a Gorrani sandglass." He motioned to where the clock sat to one side, sand falling from one tray to another through a pinched hourglass, the tray beneath slowly lowering as it grew heavier. "I was hoping you'd be able to take a look while I finish the work on this piece."

"Da?" Her voice cracked and she coughed and cleared her throat. "Da, there's someone here."

Metal clattered against metal and her father swore, too softly for her to hear the words. Straightening, he sighed and pushed the ley globe aside, spinning in his chair. "What did you sa—?"

He stilled when he saw the brown robes of the gardener, the weary smile that had started to form freezing, then slipping into a tight frown.

"He stopped me in the street outside Halliel's Park," Kara said, a shiver of worry slicing into her gut. "He said he needed to speak to you."

A long moment of silence stretched, and then the gardener shifted behind Kara, one hand falling onto her shoulder. "It's about your daughter, actually."

Her father nodded. "I see." His gaze dropped from the gardener to her and he attempted a smile of reassurance. "Why don't you go into the kitchen and get us something to drink, Kara? I think there's still some tea left in the pitcher on the sill."

Kara nodded, more than happy to slip out from under the gardener's hand. Even here, when he touched her, she could feel energy passing back and forth between them, although it wasn't as intense as it had been at the park.

She heard the gardener and her father speaking as she found the pitcher, some cups, and loaded them onto a tray.

"I'm simply concerned for your daughter," the gardener was saying as she returned. Neither one of them appeared to notice her. "For her to be manifesting so strongly this early . . . it could be dangerous. Not only for her, but for you and those around her as well."

"What do you mean manifesting?" her father said sharply. Kara had never heard her father speak in such a harsh tone, tinged with fear, and dread shot through her back. Her hands tightened on the edges of the tray.

The gardener snorted. Then his eyes narrowed. "I am a Tender of the stones in Halliel's Park," he said purposefully. "That means—"

"I know what that means! And I know what you are, who you were!"

The gardener straightened, arms crossed over his chest. "Then you know that I speak the truth and that the concern is real."

Her father glared at him. For a long moment, neither relented. Kara set the tray down in a free space on the desk, next to the sandglass, and poured two cups of tea. Her hands shook, but she didn't spill any.

Finally, the stiffness in the gardener's shoulders relaxed. He let a breath out through his nose and shook his head. "You are deluding yourself if you think this can be ignored. You must have seen signs." He glanced toward the ley globe that hung above the desk. "How did you know it was Kara at the door when we arrived? You didn't turn."

"I assumed—"

The gardener's eyes narrowed and her father halted, mouth open, then bowed his head.

"I knew because the globe brightened."

The gardener nodded. "And have you seen other manifestations like that?"

Grudgingly, as if dredging the admission up from long buried depths, her father said, "Yes." He glanced toward her and she stepped forward and handed him the cup of tea she held. He pulled her in closer, one arm holding her protectively, and somehow that gave his voice more strength. "We—my wife and I—have seen her repair the globe when it flickers. I don't even think Kara's aware she does it. She just . . . reaches up and touches it and it steadies. When customers bring in ley clocks, they seem to burn brighter, even before I repair them." He hesitated, then added, "And then there's what happened during the sowing."

This caught the gardener's attention. "Something happened during the sowing?"

"She fainted. The healer said that the excitement of the sowing overwhelmed her, and my wife and I want to believe him . . . but we think it was something else."

The gardener's gaze dropped to Kara and he studied her for a long moment. Her father's arm tightened where it draped over her shoulder, making her fidget. Then the gardener knelt, so that his eyes were level with Kara's.

"Tell me what happened, Kara. What did you feel during the sowing?"

Kara shifted uncomfortably beneath his gaze. "I don't know. My body tingled, and I could feel the ground, as if something was drawing something from inside me out through my feet and into the ground, sort of like what it feels like when you touch me."

The gardener's eyebrows rose. "You can feel the energy when I touch you? Flowing through me to you?"

"Yes. But more of it's flowing from me to you."

The gardener grunted, thought for a moment, then asked, "What else happened at the sowing? There must have been something else, or your father wouldn't have felt the need to call a healer."

"The tingling got worse. I couldn't move. And then when it ended, when the tower was finished, the tingling stopped, but I felt weak. I couldn't stand up anymore."

"She fainted," her father said roughly. "She collapsed in my arms."

The gardener nodded, as if he understood. He patted her shoulder, then straightened. "I'm certain it was frightening, for both of you. But I'm not surprised that it happened. Not if what I suspect is true. I'm certain the sowing affected many others in the city."

"What do you mean?" her father said.

"You already know, or suspect." He glanced toward Kara. "And I'm certain that it's occurred to Kara as well. But there is a way to be certain, one that won't involve anyone else, in case our suspicions are unfounded."

"How?"

The gardener hesitated, contemplating Kara, then shook his head. "I don't want anything I say to influence the outcome. She's probably heard too much already. But if you want to know for certain, bring her to Halliel's Park tomorrow, after school. I'll be waiting."

A shiver ran down through Kara's back, but she couldn't keep the smile from her face.

As Kara and her father approached the gates of Halliel's Park, she felt again the energy through her feet, realized she could feel all of the surrounding people as they moved down the crowded street. But her attention was focused on the gate, on the stone of the archway and the ley globes above it.

She searched the entrance avidly and was disappointed to see that the gardener wasn't there waiting for them.

Her father paused at the entrance to the park, staring up at the globes above. He appeared nervous. Kara knew that he and her mother had talked long into the night, their voices hushed but hard. The initial argument had died down into silence, broken only by the clatter of dishes being washed from the kitchen, Kara trying to fall asleep in her bed. Then she'd heard her father's chair scrape across the floor, and the clattering had stopped.

Then, clearly, as if her mother had been facing the door, Kara heard her say fiercely, "It's too early. She's too young. We should have another few years with her at least!"

Her father murmured something in return, and then her mother again, her voice muffled this time, as if her head were pressed against a shoulder, but still too loud and choked with tears. "I don't want her to leave."

The pain in her mother's voice had dampened Kara's excitement and she'd rolled away, back to the door, drawing herself up into a ball. She thought about those few students at the school who had been tested and who had sparked light in the two clear globes the Head of the University placed in their hands. They'd gone to the University at the confluence of the two rivers the following day. None of them had returned to the school, and they were rarely seen in the district after that. She'd never thought about them much after they left, never thought about what happened to the students after the testing if either the Head of the University or the Prime Wielder singled them out. Those chosen had to study at the University or under the hands of the Wielders, but for some reason she'd never realized that meant they had to leave their home and their family behind, that they had to leave Eld. Once their studies were finished, they were posted throughout the city—the new Wielders focused on keeping the ley system running, those from the University helping with everything else.

Curled up in her bed, she'd stared at the darkness of the wall closest to her and thought about leaving her apartment, her mother and father, Cory, Justin, and all of the rest of her friends, and suddenly the thought of Halliel's Park wasn't as thrilling.

It had taken her a long time to get to sleep.

But the excitement had returned the following morning, and grown the closer she'd gotten to the stone arch and the pathways that lay beyond. Now, with the energies of the park coursing through her, her father glanced down at her and with a sad smile said, "Shall we find the gardener?"

They entered the park, something Kara had never dared to do on her own, even though the gates to the park were open to the public. She had rarely seen anyone enter other than the brown-robed gardeners, and had only heard people refer to the park when giving directions or as a reference for something else in the city. She suddenly realized how strange that was, as if the park didn't exist, even though everyone knew it was there.

Stepping onto the crushed stone path inside the entrance, Kara's breath quickened. But then her father's hand touched her shoulder in reassurance and she relaxed and began looking around.

Pathways meandered through trees and shrubs and piles of stone with no obvious pattern, curving out of sight ahead, or dipping down as the ground undulated. They moved deeper into the trees, the walls that surrounded the park and the sounds of the people on the street falling away behind them. Around a sharp curve, they found a secluded area beneath a huge willow with a bench made out of flat, stacked stones. Farther along, the path split into three sections, weaving through each other like a maze, surrounded by waist-high lilacs, their scent heavy on the air. Somewhere close they could hear the sounds of a stream, water gurgling over stone. They passed beneath a canopy of intertwined branches, leaves rustling in a breeze, and then the trees opened up and fell away.

Before them, the path wound down between huge stones, the boulders angular, edges sharp, completely unlike the river stone found throughout most of the Eld District. They paused, Kara running her hand down the striations of the nearest stone, the dusky browns and reds stacked upon each other in layers. Energy flowed through her into the stone and back again and she felt her fingers tingling, her skin prickling beneath the touch.

Ahead, the gardener appeared around a turn in the path and smiled. "I see you decided to come."

"I thought you'd be waiting for us at the entrance," Kara said.

He laughed. "I wanted to see where you'd head if you were left unattended. Not everyone finds the stone garden." He shared a meaningful look with Kara's father, then turned his attention back to her. She suddenly realized that her father had let her lead them through the park, that he'd simply been following her. "Follow me. I want you to see something."

She moved forward, the stones rising up above her head, the spaces between the rock cooler, smelling of earth and dust. Her father trailed behind. The gardener chose paths seemingly at random, although Kara realized she could sense something ahead, a strengthening of the energy, and her pulse began beating faster.

They stepped into a grotto, the closeness of the stone retreating as it opened up into a wide, roofless chamber. Water poured down from the lip of the recess in a small waterfall, pooling below before disappearing through a crevice in the stone wall. Moss covered the rock near the stream, glistening with moisture. In the center of the grotto, six stone plinths rose in a rough circle, none of them the same height, a few canted to one side. Another ring of mismatched stones encircled these, waist-high. The gardener moved toward the stones at first, then veered off to one side, closer to the waterfall, and sat down on a ridge of stone that rose from the floor to form a natural bench. The ground was littered with rocks of various sizes and colors, scattered haphazardly, some the size of Kara's fist, most smaller. Unlike the surrounding rock of the grotto and the plinths, these were river stones, smoothed and rounded.

The gardener motioned them toward seats to one side and Kara sat down beside her father. The moment she touched the stone beneath her, she felt something was wrong. She frowned, but the gardener didn't seem to notice.

"This is the heart of the park," the gardener said, nodding toward the plinths and the surrounding walls. "This grotto was discovered before Erenthrall was even a village, before anything had even been built near the confluence of the two rivers. It is believed that the local population realized the power that resided here, even if they had not yet learned to harness it as we do, and so built such stone monoliths to mark its location. There are such stellae scattered throughout the Baronies, the Demesnes, the Temerite lands, and even as far south as the Gorrani Flats and the Archipelago."

Kara found herself only half listening as she stared down at the smoothed stone beneath their feet and the scattering of rocks. The energy she'd felt outside the park flowed beneath her, beneath the stone, as if there were a large lake far beneath the surface, rivers of power sifting back and forth below, barely perceptible to her. Here on the surface, she could feel its pulse, feel the eddies as they shifted. But something had disturbed the flow.

She curled her toes up inside her shoes, then spread them out, trying to sense what was wrong, even as she heard her father ask, "Are the other stone markers in the other Baronial cities? Where the Nexi are?"

The gardener snorted in disgust. "No. The Nexi that are in the Baronial cities like Erenthrall have nothing to do with the natural structure of the ley. That network of ley—the network controlled by the Prime Wielders and Baron Arent Pallentor—is political, the Nexi created at the whim of the Primes. The Barons pay for their access to the ley and for the Nexi in their cities. Even then, those Nexi are run and maintained by Wielders who are trained here in Erenthrall and are loyal only to Baron Arent. No, that is an artificial network. This set of stones, and those like it spread throughout the continent, are markers for the natural ley system."

"The one the Kormanley wants us to revert to?"

Kara looked up at the mention of the Kormanley, saw the gardener looking at her father oddly, concern flashing across his face.

"Yes," he said as he studied her father. "That is what the Kormanley preach. A return to what is natural."

Her father nodded and the gardener relaxed, his gaze shifting toward her.

"What's wrong, little one?"

She started, grimacing as her father turned toward her sharply. "I don't know. There's something wrong with the stones. With that stone, I think." She pointed toward a white stone with a streak of red running through it. "But I can't tell what."

The gardener's attention was fixed on her completely now, as well as her father's.

"Why can't you tell what's wrong?"

She frowned. "I can't feel it through my feet."

The gardener chuckled, then leaned forward, eyebrows raised. "Then take off your shoes," he said softly, and grinned.

Kara glanced toward her father, who nodded permission. Without hesitation, she kicked off the soft leather and planted her feet directly onto the stone.

And gasped. Energy shot through her legs and into her gut, spiking a moment before settling down into a steady stream. What had felt like a single current through the stone now split into separate eddies, flowing in all directions, although still interconnected, still part of the same whole. Goose bumps broke out on her skin and she shuddered, her heart adjusting to the flow, even as the grotto came into sharper focus. Scents amplified, stone and dust and the damp, dark taste of the moss by the stream. Pollen from the trees outside exploded across her senses, along with the heat radiating up from the rock all around, heat it had absorbed during the day from the sun. With the sudden awareness of the heat, she realized the eddies and flows she felt in the stone were in the air as well, that she could sense the air, like cloth, all around her, that everything was connected—stone, stream, air, and the lake of ley far beneath her, with an upwelling there, at the center of the stone stellae. Except that a deeper upwelling had been siphoned off, diverted and centered farther away, north of here. She frowned as she tried to pinpoint it exactly, but couldn't. The energy outside of the grotto was too blurred, too vast for her to try to take in and understand.

"Can you tell me what's wrong now?" the gardener asked, and somehow the question sounded more formal, more weighted. He sounded like one of her teachers at school.

She almost told him about the energy that was being diverted away from the circle of stones—so much more energy than coursed through the stone around her now, so much more than what had once passed through here—but then she realized he meant the red-streaked stone she'd pointed out earlier.

She pulled her attention away from all of the new sensations and focused on the scattered stones at her feet, focused on the currents that she couldn't really see pulsing through the stone and air and the rocks before her.

"It's out of place," she said. "It doesn't belong there."

The gardener didn't move, didn't react at all. "And where does it belong?" When she turned to look at him, he smiled. "It's all right. You can move them around. You won't harm anything. Not here."

She slid off of the stone ridge and picked up the red-streaked stone. The flows around her changed instantly, shifting before her. She stood a moment, considering, feeling the weight of the stone in her hands, heavier than she'd expected, her fingers brushing its grit and roughness. Then she stepped to one side and set the stone down in a new location.

But even as she did so, the flows changed yet again, settling into new streams, ones that were decidedly worse than before. But she knew the red-streaked stone belonged there. She felt it, felt the eddies coursing through it.

The other stones were wrong as well.

She began moving them all, picking them up, setting them down in new locations, rearranging them. A few times, with a new arrangement, she'd step back and shake her head, then move in again. Some stones had to be stacked one atop the other, or next to each other, balanced precariously, although as soon as they were set properly she could feel the energy flowing through them and knew that they were right. Others were set to one side, solitary. Color did not matter, nor texture—or if it did, then the meaning was too complex or too subtle for her to see.

Finally, all of the stones were in place except one. The size of her fist, blue-black with swirls of white in it, she held it a long moment, contemplating the pattern before her, then turned to the gardener.

"This one doesn't belong here," she said.

The gardener raised his eyebrows in surprise. "It doesn't belong in the grotto at all?"

She bit her lower lip at his reaction, glanced down at the pattern again, then back at him. "No."

He grunted, then stood slowly and took the stone from her, gazing at it in consternation, then at the layout of stone before them. Her father said nothing, although his expression was pinched with worry and resignation.

Kara fidgeted as the silence stretched. For a brief moment, she thought she felt something else on the eddies surrounding her, another presence, but the impression was fleeting.

Finally, the gardener nodded. "I believe you are correct." He tucked the stone into one pocket and glanced toward her father. "I think the outcome of the test is obvious."

Her father stood slowly and nodded. "Yes."

"You are not surprised."

"No. As you said before, we knew. We simply . . . didn't want to admit it. She's too young." Her father caught her gaze, gave her a strained smile.

"She's young, yes, but not too young. The talent is appearing earlier and earlier as the Baron continues expanding the ley network, as it continues to grow. And with the sowing of the tower, he's increased the potential in Erenthrall itself greatly. I'm not surprised she was overwhelmed by the surge created in its sowing."

Kara's heart shuddered. Something had changed as they spoke, something had shifted, like the lines of energy had shifted as she moved the stones. A distance had opened up between her and her father, a distance she felt even when he had smiled.

"What do we need to do?"

The gardener drew in a deep breath as he straightened, brow creased in thought. "Nothing for now. She should continue to go to school as usual. I'll inform my fellow Wielders."

Kara started in surprise, glanced at the gardener's brown robes in consternation. The Wielders wore dark purple jackets, not robes. And the Prime Wielders—like the ones that came to the school for the testing—wore cloaks.

The gardener—the Wielder—studied her, then said to her father, although his eyes stayed on her, "I believe she has . . . great potential. Perhaps she will even become a Prime. She sensed that the stone did not belong, something I had not yet discovered in my own ministrations of the grotto." He touched the pocket where he'd secreted the stone, and Kara suddenly remembered seeing him at the entrance to the gardens, doing what she had done here in the grotto—adjusting stones. "I have not been a part of the politics of the Wielders for a long time, so I cannot say what her role will be, not for certain. But I will inform the appropriate people."

"Very well."

As if hearing the resignation in her father's voice, the Wielder tore his attention away from her, smiled, and grasped his shoulder. "You will have some time with her yet," he said softly. "And there will be other times afterward. Enjoy them."

Her father nodded, although he did not seem convinced.

The gardener—the Wielder—turned toward her, then knelt, meeting her gaze squarely. "And you, little one . . . you should not be afraid. You will have to leave your father, yes. Your mother and your friends as well. But you will find so much more. You are just beginning to discover the world."

He smiled and stood, but his words hadn't settled the trembling panic in her chest or the faint nausea in her stomach. She didn't like the creases between her father's eyes, the tension around his mouth.

And she didn't want to leave Cory and Justin or any of the others behind.

Ischua watched Kara and her father as they left Halliel's Park, his reassuring smile slipping into a frown as soon as they passed beyond sight. Reaching into his pocket, he withdrew the stone Kara had said didn't belong in the grotto, rubbing his thumb over its blue-black surface.

"You shouldn't have known this didn't belong," he muttered to himself. "*I* didn't know it didn't belong."

He looked up, in the direction the two had taken out of the grotto, then tucked the stone back in his pocket and headed out of the grotto and through the park, moving toward the entrance and the city beyond. As he did, he scanned the area for signs of the other Tenders of the garden, men and women who had once been Wielders but were now retired, content to work with the lesser, natural node here in the park rather than the intricate and convoluted ley lines and nodes that had been created throughout Erenthrall. He saw no one near the grotto, and only a distant figure—Terrana, perhaps—once he neared the entrance. He hesitated, watching her hunched figure as she pruned one of the hedges, but he didn't think she'd noticed his visitors.

He entered the flow of traffic on the street, weaving swiftly through the stream of people, carts, and horses toward the marketplace. He skirted its edges, delving deeper into the shops and storefronts that lined the narrower streets to the east. Here the buildings were built of river-stone on the first floor, the second and third stories of wood, part of the oldest section of the city. He made for a small door tucked between two larger shops. He glanced down the street in both directions before entering and descending the stairs into a wide basement beneath both buildings to either side. The noise began as soon as he opened the door and reached a wincing pitch by the time he entered the main room. The acrid scent of ink hit like a stone to the face, even though Ischua had been expecting it. Nose wrinkled, one hand covering his mouth, he tried to take shallow breaths as he searched through the cluttered basement for Dalton. The leader of the Kormanley was near the back, working the printing press making such a profound racket. Ischua wended his way through stacks of newsprint, tied and ready to be distributed by Dalton's crew of newsboys to the streets above, past reams of yellowish paper smelling faintly of acid and numerous desks and tables full of racks and cubbyholes with the small lettered printers' blocks in each. Dalton was hunched over one rack, slotting in tiles for the newest article with surprising speed, mumbling to himself as he scanned the scrawl of the writer's notes. He never looked up from the page, his hands finding the correct letters and fitting them into place out of habit.

Ischua shifted into Dalton's line of sight slowly, but the Kormanley leader still jerked upright in surprise, hand reaching for something beneath the desk before he registered who had arrived. His eyebrows rose—Ischua rarely saw Dalton outside of the Kormanley's usual cavernous meeting room—but he shut down the printing press so they could talk. It died with a moan and clatter. Ischua felt its connection to the ley falter, a tension against his skin lessening.

"Ischua, what brings you to my shop?" Dalton asked, wiping his hands on a cloth as he approached. His fingers were stained heavily with black ink, but Ischua didn't hesitate to shake his hand.

"Someone visited Halliel's Park today, a young girl. She's been coming to the park recently, drawn to the node there, I'd guess, and I had her father bring her into the grotto."

Dalton's eyes had narrowed. "To test her? She's manifesting early?"

"Yes."

"How did she do?"

Ischua pulled the stone from his pocket and set it on Dalton's work desk. "She aligned all of the stones perfectly, and told me that this stone doesn't belong in the grotto at all. I've been trying to place this stone correctly for four months."

"So she's powerful?"

"Definitely Prime level. Although she's only twelve. It's possible the manifestations are spiking and she'll level out below Prime, but I doubt it."

Dalton picked up the stone and massaged it that same way Ischua had inside the grotto. "Did anyone see you test her?"

"No. None of the other Tenders were present."

He met Ischua's gaze. "Then you don't have to report this to the Primes."

"I don't think so. Her parents have noticed her talent, but I don't think the school is yet aware of it. They'll find out shortly, though. I don't think she'll be able to keep it controlled on her own long enough to last until the testing at fourteen. Someone in authority will notice before then."

"You should be the one to find her and take her to the Primes for the official testing. And we'll have to keep watch once she's in the Wielders' hands. If she can be made sympathetic to our cause, perhaps she can provide us with information about what the Wielders are up to."

He'd gripped the stone in a tight fist as he spoke, but now unclenched his fingers and, after a contemplative pause, handed it back to Ischua.

He gripped Ischua's shoulder and added, "Keep an eye on her, Ischua. Let me know when she's ready to be approached by the Kormanley, and when the Wielders become interested in her."

Tyrus nearly cried out when Calven, his initial contact with the splinter group in the Kormanley, thrust the burlap sack over his head, cutting off his sight. He only stopped himself by biting down on the inside of his mouth hard enough to draw blood. As its coppery taste tainted his mouth and the itchy scent of the impromptu hood assaulted his nostrils, he heard a door open behind him and the tread of at least two pairs of feet enter. A hand fell on his shoulder and squeezed hard.

"Are you certain of this, Calven?" The voice rumbled, low and deep. The hand on his shoulder felt huge. "We know he's in tight with Dalton and the others who lack true faith."

Tyrus suppressed the urge to shudder and straightened in indignation. "I have faith," he protested.

Calven shifted closer, Tyrus straining to pick up any other sounds. His eyes had adjusted and he could see faint light through the weave of the sack. "You heard him. But we'll be cautious just the same." His voice shifted toward Tyrus. "We'll take you to this meeting, but you'll have to keep the hood on while we travel."

The man standing over him leaned down and muttered in his ear, "Don't try anything funny."

Tyrus cringed.

Then he was hauled to his feet, two of them leading him out of the room down what sounded like corridors, turning left, then right, then right again before a door creaked open and a gust of chill night air puffed through the hood. Before he could enjoy it—he was already sweating with apprehension, his own breath heating the air inside his hood—he was tossed into the back of what he assumed was a wagon. Straw crackled beneath him as he shifted and he heard a rumbling chuckle. The wagon lurched into motion with a quiet, "Tch!" The clop of horse hooves blended into the rattle of the cart as it jounced over cobbles.

Tyrus bit back a curse and rolled onto his back, not trusting himself to sit upright. He tried to control his breathing, the hood already stifling. Fear sweat broke out across his shoulders and back. He'd nearly had a heart attack during those first tentative, blundering conversations with Calven, the man's eyes narrowing when Tyrus had finally tired of the obscure word play and simply asked about the splinter group. The few moments of careful silence that followed had felt like an eternity. But then Calven had glanced around the bustling market stalls near his own booth and said, "Not here."

They'd met a couple of times after that in out-of-the-way inns and once in a park, Calven mostly quiet as Tyrus attempted to convince him of his conviction that the Kormanley needed to do more, that he was tired of Dalton's lack of action. This last time, Calven had asked a few pointed questions, then grunted and told him to meet him at the tavern tonight. He'd led Tyrus into the back room the moment he arrived and produced the burlap sack. Tyrus hadn't even seen who else was in the tavern, had no idea who the other men were who accompanied them.

The horse's tread altered, the cart rumbling over wood for a long stretch—Tyrus thought it might be a bridge—and then back onto stone, although the cobbles were smoother here. His teeth didn't feel like they were going to rattle from their sockets anymore.

The cart halted suddenly, rocking Tyrus forward. He heard muffled conversation, a bark of laughter—

And then someone grabbed his legs and hauled him out of the cart as if he were a sack of grain. His legs flailed over empty space and for a heartbeat he thought he would tumble out into the street, but someone else caught and steadied him.

"You don't have to be so rough." A voice he didn't recognize. A woman's voice. Somehow, this shocked Tyrus more than anything else that had happened so far.

The meat-handed man growled, "I don't trust him."

"Calven does, at least enough to bring him here."

A grunt and then the meat-handed man grabbed his upper arm and hauled him forward. He stumbled but caught himself and was led away. The fresh air filtering through the hood dropped away, replaced by the faint yet pungent scent of pickling brine. The man leading him said curtly, "Steps up." He tripped on the first one. They passed into a building—the sounds of their footfalls became hollow and the fresh air filtering through the hood dropped away. A door creaked open. "Stairs down." Tyrus' foot caught empty space and he pitched forward, the man wrenching his arm painfully to keep him upright.

By the time they reached the bottom of the steps, earthy scents replacing the brine, Tyrus was gasping, sweat slicking his face from the anxiety. He thought they passed through another door and then he was shoved downward with a sharp, "Sit."

He plopped down onto a wooden stool and tried to calm himself. The scent of smoke and oil from what must be numerous lanterns cut through the burlap now. Feet shuffled, more than just Calven and the two others, but then everyone quieted and all Tyrus could hear was his own strained breathing. This lasted long enough that Tyrus jumped when a new voice spoke.

"We have a potential new member here tonight. Are you certain of his faith, Calven?"

"He believes."

"Of course he does, he is part of the Kormanley already, those who are too weak to act, too afraid to take risks. Can we trust him?"

"I believe so. He was too clumsy and inept when he approached me to be a tool of the Dogs."

Beneath the burlap hood, Tyrus scowled and wondered bitterly if that was why Dalton had chosen him for this task: no one would believe he could be anything but sincere.

"Very well. Remove the sack."

The burlap hood was jerked off his head and he blinked in the sudden brightness of the lanterns. Six others stood around him in a loose circle, but he couldn't identify any of them. Each wore the white robes that had long been used by the Kormanley—the true Kormanley—but heavy cowls had been added and all six had pulled them up over their heads, obscuring their faces in the shadows beneath. The room was small, obviously a basement, shelves and tables to one side beneath some type of banner, papers littering every surface. A closed door interrupted the mudbrick of the walls behind him.

Tyrus spit the taste of the burlap off to the side and glared at the cowled figures. "You get to see me, but I don't get to see you?"

One of the figures snorted—Tyrus thought it was his meat-handed guard—but someone else, the leader apparently, answered. "You aren't part of our group yet." Then he turned to the others. "How are we progressing on our next operation? Has our new benefactor come through as promised?"

"He has. The supplies were delivered and have already been dispersed."

"Where are we on our own delivery? How close are we going to be able to get?"

The woman sighed. "Not as close as we'd like. I've bribed the city watch, so we'll be able to get the wagons into the park, but we can't get any closer than that. The Wielders and the Dogs are keeping too close a watch on the staging area itself."

"We still have some time. And there will be Dogs in the park, not just city guard. We need a cover for the wagons."

"That's one of the reasons I brought him," Calven said, and motioned toward Tyrus.

Tyrus flinched. "What do you mean? What are you talking about?"

Calven ignored him, turning toward the leader instead. "He works for Erenthrall, issuing permits for business ventures ... including vending permits for the parks."

All of those present turned toward Tyrus. The leader stepped forward, until he was directly before him. The lantern light fell in such a way that Tyrus could see the edge of his jaw and a neatly trimmed goatee.

"You want to be part of the Kormanley? You want to force the Baron to release the ley?"

Tyrus nodded and stuttered, "Y-yes." He didn't like the hint of danger in the man's suddenly soft voice.

"Then we need six permits to sell wares in the park."

Five

"WHAT DO YOU MEAN you'll be leaving?" Cory said.

Kara squirmed beneath Cory's gaze and the flatness of his voice.

It had been three weeks since she'd been to Halliel's Park and rearranged the stones with the gardener, Ischua, and her father watching. Since then, the gap that she'd felt in the grotto between herself and her father had expanded, making any time she spent at home strained. Her mother had reacted the same way, withdrawing somehow, as if distancing herself from Kara even as her parents drew closer together. It was as if she had become one of her father's clocks, one of the rare and expensive ones he'd been asked to work on, both of them nervous around her, for fear that something they did would cause her to break. Both of them tried to pretend nothing had changed, that nothing had happened, but the tension made staying home awkward. So she found any excuse to leave. She'd spent more and more time with Cory, when he wasn't helping his father with the candlemaking; when he was, she found herself returning again and again to the park to speak with Ischua.

She could smell the tallow on Cory even now, the scent much sharper than before the sowing. Everything around her felt sharper. She could feel the energies flowing beneath her and around her, although this far away from the grotto the sensations were muted, the eddies like a faint breeze brushing against her skin. They strengthened or lessened depending on where she was in the city. They were strongest near the Eld's main ley node, the short tower that connected the ley network in Eld with all of the other nodes in the districts and with the Nexus beneath the Amber Tower. According to Ischua, the nodes controlled the entire network in Eld—the flows of ley that regulated the barges and the transportation system, all of the heat and light that relied on the ley, the few ley cars in the area—everything related to the ley, including the ley clocks her father occasionally worked on. Kara had gone to the node and stared up at the stubby tower from around the corner of a nearby building, but there wasn't much to see. Maybe four stories high, it was round, built of dark gray stone with few windows, the top crenellated like the old walls of the University down in Confluence. She hadn't seen anyone on its heights, and she hadn't seen how it could control the ley throughout the district. She hadn't seen any of the ley at all. As far as she could tell, none of the ley lines that were interlaced throughout the city connected to the building.

Yet, when she was that close, she could feel the ley in the stone and in the air around her.

Now, to cover her sudden nervousness at Cory's reaction, she reached down and picked up the small ball and scanned the scattering of metal thistles that lay between them. They, along with Justin, were in a small square paved in wide flat flagstone that was perfect for a game of Thistle Snatch, since it was far enough removed from most of the markets that the traffic through the area left them mostly undisturbed. Cory and Kara had found the square three years before, after they'd first met and had begun exploring the surrounding area, once their parents were willing to let them roam alone. Kara liked the architecture of the red stone buildings that enclosed it, and the tall stone obelisk that rose from its center, benches on its four sides and urns with scraggly bushes at its corners.

Head still bowed as if contemplating the thistles, she glanced at Cory. He was glaring at her, mouth set, back against the nearest bench, exactly the reaction she'd been afraid of, the reason she hadn't said anything to Cory about Ischua or the park since it had happened.

She could feel Cory shifting away, just like her parents, and it made her sick to her stomach.

"Never mind," she said tightly. "Forget I said anything. It's my turn. How many thistles do I need to catch this time?"

She bounced the rubber ball, but Cory snatched it out of the air. "What do you mean you'll be leaving?"

Kara winced at the anger in his voice. She swallowed, something hard lodged in her throat. "The Wielders are going to come and take me away at some point."

Confusion crossed through Cory's eyes. "The Wielders? But why? You haven't been tested. You won't be tested for two years."

She shifted uncomfortably, caught Justin watching her out of the corner of her eye, his eyes wide. "I . . . I was tested. Sort of." She told them what Ischua had said to her father after Cory had left, about the trip to Halliel's Park and the grotto, about the fact that the gardeners were really Tenders, retired Wielders sent to the park to tend to the stones and the original ley system. Then she told them of the energy she felt, how she'd known where the stones were supposed to be through her feet, how she could feel it in the air and the stone and the earth deep down beneath her. Excitement crept into her voice, overwhelming her fear of how Cory and Justin might react, and when she was finished she found herself slightly flushed and breathless.

Until she saw Cory's face and then she couldn't breathe at all.

"But you can't leave." The anger she'd heard in his voice before had settled into an intense fury. "We were supposed to be . . . to be friends. You, me, and Justin! We were supposed to hang together, protect each other from the other kids, watch out for each other. How are you going to do that if you're gone?"

Kara tried to say something, but no words came. Cory's fury was shocking, but the fear that had crept into his voice as he shouted at her only confused her, along with the sudden redness of his eyes as tears began to fall down his face.

Justin fidgeted uncomfortably on his bench as the awkward moment spread, Cory and Kara staring at each other. Cory coughed up phlegm, nearly choked on it, and scrubbed his arm across his eyes, glaring at Justin defiantly for no reason at all before ducking his head as if embarrassed.

Still searching for something to say, Kara leaned forward and took the rubber ball from the limp hand resting in his lap. She held it a long moment, not willing to look up into Cory's face, uncertain what she was supposed to do or how she was supposed to feel. She'd seen something in Cory's eyes that she didn't understand, but it still sent uneasy shudders through her chest, hot and fluid, but not unpleasant.

And then Justin said, "Five thistles."

Bewildered, Kara turned toward him. "What?"

Justin shrugged awkwardly, watching her, pointedly not looking at Cory, and nodded toward the flagstone between them. "It's your turn. Five thistles."

Cory shifted beside her, the anger creeping back into his eyes, but before he or Kara could react a group of Dogs burst into the square.

All three of them gaped as the Dogs spread out, moving quietly along two sides of the square, most with swords drawn, heading toward one of the buildings opposite. The two in front halted at the corner, then motioned sharply to the remaining eight men. The men and women who'd been caught in the square on their arrival watched silently a single moment, then turned and left as quickly as possible, heads ducked and shoulders hunched, but the Dogs didn't pay attention to them. They remained focused on the building, on the door two down from the right.

When the first two Dogs hit the short steps that led up to the door, Kara turned to Cory and Justin, their eyes wide, bodies still, as if afraid any movement would draw the Dogs' attention. Kara's heart thudded in her chest, but she reached down and scooped up the scattered metal thistles and began stuffing them in her pockets. "We have to get out of here," she whispered fiercely. All of the tension from her announcement, all of the confusion over the emotions she'd seen in Cory's eyes and the heated ache in her own chest, had vanished. All she could see was the image of the Kormanley priest in the market square on the day of the sowing and the blood splattered across his white shirt as they dragged his limp body out of sight.

Cory nodded mutely. Justin slid off of the bench and huddled down next to them, helping Kara snatch up the last of the thistles. They watched as the rest of the Dogs closed in on the doorway, the two at the corner moving forward when one of them reared back and kicked the door in with a grunt and splinter of wood.

"Now!" Cory said.

As the Dogs began streaming into the building, Kara, Cory, and Justin dashed from the base of the obelisk across the square in the opposite direction. Kara's blood sang in her veins, her breath coming in harsh exhalations, burning in her chest as they ran. Cory and Justin reached the far corner ahead of her and charged beyond, but she skidded to a halt behind its protection, risked a glance back.

One of the two Dogs who had hung back had turned to watch their retreat, his face set in a deep frown. She was surprised at how young he appeared, although there was a hardness about his eyes.

His gaze caught hers and held for a long moment. Kara shuddered.

Then he turned back to the building, his fellow Dogs already inside.

Kara heard a crash, followed by a woman's scream and a man's enraged bellow. Then Cory grabbed her arm from behind and pulled her away from the corner and back toward their homes.

Allan watched as the team of Dogs charged the front door, bursting through into the interior with a splintering of wood and harsh roars as the lead, Range, ordered the others to fan out. More crashes followed, glass breaking, shifting from the front rooms into the back and up to the second story. Allan followed the movements of the men with his eyes, even though he couldn't see anything. He could picture it in his mind, though. He'd led three such raids over the past week, the Dogs stepping up their hunt for the Kormanley priests and their followers as the Wielders—in particular Prime Wielder Augustus—prepared for the upcoming unveiling. The sowing of the tower had only been the first step, according to the Wielders. The real event wouldn't happen for another two weeks.

And Baron Arent wanted nothing to go wrong. The attack and self-immolation in the tower during the sowing had sent ripples through the aristocracy and the Baron had taken his rage out on the Dogs.

Hagger nudged his arm. "Three kids just bolted toward a side street. Should I send men after them?"

Allan turned, caught sight of the three as two of them made the corner. The third, a young girl with light brown hair and a narrow face, spun back to watch, her eyes terrified. He held her gaze, then turned back to the house. He knew the question was a test. Hagger was the leader of this squad; the decision would be his, not Allan's. But he answered. "No. They're not worth the effort."

Inside, something large and solid crashed to a floor, followed by a woman's vitriolic cursing and a man's animalistic roar of rage.

"That's our cue," Hagger said, and began trotting toward the building, hand falling to the sword strapped to his side. Allan followed a few short paces behind.

They passed through the outer door and into a room whose furniture had been trashed, chairs and tables tossed to the floor, strewn with the broken glass and pottery of lanterns, plates, and what appeared to be urns. The sharp scent of pickling brine permeated the space, vinegar burning Allan's eyes. The shouts of the other Dogs were everywhere, the eight men calling out to each other as Hagger barreled through the rooms, all in as much disarray as the first. One of the men shouted, "Downstairs, downstairs!" and suddenly Hagger and Allan were pounding down a flight of steep steps into a torch-lit basement lined with crumbling mudbrick and makeshift shelves filled with sealed pots. One wall had been cleared, the shards of clay and the watery contents strewn across the floor—Allan couldn't tell what had been pickled—but the stench was horrendous in the confined space. He tried to take shallow breaths, blinked away the tears, and caught sight of the far wall.

The shelves had been torn away and were now a splintered wreck on the basement floor, exposing a narrow doorway leading into the basement of the house next door. Lantern light shone through, blocked as Hagger passed the Dog guarding the door and ducked down to enter. Allan followed.

As he straightened on the other side, Hagger stepping out of his way, he found a woman and man trussed up in the center of the room, kneeling on a stretch of carpet. The man's nose had been broken and blood covered his upper lip and dripped from his chin. A bruise had begun to form on the woman's face. As Hagger entered, she spit at his feet. The elder Dog merely chuckled and scanned the room.

Lanterns hung from the ceiling, illuminating a wall of texts, scattered tables and chairs, and a banner bearing a vertical squiggly line with a straight line branching off from it. One table held a few waterskins and a stack of parchment.

Hagger's attention returned to the two captives. Allan moved toward the table bearing the waterskins. The strange banner hung above it. One of the Dogs shifted out of his way as he approached.

"Are you Kormanley?" Hagger asked. When neither answered, he stepped forward and gripped the man by the chin, squeezing hard as he forced him to look up. "I asked, are you Kormanley?"

The man's jaw clenched in defiance, his eyes hardening.

Moving faster than Allan thought possible, Hagger released his chin, grabbed the man's nose with one hand, the back of his head with the other, and ground the broken cartilage between his fingers.

The man screamed, the sound trapped in the low room, grating against Allan's skin and making his shoulders hunch. The woman shrieked and tried to intervene, but Hagger backhanded her, the other two Dogs grabbing her and pulling her away. Allan focused on the table as the torture continued, Hagger releasing the man and repeating his question.

The papers were covered with notes and sketches of maps from different locations around the city, mostly parks and larger intersections, a few of the ley stations where people could catch barges to different parts of the city. One map appeared to be of the ley routes, starting at the central area of Grass—at least those that were visible above ground. Allan knew that the Wielders kept the true ley lines—those underground—secret. He pushed the maps aside, looking for a list of names, for something that would identify the Kormanley priests, but there was nothing that obvious among the papers.

Disgusted but not surprised—the Kormanley were adept at keeping their members secret—he spread the maps out again, rearranging them into a rough pattern of the inner city's districts, then bent over them, squinting at the scrawled notes. Most were senseless, a sequence of numbers or letters that didn't form words. Like a code.

Allan shook his head and stood back, his gaze falling on the waterskins.

Except they weren't waterskins. Not really.

Behind, the woman screamed, the sound degenerating into a whimper, and Allan turned to see Hagger thrust her away in disdain, a knife held in one hand. Her face was lined with bloody, yet shallow, cuts, and streaked with tears. The man lay on the floor, facedown, moaning.

"They're Kormanley," Allan said.

Hagger spun on him, hand clenched on his knife, a snarl twisting his mouth. Allan had seen him like this before—enraged, on the verge of a full-out brawl—usually when the interrogations of the Kormanley they did find didn't go as planned.

Like this one.

"How do you know?" Hagger snapped.

Allan picked up one of the skins. "Remember the sowing? The Kormanley who immolated himself? He was wearing one of these."

Hagger broke away from the two prisoners and approached the table.

Allan opened the one he held and sniffed the contents, grimacing, then held it up for Hagger. "Lamp oil. These were strapped to that man's chest. He split them open with a knife, then set himself on fire."

Hagger took a whiff of the skin. "Sick bastards," he muttered, then glared at the two captives. One of the other Dogs had pulled the man back into a kneeling position. Both of them were wobbling in place, the woman's head downcast, the man's face set with rage.

"They're just like all the others," Allan said. "They aren't going to tell us anything."

Hagger stiffened, then jammed his knife back into its sheath and motioned toward the other Dogs. "Take them back to the Amber Tower. Take everything in here. The captain will want to see it."

The Dogs dragged the two Kormanley outside, then began tearing the place apart. Allan scooped up the papers, folded them, and tucked them into a pocket.

Hagger gave him a funny look. "Something important in there?"

"I don't know, but there's something bothering me about it."

"Just make certain it gets to the captain."

Allan nodded, back straightening at the undercurrent of suspicion and threat in Hagger's tone. He reminded himself that he hadn't been part of the Dogs for long, even if he had caught the attention of the Baron.

Hagger watched the Dogs working, then motioned toward Allan. "Come along. We need to meet with the captain and tell him what we found."

They ducked out of the hidden room, through the stench of vinegar and brine, and back onto the street. A few people gawked at the Dogs' activity from a safe distance, but none of them appeared to be a threat. Hagger ignored them, turning north out of the small square, moving at a brisk pace. Allan's breath came in short gasps by the time they'd wound their way out of Eld and into Green.

A short time later, Hagger slowed, turning toward the base of one of the newest spires in Erenthrall. Allan tilted his head back and scanned the narrow tower's length as they crossed the plaza where the spire had been grown. It was too thin to hold any rooms, more like the bole of a tree, but it soared well over the nearest buildings. Since the sowing of the main tower in Grass, twelve of these smaller spires had been grown in different parts of the city, four in the inner city surrounding Grass, and eight more in the outermost districts, set on two concentric circles that encompassed Erenthrall. None of the Dogs knew what they were for, and the Wielders had kept silent.

Allan spotted Captain Daedallen at the base of the tower, with Baron Arent, Prime Wielder Augustus, and another man at his side. The Prime Wielder was shouting at a group of Wielders working frantically around the tower's base.

"—keep working, you fools! This subtower must be activated by the end of the day today or we'll fall behind schedule. No, no, Parl, adjust your position, you're too far to the left." Augustus heaved a sigh and stalked over to one of the Wielders, seizing him by the shoulders and shoving him hard to the left. "My left, not yours. Now prepare yourself. Use the catechism if you have to. Barthen, are the others ready on the far side? What about those from the University? Good. Have the Wielders begin calling the ley, then."

Hagger and Allan had halted a respectful distance away from the Baron, Daedallen, and the man Allan didn't know, outside of their small entourage of Dogs and Wielders. None of them had noticed them yet, but when Augustus spun around, he caught sight of them and frowned.

He moved back to Baron Arent's side.

"How are the preparations coming, Prime Wielder?" The Baron's tone was mild, but Augustus grimaced.

"As well as can be expected, my lord Baron." Augustus' eyes flicked toward Hagger and Allan and both Baron Arent and Daedallen turned to look.

Daedallen waved Hagger forward, Allan at his heels. "Report."

"We raided the house the Kormanley priest revealed to us during his interrogation and found a hidden room and two more Kormanley inside. We questioned them at the site, but they did not break. The entire contents of the room are being hauled back to the Amber Tower for inspection, along with the two prisoners. I expect they will be more forthcoming there."

"What was found in the room?"

"There were books, maps, a set of pages with notes, and a few skins of oil. We believe the skins are like those used by the priest who set fire to himself at the sowing."

Baron Arent stirred, face troubled. "So they are planning more immolations?"

Hagger bowed his head. "So it would seem."

Prime Wielder Augustus cleared his throat. "You said there were notes? And maps?"

Hagger deferred to Allan. With a nervous start, he reached into his pocket and retrieved the pages, handing them over to Augustus, who snatched them from his grasp. As the Prime Wielder began glancing through them, he said, "These were scattered on the table that held the oil. I couldn't decipher the notations, but I think there's something in the maps that I'm not quite seeing. Something important. There was also a banner over the table with a strange symbol on it."

The man Allan didn't know glanced up sharply. "What symbol?" Allan realized he must come from the University, like some of those helping the Wielders with the subtower.

"A wavy vertical line with a straight line branching off from it. Like this." Allan knelt and sketched the symbol in the dust of the flagstones of the plaza.

Augustus snorted in contempt.

"You recognize this symbol?" Baron Arent asked.

Arent addressed the question to Augustus, but the man from the University answered. "It's the symbol of convergence, of a return to the natural order. See how the straight line converges with the vertical one? The Kormanley must have adopted it as their own."

"Does it have any other meanings, Sovaan? Anything subversive?"

"Only in the sense that the Kormanley have apparently adopted it."

Augustus turned back to the pages with a dismissive wave of his hand. "It's nonsense." He rifled through them, his brow creasing in consternation as he glared at the notations. His lips moved as if he were muttering to himself, but Allan couldn't catch any of the words.

And then he stilled, his eyes going wide.

"What is it?" Baron Arent asked.

Augustus stared at him in shock. "These maps . . . they're all of the locations of the subtowers, along with a few of the ley stations and nodes."

Sovaan frowned. "Let me see."

"Which means what?" Daedallen asked as Augustus handed the

notes over to Sovaan. He had shifted slightly forward, reacting to the edge in Augustus' voice.

"It means that the Kormanley are targeting the subtowers. Or at least the Wielders who are set to guard them."

"I agree," Sovaan added. "All of their notes reference the new locations of the subtowers, even those we haven't sown yet."

Everyone remained silent as what Augustus and Sovaan said sank in.

Then Baron Arent said, "Can they disrupt the process from these subtowers?"

"Once the subtowers are activated, they could only disrupt it by destroying the spires."

"How long before all of the subtowers are activated?"

Augustus frowned. "Ten days. After that, only the main tower within Grass needs to be activated for the new network to begin working."

Baron Arent turned toward Daedallen. "I find it hard to believe that these skins of oil would be enough to bring down one of the subtowers. They must be planning something to halt their activation instead. I want an increased guard on the subtowers until the unveiling in two weeks."

"The Dogs will handle it."

"I'll have additional Wielders stationed at the sites as well, just in case."

Daedallen tensed, as if offended, but the Baron settled him with a cool look.

Barthen, the Wielder who had organized the others while Augustus was occupied, moved to the Prime Wielder's side. "We're ready to activate the spire."

Augustus immediately turned away, staring up at the tower overhead. With a quick nod of approval from Sovaan, he said, "Proceed." His voice had hardened, his attention so focused that the Baron, Daedallen, and the rest of the Dogs were forgotten. His intensity made Allan's skin crawl and he was suddenly thankful that he was not one of the Wielders beneath Augustus' hand. He would hate to have that gaze settled on him fully. The scrutiny of the Baron was hard enough.

Hagger gasped and Allan focused on the array of Wielders and University mentors beyond. All of them had their eyes closed, hands folded casually before them, and yet their faces were pinched in concentration.

Three paces from Allan, Augustus' breathing slowed and fell into a steady rhythm, drawn in through his nose and out through his mouth. The others appeared to follow suit, until those nearest matched Augustus. Sovaan had drifted to one side, scanning those from the University. Augustus may have created the Nexus, but it required the skills of those from the University to help channel such large energies into its appropriate uses.

Both Baron Arent and Daedallen had tensed and were staring up at the tower in anticipation.

"Can't you feel it?" Hagger asked, his voice a low rumble. Allan noticed that the hairs on Hagger's arm were standing on end. "It's the same as it was at the party."

Allan shook his head. "I don't feel anything. I didn't feel anything at the party either."

Hagger shivered and ran his hands up and down his arms. "It isn't unpleasant. It just . . . prickles."

Before Allan could respond—shifting awkwardly as he strove to feel something, anything—Augustus grimaced as if in pain.

Baron Arent immediately stepped forward. "What is it?"

Augustus shook his head, a curt gesture. "Something is disrupting the ley field. I can't pinpoint what or where it is, though."

"I sense it as well," Sovaan said.

Daedallen instantly scanned the people who had gathered on the plaza or were passing through, eyes darting from face to face. Hagger and Allan responded as well, stepping away, hands falling to their swords.

"Could it be the Kormanley?" Daedallen asked.

"I don't know," Augustus snapped.

Baron Arent nodded and with a sharp gesture of his hand Daedallen ordered the nearest Dogs, including Hagger and Allan, out into the crowd.

Allan split off from Hagger, but kept him in sight, the crowd parting before him, most with a sudden look of fear crossing their faces. He clenched his jaw, felt his face harden, and slid past the terrified citizens. Even though they moved out of his way, their attention was still focused on the spire and the Wielders working beneath it. One woman cried out when she saw him, jumping to one side. A young boy gasped and fled for a side street. Allan tore after him, shoved people aside with low curses, then realized the boy was merely a pickpocket. He growled, letting him go. He searched the press of people, others scattering as the Dogs worked their way through the crowd, but he saw no one in the white robes of the Kormanley priests, no one acting suspicious.

Then everyone in the group gasped, a few hands pointing upward.

Allan spun and caught the first edges of white light as it surged through the inside of the tower, bleeding out through cracks in the spire's side as it rose. In the space of two breaths, it spiked to the top of the tower and exploded outward in a flare of light that made the crowd cry out and shy away, hands raised to cover their eyes. Allan squinted, head tilted to one side, but after a few pulses the light subsided to a bearable level.

After a few moments, Allan realized that the light wasn't going to fade completely. It seeped from the cracks in the tower, making it look more like the texture of bark, and burned at the apex like the beacon of a lighthouse.

"I guess they handled the disruption," Hagger muttered, coming up on Allan's right. "I wonder what it was?"

Allan didn't say anything, suppressing a surge of fear. He suspected he'd caused the disruption himself, simply by being near Augustus and Sovaan and the others as they worked. He'd been in Erenthrall long enough to notice that whenever he was close to objects powered by the ley, they flickered or, in some cases, died completely. He didn't understand why it happened, but he knew he didn't want Hagger, or anyone else for that matter, to find out. So he kept himself as far from ley-powered objects as he could, knowing through some careful experimentation of his own that a little distance—five feet or more—usually resolved the problem. Although it did appear to be getting worse.

They stared at the tower as the crowd around them broke out into hushed conversation, some of the people scurrying away. Allan eyed them all warily, but no one approached the Wielders or the protective circle of Dogs that stood around Baron Arent and Augustus. Everyone's attention appeared focused on the spire and the white light that burned within it.

Hagger gripped Allan's shoulder and pushed him toward Daedallen. "Let's go. We're going to be busy in the next few weeks, what with the Kormanley and these subtowers to activate. There are still eleven more to go."

Allan sighed. He had hoped to make it back to the barracks and Grass in time to catch Moira as she passed through the inner gardens on her way home from work in the Amber Tower. He had only seen her a few times since meeting her at the sowing, but he definitely wanted to see her again.

Hagger chuckled and shook his head, as if he knew why Allan had sighed, then growled, "Welcome to the Dogs, Pup."

Kara felt the surge of power through her feet, energy tingling in her soles and sending shivers up her spine.

She halted dead in her tracks and turned, even as Cory and Justin gasped on either side of her. Cory grabbed her arm, so hard she winced, and pointed. "Look!"

From the street where they'd fled after seeing the Dogs, they could see one of the spires that had been grown nearly a week before. Eleven others had been grown throughout the city; she'd heard the hawkers talking about it in the market.

Now, the spire in Green glowed with an internal light, appearing cracked, like shattered flagstone. A steady light glared out of the top, like a fiery white star. Kara could feel the energies beneath her feet as they rearranged themselves, patterns shifting into new flows. The air tingled against her skin. She glanced toward the two other spires they could see from their location, but they remained empty.

She didn't think they would stay that way for long. Whatever the Wielders were doing, it was progressing fast. Not even Ischua knew what the Prime Wielder was attempting, but he claimed it was because he was only a Tender.

When it became obvious that nothing else was going to happen with the spire, Kara pulled her arm from Cory's grasp, rubbing the bruised flesh. She glared at him, saw him shrug in apology, then noticed that everyone else on the street had halted to watch the spire as well. They were close to home, only a few streets away. At the intersection ahead, a group of young mothers had been bathing their small children in the fountain, but now they stood in a small huddle, children on their hips, pointing toward Green. A merchant on horseback had halted as well and spoke to a group of younger men who stood nearby, all of them talking excitedly. One or two others had paused, but were now moving on their way again.

Then, abruptly, Kara said, "What's that sound?"

Cory, who had begun chattering with Justin, quieted. "What sound?"

"That sound," Kara said curtly. "Can't you hear it?"

She grimaced as the high-pitched buzzing noise increased. At first, it had barely registered, more of an annoyance, like a bug flying too close to her ear. But as it increased, it steadied, became a high-pitched whine. Both Justin and Cory winced, Justin covering his ears with his hands. The adults on the street and in the intersection ahead suddenly turned and began searching for the source of the sound. A couple of the infants began crying. The mothers hushed them and bounced them up and down, then began hastily gathering up clothes and bags and toys. Out of the corner of her eye, Kara caught a flare of white light, nothing more than a candle's flame. The sound escalated—

Then abruptly cut off.

Kara drew in a sharp breath and held it, turning toward where she'd seen the small flicker of light. It held there, hovering in midair, flaring once.

Before she could point it out to Cory or Justin, it collapsed in upon itself.

Tension bled through the air, caressing her skin. Pressure built as the adults glanced around, a few of the men shrugging, the women glaring uncertainly at nothing, lips pursed.

"Kara—" Cory began, fidgeting, reaching out toward her as if for reassurance.

And then the air before Kara wrenched and tore open.

She cried out and stumbled backward a step, throwing up a hand to ward away the small flare of color that bloomed where the light had been. It unfolded like a flower, arms of distortion swirling outward as it spun. It expanded until it was the size of an orange, small enough to fit in the palm of one hand, and then the coruscating arms of red and orange slowed and halted.

Kara lowered her arm, Cory breathing hard behind her, as if he'd just sprinted all the way from school to reach her. One of the men shouted in dismay and pointed, even though Kara, Cory, and Justin were far closer to the strange, colorful light than anyone else. Through the air, Kara could feel the wrongness of the light, even though it was beautiful. Like something the glasswrights would produce for one of their aristocratic patrons. Intrigued, Kara stepped toward it, reached out a hand as if to pluck it from the air, but she halted when Cory shouted, "Don't!" Even without touching it, she could sense it, the air around it somehow brittle and cold, frozen like ice.

She shuddered.

"Don't go near it!" the merchant commanded, riding forward on his horse and motioning everyone else back.

"What is it?" one of the mothers asked. A few of them had already fled from the fountain, but two remained behind. One of them ignored the merchant and stepped closer, eyes wide, hand half raised, as if enchanted by it, even as she kept her body canted to protect her little girl.

The merchant glared at her, then cast his frown on Kara, eyes glinting. But Kara saw a layer of fear beneath the glare. "I don't know," he said gruffly, "but someone should summon a Wielder. They'll know what it is, and what to do about it."

No one moved, and a moment later the strange distortion flared and pulled in upon itself, vanishing without a sound.

Someone exhaled harshly, as if they'd been holding their breath the entire time. The mother sighed in disappointment. The merchant's horse stamped its foot and snorted as its rider frowned down at where the flare of colorful light had been.

Kara turned to face Cory, his face creased in confusion and worry.

"What was it?" he asked, as if Kara would have the answer.

She shook her head. "Let's get out of here before the Dogs or Wielders show up."

Six

"WHERE ARE WE GOING?" Cory asked breathlessly. He was trotting to keep up with Kara as she led them through Eld's marketplace, Justin trailing behind doggedly. Justin's eyes kept flicking toward the crowds of hawkers and customers, head bowed, brow furrowed deep with concern. She could almost feel him vibrating with tension without even glancing back, a strange counterpoint to her own excitement.

"The ley station," she answered.

Cory paused, startled, then rushed to catch up. "Why are we going there? We aren't allowed to take the ley barges, not without our parents along. We aren't even supposed to leave Eld."

Kara didn't answer, focused on pushing through the crowd, cutting between a stall selling colorful shawls from the Gorrani Flats to the south and a man with a blanket spread on the market's flagstones to display crude pottery. But Cory snagged her arm on the far side, forcing her to halt. Justin sidled up behind them, standing closer than he normally did, ignoring them as he scanned the flow of people behind them.

"Where are we going, Kara?"

She could hear the anger that had edged Cory's voice since she'd told him she'd be leaving for the Wielders' school. She hated it—it set her teeth on edge and made the skin at the nape of her neck crawl—but she didn't know what to do or say to Cory to make it go away.

So when she answered, her tone was curt. "We're going to the Eld ley station. I heard they're activating one of those subtowers in Shadow today." When Cory's eyes widened with the same excitement she'd felt since that morning—when she'd planned their escape from her father, who thought she and Cory were headed down to the riverfront—all of her annoyance with Cory's tone fled. She grinned. "I wanted it to be a surprise, but we're going to go see it! I've got three passes for the barges and three more to get back. The subtower is supposed to be lit this afternoon, so we have to hur—"

"Wait. Shadow?" Cory barked. "You want to go to Shadow? That's three districts away! And my father says there's nothing there but thieves and cutthroats, as bad as Eastend. He won't even deliver candles to that area!"

Kara rolled her eyes and crossed her arms over her chest. "It can't be that bad. Besides, we missed the subtowers being activated in Green and Hedge. All of the rest are too far away. This is the only chance we'll get to see one."

Cory chewed on his lower lip, glancing toward Justin as he wavered.

"We'll be fine," she said in exasperation, drawing his attention away from Justin by catching his arm and pulling him toward the next row of stalls, tents, and blankets. "We'll hop on the ley barge, get off in Shadow, see the subtower get lit—it's practically being raised in the middle of Shadow's ley station—and then climb back onto the barge and head home. No one in Shadow will even know we're there." And hopefully no one in Eld would find out where they'd gone.

Whatever resistance Cory still had left vanished. Keeping Justin in sight, Kara and Cory snaked through the press of people in the market, then passed into the less dense side streets of Eld, where they trotted through the narrow alleys and back gardens until they reached the stone steps that led up to the open doors of the ley station and entered the huge mezzanine beyond. All three of them stood stunned beneath the arching pillars carved like tree trunks and the interlaced branches etched into the ceiling, but the awe didn't last. They crossed the smooth marble floor to the tunnels leading down to the ley lines and barges below, Kara handing over three chits as they passed down into the platforms.

"Where do we go?" Cory asked.

They were huddled, backs to one wall, people moving back and forth before them in a riot of activity. Kara licked her lips in uncertainty, but before she could answer a piercing whistle cut through the room and made her jump. A moment later a ley barge pulled up alongside the platform where they stood and a man in a gray uniform trimmed with weathered gold shouted, "Mainline—Leeds, Light, Shadow, and Reach!"

"That one," Kara said, then pushed forward as those waiting on the platform made for the doors.

But Justin suddenly shouted, "Wait!"

Both Cory and Kara turned; Cory spoke first. "What's wrong, Justin? You've been acting weirder than usual all day."

"That man," Justin said. He shifted nervously, not looking at either of them, but at the surge of people around them. He stepped closer, his voice dropping. "He's back. He's been following us since the market. Following *me*."

Kara shared an annoyed glance with Cory. "Where is he now, Justin?"

Justin pointed with certainty. "Right there, leaning in that doorwa—"
Justin's eyes went wide.

"Let me guess," Cory said, his voice dry. "He's no longer there."

"Oh, no," Justin said, and Kara felt a tendril of fear slipping beneath her irritation at the raw panic in those two words. Justin inched closer toward them. "No, no, no." He sucked in a noisy breath. "Where'd he go?"

Now Cory rolled his eyes. "Come on, Justin. He's not there. And we need to catch this barge if we want to see the subtower!"

"Cory's right," Kara said, her words harsher than she'd intended. But most of the people had already disembarked and others were filing onto the barge. Only a few remained on the platform. "We need to go. The doors are going to close!"

Cory grabbed Justin's shoulder and pushed him toward the barge, Kara sprinting out ahead of them. The doors nicked Justin and he stumbled into Cory and Kara with a wild cry. The barge was crowded, none of them able to move far from the door, but then it lurched into motion and Kara felt her entire body humming—from the anticipation of seeing the subtower lit and the stream of ley beneath them.

"I can't believe we're doing this," Cory said under his breath.

Kara shot him a warning glare—there were too many adults around—but couldn't keep a grin from breaking out as she steadied herself against the wall.

The barge stopped in Leeds, people shoving their way to the door to exit, others piling on. Cory and Kara were pushed to one side, Justin to the other, and Kara's heart leaped as she lost sight of him. But as the barge began moving again, Justin squeezed closer, taking advantage of his shorter size. At the stop in Light, more people exited than entered and Kara felt she could breathe again, the air not so close and tight. Cory broke out into animated conversation about nothing, not expecting a response, and her own excitement built as the barge headed toward Shadow.

Cory was still talking when they spilled out onto the platform at their stop, his hands waving in punctuation. They trotted toward the tunnels leading up to the mezzanine, Kara in the lead, when she suddenly realized that Cory had fallen silent.

"What's wrong, Cory? Finally run out of breath?" she asked as she turned . . . only to find Cory twenty paces behind her, stock still, his eyes wide in horror. Something hard filled Kara's throat, wiping the smile from her face. She swallowed the sensation down and ran back to Cory's side. "What's wrong? Why did you stop—?"

But then she realized and a pit opened up in her stomach, her legs going weak. She reached out for Cory, eyes scanning the tunnel behind them, what little of the platform she could see beyond.

"Where's Justin?" she asked, and her voice sounded hollow to her, removed and far away.

"He was right behind me," Cory said, voice cracking. "I know he got off the barge."

"Then where is he?" Kara snapped. She began moving down the tunnel, her pace increasing until she burst out onto the platform and spun, trying to search in all directions at once. The barge was gone. Almost everyone had departed, the platform empty except for a few stragglers, two men in station uniforms who looked bored, and a man asleep on one of the many benches against the walls to one side. Kara turned around twice, the pit in her stomach widening, then locked gazes with Cory.

"I don't see him anywhere," Cory said.

"He has to be here," Kara said flatly, anger seething up from deep down. "Look down to the right, I'll look left."

Cory nodded and headed right. Kara moved left, jogging, scanning behind the few columns and searching the benches. But she knew even before she reached the edge of the platform that she wouldn't find him.

As she turned back, she found it harder and harder to breathe. At the far end of the platform, Cory shrugged.

"He has to be here," she whispered to herself as they closed. Except she knew that wasn't true. Justin had warned them time and again, since that first time when he'd told them of the man watching him outside of the school. When Justin hadn't been able to point the man out, she'd decided Justin was being . . . well, Justin. Odd. Weird.

But now, all of his warnings echoed in her head, including earlier at the Eld station. She heard the terror in his voice when he realized the man had vanished and it clawed at her chest.

"He's not down there," Cory said as they met before the tunnel.

"Not on my side either."

Cory's eyes were filled with panic, with the same hollow fear and knowing Kara felt churning inside herself.

"You don't think it was . . . that man he's always talking about?" Cory asked. "Do you?"

Kara scowled, even though that's exactly what she thought. "He must have passed us somehow. He's probably up in the mezzanine."

Cory looked doubtful but followed her up the tunnel and out into the mezzanine, a less artful and much dirtier version of the one in Eld. The high windows were yellowed with dust, the stone columns gritty with blackened edges, the stone flags of the floor cracked. They searched the mezzanine for twenty minutes, Kara becoming increasingly frantic, until Cory caught her wrist and said, "The station guards are starting to notice."

She glanced toward the two guards in gray uniforms conferring with each other near the mezzanine's entrance. One of them motioned toward Kara, then they both turned, their faces lined with suspicion.

"We should tell them."

Kara spun. "We can't! They wouldn't believe us. And we aren't supposed to be here anyway." Her throat closed up and she had to swallow twice to continue. "They probably think we're pickpockets . . . or worse." She suddenly felt the taint of Shadow weighing down on her—all of the rumors, her father's warnings about leaving Eld. Tears pricked the corners of her eyes.

"What are we going to do?" Cory demanded. His fingers dug into her skin. "We can't just leave him."

Kara glanced around again, noticed one of the station guards heading toward them. She grabbed Cory's hand and dragged him back toward the tunnel. "He must have gotten back on the barge, headed back to Eld. He's probably already home."

She didn't believe it, knew Cory didn't either. They used two of the ley tickets and boarded the barge when it arrived in silence, Kara casting one last longing, hopeful glance down Shadow's platform. But she saw nothing and the doors closed.

When they disembarked in Eld, they searched the platform and mezzanine, but found nothing.

Kara stood outside the ley station's doors, staring at the wide steps, Cory beside her. Her eyes burned with tears now, and her nose felt clogged and thick.

"We need to tell our parents about Justin," she muttered, voice weak.

Cory fidgeted beside her. "Maybe he'll be at school tomorrow. Maybe we should wait and see?"

"Maybe," she said. But she didn't believe it. Why would Justin go without saying anything?

But when they arrived home, Cory dashing off to his own door with a wide-eyed glance backward, Kara halted. What if Cory was right? Justin hadn't wanted to go to Shadow in the first place, and Justin had always been different. He *could* have bolted and run home.

When she pushed open the door, her father turned from his work on a clock and smiled. For a moment, Kara felt the rush of warmth she'd always felt when returning home and finding her father at work, but then her father's smile faltered.

The wall that had formed between them since they'd visited Ischua at Halliel's Park returned.

Kara stepped into the room and closed the door behind her.

"What's wrong? Where have you been?"

Kara's breath caught in her throat. "Nowhere. We were . . . we were at the market, playing Thistle Snatch."

Her father met her gaze and held it. "What happened?" he repeated.

She drew breath to tell him about taking the barge to Shadow, about Justin, but in the end she simply said, "The Dogs showed up. They were harassing one of the hawkers. So we left."

Her father relaxed, the smile returning. But it still wasn't like before.

He motioned her forward and hugged her tight, holding her close and then pushing her back to look at her, hands on her upper arms. "You let the Dogs bother you too much. They're simply doing their job, protecting the Baron—and us. I'm certain they had a good reason to go after the vendor."

He squeezed her arms, then sighed and rumpled her hair before turning back to the clock. "You should finish your schoolwork."

Her gaze slid to the gears and other pieces spread out across the black cloth of the table. "I could help," she said, hope tingeing her voice as guilt seized her chest. Even from where she stood, she could see what needed to be done next.

But her father shook his head. "I've got it. Your schoolwork is more important."

But Kara knew what he truly meant. He hadn't asked her to help him with the clocks since speaking to Ischua, because after the Wielders came for her, she wouldn't be working on clocks. Unlike Cory, she wouldn't be taking over from her father. Or her mother.

Her father leaned over his work, intent on fitting the next piece into position. He'd already forgotten her. She shifted into the kitchen, where vegetables roasted in a low simmer in the heated ley oven, the hearty scent making her stomach growl. She stirred them, the juices in the bottom of the pot already thickening. She cut a slice of bread from the loaf on the sideboard, dipped it in the sauce, and ate it as she settled into one of the kitchen chairs, staring out into the outer room. The bread had no taste, and didn't help the empty feeling in her stomach. She didn't realize she was waiting for her father to start humming until she ate the last of the bread and it was still silent; she suddenly realized he hadn't hummed while working since they'd visited the park.

Everything was changing. The city—with the new tower and the smaller spires spread throughout its districts. Her family—her father drawn into himself, focusing on his clocks; her mother always at work, as if she were avoiding coming home. Her friends—Cory's anger, Justin's sudden pervasive fear of a man that Kara had never seen. And herself. In another few weeks, perhaps a few months, she would be part of the mysterious enclave of the Wielders.

She sighed, shoulders hunched. Then she stood, grabbed the leather strap of her schoolbooks, and headed toward her room to work. Maybe tomorrow it would feel different; maybe tomorrow it would feel normal again. Maybe Justin would be back and this entire horrible day would feel like a dream.

But the next day, Justin never appeared at school. No one had seen him since the day before. Even after Kara confessed and her father called in the Dogs, he couldn't be found. She thought she'd be punished for leaving Eld, for losing Justin. Instead, her father merely looked . . . disappointed.

Kara found that worse.

Later that evening, another one of the spires burst into life, its entire length pulsing with white light at the edge of the Rill District.

Justin woke to darkness, his breath catching in his throat again as he opened his eyes and saw . . . nothing. Panic set in with a rush of blood in his ears, loud because in this room he could hear nothing except his own breathing, his own heartbeat. He gasped, listened to the noise in reassurance, and then pushed himself up off the gritty stone floor into a seated position, back against the stone wall where he'd crouched and slept since the man had put him here. He drew his knees up to his chest, hugged them tight, and fought the tears that threatened to spill out even though he'd vowed not to let them after the first day—if it had been a day; he couldn't tell in such total darkness—of solid crying.

Sitting in the utter silence, blind, he thought about the moment the man had grabbed him on the platform in Shadow. He'd searched frantically for the man on the barge, certain he'd followed them, but Justin hadn't seen him at all, had convinced himself that the man must have missed the barge in Eld and they'd lost him. Still, he'd checked out the platform when they disembarked and hadn't seen anything.

Until the man had reached out and caught him, drawing him in close to his chest and muttering softly in Justin's ear, "Do anything and your two friends die."

Justin had choked on his scream, his terror caught in his chest, fluttering with his heart as the man lifted him and hauled him to one of the benches. They'd sat, the man's arm wrapped around Justin's shoulders, utterly still, as Kara and Cory charged back onto the platform and searched. When Justin had whimpered, tears coursing down his face, the terror now a hard knot in his throat that *hurt*, the man's arm had tightened painfully and he'd slid a knife from his sleeve. Mouth close to Justin's ear, so close he could feel the man's breath puffing against his neck, the man had whispered, "Do you want them to die?"

Justin had shaken his head, drawing in a slow breath as he tried to calm himself. His body had thrummed, but he'd forced himself to remain silent, to remain perfectly still as Kara and Cory vanished back up the tunnel, Kara's eyes frantic, then returned and boarded the barge back to Eld.

He hadn't understood why his friends hadn't seen him, but he knew it had something to do with the man because no one had seen them as the man hauled him upright and walked him to the next barge, the knife still visible. They'd left the barge in Grass—a place Justin had never been, only seen from the rooftops and streets in Eld—and entered a strange orange-red tower, descending into the lower levels, into granite passageways, into darkness and this room.

It had been pitch-black when the man thrust him forward and he'd stumbled to the floor, scuffing his hands on the rough stone. He'd heard a door close but had remained still, waiting. When he'd been certain he was alone, he'd crawled around the room, felt for the walls, the ceiling, found the rough outline of the wooden door, the pile of fresh-smelling straw in one corner, the chamber pot. Nothing else.

Not certain what to do, he'd retreated to the corner and curled in upon himself on the floor. Eventually, he'd slept.

The first time he woke to darkness, he'd cried out, then silenced himself, afraid they'd hurt Kara and Cory. But that fear hadn't stopped the choked sobs, the racking tears that suffused his face with heat as he tried to suppress them. He'd cried himself to sleep again.

Now, he pushed the terror down, stifled the fear, although he could feel it ready to bubble up again from his chest. His gasps lessened and the bloodrush in his ears faded. Eyes wide to capture light that wasn't there, he listened . . . and heard nothing. No sound at all, except himself.

But there was something else.

He concentrated . . . strained . . . and suddenly realized it wasn't a sound.

It was a smell.

He breathed in deeply, closed his eyes and focused on the scent: something clean, like the soap his mother used to wash their clothes at the river, with a hint of sweat, a prickle of . . . of oil. Not lantern oil, something sharper, harsher. The combination was familiar. He remembered smelling it before, recently. . . .

Justin jerked with recognition, eyes flaring wide, back stiffening even as he cowered back against the wall so hard the rough stone ground into his spine. "You're here," he said, the words loud to his ears, like a slap to the face.

Nothing at first, then a low chuckle. "I knew you were ready."

Justin recognized the voice as that of the man who'd taken him, who'd threatened his friends. The man who smelled like soap and oil. Justin's nostrils flared and his eyes widened further, but he still couldn't see him, even though the voice didn't sound far away. He couldn't hear him either, not even his breathing. But he could see him in his mind—the rough-looking, angular face, the hard glint in gray-green eyes, the tension in his stance even when he appeared to be leaning against a wall, relaxed, as he watched from across the street or a darkened alcove. He'd dressed like everyone else in Eld, but he hadn't acted like them. He'd been too still, too focused.

Justin had felt that stillness when the man had grabbed him on the platform, like a smothering blanket.

"Ready . . . ready for what?" Justin rasped. His mouth was dry.

"Ready to become a Hound."

Justin frowned in incomprehension, grew still. He hadn't even realized he was trembling. "I don't want to be a Hound."

The fist came out of nowhere, slamming into his face and knocking him into the wall to one side. He rebounded and flopped onto the floor, stunned. Pain radiated from his cheek, its inside flesh torn by his teeth. Blood filled his mouth, coppery and salty. He spat to one side, started to raise a hand to his lips, which felt slick, but a foot pressed down onto his chest and suddenly he couldn't breathe.

"You are a Hound. Your life belongs to the Baron. Your thoughts belong to him. You live to seek, to subdue, and to kill. That is your sole purpose. Seek, subdue, kill. Repeat it."

The pressure against his chest released enough so that he could suck in a lungful of air. He began to wriggle, trying to thrash his way from beneath the man's heel, but the pressure increased again.

"Seek, subdue, kill," the man's voice said, grating and hard this time. "Repeat it."

When the man's weight shifted again, Justin gasped in more air, then steeled himself and shoved hard away from the wall to his right, but it was useless. The man's heel dug in with bruising force.

"If you refuse to train as a Hound, your parents will be killed." His voice came from above, cold and implacable. "If you rebel, your friends will be killed next. We will bring them here and kill them before you. If you try to escape, you will die. You are a Hound. Your life belongs to the Baron. Your thoughts belong to him. You live to seek, to subdue, and to kill." The man leaned forward, the weight against Justin's chest increasing until it felt as if his ribs would crack. "Now, repeat it."

The pressure lessened, barely enough for Justin to draw in a trickle of air and wheeze, "Seek, subdue, kill."

For a heart-wrenching moment, nothing happened and Justin nearly sobbed. Then the heel withdrew and he rolled to one side, heaving in air, choking on it and the blood that coated his throat. His stomach turned and he dry-retched.

When the waves of pain receded, Justin curled into as tight a ball as he could, hands over his head, chin and knees tucked into his chest. A low whine escaped him.

A rustle came from the darkness, the first real sound Justin had heard aside from the man's voice. He reached for the sound in desperation, and as if his sense of hearing had been heightened he caught a scrape of metal against glass, followed by a hollow pop, as if a bottle had been uncorked.

Justin flinched when the man spoke again: "Tell me what you smell."

He didn't respond until he heard footsteps approaching, then he shouted, "I smell you!"

The footsteps paused. "And what do I smell like?"

"Sweat and soap and oil," he snuffled into his arms.

A hesitation. "Is that how you knew I was here?"

Justin nodded.

Silence. Long enough Justin's shoulders unconsciously relaxed. Then: "What else do you smell? What else do you sense?"

Justin began to shake with silent sobs, but he drew in a ragged breath and realized he *could* smell something else, something stronger than the soap and oil, something newer, sharper, acidic. "An orange," he cried out desperately. "I smell an orange!"

"Good. Although I think I started with too strong a scent. You're already sensitive to smells, aren't you? New Hounds usually are . . . but not always. Do you sense anything else?"

Justin thought he felt the smothering blanket again, but couldn't tell if that were true or if his chest merely ached from the bruises. He shook his head. "Nuh—nuh—nuh—nothing."

"Disappointing." More rustling, another soft pop. "Tell me what you smell."

A noisy, deep breath. "Cinnamon."

"And now?"

It was getting harder. The scents were mingling, the orange and cinnamon overpowering. Justin had to suck in air twice to catch the floral scent beneath the other two. "A flower."

"What kind?"

"I don't know."

A strike from the darkness, a stinging cuff to the head. "What kind of flower?"

"I don't know!"

Justin tensed in anticipation of another blow.

"It's called hyacinth. Remember it." A hollow pop. "Tell me what you smell."

Justin shook his head, the tears he'd been withholding coming now, harsh and hot. "I don't know. I want to go home. Please let me go home."

The man's foot drove hard into Justin's back and Justin screamed, white-hot pain lancing up into his shoulders along his spine. He arched back, then scrambled blindly away, sharp jabs from his muscles making him wince as he moved. He hit the wall, scuttled down its length until he hit the corner, then huddled there, waiting for another kick, another punch, willing the nightmare to end. But it didn't. The granite cell didn't disappear. The scents that filled the air didn't fade. The darkness didn't recede.

Instead, from the darkness, he heard the hollow sound of a bottle being uncorked and the man who'd sought him out, who'd taken him, said, "This is your home. This is your life. You are a Hound. Your life belongs to the Baron. Your thoughts belong to him. You live to seek, to subdue, to kill." A rustle as the man shifted closer. "Now, tell me what you smell."

Tyrus heard the creak of a floorboard behind him where he sat eating his lunch a moment before a meaty hand closed around the back of his neck, twisted, and shoved the side of his face into the table. He cried out and began to flail, knees hitting the underside of the table, making the crockery and his mug of ale jump, but then the hand on his neck tightened and someone leaned in close to his ear.

"What did you tell them, little snitch?"

He recognized the voice instantly, the fleshy hand a breath later, and stilled, hands clutching the edge of the table so hard his knuckles were white.

"I didn't," he gasped, "tell anyone anything. What are you talking about?"

His Kormanley bodyguard from three weeks before leaned in even closer, his breath reeking of liver and onions and pickles. "The Dogs raided our meeting place four days ago. They took Pils and Korana to the Amber Tower. I don't expect to see them alive again, and you," he squeezed Tyrus' neck hard enough Tyrus whimpered, "are the only one I can think of who would have snitched."

"I didn't—"

"Careful what you say. I can snap your neck as easy as breathe."

Tyrus swallowed hard, a shot of pure panic slicing cleanly to his already trembling arms and legs. It took him a moment to work enough spit into his mouth so he could talk. "I didn't snitch. I don't even know where the meeting took place. You took me there with a burlap sack over my head, dragged me out the same way. How could I have told them where it was? It must have been someone else."

His captor grunted, a fresh wave of onion and brine washing over Tyrus' face, but the hand pinning his head to the table relaxed. He could see the man's shadow against the wall; he'd straightened.

"Good point," the man admitted grudgingly, but he didn't release his hold completely. "What about those papers? Where are they?"

"The permits have been submitted. I'm awaiting signatures. I'll have them tomorrow or the day after."

"Good. The event is only a few days away."

Tyrus tried not to shudder at the anticipation in the man's voice.

Then the grip on his neck tightened again and in a soft but deadly tone he added, "Don't screw up. We're watching you."

The meaty hand released completely and Tyrus sat bolt upright, wincing as his neck twinged. He spun around with a barely checked snarl and caught a bulky figure striding out the gloomy inn's door into the bright afternoon sunlight beyond, vanishing immediately to the left. He thought about leaping up to follow him, but restrained himself. He needed to keep in the splinter group's good graces if he intended to help stop them. And at the moment he knew nothing, only that something involving wagons was to happen at the park in Grass a few days from now, during the Baron's latest display of his abuse of power. Dalton and the other members agreed that it wasn't enough for them to act on alone—there weren't enough of the regular Kormanley to stop all of the vendors that would be inside the park—and they certainly couldn't approach the Dogs or city watch with such sketchy information.

Tyrus turned away from the empty doorway, one hand reaching to massage his bruised neck, to find the inn's keeper standing a discreet distance away looking troubled.

"Is there a problem, Tyrus?" he asked.

Tyrus sighed. "No problem, Rell. Except I seem to have spilled some of my ale."

Rell stepped up immediately to retrieve the mug. As he retreated to top it off, Tyrus glared at the remains of his meal, no longer hungry, and wondered what exactly the splinter Kormanley had planned and how long he would have to continue the subterfuge.

Allan waited for Moira in the garden area beneath the Amber Tower as dusk settled over the city. The newest addition to the central section of Erenthrall rose into the sky not far away, its dark green outer shell textured like overlaid leaves touched orange in the fading sunset. It was taller than most of the towers that surrounded it, although it appeared lifeless in comparison. Ley light gleamed in the windows of the other towers, and Allan could see people moving on balconies and through the lowest windows. One or two rooms glowed with the yellowish light of candles. But the new tower remained dark. The Wielders had kept it sealed, awaiting the activation of the twelve subtowers, which continued on schedule. Ten of the subtowers were operating now, and the eleventh had been activated a short time ago. There had been no sign of the Kormanley protestors.

Allan's gaze dropped to the entrance to the garden as two women entered, but neither one was Moira. He shrugged off his disappointment, surprised at how strong the emotion felt. He'd managed to catch Moira only twice on her way home from working for the Baron; three other times he'd waited in vain. Since the disastrous party at the sowing of the green tower—when he'd bumped into her and caused her to drop the box of candles—they'd seen each other only five times, mostly in passing as Allan went about his duties as a Dog and she as a servant of the Baron. And yet after each meeting, Allan found himself thinking about her more and more.

He smiled as he stared down at the crushed stone beneath his feet. The bench where he sat gave him a direct line of sight on the entrance to the garden, yet was hidden from the rest of the pathways by a screen of willow trees. Their long branches rustled in a faint breeze, the last edge of the sun sinking into the horizon, and with a sigh Allan shook himself. Moira must have taken a different route home that day, perhaps had not even been working in the Amber Tower at all. Baron Arent had planned events all over the city for the night the main tower would be opened and the new ley system activated. She may have been assigned to one of the other locations.

He swallowed back the bitterness of regret in his throat and glanced up.

Moira stood on the edge of the path near the entrance, watching him, a smile quirking the corner of her mouth.

Allan stood abruptly, hands smoothing the rumpled creases in his Dog uniform, fumbling with a pocket, his belt, the hilt of his dagger, before he drew in a deep steadying breath and forced them to still, his body to relax. Moira's eyes glinted with amusement as she headed toward him and she shook her head. She halted before him and looked up into his face, one hand plucking at an amber sleeve.

"Were you waiting for me?" she asked.

Allan drew in another breath, smelled honeysuckle, knew that it came from Moira; there was no honeysuckle in this garden. The scent was intoxicating and he grinned. "Yes. I thought I could walk you home. Again."

Moira raised her eyebrows. "I see," she said, but chuckled and motioned toward the path. "This is becoming a habit."

"I'd like it to be more than that." He said it baldly, before he had a chance to think, and immediately ducked his head, cursing himself under his breath. He could feel his cheeks burning. He'd risen in the Dogs since his arrival in Erenthrall, but for the first time in weeks he felt less like a Dog and more like the Pup that Hagger still teased him about being.

When he glanced to the side, he caught Moira staring at him, her expression guarded, the lightness of a moment before gone.

An awkward silence held, Moira turning away, head bowed, until she said uncertainly, "You're a Dog."

"Yes," Allan answered, even though it hadn't been a question. His heart fell and he found his hand gripping the hilt of the sword belted at his side. "I'm a Dog. I know what everyone says about us. I know what everyone thinks. And some of the Dogs *are* cruel and vicious." He thought of Hagger and what he'd done to the Kormanley they'd interrogated, then swallowed at the sudden constriction in his throat and added softly, "But we aren't all like that."

"You aren't like that?"

"No!"

"Then why are you a Dog? Why are you still with them? Why haven't you left?"

Allan's hand twisted in the fabric of his shirt. "Because I can't." His voice came out rougher than he'd intended, remained raw even though he tried to control it. "I was raised in Canter, a small town, not really more than a village. My father was a farmer, and his father before him, and *his* father before *him*. I wanted something different. I wanted to escape, wanted to see Erenthrall. I wanted to be a Dog. So I trained, entered local contests, and when the chance to leave Canter came, I took it."

"And came here. Became a Dog."

"Yes." Allan considered this, head bowed, then said, "It wasn't what I thought. But by the time I realized what being a Dog truly meant, it was too late. The Dogs won't let me leave. Hagger won't let me. I'm too valuable to him. He never expected to rise so high in the Dogs' ranks, but now, with me at his side, he thinks he can become one of Daedallen's betas. He'd kill me if I said I was leaving."

They walked a ways in silence, Moira chewing on her lower lip in indecision. Then she halted and faced him. "I'll probably regret this, but what did you have in mind?"

Allan sucked in a breath, felt himself trembling. He hadn't planned anything, hadn't expected to blurt out what he really wanted earlier, certainly hadn't meant to tell her about Canter and his father and Hagger. "Can we meet before the ceremony Baron Arent has planned in two days?"

"I have to work—"

"So do I," Allan interrupted, "but not until later. We could meet in Wintemeer Square, stroll along the canals, find some place to eat—all before we have to report at the Amber Tower."

She searched his face, as if looking for something she could trust. He was suddenly intensely aware of the burn scar along his jawline, of the bruise near the corner of one eye, and all of the little nicks and cuts he'd gotten since he'd become a Dog. He should have cleaned himself up before coming here, instead of heading over immediately after Hagger had allowed him to leave.

But then Moira reached up and tweaked a lock of his mussed hair into place.

"I'll meet you," she said, letting her hand drop. "By the fountain in the square, an hour before midday." Before he could respond, she said sternly, "But I have to be back at the Amber Tower by the second hour or the steward will have my hide."

Allan's heart thudded hard in his chest but he nodded in agreement. "I'll need to be in the barracks by that time as well."

Moira held his gaze a moment longer. "At the fountain, then."

She turned to where another entrance to the garden led out to the street and with a few short steps merged into the flow of people along the walk.

Allan let out a pent-up sigh of relief, then grinned and headed toward his bunk in the barracks. He needed to find out everything the other Dogs knew about Wintemeer Square.

❧

Allan waited anxiously at the fountain, trying to appear calm and casual. Puddles of water from the rainstorm that morning filled the square, glinting in the sunlight that had broken through the clouds in the last hour. To one side, a pair of children screamed in delight as they stomped in one, the mother gasping in horror and herding them away while scolding them. The other patrons of the square smiled as they wove around the cobblestones and the few vendors who had taken advantage of the sunlight and already set up their wares. Across the way, the owner of a small tavern had moved a few tables and chairs out onto the edge of the walk. A few drays passed by, horse hooves clopping on stone, as overhead the black clouds continued to fray as they streamed south.

Allan saw Moira the moment she stepped into the square, her gaze searching the fountain as her hands smoothed out the dusky-colored dress she wore. She caught sight of him, smiled, and headed toward the fountain. He was startled at how different she appeared without the amber clothing of one of the Baron's servants. Her hair looked darker, her skin pale and smooth, not washed out and strained. Allan's pulse quickened as she drew near and he smelled honeysuckle.

She hesitated a step from him, a slight frown marring her smile. "You wore your Dog uniform."

Allan grimaced. "Only the shirt and breeches. I . . . I don't have anything that looks better."

Something passed through her eyes and the frown faded. She glanced around at the square, already beginning to grow crowded as people emerged from hiding from the storm. "So what did you have planned?"

Allan allowed himself to relax and smiled. "You'll see."

Her eyebrows rose, but she said nothing.

They broke away from the fountain, crossing the square and entering the maze of streets, bridges, and canals that wound through the district, the twists and turns of the pathways as illogical and random as a true labyrinth. Elongated boats drifted through the canals, carrying a few passengers from location to location, but most of the residents of the Canal District preferred traveling by foot. There were some shops, taverns, and cafés that could only be reached by boat. The deepest section contained no wagons or ley carts, the paths too narrow. They fell into an easy chatter, Allan pointing out flowers and trinkets in the shops they passed, buying a small chunk of cheese from an elderly woman with a hand-drawn cart, sharing it with Moira.

One walkway emerged onto a landing where a boat waited, tied to a tall pillar of wood carved and painted in vivid yellows and reds. A man who leaned against the pillar pushed away when he saw them, catching Allan's eye. As they approached, he motioned dramatically toward the boat and said, "I have been waiting all day for you, my lady," with too broad of a smile.

Moira glanced back at Allan, who grinned. "You can't be serious," she said.

"Oh, but I am."

She stared at him, mouth open as if to protest, then shrugged and stepped into the boat. The man held it steady for her, then for Allan, and when they were situated, climbed into the back after untying from the pillar. Using a long pole, he pushed them away from the stone walkway and into the canal.

"He wasn't lying, was he?" Moira asked. "He was waiting for us. You hired him."

"Yes."

"So our random walk wasn't that random after all."

"No."

Allan wasn't certain how she'd react, felt his chest loosen when she finally shook her head and laughed. She turned away, to look at the passing houses that butted up against the canal. The windows and balconies were done in an older style, one more suited to when the canals had been used for serious trade. Now the canals were considered quaint, and the docks and wharfs that had been the foundation of the river trade—districts like Eastend and Leeds—had fallen into squalor.

Allan watched Moira closely, could tell that she wanted to ask where they were going in the slight tension in her shoulders. But then she forced herself to relax with a sigh, leaning over the edge of the boat to trail her hands in the water.

It was the first time he'd ever seen her completely calm. At the party, in the Amber Tower, even in the gardens, an aura of wariness surrounded her, as if she were constantly waiting for a harsh word or the back of a hand. He recalled the lord at the party swearing at her when she'd dropped the crate of candles, and realized she'd grown used to defending herself against such abuse.

Allan let his own sigh escape slowly and joined her, so they were side by side. He heard the man shifting position to compensate behind them, but didn't turn.

"Look," she said, after a long, comfortable moment of silence, interrupted only by the splash as the man poled them along. "A fish!"

Allan glanced into the murky water and nodded. "Looks like a trout. Why are you surprised by fish in the canal? There are fish in the pools and fountains around the Amber Tower."

Moira scoffed. "Those are ornamental. They're small and colorful, there to please the lords and ladies and the other guests of the Baron. This . . . this is just a fish. It isn't pretty, and it's big. The biggest fish I've ever seen."

She glanced up and caught Allan trying not to laugh. He flinched as she slapped him on his shoulder, holding up a hand to fend her off. "What?" he said, as the boat rocked.

"It's not funny."

"Haven't you ever been down to the river?"

"The rivers are too cloudy and dirty. And I've never been outside of Erenthrall." She sniffed. "I suppose you have?"

"I grew up in Canter, remember? It's . . . nothing like Erenthrall. I've seen trout practically every day my entire life, in the streams that run through the hills surrounding the town. It's Erenthrall that's bizarre, with its fish kept in ponds simply to be looked at, never to be eaten."

He shifted under Moira's sudden intense scrutiny, prickles of embarrassment crawling across the back of his neck.

"Maybe that's why you're so different," Moira finally said, voice soft, as if she spoke to herself.

"What do you mean?"

She turned back to the water, troubled, the trout long gone. "I told the other servants about you, after we met at the sowing of the tower. They warned me away. They said you were a Dog, that nothing good ever came of speaking to, let along seeing, a Dog. I told them you were different, but they just laughed. Half of them expect me to return to work tomorrow with a bruise on my face."

Allan said nothing at first, let the shock sink in, even as he realized that he shouldn't be shocked. Not after what he'd seen the Dogs do over the past few months.

Then he reached forward and brushed a lock of her dark hair behind her ear, caught and held her startled gaze, and said, "I would never strike you. I told you, I'm not like the other Dogs."

Moira held her breath, then murmured, "I believe you."

Allan let his hand drop and turned back to the water. Moira did the same, but edged closer to him.

A moment later, the boat scraped up against a stone dock with another of the pillars of carved wood, this one painted yellow and blue.

"We have arrived, my lord and lady."

Moira rolled her eyes, but stood and allowed Allan to help her off the boat. The man winked at him as he disembarked. Allan slipped him a few errens in payment.

"Which way?" Moira asked. The path ran parallel to the canal, steps leading up to the right.

"Up the steps. There's a café where we can eat, but I want to show you something else first."

He led her up the stairs, ignoring the numerous paths, landings, and alcoves that branched off from them as they wound around the buildings on either side. He paused to show her the café, small enough it could only hold ten patrons inside, the rest outside on a scattering of tables and chairs in an open space not even large enough to be called a square. Then they continued, climbing higher and higher, until he ducked through an archway, drew her up a last flight of worn stone steps, and they emerged onto the roof of a truncated tower.

Moira gasped, moving immediately to the crenellated edge, placing her hands on the stone for support as she leaned out to take in the view. The city gleamed around them on all sides, sunlight glancing off of white stone buildings and the occasional fountain or pool of water. People, carts, and wagons moved on the streets in a steady stream, and barges plied the rivers and the ley lines. The noise of the city rose around them, merging into a wash of sound without component parts, while overhead the blue skies were streaked with white clouds, the storm far to the south. Slightly north of east, the towers of Grass rose like spikes into the sky, and on all sides the new subtowers glowed a faint white, subdued by the brightness of the sun. A light breeze played with Moira's hair and the folds of her dress.

She breathed in deeply and exhaled. "How did you find this place?"

Allan shrugged, suddenly aware of the time. They'd spent longer on the boat than he'd intended. "One of the other Dogs knew of it. He told me how to find it. You can only reach this part of the Canal District by boat."

He let her revel in the breeze and the sights and smells of the city until she turned back toward him, then said reluctantly, "We should go eat. It's getting late, and—"

"We both have to report to the Amber Tower," she finished for him. Her shoulders slumped, but she stepped toward him and took his hand. "But we can always come back later."

Allan grinned. "We will."

"Look!" Cory exclaimed, pointing out over the edge of the roof of their apartment building where they lay on their stomachs, staring out toward Grass, even though they couldn't see any of the activity beneath the main towers, only the towers themselves.

Excitement thrumming through Kara's skin—and a building energy prickling at the back of her neck—she squirmed farther forward. "What? What did you see? I don't see anything."

"The lights in the Amber Tower just came on, near the top."

Kara rolled her eyes, but said, "That must be the main ballroom. My mother said many of the lords and ladies will be there, although anyone with influence will be in Seeley Park below the new tower."

"Is that where your mother will be working?"

"No, she's not working today. She's coming with us to the park. She's supposed to work afterward, though." But Kara didn't care. Her mother would be with them for the main event, the activation of the tower. Everyone would be there—her parents, Cory, his family, the Tender Ischua. The only one who'd be missing would be Justin.

She frowned, her gaze dropping to the throng of people already heading toward Grass in the streets around their building. It had been over two weeks since Justin had vanished and still no one knew anything. No one even seemed to be looking anymore.

"You're thinking of Justin again, aren't you?"

Kara gave a guilty start, although she wasn't certain why. "How did you know?"

Cory pushed up, sitting cross-legged. "You get this worried, distant look, your eyes all squinched up and tight." He hung his head, hands twisting in the ties of his shoes. "It wasn't your fault. Or mine."

Kara shoved herself up and faced Cory. "We should have believed him when he said someone was watching him. We should have said something then."

"I never saw anyone."

"Neither did I."

"I thought he was just being . . . you know . . . Justin."

Kara sighed and looked back toward the towers of Grass. "I know. So did I. But we should have trusted him. We should have searched for him longer, harder."

"We did search for him. We've been doing nothing else for the past two weeks outside of school."

They sat in silence for a long moment. And then Cory said, "Kara?"

She turned, something in Cory's voice clutching at the base of her throat, making it hard to breathe. Since she'd told him of Ischua and the test in Halliel's Park, he'd been distant, like her own parents, anger simmering beneath the surface. But in the last week that had faded, until it was almost like it had been before. But she heard that distance between them in his voice now.

He met her gaze, his eyes huge. She saw fear there, a strange vulner-ability, and buried deep beneath that apprehension, but no anger.

Cory swallowed once, then said, "I don't want you to go."

She knew he was talking about the test and the Wielders, still years away, but before she could say anything, he leaned forward and kissed her on the cheek.

Heat burned up from Kara's chest and she felt her neck and ears prickling, knew she was flushed a deep red, that her eyes were wide. She knew she should say something, but her throat had locked, her entire body paralyzed.

Cory had ducked his head down with a choked sob, but he suddenly looked back up, his own face bright red and filled with terror. "I'm sorry," he whispered, and then bolted for the door and stairwell down to their apartments.

"Cory, wait!" She wrenched herself up and ran after him. He'd al-ready vanished down the stairs, and when she reached the door, she plowed into her father coming up from below.

"Hey, hey, hey," he said, catching her and holding her close, shushing her. She struggled at first, not certain why she was crying, but after a moment she buried her face in her father's shirt and clutched him tight.

A moment later, he pushed her back, gently, and knelt down before her. "Hush, Kara. What happened? What's wrong?"

Kara felt the blush returning and scrubbed at her tear-streaked face with the crook of her arm. "Nothing. Cory doesn't want me to leave."

Her father chuckled and brushed the hair from her forehead. "None of us want you to leave, Kara." His eyes narrowed as her blush deepened, the skin where Cory had kissed her throbbing . . . but then he suddenly relaxed, a smile turning the corners of his mouth, as if he knew what had happened even though she hadn't said anything. He stood and herded her down the stairs to their loft. "Everything will be fine, Kara. We still have time, a few years at least. Ischua has assured me of this. In the meantime, your mother is waiting with Ischua downstairs. You still want to go to the park, don't you?"

Kara shoved the turmoil of emotions over Cory to one side and nodded, letting the excitement she'd felt earlier on the roof build again.

When they reached the street—her mother, Ischua, and Cory's parents already waiting—she smiled at Cory and, even though the air between them throbbed with an awkward tension, she grabbed his hand and broke into excited chatter as they headed toward the park.

Seven

ALLAN HUSTLED DOWN the crowded walk, dodging the press of people as they edged their way toward the open swath of grass in the park beyond, vying for the best view of the new tower and the rumored spectacle that was going to take place a few hours before sunset. None of them knew exactly what to expect, but everyone had seen the subtowers being lit during the past few weeks and the anticipation had grown, the rumors getting wilder and wilder on the streets. Allan had paid little attention to them, too caught up in the activities of the Dogs and their attempt to find and eliminate all of the Kormanley, and on meeting and surprising Moira. But he could feel the excitement of the crowds now, coming off of the citizens of Erenthrall in palpable waves. It thrummed in his skin and traced lines down his back. His breath quickened as it began to affect him and he pushed deeper into the park, searching for Hagger and the rest of the Dogs. The general city watch was scheduled to patrol the park for the duration of the event and to check those entering the field for anything suspicious, their presence blatant and visible. The Dogs were there to search for the Kormanley and any other dangers as they mingled with the crowds.

And Allan was already late.

"Pup! Where in hells have you been?"

Allan honed in on Hagger's grating voice, already sensing the anger in it. A moment later he found himself in the empty space that separated the people of Erenthrall from the contingent of Dogs already beginning to break up and spread out around the park.

Allan headed straight for Hagger. "Have you seen the crowd? It took me forever to get through them."

Hagger snorted in contempt. "You mean you stayed with your little servant girl longer than you should have." He cuffed Allan hard across the back of his head, as if he were a child. "Don't do it again, no matter how much you want her ass. She's only a woman, and you're a Dog and will always be a Dog. The Dogs come first in everything. We're assigned the northeast corner, farthest from the main activity. Terrence is our alpha today."

"Where's the captain?"

"With the Baron in Seeley Park, along with a small gathering of extremely exclusive guests. The entire park has been sectioned off. Only the Wielders and the twenty or so guests Baron Arent personally invited are allowed in."

"But it's nearly twice the size of this one. Why not use this one and open Seeley to the rest of Erenthrall?"

"You saw the barges the Wielders have had built," Hagger growled. "They claim they need the barges directly beneath the new tower, which for some reason the Wielders have begun calling the Hub, so that means Seeley Park. Now shut up and let's find our corner."

Allan had seen the barges being built on scaffolding in the middle of the park, complete with sails, which made no sense. The Dogs had also been told what the Wielders intended for those barges, and Allan didn't believe it was possible. But that was the Wielders' problem, not the Dogs'.

Hagger bellowed and a path cleared before them as they made their way across the grass and scattered trees. They reached the northeast corner without trouble, Hagger cursing as a cart drew in front of them, the driver ducking his head within his cowl as the Dog berated him and demanded his vendor's permit; the cart would already have been checked by the city guard manning the perimeter. He noted their ranks lining opposite sides of the cobbled path that cut down the length of the park. A statue of a soldier, sword drawn and pointed toward the sky, stood on a wide pedestal at the park's corner, a line of narrow trees screening it from the base of a tower to the east. The Hub rose into the sky to the south, so close that Allan had to crane his neck and shade his eyes from the sun to see the top. It still appeared lifeless to him, the windows darkened, even the veined-leaf texture of its sides strangely flat. But from this distance, he could see the individual leaves that had grown to form its walls. Others protruded outward to form balconies, edges curled up to protect those from falling over the side. Holes gaped wide in the bulbous top.

Raised voices and the sound of thrown punches hitting flesh drew Allan's attention back to the park, but Hagger had already intervened, seizing the two young boys by the scruffs of their necks, shaking them like sacks of grain as he roared about keeping the peace or they'd face the Baron's Amber Tower. Then he tossed them to the ground and waited until they'd picked themselves up and scrambled away. Allan moved closer to the statue, noted another cart, its contents covered, making its way toward the front of the park. A third had wallowed out in the grass at the northwest corner.

He frowned and shook his head. Why hadn't they used the stone walkway?

Then a child screamed and his attention was diverted, the mother's harsh voice calling the girl back to her side. Allan began scanning faces, looking for pickpockets, for anyone acting suspicious, for signs of the white robes of the Kormanley or their newly adopted symbol. Instead, he saw elders being guided along by their sons and daughters, couples with hands clasped, and families, all drawn toward the south end of the park, most intent on getting as close as they could to the Hub before the festivities began. Performers roamed the crowd—magicians doing tricks for the children, jesters and players capering and cavorting. One enterprising man had set up a folding table and sold chunks of seared meat on sticks, claiming it was chicken.

As the excitement grew, infecting everyone in the park, Allan became more and more anxious. His hand fell to the handle of his sword and he edged backward, until he stood against the base of the statue. From this vantage, he could see most of the park. If he only had more height—

He turned to look up at the pedestal, then caught Hagger's eye and gestured his intent. The elder Dog nodded permission.

He heaved himself up onto the edge of the pedestal, kept his balance by grasping the raised arm of the soldier, then situated himself so he could see the grove of trees at the southern end of the park. Three more statues stood at the other corners, their bases nearly lost in the crush of people. At least five carts had made it to the front, where even now he could see men and women in Wielders' robes handing out some kind of sparkling sticks to those gathered. The cart that had wallowed in the grass remained behind, to Allan's right.

At least five thousand people had gathered, perhaps more. And when Allan glanced back over his shoulder, he could see thousands more packing the streets behind.

A sudden hush fell and Allan spun back, frowning as those beneath the statue touched their arms or hissed sharply to their neighbors. As at the sowing, Allan realized that nearly everyone could feel what was about to happen except for him. The anticipation doubled, all eyes turning toward the Hub, breaths held.

Then, abruptly, light fountained skyward near the base of the Hub and everyone gasped, drawing back. Allan saw a ripple in the crush of people nearest to the Hub as everyone there retreated. Those with the sticks the Wielders had handed out raised them to the sky. But the gouts of light didn't explode upward as they had at the sowing.

Instead, white light flared in the base of the tower itself, as had happened in the subtowers upon their activation . . . except this was a hundred times more powerful, the tower larger, the light more immense. The light streaked upward, threading through the veins of the leaves and bringing their lifeless forms into sharp and searing relief. The crowd cried out, half in awe, half in fear, as the light roared up the length of the tower, bleeding out of the windows and balconies before reaching its apex and exploding outward in a conflagration so bright that Allan was forced to shield his eyes. His heart thudded in his chest, pounded throughout his entire body, and all around him those gathered reacted to the unexpected brilliance. Children screamed. A few women shrieked. Men bellowed in surprise, a few cursing.

Allan's hand squeezed the hilt of his sword, but he blinked rapidly, tears forming as his vision cleared. He lowered his hand—

And found the intense white light still burning at the center of the tower's bulbous top, flaring out of the gaping holes in the tower's sides like a beacon, like a second sun. It had dimmed enough that he could look at it directly, but it still hurt his eyes. The shaft of the tower had dimmed as well, the light fading from the windows and balconies completely. Only the walls of the tower remained traced with power, the veins of the leaves throbbing with a soft yet still visible green, as if the leaves had been held up to the sun. The previously lifeless tower now beat with a pulse like that of his own heart, steady and potent.

He glanced toward Hagger uncertainly, the crowd around him turning to each other as well, looks of disappointment on their faces. A few murmured, "Is that it? Is it over?"

Allan mouthed the question to Hagger, who shrugged.

It was strangely anticlimactic. And the Dogs had been told to expect more. Had the Wielders' experiment failed? He had already seen something similar to this display at the subtowers, knew that many of the citizens of Erenthrall had seen the same over the past two weeks. The crowds had grown as each one was activated. Even though the Hub was a hundred times taller and grander, the power behind it infinitely greater, he still felt somehow . . . cheated.

He thought suddenly of his conversation with Moira about the trout and wondered if the awe and wonder of the city had already worn off for him.

And then one of the men close to Allan's position swore and pointed. "What in bloody hells is that?"

Everyone turned, necks craning, some stepping forward, hands on the shoulders of the person before them. Allan followed the direction of the man's arm, low on the horizon—

And nearly stumbled backward and off the pedestal, even though he'd been told what to expect by the Wielders. He caught himself on the soldier's arm as shock drove the breath from his lungs. In the crowd before him, men shouted in alarm, while women clutched at their husbands' arms. Children buried their faces in their parents' legs, and a few of the adults actually gasped and fainted dead away. No one moved to catch them, everyone frozen in confusion, in fear and awe.

Above the copse of trees at the southern end of the park, beneath the blazing light of the Hub, the barges built in Seeley Park were rising into the sky. Bases like the barges that plied the river and the ley lines, but with sails rigged flat across the tops instead of vertically on masts, they drifted upward and out from the tower, the sails belled like true sails, but with no wind that Allan could feel or sense. In fact, the cloth of the sails appeared to glimmer, as if suffused with ley light.

The flying boats—Allan counted seven of them—reached the copse of trees at the end of the park, the top branches scraping across the hulls. Once they cleared the branches, the people closest to the trees panicked, even though the ships continued to ascend, all seven shooting away from the Hub in a straight line, separating as they moved, like the spokes of a wheel. The crowd broke, screams rising from the distance, people turning and charging away, trying to stay clear of the ground beneath the ships. But the park was too packed, the ships moving too fast.

The excitement of a moment before peaked . . . and then twisted into raw fear.

"What's happening?" Hagger demanded, and Allan glanced down to find the Dog had moved to the base of the pedestal.

"The people are panicking. They're trying to flee from the . . ." he swallowed, ". . . from the flying barges."

The panic spread. Allan could see it ripple through those gathered, felt it when the wave hit their location. The unease of the people that surrounded them escalated, people shifting, glancing at each other in uncertainty. Most began to edge away as one of the ships headed straight toward their position. The city guard along the walk grew tense. Signal whistles pierced the air from the direction of the worst of the panic, their sound skittering down Allan's back, but nothing changed. The barge was close enough now that Allan could see people at its edge, hanging over the side and pointing down at those below.

The lords and ladies Baron Arent had invited to Seeley Park.

"We have to do something," Allan said.

"What?" Hagger demanded.

Allan shrugged. Before he could answer, someone bellowed in a deep, dark, authoritative voice, "Abominations! Look what abominations the Baron has created now! Look at how he twists nature to his own whims!"

Allan's gaze ripped from the rising ships toward the voice, toward the man who now pointed toward the skies, toward the oncoming ship, and screamed, "Sacrilege! He has perverted the very sanctity of the heavens! He has defied the gods!"

The crowd—on the verge of panic a moment before—paused in confusion, even as Allan narrowed his eyes and muttered under his breath, "Kormanley."

Before anyone could react, the man—face twisted in frenzied rage—threw his arms back and roared, "We shall pay for our hubris! We shall be punished!"

And on his last words, the cart that had wallowed in the trampled grass exploded in a ball of seething flame.

Allan ducked, the park instantly torn with screams of terror and pain, interrupted within a heartbeat by the crump of another explosion, this one distant, coming from the front of the park nearer the Hub. Two more followed, flames enveloping the entire southern side, reaching toward the sky and the ship that passed overhead. The fire caressed the bottom of one of them, the craft rocking in its wake, the wood scorched, but it didn't catch. The sails thrashed in the backwash, but held, the ship faltering only a moment. Most of the ships had already passed beyond the range of the carts.

On the field beneath, fire raged, catching in the trees to the south. Allan cursed and jumped down from the pedestal to Hagger's side. The elder Dog was yelling for the crowd to remain calm, but no one could hear him above the shouting. The city guards' whistles shrieked on all sides.

"The Kormanley have set part of the park on fire!" Allan screamed into Hagger's ear as the tumult increased. "There are bodies on the field!"

"Leave that to the city guard! What about the Kormanley?"

"I lost sight of him in the chaos! He was swallowed up by the crowd when it began to panic!"

Hagger's jaw tightened, teeth clenched. The panicked people pressed up against them, shoving them back into the pedestal. Overhead, the ship passed by, its shadow falling across them both. Hagger looked up, then focused on the pillar of smoke that billowed up from the first cart.

"Gods-damned lords and their parties," he muttered, then grabbed Allan's shoulder and shoved him away from the pedestal. "Make for the cart! We'll help whoever we can and try to bring this gods-cursed mob under control from there. Snag any of the Dogs and city patrol you see along the way. If you see any of the Kormanley, take them! I don't care what you have to do!"

Allan nodded and thrust himself into the press of people, elbowing men, women, and children out of his way as he roared for them to make room. Hagger did the same a few steps away. But he already knew that what the Kormanley had intended to do here had been accomplished. There would be no men in white robes to hunt down. Not today.

The Kormanley had changed. They were no longer content with words alone, no longer content with harming only themselves.

They'd declared war on Baron Arent and all of Erenthrall.

Kara moaned and blinked up into blurred sunlight and sky marred by black billowing streaks. Smoke. Its scent burned her nose, harsh and acidic. She raised a hand to her face, rubbed at her foggy eyes to get them clear. Her head pounded and her ears hurt. Her entire body hurt. Aches riddled her arms and legs as she shifted. Whistles pierced the air and people shouted, but the sound came from a long distance, muted, as if her ears had been stuffed with cloth.

"What happened?" she croaked. She could barely hear her own words.

Acrid smoke skated across her face and she choked and coughed and rolled to one side, tears squeezed through her eyelids. She levered herself onto her hip, grass prickling her hands, and suddenly she remembered.

The new tower, the park, the rising of the boats, Cory's excitement, her parents' unease, and then—

She twisted in the grass. She could see the gleaming tower, suffused with light, the beacon pulsing at its top in a slow, steady rhythm that matched her own heartbeat. As soon as the activation had begun, she'd felt it through the grass of the park, the working so powerful that it had thrummed in her chest. But unlike the sowing of the tower earlier, when she felt the energy pulling at her, drawing upon her strength through her feet, she'd unconsciously blocked it off. She hadn't felt faint or dizzy.

But when the boats had risen, a sense of awe had filled her. She'd met Cory's gaze, seen the same excitement there, and then the two of them had surged forward, away from the wagon where they'd halted to watch the tower. Her father had called out to her, his voice harsh, threaded with fear. Her mother had barked, "Kara!" The same panic that tinged her voice wove through the crowd around her and Cory, but they'd simply wanted to get a better view. She'd heard Ischua, the Tender, attempting to calm them.

Then a man nearby had bellowed something about abominations, about paying a price—

And something had exploded. The wash of heat had thrust Kara forward, as if she'd been shoved hard from behind. The air had been sucked from her lungs as she was flung to the ground. For a moment, the world had blacked out.

Now clouds of smoke streamed into the sky from the base of the tower. The ships floated a short distance away, now out over the city, but her attention wasn't held by the awe-inspiring spectacle anymore. It was fixed on the park.

People lay everywhere, bloody and torn, some screaming as they staggered to their feet clutching arms or legs, or holding hands to gashes on their faces. A wagon lay in splinters at their center, burning with a fierce heat, those closest not moving at all. Kara's breath choked off and she leaped to her feet.

"Da!" she shrieked, the word tearing in her throat. She coughed and lurched toward the wagon, sound solidifying even as she moved. The city guard and a few Dogs barked orders, but Kara ignored them. Someone reached for her, but she thrust the blood-streaked woman aside, crawled over a man who was missing an arm, the stump blackened, still smoldering. Her eyes latched onto a body wearing a blue shirt—her father's shirt—and she scrambled toward his side.

"Da," she gasped, then rolled her father onto his back.

Half of his face had been charred, cooked to gristly meat and bone. His remaining good eye stared sightlessly up at the sky.

Kara screamed, the sound emerging from deep in her chest. It filled her head, drowned out the chaos around her. It tore at her lungs and throat.

She heaved backward, away from her father, away from the remains of his face, even though she couldn't look away from it. She collided with someone behind her and arms enveloped her, held her tight. A soothing voice—Ischua's voice—muttered into her ear, words she didn't comprehend. Her voice broke and she heaved in another breath, screamed again as she tore her gaze away from her father only to see her mother lying two paces farther on, body also twisted and blackened. Ischua picked her up and hauled her away from the heat of the burning wagon, away from the destruction. She was vaguely aware that guardsmen were swarming the area, hustling the wounded away, that one of them carried Cory's limp body in his arms beside them.

Her second scream cracked and rattled down into heaving sobs. Tears scoured her face. Her chest ached, tight and hot and fluid. She couldn't seem to catch her breath, her mind scattered, her gaze darting everywhere.

Ischua glanced down at her, his face streaked with soot, twisted in a rictus of pain and grief. His hair had been burned away on one side, the exposed skin raw and angry.

"You're safe," he said. "We'll get you out of here."

Kara didn't react. Numbness began to enfold her, starting in the center of her chest and flowing outward. The world retreated—the sounds, the smells; Ischua's harsh breath and the jarring of her body as he carried her.

All that remained was her father's face, eaten by fire, and an empty hollow in the pit of her stomach.

PART II

Eight

K ARA SPRINTED TO the Wielders' Hall the moment she was summoned, arriving out of breath and flushed. The seven Master Wielders in their black robes waited for her at the end of the empty hall, seated at a long, heavy oaken table, their hands clasped and resting on its surface. Despair washed over her when she didn't see a purple jacket folded neatly before her adviser. Had she failed the examination? She tried to read the Wielders' faces, but they were all studiously blank or stern and creased with wrinkles.

She halted at the end of the hall, then swallowed and forced herself to walk the length of the rich purple-and-green carpet that ran down the center to the table. As she approached, the head of the Wielders' college stood, but he did not speak until she'd reached the end of the carpet and halted.

"Kara Tremain," he intoned, his deep voice filling the expanse of the hall, "it is the opinion of this gathering that you have mastered the skills required of an apprentice. We now present you with the purple jacket of a true Wielder. We expect that you will fulfill your duties at the Eld District's node with the attention and respect that you have shown during your studies here, and that you continue in your efforts to master the ley. The robes of a Master Wielder await you."

Her heart stuttered in her chest at the words—not all Wielders were invited to wear the robes of a master, some were simply given duties within one of the nodes—but before she could recover, her adviser stood, rounded the table, and presented her with her purple jacket. He did so with the rigid solemnity that all of the masters possessed, although she thought she caught a quick smile when he pulled the jacket from where he'd hidden it from sight beneath the table.

She reached out to touch it, her hand trembling, and then her adviser said softly, "Allow me."

He held it open before her as she slipped it on, then tugged it into place. He looked into her eyes, and for the first time she saw the man behind the robes. He'd guided her studies for the last two years, but she suddenly realized she barely knew him. She'd seen him only at the college, in his office, or in the classroom, spoken to him only about the ley, about her courses. She'd hated him for the last six months as he drove her harder and harder in preparation for the exam.

And now, suddenly, she could relax.

"Wear it well, Kara Tremain," he said. "Make the Wielders proud."

Kara nodded, her chest too tight for words, her struggle to hold back tears too intense. She walked from the hall slowly, speeding up as she reached the doors and pushed out into the sunlight before realizing she had nowhere to go. Not close. She thought of Cory—realizing that she'd barely seen him in the last two years, as her studies grew steadily more intense, even though they'd met on a regular basis before that—but he was three districts away, in Confluence, and besides, he'd recently tested into the University, a surprise for them all. Her heart was beating so fast and hard she couldn't simply return to her rooms, but she'd made few friends at the college, too reclusive after her parents' deaths, not to mention the two years' difference in age between her and the other students when Ischua first brought her here. Yet she still wanted to leap in joy, shout in triumph, laugh until her throat was raw.

Instead, she retreated to the nearest shadows, beneath a portico, where she knew few of the students or instructors passed. She trembled in awe, too ecstatic to move. Even breathing was difficult. She ran her hands down the fine fabric of her Wielder's jacket and tried to suppress the laughter that threatened to burst forth. After four grueling years under the hands of the Wielders, studying the ley, the stones like those within Halliel's Park, and the nodes in the city, she had finally been granted her purple jacket. Apprentices wore green jackets, to signify they were training to be Wielders and to make certain they were given the respect they deserved, but only after passing the week-long, grueling tests—both academic and practical—were apprentices granted the purple jackets of a true Wielder.

Kara had completed her exams five days before, had been hovering in alternating dread, despair, and excitement since. She knew she'd handled the practical aspects of the exam without issue. Ever since she'd been shoved into the well of ley in one of the nodes after her first month of training, she'd been connected to the ley in a way that she and the other Wielders barely understood. But the academic portions had nearly killed her. Mathematics and the underlying structures of the ley and how it was manipulated were easy; learning all of the rote historical dates and names and achievements had been enough to make her scream. Who cared which of the Barons of the surrounding lands had signed the concordance that ceded all control of the ley to the Wielders in Erenthrall under Baron Arent's hand? And who cared that Wielder Antipithus had discovered a secondary ley field in the Steppe fifty-five years ago, giving rise to the Nexus at the island-city of Severen and providing the first step of Erenthrall's expansion of control to the north? Although Kara did wonder how Prime Wielder Augustus had been around at the time to oversee the building of that node; Augustus barely looked forty. And Arent had been the Baron then as well, even though he appeared younger than Augustus! She'd asked but been summarily shut down, her adviser telling her it was information to which only the Primes were privy.

She shrugged. It had happened long before Kara was born. She didn't see why it mattered to Erenthrall today, especially not for a newly-jacketed Wielder.

She ran her hand down the purple fabric once again and shuddered at the sensation.

"Be careful, or you'll wear it out before you even step onto the streets of Erenthrall."

Kara started and spun, thrusting her hands behind her back guiltily, then glared as Ischua chuckled and moved toward her. Afternoon sunlight lanced down between the arched columns of the portico, an open square surrounded by buildings beyond. A few students were working on their studies in the light, most with green jackets. Two of the Master Wielders paced sedately through the area, passing through the shade of the porches and covered walkways beyond.

"I won't wear it out," she said with a mock scowl. "It's too new."

Ischua laughed and shook his head. "I tried to make it here before they presented it to you, but my duties kept me. A Wielder should have someone to rejoice with when they don the purple jacket. I know you have few friends here, and since your parents' deaths. . . ."

Kara's heart clenched at the old pain and a deeper hatred as Ischua's voice grew somber. She tasted the ash of the fires from the park that afternoon, glanced to where she knew Ischua's head was scarred from the explosion. He wore a simple rounded hat to cover the mark. He'd saved her and Cory that afternoon, although Cory's parents had survived.

She thought of that last night on the roof of the apartment building, Cory's flushed face after he'd kissed her, the panic in his eyes.

"My father would have been proud of me," she said roughly, to break the awkward silence.

"Your mother as well. Especially since you'll make Master soon enough. They did mention Master's robes, didn't they?"

She grinned. "How did you know?"

"Because I could sense your power back in Halliel's Park. I wouldn't be surprised if the black cloak of a Prime is in your future. Although you shouldn't rush such things. You're already two years ahead of everyone else."

She gaped at him, speechless, her arms tingling at the thought.

Ischua chuckled, then reached forward to grip her shoulder. "In any case, you should not be alone at a time like this. The purple jacket alone demands a celebration. Walk with me."

He tugged at her shoulder before letting his hand drop, a nudge that wasn't necessary. Even if he didn't wear the robes of a master, she would have come with him. The only reason she was here at the college was because of him; if he hadn't been with them at the park, she wasn't certain what would have happened to her.

They passed out of the shadows of the portico into the afternoon sunlight, chatting as Kara self-consciously caught the envious looks of the green-jacketed students they passed. Ischua guided her to the gates of the college, out into the streets of the Light District. The towers of Grass rose into the sky to the northwest, the beacon of the Flyers' Tower burning bright. Numerous flyers had taken to the skies—at least five that Kara could see—the hulls of the ships dark against the white clouds above. Their specialized sails glittered with leylight. Kara could feel the eddies the ships caused in the Tapestry if she stretched out her senses. She'd once thought that what she felt in her skin and through her feet, what she'd discovered she could manipulate, was the ley itself. She'd learned in her studies that it wasn't, that the Tapestry was the basis of reality around her, the essence of what was real, both seen and unseen. The ley—the power itself—merely flowed along the Tapestry in prescribed courses, as rivers flowed along the land through channels dictated by the hills and valleys. And like rivers, the ley lines were malleable, subject to change if the lay of the land were altered in some way. Wielders manipulated the Tapestry to force the ley into the lines of power they wanted; the Masters at the University manipulated the Tapestry as well, although they could not feel the ley structure like the Wielders.

It was one of many misconceptions the people of Erenthrall held about the Wielders, a misconception the Wielders encouraged. Like all of the specialized guilds, the Wielders held their secrets close, especially from the Masters at the University. Not even the apprentices learned everything, even those who passed the examination. Kara knew there were secrets revealed only to the Primes, such as the exact layout of the ley lines themselves—in Erenthrall, throughout the rest of the Baronies, and beyond—and the reason that both Augustus and Baron Arent appeared younger than they actually were.

"Here we are," Ischua said abruptly, motioning toward an unmarked wooden door, a small window set into it at shoulder height.

Kara glanced around the unfamiliar streets. At some point during the walk, they'd drifted off of the common thoroughfares and into the alleys and side-ways. Like the rest of the district, the buildings were built of off-white granite accented with red-and-brown stones set in patterns along the corners, around windows and doors, and with an occasional artistic flare in the middle of large walls, but here the granite was yellowed with age, the cobblestones of the walks dirtier.

"Where is 'here'?" Kara asked suspiciously.

"Come in and see."

Ischua knocked on the door and the shutter on the small window flipped inward, a man's gray eye filling the space, shooting between both Ischua and Kara before demanding, "Password."

"Copper."

The gray eye narrowed, fixed on Ischua, then vanished, the shutter snapping closed.

A moment later, the door creaked open.

Ischua motioned Kara forward. "After you."

Kara stepped into the door's shadow, caught sight of the gray-eyed man standing behind it, then moved along a short entryway and pushed through a deep red curtain into—

"A tavern?" she spluttered.

Ischua grinned as he joined her. "Not just *any* tavern. This tavern caters only to those who have donned the purple jacket." He turned to scan the few patrons at the tables and booths, all of whom were watching them even as they continued their conversations. Then the old Tender caught the attention of the burly bartender, drew himself up to his full height, and said pretentiously, "An order of the special brew, Ivens." The bartender's eyebrows rose. "We have a new Purple."

The patrons erupted in a general "Here, here!" and a round of applause. The bartender turned to a keg draped in a purple cloth embroidered in gold placed high up behind the massive bar as Ischua and Kara made their way to barstools. A few of the men and women present congratulated her on the way, one woman grasping her arm, a man clapping her on the back. By the time Kara slid onto the seat, the bartender presenting her with a mug that appeared to be made of bone, the same excitement she'd felt immediately after leaving the Wielders' Hall gripped her again. She didn't even hear Ischua order, but suddenly he held up his own mug—much plainer than hers—and toasted, "To donning the purple. May master's robes be close behind."

They clicked mugs and then Kara took a swallow of the beer, nearly choking at the bitterness of the hops, but marveling at the smoothness. She had drunk beer before, of course—no green jacket could survive four years without eventually hitting one of the many local taverns for a glass to take the edge off a particularly grueling day—but she had never had anything as potent or aged as this.

"It's a little bitter," she coughed.

The bartender shook his head and wandered away. Ischua ignored her.

"I have something else for you as well," he said, fishing in one of the pockets of his robes. After a moment, he pulled out a stone and set it into her hands.

It was the size of her fist, blue-black, with swirls of white in it.

She hefted the stone, allowed herself to sense the energies of the Tapestry that flowed around her and through it, then squinched up her face in confusion. "What's this for? Is this another test?"

Ischua shook his head. "No more tests. Not today. Don't you recognize the stone? It's from Halliel's Park. It's the stone you told me didn't belong there, nearly five years ago."

Kara's heart stilled in her chest as some inexplicable emotion coursed through her, like the energy of the Tapestry and the ley. Her hands trembled, clenched unconsciously on the stone, and she looked up at Ischua as a strange ache filled her. "You kept it? All this time?" Her voice was ragged, and her eyes burned with tears.

Ischua merely smiled. "Of course I did."

Kara didn't know what to say, but she drew the stone closer to her body protectively. It carried with it a myriad of emotions, brought back memories of her father, who'd taken her to the park that day, and Cory, who'd felt so betrayed by her leaving to become one of the Wielders, even though they'd kept in touch.

"So," Ischua said, to break the awkward silence, "where did the illustrious Prime Wielders station their newest Wielder?"

Kara ran her hands over the surface of the stone, then tucked it into one of the pockets of her jacket. "Eld District."

Ischua's eyes narrowed. "Really? That's . . . interesting."

Kara straightened where she sat, leaning forward. "Why?"

Ischua glanced at her out of the corner of his eye, raising his mug to take a slow drink. He lowered his head, as if considering whether he should answer or not, then blew out a breath between his lips. "Because the Primes don't usually allow Wielders to work in the same district where they grew up. You know how they are about keeping the Wielder secrets."

"'No Wielder can know the location of all of the ley lines, nor all of the nodes,'" Kara recited.

"Only the Prime Wielders know the true map of the ley, and most of those only know that of Erenthrall or their own city's Nexus. Only Prime Augustus knows the full extent of the ley system, and he won't share. The ley system is his creation and he intends to keep it that way."

Kara shifted in her seat, suddenly uncomfortable.

"You tried to map it yourself, didn't you?"

Kara took a hefty swig of beer, coughed harshly. "How did you know?"

Ischua chuckled. "I don't think there's ever been a green jacket who hasn't. What did you discover?"

"That the ley system we can see being used for the barges—and now the flyers—and the nodes that dot the city are merely surface elements of a much larger system underground." She sighed.

Ischua nodded. "There are nodes throughout the city, ones that the general population in Erenthrall does not know about, or suspect."

Kara thought about what she'd sensed when Ischua had tested her, the lake of ley hidden beneath the city. "Like Halliel's Park."

Ischua raised an eyebrow. "Perhaps." But then he frowned. "But placing you in the Eld District is unusual. I would have expected them to station you somewhere north of Grass, away from all of the people that you knew growing up, away from any friends or family."

"I don't have any family in Eld anymore," Kara said. "The only friend I have is Cory, and I haven't spoken to him since he was tested and sent to the University in Confluence a few months ago. I've been too busy." She thought abruptly of Justin, but shoved that memory away. He'd never been found after disappearing that day, although she knew that his parents had continued the search, that they'd even continued their attempts to enlist the Dogs. Their efforts had yielded nothing. Justin was simply gone, as if he'd never existed.

Kara shivered at the thought.

Ischua settled his hand on her shoulder and squeezed. She gave him a weak smile, then noticed that his attention had been caught by something over her shoulder.

"Marcus!" he shouted, half-standing from the barstool and motioning someone over from the opposite side of the bar. "Marcus, come here. I have someone you should meet."

Kara twisted in her seat, then stilled.

Marcus was another Wielder, his purple jacket dusty and worn with use, although he appeared to be only a few years older than Kara. His hair was a thick blond-brown, mussed up as if he'd just run his hands through it, and his eyes were a startling blue. He moved with a cool confidence, drawing away from another group of Wielders seated around a table in the far corner. His grin was easy and didn't falter even when he caught sight of Kara and a slight frown of consternation creased his forehead.

"Ischua," he said in acknowledgment.

"This is Kara Tremain," Ischua said. "Freshly risen to the purple jacket . . . and stationed in the Eld District." The gardener turned to

Kara. "Marcus Renshaw, one of the Wielders in Eld. You'll be working with him for the next few years."

Marcus held out his hand, the creases in his forehead gone. As they clasped forearm to forearm, a heady warmth rushed from Kara's hand down through her chest, settling disconcertingly in her stomach. She gasped slightly, then caught Marcus' eyes.

"Welcome to the Eld node," he said. "Find me when you arrive, and I'll show you around."

"I don't think I can do it," Tyrus said without preamble as he dropped himself into the seat across the small café table from Dalton.

Dalton glanced up from the news sheet he was reading, took in his fellow Kormanley's appearance—pale, haunted, and shaken—and immediately motioned for the server. "A shot of Gorrani wine, please, the stronger the better."

Then he turned his attention to Tyrus. The slightly younger man looked as if he'd aged twenty years since he'd infiltrated the splinter sect of Kormanley, his hair gray and face pinched and lined with worry and tension. He sat slumped in his chair, staring at Dalton but without any indication that he actually saw him, his eyes distant, locked on some vision Dalton couldn't see.

"I can't," he mumbled to himself as the server arrived and placed the tall, narrow glass of wine on the table. "I can't do it."

As soon as the server departed, Dalton asked, "Can't do what?" Although he thought he already knew. He'd given the order, after all.

Tyrus jerked, his focus snapping in on Dalton, then away as he checked to see if anyone sat nearby. They were outside one of the many cafés in Wintemeer, but Dalton had chosen a secluded section near the back, partially hidden behind a screen of dangling ivy. No one was near.

Tyrus leaned forward. "They want me to plant a bomb on one of the barges. I can't do it, Dalton. Running errands for them, passing along messages, even forging documents through my office is one thing, but this is entirely different. This bomb may kill people! Others have before this."

Dalton frowned in consternation. He nearly pointed out that forging documents and passing messages that led to the bombs the Kormanley had been setting off throughout the city for the last four years made

Tyrus as culpable as those who planted the bombs in the first place, but restrained himself. Tyrus didn't need any more doubt or guilt laid at his feet. He was already shaken up enough.

And Dalton needed him where he was, as his eyes and ears in that splinter cell. If he backed out now. . . .

"They trust you enough to plant a bomb?" he asked carefully.

Tyrus snorted. "I don't know if it's trust so much as desperation. The Dogs have been sniffing a little too close to the group lately. Calven thought he caught one following him the other day, so he doesn't dare risk it himself. Both Vanel and Ari planted the last one in Stone. Even though that was six months ago, they don't dare do another any time soon. That only leaves me, and Vanel has threatened—" He cut off suddenly, one hand reaching to massage the back of his neck. Fear leaked out through the sickening dread that had bleached his face. His gaze locked with Dalton's. "But I can't do it. I can't do something that I know will hurt people, probably kill them. What if there are women on the barge? Children?" He looked close to vomiting.

Hot anger flicked through Dalton; he reached forward and grabbed the flute of Gorrani wine. Tyrus' weakness nauseated him. This was why the original Kormanley had failed so miserably, because no one had been willing to take action, to take risks. It was why he'd cultivated the younger members when he'd noticed they were willing and able to take those extra, sometimes violent, steps.

"Don't you see what this means?" he snapped. "It means you're finally making progress. Real progress. It took over a year before they trusted you enough to remove their cowls during the meetings and reveal themselves."

"That was only because the Dogs raided and caught Korana and Pils immediately after that first meeting," Tyrus grumbled.

Dalton nodded in irritation at the interruption. "But they revealed themselves. We knew who they were. We figured out how they operated, and you were privy to some of their plans."

"Not that it helped much."

Dalton thrust the wine into Tyrus' hands, noted that they weren't trembling as much. "We stopped their attack in Wintemeer, didn't we?" Which was a lie. That had been an accident; the bomb had gone off before it could be put in place. But if the accident could be used to keep Tyrus in line, so much the better. "And now they trust you to carry out one of the attacks yourself. I'd call that progress. Slow progress, but progress nonetheless. More than the Dogs can claim. Now drink. It will help calm your nerves."

Tyrus drank absently, coughed harshly as the potent wine—made from a cactus that grew only in the Gorrani Flats—hit the back of his throat. A flush burned through his sickly pallor. "We're still no closer to finding out who the Kormanley's Benefactor is," he wheezed.

"But we know there are at least five Kormanley groups spread throughout the city, even if we don't know who their members are. One of them must have contact with this Benefactor, or at least know of someone who does." Dalton knew the Benefactor, of course, even if he only received direction from him through a courier. And there were seven active Kormanley groups in Erenthrall, not to mention the groups he'd begun to organize in other cities with the Benefactor's help.

"Calven said someone from one of the other groups approached him recently, a man named Ibsen. He said the group is planning something major and they may need our help. He didn't reveal any other details, only that it involved the Baron somehow."

A tension within Dalton released and he leaned back into his chair and picked up his own wine. So Ibsen had made contact, then. This was exactly why he needed Tyrus in that group's confidence.

And it was exactly what he needed to keep Tyrus where he was.

"You have to plant the bomb, then." At Tyrus' pained look, he added, "Even if we can't learn the identity of the Benefactor, you need to re-main inside the Kormanley group long enough to find out about this new plan."

Tyrus held his gaze . . . but then his shoulders sagged in resignation. He took a deep swallow of the wine, merely wincing at the burn. "If you think it's best."

Taking pity, Dalton asked, "Where are you supposed to plant this bomb?"

"On a barge in the ley station in North Umber, beneath one of the seats."

"If you can give me more details, I'll see if I can stop it somehow, like the Wintemeer attack."

Hope flared in Tyrus' eyes. "I'll let know you which barge as soon as I find out."

Dalton forced a reassuring smile. "You'll be fine, Tyrus. Trust me."

Tyrus finished the last of his wine with a grimace and hurried through the scattered café tables and out into the street. As soon as he passed outside of Dalton's view, Dalton frowned.

Tyrus might be a problem. He couldn't afford to push him so far that he ran to the Dogs. He knew little about the splinter Kormanley—only those members in his own group, and now Ibsen—but Dalton couldn't afford to have the Dogs nosing around at this stage. Not so close to the beginning of this new endeavor. The attacks on the ley stations, bridges, and the Baron's holdings throughout the city weren't enough; the last four years had proven that. And the Kormanley's Benefactor had grown impatient. He wanted the group to do something more significant.

Dalton was more than happy to oblige. He glanced skyward, noted two barges and one of the lords' personal flyers skimming the sky overhead, above Grass. His lip curled in derision and his stomach roiled. The Baron's abuse of the ley had become more flagrant with the activation of the Flyers' Tower. The ley was never meant to be used in such a manner. He had hoped the attacks would catch the attention of the citizens of Erenthrall, force them to see the Baron's abuse for what it was, but obviously the citizens were content to let him squander the ley's power for his own purposes. He'd certainly used it to solidify his hold on the other Barons, lords, and ladies; most were clamoring to have Flyers' Towers built in their own cities.

Not even the strange distortions that had begun appearing throughout Erenthrall over the past few years were enough to awaken the citizens' fears. The bursts of light that appeared at random made everyone pause, and there were rumblings of discontent, but usually only when the distortions forced a delay in the ley barges' schedules. Most didn't care where they came from, or what caused them, as long as they didn't disrupt their lives.

But Dalton did. Each instance of a distortion drove his fear of what the Primes and the Baron were doing to the ley deeper into his gut. He was convinced they were caused by the overuse of the ley, that they were signs of the strain on the system. He couldn't prove it—he had no intimate knowledge of the ley nodes or the Nexus—but he *knew* it was true. The distortions were a warning. And if that warning wasn't heeded. . . .

He shuddered—in fear, dread, and with a touch of ecstasy. He didn't know what would happen, but he'd had visions of Erenthrall in ruins, its towers cracked, its streets empty. Each time he dreamed, he woke soaked in sweat, his body trembling and weak. And the visions were coming more often now, had become more intense. They'd set him on this path initially—they were why he'd joined the Kormanley in the first place, in his youth—but now they'd grown urgent, as if a reckoning were coming. He had to stop it. It was his destiny to stop it.

And to do that he had to push the Kormanley harder, take greater risks. He needed to set his sights higher, as their Benefactor suggested.

Perhaps as high as the Baron himself.

Tyrus wiped sweat from his forehead with the sleeve of one arm and scuttled down the tunnel in the ley station to the platform beneath, leaving the mezzanine behind. The space before the ley line that ran through the far side of the chamber was crowded, citizens milling about as one barge unloaded and another departed. A whistle pierced the air as he worked his way toward the edge of the platform, swiping at his face again. He shifted the strap of the rucksack slung across one shoulder. It was heavier than he'd expected.

The barge that had been unloading passengers when he arrived closed its doors and pulled out, the platform clearing slightly as people made their way up to the mezzanine above. Tyrus watched them, mumbling, "Yes, yes, keep moving, out to the streets, you're safer there," under his breath.

He started when another whistle blew and turned to find another barge sliding down the glowing white ley line. It emerged from the tunnel and pulled to a halt beside the platform, a gust of air at its passage cooling the sweat on Tyrus' face. He swallowed, something hard in his throat clicking.

"This is it," he muttered to himself. A woman next to him cast him an odd look. He grimaced and followed her onto the barge, moving toward the seats at the back. He sat down heavily, body shaking. He barely noticed when the barge began moving, heading toward the North Umber District. Acid rose up in the back of his throat and he leaned back and breathed in deeply. He kept his eyes focused on an empty spot. He didn't want to see who else was on the barge, didn't want to see their faces.

When they neared the next station, he reached down and pulled a leather strap that dangled outside the rucksack, felt something tear inside. Then he kicked the rucksack deeper under the seat and stood, glancing around once as the barge drew to a halt—

And stilled, horror seizing his muscles and locking his arms in place, his eyes going wide. A Dog waited impatiently at the door to the barge, one hand steadying himself, the other on the handle of the knife sheathed at his belt. He scanned those around him, all a discreet distance away and studiously avoiding his gaze. His eyes locked onto Tyrus and Tyrus nearly pissed his pants, but then the doors to the barge were opened by the stewards on the platform and the Dog stepped out.

Tyrus stood rooted to the spot, relief coursing through him, then cried out and leaped through the doors as the steward began to close them again. The barge pulled away. Knees weak, he wanted nothing more than to collapse onto the platform where he stood and let the sickening tremors that tingled in his arms and chest fade, but he knew he couldn't stay. He needed to get out of the station, and as far away from North Umber as he could.

He'd reached the tunnel leading up to the mezzanine when the bomb exploded.

Nine

"THERE WAS ANOTHER Kormanley attack last night, this time in the North Umber District," Daedallen said.

From his balcony overlooking the center of Grass in the Amber Tower, Baron Arent Pallentor frowned at Daedallen's report but he did not turn. Overhead, the beacon of the Flyers' Tower pulsed with a brilliant white light, more visible at this height than from the ground. Numerous flyers drifted between the towers, two docking at balconies that jutted out into the open sky below him, while a third sailed past at nearly eye level.

"What did the Kormanley strike this time?" he asked, letting none of his annoyance leech into his voice.

"Another one of the barge stations. They placed an explosive device beneath one of the seats in a rucksack. Twenty people on the barge were injured, another dozen on the platform. Three passengers were killed outright. It is uncertain whether one of those killed was one of the Kormanley."

Arent turned from the window and caught Daedallen's eye. "None of them were Kormanley. They moved beyond immolation and suicides over four years ago."

"One of them died in the Wintemeer attack," Augustus said from his seat at the table, a glass of wine resting before him, untasted.

"But that was a mistake," Daedallen responded immediately. "From what we've learned, the bomb exploded prematurely. It was intended for the Fairview Bridge, not the marketplace. The Kormanley priest was the only death, everyone else was merely injured. It would have been much worse if he'd made it to the bridge."

Arent moved away from the light pouring through the balcony windows and into the main room. The captain of the Dogs glared at the Prime Wielder, face set in a sharp frown. He stood as far from the Wielder as he could without giving offense.

"How did he make it to the square in the first place?" Augustus asked, shifting in his seat to face the Dog. "Shouldn't the Dogs have found him first? Shouldn't the Dogs have discovered their plot and eliminated the threat before it hit the street? Isn't that the Dogs' job?"

Daedallen stiffened. "We've discussed this before. You know it's not that simple."

Augustus smiled thinly. "I expected the Dogs to be more effective, that's all."

"You sanctimonious bast—"

"That's enough, Daedallen." When Arent turned his attention from the bristling Dog, he caught Augustus' smug expression. "You as well, Augustus. We both know the Dogs have done everything possible to contain and eliminate the Kormanley. The group is simply too organized, and too dedicated to their cause. But again, I wonder if it is more than that."

Daedallen and Augustus halted their irritating posturing and focused on him with the statement, both wary.

"What are you saying?" Augustus asked.

Arent moved to the table, reaching for the flagon of wine and pouring himself a glass as he spoke. "As we've discussed before, perhaps the Kormanley are receiving some kind of outside help with regard to their efforts here in Erenthrall. Perhaps the reason we have not been able to locate their leader—if they have a leader—is because their leader does not reside here in the city."

"That would explain why it has been so difficult to find them, yes," the Wielder muttered grudgingly. "But we could never settle on a suspect before this. What has changed? Why rehash an old argument now?"

Daedallen stirred, as if he'd realized where Arent was headed. "We have begun getting reports of the Kormanley spreading to other Baronies. There have been two attacks so far in Farrade and one in Severen. Not on the same scale as here in Erenthrall, but nevertheless. . . ."

"The diplomats from Temerite, Gorrani, the Archipelago, and the

Demesnes to the west have all expressed concern over the Kormanley," Arent added. "They are afraid that because their main cities rely on the ley, that the priests will target them as well."

"They will, eventually," Daedallen said.

"I agree, although I have not said so to any of the diplomats. I'm hoping that we can destroy the Kormanley before that happens."

The captain of the Dogs moved toward the table, his arguments with Augustus set aside. "Who do you think is supporting the Kormanley from outside the city, then? Now that they have spread their attacks outside Erenthrall."

"Who do you believe it is?" Arent countered.

Daedallen didn't react to the subtle admonishment that the Dogs—and Daedallen in particular—should already have their own suspicions. As soon as the attacks began in these other cities, Arent had narrowed his own down to a few likely candidates, one in particular, but he was curious to hear what the captain of the Dogs thought.

Daedallen paced to the tall windows of the balcony, hands clasped behind his back as he stared out into the sunlight. A shadow passed by as one of the flyers drifted around the Amber Tower. "Nothing has changed from our previous discussion; it would have to be someone of high rank, perhaps a lord, although I find that unlikely. The Kormanley have resources that would require more funds than the lords could pull together on short notice, let alone over the course of the last four years. Besides, the lords would have no interest in attacking other cities. Their interests lie solely within Erenthrall, with you, Baron. Without your support, they would be nothing."

"Unless the attacks on Farrade and Severen are independent of the core group here in Erenthrall," Augustus said.

Daedallen turned, his irritation at being interrupted clear, but he nodded in acknowledgment before continuing. "I still believe it un-likely that any of the lords or ladies are funding the group. It is too extensive, has been acting for far too long. Which leaves only the Barons."

Arent had come to the same conclusion in their previous discussions, but he merely inclined his head and said, "Continue."

Daedallen began pacing before the window, moving from one long stretch of deep blue velvet curtain on one side to the other. "Baron

Calluin was distressed over the two attacks in his own city. I doubt he'd sanction attacks on his own Barony—he's too protective and prideful of Farrade's architecture. Baron Tavor might attack his own city to deflect attention away from himself, and with the resources of the Steppe behind him, would have the money to fund the group. But he has never shown any aggression toward Erenthrall, not since his city of Severen was joined to the ley system by the Wielders. That leaves four other Barons—Leethe of Tumbor, Sillare of Dunmara and the Reaches, Ranit of northeastern Jarada, and Iradi of Wayside."

"Ranit is too weak. He does not have the resources of the other Barons, nor the backbone to carry out such devastating attacks." Arent swirled the wine in his glass, brow creased in thought. "It must be Leethe, Sillare, or Iradi. Find out which one is behind the Kormanley before the Baronial Meeting at the end of summer."

Daedallen's eyes narrowed. "You believe it is Leethe."

Arent's hand tightened on his wineglass. "You know what it took to subdue the other Barons, what it took to subdue Tumbor in particular. A hundred years ago, the other Barons viewed Erenthrall as the weakest of the Baronies. And they were right. Erenthrall was nothing, a city lost in the middle of the plains, a trading post surviving at the meeting of the Tiana and Urate Rivers. It provided a convenient resting point for the shipments coming down the river from the northern mountains and the caravans crossing the grassland headed toward the Demesnes to the west. My *father*," he could not suppress the sneer, "was content with letting Erenthrall remain nothing more than that—a stopover to greater places.

"When he died, I seized control of the Barony and allowed Augustus to begin building the Nexus. It took me years to train the Barony's forces after that, even longer to use my new Dogs to bring the Barons to heel. The Baronies had always been unsettled, a place of treachery, assassination, and deceit, but during my rise, the plains were drenched in blood. I succeeded in eliminating the strongest of the Barons, letting weaker and younger sons take their places. I thought the Baronies were mine at that point. I meant to reshape the plains using the Barons' dependence on the ley and their fear of my Dogs as the hammer and anvil.

"But I was wrong."

Daedallen shifted where he stood. "Tumbor."

With effort, Arent forced the hand gripping his wine to relax before the glass shattered. "Tumbor had always been my strongest rival, and it was Leethe's father who revolted when the Barons signed the concordance ceding control of the ley to Erenthrall. He became a thorn, drawing blood at every opportunity. So I sent the Hounds after him. Leethe saw his father die at their hands. Even though he was only nine at the time, I do not think he has forgotten that moment." Arent had not forgotten his own father's bloody death, after all, even though it had been by his command and carried out by his personal guard.

The captain of the Dogs straightened and gave his Baron a formal bow. "May I release the Hounds now?"

Arent stilled.

After Leethe's father's death, the remaining Barons had refused to sign the concordance until Arent agreed to rein in the Hounds and his Dogs. Initially he'd resisted, but when he saw the beginnings of an alliance building against him—one that could be strong enough to defeat his Dogs—he'd relented. He could still train the Hounds, but he could only use them here, within Erenthrall. Sending them to seek out the Barons themselves, in their own lands, in secret. . . .

If the Hounds were discovered, it would be political suicide. The already tenuous hold he had on some of those Barons would shatter. The Barons would ally against him as they had threatened so many decades ago. The concordance—with himself, Erenthrall, and the ley at its center—would crumble. It would be war.

He did not have the resources or the manpower to fight such an alliance. Not now. He needed to keep the Barons on edge, tied and beholden to him—and only him—by the ley.

"No," he said reluctantly. "The Hounds must remain leashed for now. Use the Dogs only."

Arent caught the smirk on Prime Augustus' face and felt anger spark in his chest. He had been ready to dismiss the two men to their respective tasks, but now he set his glass of wine aside. He could not have brought Erenthrall to its current height of power without Augustus, but he could not allow his control of the obsessive Wielder to slip.

"There is one other issue we must discuss," he said.

The Wielder tensed as Arent's attention fell on him. "My Baron," he said.

"These . . . distortions."

Augustus grimaced. "I have had the Wielders looking into them and as of yet we do not have an explanation as to what they are or why they are occurring."

"That is not acceptable. I am receiving reports from all around the city. Since the sowing of the Flyers' Tower and the activation of the subtowers there have been twenty-seven visible distortions in nineteen separate districts. The first was reported within a month, and ten have been reported within the last year. Initially you claimed that they were a result of the ley system acclimating to the activation of the tower, that they would dissipate over time. But I fail to see how that explanation still holds, since the occurrences appear to be escalating. Even the size of these distortions . . . these 'blossoms of light' as the commoners call them . . . has increased." He leaned forward onto the table, both arms rigid. "You assured me, at the time you proposed the Flyers' Tower, that the ley system would be able to handle it. Have you changed your opinion since? Or is there some other explanation for the distortions that now plague my city?"

Augustus' back grew rigid and he shot a black glance toward Daedallen, as if somehow the captain of the Dogs had brought this upon him. But then he turned back to Arent. "So far, we are uncertain exactly what is causing the distortions. I am not convinced that it has anything to do with the Hub—I apologize, the Flyers' Tower. I have descended into the pit of the Nexus myself, searched the coils of ley, and discovered no connection between the tower and the emergence of these lights."

"Then what are they, if not effects of the Flyers' Tower?"

Augustus spread his hands and shrugged. "I have no idea. I agree that they appear to be directly related to the ley, that somehow the interaction of the ley with the Tapestry is causing the Tapestry to tear in some way. But so far these tears have been minor. None of the distortions have been larger than a man's fist. They open, hold for a moment, and then close. No significant damage has been done."

Not mollified, Arent pushed back from the table. "And yet the distortion that appeared in Wit last month tore a chunk of stone from an interior chamber of the Temerite's embassy when it closed, splintering the marble and scattering the shards across the embassy's foyer."

"Because the distortion coalesced inside the marble wall. None of the others have caused any damage."

"Because we have been lucky! What if one of them appears inside one of your nodes? What if they appear here, in the Amber Tower? Or your Nexus? What if one manifests near a person? What kind of damage will it do then?"

The Prime Wielder's mouth opened as if to answer, then shut, lips pressed thin in anger.

"I don't think you understand the magnitude of my concern," Arent said, "so let me make it clear. The flyers have become so prevalent in Erenthrall that they rival the barges of the ley lines in terms of public transportation. There are now stations at all twelve of the subtowers that support the system, even though the flyers cost dramatically more than the barges on the ground. The other Baronies are already scrambling to make offers to have the flyers established in their own cities. I expect them to demand towers of their own at the upcoming meeting. And even though I've made it clear that the flyers are only viable within a certain radius of the Flyers' Tower, the lords and ladies of the surrounding lands are already complaining that they can't have flyers on their own lands."

He leaned toward Augustus, voice hardening. "If the flyers are creating the distortions, that flaw must be repaired. I need to provide the Barons—and the lords and ladies—what they want."

He spun away, pointed toward Daedallen, the Dog still standing near the balcony. "Find out who's behind the Kormanley and stop them, whether it's Baron Leethe or not." Then he turned again on Augustus. "And find out what's causing these distortions."

Allan opened his eyes, instantly aware of Moira's warmth on the bed beside him. The small chamber glowed with the pulsing red of the fire's last embers, the tables, chairs, and the wooden crib casting strange shadows. He remained still, automatically searching the room for dangers, even though there was little that would harm them in the Hedge District. He'd learned to be wary in Erenthrall over the past four years. The Kormanley were not above bombing one of the Dogs' flats. Not many lived outside of Grass and the barracks there.

But not many had families to care for either.

He rolled over, certain the flat was safe, and curled up into Moira's warmth, kissing the nape of her neck. She moaned in irritation, her sleep disturbed, but pressed back against him, flesh to flesh. His hands traced patterns across her stomach, around her breasts, and then reached lower.

She gasped, coming fully awake, and clutched at his arms. "You're a beast," she accused, pulling his hands away. "Wasn't last night enough?"

"It's never enough."

She chuckled, the sound deep and throaty, then twisted around so that she faced him. She snuggled in closer, their legs entwined, the blankets keeping the warmth close. "Don't you have to work at the tower today? The mighty tower guardsman, protecting the Baron from the evil Kormanley."

"You mock me?" He pinched the nearest available flesh and Moira shrieked, wriggling away from him as he reached for more. He caught an arm and pulled her back into the covers, holding her tight.

The baby cried out, then hiccupped.

Both of them stilled, breath held. In the quiet that followed, they could hear Morrell rustling in her crib, making an occasional small noise before settling down into silence.

Allan had just begun to relax, his hands moving suggestively along Moira's thigh, when Morrell hiccupped again and broke into a full-fledged wail. Allan swore softly, Moira pulling away from him and heading toward the crib. He watched her pad across the floor, snatching a blanket to pull around her as she moved, then he collapsed back onto the bed with a groan.

"You could stoke up the fire," she said.

"I was trying," he grumbled. He rubbed at his sleep-gritted eyes, then dragged himself from the covers.

Moira had pulled Morrell from the crib, blankets and all, and settled into a rocking chair set to one side. She glanced up as Allan halted before them, Morrell already quieted and intent on feeding. One of her tiny hands grasped at Moira's dark hair, until Moira pulled it free. Morrell's tiny face squinched up as if she were irritated at the loss, but she continued suckling, not irritated enough to start wailing again.

"Ugly things, new babies."

Moira snorted. "You're one to talk. Besides, she's nearly ten months old. I wouldn't be calling her new anymore."

"New enough." He leaned down to kiss Moira on the forehead.

She smiled, a wicked gleam in her eye. "Aren't you cold?" She glanced down toward his naked body meaningfully as she shifted Morrell's position.

Allan faked a hurt look, but moved to stir up the embers in the ancient stone fireplace. Most of the flats in Hedge used the ley to keep the rooms warm and for cooking, but the ley never worked properly around him, its power sporadic. Allan knew it was his presence that interrupted the ley, but he'd kept quiet, telling only Moira and making her vow silence. He didn't want the Wielders or those at the University taking him away to do . . . whatever they might do. He'd made certain he stayed clear of anything related to the ley when with the Dogs or the Wielders, although he had noticed that the disruptions were getting worse. Before, the ley had flickered only if he were within a few paces. Now he would affect the ley from across the room, ten feet or more.

None of the Wielders who'd come to repair the heat had found anything wrong with the ley itself, so he and Moira had finally given up and resorted to a fire for their cooking instead. He placed some dried grass on the coals, blew on them gently until flames began, then placed kindling over those. Once the fire caught and held, he placed some larger pieces on top and backed away.

He was disappointed to find Moira already dressed.

Sighing, he reached for his own clothes and shrugged into the Dogs' uniform. The newness of the fabric and the slightly different cut from that of the Dogs that roamed the streets still felt awkward, even though he'd been transferred to the tower eight months before. He set his sword and sheath on a table. Moira had swung a kettle of water over the fire as he dressed and now poured the contents over a heap of oats in a bowl, stirring the mixture until it cooked and thickened. Allan checked on Morrell, his little girl staring at him with widened eyes while chewing on her own hand. Her legs kicked the air and she giggled when he reached down to chuck her chin.

"My little poppet," he whispered, then settled into a chair.

Moira placed a bowl of the steaming porridge in front of him, then flavored it with some honey, leaving the comb behind in a small bowl in case he wanted more. His stomach growled.

"What are you and Hagger handling today?"

Allan sighed and grimaced. "More of the same, I expect. There are Kormanley to question." He took a spoonful of the porridge, but it tasted like ash, even though a moment before it had smelled delicious. He wrinkled his nose and added more honey.

"I'd think the Dogs would try something different after all this time," Moira said, as she began chopping up carrots and onions. "Obviously, interrogation isn't working."

"It's the only option we've got," he said around a mouthful of tasteless porridge. "The Kormanley aren't stupid. For every one that we capture, there seem to be two more out there, although those we question only know *of* them, not who they are. And none of those we capture appear to be all that high up in the organization. They're pawns, sent to place the bombs or deliver messages. Nothing significant. And the Baron refuses to release the Hounds. Not that they'd be much more effective. They're best when they have a scent to follow, from what I've heard."

Moira passed by as he pushed the porridge away; it was smothered in honey, but it hadn't helped. She kissed him and patted his cheek. "They'll make a mistake at some point."

Allan glanced toward Morrell and fervently hoped so. He didn't want to raise his daughter in Erenthrall with the Kormanley around.

"Where in all hells have you been?" Hagger snapped the moment Allan stepped into the barracks. His fellow Dog looked like he'd been searching for him. The rest of the Dogs present—sitting at tables or stretched out on their bunks—glanced in their direction.

"Home," Allan snapped back.

Hagger snarled. "Your home should be in the barracks, Pup, with your fellow Dogs. Not shacked up with some woman you knocked up and your little whelp."

Anger flared deep inside Allan's chest. He let it spark in his eyes and color his voice as he asked, "What happened?"

Hagger drew back at his aggression, eyes widening, then hardening. He sucked in a breath to slap Allan down, Allan could see the intent in his eyes, but he choked back the response and grabbed Allan by the arm, spun him around, and headed back out the door and into the streets of Grass. The Amber Tower loomed before them, the Flyers' Tower beyond it. The skyboats drifted overhead, a sight Allan had still not grown used to. But Hagger thrust him forward, his grip so tight Allan's arm began tingling with numbness.

He wrenched his arm free. "What in hells happened? Where are we headed?"

"To the Amber Tower. Captain Daedallen came down on us like a sailor on a whore. The Baron thinks the Kormanley are working with one of the other Barons and he wants the Dogs to figure out which one. He isn't happy with our progress. Neither is Daedallen. He beat the shit out of Grierson when he had the gall to point out we were doing the best we could, then demanded we do more. He roared we'd better find out before the Baronial Meeting, then stormed out."

"What happened to Grierson?"

Hagger shot him a confused look. "Who cares? Someone toted him off to the healers. We've got more important things to worry about. Since we've been promoted to Tower guardsmen, Daedallen and the Baron have been expecting some results from us, and they haven't gotten them."

"I don't see how that's going to change."

Hagger grinned unpleasantly. "We brought in another follower last night, along with a cartload of those damn papers with the cryptic notes. I told everyone not to touch him, to leave him to me, and to dump the pages into your lap."

Allan nodded. This was how they'd worked their partnership for the past few years. Hagger had realized early on that Allan didn't have the stomach for the interrogations. The old Dog might have abandoned him in disgust, but he'd risen too far too fast and knew it wasn't his own work that had caused it.

They entered the Amber Tower, passing through the great round foyer, staircases rising elegantly to the upper floors like the arms of an embrace on either side, a massive crystal chandelier lit with ley globes dangling down from the ceiling overhead. But the two Dogs didn't move toward the upper levels. They crossed the flawless marble floor to a set of double doors beneath the stairs, passing through and then down into the tower's depths. This was the domain of the Dogs, where those who provoked or annoyed Baron Arent were kept. And beneath this level lay the domain of the Hounds, the elite Dogs rumored to be Baron Arent's assassins. Allan wasn't exactly sure how one became a

Hound, only that some of the more vicious Dogs disappeared on occasion, taken to train with the Hounds to see if they had what it took to become one themselves. Rumor said that if they didn't, they didn't survive the training. Allan had also overheard some of the Dogs discussing a slew of disappearances throughout Erenthrall, mostly young boys and girls, one of the men muttering about the Hounds recruiting. But the Dogs had quieted as soon as they noticed him nearby and he'd heard nothing more.

All Allan knew was that no one went willingly down into the Hounds' lair, and that even though he had only seen a Hound twice, he had no wish to see one again. They looked normal in every way, but they *behaved* differently, in a way that he couldn't quite describe and that sent chills down his back and prickled the hairs at the nape of his neck.

As soon as they descended the first flight of stairs, the atmosphere of the tower changed. The amber that made up the core of the structure vanished, replaced by smooth granite that appeared molded from the earth itself. The ostentatiously decorated doors gave way to oak banded with iron, and the delicate brass and pewter of the ley sconces were replaced with practical iron holders.

They emerged into a central room, desks, tables, and chairs strewn around the edges of the hall, the center reserved for training. Three Dogs were brawling, one of them barking out instructions as the other two grappled with each other. The granite flooring had been covered with sand, enclosed by an ankle-high, circular barrier. As Allan and Hagger circled toward a set of doors on the far side, passing other Dogs who were watching the bout, one of the men landed a brutal punch to the face that caused blood to fly. Roars of encouragement followed as Hagger led Allan into the next room.

A pair of Dogs looked up immediately, hands shifting toward swords. But they relaxed as soon as they recognized Hagger, nodding to him and Allan both.

"Here to interrogate the newest prisoner?" the Dog on the left asked. He was built as solidly as Hagger, although he must have been ten years younger.

"And to take a look at those pages," Hagger answered. "Are they in the same rooms as last night?"

"They haven't been touched, as you requested."

"Very well."

Hagger and Allan passed through another doorway, down a set of hallways, and halted before two doors directly across from each other, the corridor continuing with door upon door to either side into the distance. He nodded to the door on the left. "The documents you'll want to look at are in there. I'll start questioning our guest." He couldn't keep his contempt for Allan from his voice as he opened the door on the right and vanished inside.

Allan frowned at Hagger's derision, then dismissed it and entered the door to the left. He closed it behind him, even though he knew it wouldn't help; the screams from one room were meant to be heard by those in the other cells.

The table in the center of the room was covered with crate upon crate filled with paper. For a moment, Allan was overwhelmed. There were more pages here than they'd collected from the Kormanley for the last four years combined. He didn't know whose home the Dogs had raided, but it must have been one of the Kormanley's main bases in the city.

At the thought, Allan's heart quickened and he stepped forward, taking the nearest crate and beginning to sort through the documents. Like everything they'd discovered before this, the pages were coded somehow, covered in words and symbols and sketches of maps. Allan hadn't been able to figure it out, although he still suspected it had to do with the Kormanley's network. Not simply places they were targeting, but where their safe houses and meeting places were located. No organization could run as smoothly as the Kormanley's with its members meeting only in pairs or groups of three, with no knowledge of the other members or the next meeting's location. They must be passing along information somehow.

All he needed to do was figure out how.

He sighed, riffled through the stack, then settled into a chair and began sorting.

Ten minutes later, his concentration was interrupted by the first muted scream from Hagger's room. He glanced up at the muffled sound with a frown, shifting in his seat. He thought he'd grow used to the methods Hagger and the other Dogs employed over the years, but in the last year he'd become more and more uncomfortable with them.

As the scream died into cracked sobbing, he turned back to his stacks of parchment and tried to focus through the noise. He found another flyer, one of the daily news sheets that were handed out on practically every street corner. He'd run across twenty of them already as he sorted through three of the crates. At first, he'd thought they had merely been in the same room as the Kormanley's papers, brought there by the man Hagger was interrogating perhaps, but now he wasn't so certain. There was something about them—and how they were mixed in with the other pages—that itched the back of his brain, but he couldn't see what.

When another scream arose, he growled low in his throat and thrust the news sheet into one stack and pulled another handful of pages from the crate. Before starting in again, he scrubbed at his face with both hands, then blocked out the noises coming from the other room and leaned over them.

Two hours after that, he laid the thirtieth news sheet out in the center of the table, then surrounded it with the pages that had been above and below it; everything else had been shoved to the side. He couldn't be certain the Dogs had stacked everything into the crates in the same order they'd rested in the home where they'd been found, but he knew Hagger had demanded that they be careful with them. This news sheet had been printed the day before the recent bombing of the ley barge. He stood and loomed over the pages, looking at the cryptic numbers and letters scrawled on the Kormanley papers, then back at the news sheet. Something connected them all, something blatant that he wasn't seeing. . . .

He cursed and thrust himself away from the table, pacing around the room, then halted before one of the coded sheets. There was a rough sketch of a hawk, wings spread, head in profile with its beak open. A number was scrawled next to it. Nearly everyone who had looked at the pages believed the number was a date. This one corresponded to the date on the news sheet. After it came a series of interspersed numbers and letters.

Allan picked up the news sheet, read through the items listed yet again, shaking his head. The ley station that had been attacked had been in North Umber, and one of the items referenced North Umber, but it was about a woman who claimed she'd seen one of the distortions that had been appearing throughout the city. Nothing unusual except that she said it was the size of her head, not the fist-sized ones typically reported. The Wielders had failed to comment, of course. Nothing about the ley station or barges—

His eye caught the word "barge" in a separate article and he frowned. With another quick scan, he caught the words "ley" and "seat" and "Eastend." The barge's next stop had been Eastend.

He returned to the seemingly random set of letters and numbers, began breaking them apart, even though they appeared as one long string. He tried a few different combinations, shook his head, then began counting out words on the news sheet.

Twenty minutes later, he sank into the chair, his body trembling, his heart racing. He found it hard to breathe. He stared at the far granite wall, noticed there were dark stains on the stone, knew that it was blood from whoever had been imprisoned in the room before this. It dawned on him that he had not heard any sounds from the other room for quite a while.

And then Hagger opened the door and stepped inside. His face was grim, his uniform splattered with blood, although the dark brown, black, and red clothing made it hard to pick out without experience. The blood that stained the edges of Hagger's fingernails and the creases of his hands was easier to see. It was dark—heart's blood—and it hadn't yet had time to dry.

Allan didn't think he'd have the chance to ask the unfortunate ley priest any questions.

He smothered his reaction by declaring, "I've found out how they're communicating with each other. They're using this news sheet, *The Ley*. Their code references different words in the sheet, and when you piece them together it forms a message. This one warns them of the attack on the ley station in North Umber." He picked up the page with the hawk. "I don't know what the hawk is for."

Hagger stepped forward. "There's a statue of a hawk in the center of the North Umber station with its wings spread like that. But I've got something better." He grinned, the expression cruel and victorious at the same time. "I've got a name."

Ten

KARA RESTED HER hands on the stone lip of the pit at the center of the Eld District's ley node. She'd stared at the outside of the squat, rounded building from the street so many times, wondering what was inside, what it was that she could feel hidden here, that she barely believed she was here now, even though she'd been assigned here for the last month.

The pit lay at the center of the building, a round chamber like a well with a stairway circling down to the bottom below, where the mouths of channels pierced the wall beneath. Made entirely of river stone fitted together with the Tapestry and the ley in mind, it was one of the most natural buildings Kara had seen in all of Erenthrall. It had not been grown or manipulated or worked in any way. No hammer and chisel had touched the rock, no mortar held it together. The stones had simply been stacked precisely, all found and pulled from the river and the surrounding land and placed to create a specific pattern.

Like the stones she'd moved and placed for Ischua in Halliel's Park.

She leaned forward onto the lip of the pit and stretched out her senses. No one was in the pit manipulating the ley at the moment; she had the chamber to herself. But she didn't want to descend into the concentrated flow of the ley below either. Its eddies and currents could be powerful enough to overwhelm someone not prepared.

It had nearly overwhelmed her the first time she'd found herself in the pit four years ago.

She tensed at the memory, anger rising sharp and acidic in the back of her throat, but she quashed it ruthlessly and forced herself to relax.

Her senses stretched out around the edge of the pit on the Tapestry, dancing along the patterns created by the river stones. She could feel imperfections in the construction, flaws created when the pit was first built by Wielders who had barely begun to use their powers. Those mistakes could be corrected, but they weren't significant enough to force the issue. Most of the Wielders Kara had met couldn't even sense them.

She let the patterns of the stones flow through her, eyes closed, even when she heard the door to the pit leading to the barracks and the rest of the node open behind her, someone moving to her side.

"Hello, Marcus," she said, smiling.

"Ready for another day dealing with the ley and the demands of the citizens of Erenthrall?"

"That's why I'm here. Trying to calm myself."

He sighed. "I remember the first time I descended into the pit. It was anything but calming. I never realized the ley could be so wild, so chaotic. The other Wielders warn you, but you never really believe it can be as bad as they say."

"I was never warned," Kara said, her voice tight even though she tried to control it. She straightened and opened her eyes, met Marcus' gaze.

"What do you mean? Your instructors didn't prepare you for immersion?"

Kara shook her head, her mouth twisting in anger, hate, and regret. "They never got the chance. I came to the Wielders earlier than usual, so I was younger than the others in my training group. The others hated me for it, singled me out as being special, even though I was struggling to learn about the ley and the Tapestry. More so than the others. It wasn't coming as naturally to me as it did for them. I wasn't as connected to it, somehow. Three in particular decided that I needed to be punished—Devin, Robere, and Terese. They hounded me from the moment I joined them, nothing serious, but annoying. They made my life hell.

"The first day we were taken to a node, they had been quiet, their attention focused on one of the other Wielders. I remember being relieved and thankful, even though someone else was being tormented. I should have tried to protect him. Instead, I pushed him from my mind, tried to forget them and focus on the node. We were brought to the pit, of course, told to remain at its edge. I never even heard the three approach me, sensed them only at the last moment."

Marcus let the silence hold, still at her side as she glared down into the pit. But then he shifted and asked, "What did they do?"

Kara grimaced. "They shoved me over the lip of the pit." Her voice was rough and she cleared her throat, continuing on even as Marcus gasped. "I fell down to the floor below, landed hard, heard something snap in my shoulder. Thankfully, it was in Leeds, one of the shallow pits, not as deep as some of the others I've seen since. I remember hearing one of the Wielders shout, heard Devin laughing, but then everything—the sounds, the pain, the shock—was drowned out by the ley. It flooded into me, a torrent that drove me under, and I was swept away."

"Of course you were," Marcus snapped, his anger palpable. "You hadn't even been initiated yet! I'm surprised you weren't burned out!"

Warmth surged in Kara's chest at his anger and she smiled thinly, gratified that he cared. The urge to lean forward and kiss him swept through her, but she resisted it. Marcus had spent nearly all of his free time with her since she arrived, but she still wasn't certain how he felt about her.

Besides, he was two years her senior.

Ducking her head and turning away, she said, "It almost did burn me out. I know the Wielders expected it. They were shocked when they finally made it down into the pit to retrieve me."

"So what happened?"

Kara hesitated. She hadn't shared what had happened in the pit that day with anyone, not even the Wielders who'd pulled her from the pit, screaming as the broken bones in her shoulder ground together.

But this was Marcus. She hadn't had a friendship like this since Cory.

She drew in a deep breath to steady herself, then exhaled slowly. "I was swept away, like I said, but I struggled. The ley surrounded me, but I reached out, trying to grasp anything that I could to save myself. I felt the resistance inside me that I'd felt during all of the training up to that point burn away by the sheer brute force of the ley and I reached beyond it, surged down the paths and channels of Erenthrall looking for something stable.

"And I found it beneath the city. There's a reservoir of ley beneath the city, a lake of it. I remember sensing it when Ischua first tested me in Halliel's Park. I stretched out for it and found myself in its waters. Unlike the channels in Erenthrall, its currents were calm, and so I submerged myself in them. It allowed me to catch my breath, to center myself. I regained control and then pushed myself back through the network of ley that riddles the city, through the rapids that we've built here, and back to the pit. It helped when the Wielders jostled me and I could focus on the pain from my shoulder.

"I suppose I should thank Devin, Robere, and Terese. After that, I had no trouble dealing with the ley. Whatever had blocked me before was gone."

She turned to find Marcus staring at her strangely. Her heart thudded once, hard, and her smile faltered. "What? What did I say?"

He shook his head. "Nothing. I've never heard of anyone talk about a lake of ley beneath the city before though. I've worked the network of ley for a while now and never sensed anything like that." Kara drew up defensively and he added hastily, "Not that I don't believe you! I've just never heard of it before. Maybe it's something you learn about once you become a Master Wielder, or a Prime."

Only slightly mollified, Kara said, "I've never told anyone, not even my adviser at the college."

Marcus sighed. "Well, I wouldn't tell anyone else. You don't want the Prime Wielders looking at you too closely, not until you're ready to become one yourself."

He grinned awkwardly, then his eyes widened in dawning horror. "Wait, I remember a group getting lashed before the entire college my third year. That was Devin and the others, wasn't it? That was because of you?"

Kara grimaced. "They were lashed until their shoulders bled. They couldn't walk for a week. The Master Wielders were furious."

They both stared down into the pit, Kara reliving those horrible moments standing in front of the college as the Master Wielders meted out their punishment, Marcus merely shaking his head. Devin's glare had been the worst of it and she'd feared his retribution for weeks, but the Wielders kept them separate as much as possible and the few times they'd run into each other one of the instructors had appeared out of nowhere to intervene before the altercation had gone too far, as if someone were always watching her, even if they weren't seen. By that point, Kara could have defended herself with the ley if necessary, but she was glad she didn't have to.

"We should probably head out," Marcus said abruptly. "Someone is claiming there's an issue with the ley stream at the Eld station. We were ordered to check it out."

Kara nodded, relieved to escape the memories. "I just need to pick up my jacket."

They left the pit behind, stopping only long enough at Kara's room to grab her purple jacket. Then they descended to the streets of Eld, moving south toward the station and the Confluence District. Kara thought of Cory, now studying at the University there. She'd only seen him once since she'd received her purple, her age-old friend appearing haggard and strained with his new schedule, although still elated he'd escaped following in his father's footsteps as a candlemaker. She half expected her superiors to forbid her to see Cory again in the future, now that he was part of the University. While both Wielders and the University Masters worked with the Tapestry, most of the Masters could barely sense the ley or its intricacies. They were better at manipulating the Tapestry, while the Wielders focused on the ley, and they spurned the Wielders as practitioners of a lesser art. The rivalry between the two factions had lasted since the Wielders first began working with the ley.

On the street, the pedestrians gave way to the purple jackets, stepping to the side to let Kara and Marcus pass, even though they weren't in a hurry. A few called out to Marcus, waved or nodded, mostly shopkeepers. They passed by bakeries, a glasswright, a florist with a door draped in tied, multicolored grass from the plains, and a man who worked with metal, although he wasn't a blacksmith. They'd repaired his ley kiln the week before.

Dodging wagons and horses and a few ley carts, they crossed a street and small plaza to the front of the ley station. The edifice rose in tall arched columns from the edge of the street, narrow windows with high peaks between them. The heavy wooden doors at the top of a series of wide, low steps were all open, people moving in and out in a steady stream. Kara and Marcus ascended the steps and entered behind a mother with two children in tow.

Inside, the building was the same as Kara remembered when she, Cory, and Justin had made their illicit trip to Shadow to see the subtower activated. Kara felt the old guilt sweep through her as she scanned the massive mezzanine, the stone columns interspersed at regular intervals carved to look like the trunks of trees. Overhead, the columns gave way to intricately woven branches filled with leaves. Sunlight slanted through the windows and lit the gray stone floor, cracked in a few places, but ley globes illuminated the farther recesses and lined the corridors that angled down toward the ley lines and the barges.

As soon as they entered, Marcus searched out the station's guards, their dull gray uniforms easy to pick out from the crowd.

"We're here to see about the problem with the ley stream," he said, the guards straightening as they approached.

The elder of the two guards nodded. "Aye, the eddy. It hasn't affected any of the barges yet, but it's disturbing some of the passengers. I'll take you down right away."

He muttered something to the remaining guard, who nodded, then motioned them toward one of the corridors. They descended toward the platform below, the people of Erenthrall streaming past them in both directions. A few of them shot the Wielders curious looks, but most were too intent on reaching their own destination.

"I can't say as I've ever seen anything like this," the guard said as they hit the platform and he turned right, heading straight for the ley stream on that side. "Although I hear there have been other instances at other stations."

At the edge of the platform, he halted and nodded toward the bed below.

Kara hung back as Marcus stepped up beside the guard. The ley pathway flowed past in a deep channel, the white light bright enough to illuminate the entire platform without the need for any globes. Normally, it held steady, carrying the barges from one station to the next.

But in this stream, perhaps an arm's length beyond the edge of the platform, a vortex had formed, the light twisting and swirling like a whirlpool on water. Riptides had formed around the vortex, evident as ripples on the surface of the ley. Even at this distance, Kara could feel the disruption to the Tapestry that had caused it, like a wrinkle in fabric.

Marcus gave the guard a reassuring smile. "This happens all the time," he said, even as he shot Kara a troubled look. "It's easy enough to repair. If you'll step back next to Kara, I can handle it myself."

The elderly guard frowned, but moved back, hands on his hips as he watched Marcus kneel down and raise his arm toward the distortion. Kara wasn't certain what the guard expected to see. What Marcus intended to do wouldn't be visible to those who couldn't sense the Tapestry. He'd only see the effects on the ley stream itself.

Marcus closed his eyes and then Kara felt him reach out toward the wrinkle in the Tapestry, felt him surround it, then begin to smooth it out. It stretched from beneath the surface of the ley stream to a height at about eye level, although there were no visible distortions above the surface. Anyone who passed through the wrinkle would feel its effects—a tingling sensation that would make them shudder—but nothing else. Kara reached out herself, ready to steady Marcus if anything happened, but knew she wouldn't be needed. She'd seen Marcus handle problems much worse than this one in the past month.

Beside her, the guard's face set into a grim expression as the roiling ley began to calm down, the ripples of hidden undercurrents vanishing. The whirlpool began to lose cohesion, struggled to maintain itself, and finally collapsed. Kara expected to hear a slap of water, like a wave breaking as it hit the riverbank, but the ley wasn't liquid. It merely behaved like it sometimes.

The guard relaxed, letting out a held breath. He shook hands with Marcus when the Wielder finally stood, the Tapestry repaired. "Thank you, both of you. The passengers will be relieved."

They left the station guard on the platform, herding the few passengers who'd been attracted by the display back to their lives. Marcus' expression turned grim as soon as they reached the corridor leading up to the mezzanine.

"What's wrong?"

He glanced toward her, then away. "We need to report this to the Wielders at the node, and the Prime Wielders as well. I lied to the station guard. That . . . fold in the Tapestry doesn't happen often. In fact, I don't know if anyone had ever seen one a year ago, certainly not any of the Wielders I know of working the nodes. But this is the third one reported among the districts so far, and I don't think it's going to end any time soon."

They hustled up the corridor and emerged into the mezzanine, the illusion of trees and foliage surrounding them even though the chamber was filled with the noise and voices of the ley station patrons. Marcus headed straight for the arched doors leading out into the plaza beyond. They had almost reached them when Kara heard a high-pitched, familiar whine, the note growing in volume. She reached out and grabbed Marcus' arm, bringing him to an abrupt halt. As he turned in annoyance, she said, "Listen."

He paused, his irritation faltering as he concentrated.

A moment later, his breath caught and his eyes widened. "A distortion."

Kara nodded. "I've heard one before, before they came to take me to the college."

Marcus was already scanning the mezzanine. None of the patrons appeared to have heard the distortion yet. "It's forming right now. Look for a light. An intense white light."

They darted in among the station passengers, both frantically searching, Kara on Marcus' heels until he shouted to head left, gesturing with one hand while he angled right. Kara hesitated, a shot of fear at being alone piercing through her, but steeled herself and began working her way left. The high-pitched noise increased, patrons beginning to stop in confusion and glance around. Kara sensed a vibration on the Tapestry, a shudder that coursed through her skin, saw a few of the others shiver in discomfort—

And then someone ahead shouted and pointed. Kara followed the man's arm, saw the piercing white light hovering a hand's breadth above the heads of the nearest commuters. Most of those closest began to edge away in uncertainty, but a woman dressed in the neat clothes of a seamstress carrying a basket with small bolts of cloth sticking out one side was reaching toward the light, a look of wonder touching her face.

Panic sliced through Kara's fear and she shouted, "Don't touch it! Back away!"

The seamstress flinched, gaze falling toward Kara as the Wielder sped toward her, her arm lowering—

And then the high-pitched tone halted, as if severed with a knife.

Kara gasped, her memories of what had happened when the noise ended on the street over four years before flaring as she watched it happen again.

The light flashed once, painfully bright. Only this time Kara was more attuned to the Tapestry. She felt it shudder, felt it tear, as the light blossomed, spiraling open in coruscating whirls of color that spun outward and ensnared the seamstress' outstretched arm. In the space of a heartbeat, the distortion opened . . . and then froze, the woman's hand caught inside it.

The seamstress screamed, the sound filled with terror so focused Kara felt it shudder down her back. Those closest to her lurched away, panic beginning to spread through the crowd, a space opening up around her. Kara stumbled into the widening region, came up next to the woman, her breath ragged and hoarse. She desperately wanted to know where Marcus was, but the woman's horror was too intense for her to look away.

"What's wrong?" she asked, and was surprised at how calm her voice sounded. When the seamstress kept screaming, tears coursing down her face, Kara snapped, "Look at me!" in irritation.

The woman jerked to one side, but caught Kara's gaze, held it. Her scream died down into a soft moan. Through choked sobs, she said, "I can't move it. I can't even move my fingers." She noted Kara's purple jacket and raw hope flickered in her eyes. "You have to help me. You have to get my hand free. I can't be a seamstress without my hand! I won't be able to work! Lady Bellum will find someone else—"

"Stop it," Kara said. "It isn't helping."

The seamstress' back straightened in affront, but then she nodded.

Kara turned away, saw Marcus fighting his way through the crowd toward her. But she didn't know how much time the seamstress had. The distortion she'd witnessed before had closed after only a short time.

She chewed on her lower lip. She had only just become a Wielder. She shouldn't have to deal with situations like this yet. That's why she'd been doing the runs with Marcus.

But Marcus wasn't here yet.

She met the seamstress' pleading gaze, then sighed.

"Don't move. I'll see what I can do."

She turned her attention to the distortion, the spirals of various colors frozen in midair, the woman's hand encased inside halfway up her forearm. This one was larger than the one she'd seen when younger, nearly the size of her torso. But in all other respects, it appeared to be the same—a beautiful, delicate flower composed of blue-green light, a trace of orange threading through it.

She reached out tentatively on the Tapestry, her stomach roiling at what she discovered. Unlike the wrinkle Marcus had smoothed in the ley stream below, the distortion wasn't a fold in the Tapestry, but a tear. It had been wrenched open, the Tapestry within the distortion shredded— although even as she thought it, Kara realized that wasn't quite right. It hadn't been torn like fabric. It had fractured, as if the air itself had broken, like a clay pot dashed to the floor, or a glass window struck by a bird. She could see the shards of reality through the colors of the distortion, some of the fractures passing through the seamstress' hand, through her fingers.

"Can you do something?" the seamstress pleaded. Fresh tears lined her face.

Kara ignored her, circling the distortion instead. She heard Marcus' heavy breathing as he made it through the edge of the commuters, sensed the crowd around them growing. Marcus shouted, "Stand back!" A few of the patrons grumbled, but no one approached closer than a few paces. Marcus came up to Kara's side and whispered fiercely, "You shouldn't be this close. We don't know anything about them. We need to summon the Primes!"

"We don't have time," Kara said, meeting his gaze. "*She* doesn't have time. It will vanish before the Primes get here. I—" She hesitated, swallowed once, then said, "I think I can fix it."

Marcus opened his mouth to argue, perhaps to ask how, then closed it. He clenched his jaw and nodded once.

Kara turned to the distortion and concentrated. She reached out on the Tapestry, surrounded the distortion completely with herself, felt its shape, felt the jagged edges of the shards where reality had been shattered. Then, as Marcus had done with the fold, she began to repair the damage, melding the shards together, starting at the outside, where the fractures were thinnest, and working her way in. The seamstress whimpered, clutching her basket of cloth close to her chest with her free hand, but Kara didn't allow herself to be distracted. It was like working on her father's clocks. Each fracture had to be repaired in a specific order, the reverse order in which they had occurred as the distortion formed. Each fracture was interconnected with the others.

Sweat broke out on her forehead and she wiped it clear with one hand before it could drip down into her eyes. She needed to be able to see, but her energy was flagging already. She'd never done something so detailed with the Tapestry before, never worked with it on this level. She could feel how clumsy her touch was, as if her hands were shaking as she tried to place a fine metal gear into the back of a clock. She frowned at herself, brow creasing—

And then she felt Marcus' presence on the Tapestry, felt his energy flowing toward her, backing her up. She steadied, flushing at the intimacy of having Marcus helping her even as she reached for his aid. She didn't know how much time she had left, but the seamstress' hand was still caught, the folds of light entwined through her palm and fingers. Kara had freed her upper forearm, but she wasn't close to releasing her entire hand.

Then, working on a fracture that passed through the woman's palm, she felt the distortion tremble.

"We're running out of time," she gasped, voice strained. "It's beginning to collapse."

"Do what you can," Marcus said.

The seamstress sobbed.

Kara worked harder, dashed more sweat from her face, even as the vibrations increased. The remaining arms of color began to shift and the seamstress cried out in pain. Kara abandoned all finesse, focused on the fractures around the woman's hand, heard her own breath quickening—

And without any more warning, the distortion closed. The colorful rose of light spun shut, the fractures slicing through the air as it did so, slicing through the seamstress' fingers. It vanished, as if it had never been there.

A moment of shock filled the mezzanine, stilled Kara's heart. She reached up to touch something that had splattered against her face, her fingers coming away slicked with droplets of blood.

Then the seamstress screamed, her shattered voice joined by both men and women from the gathered crowd as she drew her mangled hand to her chest, her severed fingers lying on the ground below. Blood spurted from the stumps, stained her fitted dress as she collapsed to her knees, her scream breaking into hitching sobs and a mewling distress unlike anything Kara had heard before. Marcus shouted for someone to find a healer, to find another Wielder and summon the Primes, then grabbed one of the lengths of cloth from the woman's basket and began winding it around the wound. One of the station guards—the elderly man who'd shown them down to the ley stream—dashed off through the crowd, shoving patrons out of his way with curses.

Kara couldn't move. She stared at the blood staining her fingers, splattered across the front of her purple jacket, numb.

"I was so close," she muttered, her voice no more than a breath. "I only needed a few more moments."

But no one heard her.

Eleven

"**E**XPLAIN AGAIN HOW you tried to repair the distortion."

Kara swallowed a sob, sucked in a deep breath, even though her head ached from the unending questions, and began to answer—

But Marcus cut her off. "She's already answered that question a thousand times," he barked, and behind him the rest of the Wielders who were part of the Eld node—those not already out handling problems with the ley or down in the pit dealing with it directly—shifted restlessly, their anger palpable in the room. "She can't answer it any differently than she did the first time. I know. I supported her as she tried to free the woman, I know what she did. It wasn't that much different than what we do to repair the folds in the Tapestry. Can't you see that she's exhausted? She's practically falling out of that chair!"

The two Primes who had finally arrived at the Eld ley station glared at Marcus, one seated across the table opposite Kara, the other standing to the right and a pace behind him. Their expressions were hard and unforgiving, and Kara could tell that they both fervently wished that Marcus and the other Wielders weren't present for her interrogation. But somehow Marcus had sent word ahead to the node, so that when they'd arrived with the Primes, after dealing with the seamstress at the station, they'd all been waiting. None of them had let Marcus or Kara out of their sight since, demanding they be allowed in the room while Kara was questioned. The Primes had refused at first, but Marcus had pointed out that anything the Wielders could learn about the distortions would only be beneficial to everyone, since the Wielders at the nodes were the ones most likely to encounter them while in the field. When the Primes had still hesitated, he'd threatened to keep them from questioning Kara at all.

Kara didn't think he could do that. The Primes were higher in rank, after all. One of them—the one with the goatee, Ashton—had pointed this out by hinting they could summon the Dogs if necessary. But all of the other Wielders had grumbled at the suggestion, the atmosphere in the node's main entrance turning ugly. After a whispered consultation with his fellow Prime, Ashton had relented.

And then the questioning had begun. Kara didn't know how long she'd been sitting in the chair in one of the small rooms built around the central pit. She only knew her head throbbed and her body had grown numb, her arms and legs tingling from exhaustion, her back pinched and shoulders hunched over. Her face felt taut, the skin around her eyes gritty. She'd come to realize during the questioning that the Primes knew as little as the Wielders about the cause of the distortions— why they were appearing or how to stop them. After the first barrage of questions, they'd begun to repeat themselves, asking the same questions but with different phrasing, as if they were trying to dig deeper into what had happened. Or were trying to trick her into contradicting herself.

But there wasn't anything deeper. She'd acted on instinct, knowing that the Primes would not arrive in time to help the seamstress. She'd done nothing except what the Wielders had been trained to do when it came to anomalies with the Tapestry and the ley: she'd tried to fix it.

She'd thought the two Primes understood that at one point, but they'd persisted. Or rather, Ashton had persisted.

He shifted his glare from Marcus back to Kara and leaned forward onto the desk from where he sat. "Are you certain there is nothing more you can tell us?"

Kara trembled, hated herself for it, but said, "Nothing. I've told you everything—everything I saw, everything I did. There's nothing more."

The man's eyes narrowed suspiciously, but the other Prime—the one Kara had barely caught sight of, the cowl of his Prime's cloak pulled far forward to conceal his face—placed a hand on his shoulder. Tension drained from Ashton's body and he relaxed. "Very well. You may go."

Marcus took her by the elbow and helped her stand. Unsteady, she let him lead her out the door and into the corridors beyond, heading around the circular hallway toward the barracks. A few of the other Wielders trailed after them protectively, but halted outside Kara's room as Marcus supported her until she could collapse onto her bed.

"Wait here," he said.

As if she could move if she wanted to. She didn't know if it was the intense interrogation that had exhausted her, or an aftereffect of trying to heal the distortion. It didn't matter. She moaned and rolled onto her back, the straw of the mattress crinkling beneath her. She closed her eyes and raised one arm over her head, heard Marcus speaking to one of the other Wielders—Kyle, she thought, red-haired, with a quirky smile; or maybe it was Katrina—and then the door closed and Marcus began pacing, furious.

"Marcus, it's fine," she said, her voice drained even to her own ears.

"No, it's not," he said. "They shouldn't have kept you there so long, shouldn't have hounded you that way. Not after what happened. Especially not after you proved that something could be done about the distortions after they've formed."

"But I'll be fine. I just need some rest."

He halted, and she could sense him standing over her, looking down at her.

"You don't understand, do you?"

She sighed. "I don't understand what."

She heard him drag a chair closer, slit one eye enough she could see him as he settled, elbows on his knees, head in his hands.

"I don't think the Primes know what the distortions are, or where they come from."

"And you do?"

He grimaced. "Not for certain. But the other Wielders and I have talked about it and it seems obvious to us that it has something to do with the Flyers' Tower. The distortions didn't start appearing until after the tower was sown. Since then, the stress on the ley system has been obvious. The Primes claim that they've accounted for the additional power needed to keep the flyers in the air, make grand statements to the public about how the distortions have nothing to do with the flyers, but those of us here in the nodes know differently. We can see it when we're working in the pit."

"But you can't see everything. The Primes work at the Nexus. They know what's happening throughout the system. Not just here in Erenthrall, but in all of the ley networks in all of the surrounding Baronies and the cities beyond."

"We don't need to see the whole system to know that something's wrong," Marcus scoffed. "We can see it in the streets! In our own ley station!"

Kara flinched as his voice rose, her head pounding. Marcus noticed, for he caught himself, forced his breathing to calm.

"But that doesn't matter right now," he said, and stood. "I've sent Kyle to get some food and drink for you, and told the others to let you sleep, even though they're all dying to hear the story of what happened directly from you again. Kyle said they haven't stopped talking about it since the Primes arrived."

She could hear the smile in his voice, heard him hesitate. She opened her eyes to find him staring down at her, a strange expression on his face. For a moment, she flashed back to the ley station, to the sensation that had coursed through her as he joined her, as he passed along his strength when hers began to flag. The memory woke a warmth deep in her chest and caused her to blush. A tiny smile touched Marcus' lips and he leaned forward. Her heart stuttered as she thought he meant to kiss her, and her arm twitched as she tried to raise it to hold the back of his head as he did so. But she was so weary she couldn't lift her arm, and Marcus merely muttered, "Good job today, Wielder. At least now we know we can do something about the distortions when they appear."

Then he did kiss her, on the lips, his breath cool against her burning skin, his mouth gentle. It sent a shock through her entire body. She tasted the salt of his sweat, drew in the musk of his scent—

And then he withdrew. She didn't want him to go, wanted to reach for him, but he turned, opened the door, and left.

Within moments, despite the fire that had awakened inside her, Kara slipped into sleep.

A violent pounding intruded on Augustus' tranquility. He ignored it at first, a wrinkle of irritation forming in his brow, and sank himself deeper into the sensation of the ley flowing over his body, the tingling energy relaxing his muscles and rejuvenating his body. He'd discovered one of the side effects of immersion in the ley over long periods of time was a youthening effect, like those described by the followers of Korma, who immersed themselves in hot mud baths and applied poultices to their faces and skin. They believed that nature harbored the secrets of the universe, that it would provide cures for every disease, antidotes for every poison, and through careful application and preservation in their daily lives, right all wrongs in the universe. Most healers ascribed to a belief in Korma. The Kormanley had originally been part of the god's following, but had broken away to focus their attentions on the ley itself, rather than nature in general. And they'd been correct, at least in regard to the ley. He'd been immersing himself in a bath of ley for decades now and even though he was seventy-seven years old, he looked forty. Baron Arent had done the same and had ruled Erenthrall for seventy years already; he expected to rule for another seventy, if not a hundred. It was one of the main reasons Arent hadn't married and produced an heir. Augustus didn't believe Arent ever intended to give up his hold on the Baronies, not even to someone of his own blood.

The pounding renewed, breaking through Augustus' thoughts. He grumbled and pushed upward out of the ley, opening his eyes to the rough stone ceiling of the immersion chamber hidden behind a doorway in his bedchamber. Arent had a similar chamber in the Amber Tower, known of only by the Baron, a few retainers, and Augustus himself. Lifting himself up onto the lip of the depression, he realized the pounding came from the bedroom door. He shrugged into his Prime robes and closed the door to the secret room behind him. "This had better be good," he mumbled as he made his way to the bedroom door.

He snatched it open and growled, "What is it?"

Two Prime Wielders waited outside, Augustus' personal servant hovering a short distance away with a look of profound distress. Augustus immediately straightened, irritation slipping into confusion. He recognized the Wielder with the goatee—Acton, Ashen, something like that—but the other Prime's name eluded him.

"Forgive the intrusion, Prime Augustus, but we felt this was urgent."

"Is something wrong with the Nexus, Prime Ashing?" he asked.

"Ashton, sire. No, the Nexus is fine. But there was a distortion earlier today at the Eld ley station. And this time, a woman was caught in it."

Augustus' eyebrows rose, all of his irritation gone now. "What happened to her?"

"When the distortion closed, her hand was still trapped inside. It cut her hand to ribbons."

Augustus' stomach turned. "Did anyone witness it? Can we keep the incident quiet?" If the citizens of Erenthrall thought the distortions were dangerous and panicked, who knows what they might demand. He couldn't let them influence the Baron or threaten his ley network. The actions of the Kormanley were bad enough!

"Everyone present at the station at the time saw it," Ashton said regretfully.

"It cannot be contained," the other Prime said, his voice deep. "Word has already spread that the seamstress lost her hand."

Augustus spat a curse and stepped out into the outer room, motioning with a wave to his manservant to find wine. He began pacing as the man skittered away.

"I knew this would happen eventually, even though I didn't know exactly what the distortions would do to someone caught in them. The one that shattered the marble in the Temerite embassy was warning enough! I'll have to tell the Baron. He needs to prepare a statement, something to calm the public, something to distract them. And we need to determine what's causing these distortions and stop them. Except there's nothing wrong with the Nexus, with the system! I've been over it a hundred times." He grabbed his hair with both hands, talking to himself more than the other Primes now. "It can't be the Flyers' Tower. The Primes have checked the calculations! So what is it? Where are the distortions coming from?"

"Prime Augustus?"

He spun on Ashton with a sharp, "What?"

"There's more," the other Prime intoned.

"More what?"

"News," Ashton said. "Two Wielders from the Eld node were in the station when the distortion formed. One of them, a young woman recently raised to the purple, attempted to repair the distortion and free the seamstress." He licked his lips before continuing. "By all accounts, she nearly succeeded."

Augustus halted his frantic pacing and stared at the two Primes. "She fixed it?"

"She said she would have been able to free the woman if she'd had a few more moments to work on it, but the distortion closed. Everyone who witnessed it swore the distortion was the size of a man's torso, but after she began working, it shrank down to the size of a melon."

Augustus' eyes narrowed. His mind was already working through the ramifications to the ley system, how the Wielders could be used to counter the distortions, at least until he figured out what was causing them and could stop them at their source, and lastly how he could use this information to skew his report to the Baron.

But first . . .

"What is this Wielder's name, the one who attempted to repair the distortion?"

The two Primes traded a look. "Her name is Kara Tremain. She received her purple jacket and was assigned to the Eld node a month ago. All of those we questioned at the college said that they fully expect her to become a Prime once she completes her training at the nodes."

Augustus' lips thinned. "So she is already being considered as a Prime?"

Ashton nodded. "She is set to be transferred to another node in four years."

Most Wielders—those not thought powerful enough to become Primes—remained at the same node their entire career, to keep information about the ley network from spreading. No one Wielder was allowed to be intimately familiar with more than three nodes. However, those who might become Primes were transferred to multiple nodes during their training, to prepare them for the much more complicated task of overseeing the Nexus and the entire ley network in Erenthrall.

"Good. Make certain that we keep an eye on her. If she continues to show promise, we may want to bring her to the Nexus earlier than usual."

Ibsen Senate.

That was the name Hagger had gotten from Sedric, the Kormanley priest he'd interrogated. The Dogs had moved on Ibsen's flat in Eastend immediately. Since the collapse of the riverboat trade with the advent of the ley barges, Eastend and its docks had declined steadily, even though the district abutted Shadow and remained relatively close to Grass, the heart of Erenthrall. Ibsen was located a few streets from the decrepit docks, in a mudbrick building with no remaining glass windows, everything boarded up, a few tail ends of yellowed curtains trailing out through cracks in the boards. They'd scouted the surrounding streets, then stormed the building, crashing into Ibsen's flat to find it empty.

Or rather, abandoned. The furniture had been scattered, cupboards left open, drawers half pulled or emptied onto the floor. Most of the kitchen remained untouched, some food left rotting on the shelves. The bedroom looked as if it had been tossed, the straw from the mattress littering the floor. Only one of the ley globes that remained worked, its light fitful, cloaking the entire flat in strange shadows.

Hagger began spitting curses as soon as they entered. Allan scanned the room once, his gaze narrowing on the old fireplace in the center of one wall. He moved toward it, dismissing the rest of the flat.

"Search it!" Hagger ordered with a gesture, then crouched down beside Allan at the mouth of the firepit. "What have you got?"

"Scraps of paper, probably burned when Ibsen left." He drew a few of the scraps out of the ashes that filled the grate carefully, trying not to smear the soot or damage the paper further. He held up the largest pieces to the flickering light and the stray streams of sunlight that filtered through the boarded windows. "It looks like some of the same cryptic messages we found at the other locations."

Hagger grunted and stood. "Doesn't look like there's much left."

"No, nothing we can use." Allan stared at the long-dead fire, then the rotting food. "I'd say Ibsen left as soon as he heard that Sedric had been taken. A few days at least, probably more like a week. He hasn't been back here since. Who knows where he's hiding."

"Not us Dogs, for certain."

Allan turned, something rough and dangerous coloring Hagger's voice. He found the old Dog standing in the middle of the room, staring down at the floor, a strange smile on his face.

Hagger stooped down, straightening again with a scrap of cloth held in one hand. "Not us Dogs. But we can use the Hounds." He motioned with the cloth. His smile twisted, turning nasty. "They'll be able to find him, no matter what cesspit he's tried to crawl into, as long as it's still within Erenthrall. All they need is his scent to follow, and now we have it."

A cold sweat broke out across Allan's shoulders and he stood to hide his discomfort, aware that some of the nearest Dogs who were scrambling through the debris of Ibsen's life had paused, were listening intently. Allan didn't like the Hounds' . . . intensity. They didn't appear any different than the Dogs, or anyone else in Erenthrall, but their sheer presence was disturbing.

And they were hard to handle. He'd seen the aftermath of one that had gotten out of control, bloodlust taking over. He shuddered at the memory.

He didn't want to deal with the Hounds unless he was ordered to.

"Ibsen is pretty low on the food chain," he said.

"He's the only lead we've got at the moment."

Allan managed to keep from frowning. "What about the papers we found? There was one coded note that wasn't outdated. It referred to the issue of *The Ley* that's coming out two days from now."

Hagger scowled.

"It could be significant," Allan retorted, knowing his voice sounded too defensive. "It could be the location of a meeting, or perhaps another attack."

"And it could be nothing! They know we've captured Sedric and his papers, and they'll know we've raided Ibsen's place, even though he's already run. What makes you think they'll even use *The Ley* again? What makes you think they'll follow through with it?"

"Because over the last four years we've been closer to them than this before and they've always followed through. They aren't afraid of us. And they don't know we've figured out their code."

"They should be afraid," Hagger huffed. He glared at the scrap in his hands, stuffed it into one of his pockets, then met Allan's gaze and said grudgingly, "We'll see what this news sheet has to say, but we'll sic the Hounds on Ibsen as well. The Baron wants answers, and I intend to give them to him."

He stalked toward the door and one of the younger sentries they'd left outside. "Douglass! Send word to the Tower. I want one of the Hounds ready to track by the time we return." He spun toward the rest of the Dogs already inside. "The rest of you, rake this place. I want everything Ibsen could have touched or worn collected and ready for the Hound within the hour."

Allan watched as the elder Dog began pacing through the flat himself, tossing tables aside and scouring beneath for anything of importance that might have been left behind. Uneasiness washed through him at his partner's energy, frantic and skittish, laced with excitement and adrenaline. He frowned, thought of Moira and Morrell as he'd left them that morning, Moira already in her amber clothing for her return to work at the Tower, the wet nurse who'd care for Morrell cooing to the child in the background. The two images clashed. He suppressed a shudder, shook himself, and forced himself to begin searching the flat as well, although he stayed clear of Hagger.

Two hours later, they left Ibsen's flat, a ley cart loaded with what little they'd found trailing behind them, escorted by the Dogs. The citizens in the street parted before them, those within Eastend with furtive glances behind as they ducked into alleys or shadowed doorways, those in Shadow stepping to one side, gazing at the contents of the cart with hooded curiosity. In Grass, the Dogs and the cart were studiously ignored.

Back at the Tower, Hagger gestured sharply for Allan to follow. Passing through the main hall, another training bout in session, they descended to the interrogation rooms below, two other Dogs following them at a look from Hagger. He spoke briefly to the two Dogs on watch, then moved to one of the doors, stepping through without hesitation.

Allan halted inside the door, the other two Dogs moving to either side of him. Hagger stood in front of Daedallen, the captain glaring down at him.

"I've brought a Hound," Daedallen said, and Allan realized with a start that there *was* someone else in the room, standing against the far wall, near the corner. He hadn't noticed him, the dirty-blond-haired, nondescript boy barely coming up to his shoulders, no more than fourteen years old, possibly a few years younger. He wore street clothes, like anyone within Grass would wear, but his face was plain, his hair slightly unkempt. Like all of the other Hounds, everything about him appeared normal. His most unusual feature was his eyes, a cool gray that met Allan's evenly. No emotion showed in the Hound's face or flickered through his gaze, but the uneasiness that had begun in Ibsen's flat with Hagger's actions intensified. The most disturbing thing about the Hounds was their ability to blend into the background. When Daedallen shifted slightly forward, drawing Allan's attention away, the Hound vanished, as if the boy weren't truly there, even though he was easy to see if Allan concentrated.

"I've brought the Hound," the captain said again. "What I want to know is what for?"

Hagger stiffened. "We raided Ibsen Senate's flat. He was no longer there. He'd tossed the place, burned any evidence that could have been useful, and fled, probably the moment he knew we had his Kormanley accomplice in custody. But he left behind a few things." He pulled out the old swatch of cloth and Allan realized he hadn't let anyone else touch it, here or at the flat.

Allan watched the Hound. As soon as the cloth appeared, the boy's attention fixed on it and he drew in a deep breath, nostrils flaring. Tension thrummed through his body, as if he were a harp string that had been lightly plucked. But he didn't move, his gaze shooting toward Daedallen, his eyes narrowing, then swinging back toward Allan as if he sensed the Dog's attention.

The hackles on the back of Allan's neck rose.

"And do you feel this is an effective use of the Hounds?" Daedallen asked.

It took a moment for Allan to realize the captain wasn't speaking to Hagger.

He snapped back to attention, found the captain watching him. He met the captain's gaze, knew that Hagger was glaring at him, expecting him to repeat what he'd said back at Ibsen's flat. But he'd had enough issues with Hagger lately. He didn't need to give the old Dog another reason to despise him.

"I don't see that we have any choice. We've run out of other leads and the Baronial Meeting is a few weeks away."

To the captain's right, Hagger relaxed and nodded once in approval. The captain's expression hardened. "Very well." He turned to Hagger. "Give me the rag."

Hagger handed it over, Daedallen taking it carefully between two fingers before moving to stand before the Hound and passing it on.

"Seek," he said, his voice taking on the harsh pitch of an order, as if he were speaking to a true dog, not a youth. "Do not kill."

Irritation and regret flashed across the Hound's face and Allan half-expected to hear him emit a plaintive whine, but he merely raised the cloth to his face and drew in the scent deeply, closing his eyes. His expression clouded, and when he opened his eyes again, his gaze latched onto Hagger. Allan saw the old Dog flinch, one hand shifting toward the blade at his side. The Hound stepped forward, Hagger jerking back as he leaned in to get a good whiff of Hagger's body odor.

He smelled the rag again, appeared to concentrate, as if picking through the different layers of scent, discarding Hagger's and focusing on what was left, and then, without a word, he headed toward the door, throwing it open and vanishing into the corridor outside.

"He's found the scent," Daedallen said, his voice soft.

"Already?" one of the other Dogs asked.

No one answered.

Hagger shook himself, as if trying to rid himself of the Hound's presence. "Blasted Hounds."

Daedallen moved toward the door as well, saying, "He'll have found Ibsen Senate by the end of the day tomorrow, if he's still in the city. Let's hope he's still alive. Baron Arent won't be happy with this use of the Hounds if he isn't."

⌘

As soon as the Hound isolated the smell of woodsmoke and the under-lying thread of disease that permeated the cloth, he moved. Jogging through the Dogs' lair and up and out into the sunlight, he filtered through the miasma of scents that overlay the world in layer upon layer, his skin prickling as the thrill of a hunt settled over him. He paused once, to glance up at the sunlight and savor its touch, then flinched and glanced around, waiting for his alpha's fist to descend and punish him for the distraction. Nothing should break a Hound's focus during a hunt; nothing should keep him from his prey. Seek. Subdue. Kill. The mantra had been beaten into him since he'd woken in the darkness of the den, surrounded by stone, four years ago.

He grunted and shied from that memory, cutting away from the Amber Tower and out into the streets of the city, drawing in its scents as he slid through the morass of people, touching no one but observing everything. No one noticed him, most stepping around him uncon-sciously as he used his training to manipulate the Tapestry and divert their attention, to impress upon them that there was nothing of inter-est to see. At the same time, he focused on the scents he'd gathered from the rag. The rank odor of the Dog who'd carried it to the tower was strong and he followed it without thought, searching for the more elusive thread of woodsmoke and disease he sought, his true prey. But that prey had not passed through the immediate area in the last few months.

So he followed the Dog's scent—rancid, layered with grease and stale alcohol and old blood. He smelled the others from the room as well, the alpha's scent cutting away in a different direction, toward the Dogs' barracks. The younger Dog's scent continued to follow the older. He smelled of tallow and baby vomit, with a trace of heady perfume from his mate. He also made the Hound's hackles rise in warning. There had been something wrong about him, something the Hound had never experienced before and couldn't identify through smell. The Dog had been aware of the Hound's presence almost immediately, had been able to focus on him even when the Hound had stilled and attempted to hide with the Tapestry. His awareness had been unsettling; the Hound was used to being invisible.

The Hound shrugged the thought aside. He had a scent; he had prey. Seek.

The trail led to Eastend, a flat in a building riddled with the scent of death, decay, and the dying. He stood in the center of the room where the Dogs had been, where his prey had lived, the prey's smell permeating the contents strewn across the floor, stronger than the acrid smoke from the week-old fire or the rotten food. The Hound breathed it in deeply, locked it in place in his mind, the disease hidden in the man's sweat taking on dimension, imbued with flavor and strength. The disease was eating him from the inside out, tainting his piss. It would gnaw at his intestines, unseen and unheard, until it killed him with a final gush of blood and pain.

The Hound didn't care. He'd sunk into the hunt, his quarry's tracks located. He turned in the confines of the flat and with narrowed gaze traced the scent out of the building and into the street. The dying man had panicked, had ransacked his own den, burned nearly everything, sweated through his clothes, marked the air with his desperation. The Hound's lip curled at the fear, his hands clenching and unclenching on air. He could taste the prey's blood.

He began to run, moving silently from the building, unseen, unnoticed. The tracks led from Eastend south and west, through Swallow and Leeds, into the ley station and the platform that led to Eld. He stood in a corner of the ley barge and watched the passengers, everyone unaware of his presence. He licked his lips, tasted their unconscious fear, his blood burning hot as they shifted and sidled in apprehension. As he disembarked at the Eld station, he faltered only once as the sights and sounds and smells struck a chord of familiarity deep inside him. He thrust the uncomfortable thrum aside, his prey's scent too sharp for him to be distracted, and stalked through the narrower streets, through the marketplace, past a park where he slowed, the thrum through his core heightening. Frowning, he pushed on and halted outside a tavern. His prey had entered three days before, but hadn't exited through this door.

He reached to open it, started to step into the interior darkness, blinded momentarily, but was brought up short by a woman and man attempting to exit. He sucked in a deep breath on instinct, felt a jolt through his entire body as he recognized her scent. Laughter echoed in his ears, dredged up from memory, a young girl and boy teasing each other. Sunlight flared on the metal thistles in a game of Thistle Snatch. Dogs surged through a square. Multicolored light bloomed in air as awe sliced through his gut. An ache of fear tingled in his arms as he stumbled through a ley station mezzanine, boarded a barge. Then an arm snaked around his waist, and even though he struggled, he was lifted and pulled away, his screams stifled.

He blinked at the barrage of sensations, his dazzled eyes focusing on the woman before him. She was staring at him in open shock, the man behind her—he didn't recognize his scent—regarding him with a suspicious, possessive frown.

"Justin?" the woman gasped.

He turned and fled, dodged out the door and into the street, weaving among the pedestrians, scrambling away, people cursing at his frantic retreat. He heard the woman shout after him, the words obscured by the heady pounding of his own blood in his ears. He cut right at the first intersection, angled left at the next, then ground to a halt around a corner, hunched over, breathing hard. His chest hurt and tears blurred his vision. He sank to one knee, heard the laughter again, and lurched upright, back slamming into the stone building behind him. His breath caught in his chest, but with a painful hitch and spasm he sucked in air and seized control of himself.

He searched the street, stilled when he realized people were watching him warily. In his panic, he'd forgotten his training, had let his hold on the Tapestry go. He cringed from imagined punishment and reached out with his senses, shifting to the side along the building a few steps, then froze. Those on the street who'd noticed him frowned, glanced around in consternation, then continued on their way. Within moments, he'd been forgotten.

Breathing easier, his blood no longer thudding in his temples, the Hound took stock. His body trembled with adrenaline, not from the hunt but from raw, unbridled fear. Not fear for himself, but fear for *her*, for the woman.

For Kara.

Tears stung his eyes and he dashed them away violently, the memory of that day playing Thistle Snatch, then running from the Dogs and seeing the blossom of light in the air, jagged and sharp in his mind. Then two days later, when they'd decided to take the ley barge to Shadow, to see the subtower lit in that district. It was the day the Hound had finally taken him, after stalking him for so long. He'd snatched him from the street and when Justin had woken, he'd been in the den and his training had begun. Training that didn't allow for a past, didn't allow memory, didn't allow friends. If anyone became aware of him, of what he had become, of what he *was*. . . .

The Hounds would hunt them down. They would hunt Kara down. Cory. His own parents.

Seek. Subdue. Kill.

He straightened where he stood. He should never have remembered. His training should have held. He needed to forget, to protect her, to protect them all. He was a Hound. He belonged to the Baron. The alphas must never know what had happened.

Heaving in gulps of air, body shuddering with effort, he ruthlessly gathered the sunbright burst of memories, bundled them tight, and buried them deep. He hunted every last shred of the life he had forgotten and strangled it into silence. Seek. Subdue. Kill. Seek. Subdue. Kill.

He was a Hound. He could be nothing else.

A thin whimper escaped him.

Five minutes later, he raised his head and unclenched fists, his body calm, centered, fingers aching. He glanced around, drew in the scents of the street, caught a lingering trace of woodsmoke and disease. His blood quickened. Excitement tingled down through his arms, his stance suddenly alert. One hand rose to wipe wetness from his cheeks. He regarded the salty moisture on his fingers a moment, then flicked it away.

He began to move, a smooth, deadly lope. He'd caught the scent of his prey.

He was a Hound, and nothing could distract him from the hunt.

~~~

Kara couldn't think. She could barely breathe. Her lungs felt constricted, her chest tight, like bands of iron had been wrapped around her and they were getting tighter and tighter. Blood pounded in her ears and heat suffused her body from head to toe.

Justin. After all this time.

She blinked in the background blaze of light, managed to suck in air and ask, "Justin?" Her own voice sounded raw and weak to her.

Then the boy—Justin would be twelve now, she thought, since she was sixteen—bolted.

She lurched forward, a cry escaping her, one hand reaching to catch him. But the sunlight was too blinding after the darkness of the tavern and her hand closed only on air. She pulled herself up short just outside the door, Marcus a step behind her, hand on her back. She wiped frantically at her eyes, but saw nothing in the street beyond, except the usual pedestrians.

"Justin!" Her voice cracked and she choked on the dryness and ache in her throat. "Come back!"

Her hand clenched and unclenched before her, but then she let it drop back to her side. She swallowed against the stone that had lodged in her throat, the moment of pure joy and excitement at finally seeing Justin dampened by a renewed sense of loss.

Marcus' hand snaked around her waist and he pulled her close. She leaned into his shoulder and turned into him, even though her eyes still scanned the street.

"Who was that?" Marcus asked. She felt the words as a rumble in his chest. "Who's Justin?"

"A boy I knew when I was in school. A friend." Her voice was dull and flat. "He used to run around with Cory and me before . . . before he vanished. He was with us the day I decided to see one of the subtowers activated. I dragged Cory and him to the ley barges, took them to

Shadow. But after we reached the district, as we were heading up to the mezzanine, Cory and I turned around and he was gone. I always thought I'd failed him somehow, that it was my fault he disappeared."

"Why?"

She pushed away from the warmth and vibration of his chest, but not out of his protective arm, and sighed. "Because he told us someone was watching him, and I didn't believe him. He had always been strange and I thought his insistence a man was stalking him was part of that. But then he vanished and . . ." She groped for words, but finally shook her head. "I should have believed him. I should have protected him better."

Marcus hugged her, then rested his hands on her shoulders at arms' length and stared into her eyes. "He wasn't your responsibility. Besides," he glanced toward the street, "are you certain it was him? All I saw was the shape of a boy in the doorway, surrounded by sunlight."

Kara frowned, thinking back to the image she'd seen when the door had abruptly opened in her hand. The sun had forced her back in surprise. It had glinted gold on the boy's hair, soft and fine like she remembered, but she hadn't really been able to see the boy's features. Only the vague impression of a nose, of eyes, of an expression of shock fractured a moment later by pure fear.

"I don't know." Doubt niggled at her. "I thought so. It *felt* like him. If it wasn't him, why did he run?"

"If it *was* him, why did he run? Unless he didn't want to be found."

Kara screwed her face up in a frown. It didn't make any sense, either way. She hadn't gotten a good look, the boy's face lost in silhouette, and she had no idea what Justin would look like now. People changed so much over four years, especially boys Justin's age. He'd certainly been taller, more gangly, and thinner than she remembered.

She shoved out of Marcus' grip and began walking. "No, it was him. I know it. And even if he doesn't want to be found, I deserve some answers."

"Kara!" She didn't turn at Marcus' exasperated tone, broke into a jog when she heard him sigh and begin to follow. As she moved down the street, she glanced into the alcoves, into doorways, down the alleys and cross streets. The niches were empty, doorways vacant, the narrows scattered with people, none of them Justin. "Kara, wait up!"

When his hand closed on her shoulder, she twisted out of his grip and turned on him with a glare. "Don't."

Marcus halted, anger flaring in his eyes. "Kara, what's going on? What are you doing?"

"I'm looking for him, what do you think?" She started off again.

"That doesn't make any sense!" He mumbled something low under his breath, then followed again, coming up on her side, not touching her. "He ran off. He obviously doesn't want to be found. How do you even know he went this way?"

Kara halted abruptly, Marcus moving two steps beyond before realizing she'd stopped. "I don't," she said sharply. "But I have to do something."

"What? You can't search the city yourself, you can't even search Eld."

"I can . . . I can tell the city guard, the Dogs."

Marcus snorted. "And you expect them to do anything about a boy who's been missing for, what, three years?"

"Four," Kara said sharply, but she felt the sudden surge of energy, of hope, fading, the despair returning. Marcus was right. The Dogs would scowl at her for wasting their time, same for the city watch. They had more important people to find, like the Kormanley. Who else would care? Her parents were dead, and she'd lost track of Justin's parents in the intervening years. Ischua? Perhaps. But he'd hardly known Justin. She couldn't even remember if the Tender had ever met him.

Which left only her. And Cory. She had to tell Cory.

She met Marcus' gaze. "Why would he run?"

"I don't know." Marcus reached for her, pulled her close, kissed her tear-streaked face. "Come on. I'll walk you down along Archam Street. I know you like the shops along there. Maybe we'll even buy some of that horribly expensive chocolate imported from Temerite. We can look for Justin along the way."

Kara smiled tentatively, for Marcus' sake, even though inside she ached with a pain she hadn't felt for years. She realized that she'd let Justin slip away from her, had stopped watching for him in the crowds, stopped searching for his face. She should never have stopped looking.

Her fingers twined with Marcus' as he pulled her toward Archam, but she glanced over her shoulder one last time to scan the street for a sign—any sign—of the boy she'd lost when she was twelve.

"Cory!"

Kara's old friend spun on his stool at the tavern, nearly spilling the mug of ale he held in one hand. He squinted in the direction of the doorway in confusion as Kara shoved the door closed behind her and made her way to his table, but as soon as he recognized her, he straightened and broke into a smile. It wiped away the haggardness around his eyes. He wore the drab brown shirt of an undergraduate from the University, although the sleeves were rucked up to his elbows.

"Kara," he said as she sat down beside him. "How goes the Wielders' work? Congratulations on receiving your purples. I haven't seen you since . . ."

"Since before you were tested into the University," she finished for him. "I know. I've been meaning to come to Confluence since they positioned me at Eld, but they've kept me so busy."

Cory snorted and waved a hand. "Don't talk to me about busy. I haven't had a chance to breathe since I entered the University. It's nothing like the school we went to. There's nothing to do but go to class and study. And the Masters expect miracles! I've only been there a few months and already I'm drinking this swill." He took a large swallow of the ale and grimaced, setting the mug down with a thud before rubbing his face with his hands. "What about being a real Wielder? Is it anything like we thought when we were younger?"

Kara's eyebrows rose. "You're not even fifteen, Cory. But no, it isn't anything like what you and Brent and the others imagined in the schoolyard. It's more gruntwork than mystical attacks and fake sorcery."

Cory grinned, the boy Kara remembered emerging beneath the dirty-blond hair and weariness. "But it was so much fun!"

Kara rolled her eyes. "In any case, that's not why I found you. I saw him, Cory. I saw Justin!"

Cory stilled, his entire body rigid. The sloppy smile dropped away in a blink, his expression hard and hurt. He turned back to his ale, drinking slowly while staring off into the distance. "That isn't funny, Kara."

"I'm not joking. I saw him. In Eld. I was coming out of a tavern like this one with Marcus and he was right there. He saw me, I know he did.

He recognized me. But then he ran. I tried to follow him, but he vanished."

Cory's jaw clenched. "Who's Marcus?"

Suddenly, the awkward tension from that last night on the roof of their apartment building returned and Kara found herself fidgeting on her stool, heat creeping up her neck. "He's my assigned partner at the node. He's helping me get used to being a Wielder." She waved a hand in irritation. "That doesn't matter. What matters is that Justin is alive! We need to find him. We need to find his parents and let them know—"

"If it were Justin," Cory snapped, turning on her, "why did he run away? Why didn't he say anything to you? Justin would have said something. If he were in trouble, he would have asked for help." He shook his head. "You're wrong, Kara. It couldn't have been Justin. He would have said something!"

Kara stared into Cory's eyes, stunned by the outburst. Anger lined his face, but beneath that anger she could see tears. He trembled with the effort to hold them back.

"Why would you bring this back up?" he whispered, his voice cracked and broken. "I thought we'd left it all behind us."

Before she could respond, he shoved away from the table, so hard he nearly knocked his stool over. And then he was gone.

Twelve

WHEN THE HOUND didn't return before midnight the next day, Allan settled in for a long night. He tried to sleep, but found himself staring up at the stone ceiling of one of the cells thinking of Moira and Morrell. The stewards in the Amber Tower were working its servants hard in preparation for the Baronial Meeting, so they hadn't seen each other much in the past few days.

He grimaced and shifted his thoughts to Morrell, drawing up an image of her tiny face, snuggled in her cradle. One pudgy hand was fisted by the corner of her mouth, her face serene, eyes closed. Drool created a dark spot in the bunched-up blanket near her head.

"Maybe we shouldn't stay in Erenthrall," he whispered to himself in the darkness. "I wonder what Moira would say about that?"

Except he knew. Moira had lived her entire life in Erenthrall, in its sprawling districts with its connection to the ley and all of the luxuries that brought. She could never live in a place like Canter, his hometown. It would be too quaint, too rustic for her tastes. Not to mention the lack of ley and its amenities. Living with a fire for cooking and heat had been thrilling for her . . . but only because she could find everything else she needed in Hedge within a short walk. In the end, she couldn't envision living without the ley permanently, not like she'd have to do in Canter, or any of the other outlying towns in the Baronies.

He sighed, rolled over, and tried to force himself to sleep.

A moment later, Hagger crashed through the cell door and bellowed. "The Hound's back! Get your ass out of bed, Pup. Are you a Dog or not?"

Allan lurched up from the cot, glanced beyond Hagger to where a few of the other Dogs were hanging back, all of them older, like Hagger, and all of them vicious with their arrests and interrogations. A cold frisson of fear ran through him as he caught the danger hidden behind the seemingly innocuous question.

He met Hagger's gaze, straightened and moved to stand before him at the door. "I'm a Dog," he announced, loud enough all could hear.

A few of the men behind sneered. Hagger merely glared.

"The Hound found Ibsen," Hagger said. "He's ready to lead us to him right now." He motioned to the men behind him, who all came to attention.

"Where—" Allan began, but then he caught sight of the Hound off to one side, although standing in the open. He muttered a curse beneath his breath and vowed to keep an eye on the boy. He didn't like how the boy's gaze made his skin crawl.

Hagger frowned and searched as well, until his eyes locked onto the Hound's position. He gestured the youth forward. "We're ready. Take us to him."

The boy nodded and took off at a fast lope. Allan caught the flash of a quick grin on the Hound's face as Hagger swore and growled, "Keep up! We don't want to lose him, or the captain will have our hides!"

The Hound, trailed by Allan, Hagger, and a half dozen other Dogs, ascended to the main level of the Amber Tower and then out onto the still dark streets. He immediately headed left, to the far side of the Tower, passing through the ley-lit gardens and thoroughfares until he reached the center of Grass—the Nexus. He circled around the huge oval building sunk into a deep depression in the ground, the crystal roof glowing with an intense white light rivaling that of the Flyers' Tower. Stairs led down to the buildings from the edge of the depression, but the Hound ignored them all, breaking away from the Prime Wielders' central power and the hub of the entire ley system and out through the northern towers, winding among their bases. As they left the cluster of spires behind, Allan caught sight of the eastern horizon, beginning to lighten with the first hints of dawn. Clouds streaked the skies in bands, and the plains spread out wide and flat beneath them.

Then they were passing through the outer streets of Grass, more citizens on the roads now, although they ducked quickly out of the Dogs' way. A moment later, Allan shouted to Hagger, "He's headed toward the ley station!"

Five minutes later the Hound broke through the arched doors into the mezzanine of Grass' main hub. Twice the size of any of the others within Erenthrall, the ceiling soared high above, stained-glass windows piercing the stone. A huge fountain spewed water in a tangle of arcs in the center. The Hound headed directly toward the tunnel that led to the northeastern ley lines.

Just as the Hound ducked into the tunnel, Allan spotted a young boy to one side selling the local news sheets. He thought about the crumpled copy of the code they'd found and grabbed Hagger's arm. "Hold up."

Hagger slowed and scowled as Allan tossed an erren to the boy and snatched up the day's copy of *The Ley*, stuffing it into his pocket without looking at it. They took off again after the Hound and the other Dogs.

"Bloody waste of time," Hagger muttered under his breath scornfully. Allan ignored him.

A moment later they were on the platform, the Hound waiting patiently at one end, the other Dogs in a rough circle around him. Even then, Allan found it hard to locate the boy. His ability to blend in appeared to increase in public, when there were more people around. He simply stood still, his gaze darting through the patrons of the ley station as they moved, none of them approaching too close to the ring of Dogs, their eyes averted. The Hound's eyes settled on Allan and held, until Allan shifted uncomfortably and glanced away. He noticed the other Dogs refused to look toward him, watching the white ley line or the rest of the station instead. Even Hagger ignored the boy, arms crossed and feet planted wide, his posture screaming "do not approach."

Allan sidled closer as they waited. "We're on the northeastern track, passing through the Shadow, Cold, Plinth, and Warren Districts. Any idea where we're going?"

Hagger gave him a cold stare. "None."

Allan frowned at the coldness, but turned away as the ley barge arrived, gliding out of the tunnel and docking next to the platform, a whistle blaring shrilly. He scanned the passengers as they disembarked, searching for anyone who felt out of place, then watched those enter the front of the barge opposite the Dogs as the Hound stepped onto the barge's deck, through the outer doors, and into the interior. Nothing appeared out of place. He and Hagger were the last to board, the whistle shrieking again as the barge jolted away from the platform, shuddering at first, before recovering and speeding down the ley stream toward the next destination. Allan grimaced, thankful he hadn't completely disrupted it by simply being there. None of the other Dogs appeared to notice, merely grumbling in annoyance at the rough ride. Allan retrieved the news sheet from his pocket, along with the coded sheet from Sedric's stash, and began counting out words according to the code.

They passed through Shadow, the Hound oblivious, eyes on Allan as he worked. The Hound didn't move as the barge paused in Cold either, passengers disembarking and joining them in a cacophony of conversation, laughter, and the whistle's shriek, nearly everyone pausing and falling silent in uncertainty when they caught sight of the pack of Dogs before shuffling farther away down the barge.

When they were halfway to Plinth, Allan leaned back from the window of the barge he'd used as a surface to write on, rocking gently with the motion of the ship, and frowned down at the news sheet. Uneasiness crawled through his gut as he sorted out the message, then clenched at his heart.

Eyes wide, he shot a glance toward Hagger. "We're going to need more Dogs."

Hagger's brow furrowed. "Why?"

"Because we're headed toward Lord Gatterly's estate. In Plinth. According to this, there's a meeting of the Kormanley there, today."

Hagger sniffed derisively and Allan bristled, anger blossoming swift and hot in his chest. He took a sharp step forward, so close Hagger shifted back without thought.

In a low voice, Allan whispered fiercely, "Ibsen Senate must be attending the meeting, that's why the Hound is leading us there. Lord Gatterly has probably been protecting him since Sedric was taken!"

Hagger's mocking expression faltered, his grizzled features creasing as he frowned in thought. His gaze darted toward the Hound, then back to Allan and the crumpled pages he held in his hand.

Then he met Allan's hard stare, lip curled. "We'll see. If the Hound takes us to Gatterly's estate, I'll send one of the Dogs for reinforcements."

Blood thrummed through Allan's veins, but he bit back a retort and stepped away. The air between them hummed with tension; the other Dogs picked up on it, their eyes fixed elsewhere, but their attention on the two ostensibly leading their pack. Allan could sense their derision as well, taking their cue from Hagger. Their lack of respect tasted bitter on Allan's tongue. He spat to one side, but nothing could rid him of the acridness. He tried to ignore it, as he'd done for the past few years, ever since he'd bonded with Moira, but he couldn't. It had grown too thick.

But he'd deal with it as best he could. For Moira. For Morrell.

He straightened, caught Hagger's gaze defiantly as the barge drew to a halt at the Plinth station. He stepped from the barge before the Hound, confident he was correct, and felt a surge of vindication a moment later when the Hound followed him. A few of the other Dogs traded uncertain glances with Hagger, but he motioned them after the Hound as the boy trotted across the platform and up through the station onto the street.

The Hound darted through the maze of Plinth's cobbled thoroughfares without looking at the heavy columns and carved facades of the mercantiles and trading houses to either side, his entire demeanor suddenly intent. He paused twice, drawing in the air deeply, his body vibrating with intensity, before taking off in a new direction. The Dogs followed, cursing as they dodged through streets packed with ley carts, a few horses with riders, and the throngs of merchants conducting business in the trading houses. But the Hound didn't falter, sliding through the masses with ease, no one apparently noticing him. Allan noted they were ascending toward the estates near the plinth of striated stone that gave the district its name and the cliffs above the Urate River. He caught the same recognition in Hagger's gaze.

The Hound halted before the gates of Gatterly's manse, the building barely visible behind the wrought iron doors and the branches of the trees in the garden beyond. The boy turned to Allan and said, "Wait here."

Without waiting for a response, he skirted the walls of the estate to the left, pausing to scent the air at intervals. As soon as he vanished around a corner, Allan turned to Hagger.

"Send a runner," he said. "According to the message, they'll be meeting here near dusk. We should scatter, set up a perimeter, seize some of the surrounding houses and wait for the others, make certain we aren't seen."

Hagger almost protested, his breath drawn for a sharp retort, but he let it out in a low growl. "I'll send a runner. You figure out how we'll get into the estate. I don't want anyone who comes to this meeting to escape. I want them all." He turned to stare through the gate, and Allan felt some of the derision fade as his focus was caught by this new development. "Maybe this is the break we've been waiting for," he muttered. "Maybe we'll finally crush these Kormanley for good."

Then he spun and began issuing orders, the Dogs dispersing to either side, fading back into the streets and narrows beyond.

Allan glanced at the manse as well, wondering if they'd already been seen. But the tension in his shoulders eased as he joined Hagger and the others. They took over a home with a sightline on the gate, the owners and their servants unceremoniously locked into one of their own rooms upstairs, two Dogs on watch. Then they settled in to wait.

An hour later, the Hound returned, appearing out of nowhere, all of the Dogs on watch startled. Somehow, the boy had slipped past everyone. After his heart settled, Allan asked, "Is Ibsen inside?"

The Hound nodded without hesitation.

"Good," Hagger murmured, glancing toward Allan. "Now all we need to do is figure out how to *get* inside."

Allan frowned, still not certain how he'd manage that, but the Hound said, "I'll open the gate."

"You can get inside?" Allan asked.

The Hound gave him a withering look, but Allan merely smiled. He almost reached out to tousle the boy's hair, but smothered the urge. Instead, he said, "You've already been inside, haven't you? Report."

The Hound straightened, suddenly formal, as if Allan were his alpha, even though the Hound had shown deference to none of the Dogs before this except Daedallen. "The manse is mostly empty. No servants. Two men on the first floor, the pr—target and the owner of the house. They were eating in the kitchen."

"What about the layout of the place?" Hagger growled.

The Hound looked at Allan first, who nodded, making Hagger's mouth twist in annoyance, but the Dog didn't dare lash out against the Hound. He focused on the boy's report on the rooms and their location instead, Allan only half listening.

The reinforcements arrived, along with Captain Daedallen, a half hour before the first activity began at the estate. At the captain's nod, Hagger dispersed the new Dogs, then brought Daedallen up to speed, Allan showing him the copy of *The Ley* and the coded message. The captain eyed the estate, and Allan felt a jolt of excitement sweep through him and the Dogs with them as Daedallen's eyes narrowed and his jaw clenched. As the sun began to sink, the excitement grew, charging the air. Lights appeared in the manse through the gate and trees, ley globes firing up all along the wall. An unmarked ley carriage arrived, the gates opening slowly at some hidden command, followed a short time later by a horsedrawn carriage, the liveried servant slapping the animals forward as soon as the gates were open wide enough to admit them. He appeared nervous, eyes scanning the street when they halted. Others arrived on foot, slipping from the lengthening shadows and into the garden beyond. Allan counted ten people, some of them merchants, others in guild colors, others nondescript.

His breath quickened; his blood sang. "It's almost time," Allan said. "The meeting should begin within the hour."

Daedallen nodded. "We'll give them a little more time, let them settle in."

Allan's hands itched to take up his sword, his legs twitching even more. If Daedallen hadn't been there, he suspected Hagger would be pacing. As it was, the older Dog's fingers were drumming against his upper arms where they were crossed over his chest.

An interminable time later, Daedallen finally gave a stiff nod.

The Hound slipped from the home's front room. Allan saw the boy cross the street a moment later, then lost sight of him. Hagger sent runners to the rest of the Dogs tucked away in the houses and shops they'd seized control of earlier. Daedallen regarded the estate in silence, body still, although Allan felt the tension radiating from him.

And then the shadow of the Hound appeared on the far side of the gate.

"Go," Daedallen barked.

Hagger dodged out through the rearranged furniture of the room, out the door and onto the street, Allan and the other Dogs behind him. They all drew their swords as they neared the gate, the Hound catching sight of them, turning, then sprinting toward the front of the manse beyond. Hagger cursed, even as they were joined by the other groups, but his attention shifted away from the Hound as his hands flashed orders to spread out to the left and right. Dogs ducked into the garden, trampling flowers and bushes, Allan and Hagger heading straight for the heavy oak double doors. One was slightly ajar, the lock shattered, a slim blade sticking out from the keyhole. The Hound's work, although Allan hadn't seen any weapons on the boy.

Then they were inside, hand gestures flying, Allan sticking close to Hagger. Signals indicating empty rooms flared from both sides as Dogs ducked through doors and returned. Hagger sent another group up to the second story, then motioned Allan and three others into the back rooms. Allan noted the lack of servants, as the Hound had reported. They encountered the kitchen area, passed through to a massive dining room, a parlor lined with tall paintings, a sitting room, and what appeared to be Lord Gatterly's office, a map of the known world lined with trading routes to the east and west drawn in black on a central table, a massive desk to one side. The Dogs sent upstairs returned, the lead shaking his head and shrugging. Hagger grimaced and motioned back toward the kitchen.

They found the narrow servant door that led to stairs up and down. Ley light glowed from those leading downward, and Hagger's expression broke into a cruel grin of triumph. He waved two Dogs toward the stairs leading up, then turned his entire focus on those going down.

They descended slowly, the only noises the creak of the stairs and the sounds of the Dogs' leather armor and their heavy breathing. The stairs turned, then turned again, the ley light brightening. They opened up onto a narrow corridor lined with cut stone, two doors to one side, another straight ahead. The one straight ahead was carved raggedly with the Kormanley symbol, just as the Hound had reported.

Allan's heart thudded in his chest and sweat dripped from his face, itching in his armpits and along his chest and back. The Dogs settled around the door, listening. The murmur of voices reverberated through the heavy wood of the door, indiscernible. Hagger waited until everyone was set, meeting all of their gazes with a quick flicker of confirmation—

And then he cut his hand forward.

Allan hit the door hard, felt a moment of resistance before Hagger hit it beside him and it gave with a loud crack of splintering wood. They burst into the room beyond, the scent of smoke tickling Allan's nostrils as soon as he and Hagger spilled out onto the floor. The Dogs behind leaped over them, pouring forward with a sudden barrage of shouts and growls, the room erupting into screams and curses, a scuffle of feet as the Kormanley—all dressed in the white robes of the priests—scattered in an attempt to escape. From the floor, Allan caught sight of two men in the center of the room inside a ring of candles, one kneeling with tears coursing down his face, the other standing regally over him. The man spun on the one that knelt and slapped him hard across the face, shouting, "You bastard! You led them straight to us!" A knife suddenly appeared in the man's hand.

"Ibsen," Allan murmured.

To his right, Hagger grunted. "And Lord Gatterly." He heaved to his feet and headed straight toward the lord: the tall man with the neatly trimmed mustache and beard holding the dagger. Hagger snagged the lord's shoulder even as the lord lunged toward the cowering Ibsen, jerking Gatterly back and bringing his own sword up to the lord's throat. At the same time, the Hound appeared from the brawl that surrounded them, stepping forward and dragging Ibsen out of range, hunkering over the man with a feral look of protection on his face.

Allan surged to his feet and joined the rest of the Dogs in subduing and rounding up the other Kormanley, shoving the white-robed members to their knees against one wall. Two bodies sprawled across the floor, blood staining their robes, both taken out in the initial attack, both still alive although the one closest to the door had been trampled. Allan held his sword on the group and Hagger herded Lord Gatterly to the other side of the room, the Hound keeping watch over Ibsen, who appeared to have fainted. There were twelve others besides those two, all glaring at the Dogs who held them. Candles and chairs were scattered, a few tilted onto their sides, and bookcases lined the wall opposite the door. Maps of the city filled another wall, each district shaded in different colors. Allan recognized at least three of the most recent Kormanley attacks marked in red on it.

In the center of the map, the Amber Tower had been circled. Scrawled next to it was a date.

The day of the Baron's Meeting.

Hatred flared and he turned to face Gatterly, but the lord's attention was caught by Daedallen. The captain stood in the door to the room, his gaze passing over everything, taking it all in, then falling on Gatterly in his white robes.

Anger creased the captain's brow and he stepped to within inches of Gatterly, Hagger pressing the tip of his sword to the lord's skin hard enough that blood trickled down his neck.

"What are you planning?" Daedallen said, his voice pitched soft, but rough, like the first warning growl from a guard dog.

Gatterly's eyes narrowed and he laughed, the sound cut to a short hiss as Hagger's sword dug in deeper.

"You can't stop it," he said tightly, defiantly. "It's already been put in motion. You can do whatever you want to me—kill me, even—but it's already begun."

Daedallen said nothing for a long moment, simply stared at Gatterly, until the lord swallowed, his gaze flicking toward Hagger, whose face was impassive, uncaring. Then the captain murmured, "You won't die. Not for a long time."

He turned, scanned all the rest of the Kormanley they'd captured, including Ibsen.

"Take them," he said harshly. "Take them all to the Tower and find out what they know."

〜

Hagger thrust Lord Gatterly across one of the cells beneath the Amber Tower, the man grunting as he hit the far wall. Allan closed the door as three other Dogs fanned out around the lord. Gatterly pushed up onto his hands. Blood had smeared across his face, and livid bruises were already rising across one cheek. He hadn't come willingly, and the Dogs had shown him no mercy as they hauled him out of his estate.

Looking up from where he sprawled, Gatterly reached up to wipe the blood from his lips and sneered at Hagger.

"I'm a lord of the Barony," he said. "You can't touch me."

Hagger's resulting smile sent a shiver through Allan's spine. "You're not a lord any longer."

He glanced toward one of the other Dogs, who moved to a narrow table against the far wall and tossed down a leather case. Metal clanked, the sound dulled by the leather, but as he untied the bundle and rolled it out he made certain Lord Gatterly saw the array of knives, hammers, and other implements that were secured within. Fear shot through the lord's eyes for the first time, and Allan felt his stomach roil in distaste. He shifted where he stood by the door and Hagger shot him a dark look that he couldn't interpret. Coldness settled against the back of Allan's neck and he stilled.

Hagger's attention shifted back to Gatterly. He moved forward and knelt at the lord's side. "You already know what's coming," he said, his voice reasonable, and as if on cue a hollow scream came from one of the adjacent rooms. "Tell us what you know and it will go easier for you."

Gatterly shifted into a sitting position. Hagger tensed, although his eyes brightened, as if he were hoping the lord would try something. "I know what happens down here, yes. And no matter what I say, you won't believe it's everything I know. There's no such thing as 'easy' once you're taken by the Dogs."

Hagger grinned. "I'm glad we understand each other."

He glanced toward the two remaining Dogs and motioned with one hand as he stood. They pounced on the lord, wrestling him to the stone floor on his back, pinning down his arms by thrusting the heels of their hands into his shoulder joints. Gatterly kicked his legs out, trying to catch Hagger as he stepped away, but the third Dog stomped on the lord's stomach and sat on his upper thighs. With cold efficiency, he tied restraints around Gatterly's ankles and knees, cinching the leather straps tight, binding his legs together. He could still bend at the waist and knees, but his motions were awkward and obviously caused him pain. He snarled as the Dog stood and returned to the table.

Hagger had come to a halt next to Allan and now stood watching the lord with narrowed eyes. His hand massaged the handle of his sword restlessly. The same agitated excitement Allan had felt at Ibsen's flat radiated from him.

Easing slightly away from him, knowing that Hagger was aware of his every move, Allan said, "I should probably go organize the wagons bringing the contents of the Kormanley room to the tow—"

"No. You're staying right here. You're going to help us interrogate him."

The calm in Hagger's voice, and the finality of it, forced the coldness at the nape of Allen's neck to spread down into his shoulders. He licked his lips, drew in a careful breath—

And Hagger turned to look at him. His eyes were hard, and Allan could see the rage in them.

"Are you a Dog or not?" he asked.

Fear sluiced down through Allan's arms, tingling in his fingers, but he steeled himself, forced his expression to remain neutral. He'd done it so many times before with those the Dogs captured, and with Hagger, that it came naturally. But his stomach churned. He didn't dare move, like the hare who has just caught the scent of the dog and realizes it's already too close.

Hagger reached up and grabbed him by the neck, a hold half friendly, half brawl, his fingers digging in painfully even as he smiled and tugged him toward Lord Gatterly. "I think you should break him in, don't you agree, boys?"

The other three Dogs grinned, and Allan suddenly realized they were three of Hagger's staunchest allies, the ones he'd hand-picked that morning for the group set to follow the Hound. He should have noticed it earlier, but hadn't, too distracted by the activity as they'd arrived with the wagonload of Kormanley, the chaos as the Dogs descended on the group with ley globes blazing, Captain Daedallen barking commands in the background. He hadn't paid attention when the Dogs were split up, the prisoners separated.

Cursing himself, he let Hagger lead him to Gatterly. "Now straddle him. Keep his legs immobile." The elder Dog emphasized the order with an excruciating pinch of his neck muscles before thrusting him forward and retreating to the table where the third Dog stood.

Allan hesitated, but only for a breath, aware that the two Dogs holding the prisoner were watching him. He straddled Gatterly, the lord grimacing and wriggling until Allan dropped to his knees, captured the lord's legs between them to keep him from bucking, and then sank his weight back to hold him down. This close, he could smell the fear sweat on the lord, even though his face was twisted in disdain and defiance. He met Allan's gaze and Allan's heart wrenched inside his chest. Gatterly knew what was coming, but he was attempting to hide it.

He wasn't going to break easy.

Hagger planted his feet to either side of Gatterly's head, wrenching the lord's attention away from Allan.

"We know you're Kormanley. Ibsen's presence incriminated you, even if we hadn't found you in the middle of a meeting. What we want to know is what you have planned for the Baronial Meeting."

"As I said at my estate," Gatterly spat, "it's already been set in motion. You can't stop it."

"Then there's no reason not to tell us."

Gatterly said nothing, merely smiled.

Hagger looked up at Allan. "Hit him. Don't break his jaw."

Allan had been expecting it. His arms still tingled with numbness, but he balled his hand into a fist and punched Gatterly as hard as he could high in the face, the shock of it jangling up through his wrist into his elbow. Shock also crossed Hagger's face, there and then hidden in the blink of an eye. Gatterly's head slammed back into the floor and he cried out, then spat blood to one side. His breath quickened, but Hagger didn't give him time to recover, growling, "Again."

Allan began pummeling the lord, something inside his head slipping, separating him from the feel of Gatterly's flesh beneath his fists, removing him from the slickness of the blood and snot that coated his hands as he continued, Hagger barking commands, Allan following through without thought. He kept Moira and Morrell's faces before him, trying to convince himself he was doing it for them, knowing that it was fear. Fear of Hagger, fear of the Dogs, of Captain Daedallen and Baron Arent. Fear of what he'd become.

So he did what Hagger told him. He hit Gatterly until the lord's face was nothing more than bruised and bloody flesh, his nose crushed and unrecognizable, his neatly trimmed beard matted. But he left the lord's jaw alone. Gatterly didn't break. So Hagger brought out the knives. They began on his fingers, the lord bucking beneath Allan while Hagger and the other Dog worked. Screams filled the chamber, echoed on either side by those in other chambers. When told, Allan laced his fingers together and pressed his palms into Gatterly's chest, weight forward to compress his lungs and make it harder to breathe. He did this repeatedly, taking the lord to the edge of consciousness before Hagger allowed him to back off. Then they began on his feet.

When they started on his chest, Gatterly sobbed something unintelligible, the first words he'd muttered besides curses trapped between screams and pitiable begging. Hagger and the other Dog drew back from their work, hands and uniforms streaked and stained with blood. They shared a glance, then turned to Allan.

Choking down the nausea that roiled in his stomach, Allan leaned forward, his thighs screaming at the motion after remaining in the same position for so long. He forced himself to get close enough to Gatterly's face that he could hear his gurgled breath, could smell the coppery stench of the blood that had pooled on the floor beneath him. It lay thick on the air, enough he thought he could taste it on his tongue.

Keeping his own breath shallow, he murmured, "What did you say, Lord Gatterly? We didn't hear you."

Gatterly's breath puffed against Allan's cheek and he drew back slightly before realizing that the lord was chuckling, the sound broken. Through the mess of his face, Allan thought he was even grinning, or at least trying to, the attempt hideous.

"You . . ." he hitched, barely audible, voice thick with fluid, ". . . yo-you don't . . . even realize. . . . The Kor . . . Korman . . . Kormanley. . . . They've already . . . already infiltrated . . . the . . . the . . ."

"The Tower?" Hagger burst out, crouching down next to Gatterly's head. "Are they already within the Tower?"

Gatterly chuckled again, shaking his head. Then he opened his eyes, the steely blue and white startling in the dark red, black, and purple remains of his face. "They're already in the Dogs," he hissed, and then he laughed, choked off by pain, but laughter nonetheless.

Hagger jerked back, surprise flickering across his face before it shifted into anger edged with panic. He glanced at the other three Dogs, then turned to Allan.

For a single moment, the panic in Hagger's gaze was tinged with suspicion and Allan straightened, tensing as he prepared to defend himself. But then the suspicion faded, settling into grim determination.

"We have to tell the captain," Hagger said.

"I still believe approaching Kara about the Kormanley is a bad idea," Ischua said, raising his voice enough to be heard above the clatter of the printing presses hard at work in the next room. He'd found Dalton at work on the next edition of *The Ley* in the basement printing hall. After seeing that the press was running smoothly, Dalton had taken him to an office to one side, shutting the door behind them. It cut the noise enough they didn't have to shout.

Now, Dalton poured a cup of tea for Ischua and handed it across the disorganized desk littered with papers and notebooks and a scattering of printing blocks. He stared at the aged Tender and suppressed his irritation. "Why?"

Ischua sipped the tea but set it aside immediately. "She still associates the Kormanley with her parent's death. Every time I mention them, even in passing, she tenses and becomes belligerent. And I don't see how we can even begin to approach her about helping us with restoring the ley without bringing in the Kormanley. However . . ."

Dalton raised an eyebrow at Ischua's hesitation. "You have something else in mind?"

He watched the conflict play out on Ischua's expressive face, in the creases of his brow and the lines around his mouth. But finally Ischua's forehead smoothed and his mouth thinned. "Not something else, some*one* else."

"Go on."

"I've noticed that Marcus' hatred of the Primes has grown, especially since Kara and he encountered the distortion at the Eld station. The Primes have been keeping a close watch on Kara since. Marcus resents it. Most of the other Wielders at the Eld node do as well—they're protective of their own—but not to the same extent as Marcus. I think we should focus on him. He may not have the same potential as Kara, most certainly will not become a Prime, but he has the passion."

Dalton sat forward, elbow on the edge of his desk. "Kara and Marcus have been partnered, right?"

"Yes. They were teamed up when Kara arrived. Since then, it's grown into something more significant." He added the last with a wry, indulgent, yet approving smile. "Much more significant if the rumors coming from Eld are true."

"Indeed." Dalton massaged his chin in thought. If they could turn Marcus to their cause, perhaps he could convince Kara. Then they would have two Wielders placed within the ranks. Even if the current strike against the Baron and the Primes succeeded, they would need Wielders to break the Nexus.

"Do you want me to approach him?" Ischua asked after a long moment.

Dalton sat back. "No. You're too valuable an influence on Kara. I don't want to destroy that if something goes wrong with Marcus. I'll have Dierdre approach him. But we'll move slow. I don't want to startle him, or have him do anything rash." Not to mention Dalton was a little busy preparing the Kormanley for the attack at the Baronial Meeting.

Ischua nodded, but Dalton still sensed something left unsaid. He considered letting it go—Ischua obviously wasn't going to bring whatever it was up without some prodding—but he heaved a mental sigh and said, "There's something else, isn't there?"

Ischua waved a hand and grimaced. "Nothing of importance. But with all of the violence lately, violence placed at the Kormanley's feet, I've begun to wonder. . . ."

Impatience nudged Dalton. "Wonder what?"

Ischua met his gaze squarely. "Wonder what we—the real Kormanley, not the violent sect that's taken our name—really want. We claim to want a return to the natural order, to the way things were before Baron Arent seized control of the ley through Augustus' Nexus. But is that true? Before Arent subdued the other Barons, the world was a much harsher place. The Baronies were a bloody place to live, each Baron vying for control of the other Barons' lands. The threat of an attack hung over everyone—Baron and common man alike. They were dark times. Food was scarce, disease rampant, mortality high. Most did not live beyond forty. It was unimaginable to live as long as I have."

And how old are you? Dalton asked himself. For the first time, he really looked at Ischua, saw the age that lined his face, the blotches that marred the backs of his hands, the weariness reflected in his eyes. If he had to guess, he'd say Ischua was nearing eighty, almost old enough to have lived during the time he described.

But what Ischua had said disturbed him more. "Are you saying you think the Baron's abuse of the ley is justified? That he and Augustus should remain in power?"

Ischua hardened. "No. Obviously the ley is being misused."

Dalton relaxed. "Then what?"

"I'm saying that some good has come out of Baron Arent's thirst for power, that our lives are better in some respects. Even you use the ley, Dalton, to run your printing presses, to heat water for your tea. You would not be able to do either of those things if the ley were returned to what it was before Augustus and the Nexus. There must be some sort of middle ground between what the ley was before and what it is now."

Before Dalton could respond, they heard movement in the outer room. Both started, then stood as something outside crashed to the floor with a rattle. Dalton's hand drifted toward the left-side drawer of the desk where he kept a small knife.

A moment later the door to the office burst open and Tyrus stumbled into the room, catching himself on the desk. His left arm was stained with spilt black ink, but his body trembled with excitement. "The Dogs seized everyone in Plinth at the meeting last night!"

The words sizzled through Dalton like lightning. "What do you mean?" he spat, though he'd heard, even over the sudden increased noise of the presses. Ischua stepped forward and closed the door again.

Tyrus drew in a steadying breath, half laughed, then swallowed and said, "I heard from Calven. The cell in Plinth was captured last night. The Dogs knew about the meeting. They raided Lord Gatterly's estate and took everyone there. They have them all in the Amber Tower right now. This is what we've been hoping for! The splinter group is broken!"

Dalton bit back a curse with effort, anger boiling up from his core. He felt it coloring his face, the heat in his skin tangible. He spun away, forced himself to face the wall so that neither Ischua nor Tyrus would see the rage, and tried to think. Behind him, Tyrus babbled more details to Ischua, his excitement grating, but Dalton had to remind himself that Tyrus thought he was part of the effort to bring the Kormanley down and that this was what he'd been working for the past four years. But they were so close! The attack on the Baronial Meeting was the culmination of months of work, of careful planning, of maneuvering people into place. It couldn't be falling apart now.

Dalton gripped the edge of the desk with one hand until his knuckles turned white and concentrated on breathing. Lord Gatterly's cell had been crucial to the plan, but it wasn't the only cell he had left, and none of the members had connections to the other cells. Even Lord Gatterly's wealth, while useful, couldn't compare to what had been provided by their Benefactor. He could shift men from the other cells into the positions to be held by Gatterly's men in the tower at the meeting. Their access had already been set up, everything was in place, he simply needed to send the orders to different cells.

Calmed, he released his grip on the desk and wiped the beads of sweat from his forehead before schooling his face into a gratified smile and turned to Ischua and Tyrus. Both were watching him with odd looks of confusion.

"This is excellent news, Tyrus," he said. "Hopefully, the Dogs will be able to track down the rest of the group."

Tyrus' face lit up. "Does this mean I no longer need to deal with Calven and the rest?"

Dalton shook his head. "I'm afraid not." At Tyrus' crushed look, he added, "We want to make certain the Dogs find them all, don't we? But I don't think you'll have to deal with them for much longer."

Tyrus grunted, face twisted into an angry grimace. But he sighed and muttered, "I'll let you know what else I learn from Calven and the others about those taken."

Tyrus left and Dalton shifted toward Ischua. The old Tender held himself stiffly, the confusion of a moment before still touching his eyes. Irritation flared through Dalton's skin again—at Ischua's sudden thoughtfulness and his own inability to control himself at Tyrus' news.

"You'll keep watch on Kara?" he asked sharply.

Ischua nodded. "Of course. Marcus as well."

"Very well." The note of dismissal was clear, even though he had never used such a tone with Ischua before. The Tender's eyebrows rose in surprise, but he withdrew, the clatter of the printing presses outside loud as he left the door open behind him.

Dalton turned away, fingers drumming against the desk; the noise of the presses had long become background noise for him, almost soothing. But the Dogs . . .

The Dogs were getting too close. It was time to withdraw himself from the splinter group, to sever his weakest ties, including Tyrus—*especially* Tyrus—and protect himself. At least until he could determine exactly how badly the Kormanley had been compromised.

He'd send Tyrus with the others to the tower, make certain he was one of the casualties. Since his complicity in the bombing of the North Umber ley station, Tyrus had become a liability. It ate at him. Dalton had seen it in his eyes, had heard it in his grumbling response to the order to remain in contact with Calven a few moments before. He was close to breaking, and Dalton couldn't risk him going to the Dogs and implicating Dalton himself as Kormanley.

No, better to eliminate Tyrus and focus more on infiltrating the Wielders. Leave the Kormanley cells to finish off the current attack and then reorganize afterward.

He settled into the seat behind his desk and began to plan out the new orders. He'd have to set them in motion quickly, with Lord Gatterly's group taken. And he couldn't forget to set Dierdre's sights on Marcus. If they couldn't break Augustus' and the Baron's hold on the ley directly, perhaps they could do it from within.

"Preparations for the Baronial Meeting are proceeding well," Baron Arent said, sifting through the papers that littered the massive table before him. He picked up a sheet and handed it to Prime Wielder Augustus, standing near him at the edge of the table. There were no seats. The table was inlaid with a myriad of stones in various shades depicting all of the districts of Erenthrall, the layout of the streets, the locations of the towers and subtowers and nodes. The Urate and Tiana Rivers gleamed blue through the sundry browns, grays, and duns. Quartz glinted in the light from the ley globes hovering overhead. A few paces distant, another table mapped out the Baronies and the known world, including the Demesnes to the west and the Temerite lands to the east. The lands to the south and the western continent weren't as detailed, but the major cities were denoted and labeled, especially those that contained their own Nexi run by Wielders controlled by Augustus. The network of major ley lines between the cities were etched in white across the continents, like a spider's web across the ocean and land. "Are the Wielders' plans on schedule?"

Augustus scanned the page once and set it aside. "All of the displays of the ley's power have been set up and are being practiced and tested with Master Sovaan's approval and supervision. It should convince the Barons that they should continue their allegiance to you and the Wielders that control their Nexi. There will be the usual display of power from the Nexus itself, but the emphasis this year will be on the Flyers' Tower. We want the Barons to covet our seizure of the skies and the near limitless possibilities that it represents. We haven't had a Baronial Meeting since the tower was sown, and some of the Barons haven't seen it yet, nor the flying ships."

"I assume you have arranged a tour of the city by flyer for all of the visiting lords, ladies, and Barons."

"Of course."

"And what of the distortions?"

Augustus met Arent's gaze. "The distortions will not present a problem while the Barons visit."

Arent didn't move, but he allowed himself a small frown, allowed the hint of a threat to tinge his voice. "Then the rumors I have heard are true? The Wielders—purple jackets, no less—have discovered a way to deal with the distortions?"

Augustus straightened. "I do not know what you have heard, but yes, it would appear that there is a way to repair them once they have formed. One of the Wielders, a young girl who only recently earned her jacket, and another purple jacket, stumbled across one of the distortions as it formed. In an attempt to save a woman trapped in it, the girl heedlessly attempted to fix it. From what I have discovered, she succeeded only partially."

"She failed only because the distortion closed before she had a chance to finish," Arent corrected.

Augustus' expression soured, eyes narrowed in suspicion. "That is true."

Arent had heard much about the two Wielders involved and knew that Augustus had tried to keep the incident quiet—and not because this was the first distortion to harm someone. Arent didn't know what Augustus' intentions truly were, but making him aware that Arent wasn't blind to the situation could do no harm. Let him think that Arent knew much more. They had worked together more or less amicably for decades, but it never hurt to remind Augustus of where he'd gotten the resources to create his precious Nexus in the first place. Without Baron Arent, he'd still be a lesser member of the University, toying with the ley under the mentors' disdainful eyes, not controlling a network more powerful than anything those same mentors had ever built.

"Why did you not approach me about this incident before this?"

"It is still being investigated." At Arent's raised eyebrows, Augustus waved a hand dismissively, but shifted as if agitated. "We've spoken to the girl. Based on what she said, it appears that we may be able to repair the distortions, but *only* if we get to them before they close. I have ordered the Wielders in two districts to form up in pairs to patrol the streets, listening for the high-pitched noise that precedes the distortion's formation while searching the Tapestry for any indications that it is being torn or shredded. As yet, the patrols have not been fortunate enough to run into a distortion in time to attempt to repair it. I have been waiting to report on our progress when there is something of significance to report."

Arent held Augustus' gaze a long moment, the only sound in the room their own breathing. When Augustus did not back down, he dropped his gaze toward the map. "What two districts are you using? Show me the patrols that you've set up."

"Eld and Green. I've had the Wielders running in circuits, along here and here." Augustus traced the paths on the map and Arent grunted. They fell into discussing alternate strategies, Arent trying to shift the focus of the effort toward Grass and the districts the Barons were more likely to frequent while they were here, Augustus pointing out that some of the districts had yet to exhibit any fluctuations in the Tapestry or the ley at all, that they should focus on those that had.

In the middle of the argument, the wide double doors to the room burst open and Captain Daedallen stalked into the room and headed directly toward the table, his eyes locked on Arent, not even flickering toward Augustus. This dismissal of the Prime Wielder caught Arent's attention more than the urgency of Daedallen's step.

"We need to review all of the Dogs' assignments and placements for the Baronial Meeting. Right now."

Arent pushed back from the table. "And your reason for this upheaval? We established those orders weeks ago. The Baronial Meeting is only three days away."

Daedallen's mouth worked as if he were chewing on something bitter. He glared around the room, made certain the doors had closed behind him, then said curtly, "The Kormanley have infiltrated the Dogs."

Shock spiked cleanly from Arent's neck down through his feet and his muscles went rigid. Anger followed, as swift and cold as lightning. "You're certain?"

"I'm certain. It's been verified by at least three of the Kormanley we captured last night at Lord Gatterly's estate, along with Gatterly himself. I would have doubted his word alone, but four of them, interrogated separately?" He shook his head. "They've done it. Somehow, they've turned some of the Dogs . . . or planted one of their own among us through our training."

"Lord Gatterly was Kormanley?"

Both Arent and Daedallen turned toward Augustus.

"Yes," Daedallen said. "He kept an entire gods-damned staging room for them beneath his estate."

Augustus glowered, but before he could retort, Arent cut in. "I have the assignments of the Dogs here." He searched through the papers on the table, pushed to one side while he and the Prime Wielder went over the new patrols, his mind working fast. "We'll have to change the entire schedule, reassign all of the Dogs to different locations. The Kormanley have had weeks to prepare, to organize."

"Lord Gatterly said that whatever they are planning—and all indications are that it has something to do with the Amber Tower and the Barons, although we don't know what—has already been set in motion."

"Changing the roles the Dogs will play may halt that. Unless you have another suggestion?"

Daedallen scowled. "No. None. Except to remove anyone who became a Dog within the last five years from patrolling near the Tower that day. If the Kormanley inserted one of their own into the training, it would have to have been during that time period."

"The Kormanley have been around much longer than that," Augustus pointed out.

"They were not as organized or as active before then."

"But we've seen they have long-reaching plans."

Daedallen glared at the Prime Wielder, who merely shrugged.

"Here is the list," Arent said, spreading out three sheets across one end of the table. "We should move all of those currently assigned positions inside the Amber Tower to patrols in the outer districts."

Daedallen nodded. "And call all of those without back in."

"How many of these men became Dogs within the last five years?"

The captain scanned the list and grimaced. "Too many. We won't have enough Dogs to cover the Tower without them."

"Then select those you trust for the Tower only, those you would risk your life with inside the Great Hall."

"Done."

"Bring me the revised assignments when you are done."

Daedallen collected papers. "I'll have them finished by this evening for your approval."

"Very well. But do not advise the Dogs of the changes until the day of the Baronial Meeting."

"Have you learned who is supporting the Kormanley?" Augustus asked.

"Not yet. Lord Gatterly has not been . . . cooperative in that respect.

But we have already coerced the others into revealing more of their fellow conspirators' names."

"You're running out of time."

Daedallen stiffened, tension thrumming through his body, but Arent laid a restraining hand on his arm, turning on Augustus.

"And what of the Wielders, Augustus? If the Kormanley have infiltrated the Dogs, could they not have done the same with the Wielders?"

"Impossible!"

"Are you certain?" When Augustus didn't answer, Arent added darkly, "Perhaps we should discuss the assignments of the Wielders as well."

Thirteen

ALLAN SIDLED UP to the railing of one of the sky barges, the sounds of light conversation and the clinking of celebratory glasses behind him intermixed with the slight breeze. Gripping the rail, he forced himself to look over the edge toward the interlacing streets of Erenthrall below. The buildings looked completely different from above, roofs of all styles and varieties—slate, wood slats, curved clay tiles, flat with hanging gardens or trellises or strung with clotheslines. A few sported dove cotes, and birds wheeled beneath the ship, or fluttered from building to building beneath them as the shadow of the ship startled them.

Through the smoothed and polished wood of the railing, Allan felt the ship shudder and he tightened his grip.

Behind him, the ship's captain muttered under his breath to one of the crew, "I don't understand why it's shuddering like that. It's never done that before. We've had nothing but smooth sailing since the ships were launched. Head below with one of the Wielders and see if one of them can find—"

The voice trailed off as the captain walked away, hands gesturing curtly. As soon as the crewman dashed off, the captain turned back to the bevy of guests he was escorting, including Barons Calluin, Ranit, and Leethe, his dark frown transformed into a smile. He edged into the group to mingle with a resigned look.

Allan turned, one hand still firmly on the railing, and scanned the crowd of partyers. He knew what was causing the ship to shudder: his presence. He was interrupting the ley's power simply by being on the ship. He hadn't ridden in one since he'd realized he affected them years before, had kept himself off of any duty roster that ended up on the flying barges. But he hadn't had any say in the sudden shift of duty assignments that morning, and he hadn't wanted to approach Daedallen as he gave them out. He hadn't wanted to face the pure rage in the captain's face.

They were returning to the Amber Tower after a tour of the city, delayed because their sky barge had suffered some difficulties taking flight. The three other barges had left without them, three Wielders joining the crew to determine what had gone wrong, Baron Arent watching from the steps of the tower with pursed lips. But as soon as Allan had shifted away from the center of the ship, they'd lifted from the ground, the entire craft shuddering with the effort. Baron Leethe had made a snide comment to Baron Calluin as they breasted the glowing crystal dome of the Nexus.

The rest of the flight had been uneventful, the ship trembling only occasionally. Allan made certain he remained in the prow of the ship, the individual districts drifting by beneath, his gaze mostly fixed on the guests. The height made him nervous.

He tensed out of habit as Hagger approached, the old Dog smiling. He gripped Allan's shoulder in greeting. "You haven't moved from this spot since before we left the Tower!"

Allan swallowed, tasted ash at the back of his throat, and smiled tightly. "Because every time I try to move, the ship shudders. Man wasn't meant to fly like the birds."

Hagger snorted. "Man does whatever the Baron wants." His hand dropped from Allan's shoulder. "Noticed anything untoward?"

Trying to relax, yet still on guard—Hagger and the other Dogs had treated him differently since the interrogation of Gatterly, but he didn't trust it—Allan shook his head. "Nothing. Perhaps Gatterly was lying."

"Or the sudden changes made this morning in our assignments bollocksed things up for the Kormanley. But keep an eye out. And watch the Barons. We've still got the meeting and the dinner to get through."

Hagger wandered off. Allan flinched as the barge lurched, hard enough a few of the guests cried out, then laughed at themselves nervously or covered their gaffe with a sip of a drink.

Baron Leethe smiled and shared a look with Calluin, the Baron of Farrade frowning and dropping his gaze.

They approached the tower, rising toward one of the balconies instead of dropping to the ground where they had departed. The barge settled into place, bumping against the amber of the balcony's railing like a ship nudging a dock, crew scrambling to secure it with ties. The captain released catches and pulled back a section of the ship's deck railing while servants in the tower lifted a short set of steps into place on the balcony. Strains of music filtered out through the tall glass windows, along with the susurrus of the hundred guests already gathered from the other three barges. Allan could see ley globes bobbing in the heights of the tall ceiling, the white light mingling with the flickering yellow of candlelight, until the entire Great Hall glowed golden. The captain held the ladies' hands as they disembarked, nodding and bowing to the lords. The Dogs and city guardsmen who'd lingered at the edges of the barge and served as escort during the ride departed last.

When the guests had stepped off the deck, Allan moved forward, falling in behind Hagger. As he neared the center of the barge, it began listing to one side.

The crew cried out, and Hagger and Allan leaped forward, jumping from the deck across the gap that was opening up between the ship and the balcony. Both tumbled down the steps to the balcony, rolling to break the fall, while behind the barge lurched again and straightened.

"Is there a problem?"

Allan glanced up to find Captain Daedallen standing over them, brow creased in concern as he stared at the barge, the captain cursing the Wielders as they emerged from below deck.

Hagger chuckled. "Not for us. But the Wielders might have some explaining to do."

"Then come with me. The Baronial Meeting is about to be called and I want you two on the main doors to the inner chamber."

They both stood and brushed off their formal uniforms, entering the Great Hall behind Daedallen. Inside, the golden light was more evident, an immense chandelier hung with thousands of dangling crystals amplifying the ley and candlelight. Long tables laden with food—fruits and cheeses, biscuits and tiny sandwiches—and thousands of candles lined both sides of the elongated chamber. More candles were set on trays held aloft by the Wielders, like the barges outside. An orchestra played at the far end of the Hall, the wide space before it filled with dancing couples in all of their finery, while the nearer space was being set up by a hundred servants for the dinner service after the official

Meeting. Allan scoured the amber-clothed servants for sign of Moira, but didn't see her. He knew she was here somewhere, though, Morrell left home with the wet nurse. He hadn't wanted her to come, but there'd been no chance of convincing the steward to assign her elsewhere, not with this many guests in the tower.

He tried to suppress the nervous worry that prickled his shoulders and scoured the room for signs of trouble.

The captain of the Dogs stationed them halfway down the Hall outside the doors into the inner chamber and meeting hall. A raised stage had been built in the center of the room, separating the dance floor from the dining area, the Barons' table set upon it, Arent's seat in the middle with the tallest back, the other seats arrayed around it. The stage stood waist-high, stairs on either side, everything draped in blue cloth.

As Allan settled into place, Baron Arent stepped up onto the platform, the orchestra taking its cue and falling silent with a flourish of stringed instruments. Everyone clapped, those on the dance floor bowing toward the musicians as conversations broke out on all sides. The Baron let the talk continue for a moment before clearing his throat.

"Attention," he called, and with rustles and shushes the Hall fell silent, all eyes on Baron Arent, the tension in the air expectant, like a held breath.

Baron Arent smiled. "It is time for the Baronial Meeting."

⌁

"—believe that the system is overtaxed. I no longer believe it is safe for the citizens of Farrade to use the ley."

Baron Calluin drew breath to continue, but Arent had heard enough. "Overtaxed?"

The word came as a low murmur, and yet his baritone voice filled the austere oval chamber of the Meeting Hall. All of those seated along the length of the elongated table—all six Barons and the captains of their guard, along with Daedallen—fell silent at his voice, turned to look at him where he sat at one end of the table. His seat was elevated, so that he could see all who sat before him in the amber-and-glass chamber lit by the midafternoon sun. It was also situated at one of the foci of the ovoid room so that he could hear every murmur of conversation, every whispered word uttered by anyone sitting at the table. When everyone spoke at once, it became a roar, but he'd learned long ago to focus his attention, to pick out the voices he wanted to hear and to filter out those he didn't, although sometimes he simply let the susurrus of sound surround him.

But not today. Every voice counted today. Every word. Every nuance and inflection. The Dogs had been unable to break Lord Gatterly and the other Kormanley they'd captured, but he knew one of the Barons controlled them, the certainty in his gut. Someone had seen their potential for disturbance, for disruption, and had seized the opportunity. He intended to find out whom here, before the Barons signed the treaty regarding the ley system that would cede authority over all of the Baronies to Arent Pallentor and Erenthrall for another four years.

And he did not think Baron Calluin was the traitor.

"Overtaxed?" he repeated, leaning forward slightly, although not far enough to be outside of the foci of the room. "Overtaxed how?"

Calluin, who stood at his position, shot a glance toward Baron Leethe before collecting himself and meeting Arent's gaze. Arent leaned back, satisfied. So Calluin was Leethe's mouthpiece.

"The Flyers' Tower," Calluin said, motioning with one hand toward the windows and the view of the towers of Grass beyond, his brow knit in irritation. "I am astounded by what the Wielders have achieved—the sky barges were most impressive—but at what cost? I heard rumors of . . . disturbances within the ley here in Erenthrall, but I did not credit them until my arrival here. The sky barge I rode in our tour of the city shook and quaked for no apparent reason. The crew and Wielders aboard appeared to have no explanation, and did not know what to do to repair it. I feared that I would not make it back to land safely!"

The other Barons stirred at this, Sillare leaning forward to say, "My experience of the tour was quite different, the ride as smooth and gentle as a breeze. Perhaps it is not the ley or the tower that is at fault. Perhaps it is simply a flaw in the construction of that barge."

Conversations broke out, and Arent listened attentively, even though no one spoke above a whisper. He honed in on Leethe's voice, but the Baron was merely verifying what Calluin had stated regarding the barge ride.

"And then there are the distortions," Baron Tavor said, loudly enough that Arent winced, and catching the attention of all of those gathered. He stood and faced Arent. "Not to mention these Kormanley priests and their attacks. Before I sign any treaty regarding the ley, I want to know what you intend to do about them. They have struck my city twice more this summer!"

The Barons grumbled now, with a dark undertone that Arent did not like. There had never been this much dissension among the Barons regarding the ley. Not since he'd so bloodily and forcefully seized control of the Baronies decades before.

He needed to end this now, before it grew to more than simple words. They all needed a reminder of who was in control here.

He stood, everyone looking toward him expectantly. He waited until he had their undivided attention.

"Your concerns are noted and appreciated, however they are unnecessary." He faced Calluin, the Baron still standing. "The Nexus here in Erenthrall—the Nexus that controls all of the ley not only throughout the Baronies but the lands beyond—is not overtaxed. I have been assured of this by Prime Wielder Augustus."

Baron Leethe scoffed and Arent shot him a dark frown. But the other Barons were listening, even if they had not been convinced yet.

He rapped the top of the table before him with his knuckles, then began a circuit around the room, behind the Barons who remained seated.

"You forget that Augustus is the architect of the Nexus, the mind behind its creation and that of the network of Nexi that we have built in your cities and those of our neighbors. With this network, we have been able to solidify the power of the Baronies with the rest of the world. We have been able to seize our rightful place on the world stage, not only in trade, but in political power as well. Before the creation of the Nexus and the harnessing of the ley, the Baronies were nothing! We were trade outposts that the other nations passed through on their way to larger ports and greater lands, greater cities! Now, we have become great ourselves. Our cities rival those of the seaports and the other nations bow down to us, since without us, they would not have access to the ley. Our Wielders in their cities, sent to control the Nexi we have built there, control more than the ley. They control the very people themselves, the lords of the western Demesnes, the Gorrani and their sheiks, the trading houses of the Temerites, and the Juwari women of the Archipelago. And it is Augustus who has given us this power!"

"That does not mean that Augustus' claims are correct," Calluin muttered.

Arent paused behind Baron Calluin's seat, rested his hands on the back of the tall chair.

"Of course not. But what evidence do we have that his claims are false?"

"The distortions—"

"Have you witnessed one of them? Have any of you experienced one of these distortions in your own cities?" The Barons glanced at each other, Calluin's certainty wavering. Leethe and Tavor glared. "I didn't think so. However, I admit that there have been a few incidents here in Erenthrall."

"Including one in which a citizen was injured," Leethe interjected.

"Yes. A woman was unfortunately injured during one such occurrence. If you know of that," Arent said, letting some of his irritation tinge his words, "then you also know that Wielders were there. These Wielders were attempting to repair the distortion and free the woman. It simply closed before they succeeded. In fact, we have Wielders on patrol in the city right now in case more of these distortions appear."

"Why are they appearing in the first place? Can you guarantee that they won't begin appearing in our own cities?"

Arent pushed away from Calluin's seat and turned to face Tavor. "I can't guarantee that, no. But even if they do, you have Wielders trained here in Erenthrall to handle the situation. These distortions are merely annoyances. Rather beautiful annoyances, actually. Like a sunburst of color appearing out of thin air, no larger than your fist. But again, the Wielders have them under control.

"As for the Kormanley, I am certain you have heard of our recent arrests. We have captured one of their leaders, and he has been most forthcoming. So forthcoming," Arent said as he rounded the table and returned to his own seat, "that I have unleashed the Hounds."

A few of the Barons sucked in a sharp breath. But no one moved. Arent sensed a new tension in the air, the threat of the Hounds hanging over all of them, the memory and fear of what they had done during the bloody battles fought by the Barons seventy years before tainting the air. Arent studied each of the Barons' faces as he continued, paying particular attention to Leethe, whose eyes glinted with malice.

"I don't believe the Kormanley will be a problem for long. Not with the Hounds roaming outside of Erenthrall's limits. Were there any other concerns?"

The room was deathly still, until Baron Sillare dared to stir.

Arent turned hard eyes on him, his patience worn as thin as spider's silk.

"Before I sign the agreement, I would like to broach the subject of building a Flyers' Tower in Dunmara and the Reaches. Having the ability to soar over the rocky terrain of the mountains would be a distinct advantage for travel and trade."

Arent hesitated, allowing himself to relax. "I'm certain we can come to some sort of agreement."

He did not miss the fleeting look of disgust on Baron Leethe's face.

Outside the Meeting Hall, Allan fidgeted in position near the closed doors. As soon as the Barons had retreated, the musicians had launched into a new piece, the dance resuming as the conversation in the hall swelled louder than it had been before. He eyed the lords and ladies, watched them drift from position to position, taking in who spoke to whom, and who stepped aside for a more in-depth conversation away from the main activity. But spirits were high, now that the aristocracy could relax, with the Barons they owed liege to otherwise occupied.

Yet a niggling tension still pricked the skin between his shoulders.

Hagger caught his attention with a discreet gesture and motioned him over. His face was pinched with worry.

"Have you noticed anything?" the elder Dog asked.

"No, but something's not right."

He nodded. "My hackles are up, too. And not because of the Barons' disrespectful guardsmen." He glared at the nearest, one of Baron Leethe's men. "Let's circle the room, see what we can sniff out."

They broke away from the door, circling right, skirting the edge of the dancers, but had seen nothing out of the ordinary by the time they reached the far side of the hall near the platform where the Barons would dine. Beyond, servants were frantically setting up the last of the tables for the dinner. Allan shook his head at the number of plates, cups, saucers, spoons, knives, and forks. They ducked into the kitchens opposite the Meeting Hall, the room sheer chaos as servants and cooks dashed back and forth, bellowing orders, pots clanging, the air heavy with the scent of roasting fowl and clouded with steam. Carts were already covered with plate upon plate of the first course. Hagger nipped a small roll, still hot from the ovens and slick with melting butter, and then they returned to the outer room.

They circled the Great Hall three more times, the slanted sunlight slipping from midafternoon to evening, before the doors to the Meeting Hall finally opened. The Barons emerged, Arent last. He stepped to the front of the Barons, the lords and ladies of the Baronies shifting from the dance floor toward the entrance of the Meeting Hall.

He raised his head and waited, even though everyone had fallen silent, then announced, "We have an agreement."

Cheers erupted from the gathered aristocracy, quickly turning to gasps as white light bathed the hall, coming from outside the massive windows overlooking the balcony. This was followed by awed delight as nearly everyone streamed toward the windows and the display of ley light that fountained beneath the tower below. The Barons moved with them, Allan and Hagger following behind. Below the Amber Tower, the crystal dome of the Nexus pulsed a pale blue-white, while all around it the gardens of Grass were illuminated with streams of ley. Men and women spilled out onto the balcony, some even ascending to the deck of the sky barge that still remained tethered there, seeking the best vantage point for viewing the land below.

While everyone was distracted, the servants trundled their carts into the dining hall and began laying out the first course. By the time the lords and ladies grew bored of the Wielders' work, the servants were ready with wine, others removing the carts to prepare for the second course.

"The Barons are headed for their table," Hagger said, tapping Allan's shoulder to catch his attention. "We'd better follow. Daedallen wanted us close."

Allan nodded. As they made their way to the platform, he searched for Moira among the frantic servants, the wine already being poured, the babble of conversation rising yet again as the musicians took up a lighter background strain. The conflagration of white light continued outside as the skies began to darken, the glow of the Flyers' Tower and its beacon becoming more prominent.

From his position on the platform, the Barons to his left, kitchens to his right, Allan scanned the room with a frown, thinking about Lord

Gatterly, about the detailed map they'd found in the room beneath his estate, the Amber Tower circled in red. He thought about Gatterly himself, unyielding no matter what Hagger did to him. He could still feel the lord's blood on his hands, could see his mutilated face. During the entire interrogation, he'd insisted that the Kormanley had infiltrated the Dogs, that they'd already set up some kind of demonstration in the Tower on the day of the Baronial Meeting. But the Meeting was nearly over.

"Perhaps Gatterly was wrong," Hagger said, as if following the same train of thought.

"He never broke. He never broke because he believed we couldn't stop what would happen here. It was what kept him alive."

"Then what's supposed to happen? What have the Kormanley planned?"

Allan shook his head, thinking.

Then he caught sight of Moira.

"Wait here. I see Moira."

Hagger scowled but said nothing as Allan darted down from the platform, catching Moira as she turned from one of the tables, plate in hand, the remains of a pheasant littering the surface. As soon as she faced away, the smile plastered to her face fell away, replaced by anger. She didn't notice Allan until he snagged her arm.

"What do you want?" she spat, spinning on him. Her glare held until recognition flared and she gasped. "Allan! Shouldn't you be watching over Baron Arent?"

"I am. What's wrong?"

"Oh, these gods-cursed lords and their demands. Or rather, the ladies. They're worse than the lords. This pheasant had too much fennel. But she ate nearly all of it before deciding to complain. Not to mention the servants who arrived this morning. They're supposed to keep the carts close. Useless! All of them! And now where are they? Nowhere! Probably off somewhere watching the Wielders' display." She huffed and headed back toward the kitchens. "But I can't talk right now. And you should be up on the platform with Hagger. You don't want him getting angry at you again. Not over me."

Allan followed her. "Wait. What new servants? I thought you'd been preparing for this for days."

"We had. But someone suggested we use the carts to bring the food out, instead of doing it all by hand. The carts appeared this morning, the new servants not long after. But what good are the carts if they aren't here to be used?"

They'd reached the doors to the kitchen, but Allan reached out to halt her, pulling her up short.

"What?" she asked, irritated.

"The carts," he murmured, and his eyes darted around the room.

The carts had been scattered throughout the tables.

Including three directly beneath the Barons' platform.

He spun on Moira. "Get out of here. Now."

Then he turned and sprinted toward the platform. "Hagger! The carts! Like the wagons in the park. It's the carts!"

Hagger frowned in confusion, head spinning toward the hall spread out before him—

And then realization dawned and he moved, barking, "Captain!"

On the platform, Baron Arent turned, a forkful of pheasant half raised to his mouth, Daedallen on his other side. The captain of the Dogs saw Hagger charging toward them and reached across Arent's chest, hauling him back from the table, taking his chair with him. The captains of the other Barons were reacting as well, as looks of confusion began to spread throughout the room. Someone screamed, Baron Iradi bellowing in protest. Glass shattered as it struck the floor, followed by the sharp crack of a plate as it was swept from a table.

Only Allan saw Baron Leethe grimace with annoyance and motion toward the floor before rising and stepping back, his captain at his side.

At the signal, all of the carts exploded, those at the front first.

The air sucked inward, toward the carts, and then flung Allan back from the platform, his ears ringing, fire sheeting out in all directions as the carts, tables, and glassware from the dinner shredded, the bodies of the nearest lords and ladies and servants rising from the center of the explosion, silhouetted against the flames. Allan struck the hard amber floor of the hall, pain knifing down from his shoulder as it twisted awkwardly beneath him, and then debris began to rain down, striking the floor with dulled thuds. Plates and glasses splintered, sending up deadly shards. A mangled and bloody but elegant hand landed an arm's length away, gold rings glinting with firelight. More of the carts exploded, the *crump* of each like softened cloth in his ears, felt more than heard as the floor shuddered. Black spots skated across his vision at each flash and he blinked fiercely, tears stinging his eyes. The black taint of smoke struck his senses; not the scent of burnt wood but something sharper, biting into his nostrils. He wrinkled up his nose in distaste.

Then, debris still clattering down around him, he thought, *Moira*.

He rolled, wincing, his arm tingling with the motion, and pushed himself into a crouch. Bodies lay strewn across the hall's floor like dolls, lords and ladies screaming, the sounds still muted. A few staggered around in shock, blood staining their clothes. Fires blazed along the length of the tables, most tilted onto one side or flipped onto their tops, chairs and the remains of the carts scattered. Overhead, the ley globes, candles, and crystal chandelier swayed. The platform that had held the Barons was scorched and still burning. At least one Baron was dead—Ranit, he thought—along with a few of the Dogs and other guardsmen. Hagger's body lay on the far side, Daedallen and Baron Arent beside him, but before Allan could react, he saw Hagger stir.

Beyond them, moving casually, Baron Leethe and his captain stepped through the doors to the main entrance to the hall, flanked by the rest of the Tumbor guardsmen.

Anger pulsed through him, but Allan turned his back to both Leethe and Arent and began searching for Moira. The sounds of the hall—the crackle of flame, the moans of the wounded, and the sobs of the shocked—became clearer, no longer muffled. He flung aside a chair, knelt over a crumpled form dressed in the servant amber, but the man was dead. Moving on, he rolled aside servants, focusing on those nearest to where he'd left Moira, but she wasn't here.

He sat back on his haunches. He'd told her to run. His gaze flicked toward the main entrance, where Baron Leethe had vanished, then shook his head.

She was a servant. She would have headed for the servant stairs.

The kitchen.

He spun on his heels and began working his way toward the kitchen, noticed flames through the door beyond. A woman clutched at his legs as he passed, stared up at him with half-glazed eyes, and muttered, "Help me. Help me, please." Her arm lay cradled across her chest, a gash along her neck bleeding profusely, her finery ruined. He tugged out of her grip. Men were beginning to rise. He heard Daedallen barking orders, caught the Dogs who were mobile moving to surround Baron Arent. Servants were beginning to help some of the lords and ladies to their feet. Clusters of other guards surrounded the surviving Barons, all of them hostile and defensive.

Then he spotted Moira.

She sat up slowly near the doors to the kitchen, one hand rising to her head in pain. Her black hair lay matted to her scalp with blood and she grimaced as she moved, weaving slightly, but otherwise she seemed unharmed.

Allan heaved a shuddering breath of relief and stumbled the last few steps toward her. He trembled as he brushed the hair out of her face. "Moira, can you hear me? Are you all right?"

"My ears." She touched her hand to her hair, frowned at the blood on her fingers.

"Lower your head." She did as he asked and he examined the wound. "It's nothing. A minor cut. You'll be fine." He gripped her shoulders and caught her attention, her eyes still dazed. "You have to get out of here. Can you move?"

She considered for a moment, then nodded. "I think so."

Allan helped her to her feet, turned toward the main entrance, Daedallen, Hagger, and the other Dogs already rushing the Baron toward them, their formation tight. The other Barons wavered, uncertain. Hagger caught sight of him and bellowed, "Allan! Get your ass over here! The Baron—"

His voice was drowned out by the roar of another explosion. The floor shuddered beneath them, the entire tower trembling, and a moment later flames poured through the mouth of the main entrance. Daedallen and the Dogs dove for the floor, dragging the Baron with them. Those deeper inside the room cried out, some of the lords stumbling as the massive chandelier clattered, pieces of crystal dislodging and falling to the floor.

Allan spun toward the balcony. In the backwash of light from the Great Hall and the pale white of the ley outside, he could see the ship still berthed at the railing.

"The ship," he said, and steered Moira toward the windows, noting that two had blown outward in the explosion and the rest were crazed with cracks. The captain of the barge and his crew were already herding people toward the deck. One of the Barons—Iradi—was already there, tight in the center of his own guard. The rest of the Barons hung back.

As they picked their way through the remains of the dinner party,

Allan glanced back toward Hagger and Arent, saw them hurrying toward the balcony, the main entrance still engulfed in flames.

"Here, here, come quickly!"

Someone snagged Allan's arm and he turned back to find the captain of the barge helping Moira out onto the crowded balcony, the lords and ladies jostling for position near the railing, one of the lords forgoing the steps and leaping from the railing to the deck beyond. Panic had set in with the second explosion, arguments breaking out, tensions escalating. Someone bellowed, "Unhand me! Let the lady on first!" while someone else shoved her to one side sharply. She screamed as she vanished beneath the mob's feet, her soot-streaked face pale in the ley light.

"Steady!" the captain roared. "Steady, there's room for everyone and more ships on the way!"

Cursing, the captain let go of Moira and thrust himself through the crowd toward the railing.

Allan glanced out into the night sky, the air chill against his skin. The Flyers' Tower glowed balefully to one side, cool and white, the Nexus beneath. But the captain was right; at least two other ships were making their way toward the balcony.

His blood sang, adrenaline piercing through the numbness, the tingling in his arm, the shock.

He turned to Moira, met her eyes.

"Allan?"

"Follow the captain," he said, leaning in to kiss her, short and quick, but with fervor. "Get back to our flat and Morrell. Don't go anywhere else. Pack whatever you can."

Frantic confusion filled Moira's eyes. "Allan? What do you mean pack? I don't understand."

"Just do it. We aren't staying in Erenthrall. Not like this."

She held his gaze, still confused, her mouth pinched tight in denial. But she nodded.

Relief coursed through him and he shuddered. "I'll be there as soon as I can."

And then he pushed her toward the barge. She was caught up in the mob trying to get onto its deck instantly, and after a quick look back she began shoving forward, a look of determination in her eyes. Allan watched her a moment, then thrust himself against the throng, working his way back into the Great Hall. Hagger, the Dogs, and the Baron were almost to the balcony now, the Dogs seizing anyone in their way by the collar and tossing them out of the Baron's way.

Allan had just stepped back into the hall when another explosion rent the air.

The remaining glass windows imploded, the force of the blast shoving Allan past the balcony doors and into the room beyond. Fire scorched his back. He struck, skidded across the debris-strewn floor, heard a sharp retort, stone cracking, followed by a ponderous groan of tortured wood. As he slid to a halt, his arms and legs weak and limp, numbed but already recovering, he rolled to face the balcony.

The ship was an inferno, the flames eating into the wood and roaring up through the ley-induced sails like wildfire. Even as he watched, unable to move, it listed, the ropes that held it tied to the balcony straining at its weight. Horror engulfed him, seared into his chest. No one on the balcony was moving, the bodies lying like cordwood, those closest to the barge already burned beyond recognition.

"Moira." The name meant everything and nothing to him. He couldn't think, his head throbbing, but the horror crept through him. He struggled onto his elbows, raised himself up onto his hands and knees. "Moira!"

Then hands grasped him beneath his armpits, Hagger on one side, another Dog on the other. They dragged him back from the balcony, the ship tilting farther outward, wood moaning at the stress as fire ate into its hull. Its weight settled completely onto the ropes as the ley sails disintegrated into wisps of flapping cloth—

And with a horrendous crack the balcony gave way.

Baron Leethe glanced skyward at the final explosion, already moving through the gardens beneath the Amber Tower. He paused, Captain Arger halting beside him, the rest of his enforcers fanning out around them at a discrete distance.

"Do you think Baron Arent is dead?" Arger asked, his deep voice uninflected.

"No. Not unless we were extremely lucky. We had to set the plan in motion too early." Leethe considered the burning barge as it hung from the edge of the tower, grunting when it began to fall, the retort of the stone breaking free coming a moment later.

"Then the Kormanley failed," his captain muttered.

"Yes. I do not think we shall use them any longer. They have proved ineffective. The other Barons were not threatened sufficiently by their attacks. They signed the agreement after only a token resistance, even Calluin. In fact, they wanted the Wielders to build Flyers' Towers in their own cities." He watched the barge crash to the ground, flames and sparks shooting up into the night, mimicking the fountains of ley that still surged from the ground throughout the gardens as entertainment for the Meeting.

In his mind's eye, he saw the fires blazing in the Baronial manse in his own city of Tumbor fifty-four years ago, after he had witnessed the slaughter of his father by Arent's Hounds. He'd been nine. The Hound had turned to look at him, eyes cold, considering, his body covered in Leethe's father's blood. But then the Hound had sheathed his knife and grabbed the nearest lantern, splattering its oil about the room, lighting it with another lamp before departing.

Leethe had scrambled to escape the flames.

His jaw tightened in hatred, a throb beginning in his right temple.

"Fools," he said, turning his back on the tower. "Don't they see that Arent already has too much power? And yet they offer him more!"

He seethed. Arger remained silent.

They emerged from the gardens, a ley carriage and escort waiting in the street beyond, the Tumbor crest in gilt on the door. Servants tore their gazes away from the spectacle in the Amber Tower and sprang into action, opening doors. Arger gave orders as Leethe settled into his seat.

He stared out the window as Arger joined him and the carriage slid into motion.

"No," he said, more to himself than to Arger. "The Kormanley have failed. I need to find a different way to seize power from Arent. He cannot be allowed to dominate the Baronies with his control of the Wielders and the ley."

He turned and met Arger's flat gaze. "We need to find another way to loosen his grip."

PART III

Fourteen

THE WET NURSE screamed when Allan burst through the door into his apartment in Hedge. She clutched Morrell to her chest, body curled protectively around the small form, shoulders hunched. Her initial shock snapped instantly to anger when she recognized him.

"Don't ever barge in here like that again," she scolded.

"Get up. Help me pack." He strode across the room, pulled a trunk out from under the bed, opened it and scanned the contents, then dumped everything inside onto the floor.

The wet nurse—Janis—rose from where she sat near the fire, bouncing Morrell, who'd begun to fuss. "What do you think you're doing? Where's Moira?"

"She's dead," Allan growled, and something hard and fluid punched into his chest, right beneath his breastbone. He struggled with the sensation, fought it back—as he'd fought it back since slipping away from the chaos of the Amber Tower and fleeing here—and said roughly, "The Kormanley attacked the Tower. She died in one of the explosions."

Janis gasped, hand going to her mouth.

He began shoving clothes into the trunk haphazardly, moving about the room in short, jerky steps, his mind seething. It wouldn't take long for the Dogs—for Hagger—to realize he was missing, even with Baron Arent enraged and screaming orders at Daedallen. Once they did, they'd be after him. Hagger knew he'd survived the final explosion; he'd pulled him away from the balcony before it snapped free. They'd come here first. He needed clothes, food, protection, money. He snatched a knife from the kitchen, tucked it into his belt, stepped to the stone recess of the fire and pried a loose rock from its place, reaching into the hollow to retrieve the stash of errens in a cloth sack hidden there.

When he turned back, he saw Janis watching him, her expression set. "Just what do you think you're doing? I know you must be upset, but this—" she waved around at the scattered mess on the floor from the trunk, the rock he'd tossed aside "—is unacceptable. You're upsetting the baby!"

Allan sucked in a deep breath, then realized she was right. Morrell had begun to cry.

He grabbed Janis by the shoulders, looked directly into her aged eyes, and said, "I'm leaving. The Dogs. Erenthrall. I'm leaving, Janis, and once the Dogs figure out I'm gone. . . ."

He didn't finish. He didn't have to. Janis' eyes widened and she clutched at his arms. "But what about Morrell? Who's going to look after Morrell?"

"I will."

Janis said nothing, merely swallowed.

He gently pushed her out of the way, shifted back to the kitchen area, tossed a few pots into the trunk on top of the clothes, a sack of rice, another of oats, then grabbed an empty sack and threw in what bread they had, packets of herbs and spices, everything he saw that was portable.

When he spun, he found Janis bundling Morrell up into a swath of blankets. "What are you doing?"

"You can't do this alone, not with an infant. I'm coming with you."

He drew breath to protest, but she cut him off with a scathing glare.

"You can't protect her and care for her at the same time. It's not possible. You need someone to help. My husband died three years ago. I have nothing left here in Erenthrall. And if what you say is true—that the Kormanley have attacked the Amber Tower, the Baron—then Erenthrall isn't going to be safe for anyone. Besides," she tucked the last edge of blanket into place, creating a sling across her torso, Morrell swaddled inside, and turned to face him, "how are you going to feed her? *What* are you going to feed her? And where do you intend to go? I know of a place to the west the Baron has no control over, one he doesn't even know exists. The people there will take us in."

Allan hesitated. He had no place to run. He couldn't go back to

Canter; Hagger would send the Dogs there as soon as he lost track of him in the city. And Janis was right. Arent would explode. He'd already seen it in the aftermath at the Tower. The Dogs were scrambling. Everyone within the Tower, within the Great Hall, had been taken into custody, and the search for more Kormanley—anyone who knew anything about that attack—had already begun. As he'd left, he'd even heard Arent order Daedallen to call out the Hounds—

The Hounds.

Allan staggered, his legs suddenly weak. He leaned against the stone wall for support, felt the heat of the fire against his leg. He'd forgotten about the Hounds. Hagger would send one of the Hounds after him, if he could convince Daedallen and Arent he was important enough. And fleeing immediately after the attack would make them think he had been part of it somehow. They might even think he was Kormanley himself, especially after what Lord Gatterly had said about them infiltrating the Dogs.

His stomach twisted and roiled and he groaned. But he had no choice. He was already committed. Hagger might have already noticed he was gone.

He shoved away from the wall, swallowed down the sudden bile boiling at the back of his throat, and said, "We need to leave now. You handle Morrell, I'll take the trunk."

Janis nodded, already moving to gather what Allan had missed for the baby. "We'll have to stop by my place for a few things, but we can leave in ten minutes. I know someone in Copper who will loan us a pullcart. He can also let those in the Hollow know we're coming. They'll be suspicious of you at first, think you're still with the Dogs, but I'll convince them otherwise."

Allan watched her bustle around the room a moment, a woman twice his age, with graying hair pulled back in a bun, dressed in the simple garb of the working class. He'd have to find similar clothes before they traveled too far; his Dog's uniform might be useful at first here in Erenthrall, but it would only draw attention outside the city.

And if Hagger did sic one of the Hounds on him. . . .

Then he'd have to distract the Hound himself and leave Morrell in Janis' hands.

Daedallen and Baron Arent stepped into the shattered remains of the Great Hall, their footfalls echoing in the chamber. The amber floor was covered with debris—overturned tables, shards of glasses and plates, the remnants of the feast, a few cracked ley globes. A breeze blew through the splintered balcony windows, reeking of charred skin and acrid explosives. A crack ran across the wall between the Great Hall and the Baronial meeting chamber, the fracture catching the sunlight oddly. The bodies had been cleared out, but there were still bloodstains on nearly every part of the hall beyond the burnt remains of the raised section that had held the Barons' table.

Arent spun on Daedallen, teeth gritted. "Find the Kormanley. I want them all dead. Hunt them down and execute them. Use those we already have in custody as an example to the citizens of Erenthrall. There is to be no mercy. Every last one of the Kormanley and all of those who support them, who have helped them, must be rooted out and exterminated. I will not tolerate such blatant defiance in my own city. Search every house, every manse, every hovel. Use whatever force necessary. I want the Kormanley eradicated!"

"What about the lords and ladies of the city? They have rights—"

"No one has rights anymore," Baron Arent spat. "If they protest, seize them under suspicion. Throw Lord Gatterly's complicity in their faces. No one is exempt. The Kormanley have gone too far. I am the ruler of this city, of the Baronies, and I will maintain control!"

As if realizing he had already lost control, Arent sucked in a deep breath and clenched his fists. He cast one last scathing glance over the destruction in the Great Hall, then turned a baleful eye on Daedallen again.

In a low, controlled voice, he added, "Consider the Dogs unleashed." Then he stalked from the room.

Daedallen shifted a few steps forward, ran his hand down the smooth amber wall until he intercepted the crack. He tapped his fingers thoughtfully, plans shifting into place in his head.

A moment later, he emerged on the damaged stairwell, where numerous Dogs on watch in the Great Hall had seen Baron Leethe escape before the secondary explosion. His alphas Terrence and Branden were waiting, along with a dozen others, including Hagger. He didn't see Hagger's partner, Allan.

"Orders?" Terrence asked briskly.

"Bring the Hounds. All of them. Have them search the Great Hall for any possible leads. They are free of the leash for the hunt, but they are to bring any members or suspected members of the Kormanley back to us alive. Then organize the Dogs. We're going to track down every last one of the Kormanley, no matter what it takes."

Terrence nodded. Everyone in the stairwell shifted nervously, but beneath the unease he could sense relief as well. They were finally being given enough leeway that perhaps they would be able to root out the Kormanley and put an end to them.

"Branden," he said, stepping past his two alphas and continuing on down the stairs as he talked. "Have the Dogs ready the Kormanley prisoners we already have in custody. Clean them up as much as possible."

"What for?"

"Baron Arent wants a display of his displeasure, and we're going to give it to him."

"When do they need to be ready?"

"By tomorrow."

"Very well."

Daedallen had reached Hagger's position. He motioned the grizzled Dog to walk beside him, Terrence and Branden jogging out in front to begin carrying out their orders. The rest of the Dogs present were falling in behind. "Where's your partner?"

"He hasn't come in yet this morning."

"Why not?"

Hagger shifted uncomfortably. "His wife was killed in the explosion last night. She was one of the servers."

Daedallen halted abruptly. In the aftermath of the explosions the night before, he had been too intent on protecting Baron Arent, clearing out the survivors, and dealing with the wounded to take notice of who had died. Aside from Baron Ranit, of course. Except for the Barons, the survivors had been held in the Tower for questioning. The city guards were taking care of that, with a single Dog supervising each interview.

Because he needed the Dogs elsewhere.

"Give him until midafternoon," he finally growled. "If he hasn't come in then, find him. We're going to need the entire pack for this. Until then, help Terrence with the Hounds."

Hagger grimaced, but nodded.

"Dalton!"

Dalton glanced up from his printing press in irritation as Tyrus crashed through the door at the base of the stairs, located him in the jumble of ink, paper, letter blocks, and other supplies, then fumbled his way toward him. Tyrus' face was edged in panic, smudges of soot across his forehead, what appeared to be blood on the formal dress shirt he must have worn to the Baronial Meeting the night before. Dalton quelled the disappointment at seeing his fellow Kormanley. He had hoped that Tyrus had died in the Great Hall, a victim of proximity, especially after he hadn't reported in after the explosions like most of the rest of the splinter cells involved.

Instead, he rose from where he was leaning over the block flat for the upcoming edition of *The Ley* and plastered a smile on his face.

"Tyrus! I was worried. I heard about what happened at the Amber Tower last night—I'm trying to print a report in *The Ley* right now—but when you didn't report back in, I feared the worst."

Tyrus wove through the last desks and supplies, leaning heavily on a work stool as he attempted to catch his breath. "They kept . . . everyone who was still . . . in the Tower . . . overnight." He wiped one arm across his forehead, smearing even more soot across his brow. "They've been questioning us . . . all morning. I was only just released."

"And you came straight here."

Tyrus completely missed the dangerous undertone in his voice. "I had to warn you."

Dalton stilled, fear shooting through his arms, tingling in his hands. He'd woken up screaming that morning, suffocating on imagined ash, the filth falling about him like snow. It had taken him ten minutes of coughing to rid himself of the illusion he was choking to death on embers; he still hadn't shaken the terror of the vision of Erenthrall's destruction. "Warn me of what?"

"The Baron," Tyrus gasped. "He's unleashed the Dogs. They're going to execute all of the Kormanley they've captured in various districts tomorrow. And they're using the Hounds. They'll find out that I've been helping them!"

Dalton couldn't suppress the shudder that coursed through him. Erenthrall hadn't experienced the Hounds in force in decades, but everyone knew of the bloodshed they'd caused during Arent's seizure of power. Entire Baronial families had been wiped out, or whittled down to only a few survivors. Like Baron Leethe.

If they'd pushed Baron Arent to that extreme, then perhaps the Kormanley had succeeded after all, even if Arent himself had not died in last night's attack.

But it still called for drastic measures. The Dogs might not be able to trace the members of the cells, but the Hounds. . . .

And Tyrus had come straight here, to the production offices of *The Ley*.

It was time to abandon the newspaper front. Time to scatter the cells. He'd have to put the order out immediately, before the executions. And he needed to vanish.

He turned a cold eye on Tyrus, his fellow Kormanley taking an involuntary step backward. A knife rested on the edge of his desk, within easy reach. He could kill Tyrus, end at least one trail leading to him.

But no. The Dogs likely already knew about the newspaper. They'd discover he was part of the Kormanley even if they didn't follow Tyrus' trail here. But Tyrus would be a useful diversion. Let them hunt the clerk down while Dalton found refuge somewhere else. He wasn't certain where, or how he would elude the Hounds—he wasn't even certain of their abilities, his knowledge based on folklore, superstition, and rumor—but whatever time he could glean to escape would be necessary.

"Warn the others," he said, tension in his shoulders relaxing. "Tell Calven and the rest of that cell to disperse."

Tyrus shook his head. "No. We need to go to the Dogs right now, tell them what we were doing, tell them we were only trying to figure out who was supporting the splinter Kormanley ourselves first. It's our only chance!"

Dalton cursed himself. He'd forgotten Tyrus wasn't part of the splinter group.

He surged forward and grabbed Tyrus by his shirtfront, felt the gritty dried blood there grinding between his fingers as he yanked the weak clerk close. "Don't you see? They won't believe us. They'll think we're only trying to save ourselves. It's too late to try to convince them otherwise. We have to run while we still can."

"But—"

Dalton shook him. "Do you honestly think they'll let you go? You forged permits to get them into Seeley Park! You planted one of their bombs on a ley barge!" He pulled Tyrus close enough that he could smell the blood and ash on his shirt. "You vouched for those who brought the carts and explosives into the Tower yesterday."

Horror bloomed in Tyrus' gaze, his breath catching in his throat. "But if you verify what I'm saying—"

Dalton snorted and dropped him. He'd already dismissed him from his mind. "I don't intend to get caught."

He left Tyrus gasping where he stood, moved into the back section of the basement, where an old fireplace had been built into the stone wall. Long dead coals were scattered in the pit, from the past winter when he'd worked late and needed the warmth—there was no ley heating down here. A small stack of wood and kindling abutted the wall.

He began building a fire.

Behind, Tyrus fidgeted, then shifted forward. "What are you doing?"

Dalton glanced over his shoulder. "I'm going to burn the newspaper's office down. That may slow the Hounds." His gaze narrowed. "I'd start thinking about where you intend to run if I were you."

He turned back to the fire, used flint and crumpled paper to start the flames, shoved it beneath the wood he'd stacked, then moved toward his office. He gathered what little he thought he'd need from his files and desk into a satchel and slung it over his shoulder. When he returned to the outer room, Tyrus was gone. He grunted and began scattering sheets of parchment for the printing press about the room, stacking it near the supports of the building above, then spilled the containers of oil for his lanterns through the maze of supplies and desks, hesitating over the press itself, but ultimately splattering the oil over its intricate mechanics. He coughed as the fumes filled the room, pulled his shirt up to cover his mouth as he used a poker to scatter the now charred wood of the fire before he edged toward the stairs, making certain the flames had caught. He told himself it was the reek of oil and the smoke that caused his eyes to tear.

Ten minutes later, he stood across the street, teeth clenched, hands fisted, as the first few tendrils of smoke wafted through the cracks around the small door tucked between the shops to either side. When flames appeared, and the patrons of the two shops began pouring out onto the street, coughing, he spun and headed toward his apartments. He needed to send word to Dierdre and Darius. They hadn't associated with any of the cells, so they should be able to go unnoticed, at least initially. They could continue their work. But he'd have to let them know he'd be gone for a while. At least until the Baron's rage had cooled.

They still hadn't accomplished their ultimate goal: a return to the natural ley system, before their arrogance and abuse brought about the destruction he had seen in his visions.

❧

Hagger pounded on the door to Allan's apartment and shouted, "Allan, are you in there?" His words fell hard into the silence. He hesitated, doubt niggling at the back of his mind. He had tested Allan after all, had forced him to interrogate Lord Gatterly. Allan had done everything they'd asked of him.

And yet. . . .

The suspicion and rage overwhelmed the doubt and he bellowed, "Allan!"

He glanced over his shoulder at the two Dogs who accompanied him, both tensing and drawing blades.

Then he kicked in the door, charging through the opening into the flat, already knowing what he would find.

An empty room.

He spat a curse, motioned the other Dogs to fan out, even though there was no reasonable place to hide. They began tearing the room apart, flipping the bed, slitting open the mattress and scattering the compact straw, opening and overturning trunks, tossing the contents of the single cupboard out onto the floor. A sack of flour ripped and spread in a fan of white, a cloud rising into the air. Hagger coughed and waved a hand in front of his face as he moved to the opposite side of the room toward a firepit. He knelt, leaned forward with a spread hand. The embers and coals were cold. To one side, a stone had been removed from the wall and when he reached into the opening the space beyond was empty.

His anger ratcheted one notch higher and his chest rumbled with a low growl as he stood to find the two Dogs waiting.

"There's no one here," one of them said.

"Of course not," Hagger snapped. "The traitor ran as soon as he could. He must have been working with the Kormanley." The two Dogs traded looks, their stances hardening. He motioned them out of the room. "Question the neighbors. See if anyone saw anything, heard anything."

As soon as they left, Hagger searched the room himself but found nothing of interest. As far as he could tell, his partner had left with almost nothing. "He must have returned, grabbed some clothes, maybe some food—" he glanced toward the hole near the firepit, "—some money and the whelp, then run. But where would he go?"

He paced, brow furrowed, the sounds of the other two Dogs— beating on doors, opening a few forcefully amid cries of protest— echoing around him. Would Allan retreat back to the sticks? What was the name of that village he said he'd come from? Cannon? Candor?

The two Dogs reappeared in the doorway, the lead shaking his head. "Nothing. Although someone reported that the woman who was acting as their wet nurse is missing."

Hagger snarled, snatched up a discarded shirt from the floor—part of a Dogs' uniform—then stormed forward, brushing past the two in the doorway.

"What now?" the younger of the two asked.

"Now, we find Daedallen and ask for one of the Hounds."

❧

"Ah, Baron Leethe, I see that you've decided to join me."

Daedallen noted the simmering anger that flashed through Leethe's eyes before he forced a smile and began walking across the expanse of the meeting room toward where Arent sat behind his massive wooden desk. Daedallen fell in behind the Baron of Tumbor as they passed between the two tables that contained the maps of Erenthrall's districts and the ley system spread across the continent and beyond.

"I'm afraid that your captain of the Dogs insisted," Baron Leethe said, coming to a halt a few paces before the desk, the sound of his footfalls dampening when he reached the rug. Sunlight streamed in from the windows, glinting off the amber floor and the various knick-knacks littering the desk's surface. Daedallen was forced to squint to make out Arent himself. "You can understand why I was hesitant to come to the Amber Tower. After what happened at the Baronial Meeting, I no longer know where it is safe within Erenthrall."

Daedallen's hackles rose at the looks the two traded and he shifted quietly into position to one side.

Baron Arent motioned to a chair, but Leethe shook his head. "I don't intend to stay long, Baron Arent. Why did you summon me here?"

Arent stood, fingers steepled on the front of his desk. "The Dogs have been looking into what happened at the Baronial Meeting. Many of the guests report that you departed immediately after the first explosion, before the second sealed off escape by the stairwell. How did you know to leave then? Your timing was . . . impeccable."

Leethe grinned. "It was, wasn't it?" The smile vanished in the blink of an eye. "But I assure you, I knew nothing of the second explosion. I was simply fortunate to escape before it occurred. My enforcers rushed me out of the Great Hall before I even knew what had happened."

Arent's eyes narrowed, his lips pressed into a thin line. "I don't believe you," he said softly.

Leethe snorted. "I don't care what you believe."

"Tell me what you know of the Kormanley. I know you are working with them."

"Even if I were, why would I tell you now? Especially after what happened last night. If they were behind the attack, then they have hurt you. They have proven that you are not in control—of the ley, of the Baronies, not even of your own city. Baron Ranit paid for that lack of control with his life. The other Barons must be reevaluating their loyalties as we speak, rethinking the treaty they signed yesterday, as I am."

Arent smirked. "I've already spoken to the other Barons. They are understandably shaken, but I have solidified their loyalties. They will not renege on the treaty. And neither will you." He pushed back from the desk. "If you had anything to do with the Kormanley and the attack, confess to me now. I will find out if you were complicit. I have unleashed the Hounds."

Leethe could not hide the spike of fear that blanched his face, his skin sagging around his cheeks, his jaw. For a moment, he appeared twenty years older, his eyes trapped in long suppressed memories.

But he recovered quickly, one hand tightening into a fist, his jaw set. "I assume you will use the Hounds with suitable restraint. We wouldn't want the Baronies to return to the bloody civil war ended decades ago." His voice carried more threat than concern.

"Not unless that becomes necessary," Baron Arent said.

The two Barons glared at each other. A long, tense moment, broken by Baron Leethe.

"Was there something else?"

Arent frowned. "No."

"Then I will take my leave . . . of you and this city."

Baron Leethe shot a cold glance in Daedallen's direction, then retreated toward the door, where the captain of his enforcers waited.

As soon as they'd moved out of sight, Arent turned to Daedallen. "What do we know of the attack?"

"The Hounds are following numerous leads, but there were nearly a thousand people in attendance last night. It will take a while for them to sort out any of the Kormanley tracks from the regular servants, lords, and ladies who were here. We have interviewed nearly everyone we detained overnight and released them. A few of those questioned showed promise and we have Hounds following their scents now.

"The Dogs and city watch have hit the streets. News of the attack is spreading rapidly and they are arresting anyone who shows any sign of support for the Kormanley and bringing them here to the Tower for questioning. Violence has broken out in three districts over the arrests, but the Dogs remain in control. We're continuing to watch major plazas, marketplaces, and gathering places in force."

"What of the executions scheduled for tomorrow?"

"Arrangements are progressing without any problems. We have nine confirmed Kormanley already in custody, all of those who survived the interrogation after the raid on Lord Gatterly's estate. The first execution is scheduled in Grass in Seeley Park for midmorning."

"Very well. I'll attend Lord Gatterly's execution myself. Inform Augustus that I want him in attendance to reassure the people of Erenthrall that at no time was the Nexus or the ley system at risk."

Daedallen grimaced, but couldn't ignore the tone of dismissal in Arent's voice. "As you command."

As he reached the outer doors, Arent already seated at his desk, poring over his papers, Daedallen noted Terrence waiting and snapped, "Report."

"We've brought in four more possible conspirators in the last hour, and three arrested for protests in the streets. They're secure in the Tower below. Also, Hagger has returned and has a request."

Daedallen's eyebrows rose. "Where is he?"

Terrence nodded toward the far end of the hall. "He's waiting for you now."

Daedallen frowned as he approached. The Dog was pacing back and forth across the breadth of the corridor, his anger palpable. Daedallen could practically taste it on the air. The elder Dog halted when he saw his captain approaching, but his hands still twitched.

"You have a request?"

"Yes, Captain. I went to find my partner, Allan Garrett, as you instructed. He was not in his apartment in Hedge. Neither was his daughter. The wet nurse who looked after her has also gone missing."

"And you believe . . . ?"

"I believe," Hagger snarled, "that he was working with the Kormanley and that he's fled our retribution after the failure of the bombing last night. We need to capture him, make him pay for his betrayal." Hagger's fingers were clenching and unclenching, as if he had Allan's throat in his grip already and was strangling him.

"That's a serious allegation," Daedallen said, his voice laced with doubt. "Are you certain? Wasn't it Allan who led us to Lord Gatterly? Didn't he figure out how the Kormanley were communicating? And in the Great Hall, wasn't he the one who warned us about the carts? Why would he allow his wife to work in the Great Hall if he knew how dangerous that would be?"

Hagger's hatred didn't falter. "Lord Gatterly said the Kormanley had infiltrated the Dogs, didn't he? Don't you find it convenient that he warned us about the carts when it was too late to do anything about them?"

Daedallen frowned. "What is your request?"

Hagger's shoulders straightened. "I want one of the Hounds to follow his scent and bring him down."

Everyone in the corridor fell silent, Daedallen's neck prickling as a chill slid down his back. "You want to send a Hound after a Dog."

"If he's Kormanley, he was never a Dog to begin with."

Troubled, Daedallen turned to Terrence. "Bring one of the Hounds to Hagger. Use the one that worked with him before, the one that found Gatterly."

As Terrence left, he considered Hagger again. "Bring Allan in for questioning. I want to speak with him myself. If he did work with the Kormanley, then he'll answer to me."

Hagger grimaced in disappointment, but nodded and said, "As you command, Alpha."

Allan stepped onto the deck of the ley barge, through the open doors, and scanned those inside before setting down the trunk and motioning Janis forward. The wet nurse held Morrell's body close as she found a seat. Allan stood before her, his eyes flicking between all of the passengers even after the barge jolted and began to surge forward with a noticeable shudder. None of them were paying the two any particular attention though—most casting curious or annoyed glances at the recalcitrant barge—so when Morrell began to fuss, he relaxed.

"What's wrong?"

Janis looked up, her rounded face open, her eyes calm. She'd begun rocking Morrell back and forth. "Nothing's wrong. She's just upset because we're jostling her around so much. But that can't be helped. Unless you think we can stop for a moment to rest."

"No, that's not possible."

"I didn't think so." She tickled Morrell's nose, his daughter responding with gurgling noises.

Allan took a moment to study her, realizing he knew little about Janis. Moira—his heart clenched, but he shoved the sensation aside—had been the one to find her, as soon as she realized they couldn't live off of the errens he earned as pay. Dogs weren't expected to support a wife and child; their money was intended for only one. So Moira had looked for a wet nurse so she could return to her work at the Tower. Janis lived in the same building, had raised two of her own children. Her husband was dead, and after a brief scrutiny to make certain she didn't trigger any of Allan's alarms, he'd agreed to let her look after Morrell. But now. . . .

"What is it?" she asked, without taking her attention away from the baby. "You're watching me with a suspicious look on your face. Reconsidering taking me along?"

"You're handling this well."

"What? Abandoning my home? Leaving most of my things behind?" She snorted. "What was there left for me? I'd been considering leaving for the Hollow since my husband died."

"You mentioned the Hollow before."

Now she did turn to him, her expression taut. "The place I told you about, where the Baron won't be able to find you. Or Morrell." She sighed. "I was ready to leave when your wife came to me about looking after the baby. I refused at first. I've already raised two children. I wasn't even certain I could produce milk anymore. And then there was you."

Allan couldn't hide his surprise. "Me?"

Janis turned a caustic eye on him. "Yes, you. You were a Dog." She spat to one side. "I have no love for the Dogs. Not many people do. You serve the Baron, supposedly to protect the people, but really to protect his interests, and his interests serve the people only when serving otherwise would cause him trouble."

"Then what changed your mind? Why did you stay?"

"Moira," she said bluntly. "She convinced me that you were different. And I see now, by what you are doing, by what you have done, that she was right. I didn't want to be associated with you in any way, but I was wrong. It's the Baron I despise, not you."

Allan stiffened, a thrill of fear jerking his hand toward his blade. "Are you Kormanley?" The accusation was barely a whisper. He didn't want to draw any attention. He'd changed out of his Dogs' uniform in Copper, after arranging for the pullcart to meet them in the Field District along the western road at nightfall. As far as the passengers on the barge knew, they were simply fellow citizens.

Janis snorted, but the barge lurched as they pulled into Arrow's station and both of them fell silent, watching the doors as people disembarked and others came aboard.

As soon as they started moving again, she said, "I don't have to be Kormanley to hate the Baron. There are plenty of citizens of Erenthrall who despise him; their anger just isn't enough to make them do anything about it. But that may change."

"What do you mean?"

"Haven't you been listening?" She shifted Morrell from one cradled arm to the other, flicked her gaze around the passengers nearby. "They're all talking about what happened at the Amber Tower last night . . . and what the Dogs have been doing today. Seizing people off the street, for nothing more than rumor. Turning violent at any sign of resistance. They beat a man to death in Leeds for trying to stay their hand when they attacked a woman in the market." She shook her head. "The people's anger is growing. Haven't you noticed?"

He grunted. "I have. And I have been listening." He hesitated a moment, then added softly, "It's only going to get worse."

Janis' eyebrows rose. "All the more reason for me to leave Erenthrall, wouldn't you say?"

"Hagger, the Hound is here."

"Where?" Hagger spun, searching, eyes settling finally on where the Hound stood in a far corner of the main room of the Dogs' lair. Most of the Dogs in the room had just returned from the streets of Erenthrall, exhausted, their faces haggard. The patrols had grown steadily more dangerous as the day progressed. The prisoners' cells on this level and below were packed. Hagger felt most of those arrested weren't serious dissidents, but the orders were to hold them until after the executions tomorrow.

His eyes narrowed as he moved toward the boy. "How long have you been there?"

The Hound said nothing, simply waited.

Hagger scowled, hiding his discomfort by moving to one of the numerous desks and digging out the shirt he'd taken from Allan's apartment. He could feel the rest of the Dogs near him watching, their gazes prickling along his skin, knew he couldn't hesitate. Weakness now would be noted, and it galled him that he felt weakened without Allan at his side.

He thrust the shirt into the Hound's hands. "Seek," he ordered, recalling Daedallen's words. "Do not kill. Find the traitorous Kormanley bastard and bring him here."

The Hound stared at him long enough he finally took a step backward, uncertain why. Then the Hound's nostrils flared and he breathed in the scent of the shirt. The boy's brow furrowed as he scanned the room.

Then he was gone, as if he'd simply turned and vanished.

Hagger swore. But a moment later, he smiled. A dark, vicious smile. Within a day, maybe two, Allan would be his.

Fifteen

A S SOON AS KARA and Marcus entered the main chamber of the node at the end of their daily run across Eld, Kyle asked, "Have you heard?"

Wiping a sheen of sweat from her brow—the sun had turned brutal—Kara answered, "Heard what?"

The red-haired Wielder rolled his eyes. "About the attack at the Amber Tower last night."

"Of course we've heard," Marcus scoffed. "It's all over the streets."

Those Wielders within hearing shifted toward them, including Katrina and Timmons, the senior Wielder at Eld. Tall and thin, with a meticulously trimmed goatee, he approached with a concerned look. "What are the streets like? We've heard reports of some altercations, even riots."

Marcus shook his head. "No riots, not in Eld anyway. But the Dogs are everywhere."

"They flooded the streets around midday," Kara added. "They seem to be sticking close to the main public areas—the marketplace, Minstrel's Park, Collier Street—although there are pairs of them roaming the back streets. They're arresting anyone who even looks at them funny." She couldn't keep her distaste out of her voice. Images of the Kormanley priest she'd seen being beaten and arrested four years ago kept surfacing in her mind's eye, his blood-splattered white robes, his split lip and broken nose.

"They're only after the ones who attacked the Baron," Katrina said defensively. "The Kormanley."

"I don't think the woman they kicked so hard she vomited was Kormanley," Kara muttered darkly. "She only protested because they kicked over her potter's cart and shattered most of her wares."

Katrina frowned uncertainly. "They must have had a reason."

Kara snorted.

"They're also erecting a platform in the square," Marcus cut in. "They're planning some kind of execution tomorrow."

All of the Wielders shifted uncomfortably, even Katrina.

Timmons cleared his throat. "Is it safe to continue our runs?"

Marcus straightened. "Do we have any choice? The Primes want us searching for the distortions, right?" He shook his head. "It's safe enough, I think. But everyone should stay clear of the Dogs, whether you're on patrol or not. They're itching for a fight."

"You heard him," Timmons said, raising his voice, although by this time nearly everyone in the hall had drifted over to listen in. "Spread the word. I want all of the Wielders to keep out of the Dogs' path. Focus on the ley, nothing else."

The group broke up, Kyle snagging Katrina's arm and motioning toward the outer door—they were replacing Marcus and Kara—the rest drifting back to whatever they'd been doing before their arrival. Conversations were low and tense with worry.

"Come on," Marcus said, catching her attention. "We had a rough run. We need a break."

He headed toward the back of the hall, where the heavy iron door to the ley pit remained closed to protect everyone in the rest of the node from any surges in the ley. But he bypassed the door, moving instead to a small corridor to one side that Kara had never noticed before. It was narrow, her shoulders nearly touching on both sides, and led to stairs spiraling up around the pit itself. It was built between the outer wall of the pit and the barracks and rooms that surrounded the central chamber.

Ten minutes later, they emerged through a wooden trapdoor onto the roof of the node. A hot, sharp breeze slapped Kara in the face as she climbed the last few steep steps, Marcus closing the trapdoor behind her.

She brushed her flying hair away from her face and turned toward her partner, wide eyed. "I didn't even know we could come up here!"

He grinned. "Not many of the Wielders do, although I don't know why. There's a great view of Eld and Confluence from up here."

Kara angled toward one crenellated edge of the circular node, resting her hands on the gritty stone as she leaned out and looked over at the street and buildings below. The stone structure was only a few stories high, some of the adjacent buildings a few floors taller, but the people below still looked small somehow.

She gasped when Marcus' arms slid around her body from behind, but leaned back into the embrace.

"I would never let you fall," he said, his breath tickling the side of her neck. She smiled and let the tension caused by seeing the Dogs on the street seep away. He squeezed her once, then asked, "Why do they bother you so much?"

She shrugged. "I saw them beat up one of the Kormanley priests once, here in Eld, at the marketplace. They were brutal. And then someone said that the priest was as good as dead after they hauled him off. I'd never thought about what happened to those the Dogs took away before, but this time, for some reason, it made a difference. The priest wasn't doing anything except talking, and after that day I never saw him again in Eld."

Marcus grunted and rested his chin on top of her head. When he spoke, his voice rumbled through his chest to her back. "The Kormanley have done more than talk. From what we heard, they bombed the Great Hall in the Amber Tower. During the Baronial Meeting, no less. They killed and wounded hundreds of people."

"I know. But back then they hadn't done anything violent yet."

Marcus rocked her back and forth a long moment, deep in thought, then asked, "Do you agree with the Kormanley?"

Kara stiffened. "What do you mean?"

"I mean, do you agree with what they preach about the ley, that it should be returned to its natural order, that we're subverting it, abusing it."

She twisted in his arms until she was facing him, arms resting on his chest. "I agree we need to be careful with the ley. But to not use it? It's there, why shouldn't we use it?"

"I don't know. I just think the Kormanley have a point. The Baron does control everything concerning the ley . . . or rather, he controls Prime Wielder Augustus. Do you honestly think the Baron—or Augustus—has the best interests of the citizens of Erenthrall in mind when he makes his decisions? And we both know that they've overextended the Nexus somehow, no matter what the Primes say. Where else would the distortions be coming from?"

Kara squirmed, pushing away from him lightly. "The Kormanley killed my parents," she reminded him.

He tightened his hold on her, drew her in, and kissed her forehead. "I know. I'm not saying I agree with their methods. They've killed too many people, hurt too many others. But I don't think we should discount what they say because of that. We should at least think about it."

Kara relaxed, mollified. "I guess."

He released her. "Look at how the sun is reflecting off the rivers."

She turned, Marcus shifting to her side, and leaned up against the crenellation again. To the south, the two rivers—the Tiana and the Urate—converged, their waters a brilliant, blinding silver, the University on the vee of land where they met. She wondered what Cory was doing at that moment, still troubled over the last time she'd seen him and told him about Justin. She wondered if she should seek Cory out and apologize. She hadn't meant to upset him.

A shadow passed over them and she glanced skyward as one of the flying barges drifted by, its sails sparkling with ley. A few people hanging over the sides waved and laughter drifted down faintly. Kara smiled and waved back.

"We should get something to eat," Marcus said as the barge passed beyond the node. "Let's see if anyone else wants to head on over to the Leyline."

"Why not?" Kara said. The Leyline was the Wielders' prime watering hole in Eld. The food wasn't great, but they had plenty to drink.

Marcus grinned, then leaned forward and kissed her. She pressed into it, a heat that had nothing to do with the sun suffusing her. She laughed when they broke apart, and Marcus asked, "What?"

"Nothing." She grabbed his hand and pulled him toward the trapdoor. "The Leyline, remember?"

When Ischua rounded the corner, he found the street packed with Dogs and the two buildings that had stood above *The Ley*'s printing press were nothing more than charred heaps of riverstone and timber. He ducked into the shadows beneath a café's awning, the sun near setting, and watched in silence.

A moment later, the café's owner arrived and asked, "Would you like to be seated?"

He caught the man's nervous gaze. "I'd like a table over here, if that's possible."

"Of course, of course! Anything for a Tender." He escorted Ischua to the table, took his order, and then hurried back inside. Almost no one was seated at the small tables and chairs outside, Ischua noted. And anyone who turned the corner and saw the Dogs either hesitated and turned back, or ducked his head and skirted their activity by as wide a distance as possible.

The café owner brought his drink and vanished again. Ischua sipped casually.

The Dogs were sorting through the debris from the fire, descending into the pit that used to be the basement using the stone steps of the newspaper's offices. There were five of them, the pack leader standing outside and waiting impatiently, the others already covered in soot and ash.

When the café owner returned with his food, Ischua asked, "What happened here?"

He shifted so that his back was to the Dogs and spoke in a low voice. "A fire, early this morning. We thought nothing of it until the Dogs showed up this afternoon looking for the man who ran the newspaper. They questioned us for an hour, have been searching through the remains of the buildings for at least two." He lowered his voice even further. "The rumor is they're waiting for a Hound."

Ischua raised an eyebrow and the café owner shrugged. "In any case, they've scared away nearly all of my customers."

"Have you seen him?"

"Who? The Hound?"

"The owner of the newspaper."

The owner sighed. "Not since yesterday. He was one of my best customers."

He retreated back inside and Ischua continued to watch. Half an hour later, the pack leader gave a sudden start and Ischua realized that a man stood before him. He hadn't seen him arrive. He was too distant to make out any of the conversation, but the pack leader's irritation was clear. He motioned to the burnt-out husk of the building, pointed to a few items that the other Dogs had dragged up from the basement, and handed over what appeared to be a scrap of cloth. The Hound—Ischua judged him to be about thirty years of age, broad of shoulder but narrow of hip, with nothing remarkable about his features or clothes—breathed in deeply of the cloth, then examined each of the items before descending into the charred pit. He returned a moment later, sneezing harshly. All of the Dogs stood back from him, wary. He shook his head, scrubbed at his face, then paced up and down the street a few times. Ischua's skin prickled when he halted abruptly and stared in the café's direction, but then the Hound spun and motioned in the opposite direction. He ran off as if following a scent trail, like a true hound, the pack leader barking an order, the Dogs falling in behind him.

Ischua took a sip of his drink and was surprised to find the glass empty. He stood, leaving a few errens on the table, and turned his back on the destroyed newspaper, troubled.

The Dogs must have discovered the real Kormanley's link to the splinter cells. It had to have been through Tyrus. He'd been their only connection to the violent Kormanley since they'd severed contact four years ago. Tyrus may have led them to Dalton, and through Dalton. . . .

His steps quickened. He needed to warn the rest of the real Kormanley.

⁓

The Hound stood in the doorway of the apartment. His gaze flicked off the overturned bed, the scattered straw of the mattress, the footprints in the fan of flour that had spilled from a split bag. He drew in a deep breath, nostrils flaring, and caught the scent of the Dog called Hagger, strong. He reeked of anger, his sweat tangy, acidic, like an orange. It permeated the room. But the Hound filtered it out, dug deeper through the layers. The other two Dogs who'd been here smelled of beer and barracks and rancid butter. One of them chewed the black leaf, his scent strong with mouth rot. But beneath that—

He tilted his head, breathed in deep again. Liniment, shit, and baby vomit. Ash and coals from the fire. The kohl and lavender of perfume. Fresh breast milk. And, threaded through it all, the scent he searched for: the strange Dog, the one that sent shivers of wrongness through the Hound's bones.

His lip curled.

The man's odor was fourteen hours old. He'd left that morning, with his whelp and another woman, the one lactating. They hadn't been back.

He spun and followed their scent outside, to the darkened street. No one in Hedge stayed out this late, the narrows and alleys empty as he trotted past closed shops, ley-lit windows, the thick scents of yeast and heat from a bakery. The prey's trail led to Copper, a market square. He'd entered numerous shops, halted at many hawkers, his scent pooling on the empty cobbles where the vendors had set up their tents or blankets. Then he'd left—with the woman and whelp—and run to the ley station.

He halted on the edge of the ley line, the platform deserted, the stream of white ley blinding in the darkness.

The man had boarded a barge.

The Hound sighed. It would make tracking him more difficult. He'd have to investigate all of the stations along this line to find out where the prey had disembarked. With the barges dormant until morning, it could take the rest of the night.

Kneeling down, he reached his hand forward into the stream of ley, felt it tingling against his skin. He closed his eyes, centered himself, and reached through the ley toward the center of the city, toward the mind of the Guide, the one who heard and gave the orders to those on the hunt.

Report.

I have sought. The prey boarded a ley barge in Copper. He didn't need to identify himself. The Guide always knew what Hound's mind he touched.

A pause. Then: *Continue the hunt.*

No approval. No contempt. No emotion whatsoever. None was needed.

The Hound severed the link by drawing his hand from the ley. He shook it, as if the ley clung to him like water, even though it didn't.

Then he turned and began to lope toward the next station along the line.

"It figures I'd find both of you here. Don't you have your own room, Kara?"

Kara blinked sleep-tacky eyes and rolled toward the door to Marcus' room.

"What do you want, Kyle?" Marcus growled.

Kyle grinned. "It's nearly noon. Everyone's headed down to the square for the execution, since the Primes have ordered all of the Wielders to attend except for those on runs. You have about twenty minutes to get ready."

Marcus cursed and tossed his pillow at the retreating Wielder, then leaped out of bed and began dressing. Kara sat up and rubbed at her temples and gritty eyes. "I drank too much," she whispered, then winced.

"We both did. That's why you ended up sleeping here. You fell asleep while we were talking and I didn't want to wake you or drag you back to your room by myself."

She looked up as Kyle's wicked grin registered. "But Kyle thinks—!"

Marcus waved a hand. "Let them think what they want. Besides, would it be that bad?" He flashed his own lewd grin.

Kara flung back the blanket and sighed in relief as she realized she was still dressed, although her purple jacket was flung over the back of a nearby chair. She stood, regretted it instantly as her head reeled, then grabbed her jacket and headed for the door, trying to suppress the blush she knew colored her cheeks. "I'll meet you in the main chamber."

Twenty minutes later she emerged from the women's side of the barracks to a few catcalls and whistles, her face burning even hotter until she realized no one really cared and they were just having a little fun. After a moment, the laughter quieted into disjointed conversations. Kara's head still pounding, the group left the node for the square, Kara sticking close to Marcus' side.

The closer they came to the square, the more they had to push through the gathering crowds. Kara was reminded of the trek with her father to Minstrel's Park to see the sowing of the Flyers' Tower four years before. Excitement buzzed through those gathering. But unlike the sowing, this had a darker undertone, threaded with discontent, fear, and dissent. Expressions were uncertain, conversation tense, quieting whenever anyone passed the dozens of Dogs or city watch that lined the streets. Kara shivered as the Wielders entered the square and began shoving through the press of people toward the stage.

"I don't like this," she said to Marcus, one hand clutching his arm so they wouldn't be separated. They'd already lost sight of Timmons, Kyle, Katrina, and the others.

"I don't think many of those here do either," Marcus said, his voice grim.

"Who are they executing? And why did Augustus order the Wielders here to witness it?"

Marcus shook his head.

"It's one of the Kormanley," a woman said to one side. "One they captured before the bombing." She shook her head and snorted in contempt. "He couldn't have had anything to do with what happened at the Amber Tower, and yet they're going to kill him anyway. As an example to the rest of Erenthrall."

Her vehemence made Kara uncomfortable. "Maybe he helped set up the attack."

The woman's eyes widened, then narrowed. She brushed her long black hair back, tucked it behind one ear, a gold hoop earring glinting in the sunlight. "Are you a Baron sympathizer? Do you agree with what the Dogs have done the last two days? Beating people at random in the streets? Storming into businesses and homes and seizing people without cause?" Her gaze flicked from Kara to Marcus, although her attention seemed to be more focused on Marcus.

Those around them were beginning to pay attention. A few glared at Kara, even as she protested, "No! I've seen how vicious they are. It's just—"

The woman wasn't paying attention to her anymore. "What about you?" she asked, tone harsh. "Are you a sympathizer?"

Marcus stiffened. "No, of course not."

"And what about the Kormanley?"

"What about them?" Marcus asked, his tone careful.

The woman drew breath to answer, but someone shouted, "Kara! Over here!"

A tightness squeezed Kara's throat as she recognized Cory's voice, but before she turned, she caught the black-haired woman giving Marcus a speculative look. Marcus didn't notice, and a moment later the woman had stepped back and gotten lost in the crowd.

Kara frowned, but brushed her unease aside as she searched for Cory. "Do you see him?"

"Who?"

"Cory."

Marcus' expression darkened, but he lifted his chin, looking over the heads of those around them. "I see him, off to the right. There's a Tender with him."

"Ischua!" Kara caught sight of both of them through a break in the press of bodies and smiled as she rushed forward. Ischua squeezed Kara's shoulder in greeting, but she pulled him into a fierce hug. "I haven't seen you in weeks."

Ischua chuckled. "I know they keep the new Wielders busy. But I've been keeping an eye on you." He drew back and patted her on the shoulder. "Look who I found."

And suddenly Cory stood before her. The smile faltered as she remembered how they'd parted the last time she'd seen him. She hadn't meant to hurt him, hadn't realized that dredging up the memories of Justin would affect him so harshly.

"Cory," she said, then halted. "I . . . I'm . . ."

Cory shrugged, tried a tentative smile. "Forget it. I overreacted." He sucked in a ragged breath and grabbed her shoulders. "If you honestly think you saw Justin . . . if you think he wants to be found . . . then I'll help."

She could tell he still didn't believe she'd seen Justin, like Marcus, but she grinned. "Thank you."

Marcus stepped forward, pulled her back out of Cory's grip. The two glared at each other. "Cory."

Cory's lips quirked and he shook his head slightly. "Marcus."

Kara's forehead creased in irritation, but before she could say anything to either one of them, Ischua muttered, "Something's happening on the platform."

Everyone turned, a wave of interest and resentment passing through the crowd. Kara shifted so that she could see the raised wooden structure that had been built at one end of the square, her view interrupted by the people between her and the stage. Dogs were mounting the steps, fanning out to either side, followed a moment later by Prime Wielder Augustus, another Dog—Captain Daedallen—and then a man Kara assumed was the Kormanley prisoner to be executed. He stumbled as they led him toward where a single block of wood sat to one side. One of the Dogs grabbed him by the ropes that bound his wrists and hauled him upright before shoving him forward again, toward the block. He'd obviously been beaten already, his face a mass of bruises and bloody scars beneath his matted hair, but he didn't cry out, even when the Dog handling him kicked him and drove him to his knees before the block, facing the crowd.

Kara's stomach turned and she shifted uneasily. "What are they going to do?"

Ischua frowned, shaking his head.

But then a new figure mounted the platform, head cloaked in a black hood, a massive pike with an ax-shaped head held in his hands.

"They're going to behead him," Marcus snapped.

Bile rose at the back of Kara's throat. "I don't want to see this," she said, reaching to grab Marcus' arm for support, "no matter what the Prime Wielder ordered."

Marcus' muscles were tense, his body rigid.

"Marcus?"

"Wait," he muttered.

On all sides, the crowd shifted, people beginning to murmur beneath their breath as realization struck. The tendrils of unease and dissent she'd felt since they'd left the node grew. The emotions of those gathered on the square became suddenly thick and fluid, like an ocean, currents beginning to ripple and flow around them all, like the currents Kara felt in the ley when she entered the pit, only black and dangerous. She glanced toward Cory and Ischua, saw shock and horror in Cory's eyes, a dark disapproval in Ischua's drawn frown and lowered brow.

Captain Daedallen stepped to the edge of the platform, glaring out over everyone gathered. He waited a moment, the growing rumble from the crowd increasing, then dying out in uncertainty.

In a voice that growled out across the square, Daedallen said, "We are here today to mete out the Baron's justice, to answer the challenge the Kormanley issued two nights ago at the Baronial Meeting. Prime Wielder Augustus?"

Augustus shifted to Daedallen's side. He smoothed out his formal black Wielder's robes, his expression stern. "Two nights ago, the Kormanley viciously attacked the Barons, lords, and ladies of Erenthrall at the Baronial Meeting in the Great Hall of the Amber Tower. Dozens were killed and hundreds were injured in this cowardly bombing. Captain Daedallen and the Dogs learned of the attack days in advance, after capturing Lord Gatterly and this man, Ibsen Senate, along with a dozen other Kormanley priests," he spat the word, "on Lord Gatterly's estate, but they were unable to stop the bombing.

"But Baron Arent wants to be clear. Such outright defiance of the Barony, such blatant disregard for the Baron and those that serve him, will not be tolerated! Even though the Baron survived, and even though the Nexus and the ley system were never in danger, he will not sit back and allow such violence to wreak havoc in his city!

"Lord Gatterly, Ibsen Senate, and all of those who were captured before the attack have been charged with crimes against the Baron and threats against the safety of all of those in Erenthrall. As such, they have all been sentenced to death. By association, anyone who claims to be Kormanley, who preaches against the will of the Baron, who violently attacks in the name of the Kormanley the sanctity of the ley system or threatens the Wielders who keep the citizens of Erenthrall safe, will be arrested and immediately put to death.

"I am here acting as the voice of Baron Arent. If any of you have information regarding the Kormanley or their associates, he encourages you to step forward and inform the Dogs." Prime Augustus turned toward Daedallen. "As decreed by Baron Arent, I charge you with carrying out the execution of Ibsen Senate."

"Very well." Daedallen waited as Augustus stepped out of the way, then nodded toward the Dogs standing over Ibsen Senate. The one who'd forced Ibsen to his knees now jerked him back, twisted him around so that he faced the wooden block, then bent him forward so that his head and chest rested against its top. The Dog planted one of his heavy boots into Ibsen's back, holding him down, while the hooded guard with the ax-like pike shifted into position.

The roil of unease that had quieted as Daedallen and Augustus spoke suddenly swelled, the mumbles and murmurs from before erupting into a few scattered shouts. Someone cried out, "You can't do this!" Another shouted, "Are we just going to let them kill him right here, in front of us?" A few answered, or called out their own judgments or denials. The press of the crowd grew closer and shifted forward, Kara suddenly crushed up against the man before her. An elbow dug into her side and she grunted, pushing back, struggling as sweat broke out in her armpits. Her skin felt flushed, heated. She couldn't breathe. She swallowed against the panic, called for Marcus, for Ischua or Cory, but her words were choked, nothing more than a gasp. She couldn't see them anymore. They were lost in the crowd. On the platform, Daedallen noted the resentment of those gathered and motioned the Dogs on the stage to its edge, where they bolstered those already holding the crowd back. Then he gestured to the executioner, the motion curt.

The black-hooded Dog changed stance, adjusted his grip on the ax, and raised it high overhead, back arched. He held it a moment as the protests in the crowd suddenly surged higher, Kara shoved violently to one side. Her gut twisted and she swallowed back a sickening nausea, her entire body shivering in reaction to the black emotions that rose and fell around her in waves. Her mind was frozen. "This can't be happening," she whispered to herself. It was too barbaric, too bloody, too—

The executioner swung and before she could wrap her mind around it, the blade fell with a dreadful, wet thud, burying itself deep into the block of wood. Ibsen Senate's head popped away from his neck and thunked onto the platform as blood fountained from the stump, splashing onto the stage and splattering those who were closest to the front. Shrieks rose from the crowd, mixed with bellows of rage. Someone close by retched, the stench of vomit slamming into Kara's senses, mixed a moment later with the copper thickness of blood. She gagged in response, but kept her queasy stomach under control. The sea of raw emotions around her surged higher, the crowd pushing forward as the Dogs on the platform roared orders and bellowed for everyone to stay back. The tension was reaching a peak. She felt herself being pulled beneath the swell, her chest constricted. She was drowning, her own pulse rushing in her ears. She began to struggle, arms shoving in every direction, legs kicking—

And then a hand grabbed her shoulder and yanked her back, Marcus pulling her in tight to his chest, his musk surrounding her, overriding the vomit and blood and sweat of the crowd. She gasped in relief as he dragged her back through the press of people, Ischua and Cory falling in behind them both. Within moments, she gained her equilibrium, falling into step with Marcus. They were headed for the edge of the square, for one of the alleys, the glimpses she caught of the faces of those around them black with anger, distrust, and hate. She remembered seeing the disgust of those in the marketplace four years ago, when the Dogs had beaten and taken the Kormanley priest, but it was nothing compared to what she saw now.

Yet, when they reached the alley—Marcus stumbling around the stone corner and into the shadows, Cory and Ischua right behind them, all of them halting, panting with the effort—the people of the square had fallen silent. The shouts and grumblings that had nearly drowned Kara had died down, submerged into a wicked undercurrent. The plaza was eerily silent and still.

On the stage, Captain Daedallen had drawn his sword, pointed it now toward those assembled, his expression hard, like granite. Those Dogs holding the crowd back had drawn blades as well.

"Would you defy the Baron?" Daedallen asked, his voice a deep-seated rumble. "Would you risk his wrath?" He swung the point of his sword left and right, glaring.

No one responded.

Satisfied, he resheathed his blade and turned his back on the square, moving toward Prime Augustus.

The crowd hesitated, then began to disperse, everyone moving slowly, silently. Kara caught low muttering, a few dark conversations. Everyone's expression was tense, fists clenched, shoulders tight.

Ischua herded them up the alley.

"What just happened?" Marcus asked.

"The Baron made his intentions clear," Ischua answered harshly, "and the captain of the Dogs barely averted a riot. I knew the people of Eld were on edge after what the Dogs have done the past few days, but I didn't realize they were this close to open revolt. I thought the Dogs would settle down after a day or so, that the resentment of the citizens would recede." He shot a glance at Cory. "What is the feeling in Confluence? At the University?"

He shrugged. "More or less the same as here. The Masters at the University are up in arms about the Dogs' incursion in the district, although they haven't transgressed on University property yet. That agreement hasn't been breached. Most of my fellow students are more riled up than the Masters, but no one's done anything about it yet. We haven't had a demonstration like this execution, though. I don't know how many of us came up here to see it."

Ischua grimaced. "I saw more than a few of them in the square. And I'd say that Eld and Confluence aren't the only districts where the citizens are on edge. If Baron Arent isn't careful. . . ." He shook his head, but didn't finish.

"What should we do?" Kara asked.

Ischua caught her gaze, concern in his eyes. "Nothing," he said adamantly. "You should do nothing. Keep to your patrols. Stay clear of the

Dogs. Do whatever the Primes demand. It's the only way for you to stay safe." He caught Kara's gaze, held it. "Tell me that you'll do nothing to bring attention to yourself."

Uncertainty flooded through Kara's chest, but she nodded.

Behind Ischua, Marcus frowned and ducked his head.

"Good." Ischua glanced around them. They'd moved far enough away from the square that the streets were less packed, most of the people here going about their daily lives, not having attended the execution. "You should return to the node," the Tender said, catching Marcus' attention, "both of you. And you should head back to the University, Cory. But remember what I said."

Marcus tugged on Kara's arm. "Come on."

Cory squeezed her arm and broke away, heading to Confluence.

Kara resisted at first, concerned about Ischua, not certain why. She watched the Tender for a long moment as they drew away, until he smiled and waved, then let Marcus lead her back to the node.

"Clean up this mess," Daedallen snapped to the executioner and the waiting Dogs. He still had his back to the square, even though his flesh crawled at the violence of the crowd he'd barely managed to contain. He didn't dare turn to see what the people were doing. He couldn't show them any sign of weakness or they'd break.

"They're dispersing," Augustus muttered. The Prime Wielder was shaken. Daedallen heard it in his voice, even though the Wielder's expression was composed.

He met Daedallen's gaze. "We saw similar reactions in Grass and Plinth, although not as intense as here. These executions may have been a mistake."

The Captain grunted. "Tell that to Baron Arent. In the meantime, we still have six more to weather."

Dierdre watched Marcus retreat with Kara, a silken shawl in one hand as she pretended to shop. The Tender Ischua watched them go, then headed back toward Halliel's Park and his duties there, but not without first scanning the street, as if he feared he'd been followed. Dierdre's eyebrows rose at that, but she wasn't concerned with him, even though she knew he was Kormanley. Not part of Dalton's splinter group, but Kormanley nonetheless.

No, she was concerned with Marcus. Dalton had told her to feel him out, to test his potential for introduction into their group. She'd had her doubts when she'd run into them in the crowd, but they'd been interrupted before she could draw any solid conclusions. However, during and after the execution she'd watched him closely. His reactions then, and to Ischua's instructions to do nothing, to keep out of the Dogs' way, were promising.

She'd have to approach him when he wasn't with his partner, Kara. She wasn't certain how she was going to manage that—the two always seemed to be together; it was nauseating—but she'd manage. Dalton was counting on her.

Allan cursed as the pullcart jounced over missing cobbles along the western road. Janis—sitting in the back of the cart with Morrell—cried out, but didn't turn to berate him. She shifted her position, though, Allan compensating by adjusting his grip on the handles. His fingers already ached with tension, blisters forming on his palms and the bases of his thumbs. Both his upper and lower back muscles screamed with the unfamiliar strain. But he was determined to be outside of the city by nightfall.

He glanced up from the road, to where the sun was sinking fast into the horizon, and cursed again.

They'd picked up the pullcart in Field, exactly where Janis' contact in Copper had said he'd leave it. He would have traveled all night if it weren't for Morrell. Janis had insisted they stop for a few hours of sleep, blaming the necessity on the baby. But after finding a place to rest at a tavern—and spending errens he wasn't certain he could afford to lose—he realized he was exhausted. The stress of the last two days had caught up with him the moment he lay back on the bed. But even with the break, they would have already passed beyond Erenthrall's outermost district if there hadn't been a riot in Calder.

"They were executing one of the Kormanley," an elderly proprietor gasped as he cowered along with Allan, Janis, and Morrell behind the barred doors of his leather shop. He flinched as something crashed against the side of the building, the barked commands of the Dogs who'd invaded the street on the heels of the fleeing crowd cutting through the roars of outrage and screams of those they hounded. "Something must have gone wrong."

Allan hadn't responded, his arms trembling with the shock of seeing the Dogs this close, charging onto the street behind him. He'd thought they were after him, his heart seizing in his chest, then realized they were cutting down everyone in their path, their rage unfocused.

He'd dragged the cart—with Janis and Morrell in it—into the shop and slammed its door shut before anyone inside had realized what was happening.

They'd lost more than an hour before the streets had settled down and he'd risked venturing outside again.

Now, shirt soaked in sweat, body prickling with an unease he couldn't explain, he dug his feet into the stone road and pulled the cart forward. They were two districts away from Erenthrall's edge, and the last district—Brink—was narrow. The street was nearly empty, the bustle that Allan associated with the city left behind hours earlier. The buildings were mostly one level, with wide courtyards, gardens behind walls. Most were residences. Shops were small and sparse. Ahead, he could see where the road—what had once been a caravan route—dipped down through Brink and stretched out into the wide yellow rolling grasslands of the Baronies.

But when he passed over into Brink, the transition nothing more than a shift in the shape and style of the cobblestones, a figure stepped out of the lengthening shadows to his left, a mere twenty paces away.

He halted with a jolt, the front of the cart hitting him in the ass, something hot and hard lodging at the base of his throat. He swallowed painfully, drew in a deep breath, and set the cart down.

Behind, a rustle of cloth and then Janis asked, "Why are we stopping?"

Never taking his eyes off the figure, mouth dry, he croaked, "A Hound."

"What?" He heard the cart creak as Janis slipped off its edge and came around to his side. She was patting Morrell's back, holding her up over one shoulder. "I didn't hear—"

Her voice choked off as she caught sight of the Hound. She stilled, then took one careful step closer to Allan.

"Is that a—?"

"It's a Hound, yes." At the sight of Morrell, his little poppet coughing once into Janis' shoulder, face squinched up and wrinkled, one
fisted hand waving before settling down again, his jaw clenched in determination. He stepped forward once, reached for his blade, drew it in
one smooth motion as he said, "You need to run, Janis. Take Morrell
and run to the Hollow."

"But—"

"He was sent to find me, not you, not Morrell. If you go, he won't
follow."

"You can't let him take you," Janis snapped, angry. "You have a
responsibility."

Allan's tongue stuck to the top of his mouth, but he worked up
enough spit to say, "I don't intend to let him take me."

Janis' eyes widened in understanding.

"Now go," Allan said harshly, to hide the heated ache in his chest.
"Morrell is your responsibility now."

She stiffened as if to protest, then softened and stepped back to retrieve her satchel from the cart. She scuttled across the street, to the
side opposite the Hound, then strode along its edge toward the open
plains beyond. She kept Morrell protected against her chest, clutched
in one arm. Once she'd passed the Hound's position, she picked up
speed.

The Hound kept his eyes on Allan the entire time. He hadn't moved
to draw any of the weapons Allan knew he carried, even with Allan's
sword bared. His face was in shadow, the sun setting behind him, but
still Allan recognized him.

"You were the one who found Ibsen Senate."

The Hound shifted stance and Allan tensed. He was sweating, knew
it reeked of fear, but he couldn't seem to slow his heart. He wondered
what the Hound's orders were. Seek, most definitely. Subdue? Kill?

He licked his lips, his tongue rough and gritty. "I'm not Kormanley.
I didn't help them with the attack." The words sounded flat in his ears.
Pathetic. He grimaced.

The Hound's head tilted as if in question. Allan flinched, caught a
hint of the Hounds' nostrils flaring—

Then the Hound turned and walked away.

Allan flinched, his sword jerking forward, until he realized the
Hound was leaving.

"Wait!" he shouted. "Why are you leaving? Weren't you sent to find me?"

The Hound halted, already half lost to shadow. But he looked over his shoulder and said, his voice cracking like an adolescent boy's, "You aren't a traitorous Kormanley bastard."

Then he was gone.

Allan stood in shocked silence, completely confused. But then the import of the Hound leaving hit and his entire body began to tremble. A wave of weakness overcame him and he sank into a crouch, ass on his heels, chest heaving, head bowed down as the adrenaline crash shuddered through him. Tears coursed down his face and dripped from his chin. He couldn't seem to stop them.

He sat that way for over ten minutes, until he'd calmed his breathing and strength had returned to his legs. Then he stood, wiped the tears from his face, tasted their salt on his lips, and resheathed his blade.

He didn't understand what had just happened, but he wasn't going to wait around to figure it out either.

Grabbing the handles of the pullcart, he lifted—it was surprisingly light without Janis weighing down the back—and trotted forward. He intended to catch up to her before the sun set fully.

And then they would leave Erenthrall behind.

Report.

I have located the . . . prey.

The Guide registered his hesitation.

Explain.

My orders were to seek the "traitorous Kormanley bastard" and subdue him. The prey is not Kormanley.

The Guide did not respond. The Hound shifted uncomfortably, suddenly uncertain, the fear of a reprimand and punishment shivering through his skin.

The prey has left Erenthrall, he added. *Should I pursue?*

More silence, broken a moment later.

No. Return to the den.

Sixteen

"CAPTAIN DAEDALLEN."

Daedallen broke off his conversation with four of his alphas and spun, immediately recognizing Baron Arent's voice through the raucous noise of the Dogs' den. Others did as well, as the cacophony of laughter, camaraderie, and the clang of swords and the pummel of fists against flesh in the training pit died out.

Daedallen could not remember the last time he'd seen the Baron in the Dogs' lair. He stepped forward instantly.

"Baron Arent. Did you summon me?"

The Baron's gaze grazed all of those present, dismissing all of them except for Daedallen and those the captain had been speaking to on his arrival. "I did not summon you, no. I came to discuss your progress with the Kormanley."

Daedallen shifted into a formal stance. "I was discussing that with my alphas when you arrived."

"Then continue."

He hesitated, then nodded and turned back to the others. All four of them stiffened, their unease clear at having the Baron listening in. Daedallen nodded toward Terrence. "It's been five days since the crackdown after the riot in Calder. What's the status of that district?"

"Activity there has quieted. The Dogs say the citizens are still on edge, and there have been reports of attacks on the Dogs and the city watch within the last day. I would not recommend decreasing the Dogs stationed there for at least another few days."

Daedallen grunted. It had been the last execution. The dissent in the crowds had grown steadily at each one, the fear and anger finally snapping. Over thirty citizens had been killed in the riot that followed. Fires had broken out in five locations; one had burned down an entire block, the smoke visible from the Amber Tower for two days. The Dogs had flooded the streets and thousands of residents had fled to neighboring districts.

But not all. Hundreds had remained behind, some in passive defiance, going about their daily lives as if the Dogs weren't hovering in pairs or triples at every street corner, while others had been more forceful. Two dozen coordinated attacks on the Dogs and city watch had killed half a dozen guardsmen in the streets. At least forty had been injured by thrown rocks, bricks, and loose cobblestones, or by vicious beatings when groups ambushed the guards and dragged them into darkened alleys or closed-up shops. Daedallen feared that the majority of the attacks happening not just in Calder but all over Erenthrall were not being instigated by the Kormanley.

"Agreed. But rotate those stationed in Calder to other districts and replace them with fresh guardsmen. I don't want any of this fighting to become personal." He skipped to Branden. "What about the search for the Kormanley? We had a lead. The Hounds were searching for the clerk and the owner of the newsprint *The Ley*, weren't they?"

Branden's gaze slid toward the Baron and he licked his lips before answering. "We captured the clerk, Tyrus, two days ago. He's down in the cells. But we haven't gotten anything useful from him."

"Why not? Can't you make him cooperate?"

Branden snorted. "He's *too* cooperative. As soon as we captured him, he began spilling his guts. He claims there are two sets of Kormanley—the peaceful one he belongs to, and a second splinter group that's behind all of the recent bombings. He gave us the name of the leader of the peaceful group—Dalton, the owner of *The Ley*—but the Hounds were already looking for him. They haven't reported back yet. He also gave us the names of the members of the splinter cell he supposedly infiltrated, but he couldn't be more specific than that. He's told us everything, but it's all information we already knew or it's useless."

The Baron had shifted forward as Branden spoke. "What about their meeting places? We can send the Hounds there, have them pick up the conspirators' scents."

"He gave us those locations as well. They were all taverns or inns. One was a slaughterhouse. The Hounds are sorting through the scents now, but hundreds if not thousands of patrons have passed through each room. They're having a hard time picking out the Kormanley from all of the rest."

"What about Allan Garrett?" Hagger asked, his voice rumbling.

Daedallen ground his teeth together, the other Dogs staring at the floor. He drew breath to reprimand Hagger, but Baron Arent spoke first.

"Who is Allan Garrett?"

Hagger turned toward him, his voice tight and formal, but laced with hatred. "Allan Garrett was my partner. He ran after the bombing at the Amber Tower."

"We thought he was Kormanley," Daedallen interjected. "We sent a Hound after him. The Hound reported back that he'd left Erenthrall and," he said pointedly to Hagger, "that he was *not* Kormanley."

Hagger's lip twitched into a scowl. "Even so, he is a Dog. He cannot be allowed to run."

Daedallen felt more than his alphas' eyes on him. No Dog had ever been allowed to leave the pack, except in death. Allan needed to be found, brought back, and punished. What he had done was inexcusable, denigrated them all with its cowardice. His hand clenched on the pommel of his sword, the knuckles white.

But Baron Arent shook his head. "He is inconsequential at the moment. We will hunt him down later. Right now, our focus must be on the Kormanley and the dissent ripping this city apart." His cold eyes fell on Daedallen. "You are not being aggressive enough. I said to unleash the Dogs. *Unleash them.* Find the Kormanley and destroy them. Purge them from this city."

Daedallen frowned. "What of the resistance we met in Calder? There are signs of it elsewhere. The dissension is coming from more than the Kormanley and their supporters."

Baron Arent stepped close, glared up into Daedallen's face. Daedallen could smell the fish the Baron had eaten for lunch on his breath. "The Dogs and the Hounds were created to instill fear. That fear brought the Barons to their knees. Make the citizens of Erenthrall fear the Dogs and the Hounds, as the Barons fear them."

Without waiting for an answer, the Baron backed away, then strode from the den. The tension he'd brought with him did not abate.

Daedallen wiped the sweat from his palms on his shirt.

"Gather your men," he said to his alphas. "Double the number of Dogs on patrol and seize the owners and employees of all taverns, brothels, and slaughterhouses where the Kormanley were known to meet. If anyone resists . . ." He hesitated. He knew what would happen, but the Baron had given him orders, here, in the den, before a significant portion of his men. He could not alter those orders now.

"If anyone resists," he said again, meeting the gaze of each of his alphas squarely, "kill them."

Marcus emerged from the shop on Archam that sold expensive chocolates, his purchase wrapped up in a small box tied with a length of blue ribbon. His smile faltered when he caught sight of the group of three Dogs loitering across the street and he ducked his head as he turned in the opposite direction. The Dogs were everywhere now. He didn't know why it bothered him so much. They hadn't done anything against the Wielders at all. In fact, they appeared to be actively staying out of the Wielders' way whenever possible.

He shrugged his unease aside and pushed the Dogs and the lingering effects of the execution from his mind. He gripped the box of chocolates harder. He was running late. Kara would be waiting for him at the market, probably with that annoyed expression that quirked the corners of her mouth in that way he enjoyed so much. She didn't realize how it dimpled her cheeks. He grinned.

Distracted, he didn't see the woman until they'd slammed into each other, both cutting the corner at the end of the street. They crashed to the ground, arms and legs tangled, the woman crying out in startled surprise and affront. Marcus' heart thudded in his chest as he dropped the box. His shoulder struck the flagstone of the walk, pain shooting into his chest, and one of the woman's elbows crunched into his face, but he shoved her aside and rolled, keeping the box in sight. It clattered to the stone, came to a rest on its side. He disentangled himself and scrambled to it, snatching it up and inspecting it for damage.

"Well," the woman he'd run into said from the ground. "I see where your priorities lie."

Seeing no damage except a minor scuff mark, he breathed a sigh of relief and turned toward her. "Sorry. I just spent two weeks' worth of errens on this and—" He halted, brow furrowing in confusion. "Do I know you?"

The woman brushed long black hair off her face and reached out a hand. He grabbed it without thinking and hauled her to her feet. She smiled. "My name's Dierdre. We talked briefly during the execution last week. I accused you of being a Baron sympathizer, remember?"

Brow still furrowed, he nodded. "I remember."

"The beheading was disgusting," Dierdre said, brushing herself off. "The Dogs should never have been allowed to get away with it."

Marcus' heart leaped up into this throat and he spun to see if the Dogs he'd noticed earlier were close. They'd been arresting people in Eld for less than what Dierdre had just said, had killed a few who resisted, right on the street. No trial, no pretense of hauling them off to the Tower for "questioning," never to be seen again.

But the Dogs were gone.

Dierdre chuckled and he turned back. "I knew they were gone," she said. "I'm not stupid." She looked him up and down, her expression so speculative he blushed. "You don't strike me as being stupid either. Young, but not stupid."

"I'm not," he said.

She shifted closer, lowered her voice. Pedestrians streamed by them on either side, no one paying them any particular attention. "I don't think you like the Dogs very much either. Am I right?"

He frowned, sweat suddenly breaking out across his back, beneath his armpits. "I'm a Wielder. I have no problem with the Dogs."

She pursed her lips. "That's not what I saw at the execution, nor when you spotted them coming out of the shop just now."

He shifted back, unconsciously gripping the box harder in his hand. "I don't know what you're talking about."

Dierdre chuckled again, a low, dark sound that sent shivers down Marcus' skin. "No need to worry. I'm not working for the Dogs. I'm not an informant." Hatred tinged her voice and her gaze flicked from Marcus to the street, where the Dogs had been standing, then back. "I know many people who don't like them. Maybe you'd be interested in meeting them sometime?"

Marcus sucked in a sharp breath, then coughed, retreating two steps, three. He glared at Dierdre uncertainly. His body shook with shock, rebelling at the thought. And yet part of his mind whispered, *The Dogs are out of control. And the Primes have lost control.*

But the Kormanley had killed Kara's parents.

Was this woman Kormanley? She hadn't said anything about the ley, only the Dogs.

Confused, he said, "I'm late. I'm supposed to be meeting someone at the market."

Dierdre's shoulders sank, but she smiled. "Forgive me. I did not mean to detain you." She glanced down toward the box. "A gift for . . . ?"

"My partner."

Her eyebrows lifted. "Your partner."

He blushed again, but lifted his chin. "We run patrols together."

"I see."

He began to step away, but she grabbed his arm, a light touch, but insistent. "If you change your mind, ask for me at the Tambourine. It's a little café on Bittersly Street."

Then she let him go, merging into the bustle of the walk. He lost sight of her black hair when she rounded a corner.

He clenched the box of chocolate to his chest, then shook his head and moved in the opposite direction, toward the market.

Dalton noticed the Dogs trailing him when he paused to pick up a loaf of bread. His hand clenched involuntarily, fingers punching through the hardened outer crust into the soft warm interior. He barely heard the baker protest and demand payment, his body rigid with fear. But her shrill voice finally penetrated, and he dug hastily in his pocket for change when he realized the Dogs hadn't noticed him yet. They appeared to be watching someone else.

"Here," he said, handing over far too many errens for the bread. Her shriek cut off, but the disgruntled look on her face didn't fade, nor the glare.

When she turned her back to get change, he slipped down the street, trying to move slowly, as if still browsing the shops. He dodged pedestrians and surreptitiously scanned for whatever held the Dogs' attention.

It took him a moment, but then he caught motion out of the corner of his eye and his gaze focused on not something, but someone. A lean figure with straggly brown hair and a narrow face, a sharp nose, freckles. Slightly taller than himself, the man moved through the crowd without effort, the patrons in the streets stepping out of his way unconsciously. No one appeared to notice him at all, except the Dogs, who kept him in sight at all times.

Dalton slid into an alley—nothing more than a shoulder-width narrow between two stone buildings—and watched.

The Hound—it had to be a Hound—moved fluidly through the crowds, eyes darting back and forth, searching faces, acutely aware of every move made by those around him. The intensity of his features sent a shudder through Dalton's shoulders and down his back. His focus was inhuman, and there was something odd about his breathing. Every so often, his head would tilt and his nostrils would flare—

Dalton sucked in a harsh breath, held it. Scent. That's why they were called Hounds. They hunted by scent.

At the same moment, the Hound spun and lashed out with one hand, seizing the baker's arm as she turned from arguing with another woman. Dalton heard her gasp in pain from his position across the street. Her perpetual disgruntled expression fled, replaced with pure panic as she caught sight of who held her and the Dogs now rushing toward her position.

"Where is he?" the Hound demanded.

"Who?" she asked, then tried to jerk free. The muscles in the Hound's forearm flexed and she bit back another gasp, her arm now canted awkwardly to one side.

"The man who was just here," the Hound said, and Dalton shrank back deeper into the narrow. Icy tendrils cascaded down his legs and into his feet, his toes tingling, as the Hound continued. "Where did he go?"

The woman's jaw set, her eyes narrowing. "I don't know."

The Dogs had arrived, everyone on the street giving the baker's stall a wide berth. But even though the other pedestrians kept their distance, Dalton sensed a dark undercurrent welling up, heightened when the Hound twisted the woman's arm further and she cried out through clenched teeth.

The Dogs' alpha must have sensed it as well. He motioned with one hand, the rest of the Dogs fanning out. Some of those on the street had stopped, were glaring at the altercation. "Was he here?" the alpha growled.

The Hound's lip curled. "He was here. Within the last ten minutes."

He drew in a deep breath, turned in Dalton's direction, searched with those odd, animalistic eyes—

And caught Dalton's gaze.

Shock bolted from Dalton's brain to his feet at the ferocity he saw there and he lurched back.

At the same time, the Hound said, "We don't need her," and wrenched the woman's hand, the motion casual. Dalton heard the snap of bone as the baker screamed.

Then he spun in the narrow and dashed between the buildings, shoulders scraping on either side. A pounding filled his ears, muting the baker's shrieks from behind and the sudden uproar from those who had watched. He heard the alpha bellow a warning, heard outraged growls from the few who'd gathered around to watch, heard a fight break out. But the bloodrush in his ears dampened everything except the harshness of his own breathing.

He cried out as he burst from the narrow's other side into another street, nearly stumbling. Someone helped him steady himself, but he jerked away and staggered to the right, heading toward the market, toward the thicker crowds. He'd eluded the Dogs and the Hounds for more than three weeks. He'd thought he'd escaped their notice. How had they found him? How had they—

He jolted to a halt in the middle of an intersection as it hit him. His scent. It had taken them a while to follow his tracks through Eld, especially since he'd traversed nearly all of these streets for years, but they'd found him.

And they'd find him again. Unless he could figure out a way to hide his scent. To destroy his tracks.

A roar of outrage from the street he'd just left drew his attention. The Dogs were piling out of the narrow, spreading out. The Hound was already honing in on Dalton's direction.

Their gazes met again and the Hound smiled and began trotting toward Dalton.

Dalton shot away to the left, running flat out for the market. He needed the crowds there to slow the Hound down, needed to give himself a lead.

He needed time to think.

"Where have you been?" Kara demanded as she caught sight of Marcus through the crowded market. He wove through a gaggle of Gorrani children being herded by a matron, only her kohl-darkened eyes visible above the silk wrap that wound beneath her shawl and covered her mouth. "We were supposed to meet half an hour ago!"

Marcus ignored her bridled tone, inexplicably smiling. "I was getting this."

He pulled the arm tucked behind his back into sight to reveal a blue-ribboned box that she recognized instantly with a gasp.

"You didn't."

He chuckled. "I did. Take it. Open it."

Kara took the box—larger than any they'd ever purchased at the shop—and held it with trembling hands. The scent of the chocolate was strong enough she thought she could taste its silky texture in her mouth already. She licked her lips tentatively, her chest tight and her gut tingling, then reached for the ribbon, but hesitated, her brow furrowing.

This wasn't a gift Wielder partners gave to one another. This was too extravagant.

She looked up into Marcus' eyes. They were smiling with encouragement. But there was a tightness about the corners, as if he were nervous or uncertain.

"Go on," he said, raising his chin and looking toward the box. His voice thickened, shook slightly. "Open it."

She dropped her gaze, quelled the sudden nervousness that twisted her stomach. With a tug, she loosened the silk ribbon and opened the box.

It contained exactly what she expected: six of the chocolatier's most expensive chocolates.

"I can't accept this," she heard herself say. "It's not . . . it's too . . ."

Marcus took her wrists in his hands, pulled her closer to him. Her skin burned where he touched her, a pleasant prickling racing up her arms to her shoulders, settling in her chest. Her breath shortened, then caught as he said, "Kara. We're more than partners. You know it. I know it. Everyone at the node knows it as well. That's why they're always snickering behind their hands and whispering behind our backs. I just . . ."

He ran out of words, his mouth open as he searched for what he wanted to say. He still had her wrists in his hands. Kara still couldn't breathe. Her heart thudded in her ears, fast and quick. The bustling market swirled around them both as if they weren't there, hawkers peddling their wares, patrons haggling with the cartmen or the farmers with blankets thrown down on the cobbles. Mixed in were the Gorrani with their rounded tents and the more exotic stalls from the Archipelago. Scents assaulted her as time stretched—pungent spices, tantalizing smoked meats, the thickness of ale. She found herself yearning upward, lifting onto the balls of her feet.

Marcus gave up his search and simply pulled her tight to him, her arms—still holding the box of chocolates—crushed between them. He kissed her. Not the protective kiss he'd given after she'd been interrogated by the Primes after the appearance of the distortion at the ley station, and not the tentative, exploratory, and sometimes fumbling kisses they'd shared in the time since. This kiss reached deep, pulling something up from within her, from a reserve she didn't know she had, a reserve she hadn't realized she kept hidden and protected. She fought the exposure at first, afraid of what had been awakened, but then she released her hold, sank herself into the kiss, and found that she was pulling something from deep inside Marcus as well, drawing it up from his center. He'd opened himself to her completely, hid nothing from her. It was like the power of the ley flowing from her into the ground, into the folds of the Tapestry around them all. Except this energy passed only between her and Marcus, sizzling through her skin, warm and fluid and exhilarating. It woke every part of her, and through it she could sense Marcus as well, his entire being.

Then the kiss ended, both of them pulling back with a gasp—of needed air, of shock, of shared experience. Kara trembled, the market still whirling around them, but somehow withdrawn. Marcus sucked in steadying breaths, then released her wrists, touched her face, her hair, cupped the back of her head on both sides with his hands. "Kara, I love you."

"I—" Her throat closed and she swallowed, then finished hoarsely, "I love you, too."

They stood silently, neither one daring to move, neither one certain how the moment should end.

Then Kara looked down and, in a dazed voice, said, "The chocolate's melting."

Marcus snorted, then broke into deep-throated laughter. He pulled back from her, took the top of the wooden box and closed it before taking her hand and leading her in a meandering path through the scattered vendors. Neither of them spoke, Kara still reeling from the intensity of the kiss and caught up in the sudden ramifications of what had just happened. Everything was shifting, like the lines of power had shifted in Halliel's Park when she'd rearranged the patterns of the stones. Her view of her place in the node, of the other Wielders, of her path forward—all of it was changing.

"Timmons," she said abruptly.

"What about him?" Marcus asked.

"He's the head Wielder at the node. What will he think of this?"

Marcus smiled. "He saw it coming. In fact, he's already spoken to me about it. Or rather, warned me of the consequences."

"Like what?"

They paused before a jewelry maker whose pendants and other objects glinted in the sunlight. But when Kara looked closer, she realized it wasn't the reflection of the sun she saw, but ley light. The jewelry maker had somehow captured a sliver of ley inside each of the glass designs, so that they glowed with an inner light. When she picked one up—the glass crafted into the shape of a tiny bird—she felt the threads of power wrapped into the structure. Yet she sensed no power from the woman keeping a careful eye on her. Someone else must be creating them.

"Like the fact that you won't be staying at Eld for much longer."

Kara nearly dropped the pendant. She spun toward Marcus, asked sharply, "What do you mean?"

Marcus shrugged, fidgeting where he stood, but not looking directly at her. "He said the Primes have taken notice of you. They were probably already watching, after what happened with your parents and your early acceptance into training. But after you attempted to seal the distortion at the Eld station. . . ." He sighed, his shifting gaze finally falling on her. "They're going to move you to another node within the year. Timmons thinks they're going to accelerate your teaching and make you a Master early, and a Prime shortly after that."

Kara swallowed. "I thought I'd have four years here at Eld."

Marcus' smile twisted. "Apparently not."

Kara didn't know what to say. The prospect of learning what the Masters and Primes knew was exciting, but she had barely settled into

Eld. It was practically all she knew, having grown up here. The only other district she'd lived in had been Grass, while studying with the Wielders, and even there she had remained within the confines of the college and the nearest streets most of the time. She had little experience with any of the other districts.

Apprehension tightened her fingers on the box she still held and she blurted, "What about us? I'll have to stay at whatever node they send me to."

Marcus' grin faltered. "Not all Wielders stay at the node. You wouldn't have to stay in the barracks." He hesitated. "In fact, I was thinking. . . ." He took the pendant she still clutched and set it back down among the others, the jewelry seller frowning in disappointment. "Timmons will never let us room together at the node. There's a strict division in the barracks—women on the right, men on the left. So I thought maybe we could . . . find a place of our own, somewhere in Eld." Before she could protest, although she wasn't certain she would, he rushed on. "You can commute to whatever node they place you in. The ley barges can take you anywhere in Erenthrall, and they've gotten cheaper since the Flyers' Tower became active. With both of our pay going into one pot, we can afford a small place. Nothing much, but something." He took a deep breath, expelled it with a hopeful, "What do you think?"

Kara opened her mouth, but her throat closed and nothing came out. She felt light-headed and dizzy, overwhelmed and reeling with all of the sudden changes. The rocks and patterns were shifting too fast. The kiss, the news she wouldn't be staying at Eld long, the thought of finding a place with Marcus—it exhilarated her and terrified her with the unknown and the uncertainties.

"I—" She halted, tried again. "I don't know, Marcus." His shoulders slumped, so she reached up to grip his arm. "I want to, but I need to adjust to . . . to everything. Especially the idea that I won't be staying in Eld."

Marcus struggled with his disappointment for a moment, the pain clear in the contours of his face, but then he sighed. "I suppose it is unexpected. I just . . . don't want to lose you."

"You won't." She kissed him in reassurance. It lacked the intensity of before, but still felt different. That part of their relationship had changed permanently.

"Kara? Marcus?"

Kara started at Ischua's voice, a flush creeping up her neck as she took a step back from Marcus and turned. "Ischua!" she gasped, a little too loudly. "What are you doing here?"

Ischua's gaze traveled from Kara to Marcus and back again, measuring and weighing, taking in everything. Kara's skin prickled under the scrutiny. "It's a market, Kara. I'm here shopping." He held up a package wrapped in paper and tied with twine.

"Oh. Yes."

An uncomfortable silence followed until Ischua said with a cocked eyebrow, "Did I interrupt something?"

"We were just discussing. . . ." Marcus floundered, glanced toward Kara in panic.

She sighed in resignation. "You'll find out soon anyway. Marcus told me I may not be staying at the Eld node for much longer. We were thinking of living outside the node, getting a place of our own."

Ischua stiffened as she spoke. "You're being transferred out of Eld?"

"Timmons said the Primes were talking about moving her, after the incident at the barge station," Marcus said. "He doesn't know where yet, or when. But within the next year."

"Earlier than usual," Ischua said. Then he muttered under his breath, "I was trying to keep them from noticing your potential this soon."

"What do you mean?"

Ischua hesitated. Then: "You exhibited power early, Kara. That's usually a sign of great potential. I tried to keep your power hidden from the Primes until the testing at the school when you were fourteen, but then your parents died. At that point, the best option was to let the Wielders take you. But I still didn't tell them exactly what you had done with the stones in Halliel's Park. I was hoping you would blend in with the others, that you would be overlooked, at least for a while." He shook his head, lips pressed tight together. "The training from the Primes can be . . . harsh. They care only for themselves and for the ley system. They will use whatever—and *whoever*—they can to retain control of it. Their abuse of the power and those who wield it is what drove me to retire and become a Tender. I didn't want them to notice you until you were strong enough and confident enough to face them, to stand up to them if necessary."

Something swelled inside Kara's chest, threatened to close her throat. "You think . . . I could be a Prime?" She couldn't voice the question she really wanted to ask, but it appeared Ischua knew anyway.

He smiled, reached out and gripped her shoulder. "Didn't I say so after you received your purples? And yes, Kara, I have always and will always be proud of you." He squeezed his hand, then turned his attention to Marcus, his expression becoming grave. "As for you . . . will you protect her and cherish her? Honor her and keep her safe?" His tone was only half-mocking.

Marcus straightened. "I will."

"Hmm . . . we shall see." The words carried a veiled threat, but Ischua broke into a smile. "But for now, I give you both my blessing."

Someone spat a curse, not far distant, followed by someone else bellowing in protest and a woman's shriek.

Ischua glanced up beyond Kara's shoulder at the commotion, and an instant later his face fell, the benign smile collapsing into fear and recognition. "Korma preserve us."

Marcus and Kara spun. Kara frowned as she caught sight of a single man tearing through the market, shoving men and women out of his way, stumbling over blankets and displays of wares as he came. He was of average height, black hair, mixed with a smattering of gray. His face was lined with desperation.

And then his gaze fell on Ischua and it transformed into determination, into purpose. He altered his course, tripped over a stack of brightly colored fabric, but caught himself with one hand and launched himself forward, ignoring the merchant's protests. He plowed between Kara and Marcus, knocking them to the side, and slammed into Ischua, grabbing onto the Tender's shirt. Ischua had braced for the impact, but he still staggered back a step, holding onto the man's upper arms to steady them both.

"You have to run," the man growled. "The Dogs have found me. They're after me now, with one of their Hounds. If they found me, then they'll find the others. They'll find *you*. You have to warn them. Warn them all to get out of Erenthrall!"

At the edge of the market, fresh screaming rose and the man pushed himself away from Ischua. He gathered himself, the panic and fear Kara had first seen on his face dissolving completely as a brace of Dogs thrust themselves forward through the crowds and into the large, packed square. They were a pace behind a much leaner man that Kara found difficult to focus on. All of them were searching the market, the lean man's nostrils flaring.

The black-haired man, now composed, scowled. "They hunt by scent, Ischua. Remember that."

And then he brushed past them all, moving swiftly, but no longer crashing through those blocking his way. Kara lost sight of him within moments, turned back to Ischua. "Who was that?"

Ischua shook his head. "It doesn't matter. They do." He nodded toward the Dogs.

The patrons in the market had grown agitated. Someone shouted, "What do you think you're doing?" Others repeated the sentiment. A few called out curses or oaths. Someone spat in contempt on the ground near where Kara stood.

The lead Dog stepped forward, almost to the side of the lean man they followed. He raised his voice so that it boomed over the protests and grumbling. "There is a Kormanley accomplice hiding in this market! The life of anyone who hinders our search, resists, or harbors or aids this man in any way will be forfeit!"

His warning given, he nodded to the lean man and gestured to the rest of his Dogs. All of them drew swords, the lean man in front stepping forward, nose tilted slightly into the air.

The rumbling in the crowd increased and Kara felt the same oceanic surge of discontent she'd felt at the execution roiling around her. Except this undercurrent was deeper and deadlier than that, because of what had happened in the weeks since the beheading. Everyone knew of the riot in Calder, of the vicious retaliation of the Dogs in that district and others since. In the last week, the presence of the Dogs on the streets had doubled. A weight had settled over the city, oppressive and menacing, felt in the streets during the Wielders' patrols. Riots had broken out in other districts, the streets left behind afterward riddled with the dead. Yet nothing of significance had happened in Eld.

But now the discontent in Eld had a focus.

Ischua stepped to Marcus' side, grabbed his arm to catch his attention. "Both of you, get out of here. Head back to the node and stay there until this blows over." When Marcus bristled, he added, "Do it! To protect her if nothing else."

Marcus glanced toward Kara and subsided.

"What about you?" Kara demanded.

"I'll head back to Halliel's Park and close the gates. Now go!"

Marcus tugged her away from Ischua as the Dogs began forcing their way forward through the market's crowd. Kara resisted, uncertain why, something dark and insidious clutching at her chest. Ischua gave her a last nod of encouragement. Then he turned away, his expression hardening, his eyes glinting with anger.

"Kara, come on!" Marcus growled, pulling her along. But she refused to turn.

Beyond Ischua, the Dogs were meeting resistance. Some of the people were desperately trying to get out of their way, but others were standing their ground, shouting protests that the market was a public area, that everyone had the right to be there, that the Dogs couldn't simply force them to leave. The Dogs were tossing those who resisted to the side, trampling those on the ground, kicking aside stacks of fruit, piles of pottery, toppling small handcarts and spilling the contents across the markets' flagstone. The lean man—the Hound, Kara assumed—simply stalked forward, heading directly toward Ischua, who didn't move.

"Wait," Kara muttered, then raised her voice to be heard over the increasing tumult near the Dogs. "Marcus, wait!"

Marcus halted. "What is it?"

Kara didn't answer. Behind, someone threw a metal pot at the Dogs, the tin clanging against the lead Dog's head, making him stagger backward. He caught himself, shook his head once, then scowled. More projectiles were launched—fruit, broken shards of clay pottery, a head of lettuce—and he bellowed, "Dogs! No mercy!" Then he thrust a woman out of his way, stomping down on her ankle as she tried to crawl from his path.

Kara winced, too distant to hear the bones break or grind together. But she wasn't too far to hear the woman's agonizing scream.

Everything within the market paused, held for a single collective breath. In that moment of silence, the oceanic tide of hatred and contempt rose in a chokehold, then crested and broke in the space of a heartbeat.

The entire market exploded into chaos, men and women surging toward the Dogs with roars of defiance and hate. Those closest struck them instantly, hitting them hard, grappling with them as they tried to bring them down. But the patrons of the market didn't carry weapons and the Dogs did. The lead Dog shouted orders and swung his sword in a tight sweep, cutting two attackers across the chest, both collapsing to the ground with shocked expressions and sprays of blood. One of them writhed in silent agony, blood pouring from between his hands where he clutched his wound. The other remained still. But no one paid them any attention, the lead Dog falling back a step, the Dogs regrouping, their blades flaring in the sunlight as they began hacking at their attackers. Kara saw two more cut down, one of them a woman. The entire market had gone mad, a frenzy of confusion as people lurched toward the Dogs in rage or scrambled to get out of the way. The madness rolled across Kara's skin in waves. Her gut tightened. Her breath came in shortened, sharp gasps. Her chest ached. She was being jostled on all sides as people tried to flee, the glimpses of those who ran past her studies in panic.

Marcus seized her arm. "Kara, let's go."

"Ischua."

The Tender hadn't moved. The crowd surged around him as if he were a stone in a river, a monolith of calm.

His attention was fixed on the Hound.

Kara had forgotten about him. But the lean man had his own blade out, was carving a path of death toward Ischua's position, his motions fluid, subtle, precise, and deadly. His sword slid out to the side as he was attacked, slicing deep into an arm, a cheek, a thigh, or a gut, blade twisting and flicking too fast to be seen, but his attackers fell to either side. He kept his attention forward, shifting only to dodge the bodies or step over a moaning form. While the Dogs had nearly been overwhelmed, the Hound hadn't even been touched, hadn't broken stride.

He halted a pace away from Ischua. Kara tensed as the two stared at each other. The Hound said something. Ischua responded, and then the Hound glanced toward Kara and Marcus. Marcus sucked in a breath through his teeth, but the Hound wasn't looking for them. He looked beyond, in the direction the man who'd lurched into Ischua had run earlier. His eyes narrowed and his nostrils flared.

With a casual thrust, the Hound sank his blade into Ischua's stomach. The Tender sagged forward over the Hound's hand. The Hound caught his shoulder, yanked his sword free, and let the Tender drop to the ground. Blood coated the front of Ischua's clothes, dribbled from his mouth and into his beard.

Shock kept Kara rooted to the flagstone for one breath . . . two.

And then she screamed, "Ischua!" the Tender's name ragged at the end as something in her throat tore. She leaped toward his crumpled form, images of her parents' corpses flaring before her eyes with sickening clarity, but Marcus' arm snaked around her waist and hauled her back. She struggled, shrieking, tears blurring her vision, but Marcus held on tight. The Hound shot her a curious glance, paused in his hunt, then continued on past them, picking up his pace as the crowd thinned. Kara kept her gaze locked on Ischua, kicking and scratching as Marcus pulled her away. The Tender coughed up more blood, rolled onto his side, struggled to rise, one arm clenched across his stomach, that hand still absurdly holding the package he'd shopped for earlier. But he had no strength. Sobbing hysterically, Kara watched him collapse onto his side, curl inward upon himself, face contorted in pain—

And then their eyes met.

Across the distance, their sightline cut off occasionally by patrons of the market as they ran between them in blurs of motion, Ischua's brows knit in consternation and he frowned. He nodded once and mouthed the word, "Go."

A reprimand. An order.

Then he laid his head down against the bloody flagstone and died, his entire body going slack.

All of the strength ran out of Kara's arms and legs. "Ischua."

Marcus cursed and thrust them both through the press of people clogging the market, dragging her along beside him. Kara dangled from his hold, his arm pressing painfully up under her ribs, until Ischua's form was lost from sight. She slumped forward a moment, let her feet scrape along the flagstones, bump over debris—a blanket, the remains of a woven basket—and then she pushed against Marcus' arm, struggled to regain her feet. He squeezed tighter at first, then realized she was trying to help him and let her go, catching hold of her arm instead as she sank into a crouch.

"Kara," he said through gritted teeth.

"I know," she muttered, her voice weak. Her throat hurt when she spoke or swallowed. "I know, Marcus. Give me a minute to catch my breath."

He looked her over, then nodded, releasing her arm and standing over her protectively as the chaos of the market flowed around them.

They'd reached the edge opposite where the Dogs had entered the square. It was calmer here, although people were still racing away from the fight, or toward it.

Marcus stirred beside her, his leg nudging her shoulder. "The fight is growing," he said. "More Dogs have just arrived. We shouldn't stay here much longer."

Kara pressed a hand against her chest, above her heart, and squeezed her eyes shut. It felt as if a stone had lodged itself beneath her throat. Her breath came in hitches, her pulse raced. Her face was flushed and her sinuses clogged with snot. And she couldn't keep the last image of Ischua from appearing through the blur of her tears, that last order.

Go.

He'd died to protect her in some way. She didn't know how, didn't know why he hadn't fled for Halliel's Park like he said he would. But she knew he'd done it for her.

Gathering her strength, she pushed herself up from the crouch and met Marcus' concerned gaze.

"I'll be fine," she lied.

Marcus didn't believe her; she saw it in his eyes. She saw something else as well. Something had hardened inside him, as if he'd come to a decision, made some sort of resolution. But he laced the fingers of one hand with hers and said, "Come on. We have to warn Timmons and the node."

⬱

Dalton slipped from the market square, headed south toward Confluence, before suddenly changing his mind and angling west. The crowds of the market would only slow the Dogs, not stop them. He wasn't certain they would detain the Hound at all. As he moved, picking up his pace as the concentration of people eased, he checked back over his shoulder repeatedly. He heard the start of the uproar in the market, nothing more than a background rumble of defiance, like distant thunder. Five blocks farther on, he stepped into a shadowed alcove as whistles pierced the air and a group of five Dogs and three city watch charged past. Dalton watched as pedestrians ducked out of the way, then returned to the street to watch the distance in consternation. Hushed conversations began, most returning to whatever task had been interrupted.

But not all. Some of them shared dark glances and began walking toward the square, hands falling to where weapons were concealed in belts or boots or pouches.

Dalton edged out of the shadows, lips pressed tight. In the distance, a pillar of smoke had started to rise and it sounded as if the riot had spread beyond the square.

Perhaps what the Kormanley hadn't been able to achieve with their bombs, the Baron would bring about with his Dogs.

The thought made him smile.

Then he turned and moved on. The back of his neck prickled with urgency. He had no time to savor the violence. If he'd succeeded, his visions would end and he could finally rest. Until then . . .

Until then, he still had to escape the Hound.

He mulled that problem over as he headed toward the bridge across the Tiana, continuing to check over his shoulder for pursuit.

He'd begun to relax, still two blocks from the bridge, when his skin began to crawl between his shoulders and he spun, lowering into a half crouch. His gaze flicked between the buildings behind, passed from face to face—

Then settled on the lean features of the Hound, stalking down the center of the road directly toward him.

A wave of weakness passed down into Dalton's legs, but he stumbled back, twisted, and hustled toward the bridge. He had no weapon, knew it would have been useless even if he held one, but still wasted time searching for something of use in the shops he passed, or what his fellow citizens were carrying. It was instinct. But there was nothing. Sweat broke out as he picked up speed, crossing the first intersection. He could see the bridge ahead, the huge marble pedestals to either side depicting rearing horses, the stone arching up slightly across the expanse of the river. Ley carts and wagons clogged the entrance, but the footpaths to either side with the grand stone railings weren't as busy. He headed for the left walkway, nearly getting hit by a cart as he crossed the last intersection. The rearing horse loomed over him and he risked a glance backward, catching sight of the Hound now less than half a block behind. Breath catching in his throat, he dodged past a woman with two children in tow, skirted the stone division between the pedestrian walkway and the road, and trotted out onto the expanse.

He was halfway across, the Candle District in sight on the far side, when he realized the Hound was less than twenty paces behind.

He panicked, his heart thundering in his ears, and lurched toward the roadway, searching for a cart to jump onto, a horse to steal. But there was nothing, everyone moving too fast. He backed up, the Hound now ten feet away, a knife glinting unobtrusively in his hand. Dalton swallowed, a sinking sensation filling his chest—

And then his back bumped into the stone railing. He glanced down, the drop to the dark waters of the river making him dizzy.

Water.

He stilled.

Water hid scents. Isn't that how prey got lost during a hunt? He wasn't certain. He'd grown up in the city, had lived here his entire life. But he thought so. He thought he'd read it somewhere. But even so, that was for regular hounds. Would it work against a Hound?

He didn't know. But he didn't think about it either. It was his only option.

He glanced up, the Hound five paces distant, and smiled. "Give my regards to the Baron."

Then he leaned backward, slipped over the railing, and fell to the river below.

Kara pulled the trunk out from beneath her bed and began packing—clothes, odds and ends she'd picked up in Eld or her time in Grass, other objects she'd been given by the shopkeepers she'd helped as a Wielder. There wasn't much. The node provided most of what its Wielders needed in terms of food, accommodations, and other essentials. But she had made the little stone bedroom her own in small ways.

She moved from bed to dresser to table rotely, her mind elsewhere. She knew the rest of the Wielders, and Marcus in particular, were concerned. It had been four days since Ischua had died, two since the riots that started in the Eld market square had finally died down, although the tension and clashes within the city itself had only heightened. People were revolting in the streets, in what many had begun calling the Purge. Pillars of smoke from burning buildings and riots had become commonplace. During all of that time, Kara had performed her duties as Wielder without fail, but she'd been withdrawn. She felt as if she were removed from her body, hovering slightly above her own shoulders, watching as it lived her life for her. She'd gone with Marcus to search out a small apartment that they could afford, one not that far from the node or the ley station. Timmons had informed her that she'd be shifted to another node at the end of her second year, but he didn't know which district yet. He'd been apologetic about the transfer, but happy that she and Marcus were finally moving forward with their relationship. He still expected them to arrive for their patrols on time, of course. He'd said it with mock sternness, hoping for a reaction, but when Kara had merely nodded, he'd cast a worried look at Marcus.

She saw all of the looks, noted all of the touches of comfort that Kyle and Katrina and the others gave her, recognized their attempts to draw her out, to make her laugh. But she wasn't ready yet. Her chest was hollow. Ischua had been a surrogate parent for her after her real parents had died at Seeley Park. He'd been her support during her years at the Wielders' college, her strength, emotionally as well as academically. He'd been her . . .

Stone.

She paused, her heart wrenching as she caught sight of the stone—blue-black, with swirls of white in it. Picking it up, she rubbed her thumb over its river-smoothed surface, thought about the test in Halliel's Park with her father and Ischua watching, about Ischua handing her the stone at the secret tavern reserved only for those who'd achieved their purples.

The tears stung. She thought she'd cried herself out over the last few days, but apparently not.

Stepping back, she slumped down onto the bed, clutched the stone to her chest, and let the wrenching, hitching sobs claim her.

<hr />

Marcus moved among the patrons of Bittersly Street, mouth turned down in a frown, brow creased in deep thought. He'd left Kara packing at the node, after days of attempting to keep her active and involved. But nothing had worked. She'd participated, but her expression was vacant and dazed. She'd sunken into herself, retreated, and he hadn't been able to bring her back.

Timmons had told him it would take time, that there was nothing to be concerned about. But his skin itched and his muscles twitched. He needed to do something, something to bring the Kara he knew back, something to make everything better.

Something to make those who'd hurt her pay.

He halted across the street from the Tambourine, uncertain. He didn't know if he trusted Dierdre, didn't know if she was Kormanley or not, although he suspected she was. But even if she were, the Kormanley had never targeted Kara's parents. From everything he knew, they'd simply been in the wrong place at the wrong time. It had been an accident.

Ischua's death wasn't an accident.

And then there was the Kormanley's stance on the ley. The Primes were abusing the system, hoarding it, misusing the resources by creating the Flyers' Tower and then ignoring the consequences, such as the distortions that were still plaguing the city.

His fists clenched as he thought of how the Primes had treated Kara during their interrogation, how they planned to accelerate her ascension to a Master and a Prime so that they could use her power for themselves.

They needed to be stopped. The Baron and his Dogs needed to be stopped. And the Kormanley were the only ones willing to stand up to them all.

Forcibly relaxing the tension in his shoulders and hands, he stepped across the street and into the Tambourine. The man serving customers inside—dark-haired like Dierdre, with similar features—looked up with a smile.

"Can I help you?"

"I'm looking for Dierdre," Marcus said tightly. "She told me I could find her here."

PART IV

Seventeen

KARA KICKED IN THE DOOR, stormed into the flat she'd shared with Marcus in the Eld District for the last twelve years, and headed straight for the bedroom, touching the ley globe alight without thought. She'd known something was up, had known it for the past two years, but she'd ignored it . . . or tried to. But accidentally seeing him at the Tambourine, sitting at a table and laughing with that damned dark-haired woman—

She slammed open the trunk at the end of the bed, rifled through the contents, removed anything belonging to Marcus, then began searching the room for her own possessions. She packed her clothes in tight, tucked a few objects—the stone Ischua had given her, a blown glass bottle the woman on the corner had gifted her, a few well-worn books from Cory—into the side, then stood, hands on her hips, and scanned the rest of the room.

The bed sheets were tousled as usual, a few random clothes hanging from a chair or the corner of a table. The posts where they hung their purple Wielder's jackets were empty, although she didn't think Marcus had been wearing his at his . . . meeting; she'd come from the node and her stint in the pit with the ley, so she had hers on. The table to one side was littered with trinkets gathered or given to them from around Eld—necklaces of beads, a Gorrani sash, a pair of jade earrings that Kara retrieved and tossed in the trunk—for services rendered or simply because they were Wielders. An empty mug rested beside a plate full of crumbs from a hasty meal. More clothes were stacked on top of additional trunks, but there was nothing on the walls except a trailing vine painted in one corner long before they'd arrived.

Satisfied she'd missed nothing, Kara closed the trunk and hauled it out into the main room, letting it fall with a thunk, then began collecting items from the kitchen. Her favorite cup and saucer for tea, the packets of expensive jarkeeling from the southern continent, plates, the earthenware bowls she loved, the mug that was really Marcus' but she wanted anyway, and some of the rice and beans, just because—all of it added to the trunk. She did a run through the main room, picking out a few odds and ends, then moved to the window and stared out into the back gardens below the building, where the neighbors had planted herbs, tomatoes, peppers, and corn. Peas climbed strings running up the far wall, the one receiving the most sunlight during the day. She crossed her arms over her chest and waited, her anger growing as the sun shifted. A Gorrani woman appeared, face covered in a bright scarf, her two small children in tow. They giggled and cavorted as she tended the garden, then were herded back inside.

She heard Marcus in the hall outside, his voice loud as he spoke to someone downstairs, so she stood facing him when he entered. He noticed the trunk blocking his way first, then her standing at the window. Confusion flickered in his eyes, followed by irritation, then anger. He tossed his jacket over the trunk.

"What's this?"

"My things," Kara said, lifting her chin. "I'm leaving."

"I see. Make certain you leave the key." He stepped around the trunk and into the kitchen, plates rattling as he began preparing dinner.

Coldness sank into Kara's gut at the flippant response and she flinched. But he'd meant it to hurt. It was how he controlled her, controlled everyone around him. He would hurt her, then claim she'd hurt him first, and she'd feel guilty because she'd never intended to hurt him. She'd apologize, or break down and cry, and he'd comfort her and tell her he loved her and everything would be all right, and then somehow whatever had prompted the argument would be lost and forgotten amid all the emotions; they'd continue on as usual, nothing changed, nothing fixed. She knew it because it was how all of their arguments had ended the last few years.

But not this one. She crushed the hurt and stoked her anger.

"The key's already in the kitchen." She moved forward and grabbed his jacket, tossing it to the floor. "I only stayed long enough to let you know I was leaving."

"Why stay at all? You've obviously been thinking about this for a long time." He appeared in the door, cup in hand, and watched her struggle with the trunk. "I don't think you really want to go."

She glared at him, gave up trying to lift the trunk, and opened the front door instead, grabbing the trunk by one handle and dragging it across the floor.

"You're wrong," she huffed, already feeling tears beginning to burn at the corners of her eyes, even though she'd vowed she wouldn't cry. "I'm done. I don't want to compete with her anymore."

Marcus looked honestly confused, but then his eyes widened and he pushed away from the wall. "You mean Dierdre?"

"If Dierdre is the black-haired woman you met today at the Tambourine, then yes."

She didn't miss his guilty twitch.

"It's not—that isn't—Kara, Dierdre's nothing!"

"Nothing?" She'd managed to drag the trunk out into the hall, could feel at least two pairs of neighbors' eyes on her where she stood, her chest tight from exertion and pain. "You've been meeting with her off and on for the past two years at least, and you never mentioned her. You've spent more time with her at cafés and taverns than you have with me. That's not nothing. So tell me what it is?"

Marcus, his blondish-brown hair ruffled and out of place, his blue eyes cold and concealing, said nothing.

Kara glowered, clenched her jaw, and reached for the trunk again, hauling it down the hall. It felt lighter now, her anger taking over almost completely, but she still couldn't lift it by brute force.

"Kara," Marcus said, but she ignored him, heading for the stairs. "Kara!"

She turned back, let him see her rage, even though she knew her eyes would be rimmed with red and her face splotched. "What?"

He stood in the door to their loft, body tense. For the first time during one of their arguments, he appeared lost. He groped for a response, but the hardness in his expression never changed.

Finally, he said, "It isn't what you think."

She answered by jerking the trunk down the first step with a solid thunk.

A wave of sickening despair hit her when she reached the street, but she sucked in a deep breath and held it, used it to keep back the pain and the tears both. She needed to think. She needed somewhere to stay, somewhere away from Marcus, a place he wouldn't look for her right away, until she could get settled. A move to another district might be best, but she wasn't familiar enough with housing in any of the others to know where to go or who to speak to, not even the five districts she'd worked since the Primes had started transferring her every two years in preparation for becoming a Prime herself. Hedge—and Tallow, her current district—would likely be the best options. She knew their streets intimately, but not the Wielders who worked there or the citizens who lived there, even though she'd dealt with them on a daily basis for four years combined. Her strongest ties were still in Eld. The nearest districts—Stone, Green, Leeds, and even Confluence—were mostly main thoroughfares in her head, the only points of interest their nodes and ley stations. That was how the Primes wanted it—distinct and separate, no one Wielder familiar with enough of the ley system to be able to map the whole. Even though she'd worked more than one district, her picture of the ley was still fractured, none of the districts where she'd worked adjacent to each other. But Marcus knew Eld as intimately as she did. He'd know all of the places she might run.

Except possibly one.

"Cory."

She chewed on her lower lip, uncertain she wanted to risk giving Cory the wrong impression. They'd met on numerous occasions, but her relationship with Marcus had kept them distant. She knew he still had feelings for her. But she couldn't think of anywhere else.

She contemplated the trunk. She couldn't drag it all the way to Confluence.

"Need help with that?"

Glancing up, she met the speaker's eyes. She didn't recognize him, but he had a horse, a cart full of musk melons, and a nice smile.

"I'm headed toward Confluence. Is that out of your way?"

The man shrugged. About forty years old, his hair was streaked with gray, wrinkles just beginning to form around his eyes and mouth. "Doesn't matter. One of you Wielders saved my boy from one of those distortions a few years back. If it hadn't been for that, he'd be dead."

He hopped down off the cart, shifted some of the melons around, then hefted the trunk into the back, grunting with its weight. Dusting off his hands, he motioned her onto the seat and climbed up beside her.

"Where to?"

"Moat Street, on the edge of Eld."

The man nodded. "I know it. Outside the walls of Confluence and the University." He hied the horse into motion, the animal flicking its ears as it struggled forward under the new weight, and they merged with the traffic on the street.

He didn't ask any questions as they made their way down from the nest of streets surrounding the node into the less tangled section surrounding the walls that partitioned Eld from Confluence, but he kept up a steady stream of light conversation, as if he sensed the tension thrumming through her body. Kara let him ramble, realizing he didn't expect her to respond. She wondered if her misery was that easy to spot and scrubbed at her face self-consciously. Her fury had ebbed, simmering low and deep, replaced with a hollow emptiness. She felt untethered, listless, the juddering of the cart on cobbles somehow remote, even though it rattled her bones. What would she do now? Where would she go? She didn't want to move to Tallow. The streets were rough, the residents mostly Gorrani who'd moved in after the candlemakers that gave the district its name had moved out. The Gorrani had different views on women and their place in society; they only tolerated Kara because she was a Wielder. No, not Tallow. Besides, her two-year stint in Tallow was nearly over. She needed to stay in Eld for now. But what if she ran into Marcus on the street? What if she had to work with him? She shuddered, revulsion and rage spiking, twisted with a pang of longing and loss.

"Which way?"

She jumped when the man touched her arm and suddenly realized he'd been speaking to her. They'd reached Moat Street, the wall that had once been the limits of ancient Erenthrall—back when it was nothing more than a town and a baronial estate—rose before her, one of its gates standing wide as people streamed in and out around them. She glanced toward the old stone of the gate's arch and noted the crest at the apex—a horse rampant, the tertiary gate—and oriented herself. "Left. It's only a few streets beyond the gate."

Twenty minutes later, the man waved as his horse cantered off down Moat Street, leaving Kara at the bottom of a short flight of steps leading to another set of flats. The building was old, perhaps as old as the walls themselves, but nearly everything this close to Confluence was.

Made of quarried granite, with small windows and carved sills, intricate stonework edging the roof, Kara thought it must once have been a trading house. She glanced down the street, noted the University scholars in their variegated tan- and dun-hooded robes mixed in with the regular inhabitants of Eld, then sighed and dragged her trunk up the steps and into the building. Cory lived on the second floor.

By the time she'd reached his landing, she was sweaty and the anger had returned. She was not surprised to find Cory was not home.

Hours later, she heard the door below open and feet trudging up the stairs. She raised her head and watched as Cory emerged on the landing, his dirty blond hair too long and curling out from the sides of his head. His brow was furrowed in thought and he didn't notice her until he'd almost reached the door.

"What in hells—" He jerked back, nearly dropping the books and papers he carried in one hand. He caught them with an awkward grab and curse, then straightened as Kara stood. "Kara? What are you doing here?"

"I didn't know where else to go. I left Marcus."

Cory's gaze dropped to the trunk and Kara watched the emotions cross his still boyish face, even though he was now twenty-five— puzzlement, realization, a sudden spike of hope and glee carefully hidden beneath a thick layer of genuine concern. "I see." They stared at each other a moment, the air between them crackling with the unaddressed, impulsive moment on the rooftop fifteen years before when he'd kissed her, and then Cory ducked his head and shifted the weight of the books so he could reach out and touch the lock of the door. Kara felt a knot of tension in the Tapestry loosen and release. Cory opened the door and held it, motioning her inside with his head. "Come on in."

She pulled her trunk in behind her.

The flat comprised two rooms. The first large, with an area to the side that served as a kitchen, chairs around a table covered in papers and books in the center, another table against the far wall beneath a window serving as a desk. A door led to the second, what Kara assumed was a bedroom. Even though she and Cory had stayed in touch during her years at the college and her time as a Wielder, she had only ever met him here once or twice before heading out to a local tavern or café.

Cory crossed the room and dumped his books and papers on the chair to the desk while she hovered by the door, glancing around at the mess. It wasn't the same type of mess left by Marcus, with clothes left lying and dishes sitting unwashed. Everything was in its place here except the books and papers, materials she assumed Cory needed for his graduate studies at the University.

"Would you like something to drink? Or eat? I'm not certain what I have. . . ." Cory moved into the kitchen and began searching through drawers and cupboards. The Tapestry pulsed as he set a kettle onto the ley's heating stone. "Grab a seat."

"They're all covered in books."

She caught Cory's wince from the corner of her eye. "Oh, don't worry about that. Just move it out of the way. I'm certain I'll be able to find what I need again later."

He didn't sound certain, though. Kara shifted into the room, the old wooden trading floor creaking beneath her, and freed one of the chairs around the table of its burden.

"So, um . . . what happened?"

Kara leaned back heavily. "I saw Marcus with that black-haired woman again."

"Oh." The kettle began to rattle. "What are you going to do?"

Kara's chest tightened. "I don't know. I can't go back. I won't. Not this time."

"But you'll still have to deal with him, right? You'll have to work with him, even if you're in Tallow."

"I know."

The kettle began to shriek. Cory lifted it from the stone and poured the water into a jug serving as a teapot. He dumped something into the jug, then picked up a cup and small bowl he'd filled with grapes and brought it over to the table, hesitating before setting them both down on top of some of the books and papers. Kara leaned forward and grabbed a handful of grapes.

"So what are you going to do?" Cory repeated, beginning to shift books off the table to make room for the tea.

Kara picked up one of the pages and stared at the scrawled notes. "Not much I can do. My stint at Tallow is coming to an end in another few months. Hopefully, the Primes will transfer me to a node away from Eld—North Umber or Plinth perhaps. Some place where I can move and live without fearing for my life. At least I know Marcus will be stuck in Eld." She frowned at the paper she held. "What's this? It looks like it has something to do with the ley, but no one at the University is allowed to manipulate the ley. Not in any significant way."

Cory snatched the paper from her. "It's nothing. Something my mentor and I are working on. Ignore it." He shuffled it into another stack of papers and dropped it all to the floor nervously, not meeting Kara's eyes. "The tea should be ready."

She watched as he strained it back into the kettle, then brought it over to the table and settled down into his own chair.

"Can't you request a transfer to a particular node? Or even ask for one away from Eld? I don't see why they wouldn't take that into account."

Kara scoffed. "You don't understand the Primes. They're too damned protective of the Nexus and their power. They don't care what's happened between Marcus and me. They don't care about any of the Wielders. We're worker bees to them. They don't even listen to us when we tell them that the distortions and the recent blackouts in the ley are caused by overuse. They're suspicious of everything that the Wielders do and barely allowed us to repair the distortions when they first began appearing. Only the Baron and common sense forced them to see that there weren't enough Primes to handle all of the distortions. They aren't about to listen to my own personal problems and take those into account when deciding what node I'll be shifted to next."

"Are you certain? Has anyone ever asked?"

Kara drew breath to retort, but caught herself. "Not that I know of," she finally admitted.

"Then ask. It couldn't hurt. The worst they can do is say no."

She plopped a few more grapes in her mouth, chewing on the bitter seeds, then sighed. "I still don't have a place to stay for the next few months."

Cory stilled. The possibilities hung in the air, awkward and potent, and she girded herself to reject his offer to move in with him, but he surprised her.

"I know of a few places that are available. One of them is even near where we used to live."

Her relief was palpable. By Cory's grimace and lowered eyes, he'd noticed. She hated herself for it, but said, "That would be great," and reached for the tea.

Cory stood abruptly. "You can stay here for the night and we'll see about the other place tomorrow. Right now, I think we both need something stronger than tea."

Cursing herself, but not knowing what else to do, Kara agreed.

Kara spoke to Karl, the current senior Wielder at the Tallow node, about her upcoming transfer. He was skeptical, but said he'd bring the issue to the Primes' attention. For the next few days, he paired her up with Yvar for the street work. He squeezed her shoulder in sympathy as she left his office. Yvar was a quiet girl, competent but uninteresting. Patrols were uneventful.

She spent her time off with Cory, settling into the flat he'd talked about and drinking at The Golden Oak, a tavern near her place that refused to use the ley for heat or cooking, even though the use of hearths was a fire hazard that most of those living in Erenthrall refused to risk. Eld was one of the only districts where it was still allowed.

She saw Marcus twice, both times from a distance. The second time, he was with Dierdre again, both of them walking down Carver Street, heads together in intense conversation. Kara ducked into a shop selling shawls from the Archipelago, the colors bright enough to hurt her eyes, the scent of perfume cloying. She caught a snatch of their conversation as they passed the open door, something about shifting the pattern of refraction . . . and then they were gone. Kara's chest had tightened so hard she thought she would choke and she fled the shop as soon as she could, sucking in the fresh air outside to steady herself. She wiped her eyes fiercely, cursing the heavy, biting fragrances of the shop, and headed back to her new flat.

As she closed the door behind her, glancing over the sparse furniture, the scattered odds and ends she'd managed to unpack from the trunk, and the empty room with the large windows that gave her a spectacular view of the towers of Grass and the city between and beyond, a wave of loneliness overcame her. She shrugged it off by moving to the kitchen to boil water for rice, her hands trembling as they held the pot.

The next day, Karl informed her that the Primes had responded. She was no longer part of Tallow; she'd been transferred to Stone. Her heart sank. Stone was adjacent to Eld; she'd be closer to Marcus than she had been for her last two assignments. She'd likely have to work with him because Stone and Eld cooperated in so many ways when it came to the ley.

As she sank into a nearby chair in despair, a bitter laugh escaped her. At least she wouldn't need to move. The flat Cory had found for her would be perfect for working at Stone, and moving to Stone wouldn't push Marcus any farther away.

She ignored the niggling relief that prickled her skin.

She'd enjoyed the last few days with Cory far too much.

Marcus started when Dierdre's hand gripped his own lying on the table outside the café.

"You're deep in thought," Dierdre said, squeezing his fingers. "What's bothering you?"

Marcus grimaced and pulled his hand from her grasp, then caught Dierdre's tight frown. A breeze tugged her dark hair over her pale face—stern, with harsh edges—but Marcus had to admit to himself that Dierdre had her own allure. He could see why Kara would mistake their meetings for liaisons.

He shifted uncomfortably in his seat as guilt spasmed through him, and answered Dierdre sharply. "It's Kara."

Dierdre sank back into her seat. "I see." Her words were as curt as Marcus' and they sat in mutual tension until Dierdre finally sighed. "Perhaps it's for the best."

"Why?"

"Because you and I and the Kormanley have important work to do. You can't be distracted—by her or anything else. If she's gone, you can focus on what matters."

When Marcus didn't immediately respond, she added with a sneer and narrowed eyes, "Unless you don't think the restoration of the natural ley matters anymore. Perhaps you think that Augustus and his Primes are right, that the ley should be abused and manipulated at the sole whim of our esteemed Baron."

"You know I don't believe that, especially after the Purge," he spat, loud enough a few of those seated near them glanced in their direction.

He lowered his voice and leaned in toward Dierdre. "The Baron, Augustus, and the Primes need to learn that they can't control us, not with the Dogs and not with the ley. But—" His vehemence faltered.

"But what?"

Swallowing back the lump constricting his throat, he said, "I just wish it hadn't cost me Kara. Perhaps I should have told her about you, about the Kormanley."

Dierdre grabbed his upper arm hard, her frown severe. "You said yourself we couldn't tell her. The Kormanley would love to have one of the Primes sympathetic to our cause, but if we can't trust her. . . ."

"The Kormanley killed her parents. And the Dogs killed her friend and mentor, Ischua, during the Purge, in the Kormanley's name. She'd never get past that. Even if I could convince her that we aren't violent anymore."

"Then you have to let her go. You can't risk what we've started for her sake. Sacrifices have to be made. Think of all of those who died during the Purge. Think of all of those the Dogs slaughtered, Kormanley and innocent alike, because of their fear. We're doing this for them, to avenge them, to make their sacrifice meaningful. We can't do this without you."

Marcus stared into her eyes, drew strength from the conviction he saw there, used it to quash the guilt and heartache over Kara beneath his own resolve. He knew what the Kormanley were attempting was right. The Baron and the Primes were out of control, were overreaching themselves in their greed and lust for power. The distortions had been the first sign, but they'd chosen to ignore it. It was time to force them to face their creation, to see how little they really controlled.

He reached out and covered Dierdre's hand with his own. "What do you need me to do next?"

Eighteen

KARA WALKED INTO the Stone node and halted, glancing around the front room. It was surprisingly similar to Eld, the interior nearly identical, although it had been built of a reddish stone like the rock of the outcroppings to the west. Both Hedge and Tallow had been significantly different, although both still had the central pit that allowed direct interaction with the ley lines.

A group of three Wielders were standing over a worktable in the room beyond the small foyer, pointing and arguing over a couple of maps. Kara halted in the doorway and watched until one of the Wielders—a woman with short-cropped brown hair and intense dark eyes—saw her. The dark-eyed woman made a motion with her hands and the other two, an older man with gray-streaked brown hair and another woman about the same age, cut off and turned toward Kara.

"Can we help you?" the dark-eyed woman asked, her voice irritated.

The older man straightened. "Illiana, behave. You know we have a new Wielder arriving today. Are you Kara Tremain?"

"Yes, I've been transferred here from the Tallow node."

"So we've been told."

"What did you do? Piss off your senior Wielder?" Illiana crossed her arms over her chest, one eyebrow raised. "Sleep with him, perhaps?"

The other woman quirked a smile, but the older man rolled his eyes and stepped forward to shake her hand. "Ignore her. Although you'll probably get numerous questions about why you were transferred early, and why you've been transferred so often. I'd suggest you come clean as soon as possible, or the speculation will run rampant. I'm Steven, the senior Wielder here. This is Illiana and Savion, the senior Wielder in Eastend."

Savion nodded with a quick greeting, but Illiana's eyes narrowed. "You still haven't answered my question."

Kara bristled. "I asked for an early transfer for personal reasons."

"So you *did* sleep with him!"

"I did not sleep with Karl."

Illiana pouted, still eyeing her. "Maybe not with Karl, but you slept with someone. That's always what 'personal reasons' means."

Steven glared at her. "Are you finished, Illiana?"

She hesitated, then growled, "For now."

Savion motioned Kara to the table. "We were discussing the recent blackouts that have been occurring throughout Erenthrall."

When Kara drew close enough to see the map, she realized it was highly detailed, streets marked off with black lines of varying width, the thickest representing the major thoroughfares, the thinnest alleys and narrows. The Urate and Tiana were shaded in blue, different districts outlined in red. The ley lines connecting the stations were yellow, nodes and some of the smaller loci in orange. She had never seen a map with so many of the nodes and loci represented throughout the city, but she realized that all of those on the map were above ground and easily visible. Anyone, Wielder or general citizen, could have produced this map. The nodes and loci that were not easy to see—those known only to the Wielders who had worked in those districts and the Primes— were not drawn. Steven, Illiana, and Savion probably knew the ley system in Stone as intimately as Kara knew Eld, Hedge, Tallow, and the other districts she'd worked in, but none of them wanted to invite the Primes' wrath by displaying it on a map.

What caught Kara's attention, though, were the shadings that appeared at random around the city. She recognized the one that covered part of Eld.

"You've shaded all of the areas that have experienced a blackout?"

"And dated them," Steven said. "We've been trying to determine if there's a pattern to them, but so far we haven't noticed anything. What do you see?"

Kara leaned forward, wondering briefly if this was some sort of test. The blackouts had only begun a few years ago, with a street or small section of a district suddenly and inexplicably losing its connection to the ley, everything—ley globes, carts, barges—going dark and falling silent. The blackouts were sporadic—less of a nuisance than the appearances of the distortions, which had been a constant and growing threat since they first appeared—but the blackouts were relatively new, and were growing worse. Kara could pick out the few streets where the first blackouts had appeared on the map easily—Lavendar Street in Hedge and Murk Street in Eastend—because every Wielder had talked about them when they occurred. But the rest of the blackouts. . . .

Her eyes flickered across the map, her mouth pinched, as she realized their extent. She hadn't been paying that close attention to them, too caught up in those that were affecting her own districts . . . and her own personal problems. But now, seeing it laid out so completely, she realized that nearly every district had been affected at some point, a few sections more than once. She traced the progress using the dates scribbled near each shading, then leaned back.

"I don't see any pattern except that the blackouts appear to be worsening over time. The first few affected only a few streets, but the most recent have plunged entire sections of a district into darkness. The most recent in East Forks covered a third of its area."

"That's all that we've come up with as well," Steven said with a sigh. "Did those in your other districts have any theories as to what was causing them?"

Kara shook her head. "Nothing except the usual overuse of the ley system, which we've been complaining about since the distortions began nearly fifteen years ago."

She thought of Marcus, the most adamant Wielder in Eld regarding the misuse of the ley. He'd fought the Primes on the issue repeatedly. His protests had died down during the Purge, when the entire city had been held siege by the Dogs, everyone afraid that one of the Hounds would be sicced upon them, or that the Dogs would appear and drag them off to the Tower. But Marcus' protests had begun again with the first few blackouts.

Steven grimaced. "The Primes have denied that theory as soundly and flatly as they can. Trust me, it's been brought up by the senior Wielders at the Nexus more than once."

"So either they're lying—" Savion began.

"Or they don't know what in hells is going on," Illiana finished. "This is useless. Leave it to the Primes. We have work to do."

"Very well. Why don't you take Kara out on your patrol, help her get to know the Stone District a little better."

Illiana shot Steven a betrayed look, then huffed and glared at Kara. "Follow me."

Illiana was shorter than Kara and moved fast. She led her around the node, showing her the pit and the Wielders' rooms, for those who chose to stay at the node instead of finding their own rooms elsewhere. The layout was the same as at Eld, except the Wielders' rooms were on the opposite side of the node.

As soon as they stepped back onto the streets outside, Illiana's mood changed. She smiled up into the sunlight, breathed in the fresh air, and then caught Kara's startled look and smiled. "Steven knows that I prefer working patrol rather than being stuck down in that gods-forsaken pit for hours on end. But I wouldn't want him thinking I appreciated it, now would I?"

Laughing, she led Kara into Stone.

They worked the main streets first, Kara laying out the main thoroughfares and branches in her head. Some she knew from traversing the city on her time off, with Marcus or Cory or the other Wielders, but she suddenly realized she hadn't roamed away from Eld much. As soon as Illiana turned off of the main streets, she grew lost. A bell tolled, marking midday, the sound jarring and unfamiliar. She'd spent so much time in Eld that she no longer really heard the various sounds that marked out the length of the day there. Illiana saw her jump and frown and halted at the next intersection.

"Give it a moment," she said when she caught Kara's confused look. "The mason's belfry is always a few minutes late."

Before she'd finished speaking, another bell rang out, this one closer, but with a deeper intonation. As it faded, Illiana turned down the next street and motioned Kara to follow.

"You'll get used to the bells," Illiana said. "As you've probably noticed, the streets are different here than in Tallow as well."

"They're curved more, and wider. Tallow doesn't really have streets, more a complex network of alleys and one-lane streets that barely allow horsecarts through. Before that I was in Hedge, which is like Eld. Both of their layouts are gridlike, the streets straight for the most part."

Illiana grinned. "That's because Stone wasn't quarried and laid out like Eld or Hedge or any of the other districts. It was created by the Primes, when they were first experimenting with the ley, before the Nexus, when the ley was channeled naturally. There used to be streets like Eld here and buildings mostly made of wood. But then there was a great fire and the entire district burned down. No one knows how many lives were lost. When the Baron ordered the district rebuilt, no one wanted to use wood and so he made the Primes come up with another option. They figured out how to mold stone, how to make it flow, and so the streets and buildings are more naturally curved. They could have forced the stone into more linear forms, I suppose, but I like how sinuous it is. Like currents in water, but frozen in place."

Illiana gestured with her hands, but it was the passion in her voice that caught Kara's attention. She watched her as she moved, realized Illiana was probably only a few years older than her, somewhere in her early thirties, although she looked younger with her lithe frame and shorter stature.

Then the Wielder halted, body going rigid with tension, the cool grin gone in the space of a heartbeat. Kara halted as well and without thought wrapped the Tapestry around her.

She felt the dissonance a heartbeat before Illiana said, "Distortion."

Illiana broke away, moving before Kara had pinpointed the location in the Tapestry. But she didn't wait, sprinting after the Wielder's thin form as she insinuated herself past the people on the street. They dodged carts and sidestepped wagons and traders with wares spilling out onto the sidewalk. Most of those who saw them coming stepped out of their way hastily, glancing toward the air in apprehension, but there was nothing to see yet.

But when they rounded a corner, Kara on Illiana's heels, they could suddenly hear the high-pitched intonation of a distortion beginning to form. Illiana cursed and motioned across the street to where it opened up into a small square. A large pool stood in its center, water spilling down the jagged ledges of rock from a fountain to one side. Children splashed at the pool's edge, parents nearby. Hawkers had set up makeshift tents around the square's perimeter. The entire plaza was filled with people.

"It's forming in the square," Illiana growled. "We'll never get everyone out in time."

"You warn them, I'll handle the distortion."

Illiana frowned at her, the high-pitched tone increasing in volume as she hesitated. Then she nodded. "Go!"

They split, Kara heading toward the sound and the dissonance on the Tapestry that grew even as she ran. It trembled all around her, and she noticed others not as attuned to the world beginning to glance up and look around. To one side, Illiana shouted a warning and Kara saw her climbing up onto the edge of the pool, motioning frantically. But the people were reacting too slowly. The distortion was going to form before they were ready. She could feel it in the vibrations in her skin.

She halted near the northern edge of the square, a black stone building rising before her, its sides glittering with quartz in the sunlight. Behind, people were beginning to panic, the high-pitched squeal of the distortion now audible to everyone. Illiana roared for them to move. Before her, the hawkers halted selling their wares, stared at Kara as she focused her attention on a point in the air above their heads, and then they and their customers scattered, leaving everything behind.

Kara drew in a steadying breath, another, and murmured under her breath, "Not a big one. About the size of a wagon."

She tested the dissonance, tasted the air around her, smelled a sudden acrid scent, like lightning, then took two careful steps backward.

And the high-pitched squeal ended.

Before she could suck in a breath in anticipation, the distortion opened. White light flared and then blossomed outward, whirling wide and wider, the arms spiraling out like a reverse vortex. Its colors were stunning, golds and oranges and reds with a hint of intense green at the edges. Its center formed about ten feet above the tents, and it expanded enough that it caught part of the obsidian building and the tops of the tents in its grasp.

And then it halted, the spiraling arms freezing in place. Kara felt reality within the distortion shatter, felt the world fracture, like ice cracking at the end of spring before a thaw. It set her teeth on edge.

But then it was over.

She let her pent-up breath out in a heavy sigh. No one had been caught in the distortion. Her heart began pounding again, hard in her chest. With every distortion she encountered, she relived the incident at the ley station with the seamstress and the bloody loss of the woman's hand. She'd saved countless lives since then—and lost a few as well—but it was that woman's face that haunted her, her shriek as she realized she'd been maimed.

She shoved the image aside with long practice and focused on the distortion, beginning to hum, the sound rumbling in her chest. The sound was unnecessary—none of the other Wielders used it—but it grounded her, the vibrations in her chest soothing. Behind her, she heard Illiana fighting her way through the crowd, demanding they step back and let her get close. But Kara didn't wait for her. She reached out with her senses and surrounded the distortion, began piecing reality back together again starting at the edges, even though part of it was locked inside the stone of the building and couldn't be seen. She didn't need to see it visibly; she used the Tapestry to sense its jagged edges. Like that first distortion she'd begun to heal, the fractures were intricate, interconnected, and deadly. But she'd had practice since then, knew what she was doing. The shards of reality inside the distortion began piecing themselves together under her guidance, merging back into the correct shape.

She had healed a third of the distortion by the time Illiana made it to her side, had nearly freed it from the building. A moment later, she felt the Wielder enfolding her, lending her strength without interfering, as Marcus had done so long ago. Her concentration wavered only a moment as she thought about him, the rhythm of her hum breaking, but she knew Illiana sensed the hesitation. She redoubled her efforts, Illiana watching her, judging her. For a brief moment, she felt like she was back at the college, testing before one of the Masters.

She let the anger this thought sparked drive her. Behind, those in the square gasped as the distortion shrank, slowly at first, then faster, its edges rippling as if with heat. It pulled free of the building and Kara relaxed, certain now there would be no damage if it did collapse before she was done. But by the time it had shrunk to the size of her fist, Kara knew they would seal it before then. None of the signs of an imminent collapse were evident—the trembling of the spiraling arms, the resumption of motion, however small.

A few harsh breaths later, the distortion vanished, sealed away completely, reality restored. She staggered back, gasping, felt Illiana's hand at the small of her back, supporting her. She drew her sleeve across her face, surprised at the amount of sweat that stained the cloth. Her arms trembled with exhaustion, but it was a good sensation, like that after a long run, body weak but euphoric.

The crowd in the square—hawkers, patrons, parents, and children—broke into scattered shouts of approval, whistles, and applause. Those nearest swept in and clapped both Kara and Illiana on the back, a few of them thanking Illiana by name, others asking for Kara's name, having never seen her before.

In the midst of all of the activity, Illiana caught Kara with a considering gaze.

"Kara, huh?" She pursed her lips, then nodded. "You'll do."

Kara ran patrol with Illiana for the next three weeks, until her fellow Wielder finally threw up her arms in exasperation in the middle of a meeting at the node and shouted, "She doesn't need a nursemaid! She's better than half the Wielders here, Steven. Give her to Colt or Terry. I'm done with her."

The outburst might have stung if Illiana hadn't thrown Kara a wink and smirk as she stormed off, leaving a slightly stunned Steven behind. The senior Wielder had shrugged an apology to Kara and then ordered Colt to partner with her.

She'd been running with Colt for the last week. Younger than her by nearly ten years, he was skittish, but he knew Stone better than she did and had a firm grasp of the Tapestry and its uses. He wasn't polished yet—she'd been forced to support him too much when they'd run into the fist-sized distortion two days before—but he'd learn. His shock of brown hair and blue eyes reminded her of Marcus, but his stance and the way he ducked his head dredged images of Justin from memory.

Now, sitting across from him at a tavern as they waited for their trenchers of pork to arrive, ale already served, he looked up at her briefly and then away.

"Why did you wince?" he asked.

She reached for her ale in surprise. "I winced?"

He nodded. "You've done it a few times over the past week. And you get this distant melancholy look."

Kara stared down into her ale, then took a deep swallow before setting it down. "You remind me of someone I once knew, a young boy named Justin. You don't look like him, but you act like him. We went to school together, before . . . before the Wielders came to take me to the college."

"What happened to him? You wouldn't wince if something hadn't happened."

She sighed. "I don't know what happened to him. I convinced him and Cory—another friend—to take the ley barges from our home district to Shadow, even though our parents didn't allow us to leave Eld, and he disappeared. Cory and I searched for him for weeks after, but he never turned up. I saw him once after that, coming out of a tavern, but he ran away and I haven't seen him since, even though I've watched for him."

Colt remained silent a moment, watching her. "Do you want to run with someone else?"

Kara laughed. "No, Colt, I don't need to run with someone else."

He looked relieved and she shook her head.

Their trenchers arrived, the serving maid setting them down on the table with a thunk, knives and forks rattling. "Your food," she said, glancing at them both, then toward their glasses. "More ale?"

Before Kara or Colt could answer, the ley globes throughout the tavern flickered. Both of the Wielders glanced up with a frown, Kara automatically reaching for the Tapestry. Something surged around her, the globes sputtering in reaction—

And then they all went out.

Colt shoved back from the table and stood, eyes wide. Around the tavern, patrons cried out, a few muttered curses.

Their server merely glanced around with a frown. "What happened?"

"A blackout," Colt said, excitement tingeing his voice. He shot a glance toward Kara. "I've never experienced one before."

Kara sighed, contemplated the trencher with regret, sucked in the heady, thick aroma of the meat and gravy . . . and then stood. Taking another deep swallow of the ale, she turned to the server. "Save it for us?" At her nod, she motioned to Colt. "Come on. Let's see how extensive it is."

They emerged into the half-light of dusk to find the blackout extended up and down the street, but that the white glow of the ley could still be seen in the towers of Grass. Kara scanned the area, eyes narrowed, most of the citizens in sight looking around in confusion, a few shrugging and continuing on their way. A horsedrawn carriage rambled by, the clatter of the wheels on the cobblestones loud. She'd kept her senses extended on the Tapestry, but the warp and weave had settled. Yet her skin still tingled, prickling with dissonance. She could sense the ley line as well, throbbing with power, the station for Stone not that far away.

"Should we head back to the node?" Colt asked uncertainly.

She shook her head. "No, not yet. It's too far. The blackout might end before we get there. I want to see what we can find at the ley station."

Colt's eyes widened in surprise, but he fell in beside her as she took off for the station, cutting across the street, through an alley, and the square beyond. She stretched out her senses, trying to determine what had caused the blackout and how to repair it. None of the Wielders who'd been around during a blackout had found anything like the wrinkles or the rifts that caused the distortions, but something was affecting the Tapestry and the ley. Perhaps with access to the ley line itself, she could find out what.

As they came close to the ley station, Kara felt a sudden shift in the Tapestry around her, an escalation of the tingling against her skin. At the tavern, it had rippled, as if someone had grabbed its edge and snapped it, like shaking dust from a blanket. She could smooth out that dissonance around her, but it wouldn't hold, because the source of the disturbance was coming from elsewhere. She needed to find the source.

As they passed through the gates and into the nearest station, she sensed the ley line throbbing in its path. Normally that pulse was steady, soothing, somehow inherently natural. But now it felt . . . erratic.

The blackout had disturbed the ley line. Now that she was closer, its effects were worse.

She grimaced.

"Kara?"

She turned to Colt, realized she'd halted within the front doors of the station. Like the one in Eld, Stone's station had vaulted ceilings and tall, narrow windows on all sides, but instead of stone carved to resemble trees, here the ceiling hung with stalactites, giving the impression of a cave, especially with the ley globes dark and the room filled with shadows. People were standing around in the fading sunlight, a few pushing past her and exiting with irritated expressions, but mostly the station was empty. It was dusk. Nearly everyone had already returned home.

"Is everything all right?" Colt asked.

"The ley line," she said. "Can't you feel it? It's throbbing. It's giving me a headache."

"Thank the gods, a Wielder!"

Colt and Kara turned as one of the station's guards walked toward them from across the darkened mezzanine, his boots thudding loudly on the flagstone floor. He tugged at the long gray coat of his uniform, his gaze sliding over those nearest with a frown before settling on Kara. His eyes were a dark brown, beneath lighter brown hair with a sprinkling of gray throughout, his face hard, marked with a few scars, his stance rigid. When he spoke, his voice was rough, and his hand settled familiarly on the hilt of the sword at his side.

"Are you here about the line?"

Kara nodded. "I've come to take a look, yes, but I doubt I can do anything about it from here."

He looked her over with narrowed eyes, then grunted. "Come with me. I'll take you down to the pathway." He caught the attention of another of the station's guards waiting at the far end of the room, gave her a nod, then motioned Kara and Colt forward. He led them past an amorphous stalagmite growing from the floor, down a flight of wide steps, through a darkened corridor where their footsteps echoed against the stone walls, and onto the ley line's platform. There were fewer windows here, light slanting downward in shallow angles, most of the platform in shadow.

"We were hoping someone from the node would come," the guard said as they moved to the edge of the platform and halted. "Thankfully the main rush is over, most of the people home, but those who were here waiting when it happened are growing impatient. Enough I've sent someone to call in more guards. If you and the other Wielders could get the ley lines back up and running before they turn into a mob, I'd appreciate it."

But Kara wasn't listening anymore. She knelt down at the edge of the line's path, stared down into its depths with a frown. Like the bed of a river, the stone pathway stretched out to either side, nearly twice

Kara's height in depth and twice as wide. But she shouldn't be able to see the bed; the pathway should be flowing with the ethereal white light of the ley.

The ley lines formed the infrastructure of the entire ley grid, all converging at the Nexus. To see one of them empty, dead. . . .

Kara repressed a shudder.

She reached out with one hand to where the ley usually ran, reached out even further with her senses, saw the fine hairs on the back of her outstretched arm rise as she moved it back and forth. There were no barges at the platform at the moment, so she had a clear sightline down both sides of the path, but she wasn't using her sight as much as she was using the Tapestry itself, *feeling* the ley, letting it wrap around her.

The station guard knelt down beside her. "So can you get the ley back?"

"I don't have to get it back," Kara answered, still distracted. "It's still there, still flowing down the path. See?" She motioned to where the hairs stood up on her arm. "You can feel it."

The guard frowned, then tentatively reached out like Kara. His uniform covered his arms, but Kara saw the hair on the back of his hand rise. He shivered as his skin prickled with gooseflesh, then pulled his hand back sharply. Colt moved to Kara's other side and held out his own arm, swirling it around and watching his own body react, his face set with an intense concentration, his lips quirking up in a tight smile.

Youth, Kara thought, and shook her head. Always experimenting.

"Then why can't we see it?" the guard grumped. "Why aren't the barges working? We should have had a barge arrive five minutes ago."

Kara sighed, pulling her own arm back and resting her hands on her knees. "Because for some reason the ley has been . . . suppressed. Or dampened. There's something wrong with the flow, something obstructing it. Its power has degraded so far that it can no longer be seen."

"Unless you're a Wielder," Colt added.

Kara shrugged and stood. "Of course. Along with anyone else who has enough power. In any case, there's nothing I can do here. Whatever's keeping the power of the ley dampened isn't occurring here." She rubbed her forehead and stepped back from the edge of the platform, moving toward the corridor and the mezzanine beyond. The guard followed her, Colt staring out at the invisible ley line longingly before turning and catching up. "You should tell your passengers that the barges probably won't be working—"

Behind her, a sudden pulse rippled down the ley line, a force that shoved her from behind hard enough she gasped and stumbled on the steps leading up to the mezzanine. Colt and the guard reacted as well, the guard's hand falling to his sword, a hand's span of blade showing even as he ducked. But both of them froze as a line of crackling light surged through the chamber, a strange purplish-white, pressing outward from the line itself. Immediately after the purplish light passed through them and up toward the mezzanine—gasps and startled screams echoing down toward the platform—pure white light spilled down the path in a flood, the ley reestablishing itself, filling the chamber with radiance.

"—until the ley line returns," Kara finished with a frown.

The three stood motionless in the silence that followed, the ley globes hanging suspended all around them and up through the corridor flickering back on.

Kara turned to Colt. "We need to report back to the node."

When Colt and Kara hit the node, trenchers from the tavern in hand, they found their fellow Wielders standing, sitting, and pacing in the main room, faces pinched with worry, gazes darting toward the corridor that led to the barracks. Kara halted inside the entrance, felt the tension prickling the air, and immediately headed for Illiana.

"What happened?"

"There was a blackout—"

"We know," Colt cut in excitedly. "We were there."

Illiana shot him a cutting look, muttered, "Good for you," then turned her attention back to Kara, ignoring the hurt expression that crossed Colt's face. "Tanek, the idiot, decided to stay in the pit, even though he knew there would be a backlash when the ley was restored. He's in his room, carried there by Steven and being tended to by Chaz."

"How is he doing?"

"I don't know," Illiana snapped.

Kara bristled, but Illiana's concern was too strong for just a fellow Wielder. Tanek must mean more to her than that. "He'll be fine."

Illiana glared at her. "You don't know that. He was unconscious when Steven retrieved him from the pit. He could be burned out."

Kara held her gaze, noted the worry beneath the anger, and turned, taking Colt's arm to lead him away. His muscles were stiff beneath her hand and she realized he still felt wounded by Illiana. "Ignore her. She's afraid for Tanek. It had nothing to do with you."

He tensed, then relaxed in her grip. She let him go and they settled in to wait. They needed to speak to Steven, but she knew he wouldn't be approachable until he'd done whatever he could for Tanek. Colt dug into his meal, but Kara found she wasn't hungry anymore. She'd seen burn-out before, had come close to burning out herself when Devin and his two cohorts had shoved her into the pit. The victim's body was still alive, still breathing, heart pumping, eyes open, but there was no one there. Their gaze was vacant, the space behind empty. It was worse than death.

She couldn't imagine Tanek in such a state. She hadn't known him for long, but he was quick to laugh, easy to anger, his emotions open beneath his fiery red hair and freckled cheeks.

Two hours later, Steven emerged from the barracks' corridor, his face drawn. Illiana leaped up from her seat and he smiled wearily. "He's awake."

Illiana didn't wait for more, dashing past him and into the barracks beyond with a choked, "I'll kill him."

A few other Wielders followed her, sighs of relief and conversations breaking out on all sides. Colt stayed near Kara, who watched Steven accepting pats on the back and other nods of encouragement before he caught Kara's look.

His eyes narrowed, and as soon as he could, he approached. "Problem?"

"Colt and I were at the site of the blackout," Kara reported. "We went to the ley station and I touched the ley line."

Steven's expression became guarded. "What did you learn?"

"That the disruption that causes the blackout, whatever it is, isn't local. It's not being caused by a flaw in the Tapestry, like the distortions. There's some external force that's causing it. And whatever it is, it's somehow dampening the ley. It's a problem with the ley itself, with the flow of the lines. There's something wrong with the system, perhaps even something wrong with the Nexus."

Steven listened silently, gaze grim. After she finished, he flicked a glance toward Colt, who nodded confirmation, then toward the rest of the Wielders still hanging about idly, or waiting to see Tanek.

He motioned them toward a more secluded section of the room. "I'll have to report this to the other senior Wielders, perhaps even the Primes. But what you're saying corroborates what Tanek said. I didn't give his account much credence—he's still groggy from the backlash and isn't exactly coherent—but if what you say is true, and what he noticed while in the pit is correct—"

His lips tightened into a thin line.

"What did Tanek see?" Colt asked.

Steven hesitated, as if uncertain he should share any more, then shook his head. "He tried to trace the disruption up the line, back to its source. He'd nearly found it when the backlash hit. But he did sense something just before he blacked out. The ley hadn't been dampened. He said it felt more as if the ley had been . . . diverted somehow."

⌖

"Diverted?"

The word came as a low murmur, yet everyone in the Meeting Hall in the Amber Tower heard the Baron speak. The last large-scale attack of the Kormanley nearly twelve years before had cracked the amber wall of the room, but it hadn't affected the special acoustics of the chamber. Because of this, Arent had commanded the fissure remain intact, even though the Primes could have repaired it, as they'd repaired the balcony in the outer hall and the damage to the corridor and stairs at the entrance. He wanted those seated at the table—Prime Wielders, lords, ministers, directors, captains, and clerks—to remember that day, to remember the retribution he'd inflicted on the Kormanley afterward.

Power had shifted during the Purge, as lords and ladies vanished, either fleeing the Hounds or sucked into the maelstrom of bloody violence that followed as accusations of complicity flew. Arent knew that many had used his wrath as a way to gain political advantage, lying or merely insinuating collusions with the Kormanley that did not exist, but he hadn't cared. Baron Ranit had been killed in the initial attack, along with countless nobility from the surrounding Baronies, and the remaining Barons had demanded nothing less than a massacre. He had been more than willing to give it to them.

And the period of blood and brutality had worked. The Kormanley had been purged from Erenthrall, their taint rooted out. A few attacks had occurred during the Purge, but nothing on the scale of the attack at the Baronial Meeting. Within two years, there were no longer any attacks at all, and the massive riots had been quelled. The white robes, the symbol of convergence the Kormanley had adopted as a sign of the return to the natural order, the rhetoric of the priests on street corners—all of it had disappeared. Stability had returned to Erenthrall.

Until recently.

Baron Arent's hands gripped the arms of the seat so hard the knuckles were white, but he kept his rage in check, barely allowed it to color his voice, although everyone in the room flinched when he spoke.

"Diverted where?"

His gaze fell on Augustus.

Augustus stood in the deathly silence, his chair legs scraping backward on the amber floor. He folded his hands before him, composed his ancient features, his robe rustling. A tic at the side of Arent's mouth twitched. The Prime Wielder had aged in the past few years, his face lined and haggard, gray hair pulled back and tied at the nape of his neck. The architect of the Nexus had been kept busy as he and his Primes stormed through Erenthrall, establishing Flyers' Towers in all of the major cities. Not only in the Baronies, but in the surrounding nations to the east, west, and south as well. He'd even extended the ley network to the western and southern continents.

But the progress had come at a price, visible in the Prime's hunched shoulders and heard in the gravelly timber of his voice. Not even the life-extending properties experienced by submersing himself in the ley—as Baron Arent did too, with his own secret ley bathing chamber connected to his rooms—had been able to counter it.

The arrogance remained, though, an arrogance and pretension Arent had learned to tolerate. It was a fair price to pay for complete control of the ley.

"I'm afraid, my Baron, that we do not know."

"You don't know."

A statement, flat, no inflection whatsoever. If his seat had not been made of marble, the chair arms beneath his fingers would have cracked.

Augustus shot a glare toward Arent, nearly a challenge. "We don't know."

"How hard have you looked?"

"The better part of the last year!" Augustus barked. Everyone in the room flinched. No one raised their voice in this room, not with the Baron present.

Augustus closed his eyes and for the first time Arent began to wonder if perhaps he spoke the truth. He had not believed the Wielder ten months ago when parts of Confluence went dark, had been certain the Prime lied after East Forks.

But now a niggling doubt slithered beneath his anger, slid down into the core of his chest, down beneath his breastbone, and bit down hard. Perhaps this wasn't a power play by the Primes, as he'd assumed. Perhaps he'd let his hatred of the Primes—of his dependence on them for the continued use of the Nexus—color his judgment. The recent instability in the ley had only emphasized that dependence. If the ley were faltering. . . .

The thought sent a lick of fear in the wake of the doubt.

"—thought we'd backtracked the fluctuation in the Nexus that produced the outage in Confluence and East Forks," Augustus was saying in a tightly controlled voice. "It appeared that someone had tampered with the alignment inside the Nexus—"

"Who?"

Augustus' eyes narrowed angrily at the interruption. "I don't know."

Lowering his voice, Arent asked, "Who could have made such an adjustment? Who would have the power, the skills?"

Augustus stilled, lips pressed tight together. He didn't want to answer, even though everyone within the chamber knew. "Only a Prime could alter the alignment with such precision. Only a Master."

Arent straightened in his seat. "One of yours? One of the Primes?" You yourself, he implied with his tone.

Augustus struggled to choose his words as the rest of the Primes in attendance shifted uncomfortably in their seats. But finally he raised his head, saying grudgingly, "I would have argued otherwise until today. But now. . . . To make most of Stone, along with parts of Eld and Green, go dark, the alignment would have to have been changed from within the Nexus itself, and only Erenthrall's Primes have such access." He said nothing to Arent's unspoken accusation, but Arent saw that he'd heard it by Augustus' look.

"We have a traitor in our midst."

Everyone turned toward the new voice. The Primes straightened in fear. All except Augustus, who merely pursed his lips.

Arent felt the niggling doubt begin to grow, coldness seeping outward from beneath his breastbone, touching his lungs, his heart. "Captain Daedallen," he acknowledged.

The captain of the Dogs turned his gaze on Arent and the Baron's eyes narrowed.

"Everyone is dismissed except for Prime Augustus and Captain Daedallen."

Simple and clear, the command emptied the room within moments. As soon as the last person departed, Arent stood and descended from his seat, motioning Daedallen and Augustus to one of the wide windows. Sun slanted off of the amber floor, made it semi-transparent, the thick glass that protected them from the winds at this height perfect, without a single bubble or distortion, made so by the Tapestry and the ley. Arent sidled up to the glass, stared out from the height at the surrounding towers of Grass.

And in the center of them all. . . .

Arent turned his attention to the heart of Grass, where he could see the nearly blinding, pulsing white light of the Nexus. He knew a building stood in the center of that white light, although he couldn't see it. The heavy, thick crystal of the dome that covered the Nexus amplified and intensified the light, making it impossible to see into the Nexus from above.

Behind him, he felt Augustus halt a few paces away, knew that Daedallen stood behind the Prime, ready in the event Augustus did anything . . . interesting. Although now Arent thought that possibility slim; he believed in Augustus' sincerity, even though he knew Daedallen had his own suspicions.

"If you have been searching since the incident at East Forks," Arent said calmly, "then you must have discovered something. I find it nearly impossible to believe otherwise."

Augustus heard the warning. And the threat that underlay the simple words. "Of course, my Baron."

"Who?"

"As I said, I don't know. One of the Primes, assuredly, but—"

Arent turned, stopped Augustus with a look. The Prime had heard the threat but he'd ignored it, too secure in his power over the ley, in the city's reliance on it. In the Baronies' reliance on it and, steadily growing, the nations beyond. Which is why Arent had grown to hate the Primes; he knew he relied on their cooperation too much. The Wielders had grown so strong that he was no longer certain the Dogs were enough to keep them in check, to keep them complacent. Even after the viciousness of the Purge.

Arent tried not to grind his teeth at Augustus' knowing face.

"You misunderstand me," he murmured. "On purpose, I think."

Augustus merely straightened, so Arent continued, turning away, back toward the cityscape.

"One of the Primes, yes. But even a Prime would not attempt something of this magnitude alone. They have nothing to gain from it. They must be aiding someone else, and there are only six others within the Baronies who would dare to meddle with the ley lines. They are the key to the Baronies' dominance of the continent, to the known lands beyond. Only six would have the means and the ability to infiltrate the Nexus, to place one of their own within its walls. It must be one of the Barons." Arent drew in a steadying breath, anger and fear so close to the surface that he could hear it vibrating in his voice. Once again, as with the Kormanley, it came back to the Barons. Except this time, the attack was more subtle, harder to deflect, harder to discern. He would have to rely on the Primes, on their cooperation, when their allegiance was already in question.

But he could not let Augustus see that doubt, that fear.

"So I ask you again," he said, voice quiet but firm. "Who?"

Augustus shook his head. Arent could see his reflection trembling in the glass before him, knew that it was not in fear of his Baron, nor fear for his life, but anger. Anger that someone had dared to disturb his Nexus, had dared to upset his balance of power.

"I don't know for certain," the Prime Wielder rasped, his breath barely a whisper. "The disruption came from the south, so one of the southern barons."

"Who?" Arent repeated, with force.

Augustus sighed. "If I had to choose a prime suspect, I would say Baron Leethe."

Nineteen

"AUGUSTUS HIMSELF COULD be the one who adjusted the alignment," Daedallen muttered as Augustus stormed out the door of the chamber, leaving them alone.

"I don't believe so. He's too visibly angry to be the traitor himself. No. Someone has infiltrated his Nexus, has intruded onto his exclusive domain, and he wants to know who as much as I do. He will spend all of his energies finding the traitor and figuring out a way to stop them—of stopping Leethe—of that I'm certain."

Daedallen considered the vacant doorway, mouth twisted into a frown, eyes narrowed. The expression accentuated the scars on his right cheek where a dog had mauled him; it made his face dark and ugly.

He turned back to Arent. "What do you want me to do?"

Arent placed his hand against the glass, felt its chill as he stared down at the glow of the Nexus, brow furrowed. "One of the Barons is meddling with powers they have no right to touch. I need to know which one. Send the Hounds to all of the Baronies, not just the southern ones. Tell them to find out which Baron has betrayed us. And what that Baron is doing with the ley. With *my* ley."

At Daedallen's silence, he looked over his shoulder. "You wish to say something?"

"We already know it is Baron Leethe," Daedallen growled. His anger was barely restrained, his hand flexing near his sword. "We've known he works against you since his miraculous escape from the Amber Tower during the Kormanley attack. We should have sent the Hounds after him then!"

"Baron Leethe was behind the Kormanley, yes. But the Barons banded together after the attack in the tower. If one of them had died at the hands of a Hound, nothing would have stopped them from tearing Erenthrall down stone by stone." Daedallen bristled, but Arent cut him off. "You know we cannot stand against their combined forces, even with the Wielders under our control. The Barons would overwhelm us. I barely managed to distract them from their rage with the Purge here in the city. By the time that ended, there was no longer a reason to release the Hounds. The Kormanley attacks had ended."

Daedallen's jaw clenched and he turned away.

Arent sighed and forced himself to relax. "You know all this. We've had this argument before. We cannot take Baron Leethe down unless he stands alone. His death, suspicious or not, would only drive the Barons into an allegiance against us. I spent too much time using the Hounds and the Dogs to break the Barons down and seize control in my youth to let it all fall apart now. And I am not convinced he is acting alone. He may have one of the other Barons behind him already, perhaps Calluin. I need to know who he is working with, and what it is they intend to accomplish by disturbing the ley. Enough time has passed that I feel the Hounds can find this out for me, without rousing the Barons from their complacency."

Daedallen considered this in silence. He clearly wanted to protest, but refrained, asking instead, "And what of the traitor here? The Prime?"

Arent grimaced and shoved away from the glass, motioning Daedallen to fall into step beside him as he exited the amber Meeting Hall at a slow walk. "We don't have access to the Nexus, to the Primes and their inner workings. We'll have to leave finding that traitor up to Augustus."

Daedallen's expression soured. "Even if he does discover who the traitor is, I don't trust him to reveal that to me. Or you."

"Then sic the Dogs on him. On all of them. Follow the Primes. Follow the Wielders if you want. Track their movements and find out who the traitor is yourself first.

"And when you find him, bring him to me."

The Hound stood on the station's platform, perfectly still, his eyes ranging over all of the passengers waiting for the next barge, taking in their clothing, their facial expressions, their scowls as they glanced up toward the sunlight to judge the time before craning their necks to peer down the pulsing white line of the ley, searching for the next barge. The station lay in Grass, so the clothes worn were fine, the women dressed in linen and silk, the men in tweeds and wools, not the coarse sackcloth of those from the lesser districts in Erenthrall. The Hound wore wool, in a quality a shade less than those around him, although no one would notice the distinction. His jacket hid the daggers at his wrists, the knives at his waist; the folds of the hood hid the bulge of the short blade strapped to his back.

Catching movement out of the corner of his eye, he turned, the motion measured, one hand sliding beneath the jacket, but paused when he saw the boy staring up at him. His shock didn't register on his face. Most people never noticed him. He made certain he blended in, his manner and demeanor forgettable, melding into the flow of the everyday around him, tweaking that unawareness with a push and a suggestion on the Tapestry. He'd trained for this, had excelled at it. The fact that the boy had picked him out of the surrounding bustle meant the boy had talents his parents would likely never realize and he would never use, talents the Hound had honed.

"Who are you?" the boy asked. He wore a small cap, his hands tucked behind his back as he rocked back and forth onto his toes and heels. His eyes were innocent and wide, staring up at the Hound in pure curiosity.

The fact he knew the Hound was different meant he was intelligent as well, even though he couldn't be more than eight years old . . . about the same age as when the Hound had been taken himself.

The Hound glanced toward the boy's mother, two steps away, her arms loaded with bundles and a basket, her attention on the ley line. He could take the boy now and she'd never know, steal him and return to the den with him so that the other Hounds could train him, mold him, teach him to use his talents, as the Hound had been taught.

But that wasn't his purpose at the moment. He had a task, one that could not be delayed. He had a scent and a destination: Baron Leethe in Tumbor.

The Hound turned back to the boy and smiled. "I am no one."

The boy frowned, brow furrowing, another question rising to the surface—

But a bell clanged, announcing the arrival of the next barge. It surged down the ley, faster than a horse and cart run wild, slowed suddenly, those on board lurching, and glided to the edge of the platform. Shaped like a ship but with a flat bottom like a raft, its side gates opened and people spilled forth, those on the platform stepping forward.

The mother turned sharply, her mouth pursed in irritation. "Sam, what are you doing? Come here, the barge has arrived."

She never looked up at the Hound. He doubted she even realized he was there, even when he motioned Sam forward. Hounds were not meant to be seen until it was too late.

The boy trailed after his mother as they climbed onto the barge, glancing back once. The Hound slid onto the same barge through a different gate, distancing himself from the boy, feeling the presence of the ley throbbing beneath his feet.

When the barge lurched forward, picking up speed, all thoughts of the boy vanished. It would take merely four days to reach Tumbor by barge, a costly journey. But he'd been told speed was of the essence. What he would find there he did not know.

But he was prepared for anything.

Dalton lurched upright, a cry escaping his lips as the last tattered white remnants of his dream surged through and overwhelmed him. He flailed in the blankets wrapped around his arms and torso, trying desperately to escape the fear that seized his chest, his heart thundering in his ears. His legs swung free, out over the edge of the bed, and with another startled cry he tumbled out onto the floor.

He sobbed into the warmth of the blanket pulled tight across his lower face where he landed. His limbs trembled, as they always did now after a dream—with fear, with hatred, with terror.

He heard someone scratch softly at the door to his room, call out, "Father? Are you all right? I heard something fall." The door began to creak open.

He stifled his next sob, choked down its bitterness, and smoothed his pain-twisted face into one of harsh implacability. He wiped the tears and sweat from his cheeks with the blanket and began to untangle himself from its grip.

"Father?"

"Here, Dierdre," he said gruffly. He disliked the remaining members of the Kormanley calling him Father, but he couldn't get them to stop. But perhaps it was appropriate. The Dogs had been vicious in their Purge, seizing members of his cells with surprising rapidity, although with unsurprising brutality. His entire network had been on the verge of decimation when—after surviving his plunge into the Tiana to escape the Hound—he'd finally rounded up those few who had survived, like Dierdre, and sequestered them away with himself in one of the many caverns where the Kormanley had held their secret meetings.

Now, the remains of the Kormanley resided in the husk of a building in West Forks—Dierdre, Dalton, and three others. The rest of those Dalton had saved from the Dogs had scattered. Dalton dared not even contact the members of the original Kormanley. Many of them, including Ischua he'd discovered, had died in the Purge, mistaken for members of the more violent Kormanley under Dalton's command. Dalton himself rarely left the flat they'd taken over. Though twelve years had passed since the attack at the Baronial Meeting, he still feared a passing Dog might recognize him.

And his work was not done. The attack may have failed, his organization destroyed, but the Kormanley were not finished.

Dierdre gasped when she rounded the bed, kneeling to help him stand. "Father! Here, let me help. Was it another vision?"

He gripped her fussing hands and caught her gaze to still her. "Yes, another vision. More powerful than the last. But unchanged." Her concern deepened and she frowned. He tightened his grip. "I'm fine. I simply woke disoriented and fell out of bed."

Her eyes narrowed and she pulled away. "Don't tell the others that. Prophets don't fall out of bed." She busied herself by returning the blanket and smoothing it out. "You learned nothing new in this vision? Nothing to aid us?"

He considered, the fragments of the dream already fading, even if their intensity didn't. He swallowed against the terror even those wisps of memory evoked. "Nothing I can remember."

"Then the plan is unchanged? Marcus should proceed as ordered?"

Dalton considered, taking into account what he had been told by Baron Leethe and his own vision. Neither Marcus nor Dierdre knew that their actions were timed according to Leethe's wishes. After the failure of the Kormanley at the Baronial Meeting, Leethe, the Kormanley's longtime Benefactor, had withdrawn his support. Dalton had been furious, but in the chaos and terror of the years-long Purge that followed, he had not been able to act on that rage. By the time events within Erenthrall had settled and Dalton had hidden the remaining Kormanley here, in West Forks, Leethe had contacted him again with a completely different proposal, one more subtle and insidious.

Dalton would have declined had Leethe's plans not coincided with his own. He hadn't determined how he could use Marcus effectively yet, but Leethe's request gave him the direction he needed. He was only biding his time, using Leethe until he could put Marcus to his own uses. He didn't know Leethe's ultimate goal, but he knew that whatever it was, it didn't include Dalton's goals or the Kormanley's. The continued recurrence of his vision proved that. Baron Leethe's plans would destroy them as surely as Arent's and Augustus'.

He realized Dierdre was still waiting on his response, brow furrowed in irritation. His lapses into deep thought and riled anger were becoming more common. He needed to push the terror the visions invoked away and focus on stopping them from coming true.

"The plan is unchanged. Marcus' orders remain the same."

For now.

Kara felt the disturbance in the Tapestry as she reached for her morning cup of tea. She stilled, then looked up a moment before the soft, steady ley globes that illuminated her flat in Eld dimmed, pulsed bright once, and died.

They did not immediately flare back to life.

"Shit."

Her eyes adjusted slowly to the darkness of her kitchen. The faint light of dawn shone through the windows on the far side of the chamber, the sun barely over the horizon, but Kara closed her eyes, drew herself inward until she could sense the Tapestry surrounding her and the ripples in its layers, just like those of the blackout a week before.

She began to hum to herself, concentrating. An old verse, something she remembered from childhood, bringing with it the faint shriek of a child's laughter, the tightening of an adult's hand in hers, and the sharp scent of new-cut grass. Meadow grass.

The Tapestry around her reacted to the song. The ripples that felt so jarring to her senses spiked, then fell into sync, until the Tapestry smoothed and settled.

Kara opened her eyes, the globes now lit again, although the light was dull. She could still sense the blackout to either side of her but didn't push her correction outward to the surrounding rooms in the building. As she'd learned with the previous blackout, the problem wasn't with the Tapestry here, it was with the ley somewhere else. Anything she changed wouldn't hold once she let her concentration slip. Besides, this was Eld, not Stone. Upkeep in this section of the city fell to Marcus and his team.

"Marcus." She huffed out a short breath, but pushed the roil of anger and hurt aside. It wasn't as easy as she had hoped it would be.

Grabbing her tea, she moved toward the front windows, stopping to add something stronger to the drink on her way, something with bite, wondering how extensive the interruption in the Tapestry and ley was this time. But when she halted before the window, tea half raised to her lips, close enough she could smell the brandy she'd mixed in with it, the world outside was dark.

Too dark. Even with dawn breaking.

She frowned, not understanding, her brain sluggish this early in the morning.

Then she realized: the entire city was dark. The surrounding neighborhood, the Stone District beyond, even the high towers in Grass in the center of the city backlit by the rising sun—all of it, all of Erenthrall, dark. Only a few lights glowed in that darkness, probably from the homes of those powerful enough to manipulate the Tapestry and the ley themselves, like her. But everything else had gone pitch-black.

Including the Flyers' Tower.

"Shit," she breathed again, more heartfelt this time. A frisson of fear sliced through her chest like a knife, followed by a sickening sense of horror.

The flyers. How many would be operating at this time of day? Would their ley-saturated sails be enough to keep them aloft?

She spun toward the ley globes that hovered behind her. None of them had crashed to the ground during any of the previous blackouts, because the ley wasn't gone completely, merely dampened.

But the sky barges weren't ley globes.

Perhaps some of those lights in the city weren't from the ley.

Already dressed, she gulped down a slug of the bitter tea, winced at the brandy, then snatched up her Wielder's jacket and dashed out her door into the awakening city, letting her hold on the Tapestry in her own loft go.

Kara cut across Eld, moving swiftly. On all sides, the buildings that had once formed the heart of Erenthrall loomed dark, gray and brown stone now worn and gritty, blackened in places by old soot and water stains. All of them contained sconces for torches, posts for oil lanterns, and stacks where chimneys rose to the sky. But none of those were in use. Even the signal fires in the watchtowers of the University had been replaced by ley globes.

Now, with the Tapestry disturbed, everything was black, the buildings somehow forbidding.

Kara paused at a corner and listened. People had begun to stir, emerging into the dawn with muttered curses as they glared at the darkened streets, others standing in their bedclothes or breeches on their stoops or balconies, staring out over the city.

Far distant, she thought she could hear shouting and screaming.

Kara shook her head and turned the corner. She had to get to Stone, check in with Steven and find out what she could do to help.

A few more people were on the street here—a young man on a horse, talking to another man outside an opened gate; a street urchin hunkered in the shadows farther down; a baker. The baker stood outside his bakery, growling and shaking his fist at the sky.

He noticed Kara and her dark purple jacket before she could dodge across the street to avoid him.

"You! Wielder!" he shouted.

Kara frowned at his thick southern Gorrani accent. She slowed.

"I know the ley is out—" she began, but the baker didn't let her finish.

"How you expect me to make a living in this city with no oven, eh?

How you expect me to live?" He gestured toward the defunct street globes, then settled his thick fists on his hips. "What's wrong with you, you can't keep globes lit, can't keep heat on? My oven no work! I canno bake the bread to make my living!"

Kara came to a full stop two steps from him, where he blocked the walk, and glared up into his eyes. He was a foot taller than her, and twice as broad, his arms thick with muscle from kneading bread and hoisting the long paddles with dough on them into the ley-heated ovens all day. His Gorrani mustache dangled down both sides of his face, the thin line of his beard trimmed and running along his jaw in the traditional style. A true Gorrani then, probably new to the city, although he'd stopped wearing the ritual saber all Gorrani youth earned upon passing their trials. She had no doubt the saber was close at hand.

Her eyes skimmed toward the open door of the bakery, where she caught a fleeting glimpse of a Gorrani woman, shawl held across the lower half of her face, before she stepped out of sight. Someone had lit a lantern or candle inside, the light flickering warm and yellow against a back wall lined with sacks of flour and sugar and shelves of unmarked containers of spices.

Kara turned back to the man, met his angry gaze, and said, "Use your damned wood oven. In this part of the city, your bakery is bound to still have one."

Shock began to register in the man's eyes at her tone, but she'd already skipped to one side and headed across the street. He spat curses after her in his own language, one hand no doubt reaching for the saber he no longer wore—Gorrani men weren't used to being spoken to so rudely by women—but she ignored him, even when he shouted, "I dunno have no wood!"

Two blocks later, she heard someone shout her name. She thought the Gorrani had followed her, had already hunched her shoulders over and bowed her head, hoping he'd assume she hadn't heard him, when the person called again and she recognized the voice.

She halted and turned in surprise. "Cory! What are you doing awake this early, let alone out?"

Cory grimaced as he came up alongside her and they continued moving toward Stone. "My mentor, the wise and all-knowing, had a flash of insight last evening while slamming back the honey mead and we've spent all night working in one of the practice rooms. When we lost power, he nearly had a seizure." He rolled his eyes. "He sent me to find out what was going on, but when I emerged from the main hall, I realized that more than the University had been affected by the blackout. It looks like it's hit the entire city!"

"So naturally you came running to me."

Cory straightened, chin up, his dirty blond hair falling across his face. Even in the faint light, Kara could see his blush.

"You *are* a Wielder," he said.

"I only patrol one district, Cory, not the entire city. And I'm headed toward Stone now."

From the street ahead, a woman appeared, running toward them, her face blank, eyes wide in shock. She didn't see Kara until the Wielder stepped out in front of her, blocking her path.

She plowed right into her, Kara reaching to catch her. The woman struggled, shrieking and clawing, Kara trying to hold and calm her as she fought, but then suddenly Kara's purple jacket registered and the woman clutched at her and gasped, "The barge! My daughter!"

Kara didn't wait for more, disentangling herself and handing the woman off to Cory, who stood helplessly as she sagged into his arms and began sobbing. Kara leaped down the street, sprinting, her heart thudding in her chest and the cool air burning in her throat. She hit an intersection, paused, zeroed in on the sudden rise of smoke a block away—smoke that hadn't been there a moment before—and dodged to the opposite corner, shouting at the few stragglers to get out of her way.

When she rounded the corner, she drew up short.

For a moment, she found herself back among the destruction and chaos of the park when she was twelve, when the Kormanley had set off the wagons, people screaming in pain, in horror, thousands fleeing as the flames leaped toward the sky and the overhanging newly-launched flyers. The memory clung to Kara like spider silk, holding her stunned, as she'd been that day on that field, the sounds around her muted by the explosion, her mind unable to comprehend what had happened. Then she'd found her father, had rolled him over to find his face—

She shook herself free of the memory, forced herself to focus on the scene before her even as she heaved in a shuddering breath and suppressed the grief that threatened to choke her. Ahead, one of the sky barges had fallen from the sky, its prow gouging into the side of a stone building, tearing through its face as it plunged to earth and exposing the rooms within. Chunks of granite littered the street. The barge had come to rest on its side, deck tilted, the mast and the thick folds of the sail belling in a low draft. Bodies were scattered, most unmoving. At least five had survived and were standing or walking around listlessly. Two were lying on the ground: one woman screaming, her leg twisted at an unnatural angle; a husky man trapped beneath a portion of the mast roaring with pain and rage.

Somewhere within the building, or perhaps within the ship, a fire had started. Black smoke billowed around the prow into the sky but as yet there were no visible flames.

She hesitated. She should be headed toward Stone. This wasn't her job; this was something the city watch should handle. Or the Dogs.

But she didn't see any of them around.

Kara swallowed, her mouth dry, then swore, darted forward, and began checking bodies. The first few—two men and a woman—were dead, and she moved on, working her way toward the pinned man and the woman. She didn't see any sign of the panicked woman's daughter. She caught sight of some bystanders and yelled, "Don't just stand there, help them!" A young man started guiltily and leaped forward. Two more men followed, along with a stocky woman. Kara heard one of them shout, "This one's alive!" and caught sight of them dragging a girl away from the wreckage. She prayed it was the woman's daughter. The smoke had increased, although she still couldn't see a fire.

She made it to the man pinned beneath the mast at the same time as the young man. She noted his build—lithe but muscular—and motioned toward the length of the mast that had crushed the man's legs below the knees. His roars had died down as they approached, but his face was livid, his teeth clenched against the pain, breath coming in harsh gasps.

"Try to lift the mast and I'll drag him out," Kara ordered.

"Get it off me," the man growled between his teeth as Kara positioned herself behind him, grabbing him beneath the armpits. Tears were streaming down his cheeks into his beard and he moaned.

The young man straddled the mast and wrapped his arms around its bulk, knotting his fingers together underneath. He paused to brace himself, then heaved upward, legs straining, the cords on his neck standing out. His face turned red, then purple, and then he exhaled and staggered to one side, shaking his head.

"It's no use," he gasped. "It won't budge."

A drift of smoke passed between them and Kara shot a glance toward the barge. Flames were crackling along the length of the prow now, and the number of bystanders had grown, their murmurs louder and tinged with fear as the fire began to spread. She heard Cory barking orders, saw three men lift the woman with the shattered leg up into their arms and carry her to safety.

"Please," the man beside her begged hoarsely, clutching at her hands. "Please don't leave me here."

His eyes glazed over and he passed out, slumping back against her. He was heavier than she expected.

Kara frowned down at him, something brushing against her face. She pulled one hand free from beneath the man's body and pushed the fold of sailcloth away, then shouted, "Cory! The fire! Get everyone to tend to the fire! We can't let it spread to the nearby buildings!"

As soon as she saw his nod, already ordering the bystanders into action—where were the damned guards?—she turned her full attention back to the man with the beard.

"Should we get some of the others to help?" the younger man said, glancing nervously toward the fire. "Maybe if three or four of us lifted all at once—?"

Kara cut him off with a sharp shake of her head. "It won't work. The mast is too heavy." She gnawed at her lower lip, thinking furiously.

The heat from the fire began to pulse against the side of her face, making her sweat. The draft from the growing blaze pushed the sailcloth against her again and she shoved it aside in irritation.

Then twisted where she knelt, still holding the bearded man's body. She snatched at the sailcloth with her free hand, felt its coarse texture between her fingers.

The sailcloth.

She gestured toward the younger man. "Take my place. When I lift the mast, be ready to drag him free."

His mouth fell open, but at her impatient, "Do it!" he darted forward.

As soon as he had hold of the man's shoulders, Kara reached for the Tapestry, humming softly to herself. Smoke choked her, stinging her eyes, and she coughed and closed them, shut out the cries of everyone around her, the crackle of the flames that were steadily growing and the heat from the fire as it ate into the wood of the barge to her right. As she'd done in her flat, she pulled the Tapestry to her, sensed the ripples that were the effect of the blackout, and smoothed them out with the rhythm of her voice.

Calm spread throughout the area immediately around her, the radius of the effect growing. Back in her flat, she'd used it to relight the ley globes. But here—

She opened her eyes and caught her breath.

Here she needed it for the sails.

Ley light played through the cloth before her, sparkling among the heavy dark fabric like stars. As the ley spread, suffusing the cloth, the folds began to rise, lifting free against the drafts from the fire, parting the smoke. The cloth was still tied to the mast and the booms, and as it lifted the rope grew taut. She heard gasps around her, saw the young man's eyes widen, but she shoved those distractions aside and focused. The ley wasn't strong here, the blackout still in effect, and like the ley globes in her apartment it flowed sluggishly in the sails. As soon as the cloth was pulled tight, it halted.

There wasn't enough power to lift the mast.

She closed her eyes again and concentrated, pushing herself to refine her touch on the Tapestry, to smooth it out even further and to widen her radius so that more of the ley could be funneled into the sails. Sweat broke out on her forehead, began to trickle down her back, but she heard the creak of shifting wood, the straining of rope. Something within the barge groaned and shuddered; when her eyes flew open, she found sparks from the disturbed fire dancing in an updraft in a mad swirl.

And then the young man next to her hauled the bearded man's unconscious body back, yanking his legs free from the mast, which had risen off the ground more than two feet, tilting part of the deck of the barge with it. Mouth clamped tight with effort, Kara held the Tapestry still until both men were safe, and then let it go with a trembling cry.

The ley light within the sail sputtered and died and with a crash the mast and splintered booms fell back to the earth. She felt their weight shuddering through the cobbles at her feet, heard something within the barge itself collapse as it settled again, another shower of embers shooting skyward. Men and women were lined up and down the street, buckets of water being passed from hand to hand at a frantic pace, but a cheer rose even as Kara felt the strength drain away from her legs.

Her knees folded and she collapsed to the street.

A moment later, hands grabbed her arms and dragged her beyond the range of the fire as it began to spread to the entire barge and the building beyond.

Prime Wielder Augustus stalked down the hall of the Nexus, moving fast but not running, his footsteps loud on the tile floor, headed toward the focusing chamber, his robes swishing around his ankles, his hands tucked into his sleeves. All of the Primes he passed in the corridors paused at the sound of his approach. Panicked conversations fell silent. Those in the center of the hall slid smoothly out of his way without a word, without a glance. Most didn't dare look him in the eye, their gaze dropping to the floor, and those who did were faced with a scathing glare, mouth tight with pure anger.

What they did not see was the stark and utter fear that lay beneath Augustus' seething rage.

He turned sharply, ignored the startled looks of the Primes in the new corridor as they sidestepped and backed away, ignored the faint flicker in the panels of ley light that illuminated the hall, his gaze fixed on the polished oak door that led to the focusing chamber. He burst through the doorway without pause, flinched in annoyance at the sudden flare of brilliant white light from the Nexus itself, and glared down into the ley-lit pit as his eyes adjusted. He'd known the Nexus was still active, and the presence of so many Primes in one location meant that the Tapestry could be corrected enough to allow the ley panels to continue operating here, at least marginally, but after the utter darkness of the outer towers—of the entire city—it was still startling.

He hadn't waited for Baron Arent to come find him once he realized the extent of the blackout. He'd come straight to the Nexus.

"What has happened to the ley?" he demanded. "The entire city is dark!"

His voice rolled around the bare stone chamber like thunder, amplified and hollow, distorted by the dimensions of the room and by the undulating tendrils of ley light that flared down from the open apertures that led to the heart of the Nexus, where the intensity of the light and the power coursing through the single node would annihilate anyone who dared to enter the Nexus itself. No one had stood within the heart of the Nexus, beneath the thousands upon thousands of hovering crystal panes that captured and refocused and augmented the ley in all of its scintillate forms, since its creation.

As his eyes adjusted to the harsh glare, Augustus picked out three other Primes, all three with panic written across their faces. His gaze latched onto the nearest, Temerius.

"Why is the city dark?" he roared, and began to descend the wide stone steps that spiraled around the outside of the rounded chamber. "What's caused this catastrophic failure?"

Temerius scowled, following him with his gaze, as the other two Primes went back to frantically manipulating the ley. "That's what we're trying to find out," he said acerbically.

"And?"

"We've found nothing so far. But we haven't had much time to look. The blackout only occurred ten minutes ago."

"Ten minutes is an eternity, when you're standing beneath the Baron's gaze," Augustus growled, coming up to Temerius' side. He cast a suspicious glare at him, but couldn't hold the man's eyes. One of the Primes was a traitor, yes, but he'd known Temerius since he was a Wielder, working the node in Eastend. He'd seen Temerius' potential even then.

"I can sympathize, but we've still found nothing. Perhaps you'd like to take a look?"

Augustus grunted, already reaching out with his senses, stretching himself on the vast cloth of the Tapestry, reaching for the edges of the pit where the contours of the walls and the power laid into the stonework gathered and enhanced his perceptions, turning them back up toward the heart of the Nexus itself. When he felt centered, his power focused and steady, creating a sheath before his eyes hazy with a diffuse yellowish tinge, he gazed up through one of the apertures and into the heart of the Nexus.

Where a moment ago the white light would have blinded him instantly, burning out his retinas and scouring deeper into his brain, he now saw through the film of yellow power folds upon folds of translucent and vibrant color, like the aurora borealis in the north, rippling across the glass-encased building above. Only this aurora was a thousand times more dense, a thousand times more active, the colors shifting fluidly back and forth across the chamber, glancing off and refracting through the crystal panes that hovered steadily throughout the massive room above. The crystals were precisely placed, so that the energies fed on each other, gathering and heightening, until they reached a peak, the measured power then shunted through the access channels that led to the ley lines and the intricate network of nodes in Erenthrall and the cities beyond. Bleed-off fed down into the focusing chamber, creating the dance of arching light around them, but it was nothing but a beautiful, secondary effect. The real power cascaded through the chamber above and out into the lines that fed the city's power grid.

Augustus' mouth tightened as he absorbed the vibrancy of the ley through the lens of his own power . . . and then he began a methodical search through the crystals, noting their position, their placement, comparing them to the memory of the positions agreed upon by the Prime Wielders during their last council session, the one thought to produce the most effective balance of power and bleed-off achievable while still producing what was necessary for the business of Erenthrall and the rest of the ley network. Height, declination, degree of rotation—he considered every facet of their three-dimensional orientation in the Nexus, skimming from one crystal to the next, his frustration growing. He'd been searching for the traitor among the Wielders since the meeting with the Baron, had spent the better part of every day here, personally, in the focusing chamber, straining to catch a glimpse of the traitor's handiwork, to find a trace of his or her manipulation of the crystals, anything that would point the traitor out and provide a clue as to how the system was being altered to affect such drastic fluctuations in the network. Only here could the system be manipulated, so it had to be one of the Primes, one of their own.

But he'd found nothing. After inspecting every crystal pane in the Nexus not once, not twice, but five times, he hadn't found a single pane out of place. Without knowing what changes were being made or how, he couldn't formulate a defense against them.

It was infuriating, the manipulations and the blackouts themselves a personal affront. This was *his* Nexus. He hadn't allied himself to the Baron and put in years of work within the city of Erenthrall itself, then suffered years beneath the Baron's oppressive hands with the risk of Arent withdrawing his support, to achieve the power he now held, only to let someone slip around his control and subjugate his own node. He'd designed it so that only he knew all of its intricacies, so that Arent could never remove him and seize control himself. To have someone else even touching the network's power. . . .

Add to that the reports he'd been receiving for the last few days of the Dogs, obviously set to trail the Wielders within the city. A blatant watch, most not even attempting to hide the fact that they were following the Primes, some reveling in it. The Dog set to watch Augustus had seated himself across the barge from him last night. Dressed in ordinary citizen's clothing, he'd actually nodded when Augustus shot him a glare, tipped his hat, and smiled!

Augustus' jaw clenched so tightly at the memory his back teeth began to ache. He would never have been on the barge—would have taken his personal flyer home—except that the flyers could no longer be trusted, not until the blackouts could be resolved. Oh, the flyers were still operating within the city, but he refused to use one himself. He knew that the ley was at risk, knew that if one of the blackouts occurred at one of the subtowers, or even the Flyers' Tower itself, the barges would drop like stones.

But he'd never expected a total blackout throughout the city. The magnitude of the event, its extent . . . it was overwhelming.

And the Baron would expect answers. No, more than that, he'd expect results.

Augustus shuddered, forced himself to unclench his jaw and focus in on the Nexus, on the crystal panes and the scintillate light.

Out of the corner of his eye, at the edge of the aperture, he caught the distinct glint of reflected light off of crystal as one of the panes shifted.

He stiffened, his entire body going rigid. For a long, held breath, he couldn't move, couldn't think, the shock coursing through his veins like cold water, tingling in his fingers, in his toes.

Then Temerius barked, "What is it?"

Augustus flinched, the heated rage he'd felt returning in a warm rush as he drew in a ragged breath and pointed. "There. There! Someone's altering the crystals, altering *one* crystal, changing its orientation."

"Who?" Temerius spat, already spreading his perceptions out on the Tapestry as he cast a scathing glare at the two other Primes in the chamber, both wide-eyed in disbelief. But even as Augustus felt Temerius reach out in the direction he'd indicated, he knew that the other two had nothing to do with the adjustment of the crystal pane. He could sense their incursion on the Tapestry and they weren't near it. No, the adjustments were being made by someone outside the focusing chamber, by someone outside the Nexus. They were being made by someone manipulating the chamber through the ley lines themselves, not through the apertures within the pit.

The revelation stunned him. He would not have thought it possible.

At his side, Temerius cried out, a sound of disbelief. "They're using the open channels of the ley lines," he hissed. "They aren't even in the Nexus, not even within the building! They're gaining access—"

"Through one of the nodes within the city," Augustus growled, still shaken, although none of that fear bled into his voice.

Temerius took a step back from him, his own eyes going wide as the implications sank in, as the ramifications shattered what he thought he knew of the Nexus. Augustus was already ahead of him, his own thoughts leaping forward. "But that means . . ." Temerius began. He caught Augustus' gaze, his mouth open, working to produce words.

Augustus nodded, jaw clenched. "That means we were wrong, that *I* was wrong. It might not be one of the Primes who is the traitor. It could be one of the Wielders."

They stared at each other a long moment, both numbed, and then one of the other Primes shouted, "Augustus! The pane has stopped moving!"

Augustus turned back to the crystal, saw two other crystals now moving into new positions, saw the undulating colored light shifting its pattern, flares of backlash and bleed-off scattering through the Nexus above and into the chamber below.

And when the last pane settled into its new position, Augustus felt his heart shudder in his chest.

"Holy Mother of Korma," Temerius breathed.

Augustus turned toward him and, in much too calm a tone, said, "Say nothing of this. To anyone. I will warn the Baron."

Above them, the Nexus flared with new light and ley surged out through the apertures and into the lines.

Through his connection to the Nexus, Augustus felt the city come back to life.

Twenty

ALLAN STOOD ON a hilltop far to the west of Erenthrall and stared out over the darkened plains toward the city. Stars gleamed overhead, and the leaves of trees shushed in a faint breeze to either side. The thin edge of dawn sliced across the horizon to the east, but the plains themselves were a black puddle, like spilled ink. He could barely pick out the nearest hills in the moonlight, even after his sight adjusted from moving away from the campfire where his daughter slept in the copse of trees at his back.

Which was wrong, he thought with a disturbed frown. He should be able to see the city if nothing else. He should be able to see its ethereal white glow even through any mist or fog that might obscure the rest of the towns and villages on the plains. He should be able to see the glow that had become the heart of the Baronies, the glow that connected the entire continent—that connected the entire known world and beyond—in a web of ley.

The fact that he couldn't sent a prickling shiver of worry down his back.

He grunted at himself in annoyance, ran his fingers through the beginnings of his scratchy beard—he hadn't done a proper shave in the last two days of traveling—and turned his gaze southward, toward Baron Leethe's domain, where the city of Tumbor would be. He caught the faintest glow of white from that direction, strained to see another patch of pale white farther out to the southeast, one he could see better by looking at from one side rather than directly on, where Farrade lay, then back to the darkness of Erenthrall. He didn't bother looking north toward Severen, Dunmara, and Ikanth on the Steppe. The glow of their ley would be blocked by the mountainous Reaches.

"Tumbor and Farrade seem fine," he murmured to himself, "so what's happening in Erenthrall?"

War? He knew the Barons were at odds, but he hadn't heard any murmurs of outright war. Most of the fighting was political. That kind of warfare never ended. That kind of warfare killed innocents like his wife, Moira.

And that kind of warfare would not leave a city dark.

He tugged at his short beard again, trying to decide what the darkness of Erenthrall meant—whether he should turn back and return to the Hollow or continue on—when he heard the snap of a twig behind him.

He didn't reach for the sword at his side, didn't even shift position, merely turned his head slightly and said, "You can come forward, Poppett."

"Dad, I'm not a poppet! A poppet is a doll. I'm not little anymore."

Allan grimaced. When had it changed from Da to Dad? Would it change to Father soon?

"I know, Popp—Morrell. I'm sorry. I was just—" Thinking of your mother, he almost said, but caught himself. Morrell had been too young to remember her mother when they fled and he knew it upset her when he spoke about the woman she'd never know.

He turned slightly, shook his head, then sat on a nearby stone thrust up out of the earth. "Are you coming out? The dawn's beautiful."

He heard Morrell sigh, then tromp forward, pushing the branches aside.

"I woke up and you weren't there. I got worried." She settled down on the dew-damp ground beside him, gangly twelve-year-old legs crossed beneath her, still dressed in her night shift. Her long, straight hair was pale in the darkness, nothing like the soft gold it appeared during the day. She immediately picked up a stick and began stripping the bark from it in thin strands. "What are you looking at?"

"Erenthrall."

"Really? Where is it? Can we see it from here? Are we that close?" All of the grumpy sleepiness and veiled worry vanished. She'd never seen Erenthrall, didn't remember any of it from when she was little, before they'd left. He hadn't allowed her to travel with him on any of his excursions to trade for the supplies the Hollow couldn't produce for itself until now, and with Erenthrall dark, he was reconsidering taking her any farther. She'd be disappointed, and the Hollow would have a rough winter without those supplies, especially the medicine, but still . . .

"Actually—"

Even as he spoke, he caught a pulse of light from the plains. The sun had risen enough the entire eastern skyline was bathed in soft gray-gold. The faintest contours—hills and valleys, rocky crags and mounds—had appeared, the black snakes of rivers and puddles of lakes cutting through them.

The pulse came from the south, from the direction of Tumbor, a blinding white-purple. Ley. Allan repressed a shudder of distaste. It streaked across the plains, hit a junction, altered course, and flared arrow-straight to Erenthrall, a secondary pulse shooting out toward Farrade, other minor branches spreading outward from smaller junctions along the way. Allan followed the main pulse with his eyes to Erenthrall, where it connected with a brilliant flare, brighter than the sun. For a moment, the entire city lay silhouetted in the backwash of white, the towers of Grass visible, soaring high over the farthest reaches of the outer districts. Something hard filled Allan's chest at the sight, prickling and hot, aching, the city beautiful. And large. Sprawling northward in the vee of the confluence of the Tiana and Urate Rivers, spilling over their edges into the surrounding plains to the north and south; to the east and west as well. The ley filtered through its conduits and spread, outlined all of the districts of the main city, then splintered farther into the outlying towns, and farther still, the entire breadth of the plains lighting up as far as he could see. For a moment, as the city lay bathed in whiteness, he heard an echo of the raucous streets, drank in the sounds of the tens of thousands of people that lived there. He breathed in the stench of so many bodies pressed so close together, totally different from the clean smells of the Hollow, where he and Morrell, Janis, and a few hundred other souls lived without the presence of the ley.

And then the flare of light faded back down to its normal level, Erenthrall now easily visible, like a pulsing of dense moonlight at the center of a lacework from the surrounding smaller towns that supported it.

Morrell gasped at the display and Allan let out the breath he hadn't realized he'd drawn, then tousled his daughter's hair. She ducked away and he smiled, the faintest hint of pain in the expression, then rose with a sigh. He couldn't disappoint his daughter. And the Hollow needed those supplies. When he, Janis, and Morrell had first arrived, those gathered there had been on the edge of failing as a community, their local resources nearly exhausted. No one had been willing to venture into the city; they valued their privacy and didn't trust those in Erenthrall, for various reasons. Reasons like his own. They'd hidden from society and didn't want to be found. Besides, no one in the Hollow besides Janis knew where to find what they needed in Erenthrall anyway.

But Allan did, and he knew how to stay hidden in its streets, as long as the Baron hadn't sicced the Hounds on him. It was the only reason those in the Hollow had accepted him and Morrell into their community. So each year, sometimes more than once, he traveled to Erenthrall and gathered whatever the Hollow needed to survive while making certain the Dogs didn't find him. He knew what would happen if they did. As Hagger had said, no one left the Dogs.

But this was the first time he'd allowed Morrell to accompany him.

He thrust his worry over Morrell's safety aside. He had survived his own excursions to Erenthrall without incident for eleven years; he would survive another. He'd simply be more careful than usual with Morrell at his side.

"Come on. We need to cook some breakfast and get the horses saddled. We're still a long way from the city."

~~~~~~

"What happened, Illiana?"

Kara tossed her Wielder's jacket into a chair in the outer chamber of the Stone District's node. Illiana glanced up from her prone position on the nearest table, one arm draped over her eyes. She looked exhausted, her usually pert face drawn, bruises under her eyes, her short-cropped brown hair sticking up in a thousand different cowlicks.

"I don't know," Illiana groaned, head falling back onto the table, arm back over her eyes, "but it's been hellish. Steven nearly burst a vein when the node went dark, thinking it was something we'd done. Or not done. We scrambled for about fifteen minutes before he went up to the roof and realized it wasn't just our district, that the entire city had gone dark."

"So where is he?"

Illiana snorted, jerking herself upright into a sitting position on the edge of the table, legs dangling, before wincing and bowing her head forward, one hand massaging her forehead. "Gods," she whispered to herself, then continued. "As soon as he saw the city was out, he left me in charge and headed off toward the Nexus to meet with the Primes, or as close to them as he could get, hoping to find out what's going on. We've had a few too many flickers in the ley lately, if you ask me, and this wasn't a damn flicker. I tried to get the node back up after he left, actually went down into the pit, but it came back on itself shortly after."

"You went into the pit? After what happened to Tanek?"

Illiana raised her head enough to stare at Kara through her fingers. "I knew what I was doing. I felt the pulse coming and disengaged. I had enough time to get out and close the shielding door before it struck. Besides, the other Wielders had begun to report in by then, so it's not like I was alone. What about you? Why did it take you so long to get here?"

Kara pressed her lips together. "I saw the city go dark from my flat in Eld. I headed here, but it's chaos out there. All of the sky barges in flight crashed to the ground, and I've heard there's been looting in some of the less patrolled districts. The Dogs have been called out to supplement the city guard." The Dogs had descended on the crashed barge she'd helped almost immediately after she'd rescued the man from beneath the mast.

Illiana's eyes widened. "And you came all the way here? What about the Eld node? Why didn't you go there instead?"

Kara shot her an irritated glance—she'd worked here long enough that Illiana knew why Kara wouldn't go to the Eld node—and didn't answer, began pacing the small chamber, taking in the desks, the work-table in the center of the room scattered with papers and reports and the large map beneath tacked to the surface with all of the ley lines in the Stone District. Pins were stuck into the map in random locations where problems or fluctuations in the ley had been reported and Wielders sent to repair them. Kara halted at the table, shoved a few of the papers aside and stared down at the map, at the array of streets, at the tacks and their positions.

"You look like shit," Kara said as she leaned forward over the map.

Illiana eased off the table. "Thanks. As if the headache wasn't enough." Kara didn't react to the snide tone.

Illiana sighed. "Seriously, there was some kind of dissonance in the ley. I could feel it even standing here in the outer rooms. Steven felt it, too. So when he left, I went down to the pit to see if I could smooth it out."

Kara nodded, thinking about how she'd smoothed the Tapestry back in her own rooms. "It didn't work."

"No. And the dissonance was worse in the pit, amplified somehow. I had a headache before I went in, and inside . . . it felt as if my head was going to split open. The flare when the ley returned at full force didn't help either. I couldn't see, even though I'd withdrawn from the ley. Nothing but a wash of yellow and an afterimage of the pit. I stumbled up here, with help from the others, and lay down, hoping it would fade." She motioned toward the map. "What are you looking for?"

Kara glanced at Illiana, saw the fear that edged her eyes and the shakiness that hid beneath her words. The experience in the pit must have been more frightening than Illiana was letting on. "Something's happening to the ley system, something more serious than a few 'random fluctuations,' as the Baron and the Primes have said."

Illiana's eyes darkened in agreement, so Kara continued.

"The Primes don't know what's going on. That's why they're constantly at the Nexus, or meeting with the Baron and his entourage. In fact, they're probably meeting with him right now."

"They are," Steven spat as he burst into the room, fuming. "I couldn't even get past the damn wardens at the Nexus, let alone the Baron's men at the Amber Tower. And I wasn't the only one trying. Lerrick and Hammond from Forks were there, and Savion from Eastend." He paused in his tirade, brought up short at the sight of Illiana. "What in hells happened to you?"

Illiana rolled her eyes and turned back to the map with Kara. "So you're thinking that if the Primes can't figure out what's going on, you can?" she asked, derision in her voice. "What do you think you'll find?"

"I don't know, but there has to be some reason the blackouts are happening, some cause."

"They aren't really blackouts," Steven said, joining them at the table. "You know what Tanek said. The ley is being diverted. It's being shunted for use somewhere else."

"How? And if it's being diverted, is it natural or is someone behind it? Who would want to disrupt the ley?"

Neither Steven nor Illiana responded, Illiana staring studiously at the ground, Steven frowning. Kara shifted uncomfortably, wary of the dark tension in the air, then suddenly realized what they were thinking and why it had forced them into silence, why the awkwardness felt so deadly and familiar.

"The Kormanley," she said. She'd meant for it to sound derisive, but as she thought about it, it made more and more sense.

Steven hissed for silence, glancing toward the doors, fear making his body rigid before he turned back to Kara and stepped forward. Voice low, he said, "We don't utter that name around here. You weren't part of the node during the Purge. There were . . . accusations here. At least half of the Wielders vanished into the Amber Tower and weren't seen again."

"I have my own reasons to hate the Kormanley," Kara muttered. "One of their attacks killed my parents. The Purge killed my friend and mentor, Ischua. But if you suspect them—"

"I do," Steven said, eyes still shifting toward the doorways, "and I've shared these thoughts with some of the other senior Wielders, and a few of the Wielders here, like Illiana. But that's as far as it's gone. We have nothing to base our suspicions on, and no one wants to broach the subject with the Primes . . . or the Baron."

"But the disruptions," Kara protested, still thinking it through in her head. "It makes sense it would be the Kormanley. They've wanted a return to the natural order since the beginning. It's what their entire philosophy—their entire religion—is based on. And isn't that what happens when the ley is diverted? The ley is still there, it simply isn't being magnified. It's returned to its natural state. Isn't that enough?"

From one side, Illiana said simply, "Do you want to bring about a second Purge?"

Kara sucked in a sharp breath, thinking of Ischua's death at the hands of the Dogs, then let it out slowly, sending Illiana a glare. "Of course not."

"Then don't talk about it." Illiana met her glare and didn't flinch.

"It doesn't matter," Steven interrupted. "We won't talk about it because no one will listen. No one wants to listen, least of all the Primes. They don't want to admit that someone—especially someone within the Kormanley—might be able to tamper with their system." He gave them both a significant look.

Illiana sniffed, but Kara turned back to the map, leaning over it, hands planted to either side, elbows locked. After a strained silence, she said, "Where's the map with all of the blackouts shaded that we looked at before?"

Steven hesitated, then moved to a second table and began sorting through the maps on its surface. Illiana threw up her hands in disgust, but paced the room behind them, unable or unwilling to leave.

"Here," Steven said, sliding the map before Kara. "Why? What are you looking for?"

Kara tapped the map. "If someone is diverting the ley—and not just the ley of one district, but the ley of the entire city—you won't discover who by looking at just the Stone District. You'll need a map of the entire system. You'll need to be able to see how everything is interconnected, and how one node is affected by all of the others."

Steven's eyebrows rose. "You won't be able to find that even here, remember? This map only shows what the average layperson sees walking the streets. Only the Primes have access to everything. And there's no way they'll let you see it. You may be on track to become a Prime, but you aren't a Prime yet. That's one secret they'd kill to keep. It's what gives them power over the Baron."

Kara frowned in frustration, because she knew he was right.

But what disturbed her more was that, looking at the two maps, the frequency of the blackouts—of all of the disruptions in the ley—and the magnitude of each were accelerating.

<hr />

"So you're saying these blackouts are being caused by one of the Wielders?"

Augustus tried to contain his frustration and failed. He had gone immediately to the Baron to report what he'd witnessed in the Nexus, but had been forced to wait as Arent dealt with a sudden influx of concerned lords, merchants, and the demands of Captain Daedallen as the Dogs dealt with the riots and looting that had sprung up around the city, not to mention the destruction caused by the flyers falling from the sky. He'd seen three fires raging from the window of the audience chamber in the Amber Tower as he waited. One of those fires raged out of control, consuming at least three sections of the Northward District.

As soon as he entered the Baron's chambers, Arent had stood, face haggard and drained but still vital. Without a word, he'd ordered Daedallen to send the Dogs to clear the gardens below, and to hold all other visitors.

They'd descended to the gardens in silence, the wait grating on Augustus' nerves. His news, and the ramifications of it, pressed against his chest. They had barely entered the first section of pathways, shielded from sight by trees, before he'd spat out the most significant news.

"Yes," he said, nearly growling at the audacity of the Wielder. "Whoever it is has entered one of the nodes and followed the ley lines directly into the Nexus itself, using the ley as a conduit. They've been manipulating the crystals within to redirect the flows of the ley for their own purposes. I believe that all of the previous blackouts have been tests of their abilities, or perhaps experiments used to determine how the ley lines would react to different settings. That's why, when I searched the Nexus myself, I found nothing—they reset the system after they were done."

"But today was different?"

Augustus ground his teeth together. "Today," he spat, "they changed the configuration of the Nexus completely. They've realigned at least three of the crystals within it. During the blackout itself, the ley was shunted to a different location, all of its power used for some other purpose, and once they were finished the traitor reset the crystals and allowed the ley to return. I can't believe the temerity of these people! To infiltrate the Nexus, to seize control of the entire system—!"

"What people?"

Augustus was brought up short by the question, seething inside as he turned to Baron Arent in mild surprise. "The people behind this catastrophe, of course. It can't be just one traitor here in the city. The ley went somewhere, had to have been used by someone else."

Arent's eyes narrowed with suspicion. "You spoke as if you knew who they were. Do you, Prime Wielder? Do you know who is behind these . . . attacks?"

Augustus halted abruptly, the stone of the garden path crunching beneath his feet. A frisson of fear sluiced through him as he recognized the cold gaze that both Arent and Daedallen had settled on him. He'd seen that gaze often during the appalling Purge, seen it leveled at lords and ladies, courtesans and merchants, at the supplicants of the Baron's court—

But he'd never seen it leveled at himself.

He swallowed, his throat suddenly constricted, and screwed up his face in condescension, waving one arm toward the city. "Do you think if I knew I would keep it from you? I would have sent the Dogs to the perpetrators' flats myself!"

Arent's gaze didn't waver. "But you have a suspicion."

Augustus wrestled with himself, but finally said, "I didn't have a suspicion until I saw the fires in the city. It reminded me of the attacks on the sky barges during their launch . . . and of the attack on the Amber Tower at the Baronial Meeting."

Arent drew back, and Daedallen sucked in a sharp breath, a glance passing between them. Augustus suddenly wondered what they knew that they were not telling him. They did not appear surprised.

"The Kormanley," the Baron said.

Augustus nodded. "They have already proven they are willing to destroy to gain what they desire, although this is more subtle than I would have given them credit for earlier. As I said, it is only a suspicion."

Daedallen stiffened slightly. "The Dogs have reported nothing regarding a resurgence of the Kormanley. If they have returned, they are no longer preaching their beliefs on street corners or in taverns. None of our sources have reported anything either."

Arent stared off into the distance in thought.

"Where was the ley shunted?" he asked abruptly.

"The south."

Arent's gaze fell on him and Augustus shuddered. "You cannot be more precise than that?"

"I did not have time to travel the ley before the adjustments were made. If I had known, if I had prepared myself—"

Arent waved him into silence, returning his attention to Daedallen. "It must be Leethe. He must be working with the Kormanley, as we suspect he did before the Purge. What is his purpose?"

"The Hounds have not reported yet."

"But one was sent to Tumbor?"

Augustus' shoulders prickled. He should not be privy to this discussion, and yet he knew that Arent would not have made such a blatant mistake. He was meant to hear this, as a warning. The Hounds had been unleashed. They were hunting outside of Erenthrall for the first time in decades.

Daedallen shot a glance toward him, then back to Arent. "Yes. One was sent to Tumbor."

Arent turned away, heading back toward the entrance to the garden, anger tightening his shoulders. "I want to know as soon as he reports in. Baron Leethe has overstepped his bounds, far more so than he did before with the Kormanley. If the Hound discovers what Leethe is attempting, and it involves the ley, have him kill the Baron."

⬱

The Hound disembarked from the barge into the glass-enclosed station in Tumbor and scanned the platform. Others who could afford the costly trip from Erenthrall spilled forth as well, rushing to meet friends or family while handlers offloaded baggage from the deck above. The station bustled with activity, people talking, children screaming as they cavorted around their parents, servants hustling as they transported the luggage to the waiting carriages and transports.

The Hound noted the station wardens in their sleek red-and-gold uniforms, motioning the patrons toward the front of the station, but his attention caught on the two men standing to one side, dressed as informally as the patrons, but with hard eyes and too casual a stance. They were watching everyone who came off the barge.

Baron Leethe's enforcers.

He headed toward the glass-walled entrance to the station at a measured pace, keeping the enforcers in sight out of the corner of his eye. One of them glanced in his direction, but his gaze slid over the Hound without pause, although the enforcer frowned as if he sensed something was wrong.

Then the Hound stepped out of the glass doors and into the square outside the station.

He didn't pause until he reached the first street corner, weaving in and out among the carriages and snorting horses. The sounds of hooves on cobbles filled the open area, along with the cries of hawkers and peddlers selling their wares out of modified wagons or on tarps spread out on the stone walk. A few tents had been erected near the fountain in the center of the square, beneath the widespread wings of a sculpted hawk ready to strike. The Hound imagined he could hear the bird's shriek as it dove, smiled tightly at the sound, then stepped into the partial shade of a building to catch his bearings.

He found himself in the middle of the old trading district. Except for the glass ley station, the buildings were made of stone, mostly granite from the surrounding mountains. Trading houses and mercantiles, massive and brooding, filled up entire blocks, their facades looming over the street and square beneath them. Encrusted with decades of weathering, they appeared dirty and dark compared to the sun-glinted newness of the glass station.

The street and square were thronged with traders from every part of the continent. The light-skinned men and women of the Steppes with their colorful and voluminous shirts and breeches mingled with the darker-skinned, bearded men of the Demesnes, their linen shirts embroidered with intricate patterns on the shoulders and down the sleeves. The Gorrani merchants carried their sabers openly here, accompanied by women wrapped in shawls so only their eyes were visible between the silky folds. Olive-skinned men from the Correllite Isles, pale-skinned folk from the eastern shores of Temerite, and the black-haired women of the Archipelago with their armored male escorts who were rumored to do more than protect—all visible from the Hound's vantage point at the corner of the square, all passing each other, conversing, conducting business, or rushing to a guild hall or mercantile or trading house.

And none of them mattered.

The Hound drew in a deep breath, absorbing the scents of the square—the sweat of a thousand or more bodies, the perfume of a passing Gorrani, the spice of a haunch of meat cooking over ley-heated stones at a nearby hawker's tent, the bittersweet incense from a Korani acolyte's brazier. All surface scents, the strongest and most powerful.

Eyes watching those passing by—noting weapons, subtle movements, expressions and hand gestures, looking for signs of danger—the Hound drew in another, deeper breath.

The amalgam of smells separated into layers, into individual threads. No longer a miasma of mingled scents, the Hound began picking through them all, searching for a hint of the one he'd been sent to track. A woman passed, her perfume—henna, myrrh, cinnamon, and juniper—overpowering everything else for a brief moment. The Hound wrinkled his nose and suppressed a sneeze. He followed her without moving as she rounded a corner, continued down that street out of sight, turned left, and entered a building, then shook his head to free himself of her scent before concentrating again on the layers around him. The deep, rich musk of horses, tallow from a candlemaker, piss where someone had urinated in a corner, rose water, camphor from a Gorrani's bound wound, smoke from a pipe, layer upon layer upon layer of scents, reaching deeper and deeper into the past as he filtered out the strongest, the most recent, digging toward the older scents, those that lingered beneath, searching for the one scent that mattered, the one person that mattered.

There.

He exhaled harshly, drew in another deep breath to verify the scent—sweat, salty and acrid, like pine sap—then turned toward where it led. Faint. Lost among the myriad other smells. But there.

Baron Leethe had been at the ley station in Tumbor about two days before.

The Hound's blood quickened and he headed across the square, brushing past the citizens of Tumbor without thought. Most stepped out of his way without even realizing he was there. A few shuddered as he passed. He blunted their awareness of him automatically now.

He'd reached the far side of the fountain, the hawk's wings spread overhead, when a pungent spike of fear distracted him from the Baron's scent.

The Hound spun, a knife in hand even as he stepped back into the shadow of the hawk and focused on the direction of the fear. His muscles tensed as four of the Baron's enforcers converged on his location, moving fast, silent and fluid, eyes hard as granite, dressed formally in armor like the Dogs, not like the enforcers he'd seen inside the station. People dodged out of their way, stumbled in their haste, the scent of their terror heightening as the gray-uniformed enforcers closed in on their prey.

The Hound relaxed, shifted so that his knife was no longer visible.

The enforcers weren't after him.

Their target was a youth, dressed in a plain white shirt and tan breeches, who slid through the crowd seamlessly, his eyes darting toward satchels and purses and the wares displayed openly by the hawkers. He smelled of opium and myrrh.

Behind him, the enforcers split, two breaking away to flank the prey.

The boy sensed their approach at the last moment, turned, eyes widening in shock. For a brief moment he froze, like the rabbit at the hawk's shriek.

Then he bolted, directly into the path of one of the four enforcers.

Someone in the crowd screamed as the enforcer, without a word, slammed a fist into the boy's stomach, and then the crowd broke. The remaining three enforcers pounced, people scattering, terror and fury and adrenaline flooding the Hound's senses. He breathed it in deep, felt it coursing through his blood, seething, hot and fervent—

And then the boy began shouting.

"Kidnapping!" he cried out, voice choked from the punch to the stomach. "Rape! What have I done? What have I—"

The enforcer grabbed his arm and hauled him upright, cutting him off. He thrashed and writhed, trying to break free. A second enforcer snatched at his free arm, and the boy heaved, strained forward, back arched as they viciously kicked his legs out from under him, driving him to his knees, knocking over the brazier of the Korani priest. Briquettes spilled from the container, sharp incense slamming into the Hound's nose like a fist, even as a third enforcer backhanded the boy, blood flying from his mouth. He staggered, the air flooded with the metallic tang of his blood, would have fallen except for the two enforcers holding him upright, his arms twisted behind him. The crowd had drawn back in a tight circle.

The boy hung for a moment, spit and blood drooling from his mouth, then recovered enough to lift his head. His eyes blazed with hatred. "I've done nothing," he spat, voice low, all of his hatred directed at the enforcer before him, the one who'd backhanded him.

The enforcer backhanded him again. His head snapped back, then lolled forward. The soldier took a step closer, hand balled into a fist, ready to strike him again, but the fourth enforcer grabbed his shoulder with a deep-throated, "Enough!" He glared around at the crowd, then growled, "Show's over. Disperse."

The crowd hesitated, but when the man's hand settled onto the hilt of the sword at his waist, they moved, breaking apart and returning to their business as if nothing had happened. The leader of the enforcers scanned them all as they departed, and then his eyes fell on the Hound.

They stared at each other, the enforcer's brow creasing with irritation and a slight confusion. No one held an enforcer's gaze; everyone lowered their eyes, or turned away.

The Hound didn't.

The enforcer finally shook himself and looked away. The crowd had returned to its steady flow, breaking around the tableau, the boy at the center.

Turning, the Hound hesitated, pushed the thick scents of the scene—the blood, the fear, the incense and terror—aside, and recaptured the sweat of the Baron.

Then he stepped out of the hawk's shadow and headed deeper into Tumbor.

The hunt had begun.

Twenty-One

KARA RACED DOWN the street, dodging carts and wagons and horses, slipping through the throng of people who milled about on their daily business in Stone, oblivious to the ripples Kara could sense in the Tapestry around them. Or mostly oblivious. A few people had stopped in the middle of the street and were looking up at the sky, eyes shaded, trying to figure out what had just sent a prickle down their backs. But they were on the outskirts of the fluctuation.

Those closer in would be feeling much more than a prickle.

Reaching a corner, she ground to a halt, bumping into an older man with a sword belted at his waist who shot her a dark look and nearly spat until he noticed her purple jacket. Eyes widening, he drew breath to apologize, but Kara didn't wait, darting across the street between two passing carts, a horse snorting and shying away from her. She could hear the formation of the distortion now, the high-pitched keen making her wince. People were moving away from the distortion's center, their fear heightened the closer she got.

When she rounded the next curve in the street, she saw people running, heard the first screams, cutting through the shriek of the distortion itself. It was louder than any distortion she'd heard before, sharper, like knives digging into her ears.

"Out of my way!" she yelled, lurching forward in desperation. "Wielder coming through!" She shoved at those blocking her path, their faces twisted with fear, sent a few sprawling to the smooth stone street—

Then she reached the next intersection and saw it.

At the same moment, before she even had a chance to draw a breath to shout a warning, the high-pitched keening stopped and the Tapestry wrenched.

Kara gasped as pain shot through her head, a tearing lance that dug in deep, then retreated. On the street ahead, the distortion flared, close to the buildings on the left. Those on the street below who hadn't fled fast enough, or had run in the wrong direction, jerked back from the light, brought hands up to shade their eyes from the glare . . . and then panicked.

Screams ripped through the air as everyone bolted. The panic spread like a ripple of water after a stone had been thrown into a pool, hitting Kara's position in seconds. She braced herself, but the crush of the crowd still shoved her back twenty paces. She bellowed for them to let her pass, began elbowing people in the ribs, the stomach, but only managed to gain a foothold by punching someone hard in the face. She felt the man's nose break beneath her fist, felt a spatter of blood. Using the break in the crush of bodies, she slid past the man as he crumpled, angling toward the edge of the street, still fighting the flow of bodies even then. The screaming continued, escalating as people were trampled.

Kara swore.

She broke free of the heaviest press of the crowd, stumbled to the edge of a building, one hand pressed to its unnaturally smooth surface. Someone had struck her in the back of the thigh, but she straightened and turned toward the distortion.

It had broken through in the smooth curve of the street, over two hundred paces distant. The glare of light had increased, pulsing, the size of her fist now, but it hadn't expanded yet, which was unusual. She could see it tearing at the Tapestry, the area around it distorted and shuddering. The stone of the nearest building rippled beneath the fluctuations, and below it people were still trying to escape its reach. Some had been thrust to the ground in the initial panic and were only now beginning to scramble to their feet, but others were trying to flee, faces strained with the effort.

They simply weren't moving. Or were moving sluggishly, as if they were fighting through mud.

Pushing away from the wall, Kara stepped forward, began humming low in her throat. She didn't have much time, not if she wanted to stop the distortion before it expanded.

Reaching out, she let the Tapestry envelop her, let it settle over her shoulders, seep into her, until she felt the throb of the distortion in her skin. It thrummed through her, the fine hairs on her arms and neck standing on end. Its vibration dug deeper still, shuddering painfully through her bones. She shrugged the ugly sensation aside and focused on the thrum, tried to match the tenor of her hum to it. The two began to meld, the Tapestry sinking into her as they joined, as she began to get a feel for the distortion itself, for the flaw that was at its heart. If she could wrap herself around the rent in the fabric, if she could absorb all of its edges, she could halt it.

She had nearly matched her humming to the shape of the rent when she felt it twist.

"No," she whispered, and unconsciously reached forward.

Before she could withdraw herself from the rent, it shuddered—

And tore wide open.

On the street, the white light collapsed in on itself for a single breath . . . and then it exploded in a vivid burst of color. Arms of distortion arced outward in swirls, vortices spinning away like mad tops, sending out their own arcs. The entire display expanded for a breath, two, flaring impossibly wide, capturing those in the street beneath it in its grip. It arced out in Kara's direction, one of its arms snaking toward her in a coruscating flare of blue—

And then its rotation slowed and halted.

Everything within its reach halted as well. A woman struggling to her feet, one arm supporting her weight as she thrust herself upward, now still as a statue. A man helping a younger man to rise. A dog on its hind legs who'd been barking fiercely at the distortion, its master trying to draw it away, the boy no more than ten. Another man hunched over a young girl protectively, as if to shield her from the distortion itself. All of them frozen, trapped, unmoving.

Kara let her held breath out in a hiss of anger and frustration, found it hard to take another. A surge of fear coursed through her. When she tried to step backward, her legs felt as if they'd been embedded in stone, so she stopped trying, focused on the distortion instead, on the arm that had halted before her, close enough she could reach out and touch it if she wanted to put the effort into making her arms move. She'd been too close to the distortion when it expanded, had been caught in its outer edge. But it was so large! Certainly the largest she'd ever witnessed, encompassing nearly the entire width of the street and the buildings to one side.

She needed to escape and repair it, before it collapsed. Or everything within its grasp, including her, would be lost.

Like the seamstress' hand.

Her heart leaped in her chest and she swallowed reflexively against the memory. Forcing herself to draw in deep, even breaths, she quieted her racing heart and swallowed down the taste of fear, of remembered failure.

Slowly, her tensed muscles loosened and the bitterness on her tongue retreated. The distortion's grip on her loosened as well.

Calmed, she began to hum again and reached out on the Tapestry as she had before, encompassing it, searching out its edges. Not only was the distortion larger than any she had seen before, it was also more complex. She seeped into its fractures, wrapped around the shards, reality shattered like a mirror, only in three dimensions. Some of those fractures coursed through the people trapped below and she grimaced, but pushed the thought of what that meant aside.

Outside the effects of the distortion, she saw people moving, nothing more than vague shapes, oddly warped, as if she were watching them through flawed glass. She caught a flash of deep purple, the hue of a Wielder's jacket, and wondered who had arrived.

A moment later, she knew: Marcus.

She sensed him as he reached out on the Tapestry, as he began enfolding it as she had done already, his essence mingling with hers. She shuddered beneath the touch, jaw clenched. She didn't know why he was here, in Stone, but his presence on the Tapestry, brushing against her, caressing her, felt like steel scraping down glass.

Suddenly angry, she thrust him away, felt his initial confusion surge into anger, then blocked him as she focused on the distortion again. She could do this herself. He stalked her, his purple cloak flashing around the outside of the distortion as his essence lashed against her barrier. Sweat broke out on her forehead under the onslaught. She knew she should welcome his help, his strength—

"Kara! Remember the seamstress!"

She flinched, his words distorted and muddled, but still clear.

Jaw clenched, she released her block on the Tapestry.

Marcus' presence surged forward, offering her support while focusing on the opposite side of the distortion, where the two men were caught. "It's about bloody time," he spat.

Kara didn't respond; she didn't waste the time.

Then she noticed movement. Not from outside the distortion. From inside.

She stiffened in panic. Her hum faltered, the barrier wavering but holding, afraid that she'd taken too long, that the distortion had begun to collapse again, that it would take her with it—

But then she realized that it wasn't the distortion at all. It was the man shielding the young girl.

He'd shifted. Not far. Only his head had moved, tilting so that he could see the effects of the distortion around him. He murmured something, his frown tightening as he scanned the others trapped in the fluctuation, but Kara was too far away to hear what was said. The girl he sheltered squirmed, but he drew her in tighter, quieting her.

And then his gaze fell on Kara. He stilled as their eyes met, as he recognized her jacket. Fear flashed across his face, tainted with hatred, followed immediately by determination and resolve. It hardened his face, drew it in sharp lines, highlighting the scars from burns across his cheeks.

He shouldn't be able to move, not trapped in a distortion.

Kara resumed humming, more intently now, aware that the distortion hung poised around her. She spread herself toward the man and girl, but found that the fluctuation had formed itself around the two. None of the fractures penetrated them, halting abruptly, close to the man's body.

Before she could investigate further, the vibration in the distortion changed. A subtle note, not in sympathy with her hum. Pushing the strange man and girl aside, she focused in on the heart of the fractures, on the original tear. She began to draw her outstretched senses inward toward that tear, pulling on the Tapestry, drawing it over the fractures, healing them as she worked. The blue arc of light before her flickered, then began to fade. The closeness pressing against her chest eased. Vortices whirled backward and closed. The edge of the distortion pulled away from her, the crowd and the dark purple of Marcus' jacket coming into focus, his face twisted with concentration as he worked. She stepped forward, her hum increasing, the distortion trembling as she freed the woman already halfway to her feet. She lurched upright, stumbled, then scrambled away from the distortion and into the waiting arms of the crowd, gasping.

Kara's hum tightened in pitch. The boy and his dog were next. The vibration in the distortion increased. Sweat burned in Kara's eyes, trickled down her neck, tickled as it seeped between her breasts beneath her clothes. She raked her arm across her forehead, blinked as her vision blurred. The distortion was too big; even with Marcus' help, they weren't going to be able to close it completely.

The dog came free easily—it shook itself savagely, barked, then pressed as close to its master as it could with a whine—but one of the largest fractures ran straight through the boy.

The vibration intensified.

Behind her, Marcus stepped forward, muttered, "Kara," in warning. She felt him working furiously. He'd freed one of the men. But the other . . . and the boy. . . .

"Kara!"

With a shudder, the distortion began to move.

Kara wrenched herself free of the Tapestry with a harsh cry, felt Marcus' hand fall on her shoulder to steady her even as he did the same. She jerked away from him with a bitter, "Don't," ended up in a crouch, one hand against the stone cobbles of the street.

Those gathered a safe distance away gasped as the distortion flared and collapsed back into itself, the whorls and arms withdrawing with a shivering hiss, like ice cracking—

Or a blade slicing the air.

A few women screamed as the scent of fresh blood struck Kara hard.

"No!" Kara barked in denial, shoving herself upright, Marcus suddenly holding her, trying to comfort her, his scent close, so familiar, twisting in her chest like a knife.

"You don't want to go over there," he muttered.

His voice reawakened her rage and she began to struggle. With a visceral growl, she broke free, staggered forward, collapsed to the stone of the street next to where the boy had fallen. She reached out a hand toward his slack face, the dog snuffling his blond hair, nudging him, licking his cheek as it whimpered. Its paws left bloody tracks on the stone as it circled around to Kara's side and pushed against her outstretched hand. The pool of blood from the slice across the boy's chest—from right hip to left torso, where the fracture had been—grew sluggishly, black-red and viscous.

Kara let her hand drop to her thigh. The dog—a mangy thing, standing no higher than her knee—pushed its head into her lap beneath her arm and whined.

Marcus' heavy footsteps sounded near her, moving to check the other man, but she couldn't tear her gaze away from the boy's dead brown eyes. Not even when Marcus returned and settled into a crouch beside her. "The other man is dead as well. Neither of them had much of a chance. They were too close to the source. The fractures had pierced them in multiple places."

There was no accusation in his voice, but she felt a nauseous wave of shame anyway, of guilt. If she'd let Marcus help her earlier, as soon as he arrived, they may have been able to save them all, may have been able to heal the distortion before its collapse.

"What about the man and girl?" Her voice sounded foreign to her, rough as gravel, dry. She coughed.

"The other two? They ran into the crowd as soon as you freed them."

That brought her gaze up. She stared into Marcus' face, into his blue eyes, the skin beneath bruised with lack of sleep. His thick hair stirred in a small gust.

Her heart lurched in her chest.

She drew back, knew her face had hardened, had turned bitter.

Marcus' eyes darkened. "What's wrong?" he asked. "What happened with the other two, the man and the girl?"

She scanned Marcus' confused face, then grunted and stood, searched the area, stepping away from the boy's body, the dog following at her heels. The body of the other man lay crumpled at the edge of the street. The smooth surface of the building behind had cracked, splinters of stone jutting out at odd angles where it had been touched by the distortion. Parts of the street were the same, as if the stone cobbles were mud churned up by the passage of too many carts. Except in one spot, where the man had shielded the girl from the distortion.

Kara halted over the location, stared down at the untouched stone of the street.

"Kara. What's wrong?" Marcus' voice was hard, demanding, angry that she'd shut him out. But it didn't affect her. She'd grown used to it in the last few months they'd been together, had inured herself to it.

She glanced up, caught his gaze before turning to scan the surrounding faces in the crowd, most horrified by the blood staining the street, eyes sad with sympathy, others weeping openly. A few were watching her with accusatory scowls, as if they knew she hadn't allowed Marcus to help her, knew she hadn't done everything possible to save the man and the boy. She didn't see the other man or the girl anywhere. She swallowed down the hard stone that had settled at the base of her throat.

"I didn't free them," Kara said roughly.

"What?"

"I said I didn't free them! I didn't have time. I managed to free myself, the woman, and the dog. No one else. But I did see him move. Both of them, the man and girl."

Marcus' brow furrowed. "Then perhaps they weren't caught in the distortion."

"No. You can see where they were crouched." She motioned to the only section of the street that didn't look as if it were churned mud. "They were inside it. It surrounded them. It had enfolded them completely."

"How is that possible?"

Kara shrugged, her gaze glancing off of the dead boy and away sharply. She didn't want Marcus' help, even though he hadn't yet mentioned that she'd blocked him. Her stomach threatened to roil and she felt herself beginning to tremble. Reaction to the effort it had taken to repair what she had of the distortion. "I don't see him or the girl anywhere in the crowd. They must have fled as soon as they were free." She thought again about the odd look the man had given her while still trapped, the fear followed by hatred and defiance.

Not what she would expect from someone caught in a distortion with a Wielder, with someone who could possibly save him. In fact, nearly the opposite.

Her knees suddenly felt weak. A wave of dizziness swept through her and the next thing she knew, Marcus was holding her upright by the arm, cursing, and she didn't have the strength to pull away.

"We'd better get you back to the node," he said, his voice sounding rough but distant. She heard the sudden thundering of boots, the harsh shouts of soldiers. "The city watch has arrived. We'll let them sort this out."

And then he was leading her away, a path opening up through the crowd before them.

Shit, shit, shit!

Allan moved as soon as he felt the hideous pressure of the distortion retreat, scooping up Morrell into his arms even as the scent of blood slammed into his senses. He heard Morrell cry out, knew she'd seen the distortion rip the boy and the man to shreds. He buried her face in his shoulder and lurched toward the crowd that had gathered at the edge of the distortion. The shocked and horrified faces didn't part before him, so he plowed into them with a low growl of anger and frustration, heard someone yell as they were thrown to the ground, and then he broke through the back into the mostly empty street.

He ran, his heart thundering in his chest, pounding in his ears. Morrell shuddered against him, her arms wrapped around his neck, clutching him tight as she sobbed, nearly choking him. He hefted her weight as he reached the first corner, grunting with the effort, risking a glance behind as he slowed to turn.

No one pursued them. Not anyone from the crowd, not the Wielder. He didn't even hear shouts for the Dogs.

He frowned, some of the tension dissipating from his shoulders.

He'd seen the Wielder's eyes narrow, seen the look of confusion cross her face. She'd recognized him. He knew it. After twelve years of avoiding detection coming to Erenthrall, he'd finally been discovered.

He heard the thunder of boot-clad feet and ducked behind the corner of the nearest building as the city watch charged toward the crowd. Back pressed against smooth stone, he listened to the shouts as he calmed his breathing. Morrell hung in his arms like a lead weight, so when she began to squirm, he set her down on the ground and knelt in front of her, smoothing out her ruffled hair and wiping the tears from her face.

"You're fine, Poppet."

He watched her try to pull herself together, the struggle to act like an adult fighting the twelve-year-old child still inside her. "But the boy . . . the lights . . . the blood . . ." Her rough breathing began to hitch, tears threatening again as her face twisted into a tangle of horror and fear.

"I know, I know." Allan hugged her close, kissed her forehead. "But you're fine, the lights can't hurt you now. They're gone." On the street around the corner, the city watch began shouting orders to disperse the crowd. It didn't sound like they were searching for anyone, but he didn't want to take any chances.

He looked Morrell in the eye. "We need to get out of here. Can you walk on your own, or do you want me to carry you?"

She searched his face, some of the fear ebbing away, her mouth setting into a determined line as she gathered herself and forced the horror back. "What was the light?"

"It's called a distortion. They happen here in the city sometimes. It's one of the reasons I took you away to the Hollow, and why I never brought you to the city with me before."

A high-pitched whistle pierced the shouting on the streets and Allan jerked upright, one hand falling to his daughter's shoulder.

Morrell clutched his hand. "What is it, Dad?"

"The Dogs have arrived."

Allan watched grimly as the crowd began to scatter, leaving the ignored city watch and the sliced-up bodies behind. He didn't see the Wielder at all, but the Dogs thronged the scene, seizing control, closing in on the head of the watch and hiding the bodies and everyone else from view. Their rough leather armor mixed with bracers and armbands made the black uniforms of the watch look pristine. He scanned the Dogs' faces, looking for anyone who might recognize him, anyone familiar. But they were all too young to have known him when he was a Dog.

And then he saw Hagger. The elder Dog looked even more grizzled and vicious than Allan remembered as he ordered the younger Dogs around, shoving those in the crowd moving too slowly for him, kicking one to the ground. He snarled, his face lined with old anger, old hatred, then spat to one side, his gaze sweeping across the scene, searching.

Allan pulled back behind the corner, hand gripping the pommel of his short sword so hard the knuckles were white. He pried his fingers loose and glanced down toward Morrell, saw her watching the Dogs curiously. When she looked up at him, he could see her thinking. The shock from seeing the boy's body and the blood had faded, although he could still see it haunting the corners of her eyes. She'd have nightmares tonight. He needed to distract her, before the memory of the boy's death returned, before she began asking questions, such as why the distortion hadn't touched them. It had to be a consequence of his nullification of the ley, but he hadn't known that when he'd ducked to protect her. Before fleeing to the Hollow, he'd canceled out the ley's power within a radius of ten feet. Experimenting in the years since, he knew his power had grown. He'd caused ley globes to flicker as far as twenty-five feet away.

The distortion had gotten much closer than that. But then his impression was that the distortion was also much more powerful than a ley globe or heating stone.

"Let's go. We missed the meeting with the blacksmith, but we can still look for the cloth Tobias wanted for his daughters. Remember? You promised to pick out something special for them."

She nodded, still thoughtful.

As they turned away from the corner, heading down the second street, the Dogs and the area of the distortion out of sight, Allan's hand dropped back to the pommel of his blade.

He'd have to be more careful in the next few days. He had to assume that Hagger would question the Wielder, that she'd report what she'd seen, that the Dogs would know he was here now, that they'd be looking for him. Which meant he'd have to cut the trip to Erenthrall short. Time to reevaluate the supplies needed for the Hollow, gather only what was absolutely necessary for the winter in order for the community to survive.

And then get the hells out before Hagger and the Dogs caught up to him.

"Move it! Nothing to see here! Get out of the way so us Dogs can do our job!"

Hagger emphasized the last word with a hard kick in the ass to one of the slower-moving oglers in the crowd. The man toppled over and hit the stone hard, scraping up the side of his face. Smiling tightly as the man scrambled away, he surveyed the scene, taking in the remains of the bodies left behind with a grimace, then scanning the crowd. Some of the Dogs had captured a few of those who'd gathered and were questioning them, but the rest appeared to be scattering reasonably fast. He grunted to himself in satisfaction, eyeing their retreating backs.

His eye caught an odd movement at the nearest intersection and he instantly focused in on a girl peering around the corner of the building. Dressed in a white shirt open at the collar and rugged pants, she watched the scene with a tight frown, then turned and looked up toward someone Hagger couldn't see. A man's hand reached out and drew her out of sight by the shoulder.

Hagger frowned, something in the girl's face somehow familiar. He didn't know any girls her age, not that he could recall, but he couldn't shake the nagging feeling he knew her.

And then he caught a snippet of the conversation nearest to him.

"—there was a man caught in it. It didn't look like the Wielders had freed him, but they must have because as soon as the distortion collapsed, he snatched up the girl and plowed into the crowd."

Hagger spun toward the sound of the woman's voice. At least forty years old, hair pulled into a tight knot at the back of her head, she was plain of face, dressed like any other citizen of Erenthrall, although her hands were callused from hard labor. She held herself confidently, and didn't appear afraid of the Dog who was questioning her.

She caught him watching her as she said, "The rest of them never had a chance, poor bastards. The distortion was so big! I was surprised the Wielders managed to save anyone at all."

Hagger moved toward her, noticed that she didn't flinch or back away, her gaze holding his almost defiantly. "You said there was a man caught in the distortion? But he wasn't affected by it?"

"Yes."

He scanned those they'd kept behind for questioning. "Is he still here?"

The woman looked as well, finally shaking her head. "No. As I said, he grabbed the girl and ran."

Uneasiness slid through Hagger's gut and he rolled his shoulders.

He turned to Ricar, the Dog who'd been interviewing the woman. "Have any of the Dogs reported in yet? Was anyone following the two Wielders at the time the distortion formed?"

Ricar shrugged. "Not yet."

He hadn't thought so. They didn't have enough Dogs to cover all of the Wielders, no matter how adamant Daedallen and the Baron were that one of them was a traitor. No one had caught their attention yet, not from the Stone District.

But still . . . something bothered him.

He growled in irritation. First the girl, now this—

The girl.

His eyes widened and he turned on the woman, so sharply that she gasped, then hardened as if angered by her own reaction. "You said he grabbed a girl. Young? Around . . ." he counted the years, surprised at how long it had been, ". . . twelve years old?"

"Yes, that would be about right, she wouldn't have been much old—"

Hagger grabbed the woman's upper arm, his grip so tight she winced and tried to draw back. "Describe him." When she hesitated, he shook her arm and repeated, "Describe him!"

"He was br-broad in the shoulders," she stammered, fear in her eyes now. "Muscled, like a . . . like a Dog. And he had a scar on his face."

"A scar? Like mine?"

She shook her head. "No, it wasn't from a blade. It was from a burn. It covered nearly half of his face." She glanced down toward the hand that held her. "Please. Please let me go."

He released her and turned toward the corner where he'd seen the girl. She wasn't there, of course, but her face, the long pale hair, something about the eyes, the structure of the face—

Hagger smiled slowly and his jaw clenched, eyes narrowing.

"So, you returned after all, old partner. You returned after all."

The woman beside him shuddered and rubbed at her bruised arm.

Twenty-Two

K ARA WOKE SLOWLY to a throbbing headache and the familiar scents of musk and someone making tea. She moaned, rolled to one side without opening her eyes, and drew the pillow and blankets filled with the musk to her face. She breathed in deeply, the scent helping to dispel the headache—

And then the scent penetrated her lethargy. A man's scent. Marcus' scent.

She lurched upright with a cry and stared wildly around Marcus' chambers. A dog—the boy's dog, she realized, the one from the distortion—raised its head and watched her from the far corner, near the door.

Marcus' room was exactly as she remembered it. Clothes scattered on every available surface, globes set to their lowest setting, a few glass objects from the southern climates on the side tables and chest in one corner. His purple Wielder's jacket had been tossed haphazardly onto the end of the bed, her own next to it.

Breath catching, she jerked the blanket away, but she was still dressed in her own clothes. In fact, she lay on top of the blanket. She must have pulled the opposite side over herself while she slept.

Relieved, but with anger stiffening her shoulders, she slid out of bed, grabbed her jacket, and stepped into the outer room, the dog rising to stand beneath her feet.

Marcus looked up as she entered, in the middle of pouring himself a cup of tea. Jarkeeling by the smell of it. Her favorite. He smiled, the expression weary and wary, as he reached for a second cup. "The dog followed us from the site of the distortion. He nearly bit my hand off when I tried to take him away from you."

"I thought you were taking me to the node," Kara said flatly, her voice grating. She cleared her throat but didn't move to accept the cup Marcus offered.

He grimaced and set it back onto the table, pushing it toward her before retreating. "I intended to, but then you blacked out. So I brought you here instead."

Kara bristled. "You should have taken me home."

"I don't know where you live now."

"Then you should have taken me to the node!"

"And *you* shouldn't have blocked me at the distortion!" He started to say something more, the anger flaring in his eyes, setting Kara's teeth on edge. The dog emitted a low uncertain growl, then stopped. Marcus backed down, but she knew what he'd been about to say: that the boy and the man might still be alive if she'd allowed him to help earlier, if she hadn't hesitated.

She winced. "What were you doing there in the first place? You don't work in Stone."

He turned away, but not before she saw irritation cross his face. "I'd gone to see the Primes, to see whether they'd learned anything about the blackout. I felt the distortion on my way back to Eld. I thought I could help."

Kara frowned. A bitter taste filled her mouth, fresh and yet so old, so familiar.

Marcus was lying. About what she couldn't tell, but she hadn't spent twelve years living with him without knowing the signs: the inability to face her, to look her directly in the eye; the defensive anger and bitterness, to distract her; the irritation. All manipulations to make her back down, to give in.

But she was done with him now. She didn't have to back down or give in.

She could simply leave.

She pulled her jacket on and moved to the door, the dog on her heels. Her mouth tasted awful, but she'd be damned if she'd drink his tea.

When she reached the door, he stopped her cold with a curt, "What? No thanks for helping you?"

She glanced over her shoulder and in a dry voice without meaning said, "Thanks."

Then she stepped out of Marcus' apartment. She needed a drink. A real drink.

"Kara! What are you doing here?"

Kara raised the glass of fine Severan wine to her lips and ignored Cory's outburst, surprised he'd found her, even though they'd hung out here before. It was a little early for him to be away from the University. The Golden Oak usually attracted a quieter crowd, not students. She liked it because of that, and because it hadn't completely embraced the use of the ley or the Tapestry for everything. A wood fire roared in the hearth. A few lanterns with actual wick and oil hung from the rafters. None of the ley globes were in evidence. Even the food was cooked over real flames. Some of the surrounding businesses and building owners grumbled about the fire hazard, but the tavern's owner didn't care.

Cory clumped across the mostly empty common room and sat down at the stool next to Kara, nudging the scrappy dog lying at her feet to one side, his grin turning to concern as soon as he saw her face. "What in hells happened to you? You look awful."

"Thanks. You always know the perfect thing to say to cheer me up."

The bartender snorted but didn't look up from where he washed glasses at the far end of the bar.

Cory ignored them both. "What's wrong?"

She looked him in the eye, saw he was truly concerned, and sighed. "One of the distortions opened up in the middle of the Stone District midmorning. I was on call. I arrived too late, got caught in it when it quickened." Cory said nothing. The bartender stopped cleaning to listen. "I managed to pull myself out of it, along with another woman and a dog. This dog," she nodded toward the floor, and the mutt looked up at her, "who hasn't left my side since. But the distortion closed up before I could save the other people trapped in it."

"And you came here, rather than going to the node to report or home to rest."

She frowned at him in annoyance, turning away to hide the flash of guilt she felt certain was written blatantly across her face. Guilt over the deaths of the man. And the boy.

But she certainly wasn't going to tell him she'd ended up at Marcus'.

"My head hurts," she said, too harshly. "And I've found that a glass of good Severan helps. I can almost taste the Steppe's frigid air, the icy waters of its lakes and snowmelt streams." She waved her glass, wine sloshing, and as she did, realized that perhaps she'd had a little too much, even though it was only her third glass.

Cory rolled his eyes. "I'll have the icy lake water and snowmelt streams that she's having."

Kara smiled, a rush of warmth toward Cory suddenly suffusing her. She didn't know if it was real or the result of the wine, but it didn't last. She set her glass on the bar, ran her finger around its rim. As the bartender thunked down a glass and poured Cory his wine, her mind turned back to the distortion and the boy. For a moment, the scent of the tavern—lantern oil and oak and ale—was overlaid with the iron scent of blood.

She shuddered, and caught Cory watching her.

"So why are you really here?" he asked.

She almost told him, almost blurted out Marcus' name, almost admitted that if she hadn't been so damned stubborn that perhaps he would have been able to help her sooner and the boy would still be alive, would be running with his dog through the streets of Erenthrall instead of his blood staining the Stone District while his dog lay at her feet.

She shoved the image away, the pressure of tears burning behind her eyes, and took another sip of her drink, Cory waiting patiently.

She frowned. He wasn't going to let it pass.

With a sigh, she said, "You and your mentor study the Tapestry, right?"

Cory leaned back in his seat, caught off guard by the question. "We use the Tapestry, but not the same way you do. Or at least, not for the same reasons. Why?"

"Something strange happened with the distortion today and I can't figure it out. Maybe you can help."

Cory frowned, suddenly wary, as if he didn't know whether he should be talking about what he did at the University at all. "What happened?"

"When the distortion quickened, it caught this man and a young girl inside it. The man crouched over the girl, shielding her from it—"

"Which never helps," the bartender interjected.

"—which *normally* never helps," Kara continued, with a glare. "But for some reason the fractures in the distortion didn't touch him, or the girl, even though it surrounded them. It appeared as if they were protected by something. I didn't have enough time to free them before the distortion collapsed, but they vanished into the crowd as soon as it closed, unhurt as far as I could tell. Have you ever heard of someone surviving a distortion once they've been caught in it? Without having been freed by a Wielder?"

Cory's brow furrowed and he took a deep slug of wine, swirling it around his mouth before swallowing. "I've never heard of anyone surviving, no." He turned toward the bartender. "How about you?"

The bartender shook his head. "Never. Until now. And bartenders hear everything."

Cory shifted back to Kara. "What is it that was protecting them? What did it look like? Or feel like?"

For the first time, Kara noticed that Cory was tense, that he'd arrived tense and had only been distracted by how awful she looked. Now, looking at him directly, she could see the tightened skin around his eyes, the way he steadied his hand on the edge of the bar, how he couldn't keep still, fidgeting on his stool. She should have noticed it earlier, but she'd been too preoccupied with her own guilt and the emotions churned up by Marcus.

Cory hadn't found her by accident today, but he obviously wasn't going to talk about what had brought him to her here, in front of the bartender.

Turning back to her drink, she shrugged. "I don't know. It's hard to explain. I didn't see anything exactly. The fractures of the distortion just . . . stopped. As if they'd run into a wall of some sort."

Cory shifted in his seat. "Was the man doing anything with the Tapestry?"

"No. Not that I could sense anyway. He didn't seem to be doing anything at all except protecting the girl."

Brow still furrowed, Colin thought for a moment, then shook his head. "I don't know of anything that would disrupt a distortion. I don't think any of the other students have heard of anything either, or someone would be studying it. But maybe my mentor knows of something. We should go ask him."

He said it casually, but he didn't look at her, stared into his glass before swallowing the last of the wine instead.

Kara did the same, setting the glass on the bar. She could feel Cory's tension as she slid off her bar stool and drew her purple Wielder's jacket around her. She didn't know what Cory was anxious about, but it would keep her from returning to her empty loft with only Marcus and the dead man and boy to think about.

Touching Cory's shoulder, she said, "Then let's go ask."

As they wound their way through the Eld District, Kara let Cory take the lead. He didn't seem interested in talking once they left the tavern. The tension she'd sensed inside had changed to excitement. He moved fast, dodging through the crowded streets, past hawkers and peddlers and around carts laden with vegetables and fruits from the fall harvests. He was moving fast enough that Kara had to pick up her own pace.

Which is when she noticed the Dog behind them.

He wore ordinary clothing, not the armor and uniform of a soldier, but he couldn't hide the fact he was a Dog, not once he started moving fast enough to keep up with them. After watching him for a moment, Kara realized he was following her, not Cory. Something cold dug into her chest—no one in the city wanted the Dogs after them, or wanted the Baron interested in them, not after the Purge—but she continued to follow Cory, keeping one eye on the Dog, memorizing his rather plain face: light hair, brown eyes, a few signs of pox on his cheeks. He didn't seem intent on catching up to her; he merely wanted to keep her in sight.

Cory reached the gates to the University, what had originally been the Baron's stronghold before he moved to the towers of Grass near the Nexus. The old fortress had been taken over by the academics. The University frowned on anyone from the city entering the grounds, including the Wielders, although they'd been called in on occasion despite the rift between the two groups in order to handle . . . problems.

"Come on," Cory said, motioning her forward. "I think my mentor will be in his office at this time, but not for long. He's got a class in less than an hour."

Kara nodded and joined the throng of mentors and students— undergraduates dressed in a drab brown, graduates like Cory in tans— passing in and out through the gate. She took a surreptitious glance behind her as they reached the inner yard. The Dog had halted at the gate. He glanced in, scanning the students, then spat a curse before sinking into the shadows beneath the outside of the gate to wait.

Smiling tightly to herself, Kara followed Cory past the old barracks—now student dormitories—around the stables and training grounds, to a set of halls in the back, behind the main manse. She could feel the Tapestry in use all around her, the lines of the ley beneath the grounds pulsing, tingling against her skin, even when they entered one of the halls. The interior foyer and main corridor were lit with only a few ley globes. The scent of old wood, soot, and musty parchment permeated the building, the stone solid but with the scuff marks of use and age, the wood paneling polished but scarred in places. Cory led her down the main corridor, past a few turns, then halted in front of a door and knocked.

The door opened without warning. A short man with a scraggly salt-and-pepper beard nearly a hand's span in length glared out at them. His skin was darker than Kara's, but not as dark as the Gorrani from the south. She thought he was from across the western mountains, from one of the Demesnes, although she couldn't determine which one since she couldn't see the tattoos on the backs of his hands. The fact that he was here, in the University, was surprising. Those from the Demesnes rarely left their lands, especially those that could wield the Tapestry or the ley. He was dressed like someone from the Demesnes as well, in a linen shirt with embroidery along the upper torso and shoulders, breeches cut off at mid-calf, stockings and leather shoes beneath.

"Ah," he said, dismissing Cory completely, focusing on Kara. His voice was soft, but forceful. She found herself shifting uncomfortably under his scrutiny, his gaze slicing through her, everything exposed, as if he could see her every thought. "I see you convinced her to come."

"She actually has a question for you, Mentor Hernande," Cory said. "I haven't told her anything about the sands."

The mentor's brow furrowed. "A question? Then perhaps we can help each other."

He turned away, vanishing inside his rooms, leaving the door open. With a shrug, Cory entered.

Kara shot Cory a dark look as she followed. "What about the sands? What *are* the sands?"

Every surface in the room was covered with books and parchment, materials stacked on the large desk against one wall, all of the myriad tables, the shelving to either side, the chairs strewn throughout the room, and the floor. Paths wound through the books, and a few plants hung in clay pots from the ceiling. A doorway led into another room, which appeared as cluttered with books as the first from what Kara could see, although she caught the end posts of a bed with rumpled blankets draped to the floor before the mentor reappeared.

He'd donned a dun-colored mentor's robe over his Demesne clothing, but hadn't tied it in front.

"The sands are where the mentors train us to use the Tapestry," Cory said.

"And where we perform our experiments," Hernande added.

"What do they have to do with me?"

"It's not the sands themselves that are of interest, but what we've done with them. I asked Cory to bring you here so that perhaps you could verify a hypothesis I have regarding the outcome of our latest experiment." He hesitated, catching Kara with that penetrating stare again. "If you are willing."

"What about my question?"

"I'd consider your question regardless of whether you're willing to help me or not. You are, after all, a Wielder. Shall we retire to the sands?" he asked, motioning them out the door again. "We can discuss your question as we set up."

"To the main field?" Cory asked.

"No." Kara caught the look of disappointment on Cory's face, but Hernande continued. "For our purposes, we shall only need the sands in one of the training rooms."

They entered the back of the old manse through what must have been a servant's entrance. Here, the corridors were narrower, stairs smoothed, with dips in the center from long use. When Kara ran her hand along the stone, she could feel the grit and, beneath an old sconce, a layer of soot and grease. Hernande led them out of the servant's section, across a wide corridor, and into a different wing, this one lined with identical doors evenly spaced along one side. Kara received a few odd or curious glances from the students they passed, and Hernande nodded to fellow mentors in their own dun-and-black robes, but otherwise they were ignored.

Hernande paused at one door, listened a moment, then tried the handle. It opened easily and they stepped into a small room. The rough

stone walls were bare—no sconces, no wood paneling, no tapestries—
but they were covered with scars. Some were from obvious sources, like
fire, swaths of soot and char etched on the stone. In one section, the
stone appeared to have melted and dripped down like candle wax. In a
few places, chunks of stone were missing, as if they'd been struck by a
sword, the raw stone beneath exposed.

Kara turned a raised eyebrow on Cory, who shrugged. "These are
the practice rooms. Sometimes experiments . . . don't go as expected."

"'Sometimes' is misleading," Hernande muttered. "'Often' is more
precise."

All three turned to the center of the room.

A stone walkway surrounded a set of three steps that led downward
on all sides to a shallow pit. The pit was filled with sand, the granules
of mostly beige stone glittering in the white light of the ley globes that
hovered high above, near the ceiling. Depressions riddled the sand,
footprints, as if someone had fought here recently. The room was dry,
but not dusty, and smelled of salt.

"This isn't sand from the rivers," Kara said, moving forward. "Where
does it come from?"

Hernande grunted. "This sand is from the beaches off the Galicia
Demesne, my homeland, which is why I prefer to work in this room
when it's available. Other rooms contain sands from other areas—the
obsidian sands of the Correllite Isles, the white sands off the cliffs of
Warten to the east, even the rare pink silt from the Qumar River near
the equator." He breathed in deeply, catching Kara's eye, his own lit
from within as he smiled. "That is the scent of the Murcia Ocean. I
lived in a villa on the ocean, played in this very sand as a child."

His obvious joy made Kara wonder why he'd left. Or what had
forced him to leave.

Before she could ask, he clapped his hands together and said, "Now,
Cory, please smooth the sands while I prepare. Then send someone to
cancel my next class, since I will obviously be occupied here."

"And what should I do?" Kara asked.

"Ask your question. Then I have something to show you."

Kara settled down on the steps while Cory left the room, returning
a moment later with what looked like a rake with small tines. But she
couldn't remain seated, a strange nervous energy coursing through her.

As she watched Cory begin smoothing out the dunes in the sand, she began pacing. "Have you ever heard of someone surviving a distortion once they've been caught in it?" she asked.

Hernande had pulled small incense holders from his pockets and began placing them at the four corners of the sand pit. "Of course. You and your fellow Wielders save people from the distortions and all of the other anomalies caused by the misuse of the ley on a daily basis. It's your job."

Kara gave the mentor an irritated look, noticed the smile touching his eyes. "I mean survival without the interference of a Wielder, after the distortion has quickened, then closed."

"Why do you ask?"

"Because this morning, a man and a young girl were caught in a distortion and it collapsed before I could free them. They left unharmed, and while we were caught in the distortion, I saw both of them moving."

Hernande halted his preparations and stared at her over the sand pit with one eyebrow raised. "You were caught in the distortion yourself?"

"It quickened while I was too close. I was only caught in its edge."

He grunted. "Still . . . it would be interesting to discuss your perceptions while inside the distortion. Some of my colleagues have theorized that the distortion actually fractures time and space. Perhaps you would have some insight into their theories. But that is not what you came to discuss." He shrugged the tangent thoughts aside and paced back and forth across the length of the sands, one hand stroking his chin, elbow cupped in his other arm, head bowed. Every now and then he pulled his beard up and chewed on the end thoughtfully, which made Kara grimace.

Finally, he turned to Kara with his penetrating stare. "I cannot recollect an instance where anyone survived a distortion without some form of outside help. Are you certain—"

"Yes," she said, cutting him off.

He nodded. "Ah. I'll have to do some research, look into accounts of the distortions, especially the earliest ones. However, I'd hypothesize that whatever this effect is, it doesn't originate with the distortion."

Kara straightened. "Meaning what?"

"Meaning that it wasn't the distortion that skipped over the man and girl," Cory answered. He finished with the last of the sand, the pit now smooth. He wiped sweat from his forehead. "Whatever caused it to stop came from the man."

Hernande nodded. "Or the girl."

"I don't think he realized what was happening. Not at first."

Hernande shrugged, his attention shifting from the conversation to the sands. "More evidence that it may have been the girl. It may be an unconscious manipulation of the Tapestry, something he or she has no control over. Or it may have nothing to do with him or the girl." With a wave of his hand, Hernande dismissed the question. "I'll need time to think on it. Now, I have something to show you."

Irritated by the dismissal, Kara began, "But—"

"Don't," Cory said quietly as he came to a halt at her side. "He's already thinking about it, even if it doesn't appear that way. And he needs to focus for this to work."

"I don't see what anything you two are doing would have to do with me." She pitched her voice loud enough to carry to Hernande where he had crouched, concentrating on the sands.

"It might have nothing to do with you. But I think it does," Cory said, his voice low as he watched Hernande. "This is what I was telling you about the other day, what we were starting when the ley went dark."

Kara frowned as she felt Hernande reaching out to the Tapestry, drawing it in and focusing it. A Wielder's job was to smooth out the Tapestry, to iron out the wrinkles and repair the tears and rents in its fabric caused by the ley or the misuse of the Tapestry by those untrained with their own abilities. But what Hernande was doing was different. Instead of smoothing it out, he was gathering it in folds, drawing it together and twisting it in such a way that no tears or rents appeared.

Then Kara felt him reach up to the ley globes, felt him form a connection between the two, drawing some of the ley down into the folds he'd created. The globes above dimmed as he drew from their power. Ripples spread outward on the Tapestry, but dissipated before they'd traveled too far.

Hernande looked up. "Everyone knows there's a connection between the ley and the Tapestry. We can see the consequences of that connection in the distortions, which only began appearing when the ley was subverted by the Primes and the Barons into the current ley system. However, we don't know what the connection between the two is. I've been studying the ley and the Tapestry for the last thirty years with the help of my graduate students, like Cory, trying to find the connection between them. This is what I've found most recently."

Without moving, he threw the gathered folds of Tapestry and ley out over the sands, the entire construct spreading like a fisherman's net and settling slowly, its corners tied to the incense burners Hernande had placed at the edges of the pit. Kara stepped forward as it began to sink into the sands, the grains and ley and Tapestry comingling, until she couldn't see the folds anymore, could only sense them hidden underneath.

For a long moment, nothing happened.

But then the sands began to move, like water, shifting and flowing in set patterns. It started in the center of the pit and spread, channels snaking outward like a web.

Kara tensed, Hernande watching her intently.

When the moving sands reached the stone edge of the pit, they halted. After a moment, everything settled and Kara began to pick out paths in the pattern. Some of the eddies were moving faster than others, appeared stronger and wider, thicker. Others were narrow and moved slowly. Still other sections of sand weren't moving at all.

"It's like the currents in a river," she said, moving around the corner of the pit toward Hernande. "In some sections, the current is stronger than others."

The mentor nodded. "Yes. Tell me what else you see. What you sense." He didn't say anything more. Cory started to speak, but Kara saw Hernande motion his student silent with a subtle gesture.

A quarter of the way around the pit, Kara halted abruptly.

Something in the flows seemed familiar.

She focused in on one particular section, tilted her head slightly to change her orientation, brow furrowed. Her heart beat in her chest, throbbing in her skin, the nervous tension she'd felt earlier prickling along the hairs on her arms, although that could be coming from the Tapestry and the ley, an aftereffect of the construct Hernande had created. She shrugged the sensation aside and concentrated, focusing on the section that had caught her attention, that seemed vaguely familiar. Hernande and Cory waited, their breath held.

Then she gasped and glanced up sharply. "That's the Eld District, and that's Stone. These are the ley lines. This is the ley structure for the entire city of Erenthrall. All of it, what can be seen above ground and what's hidden below."

Hernande nodded with a tight smile, eyebrows raised. "It extends a little beyond Erenthrall as well."

Kara held his gaze, her mind racing, thinking back to the discussion she'd had with Illiana and Steven in the node, back to the map tacked to the table, the implications and ramifications of what Hernande had constructed penetrating with sudden swift force, like a blow.

"We can use this," she whispered, excitement already creeping into her voice. "We can use this to find out what's wrong with the ley system."

Hernande frowned. "But if this is what you say it is, if this is a true map of the ley system and its current flows, and the Primes find out we have it. . . ."

Kara felt something choke off her breath, cutting off her excitement in a death grip. She thought of the Dog who'd followed her to the University grounds. "They'll kill us all."

"Why?" Cory asked. "Why would they kill us? We could have the key that helps them solve the problems with the ley."

"They won't care," Kara said, beginning to pace again. "The ley system is how the Primes keep their stranglehold on the Barons. They knew when the ley system was created that it would become the basis of power within the city, and they knew that they could control that power. They'll eliminate any threat to that control. If they discover that we have access to their system, to the ley's secrets—"

"They will attempt to contain us," Hernande finished. "Especially us. The rivalry between the Primes and the mentors at this University is . . . historic."

"They've kept this secret from the Wielders as well," Kara added. "Only the Primes have access to the Nexus. Only the Primes know how the entire system works. The division between Prime and Wielder is sharp. They do not react well when a Wielder treads on their turf." She thought back to the interrogation the Primes had put her through after she'd worked with the distortion at the Eld ley station, and she had already been slated to become a Prime herself. If Marcus and the other Wielders hadn't been there to protect her. . . .

She shuddered and glanced up to find Hernande watching her, his eyebrows pulled down in concern.

"What I fail to understand," he said quietly, "is why you are so anxious about the Primes at the moment. They do not know what we have discovered. Only you, Cory, and I know of this. I have not shared this with any of the other mentors."

She held his gaze a long moment, then said, "One of the Dogs followed us to the University."

Hernande's eyebrows rose in surprise. "That . . . is unexpected." Then he frowned in thought, hand traveling to his beard. He chewed on it as he began moving around the pit of sand, coming to Kara's side. "Is it possible the Primes have detected the construction of the map?"

"I don't think so." Kara closed her eyes and spread herself out on the Tapestry, her senses encompassing the room first, then passing beyond, feeling the energy flows around her. Someone was working in the room two doors down—she could sense the use of the ley and Tapestry there—but once she passed beyond a certain distance all signs that anyone was using the ley in this room faded into the background.

She opened her eyes and shook her head. "I don't see how they could know about it. The power you use for the map is too localized. It's lost in the background outside twenty paces of this room. Besides, the Dog was following me, not Cory or you. And I didn't know about the map yet."

"Why would the Dog be following you?"

"I don't know. And I don't know how long he's been following me. I only noticed him on the way over here, but he could have been watching me for a while now. Either way, it doesn't make sense." She thought about the barge crash, how the Dogs had arrived before the city watch. But if they'd been following her since then, why hadn't they appeared immediately after the distortion this morning?

And hadn't a few of the other Wielders mentioned seeing the Dogs more often lately while chatting around the node?

Kara traded looks with Hernande, who shrugged. "It doesn't make sense. They can't possibly be aware of the map."

They both turned to look at the flowing sands, Kara kneeling down at the edge of the bottom step. This close, she could hear the grains moving against each other with a faint hiss. The smell of salt was much stronger now than when she'd first entered as well, as if churned up from the sand pit's depths.

"Do you see anything?"

"No. The patterns match what I know of those two districts, and Hedge and Tallow and all of the other districts I've worked in. But beyond that, I can't tell. The Primes don't like us to know too much about the rest of the city."

"Then it may take some time to find any anomalies in the system. We'll have to study it, look for discrepancies. We'll need to take note of the directions of the flows, their strength, whether they ebb or increase at specific times of the day, if they fluctuate at all." He began wandering away, his attention shifting to Cory. "And we'll need to try to expand the map to include places other than Erenthrall."

Kara reached out toward the shifting sand near her feet, nearly touched it, but pulled back and stood. "I'll help, when I can."

"What will you do in the meantime?" Hernande asked.

She smiled grimly, pulling her attention away from the sands. "I'll watch the Dog, see if I can find out why he's watching me."

"And what if we find something here?" Cory asked. "How are we going to tell the Primes if we can't reveal we have the map?"

"We'll deal with that when we come to it," Kara answered, although she had already begun planning. Steven had contacts within the Nexus. And the Wielders themselves could act, if it came to that.

The Primes couldn't kill all of them. Not when the Wielders were the ones who maintained the ley out in the streets.

"I can help you with some of the equipment on your list, but the supply of medicinal herbs—the coraphile and bloodbane," Vanter tapped his finger against the sheet of parchment, "that's hard to come by. Costly as well."

Allan scrubbed his haggard face with both hands, then grimaced. "What can you get on that list? And how much will it cost?"

Vanter shrugged his massive shoulders and moved back behind the long table that separated the front of the room from the dark recesses in back. Allan could see stacks of crates, labeled and categorized, straw sticking out of the cracks between the wood, along with heaps of burlap sacks, rounded casks, sealed clay urns and pots, and a hundred other assorted containers within the first thirty feet before the rest was swallowed up in shadow. The illicit dealer's room reeked of hay, dust, animal feed, and some type of oil that must have been spilled recently. The overall effect was rather pleasant, somehow clean, especially considering that Vanter's establishment was in East Forks, one of the worst districts in Erenthrall.

Which was why Allan knew that the two of them weren't alone. There were at least three others hidden in the darkness of the warehouse, there to guard the supplies from the denizens of East Forks and to keep an eye on Vanter's customers. Allan could feel their eyes on him, even though he couldn't see them.

Vanter himself was huge, at least a foot taller than Allan, with a broad back a hand wider and certainly more muscular than Allan's. None of his bulk was from fat. He wore a beard trimmed down to a thin line along the jaw in the current Temerite style, although Allan thought he came from Erenthrall itself originally. Allan had dealt with Vanter before and while he was straightforward and trustworthy when it came to the items he traded, the cost was typically exorbitant.

Vanter studied one of his ledgers, flipping back and forth, making notations on a separate sheet as he went. "I can get you the plows and the hitches easily enough. The leather materials will take a few days. Most of the rest of what I've marked here—the bags of grain seed, the oils and bronze ingots—are already here at the warehouse."

He handed back Allan's sheet, a check near the items he could supply.

Allan scanned it and tried not to grimace. Not nearly enough covered, and this was the pared-down list.

He looked Vanter in the eye. "How much?"

Vanter leaned back, hands behind his head. "Rumor has it you come with a list every year, yet you've only come to me . . . what? Three times in the last ten years? Why is that?"

Anger tightened Allan's grip on the sheet of paper, but he didn't drop his gaze. "You're too expensive."

"I see. The rates do get cheaper with repeat customers, as I'm certain you're aware. You only come to me when you're desperate." He paused in contemplation, his eyes not wavering, then he grunted. "One hundred errens for the lot."

Allan's stomach clenched and he gazed back down at the sheet of paper, noticed that it shook. He mentally tallied what he'd brought with him to pay for the supplies—what the citizens of the Hollow had sent him with—and felt sick.

He straightened and met Vanter's flat stare. "Seventy-five."

Vanter snorted. "I could get twice that for half the supplies on your list." But his gaze narrowed. "Ninety."

"Eighty."

"How do you intend to transport all of this? Plows aren't light. Neither are the rods for your blacksmith."

"I have transport already arranged. Eighty."

Vanter frowned. "Eighty-five. Take it or leave." His voice had taken on a dangerous, dismissive tone.

Allan thought of the Wielder at the distortion, of Hagger and the Dogs he'd seen all over the city since. More Dogs out than he had ever seen during his stint in the Baron's pay, let alone the last twelve years he'd come to Erenthrall for supplies. They were looking for something. Or someone. He could feel it in the prickle on the back of his neck, in the sense of urgency building in his gut.

"Done." He retrieved forty errens from the pack slung around his back. "Forty now, the rest on receipt and delivery of all of the supplies."

Vanter nodded, leaning forward to take the money. "Agreed. I can have it ready to go in three days."

"What about the medicine, the coraphile and bloodbane?"

"What about it?"

"You only said that it's hard to come by. Does that mean you can get it?"

Vanter hesitated. Allan could see him calculating its cost against Allan's desperation. "Let me ask around. I may be able to get it for you. How do I get in touch with you?"

Allan frowned. The prickling urgency in his gut passed through him in a wave. "You don't. I'll stop by in a day or two."

"Fair enough." Vanter scratched out a receipt—which Allan had always thought odd for someone who dealt on the black market—and handed it over. "Pickup will be at the docks, as usual."

Allan halted in the street outside, scanned the surrounding rundown and decaying buildings—what had once been the thriving docks and warehouses of the city until the arrival of the ley lines—but saw no

Dogs through the faint drizzle. The few people on the street ignored him, and those partially hidden in the alleyways and alcoves of doors that preyed on those in the streets sidled deeper into the shadows.

Allan shrugged his shoulders, but the prickling tightness at the base of his neck remained.

He headed toward the bridge leading to West Forks, head bent against the chill rain, shifting his cloak enough so that the pommel of his sword was visible to discourage the gutterscum, but the sense of urgency in his gut didn't abate. Picking up his pace, he caught occasional glimpses of the Tiana River between the buildings, suddenly concerned about Morrell, left alone in the small room he'd rented for their stay in Erenthrall. She would have drawn too much attention in East Forks if he'd allowed her to come with him, both from the Dogs and from the gutterscum. But now, a cold, thin mantle of fear settled over him, shivering in his skin. What if the Dogs had tracked him to the room? What if they were desperate enough to bring one of the Hounds to bear to find him?

He shuddered. Even after the Hound had let him leave Erenthrall, he'd expected them to hunt him down. When over two months had passed, he'd assumed that he wasn't important enough. Then he'd heard about the Purge and realized that the Dogs and Hounds were too busy controlling those within Erenthrall to worry about a lone deserter. But maybe something had changed. Maybe there was more going on here than a Wielder recognizing a former Dog who'd fled after the death of his wife.

Maybe the Wielder hadn't recognized him at all. What if her strange look had been about something else entirely?

His pace slowed with the sudden thought, and new fear jolted through his back.

He lurched forward as the fear seeped inward, his heart pounding, nearly moving at a run. The reek of the district burned in his lungs, people dodging out of his way, cursing. All he could think about was Morrell, her sulking face when he told her she couldn't come with him, that she'd have to remain inside and out of sight until he returned.

He never saw the men. The board swung out of the shadows of an alley and connected with his gut.

Pain exploded in blinding whiteness as he folded over the board, curled and twisted, hitting the ground hard with one shoulder and ripping the board out of the attacker's hands. He heard someone curse, heard a short burst of laughter, followed by shuffling feet. His stomach clenched in agony, making it hard to breathe, hard to focus. He hissed through gritted teeth and rolled onto his back. The board clattered to the stone of the street.

He lay there gasping, blinking his eyes to clear his vision—

And a hand reached down out of the receding whiteness, grabbed a handful of his shirt, and hauled him across the stone, new pain exploding through his chest. Sounds grew muffled as they entered the alley. Allan winced as the man dropped him into the middle of the sludgy runoff from the rain, then retreated. Jolts of pain shot through him at every movement, so he remained motionless, willing the aches away with every gasped breath.

He needed to be able to move if he was going to get out of this and back to Morrell.

"Stop cursing and help me," one of the men growled.

A figure knelt down beside him. He couldn't see the man's face, but he could smell him. He reeked of the river, of fish, and the shit and slime of the alleyway.

"I'm bleeding. The board cut me up good when he ripped it away."

"That's your own damn fault," the man kneeling beside him said, then glanced up. Allan caught the profile of a broken nose, a cheek scarred and pocked, with ragged stubble. "Are you holding him, Tery?"

Something pressed down on Allan's chest and arms, as if a heavy blanket had been thrown over him, although none of the shadowy figures Allan could see had moved.

"Well?" the leader spat.

The figure at the edge of Allan's vision shifted. "I've got him. I think."

"You think?"

"I've got him, I've got him! Just get on with it."

The leader grunted and motioned the third man forward. "Let's see what this bastard has for us, shall we?"

As the third man settled down on Allan's other side, shaking one hand and still wincing in pain, the leader began sorting through Allan's clothes.

Allan tensed, clenched his jaw as the leader reached into an inner pocket—

And then he heaved up, throwing off the heavy blanket, a fist shooting out, catching the leader with the broken nose hard in the face. Bone cracked and blood splattered as the leader roared in surprise and fell backward, but Allan didn't wait for him to land. His other hand had gone for the short sword at his side. He drew it and swung as he rolled into a crouch, cutting the third man, the one who'd nailed him with the board, across the stomach even as the man cried out and lurched away. Allan felt the blade bite deep, then turned his attention to the leader and the other man who'd hung back near the edge of the alley.

"Who are you? Who sent you?"

The leader held one hand over his face, blood gushing from between his fingers, his breath coming in harsh, fluid heaves. He glared at Allan, his hatred tight across the skin beneath his eyes. "I thought," he said, his voice low, like a growl, "you had him held down."

"I did," Tery said from behind him.

"Obviously not!"

"I did! He slipped out of it somehow. The ties I used to bind him just slid free. They rolled right off of him!"

To one side, the third man had fallen onto his back and now lay still, emitting short, ragged gasps as he whimpered and mumbled to himself. Allan risked a quick glance in his direction, saw him clutching at the wound in his stomach, his face strikingly pale in the gloom, beaded with sweat and rain, his clothes stained black. The sharp scent of blood and stomach acid lay beneath the drizzle, tainted with an underlying reek of shit. A dark pool began to spread from underneath his body.

"Oh, gods, Lars, it hurts! He cut me good! Lars? Lars, it hurts bad, it—"

He drew in a sudden deep breath, as if surprised, and let it out in a long slow sigh. One hand slipped from his stomach and fell to the alleyway with a thick slap.

Allan turned back to Lars. "Who are you and what do you want with me?"

Behind, Tery grew still and gasped, "Baron's balls, Lars, he's a Dog."

Lars' eyes flew wide, true fear crossing his face, settling in the corners of his eyes, but then those eyes narrowed, took in Allan's clothes, his sword, his stance. "No, not a Dog. Why would the Baron send his Dogs to East Forks? There's nothing here the Baron's interested in."

"But they've been seen all over the city lately, even in Tallow. What if they've sent someone in to sniff things out? What if—"

"Enough!" Lars spat. "He isn't a Dog!" But the fear in his eyes hadn't abated. He smiled uncertainly. "But he was a Dog once, wasn't he?"

Allan's hand clenched on the handle of his sword. He brought his other hand across his bruised stomach with a wince, then swallowed, tasting a sourness in his mouth. "Leave," he said, and heard the tremor in his voice.

Lars heard it as well. His smile widened and he pulled the hand covering his nose away from his face, glanced down at his own blood and snot coating his fingers, then back at Allan. New anger sparked beneath the fear and he wiped his hand on his breeches. "I don't think so. You've killed my friend here, and I think you need to pay for that."

He drew his own sword, the blade narrower than Allan's, with a slightly longer reach, but older and not as well taken care of judging by its dullness and the nicks in its edge. The style of the hilt suggested it was from the Demesnes, which made Allan wonder how Lars had gotten his hands on it.

Perhaps the same way he'd managed to get Allan cornered in this alley.

Allan rose from his crouch, hand falling away from his stomach. Fresh pain flared, but he could already feel himself sinking into a calmed state, his breath slowing, aches and bruises receding into the background, his body already slipping into the default stance of the sword. Lars slid into a similar stance—

Then he moved, unexpectedly, sword striking in a classic Temerite style, fluid and swift. Allan reacted without thought. Training kicked in even as he registered a moment of surprise and a thin frisson of fear—Lars was trained—then he seized the man's movement and used it to his advantage, parrying the sword with a clash of metal on metal and carrying the force off to the side, slipping beneath Lars' defenses and slashing hard across Lars' other arm. Lars hissed as Allan's blade bit into his bicep, deep enough to draw instant blood, but he stepped forward, raised his free hand and shoved Allan hard, bringing his sword around and cutting low along Allan's thigh as he stumbled back.

Allan came up hard against a stone wall with a grunt, then pushed away, raising his sword to block another strike as he lurched toward the center of the alley, seeking space to maneuver, room to fight back. He felt a twinge in his side as he spun and caught Lars' sword again, metal scraping as he drove the strike down and away. Even as he moved, feet slipping in the mud of the rain-slicked alley, his fist drove forward for another punch to Lars' bloodied face.

He missed Lars' nose, struck his cheekbone instead, but it staggered him. He stumbled back with a howl, Allan seizing the moment to take control of the center of the alley. Tery had moved to the far end, near the entrance, his back up against the wall, his face open with blatant fear. He didn't look like much in the greater light near the street—tall, thin, dressed in clothes as worn and ragged as Lars'. He didn't appear to be carrying any weapons larger than a knife.

Allan brushed him from his mind, focused on Lars again. The thug had regained his balance and now glared at Allan from his own position, seething, rage replacing everything else in his expression, all of the fear and hesitation gone. He was pissed, and not because Allan had killed the other thug. He was pissed because Allan had bested him. And he'd done it in front of Tery.

They glared at each other, both breathing heavily, Lars' more phlegmy and less controlled, but Allan's strained. His bruised abdomen had begun to take a toll.

"Leave," he said again, the word harsh, filled with command.

Lars sneered, then attacked. Not a charge—his training wouldn't permit that—but Allan countered, grunting with the effort, his strength ebbing. Swords clashed, strike and feint and parry, and at every opportunity Allan drove his fist into whatever opening presented itself: a thigh, lower back, chest, upper arm. Lars cried out, managed to slice Allan again across the chest, the wound barely drawing blood, and Tery watched it all from the entrance to the alley.

"Help me!" Lars barked at one point. "Help me, you bastard!"

But Tery only shook his head and muttered, "I can't. It just slips off of him. I can't hold him. I can't even touch him." His voice shook with effort, sweat and drizzle rolling down his face.

Then Lars slipped in the mud of the alley and Allan seized the opening, driving his sword down into the thug's side, an inch beneath his ribs.

Lars gasped. His free hand rose halfway toward the blade embedded in his side, his eyes catching Allan's one last time, still burning with hatred.

Then he collapsed, Allan's blade slipping free. He tried to roll away, body arching. His sword dropped from his weakened hand and Allan kicked it away, but the action was unnecessary. Lars was already dead.

Allan turned slowly toward Tery. The thin man watched him warily from the alley's entrance, still breathing hard. Allan felt a pressure against his arms, his chest, his neck, but at each fumbling push the pressure slipped away, like folds of silk brushing across his skin.

"You can't touch me," Allan said. "Not with the ley, or whatever it is the Wielders use."

The pressure stopped. Tery swallowed once, eyes widening even further—

Then he bolted into the street.

Allan let his sword lower, watched the entrance to the alley for a long moment, listening for a shout, for a call to the city watch, but heard nothing except the dripping of the misty rain.

Morrell.

Heart leaping, the urgency from before the attack returning with a spasm in his chest, he wiped the rain and sweat from his face, cleaned his sword and searched the two bodies perfunctorily, taking a few coins but nothing else. Then he returned to the street, pausing only at the entrance to the alley to scan for threats.

Then he moved, fast, but not as reckless as he had before, his senses heightened. His stomach ached, the two cuts burned, but he shoved the pain aside, moving out of East Forks, across the bridge over the Tiana into West Forks, passing through streets and narrows. At a corner, he slowed, head bowed, as a group of Dogs passed by, and then he darted down the street behind the building where he'd rented a room. Entering through the courtyard gate in back, he moved through the hall to the front of the building, scanned the street outside but saw no one watching.

He turned to the stair and ascended to the second floor. When he opened the door to their room, Morrell turned from where she was sulking on the bed, her eyes angry and pensive, ready to protest her seclusion, but her indrawn breath caught in her throat as she took in his shirt stained with blood.

Her eyes widened, and she leaped from the bed with a strangled cry of "Da!"

"It's all right, Poppet, I'm fine," he said, letting her hug him tight around the waist a moment before pushing her away slightly and moving to the single window, gazing out at the street below.

Morrell followed him, not willing to let go of his hand. "I don't like it here," she said in a soft voice. "I want to go home."

Allan glanced down, saw the tears streaming down her face, the vulnerability there, and his heart twisted in his chest.

He should never have brought her with him.

Kneeling down, he wiped her face dry and kissed her on the forehead, hugging her close to his chest. "Three more days, Poppet. We can leave in three days."

Twenty-Three

THE HOUND HAD found Leethe within three hours of disembarking in Tumbor, had been following him for the past week. Most of the Baron's activities had been uninteresting, duties that took him to various districts throughout Tumbor. The Hound had seen the old wharf, the massive trading grounds to the east, where caravans had once gathered for protection and to conduct business, the trading houses that surrounded the new ley stations, and the hulking granaries where Leethe and the other nobility stored most of their export goods. He'd investigated all of these locations thoroughly and found nothing. He'd searched the palace, the mistress' residence, even the estates of the lords and ladies Leethe had visited since his arrival. Nothing.

Until yesterday.

Yesterday, Leethe had deviated from his normal schedule. Instead of rising and attending to the mundane details of his responsibilities in Tumbor—passing judgment and mediating quarrels—he'd ordered a carriage and departed the palace for an unknown location along with an escort of enforcers and his chief enforcer, Arger. The Hound hadn't been able to keep up with the carriage, hadn't even tried. He'd followed Leethe's scent to the base of the Flyers' Tower instead, and discovered that the Primes and Wielders who had been sent to Tumbor to oversee the ley network in Leethe's city had allowed the Baron to enter.

The shock when he realized Leethe's scent passed through the tower's doors had set the hairs on the nape of his neck prickling. He'd stood in the tower's shadow, mouth twisted into a snarl, staring up at the subtle folds of vine and leaf that had been sown to create it. No one but the Primes and Wielders were allowed access to the towers or the

Nexi, not even Baron Arent. The argument over access had been harsh and loud, but Prime Augustus had refused to back down and eventually, grudgingly, Baron Arent had agreed. The Nexi and the ley were declared sacrosanct. All Wielders and Primes swore fealty to Augustus, and through him Baron Arent. It was the only way to maintain the integrity of the ley system and to retain control of the ley for Erenthrall and Arent.

For Baron Leethe to have gained access to the Flyers' Tower, he must have subverted some, if not all, of the Primes within Tumbor. It was the only explanation.

He needed to gain access to the tower. He needed to find out what Leethe and the Primes here in Tumbor were doing.

By the time he reached the base of the Flyers' Tower, the sun had set, darkness settling over the city streets. Here in the heart of Tumbor, the walks were mostly empty, those who worked in the palace and the nearest trading houses already returned home. Ley globes lit the thoroughfares, the white lights steady, but the Hound kept to the shadows, halting only when the occasional group of pedestrians or Prime Wielders walked past. He didn't halt for ley-driven carriages or carts, trusting the occupants to be preoccupied.

He contemplated the tall main doors, shaped like a leaf, coming to a point at least thirty feet overhead. He'd never attempted to enter the Primes' precincts, not even in Erenthrall. He didn't even know if the doors opened in the traditional manner.

With one last glance up the tower's side, the entire building glowing with veins of pale white tinged a slight green, he ascended the wide steps, keeping to the rounded half-wall on one side, where the shadows were deepest. When he reached the tower, he paused, scanning the street below in both directions, then slipped to the center of the doors.

The handle was in the shape of a curling vine, even though it had petrified after its sowing. He reached forward, gripped it tight, then pulled.

The doors didn't move. But he felt a tingling in his hand, one that was familiar.

The Tapestry.

He sent a small surge into the handle of the door, felt the power within hesitate, as if testing him, tasting him, and for a moment he thought what little power he had would not be enough.

But then the door gave, nudged outward by the pressure he'd exerted.

He pulled it open enough to slide through, then closed it behind him.

Inside, he shifted to the edge of the room as he scanned the interior. A single huge ley globe hovered far overhead, near the apex of the arched and vaulted ceiling. The round foyer contained three doors, the stone floor a smooth pattern of twisting vines. The Hound drew in a deep breath, scented the hundreds of people who had passed through the room, along with all the varied incense and other odors that had mingled here. He filtered through them all, found the one that mattered—Baron Leethe—and stepped toward the door on the left.

It led to steps heading down. The Hound paused to listen, heard the murmur of voices from behind, beyond the foyer through one of the other doors, but nothing from below. He descended, his hand loosening one of the knives hidden about his body. He breathed in and out steadily, concentrating on the scents. His blood heightened. He recognized a few of those who had accompanied Leethe: Chief Enforcer Arger the most prominent; a few of the other enforcers that Leethe kept close. He growled low in his throat at this further betrayal by the Primes, but continued, ignoring the corridors that opened up on a few landings. He judged he'd circled to the northern edge of the building before the Baron's scent broke away from the steps into a central room.

The Hound hesitated, breathing in deeply, but no one had passed through here recently. He stepped into the new room, realized that the architecture had changed. The walls were formed from the reddish-brown rock of the surrounding lands, molded by the ley, not the sown and petrified vines that had been used for the tower. Vertical slivers of ley light illuminated the room at regular intervals. Three more corridors branched off from this room, but the Baron had only traveled through one of them.

The Hound frowned. If his sense of direction hadn't been thrown, this new room and the corridor beyond led away from the tower.

He glanced back up the stairs, then started toward the new corridor, halting at the edge of the door when he heard voices approaching. He slid to one side, back against the wall, knife now cupped loosely in the palm of his hand, and quieted his breathing and heart. There were no shadows here, no places to hide. He would have to rely on inattention and his skill with the Tapestry.

A heartbeat later, two Primes emerged from the corridor, arguing intently. The Hound tensed. But neither Prime turned, too focused on their argument. They passed through the room and into the tower beyond without turning, their voices fading as they ascended the stairs.

Relaxing, the Hound headed down the corridor, lit in the same manner as the room, moving swiftly. He wouldn't be able to remain unnoticed if someone came down the corridor now; the hallway wasn't wide enough. As he moved, he estimated his location in relation to the tower, realized the underground passage led across the thoroughfare to the north of the tower and beneath a park. He hadn't paid much attention to the park in his attempts to follow the Baron, except to note that the gates to the park had been closed and sealed. Now he wondered why.

He slowed as the hallway came to an end, sensing a massive chamber beyond, lit with a much more intense source of ley than that in the corridor and shivering with an immense power he could feel vibrating in his bones. He shielded his eyes, heightened his sense of hearing and smell, and stepped to the edge of the room.

The corridor ended in a short landing that circled around a massive cavern, the floor dropping down to another, wider ledge of stone encircling a pit. Stairs led down to the lower ledge on the left and right.

But it was the pit that held the Hound's attention. It was filled with ley light, so intense he couldn't look at it directly. But he could see sheets of ley undulating back and forth, arching outward and curling back, captured and refracted through prisms of crystal, edged in various colors as it moved and shifted. It was like nothing he had ever seen before, exotic and beautiful and pulsing with so much power he could feel it throbbing in his blood, crawling across his skin. All of the hairs on his arms were standing on end, tingling, and his teeth shuddered, the sensation excruciating. He clenched his jaw and forced himself to look away from the mesmerizing lights, scanning the ledge below, noticing Primes scattered about, their attention fixed on the display before them. Some had their eyes closed, their brows creased in concentration; others appeared to be meditating. A few were arguing as they motioned toward the pit.

And then it struck the Hound what he was seeing, what this display of ley must be: another Nexus, one to rival that in Erenthrall. Tumbor had its own Nexus, of course, built by Augustus and the other Primes when the ley was first harnessed here in the southern city, but that Nexus lay in a different part of the city, and from what the Hound had seen from the outside, was perhaps only half the size of this one.

His grip tightened on the knife in his hand and he struggled with the urge to descend to the ledge below and begin killing the Primes immediately. He'd taken two steps toward the stairs before he seized control, his plan of attack on the Primes already half formed. But his orders weren't to kill. Not yet. His orders were to gather information.

His lip curled into a snarl of disdain. Hounds were not meant to be spies, they were meant to destroy. His nose twitched at the remembered scent of blood, at the ecstasy that overwhelmed him when the prey was located and the bloodlust took over. He shuddered as he suppressed that urge yet again, growled as he twisted himself away from the pit and the victims below, retreating back down the corridor toward the tower.

He needed to find a ley station. He needed to touch the ley lines so he could report back to his handler. Baron Arent would want to know what Leethe had done, what he had created.

And then, the Hound thought with a vicious smile, perhaps he would be fully unleashed.

He could smell the Baron's blood already.

Allan drew the flatbed wagon to a halt before Vanter's warehouse, scanning the street on all sides as he did so. One of the two horses snorted and stamped its foot, not liking the stench of East Forks. Allan agreed. He also didn't like the shadows in the alleys created by the heavily overcast day. It wasn't yet noon, but the cloud cover darkened it to nearly dusk. Rain threatened, but so far the black clouds hadn't broken.

He shifted in the wagon seat, making certain that the eyes he could feel prickling against his neck knew he carried a sword, then jumped down to the broken cobbles of the street and rapped on the wide loading doors of the warehouse. Movement registered in one of the alleys, and he thought he caught the glint of a blade. A frisson of fear and the stark memory of the attack three days before returned, tightening his shoulder blades and making him shudder, but then the doors rattled partway open and Allan turned to find Vanter peering out.

The broad-shouldered man grunted as he recognized Allan, surprise flickering across his face even though Allan had returned the day before to ask about the medicinal herbs and to verify he would pick up his other purchases today. Vanter had appeared nervous and distracted, but he'd found the herbs and everything was set for the pickup. Now, the black market dealer glanced up and down the street, ignoring the alley where Allan had seen movement, before locking gazes with Allan.

"You've got transportation, I see," he said, but he didn't move to open the door further.

Allan touched the pommel of his sword and frowned. Something wasn't right. He thought of Morrell, hidden in the flat in West Forks, of the rest of those in the Hollow who were depending on him to bring back what they needed for the winter. He'd already sunk most of his remaining funds into this deal.

Swallowing his unease, he said, "And the money. Are we going to deal or not?"

Vanter grimaced, but pushed the door open further, motioning him inside. "Bring your wagon inside. We'll load it up for you."

Allan nodded and climbed back into the seat. He flapped the reins and tsked the horses into motion, shooting one last glance at the shadowed alley before passing into the warehouse. Two of Vanter's guards pulled the doors closed behind him, Vanter waiting at the far end, beside his desk. The goods that Allan had purchased were stacked before him. Allan pulled the wagon to a halt again and slid from the seat. As he moved toward Vanter, three of the man's guards emerged on Allan's right side, the two who'd closed the doors coming up on his left.

Allan's eyes narrowed and he fixed a hard look on Vanter. "What's going on, Vanter?"

Vanter smiled. "A business transaction, nothing more. Just . . . not the transaction you were expecting."

He stepped to one side, and from the deeper shadows of the warehouse, Hagger appeared.

Allan's reaction was instantaneous. Even as his stomach lurched with dread and horror tightened his chest, he reached for his sword, drawing it in a smooth, soundless motion while dropping into a defensive crouch. He backed up against the wagon, gaze darting toward Vanter's men. But none of them made a move, their expressions blank, their gazes fixed on the floor. None of them looked at Allan, or at Hagger.

The older Dog laughed, the sound hollow in the cavernous ware-house. "Good to see you, too, old partner," he said, but his voice was dark and promised blood. "I never expected you to return to Erenthrall. I was shocked when you fled—all of the Dogs were—but none more so than me. I sent a Hound after you, after your betrayal, but he claimed you weren't part of the Kormanley. And the Baron was too busy de-stroying them to worry about a deserter Dog. After the Purge, no one cared anymore about a traitor who'd already fled the city. No one ex-cept me. And now here you are." His voice hardened. "Didn't I warn you that no one—*no one*—ever leaves the Dogs?"

Allan tensed as ten other Dogs stepped into the lantern light. Behind Hagger, Vanter grimaced. He shot a glance toward his men, who began shifting out of the Dogs' way.

The black market dealer's face settled into distaste as he caught Al-lan's eyes. "He came to me," he said apologetically. "And I have a busi-ness to run."

Then he turned and motioned his own men into the shadows of the warehouse.

Allan spat a curse, searching frantically for a way out. The main doors were clear . . . but he knew that Hagger would never have left them uncovered. The movements in the alley must have been Dogs waiting to close the trap, not the gutterscum he'd assumed. Which meant Hagger wanted him to run, wanted him to try to escape. The street outside must be packed with Dogs.

He turned away from the doors and gripped his blade tighter. He'd trained hard while in the Hollow, but not enough to best this many men. Yet he couldn't lose; he had to get back to Morrell.

Some of the other Dogs had edged forward. The two horses sensed the tension in the room and snorted, shying away from those closest, their feet pawing the rough stone floor. Allan ignored them and the Dogs, focusing on Hagger.

"What's wrong, Hagger? Your pack seems hesitant."

Hagger scowled and gestured with one hand.

Three of the Dogs moved in instantly, the youngest of the group, their faces only minimally scarred, but their eyes dark with hatred. Allan's stomach roiled sickeningly—Hagger wanted to play, otherwise he'd send them all in at once—but then the one on the right struck.

Allan moved, stepping forward into the swing, catching the Dog's blade with his own even as he twisted inside the youth's guard and slammed his elbow into his gut, then rotated his clenched fist up into his face. The Dog gasped and staggered back, but Allan had already turned to the other two, coming in hard. He parried the first's blade, kicked his knee out from beneath him, and barely managed to turn the second's sword. He wrapped his free arm around the second attacker's throat, slipping in behind him and leaning him backward, then spun both of them around to face the rest of the Dogs.

None of them had moved. Of the three who'd attacked, one lay on the floor moaning. The other climbed to his feet, favoring one leg, his grimace vicious.

Allan tightened his hold, the Dog flailing, back bent into an awkward stance. His face began turning red and his breath escaped in harsh, desperate exhalations.

A moment later, his struggles increased and his eyes began to flutter. Then his body went limp, his sword clattering to the floor from his loosened grip. Allan eased his body to the ground and stepped to one side, the wagon again at his back.

"You aren't training them as good as you used to, Hagger," he said.

Hagger glowered. "You've had more practice."

The remaining seven moved in suddenly, joined by the one remaining, limping Pup. Allan met them head on, swords clashing, men grunting as blows were landed, blades slicing into skin. He'd tried not to harm the Pups, but he released himself on the Dogs, taking every advantage presented. He cut clean through one Dog's guard, his blade sinking into the man's chest, but as he roared in pain and reared back, someone cut in along Allan's thigh. The sting of the blade made Allan hiss, but he turned, flashed his blade across the Dog's face, and punched hard with his left hand. Pain flared in his lower back—another cut, another slash of blood—followed by one to his upper arm. A glancing blow numbed his sword arm. He felt his blade tumble from his fingers, closed them into a fist and began to brawl, punching hard left and right, aiming for faces, for kidneys. He heard Hagger bellow something, felt the Dogs shift patterns, swords giving way to fists. He sucked air through his clenched teeth as blows landed hard, coming from all sides. A punch caught him on the jaw, another driving into his lower back, and as he bent into the pain, someone hit him with a sharp upper cut.

His head snapped back and he fell, dazed, the world tilting around him, the lantern light blurred. Stone slammed into his face and he tasted blood as he bit the inside of his mouth. Fists shifted to kicks, boots slamming into his gut, and he unconsciously curled to protect his stomach. His ears rang, the sounds of the beating muffled, and as the taste of copper and salt filled his mouth he thought of Morrell. What would she do when he didn't return? Would she flee back to the Hollow? He wasn't even certain she could find it on her own.

At least he hadn't brought her with him.

Then, dimly, he realized the Dogs had stopped.

He opened his eyes—didn't remember closing them—and blinked through the haze of pain. He heard heavy footfalls, rolled his head back and rocked half onto his back to see Hagger approaching, his old partner halting to stare down at him. He grinned, then knelt, reaching out to seize Allan's jaw with one hand, pinching hard to keep Allan focused.

"I think that's enough for now," Hagger said.

"What if he doesn't cooperate?"

"Oh, he'll cooperate." Hagger released his jaw and motioned to one side. "Won't you, Allan?"

Allan concentrated, blinking the haze from his eyes—

And then his chest seized, his body going still, his eyes wide.

From the depths of the warehouse, two Dogs appeared, shoving Morrell before them.

Hagger stood. "Take them to the Amber Tower."

⟞⟝

Dalton read the orders from Baron Leethe one more time, controlling the tremors in his hands with effort, then set the single sheet of thick paper onto the table before him. The Baron's representative stood on the other side, watching him through narrowed eyes. He wore street clothes, nothing that would make him stand out in West Forks, but he'd recited the correct code words, and the paper the orders from Leethe were written on was of the same coarse stock Dalton had given the Baron for use in communications. But still Dalton hesitated. There was tension in the air. He could feel it pressing against his skin, against the inside of his head, like the approach of a storm. He sensed it in his visions.

"Are the orders clear?" Leethe's messenger asked.

"The orders are clear."

"Then your Benefactor expects you to carry them out." The messenger turned to leave, reaching for the door.

"How much longer will he need our services?" Dalton asked.

The messenger halted, half turned back. "I do not know his wishes. I am simply a courier." But there was a hint of warning in the man's voice, that perhaps Dalton had overstepped his bounds. It said that the Baron's wishes were his own and none of Dalton's concern.

But Dalton thought the Baron was nearly finished with them. The courier had been too abrupt. And then there was the tension and his dreams.

He realized the courier was waiting for a response. "Tell the Benefactor I await his next message."

The messenger nodded and ducked out through the door into the hallway beyond. He had been escorted to the room by Dierdre, the woman closing the door behind him without entering herself. But Dalton knew that Dierdre would have wound her way through the building's halls to listen at the door behind him. When he heard it creak open, he was not startled.

"What does the Benefactor want?" Dierdre asked as soon as they heard the outer door close behind the courier.

"What he always wants," Dalton answered, handing the sheet of paper to Dierdre. "Tell Marcus to implement these changes in the ley as soon as possible."

"All of these changes? What about our own plans? Isn't it time to begin bringing down the Nexus? Marcus says he thinks he sees how it could be done. His experiences manipulating the Nexus have given him some insight into how it works. You said yourself it feels as if everything is coming to a head now. Perhaps this is our opportunity to interrupt the Benefactor's plans and take out the Nexus."

Dalton nodded, his eyes still on the empty hallway before him. "The culmination is near. The visions proclaim it, and I feel it in every sinew in my body."

"But?"

He raised his trembling hands before him, willed them to stillness, but the doubts that plagued him and the terror of the visions wouldn't allow for calmness and they continued to shake. He let them drop to the table again. Was this their opportunity? If he didn't act now, would the Baron succeed in whatever it was he intended? Or was it too early?

He didn't know. He couldn't tell.

"It is not yet time. Tell Marcus to make the indicated changes, as written."

Dierdre hesitated. Dalton could taste her doubt on the air, acrid and bitter, but she turned and left, the coarse paper rustling as the door closed behind her.

Dalton bowed his head, a wave of regret sweeping through him. For a single moment, the fires of his vision consumed him to his core, seared him with the certainty that he had made a mistake, that he had let his chance pass by.

But then the fires faded and he was left only with his fears.

Baron Arent cut through a section of lamb, the meat tender and perfectly cooked. Captain Daedallen sat to his left, looking uncomfortable at the formal setting, as if he wasn't certain which fork to use, or what the shallow bowl of lavender-scented water to one side was for, although he had attended formal dinners before. The rest of the lengthy table was empty, although a seat awaited the arrival of Prime Augustus to Arent's right.

The two ate in silence, Daedallen having already delivered his report. Arent hid his own rage in the meticulous slicing of meat. He could not quite control the tic near his temple.

Twenty eternal minutes later, the door on the far end of the room opened and Prime Augustus entered, pausing as he noticed Daedallen, then moving down the length of the room toward them.

Arent's rage faltered only a moment when he saw how exhausted Augustus looked, his eyes sunken in their sockets, his face drawn and haggard. He motioned toward the empty seat.

"Join us. Eat. Daedallen has heard back from the Hound sent to Tumbor. You need to hear his report."

With a small nod from Arent, Daedallen set down his fork and focused on Augustus. "The Hound believes Baron Leethe has been behind our recent troubles with the ley network. He has discovered that Leethe, with the cooperation of the Primes in Tumbor, has created his own secondary Nexus, one to rival that of Erenthrall."

Arent watched Augustus closely. The Prime Wielder stared at Daedallen in incomprehension, back hunched over.

"He has created a new Nexus," Arent said, barely controlling his anger. "He has forsaken the contract with Erenthrall, with you, with *me!*"

Augustus gaped, as if Arent's rage had finally pierced through the weariness that lay over him like a shroud. He straightened, glanced toward Daedallen, who remained silent, his expression clouded, then back toward Arent. "A new Nexus? Leethe?"

"Is it possible?" Arent snapped. "Is it possible that the Primes in Tumbor have turned traitor? Is it possible they could construct a Nexus equivalent to that here in Erenthrall? Could Leethe seize control of the ley?"

"I . . . I don't . . ."

Arent slammed his palm down on the table, glassware and silverware jumping, the sharp sound startling in the elegant silence of the room. "Gods damn it, Augustus! Wake up! Is it possible for Leethe to take control of the ley?"

Anger flared through Augustus' eyes and he clamped his mouth shut, teeth grinding. Arent didn't care, as long as it brought the Prime out of his lethargy. He needed answers. He needed confirmation.

He needed to take back control.

"I don't think so," Augustus snarled, his back rigid now, but doubt marred his expression. "But . . ."

"But what?"

"But if someone were to attempt it, it would require massive power. They would have to draw from the main network—"

"Meaning Erenthrall," Daedallen said.

Augustus shot him a dark look, but Daedallen didn't respond. "Yes, meaning Erenthrall. And they would have to overcome the protective security measures I've put in place—" His eyes widened with sudden realization. "No, they wouldn't. Not since they have someone in Erenthrall manipulating the Nexus from within. That person's already inside the main security measures. They've already circumvented them."

His voice had risen as he spoke, all of the exhaustion gone. He shoved back from the table, hard enough to knock his wine over, but Arent clamped a hand down on his forearm and he lurched to a halt.

"Can you place these security measures on the Nexus itself? Keep the infiltrator from accessing the Nexus from the nodes?"

"What do you think I've been trying to do since I discovered what they were up to?" Augustus spat. "But I can't restrict the access from the nodes without cutting the power flowing out of the Nexus! Erenthrall needs that power. Without it, nothing will work, as we've seen with the blackouts. And that power flow is exactly what they're using to create their own Nexus. They're altering the orientation of the crystals here to shunt the power to Tumbor. That's what's causing the blackouts. It might even be the cause of the distortions."

"What about cutting Tumbor off from the Nexus? Cut the flow of ley to Leethe's city?"

"We'd be cutting off the flow to other cities as well. The network is too interconnected to isolate only Tumbor. It's a flaw in the system, something I didn't anticipate." Augustus grimaced at the admission. "You would risk angering Baron Calluin, along with relations with the Gorrani, the Archipelago, the Horn. It's possible, but the collateral damage to Farrade and the other nations would be significant."

"How do you intend to stop them, then?" Daedallen asked.

"I can't stop them unless I'm inside the Nexus. I have to be present when they attempt to alter the alignment of the crystals. It's the only way short of cutting the power to Tumbor completely."

He met Arent's gaze, their eyes locking, Augustus' filled with rage, his arm still trapped in Arent's grasp. Arent tightened his grip, but the Prime Wielder never wavered, his jaw locked rigid, the exhaustion setting the bones of his aged face in stark relief. He hadn't been immersing himself in the ley baths, Arent realized, not as often as he should have been. This trespass on his domain, this infiltration of his Nexus, had consumed him.

Arent released him.

Augustus straightened, then spun and headed stiffly toward the doors of the dining chamber. Halfway there, he announced, "I won't give up my network. I won't give up my ley." Then he stalked out of the room.

Arent gripped the edges of the table hard, knuckles white. His glare dropped to the table, to where the dark red stain of Augustus' wine grew, the liquid nearing the edge of the table. In a tightly controlled voice, he said, "Order the Dogs to collect everyone they have been following. Everyone. No matter how trivial their suspicions. We can't count on Augustus stopping this Wielder from inside the Nexus. I won't place all of my trust in him alone. We have to find this traitor ourselves. And have the Hound kill Baron Leethe. He's violated the compact with Erenthrall. Not even Baron Calluin would dispute his transgressions now."

Daedallen reached for his knife and fork. "Already done. The Hound is unleashed, as you ordered. And the Dogs have already been sent."

Arent sent the captain a harsh look, irritation at the anticipation of his orders about the Dogs roiling upward from within. He would have given vent to them, had already drawn breath to berate the captain, when the ley globes that illuminated the entire hall flickered—

And went out.

Twenty-Four

KARA SCRUBBED AT her face where she sat cross-legged at the edge of the sand pit at the University, feeling the grit around her eyes and the strain of using the Tapestry and manipulating the ley all day. But she stifled the yawn and subdued her weariness and tried to focus on the sands before her. The shifting granules hissed, a noise that had grated on her nerves at first, but after spending hours with Cory and Hernande in the practice rooms over the last week— every hour she could spare from her duties at the node—she'd grown accustomed to it, almost found it soothing.

She noticed Cory watching her from across the pit, brow furrowed in concern, so she smiled. "So what have you two learned since yesterday?"

To one side, Hernande grunted. "We've been able to extend the range of the pit out to a radius of about two days' travel."

"But at that range," Cory interjected, "the details of the ley system are lost. You can only see the major ley lines, those used for shipping, or those that connect to the major ley sources surrounding Erenthrall."

"The finer details, like the lines that form the network here in Erenthrall, are lost."

"We've spent most of our time studying the interactions of the lines here in Erenthrall, trying to determine what is causing the distortions and the blackouts," Cory said. He hunkered down close to the sands, pointing out aspects as he spoke. The pit was currently set on Erenthrall, on the districts surrounding Stone, and Stone itself. "Since you're most familiar with Stone and Eld, we've reset the map on that area. I think we've watched it closely enough to determine the normal flow of the ley in general. Most of the activity is centered at the nodes, of course. We noticed a fluctuation here, near the ley station—"

Kara nodded. "There was a wrinkle in the Tapestry earlier today. Illiana was sent to repair it."

"—and a disturbance on the edge of Green."

"A distortion. Normally I wouldn't have known about that, but it was close enough to Stone that one of our Wielders crossed into Green to help."

"Then it would seem," Hernande said, both Kara and Cory looking toward where he stood contemplating the map, "that the sands react almost instantly to changes in the ley. This could be invaluable to the Primes."

"It would be invaluable to the Wielders. Our patrols don't catch all of the distortions. We never know when or where they will happen. If a Wielder isn't close enough to sense the disruption to the Tapestry, we often don't even know a distortion occurred until someone reports it. With this, we'd be able to locate one from the node as it was forming, then send someone directly to it to deal with it." She shook her head in angry regret. "But the Primes would never allow it."

"There has to be a way," Cory said.

"I don't see how. Not with all of the tension between the Primes and the Wielders. Especially now."

"Why is that?" Hernande asked quietly. He was chewing on the end of his beard again, his gaze intent.

Kara scowled. "The Primes seem to think the Wielders are causing the blackouts. Or at least one of the Wielders."

Hernande's eyebrows rose in surprise. "Is it true?"

Kara shifted uncomfortably. She'd been thinking about it ever since the Wielders had noticed the shift in the Primes' attention and Steven had returned from one of his visits to the Nexus in a fit of anger. "I don't know. I don't see why."

"But you do see how." Hernande made it a statement, not a question, and once again Kara fidgeted in discomfort. She had grown to like him, but he was too perceptive.

She almost lied and denied it, but sighed and said, "Yes. I can see how it could be done using the nodes. But I still don't see why. The Wielders are sworn to preserve the ley, to repair the Tapestry."

Hernande grunted. She expected him to ask for details, but he didn't.

Instead, he said, "Do not forget the Kormanley. They intended to protect the ley as well, yet they instigated significant damage—and death—in the name of their cause. Does it not seem possible that a Wielder would be willing to cause destruction in order to protect and preserve the ley?"

Kara frowned, unable to answer. It didn't make sense to her, but she had never understood the Kormanley, could barely repress her anger and grief at the mention of their name.

But she knew Wielders who were passionate about the ley, about the Tapestry and the protection of the network. She worked with them on a daily basis. Illiana rose instantly to mind. And Marcus. Even herself. It was their work. For some of them, it was their entire life.

As she struggled to comprehend what Hernande had suggested, the mangy dog that had attached itself to her lurched upright from where he'd lounged in a far corner, ears at attention, a low growl coming from deep in his chest. Cory suddenly glanced up from the map toward the door, then stood.

"Something's happening," he said sharply.

The warning in his voice caught Kara's attention.

Outside the room, she heard the muffled sounds of a struggle, the harshness of boots against stone. A voice rose, loud and demanding, cut off by the sound of a fist hitting flesh, followed by a cry. Her dog barked once in warning. Kara rose to her feet, but Hernande had already moved around the pit. He flung open the door to the practice room and glared out into the hall, and in the next breath roared, "What is the meaning of this? What are you doing here? Dogs are not allowed on University grounds!"

Two Dogs appeared in the doorway, their angry gazes falling on Kara. One of them sneered in satisfaction, then shoved past Hernande, the mentor slamming into the wooden door. Her own dog scrambled to her side, barking fiercely.

"Dogs go where they wish," the lead Dog growled, "by the Baron's decree." He pointed toward Kara. "We've come for you, Wielder."

Kara's heart lurched in her chest and she swallowed back the taste of bile rising up in her throat. She didn't dare glance down at the map, the shifting of the sands suddenly loud in her ears. "What for?"

"Does it matter? The Baron wants to speak with you."

He started forward, two more Dogs appearing behind the second waiting in the doorway. Shouts came from the hall, mentors and students exclaiming in outrage, some voices tinged with authority, others with fear. Kara took a step back as the lead Dog advanced, tried to restrain her own dog, now barking wildly and dancing protectively around her.

Suddenly Cory stood between her and the guard. His face was locked in determination, edged deeply with fear. "You can't—" he began.

But the Dog reached out, grabbed him by the shoulders, and flung him aside. He hit the wall of the practice room, crumpled to the stone floor, rolling to the edge of the pit. Kara didn't even have time to protest before the Dog's hand latched onto her arm, fingers digging painfully into muscle. He jerked her forward, began hauling her toward the door. Her mutt growled and lunged at the Dog's heel, but the guard kicked it aside viciously. It hit the wall with a yelp and lay motionless. Everything was happening too fast. It didn't make any sense. If they were here for her, because of the map, then why weren't they seizing Cory and Hernande? The Dog hadn't even looked at the map. But if they weren't here for the map, what did they want her for?

Then Cory gasped, "Kara, look!"

She twisted in the guard's grip, saw Cory at the top of the stone steps that led down to the sands. He pointed toward the map, toward a particular section.

The Dog hauled her forward, but she dug in her heels, resisting, even though the Dog wrenched her arm painfully to one side in reaction. She focused on the sands, realized that something was wrong, something had changed. The normal flow had altered, the sands in one part running in the opposite direction, running from one of the nodes *back* toward the Nexus. She sucked in a sharp breath, held it as the pattern solidified, as something within the swirling eddies of the Nexus changed—

And then, even as the sands settled into the new pattern, the ley light within the practice chambers guttered and went out. With a rustling sigh, the sands of the map halted. All of the protests in the outer corridor, all of the demands, fell silent.

"Blackout," one of the Dogs muttered in disgust.

The single word broke the tableau.

"Let's move!" the Dog holding Kara roared. His grip tightened and he dragged her toward him in the darkness of the room. "Go, go, go!"

he barked, the sound so close Kara winced, and then he pushed her out into the hall where the other Dogs were bulling their way through the mentors and students. All of their protests had died in the blackout, everything chaotic. Kara stumbled over people, bumped into bodies, hauled forward relentlessly by the Dogs down hallways and corridors, until suddenly they spilled out of the servants' stairs and into the harsh afternoon sunlight.

She blinked, her mind refusing to think. Because the Dogs were still herding her forward, moving fast, cutting through the clusters of University people in the quad out front, heading toward the gates. Because even in the daylight she could tell that all of Erenthrall had been affected by the blackout.

And because the disturbance she had seen in the sands, the disturbance that had affected the Nexus, that had caused the blackout . . .

That disturbance had originated in the Eld node.

And she knew, with sudden and undeniable gut-wrenching certainty, what that meant:

"Marcus."

Hagger drew the edge of the blade down along Allan's shoulder, to the armpit and across to his lower back, drawing out a thin line of blood. He wasn't pressing deep, even though he wanted to—oh, how he wanted to, his rage making his hand tremble—but the sweat and blood that already slicked Allan's back salted the wound and Allan's breath quickened as it hissed through clenched teeth. His entire body shuddered, even though Hagger knew he was trying to control it, trying not to react. Hagger knew Allan had seen enough of these sessions—participated in enough of them—to know that reacting fed Hagger's need. He grinned as he thought about everything he intended for this lying, cowardly traitor. He'd only just begun.

And the best part was that none of the other Dogs cared what happened to him, not even the captain. Hagger could do whatever he wanted, prolong it as long as he wanted. He needed nothing from Allan.

He finished the slice with a vicious jerk and stepped back from the table, Allan's arms tied underneath it, his legs strapped down behind him. By now, Allan's arms would be numb, perhaps his legs as well, depending on how tight the other Dogs had drawn the straps. Allan's attention would be focused exclusively on his back.

Hagger examined his work in the ley light, then moved around to Allan's far side for the next cut. The bruises from the arrest at Vanter's marred the work, but he expected they would fade before he was finished.

He intended to keep Allan alive for a long time.

"What . . ." Allan croaked; Hagger hadn't given Allan any water since his arrest. "What . . . do you want . . . Hagger?"

Hagger grinned. "I want you to suffer."

He placed the knife against Allan's skin again, making the cut smoothly and cleanly, a little deeper this time, as Allan juddered against the table. Satisfaction curled through his anger, and as Allan tried to swallow his gasps, Hagger leaned forward, close to Allan's ear, and allowed his rage to color his voice. "No one leaves the Dogs," he growled.

Then he backed away, watched Allan try to follow his movements even though he couldn't move his head far. "Why did you leave, Pup?" The question came out hard, curt, even though he didn't really care. It didn't matter. But he was curious. "Was it because your last Kormanley attack failed?" he sneered. "Did you run because you were afraid that we'd finally catch on to you?"

"I wasn't . . . Kormanley."

"Then why did you run?" he shouted.

"They killed . . . Moira," Allan barked. "I ran . . . to save . . . Morrell!"

Hagger frowned, seething inside. It made sense, in a cowardly way.

He set the knife down on a separate table, picked up a small hammer.

Time to break some bones.

The ley lights flickered and went out.

He glanced up, even though the room had plunged into utter darkness, and swore harshly. Hammer in hand, he turned toward the door, stepped forward and rammed his foot into the leg of the table holding his tools. Steel clattered against steel as the various knives and hammers jounced, but he bit back the sharp retort that rose at the pain in his foot and reached out for the wall, his hand settling against the rough granite blocks, steadying him. Behind, he heard Allan struggling with his ties, but he ignored the traitor, slipping along the wall until his hand encountered the rough wood of the doorjamb.

Fumbling for the latch, he flung open the door and found the hallway outside pitch-black as well. To the left, he heard the scrambling of the Dogs in the training pit, orders being shouted left and right in a chaotic jumble. He swore again, then charged along the wall, one hand out for guidance. The sounds of the pit grew louder as he passed door after door, and then suddenly the wall to his left vanished and he took two steps into the large chamber that the Dogs had claimed for their own ages ago.

Sucking in a deep breath, he roared, "Silence! Nobody move!"

The curses and shouts died down, along with the scrape of armor against stone and the rustle of cloth. Someone was gasping in pain, from the direction of the training circle itself, and everyone was breathing heavily.

"Who's there?" someone demanded.

"Hagger. Alpha. Now shut up. Are there any other alphas here?"

Silence, broken a moment later by the same voice. "None. They're all out collecting the rest of the Wielder suspects."

Hagger rolled his eyes. "I said shut up. Who's on duty at the desk?"

"I am," another voice said, from the direction of what Hagger thought was the front of the room. "Drew."

"We need light. Aren't there some of those damned candles in the desk? We put them there after the last blackout."

He heard drawers opening, a clatter of junk as Drew rooted around, then a cry of triumph. "I found them."

Hagger swallowed down impatience. "Then light them."

A moment of hesitation, and then: "I don't have any flint."

Hagger felt the urge to crush something with his hammer, but before he could act the main entrance doors burst open and a slew of Dogs rushed into the room, the lead carrying lanterns, the strange gold light washing through the chambers and highlighting the rest of the Dogs in various tentative poses. Hagger was happy to note that not all of them were frozen in shock, that at least twenty spun on the new arrivals, swords already drawn or hissing from sheaths as they turned. The Dog who'd been harmed in the training pit when the ley died moaned and Hagger noticed blood coating his hand where it clutched his side.

"Drew, see to the wounded. And get those candles lit!" He stalked across the room, directly toward the new Dogs. "What's happened?"

The leader turned to Hagger, face tense. "The entire city's out. Again. We found lanterns and came straight here." He motioned toward a young man the Dogs were holding captive behind him. "We brought one of the Wielders."

"Put him in one of the rooms," Hagger said, "then get back out here. We're going to need all the Dogs we can get."

The grizzled alpha nodded. "There'll be more of us coming in with Wielders."

"I don't care. We need to get everyone out on the street and into the Tower. Where's the Baron? Where's the captain?"

The other alpha shrugged, already halfway across the room. "In the Amber Tower, last time I heard."

Hagger shook his head, then glared around at the rest of the Dogs in the chamber. "Form up into packs! Now!"

The Dogs scrambled, those out of uniform racing to get into armor, everyone else forming into groups of ten. Hagger began dispensing orders, Dogs rushing out into the tower. He didn't know the situation outside, but he knew what had happened the last time they experienced a full blackout. He sent them to secure the area immediately surrounding the tower. Protecting the Baron was imperative. Everything else could wait.

Even as packs left, new Dogs arrived, another Wielder behind them, this time a woman.

"We brought her from the University," the alpha reported, even as he motioned the Dogs holding her toward the cells.

Hagger's eyebrows rose. "What was she doing there?"

The man scowled. "I don't know. Something in one of the practice rooms. Something to do with sand. She's spent an inordinate amount of time there in the last week."

Hagger followed the woman with his eyes as she was taken away. She appeared stunned, but pissed off as well. She struggled only when the Dogs holding her used force.

She knew something, though. Hagger could see it in her eyes.

He raised the hammer still clutched in his hand, anticipation boiling in his blood, then lowered it with regret.

He could question her later. Right now there were more important issues at hand.

He motioned to the new alpha. "Follow me. I need to see what's happening outside."

They trotted up the stairs, another group with a Wielder passing them as they climbed, and then they broke out into the main chamber. Lanterns had been lit, imbuing the room with an orange amplified by the amber walls. All of the ley globes were out, but still hovered overhead. Servants were scattered, running to and fro, half panicked, but Hagger was glad to see that ten Dogs guarded the stairs leading higher into the tower on either side, another five inside the main door.

He nodded as he and the other alpha burst through to the outside steps.

Dogs lined the stairs, keeping all but fellow Dogs from entering the Amber Tower. As Hagger shielded his eyes from the sun's glare with one hand, blinking rapidly, his attention was caught by the harsh white glare coming from the Nexus.

He halted in his tracks and turned on the other alpha.

"It was like that when we came in," the alpha said.

The city might be dark, but the Nexus certainly wasn't. In fact, the ley appeared to be shooting out above the building itself, at least half the height of the Amber Tower. Unlike the displays of ley Hagger had witnessed at the sowing of the Flyers' Tower and at the Baronial Meeting, though, these jets of ley were chaotic. Beautiful, but uncontrolled.

Hagger swallowed, and for the first time in decades tasted the bitter acridness of fear at the back of his throat.

❦

When the ley died, Augustus halted, already halfway down the steps from the Baron's dining hall in the Amber Tower.

Then he ran.

He plowed through the clog of panicked servants and Dogs at the entrance to the tower, shouting "Prime coming through!" then spilled out onto the steps, tripping and falling down to the street below. Carriages lay dead, not even hovering above the ground, and he cursed as he picked himself up. Pain shot through his hip, but he shoved it aside. If the carriages were no longer hovering, then the ley that supported them had nearly vanished.

He staggered away from the street, cutting through the park to the left and emerging at the edge of the wall that surrounded the Nexus. It was housed at the base of a wide depression in the ground, stairs descending to the main building from four different directions. Primes were running toward the building, their figures casting long shadows as the throbbing white light of the ley fountained upward from the center of the building.

"It shouldn't be doing that," Augustus muttered to himself as horror pressed against his chest. "It shouldn't have escaped the confines of the building."

For a moment he faltered at the top of the stairs. He considered fleeing, the thought seizing his mind with conviction. He had already half turned back to the open gates—

But he halted with a shudder. His exhaustion returned, but he drew in a steadying breath and began descending toward the building, picking up speed as he went.

Erenthrall's Nexus was his. He'd be damned if he allowed anyone else control over it.

He stalked through the outer rooms and halls, summoning Primes as he went, until he had a group trailing behind him, all of them talking, all of them shaken. When he reached the doors to the inner chamber, he shoved through them without hesitation.

He found the center of the Nexus in turmoil.

The entire chamber was flooded with white light, so intense Augustus raised one hand to shield his eyes. Through his splayed fingers, he caught movement on the main floor. Gouts of ley fountained up from the central pit, splashing against the crystal dome overhead and spilling down onto the edges of the shallow tiers that surrounded the pit. He could see the fallen figures of Primes who had been too close, their bodies black silhouettes against the ley's fury. Other Primes were scattered on all sides, hands overhead, and even without reaching for the Tapestry, Augustus could see the wards they'd raised to protect themselves, the ley coursing down the invisible walls in front of the Primes like water sheeting down glass. The air in the chamber throbbed with power, thrumming in his skin. Before Augustus could step forward, one of the Primes holding the ley at bay cried out, falling back as his shield collapsed, the white ley he'd held at bay claiming him.

Augustus gestured toward the dozen Primes behind him and shouted, "Help them! Try to contain the ley as much as possible!"

The Primes spread out around the pit, dodging the licks of ley as it wreaked havoc throughout the chamber. Augustus ducked left, hurrying to the steps that led down into the lower chambers.

The lower pit was worse, bodies strewn everywhere, the ley breaching the overhead holes that looked out onto the heart of the Nexus, where the crystals within centered and augmented the network. At the heart of the Primes who had survived, Temerius shouted orders, his voice ragged and hoarse and threaded with fear. Augustus headed straight toward him, reaching for the Tapestry as he did so.

He found the Nexus in complete chaos, the Tapestry shuddering and rippling in waves. The crystals above spun out of control, no longer even remotely set in their usual positions. He could see Temerius and the others frantically trying to reset the crystals, but there were too many out of alignment, too many shuddering under the pressure of the ley as it raged.

He stepped forward, snagged Temerius' arm as the Prime bellowed, "Ventris! Shift that crystal to the left! Now, Leigh, twist the other to the right, like that, yes!" Temerius shot a black look back, eyes widening in surprise as he recognized Augustus. "Augustus! Thank all of the gods. It's spinning out of control. I don't know if we're going to be able to correct it."

Everyone was shouting, even though there was no real noise. But down here, the throbbing in the air was amplified to a painful pitch. It carried a high-pitched whine at its edge as well, making Augustus grimace.

"Let me see what can be done."

Temerius nodded, stepping back and releasing control of the Tapestry to Augustus.

He skimmed the entire Nexus, took stock, noticed the work the other Primes were doing to bring the crystals back into alignment, sectioning off the worst problems, planning an attack.

And then he noticed something else: even as one of the Primes corrected a crystal and moved on, someone else came behind and set the crystal spinning again. Someone was actively keeping the system in chaos.

The traitor. The Wielder.

He drew breath to report to Temerius, his anger flaring high, but a sudden hissing, as of ice cracking, resounded throughout the entire building. He glanced up, even though he couldn't see the ceiling of the upper chamber above him. The hiss escalated into a groan, the sound shuddering through the stone floor. Some of the crystals in the Nexus whined in sympathetic vibration—

And then something above cracked, the single retort deafening. Augustus staggered as the entire building shook, catching himself with one hand against the floor in a low crouch as the rest of the Primes were flung to the ground. He heard cries of distress, shouts of surprise, but they were all muted, his head ringing with the explosion. More rumbling followed, and after a moment he recognized it as debris falling to the ceiling overhead, and he realized what had happened.

Someone grabbed his arm and helped him rise. He turned, and as if through a blanket heard Temerius shout, "The crystal dome! It shattered!"

He nodded agreement, then shrugged Temerius' supporting hand aside, motioning toward the Nexus. "It doesn't matter. Someone's creating the chaos. Focus on the Nexus and get it stabilized. I'm going after the traitor."

Augustus didn't wait for Temerius' reaction, spinning toward the Nexus and reaching out along the Tapestry toward the channels branching out from the core and into the city. The ley in each channel had been dampened, nearly to the point that it didn't exist anymore, slowing down Augustus' search. He could manipulate it more easily if there were more of it around, but he plowed forward, using his rage to bull his way down the pathways.

He found all of them inactive . . . except for one, the Eld node. Someone was in the pit there, and had accessed the Nexus through the line.

Augustus trembled at the affront, at the audacity, but shoved the emotions aside. If they were to regain control, he needed to shut the traitor down. Now.

Seizing the ley, he tried to slam a wall down between the Nexus and the channel to Eld, to cut off Eld's access to the ley. Except the wall met resistance.

The traitor had put up a block. Augustus stepped back in shock, then narrowed his focus on the section of ley that kept his wall from cutting

Eld off from the source. As he began sensing the folds in the Tapestry that kept it in place, began prying them loose, the traitor's presence surged forward and slapped him back from the block, using the ley as a weapon. Augustus gasped at the temerity, then clenched his jaw.

"You want to fight?" he murmured to himself beneath the roiling Nexus. "Then we'll fight."

He gathered the faint traces of ley in the channel around him, then charged toward the traitor's presence.

The Hound could hear Primes shouting from the end of the long corridor that cut under the street above and led to the illicit new Nexus. He halted, drawing in the scents around him as he pulled two knives from their sheaths. The orders from Erenthrall had been explicit: kill Baron Leethe. The Hound assumed that meant the Primes who had turned traitor to Arent were also fair game. He could smell at least twenty of the prey who had passed through the corridor recently, including the Baron and his chief enforcer, Arger.

A smile of anticipation broke the Hound's expression. He intended to enjoy himself.

He began loping down the hall, moving fast and silent, the shouts getting louder. As he neared the end of the corridor, a pressure from the room beyond tingled through his skin, tasting of the ley, but he ignored it, focusing on the scents, on the sounds, a picture of the chamber beyond and the placement of his prey already forming in his head.

Then he slid through the opening into the new Nexus. Two enforcers stood to either side of the door, but their attention was focused on the cascading white light of the ley in the center of the room. The Hound slit both of their throats in two smooth moves, the second enforcer's eyes widening even as the Hound's knife drew across his neck. The thick tang of blood thrilled the Hound to the core, exhilaration shuddering through him. He spun as the bodies slumped back against the wall in two sprays of blood, but none of the others had seen him. The sheeting white light of the ley caught and held them all, the Primes frantically trying to control it, Baron Leethe and Arger standing behind the head Prime as he bellowed orders right and left. Two more enforcers stood behind Leethe and Arger, the closest people in the room to the Hound.

He moved up on the two enforcers as the head Prime growled, "No, no, to the left! A little more. A little more. Now, Retellus, skew the next crystal to the right and up slightly. Yes! Oretus, adjust yours to compensate! Capture as much of the ley coming in from Erenthrall as you can. We need to break free of Erenthrall's control today. We'll only get one shot at this, so move!"

The Hound punched his knife up through the left enforcer's back, reaching around to stifle the man's grunt, but the other enforcer turned, a look of confusion on his face. It shifted immediately to horrified realization and he reached for his blade, but the Hound was already moving, letting the body he held slip behind him as he crouched low and brought his second knife up into the enforcer's gut. He couldn't dampen the man's barked warning, so he twisted his blade savagely, blood already coating his hand, as he spun in behind him, using the enforcer's body as a shield. Both the Baron and Arger turned, Arger's sword already snicking from its sheath. With one glance, Arger noted the dead enforcers at the entrance and the one writhing on the floor to the Hound's left, a pool of blood already forming beneath him. His face narrowed with sudden tension. Behind him, Leethe stiffened in rage. But he didn't step back either and didn't retreat behind the protection Arger offered.

He glared at the Hound instead. "Who are you? Who sent you?" He glanced toward the two dead enforcers near the corridor and his mouth tightened. "A Hound. I knew Arent would send one of you. But I didn't think he'd have the conviction until after we'd activated the Nexus here."

He turned to the head Prime, who had halted his orchestration of the other Primes and now watched the Hound with unadulterated fear. "You guaranteed that Augustus would not find out about the Nexus here. You said he would think the traitor came from within Erenthrall, that he would think it was a resurgence of the Kormanley."

"He d-did," the head Prime stuttered. "My latest intelligence from our sources in Erenthrall stated that Augustus was looking for our activist in the city. It was already set up. He doesn't even know he's working for us. He thinks he's working with the Kormanley, trying to bring the ley back to its natural course!"

"It wasn't enough," Leethe said dryly. He motioned toward Arger. "Take care of him. And you," he spat at the head Prime, his face reddening with fury, "get me my ley!"

The Hound met Arger's gaze. "I only came for Leethe."

Arger's mouth twisted in a grim half smile. "I find that hard to believe."

The Hound flung the dead weight of the man he held forward and dodged to the side as Arger leaped toward him. Arger stepped onto the dead enforcer's body without pausing and the Hound felt the tip of the chief enforcer's blade tug at the back of his shirt. He scented the man's fear, but none of it showed in the enforcer's face. The pulse of the Nexus throbbed in the Hound's temples and the heady aroma of blood intoxicated him, making his movements fluid as he ducked and spun, Arger lashing out after him, herding him across the room and away from Leethe. The Hound kept just out of reach, teasing him, goading him, trying to draw out his anger and irritation so he'd make a fatal move, but Arger was too well trained. The skin around his eyes tightened, but that was his only reaction.

So the Hound changed tactics. With a shrug of his shoulders, he turned on the pad of his foot and sprinted toward the nearest Prime, the man's attention completely focused on the coruscating wall of light before him, his hands raised and moving in subtle and obscure motions. The Hound had no idea what the Prime was doing, but he knew it was important.

He stabbed the Prime in the side as he sprinted past, a quick thrust and then away, barely pausing as he headed toward the next Prime farther down the rounded chamber. The man behind cried out, followed by a curse from Arger. The Hound grinned, even as he punched his second knife into the next Prime's back, the man collapsing to his knees, his outcry garbled as he choked and coughed up blood.

He rounded the central flare of ley. Arger charged behind, his boots thudding against the stone floor. The Hound focused on the next Prime, a woman, her black hair streaming behind her in the pulsing wake of the ley. From much farther away, the head Prime yelled, "Stop him!" His panic was an acrid taint in the Hound's nostrils. Then, to the remaining Primes, "Hold them! Hold the gods-damned crystals steady, you bastards!"

The Hound cut low along the woman's side, ducking beneath her hair. As he spun away, he saw the struggle on her face to keep control of the ley even though she'd been wounded, her lower lip clenched so tightly between her teeth she'd drawn blood. But her face was already pale and she stumbled as the Hound's attention shifted toward Arger.

The chief enforcer had nearly reached them.

The Hound gripped the woman by the arm and flung her into Arger's path. The chief enforcer dodged out of her way as she screamed, but she was already too weak to react. She hit the floor hard, rolling, leaving a trail of blood behind her—

And then Arger swung, grunting with the force behind it. The Hound focused on the dance, on the swift movement of dodging and ducking the longer blade, waiting for his opportunity. They whirled around the Prime as she raised herself to her elbows and tried to drag herself away from them, but she was too weak to move, slumping over a moment later. The Hound felt Arger's blade nick his shoulder, his thigh, but shoved the silvery white-hot pain aside, allowed the coppery scent of his own blood to mingle with that of the rest. It drove him harder and he pushed himself, felt his muscles beginning to burn, aware that Arger was flagging as well. The chief enforcer's breath came in harsher gasps, but his blade never wavered. His frustration grew, though; the Hound could smell it. The Hound wasn't attacking, all of his efforts going toward evasion, knowing that an opening would come.

And it did.

Arger swung hard, too hard, his blade dipping too low, the tip scraping along the stone floor and throwing off a smooth recovery. It was a subtle mistake, Arger correcting in a heartbeat.

But a heartbeat was all the Hound needed.

His knives dove in, one high, buried in Arger's armpit, the other low along the fumbled swing and into his side.

Arger gasped and staggered back, helped by a shove as the Hound withdrew his blades. His mouth opened, as if he wanted to say something, and then he fell, his body hitting stone with a heavy thud. His sword dropped from his fingers with a faint clatter.

The Hound turned back to the Nexus, noticed a strange shudder in what had been a steady pressure from the ley. The trail of bodies led in a smooth arc toward Baron Leethe and the head Prime, around the curve of the room. The Baron watched him, the Prime's attention riveted on the Nexus. The Prime's hands were raised, like those of the Primes the Hound had killed, his face tortured with concentration, pale and sheened with sweat.

The Hound began walking toward the Baron, his pace steady, not rushing. The Baron gripped the handle of a knife thrust through his belt, but the Hound ignored the gesture. It wasn't a fighting knife. It was decorative, and as the Hound advanced, the Baron's hand fell away from the blade.

"We can come to some agreement, I'm certain," he muttered when the Hound was twenty paces away.

The Hound shook his head, raising the bloodied knives before him.

The Baron raised his chin defiantly.

To the side, the head Prime gasped at the strain, sweat dripping from his chin, his hands trembling. Before the Hound could advance on the Baron, the head Prime wheezed, "I . . . I can't hold it."

Something deep inside of him audibly tore and he sighed, a trickle of blood coming from his nose. His arms dropped, and then he collapsed to the floor, his head falling to face the Hound. He was already dead, his eyes wide, one of them bloodshot and skewed in the wrong direction.

The Hound and the Baron looked down at the body, toward each other, then at the Nexus.

The white light fountained out of the control, the remaining Primes crying out and collapsing on all sides, some succumbing to the waves of ley that roiled out from the center.

The Hound felt the pressure from the Nexus triple, the strange shudder amplified, shivering in his bones and pressing hard against the inside of his head. In sudden realization, he lunged toward the Baron, knives raised.

He never made it.

The Nexus exploded, the ley breaching its containment in a wave of pure, hellish light. It consumed the Baron and the Hound in less than a heartbeat, seared the Primes and the bodies of the enforcers from existence, and tore through the ceiling of the chamber and the park above. It rose into the sky and expanded outward, engulfing the Flyers' Tower, the Baron's palace. It engulfed the entire central city, and still it expanded, burning through the Ganges and Tiana Rivers, water vaporized, and then deeper into Tumbor. Sky barges were scorched from the air, and the ground shuddered beneath the onslaught, the red stone of the surrounding strata cracking.

And even as the white fire raged above ground, even as the earth shook, the fire within the Nexus channeled itself into the ley lines that connected Tumbor to the entire network and sent a pulse outward in all directions, toward Farrade and the Temerite coast to the east, the Archipelago and the Gorrani Flats and Horn to the south, the Demesnes and the lands farther west—

And to Erenthrall and the rest of the Baronies to the north.

Augustus tightened his grip on the ley, his anger coloring the Tapestry around him, and flung the presence of the intruder up against the rounded stone tunnel of the ley conduit. He'd come to the conclusion the traitor *was* nothing more than a Wielder; he wasn't powerful enough to be a Prime. A Prime would have put up more resistance, would have been able to keep Augustus at bay longer.

But this Wielder, this insufferable, disastrous interloper! This meddler, who'd somehow managed to weaken the network so easily, with so little power—!

Augusts gritted his teeth, seized the nuisance, and drove him into the ceiling. He could feel the Wielder weakening, the hold on his block at the entrance to the conduit wavering. He'd break any moment, Augustus having wasted precious seconds dealing with him, seconds he could have spent bolstering the Nexus. The thought infuriated him. He seized the presence again and slammed it into the bottom of the channel, holding him there, increasing the pressure as the interloper struggled. Back beneath the Nexus, he could hear his own breath hissing through his teeth, could feel his face throbbing with his rage, but he didn't let up. He wanted to strangle this man, this heathen, this peasant with pretensions of power.

But then something throbbed through the entire system, an unsettling shiver. He glanced up, his attention within the conduit faltering. The traitor slipped from his grasp and fled, back toward Eld, like a dog with its tail between its legs, but Augustus could only spare a moment of derision for him. As the traitor fled, the block he'd placed on the conduit dissolved, the Tapestry slipping back into its natural folds. Augustus shot toward the Nexus, closing the conduit behind him with a snap, sealing off Eld's direct access to the heart of the network. As he returned to his body, he barked, "What happened?"

Temerius spun around, startled. "I don't know. But we've managed to stabilize nearly half of the crystals. No one appears to be working up above. We haven't felt any activity from the Primes up there."

"Most are probably dead," Augustus said. "From the dome's collapse."

Temerius flinched.

Augustus ignored him, beginning to pace back and forth before the Nexus. The shiver disturbed him. He'd never felt anything like it on the ley before, and it had shot through the entire network, hitting every node, every locus in the outer reaches. It was as if the entire structure had been seized and shaken.

The image didn't hearten him.

"Something's wrong," he muttered, but before Temerius could respond, he dove back into the ley, began methodically checking the integrity of the conduits. Not the ley itself, but the actual channels and corridors that the ley traversed, the stone and bedrock.

He felt the pulse while in East Forks. It roared through the massive conduit connecting Erenthrall to Tumbor without a sound, but it roared nonetheless. The river stone that had been used at this ancient node trembled, the earth quaking as the pulse approached, the pressure inside the conduit increasing exponentially with each passing heartbeat. Augustus had time to think that it felt like the approach of a storm, the ley receding in a sudden rush—

And then it hit. Augustus' mind was incinerated in East Forks, his body collapsing in the Nexus as if it were a puppet whose strings had been cut, still breathing, heart still pounding, nothing but a husk. Temerius stared in confusion, the crystals above beginning to quake.

They shattered simultaneously, the shards of glass splintering and needling the Primes, those closest flayed instantly. The shards peppered Temerius' skin and he gasped, but before he could truly sense the pain, the Nexus exploded.

Ley surged through the conduits, blossomed out through the dome, and expanded rapidly. The ground shook. The citizens of Erenthrall nearest the Nexus had a moment to turn, to gape, and then the ley burned them from existence. The towers of Grass snapped near their bases, debris flung toward the sky, pushed by the ley as it expanded. It consumed Grass, seared everything living and unprotected from existence, then swallowed the surrounding districts, rising higher, the radius of destruction increasing with every heartbeat. The buildings of Stone cracked and fractured. The water of the channels in Canal and the Tiana and Urate Rivers evaporated, and still it pushed on.

Then, when its edge began to reach the outermost districts, it began to slow. Its fury dissipated, the piercing white light of the ley fading into the air. Nothing exposed to the direct power near its heart remained alive, the streets and alleys, bridges and towers swept clean. Only those who had been protected by buildings that had not crumbled in the ley's wake survived. Farther from its center, bodies littered the streets, the power of the ley enough to kill but not incinerate. Those farthest away lived, but were stunned, a few driven insane.

When the earth settled, the pulse continued on beyond Erenthrall. But when the roar of debris and destruction had faded, there wasn't stunned silence, like a held breath.

Instead, there was a high-pitched whine that shivered in the bones of the earth, coming from directly over the remains of Grass.

PART V

Twenty-Five

KARA WOKE AND moaned, her entire body aching. Her first breath was choked with stone dust and she gagged, coughing, making every ache worse. Her head pounded. Not the thud of a headache, but something deeper, as if her brain had been bruised at its core. She winced and tried to take a shallow breath, the dust tasting gritty and bitter in her mouth. She opened her eyes—

And saw nothing but darkness.

Her eyes widened, as if seeking more light, but there was none, and the grit in the air stung and made her tear up. Her other senses kicked in. Pebbles rattled against each other as something shifted in the darkness. Small stones rained down from above, striking her shoulders where she lay on the floor. Nearby, the sound muted, she thought she heard someone screaming, but she couldn't tell. It was too faint. She smelled nothing but crushed rock, her nose already filled with grit. It covered her face, her arms, her entire body.

Clenching her teeth, she moved her arm, raising herself onto her elbow. She hissed at the pain, but as she shifted into a sitting position the aches began to work loose. She reached out to either side of the cell the Dogs had placed her in and felt the wall to one side, the wall that had been at her back when she'd sensed the hideous pulse of power descend on the city. The earth had heaved after that, a crack that shook the heavens flinging her to the floor, even as she felt the Tapestry around her convulse.

She hadn't even had time to roll onto her back before she'd blacked out.

Raising one hand to her head she touched her temples, the throbbing intensifying for a moment. The convulsion must have knocked her out, and the headache was the result.

Tentatively, she tried to sense the Tapestry, her breath rushing out in relief when she could. She'd thought she'd been burned out by the wave of energy. But the Tapestry was there.

Except something was horribly wrong. The patterns were distorted, twisted . . . *off.*

Keeping one hand above her, she rose into a crouch, then stood and began feeling her way along the wall. The cell wasn't large, but before she'd taken two steps her foot hit something hard on the floor. Reaching down, she found a huge chunk of stone. She felt all around her and discovered a rockfall and realized one of the walls of the cell had collapsed.

In horror, she scrambled around the edge of the fall, desperate to find the door, hoping it hadn't been where the fall was. A puff of air pushed against her face a moment before her hands found a massive crack in the wall. Farther along, she found the door, cursing as splintered wood jabbed her hand. The door had folded near its center. Feeling upward, she realized why.

The ceiling was lower. She could touch it with her hand, her arm not even straightened. The Amber Tower had collapsed.

She suppressed a shudder and swallowed a dry sob, the weight of the building above suddenly pressing down on her. She forced herself to remain standing and felt around the edges of the door. A gap appeared where the lock had once been, the crack in the wall intersecting with the doorframe there, but when she tugged on the door it was lodged tight.

She moved on, exploring the rest of the cell in short order. The remaining walls were solid. The only way out was through the door.

Returning, she tugged on it harder and felt it give. But something above her groaned and a spill of debris cascaded onto her back. Her breath quickened, but the stone quieted, the spill reducing to a fall of silt.

Turning back to the door, her eyes narrowed. Placing one foot against the jamb, she gripped the upper part of the splintered wood—the part that had shifted—and heaved.

It came away with a screech of wood and another, larger rain of stone, releasing so sharply Kara fell backward, hitting the floor hard. But the groan of stone from above escalated, so she scrambled forward, ignoring the pain in her butt. As larger chunks of rock began to fall, hitting her shoulders, she thrust herself through the opening she'd made, kicking her legs out as she shoved with her arms. Wriggling, she slipped through a moment before something above her gave, the ceiling of her cell collapsing inward behind her with a horrendous crash of stone and another wall of choking debris. One arm raised to cover her mouth, she still couldn't stifle her coughing, turning away from the unseen cloud even as it rushed over her. She hunched her shoulders, certain she'd feel the ceiling in the outer corridor caving in any moment.

But the groans of stressed stone faded.

"Hello? Is anyone out there?"

Kara turned and squinted into the darkness. There wasn't any light here either, but the breeze she'd felt inside her cell earlier was stronger, coming from her left: the way out.

The voice she'd heard came from the right.

The sound she'd thought was a scream was louder here as well. Only it wasn't a scream, she realized. It was too consistent, too even. A steady throbbing whine.

"Hello? Please? Is anyone there?"

This time, the voice wavered, breaking into low coughing at the end. It sounded young, although it was hard to tell.

Kara picked herself up and said loudly, "Where are you?"

A hesitant silence, and then: "Here! I'm here! The Dogs took me and captured my father and dragged us here and I haven't seen him since! And then there was this crack and I think the tower collapsed, but the door's still locked and I can't see anything and . . . and . . ."

"It's all right," Kara said, feeling her way down the corridor toward the voice. Her feet kicked stones out in front of her, but the wall to her left was intact. A moment later, the girl's voice breaking down into sobs, the stone ended and Kara's fingers found the wood of another door.

Locked. She knocked on the door. "I'm right here. But I don't have the key. I was in one of the cells as well. I'm going to find the key . . . or another way to get you out."

"Wait! Wait, don't leave!"

Kara pressed her hand against the door, bringing her face close enough she could smell the wood. "Don't worry. I'll be back."

She fumbled back in the direction of the draft, until she passed her own cell, then slowed, feeling her way with every step, cursing the darkness. She passed another door, knocked but heard nothing in response, so continued. Ten steps later her feet encountered another rockfall, half the corridor blocked. As she felt her way around it, her hands came upon something soft and sticky. She prodded it with a frown, until she encountered fingers and sucked in a harsh breath, staggering back a step, choking back bile. She scrubbed her hands against her breeches but couldn't dispel the stickiness of what she assumed was blood. Trembling, she forced herself to reach forward and test for a pulse, even though she knew the person was dead; the flesh wouldn't have been so cool when she'd first touched it. Then she steadied herself and searched the parts of the body that weren't buried, looking for keys. It was definitely a Dog by the bulk of the body and the armor beneath the clothing, but she found no keys.

She gathered herself, drew in deep breaths of the clean, cool air gusting against her face, and continued, climbing over the edge of the fall, following the breeze. She stumbled upon two more bodies as she progressed, both Dogs by the feel, both killed by falling debris. After passing the collapse, she began to hear noises, moans and the sounds of someone weeping. She found the weeper behind another cell door and promised to return. The moaner was another Dog, legs trapped beneath stone, barely conscious. He didn't respond to Kara, even when she slapped him lightly. But she couldn't see his face, only felt the stubble of his beard and a few cuts along his jaw.

The next door had stove in, like her own, although the ceiling wasn't raining debris. She called out, "Anyone in here?" She considered entering, but more noises came from farther down the corridor, a few muted voices, even the sound of someone stumbling about. The whine had increased as well.

Someone moaned in response, then bit back a curse. "Here." The voice was weak. "Are you a Dog?"

Kara snorted in contempt. "I'm not a Dog," she said, then shoved the crack in the broken door open further and slipped inside. "I'm a Wielder. Where are you?"

"Here. I'm tied down to a table in the center of the room."

"Keep talking so I can find you."

"It shouldn't be that hard," the man said, then coughed and groaned. "There's not much else in the room."

Kara's hip hit the edge of something hard and she heard metal utensils jouncing against each other. She reached down and felt the edges of a table, the cool metal of many objects lined across its top, set on a fine piece of cloth, all now covered with dirt, stone chunks, and dust. For a moment, her mind flashed on the black cloth of her father's worktable, the gears of the clocks laid out in careful precision. But these weren't the innards of a clock, she realized, as one of the knives cut the pad of her questing finger.

She hissed and automatically brought the finger to her mouth, tasted the copper of her own blood.

"That's the interrogator's table," the rough, grating voice said from the darkness. "Those are his tools."

Kara shuddered at the snide casualness of the statement.

"Take one of the knives. You'll need it to cut through the ropes."

Kara picked up one of the knives automatically, then hesitated. "Why should I set you free? The Dogs had you for a reason."

The man laughed, the sound harsh and derisive and threaded with pain. "No real reason," he growled. "I was a Dog once, but I left. Before the Purge. They caught me."

Kara sensed he held something back, but she shifted forward anyway. The noises outside were growing, more and more people moving around as they recovered. She wondered how many were dead, wondered what had happened in the first place, the persistent whine nagging at her.

Her legs bumped against another table and she halted, reaching forward. As her hand touched bloody flesh, the man hissed in pain and she felt him jerk beneath her fingers, the table shuddering.

"What did they do to you?"

"Interrogated . . . me," he muttered through clenched teeth.

Kara swallowed. "Hold still."

She ran her hands over his back, down his arms, and found his wrists tied beneath the table. His breath came in harsh gasps as she did so. But she didn't free him. Instead, she returned to the top of the table and traced out his legs, found the cords that bound his lower body to the table as well.

Then she moved away, back toward the smaller table with the knives and other tools.

"Where are you going?" the man barked.

"I'm looking for keys," she said. "And I can't see you. I don't know who you are, or why you're here. I don't know if I can trust you."

The man cursed in frustration and she heard him struggling against his bonds. She ignored him and felt along the table, looking for keys, the knife still clutched in her other hand. She frowned when she realized there was nothing on the table but knives and hammers, then began moving back toward the splintered door.

"Wait!" the man called out, his struggles halting. "Wait, I think there was a ley globe in here."

Kara halted, one leg already through the opening. "What do you mean?"

"There was a ley globe hovering against the far wall. It might still be there. I don't remember hearing it shatter, so maybe it didn't fall during the blackout and what happened after. If you're a Wielder, maybe you can make it work."

Kara's eyes narrowed in suspicion, but the chance of getting some light was too tempting. She shifted back into the room. "Where was the globe?"

"Against the wall opposite the door."

Kara circled the room, her skin prickling as she sensed the man's eyes on her. She couldn't remain silent. There was too much debris on the floor, chunks of stone grinding beneath her feet with every step. She reached the far wall and stretched up to a globe's usual height and found it. It was hovering just over her head, and the moment her fingers brushed it, she could sense its connection to the ley. She reached for the Tapestry and searched for the ley lines around her, again disturbed by their chaotic flows. Even as she tapped into them and the ley globe sprung into weak life, she realized why.

The ley network that she was familiar with, the structured lines all centered around the Nexus and branching outward from that source, were destroyed. All of the familiar touchpoints—the nodes, the ley stations, the channels—were gone. What remained was a chaotic jumble of what the system had once been . . . and what she guessed had been the natural lines of the ley before the Nexus had been created. The lines were still reshaping themselves, shifting and fluctuating as they sought out new paths.

But there was something keeping them in flux, something drawing on their power with hideous strength. Kara didn't know what it was, but it felt vaguely familiar, like the incessant whine that prickled in her ears.

Even as she turned, that familiarity—the whine and the tug on the ley system—clicked, and she gasped and stilled.

"What is it?" the man asked, and she dropped her gaze to the table, flinching back from the sight.

The man had raised his head and looked up at her from a face caked in blood and grit and bruises. His back was a pattern of lacerations, the blood and sweat dried in trickles down his sides. The thick cords that bound his legs cut cruelly into his flesh, mitigated only by the cloth of his breeches. Nearly every square inch of his exposed back, arms, and sides were riddled with bruises.

"Why did you gasp?" the man demanded.

She focused on his eyes, swallowing against the tightness in her throat. She thought about the Kormanley priest she'd seen the Dogs drag off the public square when she was younger, thought of all of the people who had vanished during the Purge, and her stomach twisted, sourness burning at the back of her tongue. In the back of her mind, she'd known what had happened here beneath the Amber Tower, in the Dogs' lair, but she had ignored it.

Looking at this man's eyes, she couldn't ignore it any longer.

"Tell me why you gasped," he said.

She licked her lips and worked spit back into her mouth. "Because I recognize that high-pitched whine now. It's a distortion. Somewhere nearby, a distortion is forming."

"Close enough to harm us?"

"I don't know. The ley . . . it's in turmoil. It's hard to tell. But close." The man considered this. Then his face hardened.

When it did, Kara recognized him.

"Get me out of here," he said, voice low and dangerous.

Kara stepped forward. "I know you," she said. "You were the one caught in the distortion earlier. But it didn't affect you, or the girl. You were immune to it. How?"

Fear flickered across the man's face, replaced a moment later by determination. "Get me out of here. I have to find my daughter. We have to get out of Erenthrall."

Kara's hand tightened on the knife she held, the other still raised toward the ley globe. She stared at the man, long and hard, uncertain—

And then she pushed the ley globe closer to the table and knelt, letting it hover above them. It flickered and dimmed as it drew closer, but she ignored it. Her hands fumbled toward the rope that had cut into his wrists as he struggled, slicing through it with the knife. It was easier than she expected, the blade sharp. His hands broke free with a snap and he cried out in triumph, Kara stepping back as he writhed on the table. But he couldn't move far; the rope around his legs still held him. She moved to cut him free as he flailed, his arms obviously numbed. He gasped as the last of the ropes fell away and she helped him roll onto his back. He lay there twitching, moaning whenever he moved his legs or arms, but Kara could see his coordination returning. She stood, back against one wall, watching him warily.

When he sat up, massaging his thighs with his hands, grimacing in pain, she tensed.

"I think I know where your daughter is," she offered.

He stilled. "Where?"

"In one of the cells. But the door's locked."

He eased off of the table, stumbling toward the interrogator's tools and retrieving a few before turning toward her. The intensity in his gaze, the raw hatred and focus, made her draw back.

"Show me."

—⟫—

Allan followed the Wielder through the hall, the ley globe held out in front of her. Shouts came from the direction of the Dogs' training pit, and he kept his eye on the darkness behind them. When the Wielder halted at a door, someone sobbing on the far side, he shook his head and said, "My daughter first." He wasn't certain he believed her, his hope nearly choking him, and he didn't trust the sounds from the training pit. He didn't think Hagger would have had time to hurt her yet—he'd been too focused on Allan—but he needed to know for certain. The fear that Morrell was dead, that the Dogs had turned on her—

He sucked in a half-choked breath and calmed himself, his body throbbing with the bruises and lacerations that riddled it. His legs still tingled with the returning blood flow, meaty and heavy, his arms not faring much better. But he could grip the blade he'd taken from the table, even though his fingers were caked with dried blood, and the hammer and second, thinner knife were clutched in his other hand.

They passed a few bodies, mostly Dogs, Allan paying attention only long enough to note that none of them were Hagger. At one of the bodies, the Wielder knelt, then looked up at him. "He was alive when I passed here earlier."

He couldn't think of anything to say, and after a moment she moved on with an irritated frown.

Finally, Allan's attention still fixed on the corridor behind them, she said, "Here."

He stepped forward, hand against the door. "Morrell? Is that you?"

"Da!"

Allan's legs grew suddenly weak, his entire body trembling in relief. He leaned his forehead against the wood of the door.

"Da, the Dogs came to the room," Morrell said, her voice cracking. "I didn't let them in, but they broke down the door. I couldn't get away. They grabbed me—my arm still hurts—and then they took me to that warehouse and made me wait, and I tried to warn you, but one of them put his hand over my mouth and I couldn't breathe—"

"It's all right," he said, and his voice shook. "It's all right, Morrell. I'm not angry with you. We'll get you out of there in a moment. Hang on."

He knelt, setting his blade on the debris-strewn ground and bringing up the thin knife and the hammer. He placed the end of the knife into the keyhole, felt it strike metal inside, then used the hammer to pound the blade into the locking mechanism with two sharp blows. Metal snapped and he pulled the blade out and shoved at the door.

It swung open and Morrell spilled out, suddenly clutching at him, her face caked with dust, tears trailing down through the dirt. He hissed at the pain in his back as her arms latched around his chest, but he didn't care, savoring it as he pulled her in close. His eyes blurred and phlegm clogged his throat and chest as he murmured, "It's all right, Poppet, it's all right."

And then the Wielder barked, "Dog!"

He spun on her, ready to snarl, thinking she was talking about him—

But she wasn't.

One of the Dogs stood near the edge of the rock fall farther down the corridor. He glared at Allan, his sword raised, a sheet of blood coating one side of his face from a wound near his temple. "You." He spat to one side. "Did you have anything to do with this?"

Allan pried Morrell's arms from around his chest, picked up the knife he'd set on the floor, stood, and eased his daughter behind him. "I had nothing to do with . . . whatever happened."

The Dog's eyes narrowed, shot toward the Wielder and Morrell, then returned. "Get back into your cells. All of you." He waved his sword, but kept his eyes fixed on Allan.

"No."

Allan was surprised at the defiance in the Wielder's voice. The other Dog was as well, shifting uncomfortably, his sword wavering.

"The Baron—"

"I don't think the Baron's in control right now," Allan growled, shifting forward, "if he's even alive."

The man started as Allan moved, raising his blade. "Don't—"

Allan didn't let him finish. With only a minor twinge from his muscles, he grabbed the hesitant Dog's forearm and punched him hard in the face. The man's head rocked back and he crumpled to the floor. Allan took his sword and motioned Morrell and the Wielder forward. "Be careful. He was dazed. If we run into others, they might not be easily distracted."

"I'm not leaving until we free the others."

He turned toward the Wielder in disgust. "We don't even know who they are."

"The Dogs were collecting Wielders before the blackout. That's why I'm here. I'm betting that a good portion of those here are Wielders as well." Her mouth firmed up. "Besides, I control the light."

Allan huffed with impatience. "Morrell, grab that hammer and knife. Be careful with the blade. It's sharp." His daughter scrambled for the implements. "Now let's move."

The Wielder insisted on checking the back of the corridor, opening every locked door. They found two dead, managed to bring one Wielder, a man about twenty-five years old, around after finding him unconscious on the floor. One room was filled with stone. They heard another Wielder pounding desperately before they reached the door, her hands bloody and her voice raw from shouting. On the way back out, they released four more, including the one who'd been sobbing.

As a group, a few holding each other up for support, they emerged into what had once been the Dogs' training pit, the Wielder's ley globe revealing a room ravaged by the collapse of the ceiling. The entire central pit was covered with chunks of granite, splinters of amber scattered on top.

A group of Dogs turned, weapons raised, as they arrived. "Halt where you are!" one of them shouted.

"Don't be ridiculous," one of the rescued Wielders snapped. She was older than Allan, than any of the rest, at least fifty. Her gray-streaked hair was disheveled and floated around her head in wisps. "We're getting the hells out of here, before the entire tower comes down on us."

They moved toward the tower's entrance, Allan keeping himself between the group and the Dogs. All five of them gripped their swords tightly, the leader stepping forward, jaw muscles clenching, but he didn't attack. Those behind him shifted uncertainly, until he motioned them to follow the Wielders at a discreet distance.

They worked their way up the cracked stairs, the Wielder who'd cut him free in the lead with Morrell, Allan at the back, trying to keep his eyes on the Dogs behind and whatever they'd encounter ahead at the same time. The urge to snatch Morrell and vanish, head back to the Hollow, was strong, skating along his skin and prickling the back of his neck, but he didn't know what had happened yet, and from what he'd seen, he thought there might be safety in numbers.

As they ascended the stairs, the high-pitched whine grew, piercing into Allan's skull. The others winced as they picked their way over chunks of the stone ceiling. A moment later, they emerged into the open foyer of the Amber Tower, granite giving way to the gold-toned amber that gave the building its name. Cracks ran through the lustrous walls, like the cracks in ice, and splinters and slivers of the amber littered the main floor. One of the curved staircases had collapsed, along with a portion of the ceiling, a gaping hole leading up to the upper floor. Allan caught the Wielder turning Morrell's head away, shielding her from the bodies strewn around the room. As the group moved across the floor toward the open doorway and the sunlight streaming through it, Allan caught furtive movement in the upper rooms, a figure ducking into shadows. His grip tightened on the handle of his sword, but he followed the Wielders out onto the tower's landing.

As soon as they stumbled into the sunlight, the Wielders halted. The older woman gasped, raised a hand to her mouth, her eyes wide. A few of the others whispered prayers. One woman's legs gave out beneath her and she crumpled into a seated position, one arm holding her upright.

"What's happened?" one of the men murmured. "What—?" He couldn't finish.

When Allan stepped out of the shade of the tower after them, he saw why.

His heart constricted in his chest and he suddenly felt weak. Morrell snatched his free arm, clutching tight with a muttered, "Da." But Allan could not tear his eyes away from the destruction before him.

Grass was gone, the towers that had risen into the sky on all sides shattered, sheared off near their bases, a few only a couple of stories high, others a little higher. Boulders that had once been part of those towers covered the street, carriages crushed beneath them, other carriages flung up against the base of the tower. Allan recognized the distinctive leaf pattern of the Flyers' Tower on one chunk of green stone the size of a house. Dust covered everything, swirling through the street and the remains of the park beyond in the breeze. None of the trees remained, none of the brush or decorative plants, the ground of the park scoured clean. Even the huge urns to either side of the tower's entrance were empty, the ornamental shrubs gone.

And then Allan noticed a sword on the wide step to one side, one edge of its blade bared and glaring in the later afternoon sunlight. The dust was so thick it had drifted and covered the hilt . . . and the armor to one side. His eyes scanned the steps and found more signs of the Dogs and servants who had stood on this spot when whatever had happened occurred. But there were no bodies, just as there were no trees.

He pulled Morrell closer to him.

"Where is everyone?"

Allan turned toward the leader of the Dogs who'd been following them, raising his sword, but the Dogs stood in loose formation, gazing out over the destruction in shock, none of them paying any attention to Allan or the Wielders.

The Dogs' leader licked his lips and dropped his gaze toward Allan. "Where is everyone?"

"Dead," Allan said, then used the point of his sword to nudge the blade he'd seen into view. Dust skirled away as he motioned toward the remains of the armor. "I think they died right here."

But not all of them, he thought, as he caught more furtive movement in the shadows of the tower behind them.

"What do we do?" the elder Wielder asked. Beside her, the Wielder half her age who had been sobbing before had switched to a low moan, the sound somehow desolate. The older woman searched the Dogs' faces, then settled on Allan. "What do we do?" she demanded.

Allan didn't know. He couldn't think, his mind numb, his body exhausted. He wanted to sink down onto the steps and simply rest, let the wind press against him, let the dust settle over him. He ached from head to toe, his back on fire from the lacerations Hagger had made; he knew he should get them treated. And now this. He couldn't comprehend it, his mind insisting it must all be a dream, perhaps fever-induced. Perhaps he was still strapped to the table in the cell beneath the Amber Tower, his mind destroyed. Perhaps Hagger had finally broken him.

And then his roaming eye caught sight of the Wielder who had rescued him. She wasn't staring out over the destruction of Grass, over the crumbled towers and the rubble they'd left behind. She wasn't even looking beyond, to where he could see the rest of the city in shambles, buildings collapsed, even a few columns of smoke from fires rising against the horizon.

Her attention was fixed above, her eyes shaded with both hands, the ley globe floating forgotten to one side. He noted a few of the other Wielders were staring straight up as well.

Squinting, he followed the Wielders' gazes.

Overhead, nearly straight above their position, a fiery ball of white light roiled against the vivid blue of the sky. Allan grimaced, his eyes watering even though they were narrowed down to slits. The light was more intense than the sun, seemed larger than the sun as well, and with a start he realized that it was the source of the piercing whine that grated against his ears and shuddered in his bones.

"What is it?" he asked.

The Wielder who'd rescued him dropped her hands and looked at him, her face lined with dread.

"It's the beginning of a distortion."

The older Wielder looked skyward and gasped. "It's bigger than anything I've ever seen."

The Wielder nodded. Then, in a strangely flat, matter-of-fact voice, she proclaimed, "If this one quickens, I think it will consume the entire city."

Twenty-Six

"WE HAVE TO REPAIR IT," Kara said.

The older Wielder with the wispy hair snorted. "How? It's too big. We'll never be able to surround it."

"She's right," one of the other Wielders said. He shook his head, his eyes wide in wonder as he stared up at the pulsing white light. "I wouldn't even know how to begin."

Kara frowned in irritation. "We can't do it as individuals, no, but if we work together. . . ." She let the thought trail off, then spun around and indicated the Wielders who'd climbed out of the cells of the tower, focusing on those who were older, more experienced. Most were around her age—late twenties or early thirties. Only one appeared to be newly released from the college. "There are seven of us altogether. If we link up, support each other, we can stop it."

The older woman's jaw tightened. "I'm not certain it will work even then."

"We have to try. Otherwise—"

She didn't get to finish. With a slow, growling rumble, the earth beneath them shook, throwing nearly everyone to the ground, men and women crying out as the stone beneath them heaved. On the far side of the park, part of a dull brown tower that had remained standing after the initial blast collapsed with a roar. Dust rose all around them as the earth shifted, and a few shards from the remains of the Amber Tower cascaded down and shattered, peppering one of the younger Dogs. He screamed, cuts riddling his face as he staggered, stumbled, and rolled around on the ground, hands raised to cover his eyes.

A moment later, it stopped, the rumble fading into the distance, the ground settling.

Kara picked herself up to find the ex-Dog who'd been tortured crouched protectively over his daughter, exactly as he had been when caught in the distortion. As soon as the earthquake faded, he stood and grabbed his daughter's hand, heading down the steps toward the street and the city beyond.

"Where are you going?" Kara called out, apprehension rising in the back of her throat. She didn't want to be left alone with the Dogs and the other Wielders; she didn't want to be left alone at all.

Without turning, the tortured Dog barked, "Away!"

"You won't make it," Kara cried, taking a step forward. "You don't have enough time to make it out of its range. If it quickens, it will enclose the entire city!"

That brought the Dog up short. He spun back with a snarl. "You said I was immune!"

She realized he was right. If the distortions didn't affect him, as they hadn't before, he might be able to escape, even if the Wielders weren't with him. He might be able to leave whenever he wanted.

"I don't know that for certain," Kara countered, trying not to let desperation creep into her voice. "What if the distortion doesn't affect you when it forms, but then you're trapped inside it? Can you move around inside one after it's formed?" That caught his attention; Kara saw him frown. He didn't know, or at least wasn't certain. She pushed the advantage. "Maybe you're immune, maybe you're not. But I *know* we aren't. None of us are."

"That's not my problem." He tugged on his daughter's arm and started off again, reaching the edge of the street, turning toward the west.

"It *is* your problem," she shouted. "You're going to need us. I don't know exactly what happened, but I know it involved the ley. The entire system is in turmoil. You might be able to protect your daughter from men like these Dogs, or whatever else might be out there, but can you protect her from what's happening to the ley? Can you protect her from the distortion? Think about her. You don't know what's out there!"

She knew the argument was weak, but he halted. He'd made it to the nearest intersection, now blocked by a massive chunk of gray stone. As if she'd planned it, something in the northern part of the city cracked and a plume of white ley light rocketed into the sky like a geyser, sheets of light breaking away from it in the wind and skirting west like spray. Parts of it shimmered like a prism, the light broken into reds and greens and gold. She saw the ex-Dog turn toward it, the muscles working in his jaw, his eyes narrowed. His daughter nudged his arm and he looked down, listening with a frown as she spoke. Kara was too far away to hear what she said, but the ex-Dog looked toward her, his expression angry.

"You'd better come with us," he said grudgingly, his eyes shifting to include all of them, even the Dogs. "I don't know what we'll find out there, but it would probably be better to meet it as a group." He shifted toward the tower and raised his voice. "That includes whoever is hiding out in the tower!"

Kara sucked in a sharp breath, everyone stilling to listen. The whine from the distortion continued, although Kara was growing used to its piercing tone. No one emerged from the tower.

Arguments broke out among the Wielders and the Dogs. Kara caught fragments, some urging the others to break away, one woman desperate to find her family. The Dogs were grumbling, eyeing the ex-Dog with hooded eyes as two of them dealt with the one who'd gotten splinters of amber in his face.

The older Wielder with the wispy hair shifted toward her and murmured, "Do we really need him?"

Kara exhaled, unaware she'd been holding her breath. "He's right. The city's quiet now because the survivors are still in shock. But once night falls?"

Both of them turned toward were the sun rested above the horizon.

"I trust him more than I trust the Dogs," the woman said. "And we aren't safe here."

"I don't think we'll be safe anywhere inside the city, not once everyone shakes off their fear and begins moving," Kara said, then shot a look toward the pulsing light of the distortion. "We're going to have to deal with it eventually."

"Agreed. But not right now. We need time to figure out what happened. And maybe we'll find someone else who knows more than us, one of the Primes, perhaps."

Unease roiled in Kara's stomach as she watched the distortion, but she turned toward the ex-Dog and shoved it aside. It was too close to nightfall, and she knew nothing about the ley system at the moment, how damaged it was, how extensive the destruction. She knew nothing about distortions of such size either. It could quicken within moments, or it could remain stable for days.

She drew herself up, steadied her trembling hands, and said, "I'll come with you."

The ex-Dog nodded and turned toward the others. All but one of the Wielders, in his mid-thirties, drew up near Kara, but after a long moment, even he joined them. The leader of the Dogs gazed at them, eyes narrowed, then flicked a quick assent toward the ex-Dog. "We'll come." For now, his tone suggested, even though he didn't say it out loud. Some of his fellow Dogs didn't appear to like the idea.

The ex-Dog said nothing, merely turning back in the direction he'd been headed. Kara started out after him, the Wielders and Dogs trailing behind at a slower pace.

"What's your plan?" she asked when she caught up with him.

"I have no plan," he said, and for the first time Kara heard weariness in his voice. He glanced down toward his daughter. "I just want to get my daughter out of Erenthrall."

Kara frowned. "You won't make it out before nightfall."

"Then we'll find some place to spend the night," he snapped.

Kara drew breath for a biting retort, but someone behind her gasped and she glanced up.

They'd moved away from the cover of the towers, Erenthrall now spread out before them. The southern part of the city was ablaze, the fire raging out of control, the columns of smoke so thick and black they covered at least three districts. The wind blew it west, the ash and embers settling across the river along Tannery Row and West Forks. The fire was a distant roar, like a wind. Kara stared down toward the University, her heart clenching as she wondered what had happened to Cory and Hernande, to all of the mentors and students, even the stupid little dog who had attached itself to her after she'd rescued it from the distortion. The geyser of ley to the north had ended, those districts strangely quiet, although they could hear an occasional unnatural howl rising somewhere from its depths that sent a shiver down Kara's spine. Bizarre lights played across a few of the districts, shimmering and fading like the northern lights that could sometimes be seen above the Steppe.

"What was that howling?" the ex-Dog's daughter asked. She was staring off to the north, her face troubled. Kara judged her to be about ten years old, maybe a little older. She was handling the situation better than Kara would have expected, her expression shocked and frightened, but serious, compared to one or two of the Wielders, who were nearly catatonic, barely functioning enough to follow along with the group. Only the death-grip on her father's hand revealed her age.

"I don't know, Poppet," her father said, "but it's far enough away I don't think we need to worry about it."

Kara wasn't so certain.

"What's your name?" she asked the girl as the ex-Dog nudged them back into motion.

The girl shot a questioning look toward her father, who shrugged. "Morrell," she said uncertainly, then added with a fierce frown. "Not Poppet."

Her father smiled.

"My name's Kara. I'm a Wielder." She let her gaze settle on the ex-Dog expectantly.

After a moment, he glanced sideways, then grumbled in irritation, "Allan."

Kara motioned to the lacerations and bruises that marred his back, a few of the deeper cuts actively bleeding. "You should let someone take a look at that."

Allan tensed, then forced himself to relax. "Later."

Another howl rose in the distance, joined by two others, much closer. The Dogs behind stared into the distance, grips tightening on their swords. The Wielders drew closer together.

"What's happened to this city?" the older Wielder muttered. "What's happened to Erenthrall?"

No one answered.

⌁

Dierdre burst into the main room of the building in West Forks, backlit by a hellish haze of ash and the pulsing blood-orange of fire until she closed the door. The acrid scent of smoke jerked Dalton out of his daze, his attention fixating on Dierdre.

"We have to move. Right now. The fire's blowing this way."

Two of the other Kormanley in the room—Michael and Brendan, both young, about Dierdre's age—began pulling the backpacks they'd assembled earlier over their shoulders. Darius, Dierdre's older brother, did the same as he asked, "Where are we headed?"

"I don't know, but we can't stay here. One of the northern districts. It looked like they were untouched, but it was hard to tell through the smoke. People are fleeing the fire. We can hide ourselves in the confusion."

Dalton frowned but said nothing as Darius grunted and motioned the others to the door. Dierdre headed toward Dalton, knelt at his side.

"We have to leave, Father. It isn't safe to remain here any longer."

She spoke to him as if he were a child. But then, since the horrendous explosion that had rocked the foundation of the building, collapsing the upper floors, he had sunk into a stupor. His first sight of Erenthrall through the upper windows as Dierdre herded the entire group to the lower floors had caused him to stumble in shock, his chest seizing so hard he hadn't been able to breathe. His mind had frozen, Dierdre cursing as he fumbled his way down the stairs with her help. He had known something horrible had happened when the world flashed white a moment before the quake—had known it was the advent of his vision—but he couldn't have imagined how staggering it would be to see it. The entire world had changed in the course of a moment; everything he had foreseen had come true.

And he could have stopped it.

That thought alone had paralyzed him with unadulterated guilt and horror. He had seen what would happen, had been warned, and he had still faltered. No, worse—he had *failed*. And there was no way to fix it.

He stared at Dierdre as she knelt beside him. Then she sighed in irritation and grabbed his arm, intending to haul him to the door and out into the decimated streets of Erenthrall.

He jerked back and barked, "No!"

Galvanized into action, he stood on his own, Dierdre staring at him in shocked surprise, the three others at the door turning. He met all of their gazes, his stance hardening in defiance, then turned to Dierdre again.

"No. You're right, we need to move. Even if there were no fire, we would need to move. But not to the northern districts. Not to any district. We need to leave Erenthrall altogether."

"What do you mean?" Brendan asked, his voice cracking with fear. He swallowed with a grimace, turned widened eyes on Darius.

"We can't leave Erenthrall," Dierdre's older brother said. "Where would we go?"

"Don't you see?" Dalton said. Outside, he could hear the howl of the fire growing closer. The building creaked around them and the men at the door shifted nervously. Dalton motioned Dierdre forward, grabbed one of the remaining packs himself and shrugged it over one shoulder. He headed toward the door. "Erenthrall is dead. The Baron's subversion of the ley, and Augustus' twisting of it, has ended. This was the price."

He opened the door, flinched back from the heat of the fires raging a few blocks away and the swirling embers and ash that assailed him. He raised a hand to shield his face and stared out into the street, out beyond the fire to the cracked and toppled towers in the distance. Above it all, a ball of white light blazed, obscured a moment later by the thick smoke. The wind kicked up by the near inferno forced him to raise his voice as he half turned back to those clustered behind him.

"This is what I foresaw! The destruction of the Nexus; the release of the ley. This is retribution for the Baron's arrogance, for Augustus' belief that we could control nature. The work of the Kormanley here is done."

Then he stepped out into the edges of the fire. Heat burned his lungs, turned his skin waxy. Embers pelted him as hot ash rained down on all sides, the streets already covered in a thick layer of gray-black.

Without looking back to see who followed, Dalton pulled his hood up to protect his face and turned away from the ruins of Erenthrall, away from the fire, and headed southwest.

A moment later, he was lost in the smoke, only a faint trail remaining in the ash.

⟡

Kara woke with a start, blinking at the darkness of the room in the building the group had finally taken shelter in. She automatically reached to light a ley globe, then winced in regret; she'd left the one she'd found in the cells back at the tower and hadn't seen an unbroken one since.

On the opposite side of the room, a window was limned with the ethereal white light of the distortion. A figure stood there, watching the street below.

They'd stumbled for two hours though the ruins of Erenthrall, the streets of Grass choked with the debris from the collapsed towers. The fire continued to burn to the south, spreading across the river, the wind shifting direction and carrying the ash out onto the plains to the southwest. Tremors still shook the earth at odd moments. Ley continued to spout from the ground in various locations, and the sheets of undulating light drifted over parts of the city at random. One had nearly swept over them as they crawled over the rubble at the edge of Grass, one of the Dogs calling out a warning a moment before it coruscated overhead. Kara had felt drawn to its shimmering dance, even as her stomach twisted in revulsion. Where it passed, the stone of the remaining buildings looked churned and warped.

They saw no one in the streets they traversed, but Kara swore that the shadows moved in some of the buildings as they passed, and once she heard someone's voice calling out, the sound muffled before she could locate the cry. She knew that people were watching them; she could feel their eyes prickling the skin at the base of her neck. Allan confirmed it with a nod when she sent him a questioning look. She was relieved there were other survivors, more than she had initially thought based on the signs, but it still kept them from searching the houses for food or water. Farther out, beyond the radius of damage caused by the initial explosion, she could see others moving, in groups on the streets, or clustered on the roofs of buildings. The greatest number of deaths had obviously occurred near Grass.

At one point, Kara noticed that the Wielder who had held back earlier had vanished. She hadn't even learned his name. She assumed he'd decided to head off on his own. Allan merely shrugged when she pointed out his absence.

When the earth shook again two hours later, the sun setting low on the horizon, the clouds above tainted a deep orange, Allan finally called a halt. The Dogs scattered at a word from their leader, Bryce. They'd checked the surrounding buildings, a shout drawing the group to the three-story building where they now slept.

Kara rubbed at her eyes and rose carefully, picking her way through the huddle of Wielders, Artras, the older woman, opening her eyes to watch her as she passed before settling back down. The Dogs had taken the perimeter, two on watch. Kara noted Morrell sleeping near the Wielders, but didn't see Allan, realizing he must be one of those on watch. As soon as she was clear of those sleeping, she moved toward the window, Allan turning as she approached.

"What's it like out there?" she asked, settling in beside him.

Allan shook his head. "Not good."

The night was cold, colder than she'd expected. But then she realized that there was no ley to warm the flat they were using. Even the glass of the window had been blown out by the explosion. And it had been an explosion, centered at the Nexus. Kara had visited the roof of the building before the sun vanished completely. Even from that height she could see the pattern in the destruction of the city. The towers had fallen in radii from the Nexus, like the spokes from the center of a wheel. Debris had been blown outward from that center. Buildings had imploded, or crumbled in the quakes that had followed. At least a third of those they passed had been reduced to nothing but rubble. Some districts, like Stone, had fared better than others. Eastend looked completely demolished.

A search of their building had yielded little to no provisions. Everything organic this close to Grass—clothes, blankets, food—had been burned away. They'd scavenged what they could, seen to the wounded, Kara bandaging Allan's torso with Artras' help, and then most had collapsed in emotional exhaustion.

A series of howls rose into the night, so close Kara caught her breath. She thought maybe the howls were what had woken her.

"How close are they?" she asked.

"Close. Maybe five blocks away."

The howls cut off and Allan stilled, listening. The sword he'd taken from the Dog in the tower rested across his lap. He kneaded the handle with one hand.

"They're hunting," he said.

Kara shifted closer to the window. "What?"

"People." At Kara's startled glance, he motioned with his free hand into the distance. "Look."

Kara followed the direction of his arm and saw firelight in the distance. Not the ruddy red glow of a fire raging out of control, but the pinprick light of torches. As she watched, she realized they were moving, a group of people hurrying along a street, heading out of the city.

She couldn't make out individuals, but the torches spread out into a narrow line, a few trailing behind.

The howls rose again and the hairs on Kara's arms prickled. The line of torches halted a moment, and then those in front began to bounce as their bearers began to run. She thought she heard vague shouts, a scream. The torches trailing behind suddenly gathered together, cut off from the rest, and a moment later the baying broke into vicious snarling.

The small group of torches left behind wavered . . . and then went out.

Kara shivered. "Shouldn't we help them?"

"We'd only draw the . . . wolves to us."

Kara didn't like his hesitation. "They aren't wolves?"

Allan stared at her a long moment in the pale light thrown by the forming distortion. "I grew up outside the city, have lived the last twelve years there with my daughter. I know the howl of a wolf. These creatures are not wolves. But I don't know what else to call them."

Kara didn't know what to say, fear and horror locking her throat. So she said nothing.

They sat in silence, Kara watching the darkness, catching more signs of life like the torches. Most of those were moving away, leaving Erenthrall behind. But not many. Not as many as she expected. And those signs were all distant.

The howls continued, but sounded farther away.

Finally she stirred again, disturbed. "The city . . . it's too dark. Even with the white light of the distortion highlighting everything, it's too dark. There should be ley light everywhere. There should be ley globes in the streets, ley illuminating the towers, a shimmer of ley in the sky above from the sails of the ley barges. Without all of that it looks—it *feels*—so empty. Where are all the people? Especially here, closer to Grass?"

Allan hesitated, then said bluntly, "Dead."

Kara's breath halted, her chest tightening. In the back of her mind, she'd known they were dead, but she hadn't wanted to accept it, still didn't want to accept it. "What do you mean?" she said, forcing herself to breathe. Slowly. Inhale, exhale; inhale, exhale. But the tightness across her chest didn't ease.

"They're dead," Allan said. "Whatever happened, it killed them."

"But what about the bodies? Where are they? What about us? How did we survive if they didn't?" She didn't like how strained, how thin, her own voice sounded.

Allan shrugged. "You're the Wielder. You tell me. Because whatever happened, I think it's obvious it involved the Nexus and the ley."

Kara's brow creased in thought. "I don't know. I'm not a Prime. But I do know the ley wouldn't destroy bodies—we submerge ourselves in the ley when we climb down into the pit."

"That's not true," Allan said sharply. "I remember the ley killing people during the sowing of the Flyers' Tower. I can still see the idiots on the balcony of one of the other towers when the ley splashed over them. They died, their bodies crumpling. I heard that those who were stupid enough to be out in the open, but were close to the base of the tower, simply vanished. Nothing was left behind except jewelry— brooches and clasps, buckles."

Kara swallowed down bile. She'd noticed the scattered metal objects hidden beneath the layers of dust in the streets on their walk here, but she hadn't really thought about them, only registered how odd the pieces were, lying in the streets. But now. . . .

She coughed at the acid burn at the back of her throat. "I didn't real- ize." Her voice was rough. "I knew that the ley could burn out our minds if we were caught inside the node during a particularly bad surge, but no one ever said that it could incinerate us as well. It must have been something you learned as a Prime."

"I only ever heard of such deaths at the time of the sowing," Allan said. "And we were told by Captain Daedallen to keep the deaths quiet."

Kara considered this silently. Then: "It must be the amount of ley involved. To sow the Flyers' Tower, the power would have been im- mense, much greater than that needed to run the nodes or the ley sta- tions. Which means that whatever happened at the Nexus must have involved a massive amount of power, something that would annihilate everyone in the city."

"Not everyone. We survived."

"Because we were underground," a new voice muttered.

Kara started, but she noticed Allan didn't even flinch. She looked over her shoulder, picked out Artras from the darkness. The older Wielder shifted closer and stood behind them, gazing out the window.

"What do you mean?" Kara asked.

"We were in the cells beneath the Amber Tower. I think we were protected from the blast. Only those who were inside buildings—deep inside, where the ley couldn't reach—or who were sheltered somehow from it, those are the people that survived. Eastend and Shadow were destroyed because the buildings there were old, made mostly of wood. The buildings here in Green and in Eld are old, but they're mostly stone and mortar, solidly built. Those in Stone are newer, and created by molding the earth itself. Most of those who survived this close to the source are going to be from the older districts, or were somehow in the lee of the storm when it struck. Those farther away from the Nexus probably survived as well. I'm certain the power of the explosion dissipated with distance. I could see buildings in the outer districts still standing, when others closer in and in sturdier condition didn't. The farther we travel, the more people we'll run into."

They contemplated her words in silence, until the Dog in position on the far side of the flat suddenly gave a startled bark, then turned. They could see his silhouette against the window as he whispered, "Look!"

"What?" Allan demanded quietly as the three of them skirted the sleeping figures to join the Dog at the window. He was the youngest in the group, barely twenty. He gestured frantically out the window.

"To the south, near the University. It's a light!"

Kara gasped when she saw the beacon, made from ley light, not fire. For a moment she couldn't place it, too used to the rest of the city lights being lit to orient herself, but then she realized it was one of the giant ley globes that rested on top of the walls of the University. It flickered and guttered for a moment, everyone at the window holding their breath, but then it caught and held.

"So someone's alive at the University," Allan said.

Kara's heart stuttered. Cory? Hernande? It was possible. When she'd seen them last, they'd been in the practice rooms, deep inside the main keep, surrounded by walls of stone. If they had stayed there when the Dogs came for her, perhaps to work with the sand further. . . .

She cut off that line of thought, dared not let herself hope.

As if in response, another tremor shook the building, its rumble growing like thunder in the distance, then sweeping over them. Kara clutched the side of the window, and some of those sleeping jerked awake, flailing or crying out. But then the earth settled. Those now awake joined them at the window and exclaimed at the sight of the beacon.

"We should head there in the morning," Artras said, voice hard, resisting argument.

Allan's eyes narrowed in irritation, but he said nothing.

The next morning dawned bright but chill, Kara shivering in the autumn air. Bryce walked among the sleeping bodies and roused them with a sharp, "Get up!" or a nudge in the ribs. Nathen, one of the Wielders, shot him a vicious glare that he didn't see, but sat up with a groan.

The first words out of Morrell's mouth were, "I'm hungry."

Kara watched as nearly everyone looked to the floor while Allan spoke to his daughter, his voice a low murmur. Kara's stomach growled and she pressed her hand against it, trying to halt the sound. She hadn't seen anything edible since they'd climbed from the tower, although some food must have survived the blast somewhere; they simply hadn't taken time to do an intense search. She hadn't seen any viable water to drink either; what was left of the rivers ran nearly black with mud and debris.

"Are we ready?" Bryce asked. It was barely a question, almost a demand.

Kara felt something subtle shift in the air, Bryce and Allan watching each other with hard expressions.

After a long, tense moment of silence, Bryce huffed out a breath and said, "Then let's move. I want to be at the University by midday, see what this light is all about."

As soon as they stepped outside, the Dogs grew grim, their expressions hardening. They fanned out around the Wielders protectively, surprising Kara, until Artras muttered, "You said it yourself. Us Wielders are going to be as priceless as errens, at least until the city settles, perhaps longer. Who knows how many of us survived? Who knows how extensive the damage is? And who's going to be able to repair it, to make sense out of it all?" She nodded toward the distance, where plumes of ley had sprouted in what looked like the Canal District. "No, if the Dogs are smart, they'll keep us close, try to keep control of us."

Kara frowned, not liking the weighted sensation that settled over her shoulders with the woman's words, like a yoke. She eyed the Dogs in a new light, wondering how they would break free of them, if they needed to at some point.

They'd made it almost to the University, its beacon still blazing even in daylight, when they saw their first survivors.

They stumbled out of a side street, a woman helping a man along, his arm slung over her shoulder. Four others trailed behind them, all of them with makeshift weapons, all of them scrambling away from something behind them. The woman's face was open and desperate, half dragging the man she held, heedless of his stifled cries of pain as his right leg snagged against debris. The muscles in his neck stood out in stark relief as he bore it. Kara didn't understand what was wrong with him at first, but then she realized that her eyes weren't blurry. The man's right side was smeared, his flesh and the bones beneath slightly out of place, even the clothing that covered him stretched somehow.

But she didn't have time to wonder why. As soon as the group appeared—the four fanned out protectively behind the other two, shouting orders to each other—Bryce brought Kara's group to a halt with a hand gesture. He waved frantically for them to retreat, but he was too late. The woman saw him, hope infusing her face with a terrifying light.

"Help us!" she screamed, veering toward them, the man she held groaning as she slewed him about, his legs kicking dust up from the road. "Help us, please!" Her hope broke into choking sobs. "They're following us! They're right behind us!"

Bryce swore under his breath, shouted an order to the Dogs that Kara didn't catch—

And then three black wolves appeared, the four other men with the woman and man backing away as the creatures loped down the street behind them. The men in the other group—three in their twenties, the fourth maybe fifteen—swerved their retreat toward Bryce. One of the wolves leaped onto a pile of stone from a collapsed wall, joined a moment later by another that skulked out of the shadows from the interior of the building. As it lowered its head, the lips of its muzzle pulled back in a silent snarl, Kara realized that Allan had been right: it wasn't really a wolf. It was too large, as tall as a man, its limbs and hip movements subtly wrong, its face too flat. Its black fur glistened with a slight iridescence and its eyes were bloodshot and an odd shape.

None of them were wolves.

"Back up to the building," Bryce ordered, the others still fleeing toward them. "Get back. Get back into the shadows! Move, move!"

He grabbed Artras' arm and shoved her toward the building behind them, but Kara stood transfixed, her breath coming in short gasps, her mouth dry. Three more of the wolves had appeared, one or two with streaks of gray or brown in their fur. She thought she caught more shadows moving in the recesses of the buildings beyond. "There's so many of them," she murmured.

Allan snatched at her arm and hauled her back, snapping her out of her trance. She tripped on the cracked stone of the street, hissing as she scuffed her hands on the dirt, but swallowed back the pain and sprinted in Allan's wake. He was shoving Morrell before him, thrusting her into the room beyond and then spinning, his sword already drawn. Kara caught his gaze as she skidded past him, but then his focus shifted toward the street outside. "Check the back for other entrances," he said, his voice unnaturally calm. He stepped back out the door.

"Artras," Kara said, turning.

"Already on it," the older Wielder muttered, and Kara saw her hurrying into the depths of the room, ordering some of the other Wielders in the opposite direction. Morrell stood in the middle of the room, uncertain, but then she hardened, stepped up to Kara's side, and looked out one of the windows.

A moment later, the woman carrying the man burst through the door, breath ragged. Sobbing, she staggered to the side wall and dropped the man unceremoniously to the ground, then collapsed herself. She raised herself onto one knee and her hands reached for the man's face. "Devitt. Devitt, can you hear me? Are you all right?"

"Of course I can," Devitt spat, swatting away her hands. "And I'm not all right." Grimacing, he hauled himself back and propped himself up against the wall with his left arm. His right remained twisted, shaking uncontrollably, as if in seizure. He cursed and caught it with his left, trying to force it down by his side. "Where are the others?"

"Outside," the woman said. "We found someone who can protect us."

Devitt's eyes latched onto Kara's.

"What happened?" Kara asked.

Devitt didn't pretend she wasn't asking about his arm. "I got caught in one of those lights. I was lucky. It just nicked me. Trev, my son—" His face grew pinched, but he didn't finish.

"It took him," the woman said viciously. "It took our Trev and transformed him. Into one of those *things*."

Kara stilled a breath in shock, then spun to face the window, suddenly realizing why the wolves' movements were off. Their legs . . . they were too long for a wolf, too narrow.

Because they used to be human arms and legs.

Outside, Allan had joined Bryce, the Dogs, and the four others in a rough circle around the entrance to their building. The unnatural wolves were pacing back and forth a short distance away, loping from side to side, lips drawn back from jagged teeth. Their breath puffed in the air before them, hotter than the surrounding late autumn air.

Kara counted thirteen of them and felt her stomach twist. "We can't beat them," she muttered to herself. But Morrell heard and spun toward her, her jaw jutted forward in anger.

Kara pushed back from the window. "Artras," she shouted into the building's depths, "what have you found?"

The older Wielder cursed as Kara heard her returning through the dark. "Not much. But I think we can escape through the back. It leads to what must have been a garden before the explosion, trapped between the surrounding buildings. One building has collapsed completely. There's no way we can get through that, but the Wielders are checking out the others."

"We're going to need it. Take these two and head through to the far street if you can. The Dogs won't be able to hold the wolves long. We'll have to run for it."

Artras nodded grimly.

"Leave me—" the man began, but Artras cut him off.

"Don't be stupid. Now get up, both of you, and move!"

Kara turned back to the window, one hand settling on Morrell's shoulder. The girl jerked back from her with a glare. "I won't leave my Da."

Kara pressed her lips together, but movement outside drew her attention away. "To the right," she barked, her fear nearly choking off her warning.

The men guarding the right spun, but they were too late. The wolves who had bolted from the vacant windows of the building next door hit two of the Dogs and one of the new men from the side. A Dog screamed as the wolf's teeth clamped down hard on his rising sword arm. The other grunted as he was driven to the ground, his blade slicing up into the wolf's torso, the animal shrieking with an eerily deep and penetrating growl even as its jaws closed down on the Dog's throat. The third man never made a sound as he fell beneath the onslaught of two wolves at once.

At the same time, the rest of the wolves charged the remaining men, two of them distracted by the attack to the right.

The fifteen year old spun and bolted toward the building at his back, the rest cursing as they braced for the wolves' charge. Bryce shouted orders. As the two groups met, Kara reached for Morrell's arm and gripped it, dragging her back. "We're not staying here," Kara snapped. "Now move!"

Morrell resisted for another breath, then whimpered and ran for the interior of the building, Kara at her heels. Screams and howls rose from the street outside, cutting through the bark of orders and curses from the Dogs. As Kara ducked from the room, she heard Bryce roar to retreat.

And then she was plunged into the muted darkness of the interior building. One hand on Morrell's back before her, the sounds of both of their gasps filling her ears, she called out, "Artras! Artras, where are you!"

"Head straight back." The older Wielder's voice came from a distance. "Ignore the stairs and any intersecting hallways. Once you reach the back garden, angle right."

The sound of men entering the hallway echoed from behind and Kara shouted, "Straight back! Head for the garden behind the building!"

Kara's heart shuddered as the growls of the wolves filled the hall.

Morrell suddenly spilled out the back door, sunlight slanting down in a blinding glare, but even as she blinked, Kara caught sight of Artras and Nathen motioning frantically to one side. She steered Morrell in their direction, turned back to see two Dogs, two of the other men, Bryce, and Allan fleeing down the hall behind her, the wolves black shadows behind.

"Go, go, go," the nearest Dog snarled, blood dripping down one side of his jaw. His eyes were feral.

Kara leaped from the door and across the dead garden, past Artras and Nathen, who fell in behind her with a calm, "Straight, then left, then right."

Kara ran. She didn't think, didn't plan, just moved. Within moments, she caught up to Morrell, the young girl sprinting down the hall, but slowed by uncertainty until Kara came up behind her. They followed the shouts of the Wielders who'd scouted out ahead, hitting the end of the hall and bearing left, then right a short time later, the Wielders' shouts growing louder.

They spilled out of the building and down a short set of steps into another street, the University's wall visible below them, still blocks away, the beacon of ley light shimmering high on one of its walls. The remaining Wielders were strung out down the road and Morrell and Kara headed straight for them, air burning in Kara's lungs now, her legs beginning to ache with exertion. A stitch began to form in her side, but she ignored it. Bryce issued new orders behind her as the guards spilled from the building. The woman and the man, Devitt, were scrambling as fast as they could go, far ahead on the street, heading straight for the University gates still hidden beyond a turn in the road.

Halfway down the street, Morrell screamed and pointed off to the right. The Wielder they were approaching turned—

And a wolf streamed out of a cross street and struck him hard, throwing him to the ground in a splash of blood, tearing into the Wielder's torso as the man shrieked. Morrell slowed, but Kara shoved her from behind with a harsh, "Keep moving," and they charged past the struggling pair, Kara trying not to listen to the sounds of tearing flesh and gurgling blood. The Wielder beyond—Dylan, Kara thought—stared at the carnage in shock until Kara snapped him out of it with a sharp jab to his chest as she passed. He stumbled back with a grunt, then spun and followed them.

They were quickly catching up to Devitt and his wife. Ahead, on the University wall, she saw movement—men were pointing down at them, shouting in the direction of the gate. But the wall was too far away for Kara to catch anything. Listening to the sounds of retreat from behind, Kara felt a hand clench her heart and squeeze.

They weren't going to make it. The gate was too far.

Devitt and his wife reached the corner and vanished from sight. Kara slowed as they came up to the turn, let Morrell outpace her and shoved Dylan after her. She spun to look behind—

And found the guards charging toward her, no longer even attempting to keep the wolves at bay. They were flat-out sprinting, Bryce and Allan at the back, their faces flushed red with effort. The wolves were spilling from the building they'd retreated through, scrambling out of doors and windows and tearing after them. A few raised their muzzles to the sky and howled. Kara shuddered.

Then something pressed down against her on the Tapestry from above and she glanced skyward, eyes opening wide. A sheet of the coruscating light, like that seen in the north, wavered over them, pulsing between green and yellow, tendrils streaking across the sky. Kara reached instinctively upward with her power to protect herself as it pushed down on her, thinking about what Devitt had said about the lights transforming him, taking his son. The light reacted, flowing away from her, and with sudden desperation she shoved it toward the street. It was unwieldy, her control limited, the light resistant, so she cupped her hands over her mouth and screamed, "Run, you bastards! Run!" even as she heaved against the light's pressure, forcing it down the street, above the guards' heads. But it was too heavy. She swore as it dipped, both Bryce and Allan glancing up as it roiled toward them.

A moment later, it swept downward, Kara's control lost.

Both Bryce and Allan flung themselves forward, hitting the stone of the street and rolling beneath the wave of light. It struck the ground behind them and rebounded into the wolves slavering on the guards' heels. Those in the lead yelped and twisted back, but they were too late. The light caught them and through the haze of green and streaks of yellow Kara saw their bodies contorting, smearing and changing into impossible configurations. Legs bent and fur shifted from wolf to human skin and back again. Bones cracked and popped. Howls rose, then changed to whimpers and snarls. The wolves behind pulled back from the shimmering light and paced, snapping at the air in frustration as Bryce and Allan both scrambled to their feet and lurched toward Kara with the rest of the guards.

Before anyone reached her, though, a piercing whistle cut through the air, and the wolves beyond the veil of light fell silent, ears pricked. Kara watched as they halted their pacing and bounded toward a man emerging from the confines of the buildings beyond, circling him in excitement. He was dressed in armor, his body distorted like Devitt's, his face twisted into a snarl, half human, half wolf. He glared at the retreating guards, one hand held out to the wolves that capered about his feet. His eyes were locked on Allan.

The Dogs and remaining men from Devitt's group tore past, Bryce and Allan slowing as they reached Kara.

"Did you do that?" Bryce demanded, chest heaving as he gasped and tried to recover from his run. His hand waved toward the shimmering wall of light.

Kara shook her head. "I didn't cause it, but I did push it a little. It was too strong for anything more."

Bryce broke into a hacking cough and leaned forward onto his knees; Allan also sucked in huge gulps of air. The ex-Dog she'd rescued shook his head and said hoarsely, "Doesn't matter. You used it. Saved us all."

Kara didn't respond to the praise, merely nodded toward the far figure. "Who is he?"

Allan turned with a frown, still recovering—

And then he stilled, his entire body going tense. Kara saw him consider lying, the muscles of his jaw twitching, but then he said grudgingly, "His name was Hagger. I don't know what he is now."

Then the ex-Dog headed toward the open gates of the University with a tight, "Where's my daughter?"

Twenty-Seven

"WHAT'S HAPPENED?" Bryce demanded. "What in living hells happened?"

The mentors and students who had rushed them through the gates of the University walls had led them to a room deep inside the main buildings on University grounds, where Kara and all of the rest collapsed. Of the fourteen people who had stumbled from the Amber Tower with Kara, one had vanished on the way here and three had died at the hands of the wolves. Two of the six survivors they'd met had fallen. Everyone else had collapsed into chairs in exhaustion, accepting water and food brought by the students at the mentors' orders. Blankets and clothes appeared. The Wielder Kara had found sobbing in her cell in the tower, and who had remained in shock the entire trek to the University, finally broke, rocking back and forth with the blanket clutched tight to her shoulders, her expression lost. A few of the University people were attempting to soothe her.

As she drank from her own cup, Kara had searched the people entering and leaving, but she had not seen Cory or Hernande. After a while, she stopped looking, and noticed that not everyone was a student or a mentor. Some of those helping them settle in had obviously found sanctuary at the University, just like Kara and the others. Men and women, even some children, drawn to the beacon. All of them appeared haggard.

At Bryce's sharp words, a few of the helpers looked up. But it was one of the mentors in dun-colored robes who answered, handing off a bowl of soup to Devitt's wife before standing and facing the Dog.

"We don't know the particulars, but I think it's safe to say that it was a catastrophic failure of the ley system."

Bryce's anger shifted toward the mentor. "And who are you?"

The man's brow furrowed. "I am Sovaan, mentor here at the University."

"Are you the one in charge?"

Sovaan bristled. "I am one of those in charge here on University grounds, yes."

Before Bryce could respond, Artras said briskly, "I think what the Dog is trying to say is thank you." She shot Bryce a glare. "For bringing us into the safety of your walls. And I believe, like all of us, he's shaken by what's happened and would like to have any information you have about . . . about Erenthrall."

Sovaan appeared mollified, even if Bryce did not. The Dog remained silent, though.

"We likely know as little as you. The explosion destroyed nearly the entire city, only the outskirts spared as far as we can tell from our walls. Those outside the radius of destruction appear to have fled into the surrounding lands. Those who survived inside the city have been struggling to leave, even as they become victims of the chaos the ley network has unleashed. Once we realized that the survivors were being attacked and needed shelter and food, we set up the beacon in hopes they would come here. So far, it appears to be working. We have brought hundreds behind the walls, although it is obvious that many, many more are simply abandoning the city. We've seen thousands leaving by wagon or horse, in groups as large as a hundred, most of them farther away from the center of the explosion and not inclined to head deeper into the devastation. And those were during daylight. Who knows how many left in the dead of night? Who knows how many more are simply hiding in the ruins, afraid to move at all?"

"The beacon was Hernande's idea," one of the undergraduate students near Sovaan added.

Sovaan grimaced, as if Hernande's name pained him. "Yes, Hernande."

Kara caught her breath, then blurted, "Hernande's alive? What about Cory? He was a graduate student here."

"Yes, yes, they survived. They were in one of the practice rooms when the explosion occurred." Sovaan dismissed Kara with a wave, but then his attention jerked back to her, his eyes narrowing in recognition. "You were the one the Dogs came for, right before this happened." His gaze flicked over Bryce and the others, then returned. "What did they want? What did *you* have to do with this?"

Kara scowled. "I had nothing to do with this. The Dogs captured numerous Wielders, not just me, and took us to the tower. I don't know why. But that's why we survived. We were in the cells beneath the Amber Tower."

Artras, Nathen, and Dylan nodded, but not the woman, who had begun mumbling to herself under her breath, the same phrase over and over. Kara couldn't tell what it was she said and didn't care.

Instead she winced in memory, then sighed. "But I think I know who may have caused it. Or at least played a part in it."

Everyone's attention was on her, but it was Sovaan who straightened and asked, "Who?"

"Another Wielder. A . . . friend of mine. His name was Marcus."

Kara felt something in the room shift, an uncertain and tremulous fear solidifying as it latched onto someone to blame. She could feel it transforming into anger, knew that it could escalate if she didn't stop it somehow now. Blaming Marcus was fine, but they couldn't let thoughts of revenge or justice or retribution distract them from the real problem: the distortion that hovered over Grass. Marcus was more than likely dead, but the distortion continued to feed. They had to find a way to stop it.

"How it happened isn't the issue right now," Kara said, setting her cup aside and standing. "The distortion is."

Sovaan snorted. "We have no hope of stopping the distortion. The ley field is in chaos. Nothing is working as it should. That's why we are leaving. Preparations have already begun. Wagons are being loaded with whatever supplies we can take with us even now."

Kara traded a look with Artras. The older Wielder shrugged.

Kara turned back to Sovaan. "Where is Hernande?"

The mentor huffed. "In the training room, where else? He's spent nearly all of his free time there since this happened."

Kara stilled, her heart pounding harder. The only reason she could think of for Hernande to remain in the training room was because of the sands.

"I need to see him," she said sharply, hope burgeoning in her chest. "I need someone to take me there now."

Sovaan didn't have time for her, but the undergraduate student who'd told her that Hernande had suggested the beacon led Kara and Artras through the labyrinthine corridors and halls of the ancient manse to the training rooms. She chattered nonstop as soon as they were out of Sovaan's hearing, but Kara wasn't paying attention.

She wanted to see Hernande, *needed* to see Cory. She needed to verify for herself that they were alive, needed to touch them, hug them.

Artras followed silently behind.

As soon as Kara recognized the stone of the corridor and the long hall with the doors to the training rooms opening off one side, she shoved past the student and charged down to the room they'd used before the disaster. When she flung the door open, both Hernande and Cory started, the mentor pacing on the far side of the sand pit, Cory kneeling at its edge on one side. The dog she'd rescued from the distortion leaped to its feet with a low growl and yip in the corner.

Cory stood, confusion crossing the weariness that lined his face, but that was all Kara allowed him to do before she ran across the room and embraced him, clutching him to her. Tears coursed down her face, even though she wasn't sobbing, but she didn't care. She breathed in his sweat and the stench of an unwashed body, felt his arms wrap tentatively around her. The dog began barking excitedly and she could feel his paws against her legs as he yelped and bounced around them.

Then she drew back and looked up into Cory's face. "You stink," she said. Her voice cracked.

He smiled, his expression haggard and drained, but filled with an indescribable happiness. "And you're dirty."

She laughed and without thought leaned forward and kissed him, long and hard, emotions she hadn't allowed herself to feel since the collapse of the Nexus—no, since long before that—giving the kiss urgency. Cory returned it hesitantly at first, then his grip tightened. Kara's body hummed and she tasted the salt of her tears and Cory's lips and for a moment the terror of what the world had become vanished. All of the strange tension between them since that night on the roof before the horror of the Kormanley attack in the park that had killed her parents died, swept aside, *burned* aside.

It lasted until the need to breathe drove them apart. She pulled back, but not far, looking up into Cory's slightly startled eyes. Muddy brown with striations of a deep gold she'd never noticed before.

She smiled. "I've owed you that since that night on the roof, when you first kissed me."

"I didn't think you wanted anything more than friendship," he said roughly, his voice ragged.

"I've changed my mind."

Someone cleared his throat and both of them turned toward Hernande, the mentor as beaten and bruised as Cory looked, his smile as radiant. "It's good to see you alive," he said. "We had feared to hope."

"So had I," Kara said, fresh tears starting as she pulled back from Cory reluctantly. Emotions surged through her, so intense she felt light-headed, off balance, yet strangely alive. She leaned over and scratched the fur of the little dog's head as he slobbered all over her hand. His tail wagged so hard his rear end wouldn't stay still.

Then the soft sound of shifting sand penetrated through the pounding of her heart and the thrumming of her body. She glanced down to see the sand pit moving, channels of sand sifting back and forth, as they'd done before the Dogs had come for Kara.

Except everything was wrong, the patterns unrecognizable.

"Is this Erenthrall?" Kara asked. She couldn't keep the shock and disbelief from her voice.

Both Hernande and Cory shifted toward the sands with her.

"This is what is left," Hernande said. "You can see the structures that once formed the ley network here in the city—the Stone node, Eld, Candle, even a few of the ley station junctions—but most of the network is no longer intact."

Artras and the student had moved forward as well, the older Wielder staring down at the sands in consternation, brow knit. "What are you talking about? What is this?"

At Kara's nod, Cory drew breath and said, "The flows of the sands here represent the ley lines in Erenthrall. Before the disruption, we could trace the entire network throughout the city, every junction, every node, every branch to the Baronies and beyond. It was a map of the entire system."

Artras hissed out a breath, eyes narrowed. "But the Primes—"

"We know," Hernande answered. "Kara made it clear how the Primes would react. But at the moment, the Primes are the least of my worries."

Artras pursed her lips, then barked a harsh laugh. "Yes, I suppose they are. If any of them are still alive." She turned her attention back to the sands, her eyes tracking ley lines, picking out features, as Kara was doing. "So this is Erenthrall now? This is how the ley lines have rearranged themselves?"

"Yes. We've been studying them since the disruption. After regrouping with those that survived, of course. And we've discovered something troubling."

"The distortion," Kara said.

Hernande nodded, his lips pressed into a grim line. He pointed toward a chaotic section of the map, where the sands were roiling more than anywhere else, a vague whirlpool swirling around what Kara assumed had once been the Nexus. Except this whirlpool swirled upward, grains of sand lifting from the pit to form an inverted tornado. "It's drawing energy from the remains of the Nexus."

"No," Cory contradicted. "It's drawing power from something deeper." Hernande gave him an irritated look. "It has to be," Cory countered. "There isn't enough ley remaining in that area to create such an anomaly. You said it yourself: the main lines that fed the Nexus before the explosion have been interrupted!"

It sounded like an argument the two had had before, so Kara cut in. "Cory's right. It's feeding off of something deeper."

Both Hernande and Artras stared at her. "How do you know?" Hernande asked.

"Because when I was younger, before I became a Wielder, one of the wardens of Halliel's Park tested me using the stones in the central grotto there. I sensed that there was something hidden deeper beneath the city, something that the Nexus had tapped into." She motioned toward where the spike rose from the sand. "The distortion must be tapping into that lake of ley as well."

Artras nodded grudgingly. "If this is an accurate representation of the system at the moment—"

"It is," Cory said.

"—then I agree." She tilted her head at the sands, then knelt down near the pit's edge. "In fact, now that you've mentioned Halliel's Park, I'd say that the ley is trying to revert back into its original flows. See there? That's the park, one of the more stable sections of the map. And this here is Oberian's Finger, another park with a plinth of stone rising from the hill at its center. Both were considered sacred in ancient times, long before Erenthrall became the city it is—*was*—today."

"That would make sense," Hernande muttered. "Now that the strictures we imposed on it have collapsed, it's settling back into its old patterns."

"But not quite," Kara countered. "The distortion that's forming is disrupting that. Look." She circled to the far side of the pit, the dog on her heels. "It's warping the new lines, drawing them toward it." She stared at the entire system a long moment, then glanced up at Cory and Hernande. "The entire system is unstable. It's going to remain unstable as long as the distortion continues drawing energy from it."

"And the longer it draws energy, the more it will consume when it finally quickens," Artras added.

Silence held in the room, interrupted only by the susurrus of the sand and the panting breaths of the still excited dog.

Finally, Cory stirred and asked, "Can you stop it?"

Kara clenched her jaw. "Someone has to try."

⌐⊂⊃

"You're insane," Sovaan announced. He glanced toward Hernande, Cory, and Artras, the rest of those in the room staring at the entire group as the tension rose. The student who'd escorted Kara and Artras to the training room bristled to one side. "You're all insane. The distortion is too large, it can't be fixed, can't be repaired. We have to flee."

"No one said we shouldn't flee," Hernande said. "Merely that an attempt should be made to halt the distortion before it quickens."

"Wielders have done it before," Kara added. "If we arrived in time, we could sometimes repair the distortion before it quickened."

"This isn't like any of the distortions you dealt with before," Sovaan snapped. "It is a hundred times larger, a hundred times more powerful—"

"And at the rate at which it is feeding, it will be a thousand times more deadly," Hernande interrupted, his voice taking on a dangerous tone. "If you left now, you would still not have time to escape its radius when it quickens. You cannot outpace it, even with horses, certainly not with wagons and carts and a group of refugees."

Low murmurs of fear threaded through the room and Sovaan

frowned as the tension in the room escalated. "How can you possibly know this?" the rival mentor asked.

"They have a map of the ley system in the sands of the training room," the undergraduate student blurted out, awe in her voice.

Cory and Kara glared at the young woman. Sovaan's eyebrows shot up. "A map of the ley?" He turned on Hernande. "And you did not see fit to reveal this to your fellow mentors?"

"It was only just discovered," Hernande said, his voice calm and unconcerned. "I would have revealed my findings to the University council eventually. At the moment, we have more pressing concerns, such as evacuating those in the University as quickly as possible."

"What about food? And water?" someone murmured.

"And where are we to go? I've never lived outside Erenthrall!"

"What about those wolves?" Devitt shouted above the growing tumult in the room.

The group got quiet, all eyes turning toward Sovaan, Hernande, Bryce, and the Dogs. Nathen and Dylan even looked at Allan. The anxiety and uncertainty in the room was overwhelming, the beginnings of a headache starting behind Kara's temples. She raised a hand and rubbed her eyes, felt the grit of exhaustion there, the result of the sleepless night and the escape to the University. A tremor pulsed through the ground, a few of those crying out, but the jolt was minor compared to what they'd experienced before.

But it was a reminder that they had little time. The longer the distortion was allowed to feed, the worse it would be when it quickened. And the longer it fed, the more unstable the area around Erenthrall would grow.

She looked up, met Cory's eyes with a silent question. He frowned, but nodded agreement. Then she turned to Allan. "I'm a Wielder. I'm going back to the Nexus to repair the distortion, wolves or no wolves. I could use someone to protect me on the way." She shifted her gaze to Artras. "And someone to help me when I get there. I don't think I can do it alone."

Artras pursed her lips, then nodded. "I'll go."

"So will we."

Kara turned toward Dylan and Nathen, who looked toward the other Wielder they'd found in the cells.

She shook her head as she continued rocking, fresh tears coursing down her face. "I can't," she whispered. "I can't."

"You'll never make it," Bryce interjected. "We barely made it here."

"We'll need protection," Artras said. "Someone to watch our backs. What about you Dogs?"

Bryce grinned, the expression sending a shudder down Kara's spine. "It won't work. Not even if all of us Dogs go with you. The wolves know we're here now. They'll be waiting. They'll attack as soon as we leave the protection of the walls."

"He's right," Allan muttered. "Especially if they're being led by Hagger."

Kara began pacing in frustration. "We can't cower in here until the distortion quickens. We'll all be trapped then. We need to do something!" She grasped at the empty air as she paced. "We need . . ."

"A distraction," Hernande said. He was chewing on the end of his beard, brow creased in thought. He considered, head bent forward, and then he looked up. "We'll have to be the distraction, the few hundred we've gathered here at the University. We'll leave—with the carts and what provisions we have—and we'll make for the grassland, to the south."

Allan hesitated, glanced toward his daughter with a strange look on his face, then he shook his head. "No. West. There's a place in the western hills called the Hollow. I've lived there for the past twelve years. It's isolated and can be defended, if necessary. Not many know of it, but I have a feeling that we're going to have to band together if we're going to survive the aftermath of the ley's destruction."

"Then west," Hernande said.

"You are all insane," Sovaan spluttered. "Why should we be a distraction for them? Why shouldn't they be a distraction for us?"

For the first time, Hernande's eyes narrowed in anger. "Because they are risking themselves to save us. And because if they fail, it will not matter how fast we run, we will be caught in the distortion."

Another tremor shook the building, crumbling mortar drifting down from between the wooden beams of the ceiling overhead.

"The tremors are getting worse," someone nearby muttered. Those in the room shifted restlessly, looking toward the ceiling.

When no one said anything more, Sovaan's expression angry and grim, Hernande pointed toward Cory. "Go down to where the carts are being loaded and tell them to get as much ready as they can by tomorrow morning. You," he switched to Bryce, "go with him and see what can be done about protecting the people and the supplies from those wolves and anything else we might encounter. We've already attempted to plot a course out of the city based on what we can see from our walls, but we'll have to modify that if we're going to head west instead. Emil, Brant, and Hera, get up to the rooftop and see about that. The rest of you, gather what you need and get it down to the carts. And search the rest of the University for any essentials we'll need once we're away from here. Spread the word. We'll be leaving at sunrise."

The room began to stir, people rising and leaving. Emil grabbed Brant and Hera, the students rushing from the room as others began fretting and bundling up their things. Fear was the dominant emotion, but now it was fear with a purpose.

Hernande watched in silence for a long moment, then rounded on Kara. "You need to convince the Dogs to accompany you and the other Wielders. We can distract them while you leave by a secondary gate, but I don't know how much time we can give you. You'll need to move fast. But for now, you and the other Wielders should rest."

He moved away before Kara could respond.

⟜⟝

Allan knocked on the door before he opened it and stepped into the training room beyond. For a moment, the scent of sand brought back bitter memories of the pit in the center of the Dogs' den at the base of the Amber Tower—he'd lost and spilled blood in those sands during his time as a Dog—but it was only a flicker, a tightening of the gut, nothing more.

Two ley globes revealed the Wielder—Kara—seated at the edge of the central rectangular pit, her eyes bruised with exhaustion, her face haggard. Before her, the sands of the pit shifted, coursing back and forth, but she'd glanced up at his knock. A runt of a dog lay beside her, head lifted and ears cocked back as he sniffed the air. He began to growl until Kara's hand stroked the top of his head. Then he settled, although his eyes stayed on Allan.

No one else was in the room.

They looked at each other in silence, until Allan said, "You should be sleeping."

Anger creased her forehead. "I couldn't. There's too much activity, too much movement."

"So you came here?"

She drew breath as if to snap an answer, but caught herself, her eyes narrowing.

Allan suddenly realized he'd begun interrogating her, as if he *were* a Dog and this was a room beneath the Amber Tower. He sighed and shook his head with a rueful smile. "Sorry. Old habits die hard."

She nodded. "How did you find me?"

"Cory. He said you'd asked him to set the map in motion and that he'd left you here. Then he told me how to find the room."

Kara motioned toward the map with one hand. "I thought I could study the ley lines, prepare myself for tomorrow, but I can't. The lines are shifting too dramatically and unpredictably. I don't know what the Nexus will be like once I get there. I don't know whether I'll be able to halt the distortion. And I don't know whether I'll be able to repair it." She raised a hand to rub at her eyes, blinking and scrubbing her face afterward as if she'd just woken up. Her gaze settled on him again. "Why did you want to find me anyway?"

Allan shifted in indecision. He could still change his mind. But looking into the Wielder's eyes he realized he'd been right to come here, to seek her out.

"I came to tell you that I'll be going with you."

The Wielder stilled in confusion. "What about your daughter?"

Allan grimaced. "She's twelve. She can take care of herself. And she'll have the rest of the University mentors and students—Hernande and Cory—and the Dogs to protect her."

He could tell by Kara's frown that she suspected he wasn't telling her everything. But she said nothing.

Allan drew in a breath. "I've managed to convince a few of the other men—not the Dogs, but some of the others—to come with me to protect you and the other Wielders. Most, like me, think that if you fail, we're lost anyway. It isn't much, but I'd rather leave the Dogs to protect the others when they run for it. Hagger won't fall for it if he doesn't see the Dogs."

"How will the group find this Hollow if you've been killed?"

Allan's lips thinned. "Morrell will be able to lead them there. I explained where she'd need to go once she was outside the city. Once she's close enough to recognize some of the landmarks, she'll be able to find the Hollow."

But he didn't expect it to come to that. He expected that the University group would make it out of the city; Hagger wouldn't be fooled by the diversion for long, and once he knew there was another group, and that Allan was part of it. . . .

Allan was the true diversion. He just hoped that the University group distracted Hagger and his wolves long enough that Kara and the others could stop the distortion.

Kara was watching him. He wondered how much she read in his face and shifted uncomfortably.

"What time is it now?" she finally said, beginning to rise. The dog hopped up and looked up at her expectantly.

"Two hours before dawn. Hernande intends to start his diversion an hour after that."

She nodded, made her way to the door, the dog trotting along behind her. When she brushed past him at the door, he asked, "Where are you going?"

She paused, looked him directly in the eye. He could see in her eyes, beneath the determination, that she didn't expect to survive whatever happened tomorrow. "I'm going to spend these last few hours with Cory."

Then she left.

Allan thought suddenly of Morrell.

He found her sleeping with a group of the others who'd fled to the University, right where he'd left her. She frowned and groaned as he settled into a seated position beside her, back against one wall, but when he began stroking her hair she curled in toward him, one arm reaching to clutch his legs. He smiled and tilted his head back against the stone.

He stayed with her until dawn.

Twenty-Eight

"A S SOON AS the beacon goes out, we run," Allan said. "Don't look back, don't hesitate, just head straight for the entrance to that building, the one with the red shutters on the windows."

"That's a cloth shop," one of the men Allan had convinced to come with them said. Allan thought his name was Keith. He held a short sword, his grip unprofessional, but competent. "My wife used to spend hours in there, searching through the bolts of fabric."

Allan felt a twinge of worry—he didn't need his guards falling apart on him—but the man, probably in his forties, caught his gaze and shook himself, giving Allan a grim, reassuring smile. "Even if we do stop the distortion, we won't be returning to Erenthrall, will we?" he asked.

"Not Erenthrall as it was before, no."

They stared out through the narrow slit of the window above one of the University's secondary gates at the remains of the city beyond. It was eerily quiet, only the faint, persistent whine of the distortion itching at the back of Allan's skull. He'd managed to shove it from his conscious mind since leaving the area around the tower, but suddenly he couldn't drive it away.

He scanned the rest of the group: three other men besides Keith, one Keith's age, the others late thirties, all clutching swords; Kara; and the other three Wielders. Not much of a guard, especially considering most were barely trained to hold their weapons, let alone use them.

Nathen cleared his throat. "What should we do if we get attacked? Us Wielders, I mean."

Allan locked gazes with him. "Run. Head straight for the Nexus and don't look back."

Nathen swallowed, his eyes edging open a little wider. He glanced toward Dylan and Artras, but both of them merely nodded, faces hard.

At a window on the opposite end of the room, Kara suddenly stilled, then turned. "The beacon is out."

"Then let's move." Tension stiffened Allan's shoulders as he motioned three of the men out in front, the Wielders falling in behind them. Allan and Keith brought up the rear. Their boots were loud on the stairs as they descended to the gatehouse below. Allan had already spent the last few hours watching the streets for movement, but he snapped a warning to halt before the first guard could push the gate open. Shoving through to the front, he slid aside the small window at eye height and peered out onto a street filled with the slanted sunlight of sunrise. Nothing moved in the gaping windows or doors across the way, and nothing but dust and scattered debris shifted on the road.

Without a word, he stepped back and gestured to the door. Two of the men—a rugged blacksmith named Ryant and a lean but strong man named Trace—drew back the bolts and raised the heavy plank out of its braces. The latticed iron gate had been raised earlier, to keep the noise of their departure to a minimum. At Allan's nod, Ryant pushed open the heavy, banded door and slid outside, the rest following as quickly as Allan could move them. He followed Keith, not bothering to pull the door closed behind them. No one remained in the University; all of them were with the wagons or here in Allan's group.

He sprinted across the street, nearly treading on Keith's heels, his gaze sweeping the road to either side. "Faster, damn it," he hissed, and Keith put on a burst of speed. Ahead, Ryant and the other guards reached the red-shuttered building, framed its doorway as they ushered the Wielders inside, Kara last. Allan wondered if those at the wagons had had the courage to face the wolves. He wondered if they'd opened their gates yet. He wondered if Sovaan would convince the ragged band of refugees to stay behind the University's walls instead.

A moment later, he got his answer.

As he reached the door, the other guards ducking through the opening ahead of him, the howls of the wolves shattered the morning stillness. He thought of Morrell and prayed for her, for all of them.

He paused and listened, heart thundering in his chest, hand gripping the hilt of his sword so hard the knuckles were white.

None of the baying was close.

He met Kara's eyes in the shadows of the interior room. "It's working. Let's move."

⬤

As soon as the beacon went out, Hagger knew they were going to move. A growl of anticipation rumbled low in his throat and the ears of the two wolves nearest to him perked up. He unconsciously huffed out a command, the sound coming from the back of his throat. One of the wolves scrambled away, the action half fluid, half clumsy and awkward. Hagger reached up to stroke the fur that matted the side of his face, felt the elongation of his jaw. Not enough to be called a snout, but close. He grinned.

Toenails clicked on stone and his ear twitched. The wolves who had been lounging in the back rooms of the flat scattered, moving off down the street. They'd listened to the prey scrambling all night, knew from the shouts and the clattering that they were concentrating their effort on this gate. Hagger had watched figures ascend the wall and the towers inside, searching the city with telescopes and eyeing the streets. He'd kept his pack in the shadows as much as possible, ordering them to withdraw at least two blocks distant, but even he could smell the fear and anticipation on the air, growing by the hour. It wafted over the walls of the University and set Hagger salivating. He wiped at the drool and tried to control the curl of his lip without success.

His transformation had some drawbacks.

He snapped his fingers and the wolf at his heels jumped to its feet and growled. It turned and stared up at Hagger. He could see the humanity in its eyes, the intelligence there. The wolf had been one of Hagger's own Dogs before they'd run into that strange sheet of coruscating light. His entire pack had been caught in it; he'd only been hit by its edge. Which was why he hadn't been transformed completely, he assumed. After surviving the initial explosion and the destruction that followed, he thought his transformation—and that of his Dogs—only fitting. The entire city had changed after all.

A new city, a new order. He grinned.

"Wait until at least four wagons have made it through the doors,"

Hagger said, his voice more rumble than words. "Then strike. Everyone, all at once."

The wolf half nodded, half sneezed in acknowledgment, then loped off into the shadows.

Hagger turned back to the window, stepping forward but off to one side. His hand fell to his sword.

When the gates creaked open, Hagger's lips peeled back from his teeth and his heart sped up. He felt the rush of adrenaline, his nostrils flaring. Scents sharpened, the air arid, filled with dust and the ashes of the dead city, the heavy musk of the other wolves, the silvery scent of water—

And the spice of human sweat filled with dread and anxiety and the delicious expectation of death.

His snarl twisted into a feral smile and the hair on his arms and back bristled. He flexed his left hand, the right gripping his sword. Muscles cracked and popped and he suppressed the urge to howl. His breath quickened as three Dogs and four other armed men spread out on the street, tense and wary, then motioned the first of the carts outside, drawn by two horses. Hagger had enough humanity left to wonder where they'd found horses, but then their scent hit his nostrils and he didn't care. Yet enough of his mind remained that he found himself searching the faces of the men. He couldn't remember exactly why, but he knew it was important. He didn't find what he was looking for, though.

A moment later, not even that mattered. Five more wagons had emerged, all guarded by men and women brandishing makeshift weapons—knives, clubs, a few decent blades—all of them reeking of fear. A thickset man bellowed orders from the seat of the second wagon, exhorting everyone to pick up the pace. He stank more than the rest. Hagger's hackles rose, but before he could react a howl ripped through the morning air.

It carried one single command: attack.

Hagger moved without thought. He drew his blade as he charged, snarled as he caught up with the wolves closing in on all sides, seized on the sharpest scent of fear as the men nearest cried out and the women screamed—

And then he swung, his chosen prey blocking, shunting the sword to one side, his other arm rising even as Hagger snapped forward with his jaws. His teeth sank into the man's forearm and slick, metallic blood flooded his mouth as the man's scream pierced his ears. Nostrils flared, he shook the man's arm, teeth sinking in deeper as the man tried to jerk back. His terror was intoxicating, overwhelming Hagger's senses, so intense he nearly forgot about the man's sword.

He caught the blade in his peripheral vision, released his hold, and leaped backward. The tip bit into his side and he yelped and snarled, bringing his own blade back into play. On all sides, the wolves were ripping into the fleeing prey, but they weren't retreating back to the gate. The lead cart careened wildly down the street, heading toward the river, to the southwestern bridge. The rest were scrambling after, wolves taking them down at random, but there were hundreds of them and not enough wolves to take them all. Hagger caught flickers of the action as he parried and thrust, the man he'd mauled stumbling after the carts, Hagger in pursuit. He suppressed the urge to toss the blade aside and drop to all fours, waited for the man to falter instead, to make a mistake—

But then another scent filtered through the sweat and tension and blood, snagging Hagger's attention and sending a frisson of shock through his entire body. He pulled back, head raised as he drew in a deep breath. His prey tripped on the cobbles, scrambled upright, bloody arm cradled to his chest, then sprinted toward the fleeing carts.

Hagger ignored him. He knew that scent. It reminded him of . . .

Allan.

But not quite. It wasn't right. It was his whelp, his *daughter*.

Allan wasn't here. Which meant . . .

He stretched out his throat and howled, even as the wolf inside him retreated and the rage over Allan's betrayal surged forward. On all sides, the wolves' heads lifted, muzzles bloody. But they ignored their prey and bounded toward him as the call faded.

One of the wolves whined.

"Leave them," Hagger growled. "Our real prey is escaping. Check the gates. Check them all. Someone left by another route. Find their scent!"

When the lead wolf glanced back toward the retreating wagons, the easy prey, a slew of bodies left behind, including two dead wolves, Hagger barked, "Now!"

The wolves flinched.

Then they bounded off around the walls of the University in search of the gates.

⌗

Kara gasped as the group raced through the empty streets of Green toward Grass. Air burned in her lungs, but she forced herself to keep moving. The desolate buildings on either side pressed down on her, the weight of their hollow interiors threatening to crush her. She fought back tears. Even though the sounds of the wolves had fallen behind, fading with distance, her imagination was too vivid. She wondered if Cory would survive, or Hernande, even the stupid little struggling dog she'd handed over to Cory at the last moment. The mutt had wanted to come with her.

She wiped her sleeve across her eyes and forced the burgeoning emotions down. She didn't have time. None of them did.

And then the ground heaved beneath her and she cried out and stumbled, unable to catch herself. She hit the cobbles hard, stone jolting her bones, breath caught in her chest. She rolled back into a crouch, heard the others cursing and shouting as the earth continued to tremble. A block distant, a four-story flat shuddered and then gave in, walls collapsing as dust billowed up into the late morning sky. To either side, the buildings swayed, the wall nearest cracking with a sharp retort. Allan grasped her arm and hauled her away, his grip so tight it cut off the circulation to her hand, but she didn't protest as the wall smashed down into the street. The rest of the building remained intact, rooms exposed to the daylight.

As abruptly as it started, it stopped.

Kara coughed, the grit in the air settling. Allan released his hold on her arm, scanning the rest of the group. "Everyone all right?"

Before anyone could answer, Artras snapped, "Listen!"

Everyone fell silent. Wind whistled through hollow windows and doorways, the sound sending a shudder down Kara's spine. Something rumbled in a distant part of the city—another building collapsing, perhaps. She thought she caught a faint shout, from their own group or other survivors—there had to be other survivors, even this close to the Nexus—but it faded. Kara strained to hear more, but the only other sound—

Was the distortion.

She spun toward Artras, then looked up toward the blazing white light, nearly overhead now.

"What is it?" Allan asked, voice sharp.

"The distortion," Dylan answered. "Its tone has changed. It's beginning to quicken. Can't you hear it?"

Allan's face stilled, then broke into a scowl. "Keep moving, then. Unless it's already too late."

In answer, Kara sucked in a breath and began to run. Not the ground-eating steady pace they'd been using since they'd left the gates of the University. A flat-out run.

A block farther on, two of the men who'd volunteered to guard them caught up with her, faces red, breath heaving. Kara backed off, but not much, the others clustering around her, the stockier guard trailing slightly behind. They passed the edge of Green and entered Grass, the buildings changing, the debris cluttering the roadway growing heavier as they neared the area where the main towers had been destroyed. Kara clambered over chunks of stone, vaulted from rock to rock, her muscles crying out in pain, but she didn't slow. Overhead, the distortion pulsed, its piercing whine growing higher in pitch at a slow but steady rate. It dug into her ears, cut into her brain, but she clenched her teeth against it.

Ahead, the base of the Amber Tower loomed, but Kara ignored it, intent on the street and the park beyond. All traces of their passage through here two days before were gone. The wind had blown their footprints from the dust, had scoured the flat surfaces clean and deposited the dirt in drifts along the stone. They reached the low wall surrounding the depression that held the Nexus, the group silent except for harsh breaths and wheezing coughs as they followed it toward the open gates. They halted at the height of the stairs leading down to the Nexus below.

Kara took in the shattered building in the hollow beneath them and her stomach clenched. Someone moaned. The crystal dome had caved inward, only jagged edges remaining, reflecting the sun now almost directly overhead, eclipsed only by the distortion. Kara's throat tightened as she realized that the center of the building looked empty, when it should be suffused with ley. Doubt set in—perhaps the Nexus wasn't the best location for attempting to repair the distortion above after all—but she couldn't think of another place that would be better. According to the shifting sands at the University, this was where the ley was the most active.

It didn't help that she saw the same doubt and dismay in the other Wielders' eyes.

"Let's go," she said, sounding more confident than she felt even though her voice cracked on the words.

They descended the steps, leaping over massive cracks, noting those that lined the sides of the building as they approached. The earth shook yet again as they neared the main entrance, not as intense as the one earlier in Green, everyone crouching down low for stability. As soon as they entered the main building, Kara began looking for Primes, for anyone who would be able to help them, even though she knew it was hopeless. The rooms were scoured bare. Her stomach roiled as she realized that scattered jewelry, belt buckles, knives, and other metallic objects were the last remains of the Primes who had been in the building. Nothing else remained—no clothing, no plants, not even the wooden doors separating the rooms. They'd been too close to the center. Whatever had happened in the Nexus, the destruction had wiped everything living away. Not even ash remained.

"Where do we go?" Allan asked as he motioned his fellow guardsmen ahead to scout the rooms.

"I don't know," Kara said. "Wielders were never allowed into the Nexus."

"The center," Artras cut in succinctly. "The Nexus would have been in the center of the building, beneath the crystal dome."

Allan nodded. They advanced, the men checking each room before they proceeded, and reached the center of the building in short order. The stone doors to the central chamber had blown open, one cracked across the middle. Tiers like wide steps descended toward a central pit. Alcoves lined the room on all sides, broken by other entrances. Huge slabs of crystal from the collapsed dome littered the floor, surrounded by thousands of smaller shards. When the guards roamed out into the room, moving carefully, their feet ground smaller crystals into the stone floor. Kara grimaced as she crunched forward, letting Allan and the guards keep an eye on the other entrances as she, Artras, and the two other Wielders moved toward the pit. Allan halted halfway across the room, where he could see the entire chamber, all of the entrances and niches. Artras sank to her knees near the pit's edge, staring down into the darkness. A faint white light bloomed far beneath them, the shaft deep. Rounded tunnels were cut into the sides of the walls, leading out to the other nodes, Kara guessed, the channels that fed the network that had once run Erenthrall. Smaller apertures were cut higher up, but she couldn't tell what they were for. She couldn't see the much deeper, wider channels that led to the Nexi in the other cities.

"There are rooms beneath us," Artras said.

"What for?" Nathen asked with a frown. "The nodes only have a pit, nothing like this."

"It doesn't matter," Kara said sharply. "What matters is if we can reach the ley here, enough to stop the distortion."

All of the Wielders glanced up to where the white light pulsed high above, framed now by clouds. It appeared to be directly overhead, and Kara would have sworn that it had grown in size. The high-pitched whine had certainly changed since she'd first heard it beneath the ruins of the Amber Tower, sharper somehow, with a faint throb that hinted that whatever stability the light had at the moment was fading.

They were running out of time.

"How do you want to do this?" Artras said, standing. She caught Kara's eye. "You and I are the only ones who appear to be dealing with this with any sense of calm." Dylan barked a scoffing laugh. Before Kara could reply, Artras added, "I think you should be the one to repair it. You're stronger than I am, younger, more resilient. I can sense that without even trying. The rest of us will support you as best we can."

Kara glanced around at the others, saw Nathen and Dylan nod, the guards not reacting at all, focusing on the doorways into the chamber. She thought about the distortion that had killed the boy, about the seamstress who'd ended up with a mangled hand. But Artras was right: all of the others looked shaken, and none of them had been on track to become a Prime.

"Fine," she said, swallowing against the sudden dryness in her throat. She wished they'd brought water with them, but it hadn't crossed her mind. She glanced around, stepped away from the edge of the pit and seated herself on a nearby crystal, brushing smaller shards aside to make room. They chimed against each other as they fell to the floor, the notes strangely musical, but dissonant, with an edge. She grimaced as she sat, Artras positioning the others around her. Kara didn't watch the others settle in, barely noted that the guards had drawn in closer to them. Instead, she reached out to feel the surrounding Tapestry, to test it and find the ley.

She gasped as soon as she sensed the Tapestry. It was in turmoil, shuddering and twisting violently, still reacting to whatever had caused this catastrophe even two days later. It threatened to sweep her away, like the currents in the river when the storms drenched the plains and steppes to the north and flooded the city. Swollen, full of riptides, the Tapestry tugged and pulled at her, until she sucked in a sharp breath and centered herself. She heard the others react as they joined her, felt their presences appear, then recoil around her. Nathen cried out and withdrew, Artras coaxing him back a moment later.

But Kara shoved Artras' soothing thoughts away and focused her attention upward, hissing as she caught sight of the beginnings of the distortion.

It was larger than it seemed, larger than the throbbing white light hanging over the city. It stretched much farther outward on the Tapestry, a knot of tension that was drawing tighter and tighter, straining the fabric of reality around it. It was already taut, threatening to tear.

They had even less time than she'd thought. But she'd need the ley's energy to feed the repair. She'd never have the strength to do this without it.

Wrenching her attention away, she reached down, centering on the pit and allowing her essence to fall, searching for a connection to the ley as she went. The conduits that led to the various nodes throughout the city were dry, only a faint trickle of ley remaining. The system that had fueled the city for decades had been completely disrupted. As she traveled the paths, she could sense ruptures throughout the city, ley pooled in odd locations, spewing forth in geysers in others, the entire network in chaos. But the network had never been natural, the Primes and mentors forcing the ley into new channels, into new configurations. With those restraints loosed, the ley was seeking out its natural flows, some of them blocked, others altered, the ley finding new courses, like a river carving out new channels after a major flood. It was the chaos she had seen in the sands, only brought to life, with depth, with dimension, and a horrifying sense of reality. And as she dove deeper, searching for a solid source for what she needed to do, she felt the stresses of the earth around her as the ley attempted to stabilize. The ground heaved in all directions, shuddering and shaking, like a body in seizure. The trembling sickened her, even as she realized that the destruction of the network wasn't just local. The earth groaned in all directions—north, south, east, and west. Whatever had occurred had not happened only in Erenthrall. It had happened everywhere, the damage extensive, so pervasive that it threatened to overwhelm Kara's search, stretching her too thin as she felt frantically for stability anywhere. But the lines to Tumbor, to Farrade, to the Steppe—they were all ruptured, all fluctuating.

So she withdrew, returned to Erenthrall, pulling herself back and centering herself again even as she choked back despair. The formation of the distortion above her pulsed against her senses, weighed down on her shoulders, somehow black and insidious even though it writhed in white light. She sucked in ragged breaths, felt Artras' questioning hand touch her arm in concern, but she shrugged the sensation aside.

"The entire system is down," she reported. "Not just Erenthrall. Tumbor, Farrade, the Steppe, the Reaches . . . all of it. Whatever hit us here struck everywhere. The conduits have been disrupted, the pathways of the ley broken. We're on our own."

The guards gasped and broke into frantic babble, until Allan snapped, "Quiet!" Kara sensed him turning toward her, sensed his fear, calmly reined in and controlled, but there nonetheless. "Can you fix it on your own?"

"We should have brought some of the mentors at the University with us. They could have helped. I know the Primes used them for anything they built of scale, like the Flyers' Tower, but I don't know how, exactly." Kara straightened where she sat. "But it's too late for that. We'll have to try on our own."

And she dove back into the pit, ignoring the channels to either side, ignoring the larger conduits leading away from the city, heading straight down beneath the city. She hit the first significant levels of ley, the energy churning around her. She plunged into it in relief, instantly dragged in its currents to one side, barely keeping herself from being swept away. Clawing her way back, she used the Tapestry to form a link to the ley, siphoning some of it off and drawing it up through the pit toward the remnants of the Nexus. This was one of the ways the mentors helped in the Primes' constructions, she realized. They helped build channels, helped control the ley, because they were more talented at manipulating the Tapestry. But she'd have to do it herself now. Once she reached the destroyed chamber, the link trailing behind her, she opened her eyes and caught Artras' attention.

"I've forged a link to the ley. I'm going to try repairing the distortion now."

Artras nodded, her expression grim, motioning toward the others as Kara took a deep, steadying breath and closed her eyes again. She felt the Wielders' presences around her as she lifted herself upward, reaching for the distortion above. Its weight pressed down upon her, worse than moments before. The tension was escalating, faster than she thought possible. But she had nothing to compare this to, nothing to judge it against. The largest distortion she had dealt with had begun with a light the size of her fist, the one that had killed the boy, the same one that had caught but not harmed Allan and his daughter. This one was a thousand times larger.

Drawing on the others' strength and the link she'd forged with the ley, she stretched out and attempted to encircle the distortion, reaching, and reaching further. Even though she worked far above the shattered Nexus, she felt her body pulsing with the beat of her heart. The rhythm of her own life's blood felt amplified as she stretched herself thinner and thinner. It roared in her ears, filled her senses, bolstered by the other Wielders. She sank herself into the sensation, drew her own strength from it—

And then she began to work at the outer edges of the distortion.

It began as usual, her mind sinking into the intricacies of the distortion. But unlike those that had already quickened, this formation wasn't stable. The stresses it placed on the fabric of reality, on the Tapestry that held everything together, shifted as she worked, so that once she smoothed out and relieved the tension in one area and moved on to the next, the distortion would ripple, the waves rumpling what she'd already worked on. It was like attempting to fix one of her father's clocks—with all the meshing of gears and the precise movement of interlocking pieces—while the clock was still working. In smaller form, Wielders had been able to close the rifts, glossing over the ripples in one surge of power. This one was too large.

Kara felt sweat break out against her skin, knew that it sheened her face, dripped from her chin. Her breathing altered, heightening with frustration, even as she clamped her jaw tight in determination. The distortion hitched beneath her touch and she gasped, but it didn't quicken. The high-pitched whine escalated. Kara gave up trying to repair the damage with fine-tuned finesse. Reaching for the ley, reaching for her fellow Wielders, drawing up their strength, she attacked the distortion in broad waves, sweeping across its outer edges and pushing inward. Dylan grunted. Nathen began to pant, breaths hissing between his teeth. Kara felt Artras' hand grip her arm, tightening as she murmured a warning, but Kara didn't relent.

"It's shrinking," she announced, her voice strained with effort. "I need more power."

At the same moment, Nathen cried out and collapsed. Kara felt Artras shove away from her, even as she sensed the loss of support up above. Her attack wavered, the distortion pushing outward again, but she dug in, pulled hard on her link to the ley, on Dylan and Artras. Distantly, she heard Artras exclaim, "He's dead!" An ache shot through her core, but then Dylan faltered and pulled back. The foundation for her work began to crumble as the pressure from the distortion increased. She needed more strength, needed more power, or the distortion would quicken.

Dylan collapsed, the sudden cessation of support wrenching at Kara's control. Desperate, she reached for the ley, reached for the seething power of the lines hidden deep within the earth. As she drew on their power, the ley rushing toward her, she sensed the reservoir of ley hidden deeper still. She had touched the ley lines of the Nexus and those constructed by the Primes during her testing then . . . but she'd known there was something deeper, something fundamentally stronger. The source of the power in Halliel's Park, the source that the Primes and the Nexus drew upon.

With the Nexus destroyed, with the artificial lines obliterated, the ley had reverted to this primal source.

And now, her grasp on the distortion slipping, Kara lunged for it.

Power flooded through her, exploding across the link she'd forged with the remains of Erenthrall's system deep beneath the earth. She heard Artras cry out, "It's not working!" and realized the high-pitched whine they'd initially heard was now a full-fledged shriek, the sound raw. The ground began to shake—not the grumbles of a shifting earth, but a violent quaking that tossed Kara from her seat on the crystal slab. She couldn't catch herself, felt her shoulder wrench, felt shards of glass cutting into her face, but she pushed all of it aside and focused on the surge of ley as it reached her.

She screamed as the ley roared from the pit to one side, using all of her strength to funnel it up toward the distortion. Tears squeezed from her eyes as she arched her back against the searing pain. The ley shot skyward, hitting the distortion and encircling it. Cords standing out in the sides of her neck, Kara poured the raw energy from the earth into repairing the damage, felt the distortion shrinking, its edges collapsing inward. Her control began to slip as Artras dropped out of the Tapestry, pulling away from the sheer intensity of the ley's flow. Through the roaring of power in her ears, she heard Allan shouting questions, heard Artras answering, felt the earth jolting beneath her—

Then she could hold the ley no longer. She cried out as her grasp slid free, the ley fountaining upward a moment longer before it began to fall back, retreating into the depths of the pit. Kara sagged to the ground, unable to move, her entire body trembling with exhaustion. She swallowed, coughed, gasped in air, but her body was hollow, empty. There was nothing left.

And the distortion still remained. Lying flat against the floor of the Nexus, she could see it still pulsing above, the sky lit with its fire, harsher than the sun. It burned her eyes, but she could not look away. She'd failed. The ley had shrunk it down to a third of its former size, but the distortion remained.

She choked on a sob.

But then Artras shouted, "It's going to quicken! Allan, grab Kara. Hoist her over your shoulder, or carry her in your arms, I don't care. Ryant, grab Dylan. We have to get out of here."

Kara heard people scrambling in the rubble, cursing as the earth kicked beneath them. Then someone snatched at her arm, picked her up. Her arms flailed, her body limp, even though she tried to help. She recognized Allan as he hefted her up into his arms with a grunt, holding her tight against his chest, and then he barked, "Stay close."

He bolted toward the entrance to the chamber. Kara caught a glimpse of the others—Artras, Ryant with Dylan thrown over his shoulder, the other guards. Nathen had sacrificed himself, and still she'd failed. The pain engulfed her, but she did not have the strength for tears. Her body was numb, burnt out.

Allan ducked through the doorway, paused to catch his balance and shift her weight, and then they were sprinting, Kara jouncing in his grip. She could smell his sweat. His muscles strained, his skin laced with scars, old and new. His heartbeat raced, pounding in the crook of his arms, and his breath heaved in ragged gasps as they tore through the shadows of the inner rooms. Then they were outside, the sun beginning to lower. But everything was thrown in stark relief, blazing in the strange, harsh, white light of the distortion above. Kara caught sight of it as Allan raced up the stairs along the side of the depression. They would never make it. It would quicken long before they reached the edge of the city.

As if he'd heard her, Allan slowed. Kara rolled her head to one side, confused. They weren't even halfway up the stairs yet.

And then she saw them. Wolves, standing at the lip of the bowl that housed the Nexus, at the top of the stairs. Their black bodies encircled the half man, half wolf she'd seen before, the man Allan had named Hagger.

Kara had no energy left for fear or shock. She was numb, on the verge of unconsciousness. Her head throbbed, the world strangely close and removed at the same time. But as the others drew to a gasping halt around her and Allan, Ryant summed up her reaction with one word:

"Shit."

"Set him down and fan out," Allan said to Ryant, even as he lowered Kara's body gently to the ground. He could feel her trembling, but not in fear. She was trying to move, but she couldn't. Her entire body had been dead weight. She'd be useless in a fight and she couldn't run. "Protect them for as long as you can."

He didn't say that it was hopeless. He counted twenty wolves at least, suspected there were more on their way, circling around to their flank. Hagger wouldn't have left them an escape route.

His chosen guardsmen spread out on the stairs as much as possible, blocking the path down to Kara and Dylan's bodies. Artras knelt down over them both, one hand resting lightly on Kara's upper arm. She glared at the wolves as Hagger motioned with one hand and they began pouring down the wide steps, most of them beginning to growl, teeth exposed.

As soon as they began to move, Allan shunted Artras, Kara, and Dylan from his thoughts, only keeping an awareness of their location in the back of his mind. He kept his gaze fixed on Hagger, hatred for the old Dog boiling up from inside. He tried to suppress the rage as well, but he could feel his body shuddering, could hear the pounding of his blood through his veins. He'd faced off with Hagger in the training pit in the Amber Tower too many times to count and the outcome had never been certain. And he knew he'd be facing off against him again, here, on the steps of the Nexus. His old partner wouldn't let the wolves get him; he wanted Allan for himself.

Allan rolled his shoulders, fighting the tension there, feeling the cuts Hagger had inflicted that had barely begun to heal, and muttered, "Come get me, bastard."

Hagger's left ear twitched and his lip curled up into a smile, as if he'd heard. Then he drew his blade and began descending the stairs.

The wolves arrived first. Allan was waiting for them.

The front line, four abreast, split at the last moment, two surging to Allan's left toward Ryant and Trace, one veering off toward Keith and Anthon.

The last leaped for Allan's throat.

He froze for a moment in shock, and then years of training took over, his blade slashing across the wolf's torso, cutting into flesh, jarring against bone. The wolf yelped, its growl cut short. Blood splashed against Allan's shirt and hands, but the force of his blow wasn't enough to halt the wolf's momentum. It crashed into him, snapping its jaws even as its lifeblood soaked into Allan's side. He cursed and thrust the animal away, rolling down three tiers of stairs before coming to a halt, the wolf landing hard a step away before sliding off to the curved stone of the depression to one side. He heard it howl as it fell and slid down the steep grade, but he'd already pushed himself onto his back, lurching upright as the second wave hit. Two wolves attacked him at once this time, the other guards fighting to either side. Allan thrust up with his blade, grunting as it punched through a wolf's chest, the animal twisting and jerking his sword arm aside. He kicked savagely at the same time, connected hard enough to jar his hip, felt sharp toenails gouge into his thigh as the second wolf scrambled for purchase. Teeth grazed his stomach and he rolled away, yanking his blade free from the still dying wolf, and found himself in a crouch on the edge of the stairs.

He rounded on the second wolf a moment before its jaws would have snapped closed on his heel. He stabbed down, severing its spine, letting its own inertia carry it over the edge as he pulled his blade free and stepped to one side. A quick glance showed that Keith was down, body mangled near three wolf corpses, Anthon, Ryant, and Trace a few steps below fighting desperately against five more, Artras standing over Kara and Dylan behind them, a knife in one hand, waiting.

But then Allan's attention locked onto Hagger, who reached Allan's level with a vicious smile and a half-growled, "My turn."

He swung even as he spoke, Allan anticipating the strike. But he didn't expect Hagger's speed. Either the old Dog had learned some new tricks after Allan left Erenthrall, or he was already adapting to his new form. Their blades clashed, edges scraping down to the hilts before Allan thrust it away, Hagger snarling as he swiped at Allan with his free hand. Hagger's elongated nails tore through Allan's shirt, scoring along his abdomen, drawing blood. The old Dog's nostrils flared and Allan hissed at the pain, circling away from the stair's edge. Beyond Hagger, three wolves paced the steps, trapping Allan between them and the wolves attacking the other guards.

Allan cursed, but Hagger gave him no time to think, coming at him viciously, blade flaring in the light of the distortion above, his free hand raking at Allan at every opportunity. Sweat slicked down Allan's back, stinging in the wounds there as they reopened. Hagger drove him back toward the other edge, nicking his upper arm, his thigh, slicing his side, none of the cuts serious but deep enough to draw blood. Allan sensed his parries flagging, drew on his rage for the strength to thrust Hagger's blade up so he could duck under his guard, away from the ledge to the safety of the central step, punching the old Dog hard in the kidney as he did so. Hagger grunted and doubled over, snarling as he recovered, lashing out as Allan retreated. He spun, faced Allan, who gasped and cradled his side.

When he'd ducked and twisted, his side felt as if it had torn apart. Perhaps the cut there had been more serious than he'd thought.

Hagger chuckled. "I can smell your death, Pup. I can scent your life seeping from you."

Before Allan could respond, the whine from the distortion high above broke. Light flashed and flared. Hagger glanced up.

Allan didn't.

Gripping the hilt of his sword in both hands, he pulled back and—

using all of his remaining strength—drove the blade into Hagger's chest.

Hagger staggered back, gaze locking with Allan's in shock, mouth open, before he fell to the steps. Behind him, the wolves began to howl, muzzles lifted to the sky. Answering howls rose behind Allan and he turned to see more wolves pouring out of the Nexus, charging up the stairs toward Artras, Kara, and the still unconscious Dylan. The old Wielder spun, knife held out before her, then cursed.

All of Allan's remaining strength fled. He collapsed to his knees, blood soaking his shirt, his breeches, not all of it his. Despair enfolded him.

He had done the best he could, but it wasn't enough.

He lifted his gaze toward the sky, toward the white distortion and its twin, the sun, and muttered, "Sorry, Morrell."

<hr />

Kara heard the fight, heard the growls, the scream as one of the guards died, the desperate curses as the remaining guards were driven closer to them. She knew the half-man, half-wolf Hagger had joined the fight because swords clashed. She knew the battle had turned against them when Artras squeezed her upper arm and stood, looming over her, one hand slipping into a fold in her shirt, withdrawing a surprisingly vicious-looking blade.

At that point, her attention drifted to the distortion, to the pulsing light high above.

The piercing whine faltered and cracked, Kara sucking in a sharp breath in the sudden silence. Then the distortion flared. Once. Twice. And Kara tensed in anticipation. The baying of the wolves made her flinch, her held breath expelled in surprise.

And then the distortion quickened.

Kara's eyes widened at the beauty of the spray of color, even as she cried out an inarticulate warning. Like the distortions she'd repaired in the city, this one blossomed outward, multicolored arms spiraling out into the city. One—a brilliant blue-green—roared through the air directly overhead, causing Artras to duck. As wide as a street, it swung out toward the city, passing through the remains of the towers and out of Kara's sight. Additional arms struck out in all directions, reds and golds and purples, jagged white lightning laced between them. Kara sucked in another sharp breath as she felt the distortion expanding, as she felt the Tapestry tearing and shredding around her. Reality ripped . . . no, reality *fractured*, like the crystal of the dome of the Nexus. She clenched her jaw as it cracked, hissing like ice on the surface of a puddle before it breaks. The hairs on her arms, at the nape of her neck, stirred as the air vibrated and shuddered. Behind them, beneath them on the stairs, the wolves, the guards, and Artras halted in awe and abject terror. For a moment, through the reek of her own sweat, through the stench of blood thick on the air, through the dust and grit disturbed by the tremors, Kara smelled sunlight, new grass, and fresh rainfall.

Then the swirling mass of the distortion slowed. The tension in the air coalesced. The shards of the new reality within Erenthrall solidified, and on the cusp of an exhaled breath—

They set.

Epilogue

KARA BECAME AWARE of the world slowly, sound intruding first—someone's muffled breath, distorted and far away. The breathing slowly resolved. Kara's eyes were open, had been open, but her vision remained a dark blur. As it solidified into darkness—night, she realized—a face coalesced above her.

"Allan," she tried to say, but her throat wouldn't move. She realized that nothing would move—her arms, her legs, her chest. She wasn't breathing, couldn't blink, her entire body locked in place.

She panicked. But there were no signs. The fear, the desperation, the clawing for release—it was all in her head. And in her heart. Even though her heart didn't beat, her chest felt tight, confined, her emotions running rampant through unresponsive flesh.

She screamed without sound, long and hard, until she realized that Allan was speaking to her.

"—relax," he said. "You can't move now, but that will fade. Give it time. It shouldn't be more than another twenty minutes."

She tried to relax, but found herself still racing about her head, trying to find a way out, a way to *move*. She'd never felt so claustrophobic in her life.

Ten minutes later, she realized Allan was gripping her arm. His attention had drifted and as feeling slowly returned to her limbs she watched him scanning the distance, his face grim, expression hard. He knelt next to her, one knee up, his other arm resting on it. His forearm was bandaged, and there were new cuts across his face. Nothing serious, but they would add to his scars.

And then she gasped, choked in a breath. At the same time, memory returned, of the fight on the steps of the Nexus, of the baying of the wolves, of the distortion flashing above and then *expanding*.

She choked again, her body wanting to breathe, but acting as if it didn't know how. Her heart stuttered, thudded hard in her chest, then halted, thudded again painfully a moment later. Allan reached across her and held her down as she thrashed, her heart beginning to beat normally an eternity later, air flowing comfortably into her lungs once again. The tingling of her blood beginning to flow through her limbs made her clench her jaw against a scream.

"Easy," Allan said. "Easy. It will settle down shortly. Just don't jerk out of my hold."

"What—?" she grated, the word barely audible, the air catching in her unresponsive lungs.

"The distortion quickened," Allan said. "Everyone here—everyone and everything in the entire city of Erenthrall—is now locked inside it, including you. Except for me. I'm immune, remember? After checking things out, I started trying to get you out. I'll get the others who survived—Artras, Dylan, Anthon, Ryant, and Trace—out as well, once you're safe."

The seizures were lessening, but Allan didn't remove his hands from her arms, nor did he lean back from where his body lay across her stomach. "How—?" The word came out clearer, but she still had to swallow hard.

"I've never done this before. But I've discovered I have to be close," he said. "And I have to be touching you. But it's taken awhile, and based on your reaction it isn't pleasant. Here." He gripped her arms and hauled her into a seated position. She gasped as shockwaves of pain coursed through her arms and chest, reached down into her legs, but then he propped her up against him so she could look around.

It was night, but the arms of the distortion glowed in vibrant shades above and throughout the city, jagged white-hot lightning laced between them, but frozen, pulsing slightly. Stars glimmered above, and the moon sat low on the horizon, but in the faint glow of the arced light surrounding them, she could see the wolves, locked in midcharge, muzzles drawn back in vicious snarls, slobber streaming out to the side. Three of them were leaping, attacking Ryant, Trace, and Anthon, barely twenty feet away, but frozen by the distortion. Beyond them, a figure lay on the steps with a sword sticking out of his chest, another body beside him. More wolves were bounding down the stairs behind them.

"That group was attacking Ryant, Trace, and Anthon. They'd already taken out Keith." Allan nodded toward one of the bodies. "I killed Hagger just before the distortion quickened. That's when the wolves above began descending on us. And then there were the ones Hagger had sent around to flank us." He turned her, so she could see those streaming up the steps below them, where Artras stood in a defensive half-crouch over Dylan's unconscious form. "If it hadn't quickened, they'd have slaughtered us."

Kara stirred, surprised she could move as much as she did. "How long have you known the distortions couldn't touch you?"

"I knew I could affect the power of the ley, but I didn't know anything about being immune to the distortions until Morrell and I were trapped in the one you were repairing. I didn't know I could move around inside them either, or whether or not I could bring you out of its hold. Not until you started struggling." He hesitated, then added, "But before I tried to save you, I checked on the others. Those at the University . . . they made it outside of the distortion's radius. Barely. If you hadn't repaired it as much as you did, they'd be locked inside with us."

Kara wanted to ask if he would have saved them all if they had been trapped, or simply taken Morrell and left. She suspected the latter. But then again, he'd come back for her, and it sounded like he meant to save Artras and the others as well. He could have left, claimed everyone had been killed by the wolves or caught in the distortion and he couldn't help them. Maybe her earlier impression of him had been wrong.

"What about Cory? Hernande? Morrell?"

"They all survived Hagger's attack. Many of those in the group didn't. Twenty-two were killed, and there are another four that might not survive their wounds. But the rest made it."

Kara nodded. "What do they plan to do?" she croaked. "Where are they going?"

"That's the question, isn't it?" Allan shifted, jostling her, then sighed heavily. "I wasn't going to take any of you back to the Hollow. I lied. I was going to take Morrell and abandon you all."

"But now?"

"Now . . . I think the Hollow is going to need you and the other Wielders. You haven't been outside of the city yet. What's happening here isn't isolated, it's all over. Not as intense as here, but still occurring. The lights that warped Devitt, that transformed Hagger and the other Dogs into wolves, the surges of ley, the quakes. . . . It's not the same world anymore. I'm not certain what it is, but I think having a few Wielders in the Hollow would be a good thing right now."

"But you don't want everyone in the group in the Hollow, do you?"

She felt his chuckle through her chest. "No. I don't think some of them will fit in. Bryce, for instance. The other Dogs. But I also think we're going to need men like them. I think the world is going to become very rough for the next few years. The Hollow, if it's survived so far, will have to be defended. But it can't support everyone either. There isn't enough arable land around it, not defensible land anyway. And there are thousands who survived Erenthrall, scattered out into the surrounding lands."

"You've given this thought." She tried to shift away from him and he let her, although his grip on her arm tightened. She trembled in relief when she found she could move her arms and legs, although they felt heavy.

"I've had time," Allan said quietly as she stretched her arms out and rolled her head, the muscles in her neck cracking. "You've been inside the distortion for three days."

Kara couldn't breathe for a moment. She couldn't remember anything from the time the distortion quickened to the time Allan's face blurred into existence above her.

She shuddered, and suddenly the urge to move, to leave, made her muscles twitch. "Let's get out of here," she said, and tried to stand.

Only to collapse back into Allan when her legs wouldn't support her.

"Easy," Allan said. "You may have been trapped for three days, but your body still thinks you just finished dealing with the distortion. You're still weak. I'll have to carry you."

He pulled her around and swept her up into his arms as if she were a rag doll. She gasped in protest, but he'd already begun moving, climbing the stairs up out of the depression that held the Nexus.

When they reached the summit and stepped out from behind the wall that had once protected the Nexus, Kara sucked in a breath in shock and wonder, although Allan didn't slow.

The entire city was cloaked in the filigree arms of the distortion, some passing through the remains of the towers in Grass, others snaking down into the earth, Erenthrall fractured into a thousand different shards. Some of those shards glowed from within as if lit with daylight. Others appeared to be filled with ley, pulsing a hot white.

And everything was eerily silent. No sound at all, except for the noise Allan made as he moved—the rustle of cloth, his breath, an occasional cough.

They came up on one of the edges between shards, the frozen lightning a lacework along a tilted plane before them. Allan slowed, shifted her into a new position, and said, "We have to move slower through the walls. And it will feel strange."

"Like what?"

Allan simply frowned and shook his head, ducking down as he pressed forward so that he passed between two jagged edges of lightning. Kara's chest compressed and she struggled to breathe, her skin tingling as if she'd just dunked her entire body into frigid water. She shivered, a bone-aching chill settling over her—

And then the pressure against her chest loosened and they passed through to the other side. With her first indrawn breath, Kara tasted a difference in the air; it was sharper, crisper. She took it in greedily, hadn't even realized that her breathing had been stifled before. The light was different here as well, almost gray, like just before dawn.

"Wait," she said, and Allan slowed before she motioned him on again and continued. "What time of day is it? When I woke, I thought it was night, but here it almost feels like dawn."

"I don't know. I won't know until we step beyond the distortion. All of the shards appear to be caught in different phases of time, some moving faster than others. At least that's what it looked like to me. But there's still something more you need to see."

"What?"

Allan shook his head. "I can't show you until we leave the distortion. And I want to hear an untarnished opinion."

Kara pressed him, but he wouldn't relent and so she settled back and watched as they moved from shard to shard, slowing at the walls, the same pressure and coldness seeping into her bones at each. She reached out on the Tapestry and felt the distortion around her, but its sheer magnitude daunted her. Her instinct was to heal it, to fix it, but she had no idea where to begin. She tried to push the thought from her mind, but kept returning to it as they traveled.

Allan didn't head straight for the bridges or to the west. He wove through the shards, seeking out specific locations to pass through, by-passing some shards altogether. He claimed that some shards were tainted, as if rotten or decaying, while others felt as if they vibrated, making it unpleasant to pass through them. At her insistence, they stepped into one, Kara nearly gagging and slipping from his grip at the stench after only one breath. He dragged her back through the wall and moved on without a word.

By the time they reached the bridge over the Tiana River, Kara could walk on her own, although Allan still had to support her, aside from keeping in contact with her. They crossed the bridge, passing through two walls, and then into the outer districts. The shards were larger here, the walls farther apart. Kara forced Allan to stop for a rest, but when he offered to carry her again, she dragged herself to her feet and they continued. Her stomach growled. Her mouth was dry and tasted of linen.

And then they passed beyond the final wall, slid out of the distortion, moving from a shard of night into midafternoon daylight. Kara blinked up at the sun, stumbling, Allan steadying her before letting her go. The absence of his hand on her forearm felt strange.

"The others took shelter in a building on the edge of this district," Allan said, "beside the river's new channel."

"What new channel?" Kara noted the lack of surprise in her voice. She'd reached the point where she simply accepted everything as if it had always been that way. She knew it was weariness and exhaustion, but she didn't feel tired, merely . . . numb.

"The distortion blocked the rivers, so they found new paths around the city. Right now, the Tiana's churning through the streets, taking down buildings to the west. The quakes haven't stopped either, so it keeps shifting."

As if mocking him, the earth shook, but it was only a minor tremor.

It still unsettled her. She said sharply, "Where are they? I need to see them—Cory and the others. I need to know—"

—that they're real. Although she wasn't certain what *was* real any-more. Her mind felt fuzzy.

"Here," Allan said, moving down one of the streets, the buildings on either side heavily damaged because they hadn't been built of stone. "They aren't far."

Kara followed, climbing over the debris, thankful for the breeze that pushed against her face and for the chirp of birds, the hiss of sand against stone, the eerie howl of wind through vacant windows—desolate sounds, but sounds nonetheless.

She heard the others before she saw them, laughter and the shrieks of children. They rounded a corner, the building at its edge surprisingly whole, and found a stone building still standing across the thoroughfare. Youngsters were playing in the street, tossing around a leather-stitched ball in some sort of game, overseen by a few women and twice as many men, at least half of them carrying weapons and obviously on watch.

"Some of those that survived have already formed into loose groups and aren't friendly," Allan said wearily, voice low. "We've already been attacked twice."

The guards spotted them first, a warning shout rising before they recognized Allan.

And then the two were inundated with people, everyone talking, everyone trying to touch her, the kids screaming, their voices shrill. She shrank back from them, Allan forging his way through the crowd ahead of her toward the building. They ducked inside and left the majority of the people behind, only to be greeted by those inside.

Kara had reached her limit when Cory was suddenly there.

She burst into tears when she saw him, reached forward and clutched him close. The strength left her legs and she clung to him, unable to control herself. She was vaguely aware of Allan and Hernande ushering people from the room, closing the door so that only Cory, Hernande, Allan, and herself remained.

No one spoke until she trailed down into sobs and pulled back from Cory, wiping her nose with the back of her sleeve. She scrubbed at her eyes and said, "I'm sorry. I—I didn't believe Allan when he said you'd survived." She laughed, the sound odd and uncomfortable. "I don't know why."

"I think it's perfectly understandable," Hernande said, stepping forward to touch Kara's shoulder in comfort. "Nothing feels stable anymore. Nothing seems real." He glanced toward Allan. "Has she seen?"

He shook his head. "I don't think she noticed on our way here, after we left the distortion."

Hernande frowned and turned back to Kara with an uncertain expression.

"What is it?" Kara asked.

Hernande sighed. "Come see for yourself. And then you can tell us what you think."

They all shared a disquieting look, but then Hernande motioned her toward a set of stairs in the far corner of the main room. They ascended three flights, emerging on the roof of the building.

Kara could see the extent of the distortion from here, could see the edges of the city as it sprawled out onto the plains that rolled into the horizon to the north, west, and south. The distortion itself was immense, a huge dome of colored light, the remains of the buildings within appearing even more broken through the jagged edges of the shards and the vibrant white of the lightning. She wondered how long they had before it closed, wondered what the city would look like once it did, thinking of the death the much smaller distortions had caused in Erenthrall before this.

She shuddered, moved to the edge of the building, the wind blowing her hair across her face. The sun had begun to lower, the plains golden in its glow. She scanned the city outside the distortion below, saw the river where it cut its new path through the streets, could even faintly hear it. When she saw nothing unusual—or nothing she wasn't already expecting from what Allan had told her—she raised her eyes to the plains. "What am I supposed to s—"

And she saw it. A faint pinprick of white light blazing on the horizon, like a star. Except it couldn't be a star because it glistened on the horizon north of where the sun would set.

She spun, a horrifying thought filling her mind, her stomach dropping away abruptly as she saw another fiery white light burning to the south, in the direction of Tumbor. The first must have been Dunmara in the Reaches. She couldn't see anything in the direction of Farrade, or to the east, because the distortion blocked her view, but she was willing to bet there were white lights burning on the horizon there as well. In fact, if she squinted her eyes and looked farther north, she thought she could see additional lights in the Steppe, but she couldn't be certain.

She turned back to the others, their faces grim. "They're distortions aren't they? Distortions that haven't quickened yet."

Hernande's mouth pinched tight, then he sighed. "That's what we thought as well." He looked older, his face drawn. But his eyes were bright, lively, young, focused on Kara. "So what are we going to do about them?"

Kara turned away from his gaze, placed her hands on the wall of the building, and stared out to the north, toward the light over Dunmara. The stone felt gritty beneath her hands, the wind cold against her face, but her jaw clenched with determination.

"We have to fix them."